Shaun Hutson Omnibus

Relics
Spawn
Shadows

Also by Shaun Hutson

One

The knife felt cold against her flesh.

As if some icy finger were tracing a pattern over her skin, the girl felt the blade being drawn softly across her cheek.

The point brushed her lips, nudging against them for a moment as if seeking access to the warm moistness beyond. She opened her mouth slightly and, for fleeting seconds, she tasted steel. Then the knife was gone.

The girl's eyes were closed, but as she felt the point gliding down towards the hollow of her throat she finally allowed herself to gaze upon the one who wielded the blade.

He was almost invisible in the darkness but she knew that, like her, he was naked.

As were the others who stood close by, little more than pale outlines beneath the dense canopy of trees whose gnarled branches twisted and curled together, rattled by the chill October wind which whistled tunelessly through the wood. It also ruffled the girl's long dark hair, causing the silky tresses to writhe like reptilian tails.

She was barely seventeen but her body was shapely and belied her youth. Her breasts in particular seemed over-developed, the nipples coaxed to stiffness by the cold air. She shuddered involuntarily as she felt the knife being moved in a circular pattern around her aureola, brushing the puckered skin for a moment before prodding the nipple. This time she felt not only the needle-sharp point of the blade but the actual cutting edge too as it rested against the swollen bud of flesh. She closed her eyes again as the same movements were repeated on her other breast.

11

The pressure increased and she gritted her teeth, waiting for the cut.

But she felt only an icy tickle as the cold blade was drawn between her breasts, down to her navel and then towards the dark bush of hair between her legs. It parted the tightly curled down, guided with unfaltering skill by the powerful hand which grasped it.

She let out a low sigh, her breath clouding in the cold air, as the knife was pressed slightly harder against that most sensitive area. She opened her legs wider, as if to welcome the blade like some kind of steel penis.

For what seemed an eternity it remained there; then she exhaled slowly as it was eased aside.

Opening her eyes once more, she saw the one who held the blade turn slightly, until he was facing a youth no more than a few months older than herself. He was powerfully built, his head supported by a thick bull neck which he offered willingly to the wielder of the knife. The cutting edge left an almost invisible white mark as it was pressed against the boy's throat. But after a second the pressure eased and the blade found its way to his chest before plunging deeper towards his limp penis. He tensed as the cold steel brushed his organ, tracing the course of the thick veins before gliding over his contracted testicles.

A moment later it was withdrawn and now both the girl and the youth knelt, fallen leaves crunching beneath them. They were close, within arm's length.

Suddenly they caught the powerful smell which drifted on the wind.

A goat was being led towards them by a rope tied around its neck.

Another thick length of hemp had been wrapped tightly around its jaws so the only sound it could make was a low mewling deep in its throat.

The young couple lay face down on the carpet of leaves as the goat was coaxed between them. It was held firmly by the man who gripped the knife. He now moved behind the creature and straddled it, holding the blade before his chest in one strong hand. With the other he gripped the horns of the goat and yanked its head back so savagely he almost broke its neck.

The knife flashed forward, shearing through the animal's throat, slicing effortlessly through muscle and sinew.

Huge gouts of blood erupted from the massive wound, spraying into the air with the force of a high pressure hose. The crimson fluid splattered the young couple as the goat bucked madly between the man's legs, its body jerking uncontrollably. The knife-wielder watched the white clouds of vapour rising into the air as the hot blood continued to fountain from the ruptured arteries.

From either side, figures approached, all of them men. All of them naked.

They lifted the goat into the air, its struggles now becoming more feeble as its life fluid gushed away. It suddenly re-doubled its efforts as the knife-wielder thrust his blade into its exposed belly, slicing open the fleshy sac with one powerful movement.

Intestines burst from the wound like the bloodied arms of an octopus, huge thick lengths falling to the ground with a loud, liquid splat. Steam rose from the spilling entrails, the pungent odour now mingling with the reek of excrement as the goat's sphincter muscle loosened and a stream of liquid and solid waste pumped from its writhing body.

Still no one spoke, but as if a signal had been given, the young couple rolled over to face each other.

The girl closed her eyes and rolled again, allowing herself to slide into the thick mass of viscera. She felt its warmth surround her, felt the slippery wetness of the pulsing organs beneath her buttocks. She spread her legs and waited for the boy to join her. His penis was already swollen and he found no difficulty penetrating her, for she was as eager as he. They writhed amidst the blood and internal organs, now oblivious to the choking smells which surrounded them and the crimson fluid which coated their bodies. They were aware only of the pleasure which they both felt.

The man with the knife watched impassively as the frenetic coupling continued.

Blood ran down his hand from the blade of the weapon

and he gazed at the crimson droplets in fascination as one fell onto his own rigid penis, staining the head bright red.

He chuckled.

So much blood.

And there would be more.

He looked around at the other naked bodies in the clearing.

Much more blood.

Two

It was getting difficult to breathe inside the tent. The air was full of dust and the small structure was definitely too small to adequately accommodate three people. Nevertheless, Kim Nichols looked on with rapt attention as the piece of hard stone was broken open.

A fragment came free as the tracer was worked slowly around it, exposing the encased relic.

Charles Cooper picked up the small hammer which lay on the table before him and tapped the wooden end of the tracer. The chisel-like implement shaved off some more stone and the article within became more easily visible.

'It looks like a currency bar,' Phillip Swanson said quietly as Cooper prised away the last of the clinging rock. He swept the metal ingot with a small brush, then laid the rusted artifact on the white cloth before him. A number of other articles already lay on view there, including coins, a couple of arrow-heads, a brooch and a roughly hewn figurine shaped like a phallus.

'It's strange,' Kim observed, picking up the metal ingot and turning it carefully between her thumb and forefinger. 'Coins *and* currency bars used by the same tribe. The Celts usually kept to one form of currency, didn't they?'

14

'Don't forget there was trade with other tribes,' Cooper reminded her. '*Atrebates* like the Iceni and the Trinovantes would still have traded with *Demetae* such as the Brigantes and the Cronovii.' He prodded the other slim metal bars with his index finger.

'A tribe that used both forms of currency,' Swanson mused. 'It must have been a large settlement from the amount of stuff we've found.'

'Then why haven't we found any bones?' asked Kim, but she received no answer from either of her colleagues. Cooper merely sat back in his chair and ran a hand over his hairless head. It was a feature which made him look older than his thirty-five years. Apart from the tufts over his ears and at the back of his head he was completely bald. Even his eyebrows appeared to be thinning. His sad, baleful eyes looked as though they had seen all the worries of the world and still carried their imprint. It was Cooper who had initiated this particular dig.

Builders working on a nearby site had unearthed a number of artifacts and Cooper had been notified. He'd ordered an electro-magnetic search of the area which had revealed a large ancient settlement of unknown origin. Subsequent aerial sweeps had confirmed the presence of a Celtic settlement which covered an area almost a quarter of a mile square.

Kim, who worked at the museum three miles away in Longfield, the nearest town, had joined his team of twenty archaeologists and their work had so far revealed a positive treasure trove of relics. A profusion of gold torcs and other neck rings had convinced Cooper and his team that this particular site had been home to one of the most powerful Celtic tribes of the time. Slave chains and shackles had also been discovered, suggesting that the tribe, unlike their contemporaries, had used forced labour.

Bones were the only thing missing.

Shields, weapons, currency, pottery and sculpture had all been unearthed during the past two weeks. Some of the finds were not only valuable in a financial sense but priceless in their archaeological worth. All these artifacts confirmed that the settlement had been very large indeed, yet still no physical remains of the tribe who'd created the horde had been found.

Kim looked down at the relics laid out before her.

What the hell had happened to the tribe?

Three

The air was turning blue.

A thick haze of diesel fumes hung over the men and machines like a man-made fog bank. Thick and noxious.

The roar of powerful engines mingled with the screech of caterpillar tracks as a number of large earth-movers rumbled across the landscape, flattening or digging according to their individual function.

Frank King watched approvingly as a JCB was manoeuvred into position, its great metal arm swinging down to scoop up a mound of earth which it then dumped into the back of a waiting lorry. The driver was sitting contentedly in the cab smoking and he waved to King as the foreman passed, unable to hear King's comment about 'not straining himself' because of the roar of machinery.

Away to his right, King could see a group of men laying tarmac. Despite the chill in the air they worked in shirt-sleeves. Sweat was soaking through their clothes from the heat given off by the red-hot tar.

The Leisure Centre itself was all but finished. An 'E' shaped two storey building, it looked like something a child might fashion from plastic blocks. Painters still swarmed over it like so many overall-clad termites, only these termites were busy applying coats of weather-proof paint.

King stood a moment longer surveying the activity, then

turned and headed towards the yellow Portakabin close by. On entering he moved across to the welcoming warmth of a calor-gas heater and held his hands over it, meanwhile trying to catch the tail end of the phone conversation one of his colleagues was engaged in.

John Kirkland was nodding as he held the phone, his mouth opening and closing like a goldfish as he struggled to get a word in. Finally he held the receiver slightly away from his ear and cupped a hand over the mouthpiece. He looked up at King and shook his head as if signalling defeat. The other foreman smiled. Another three or four minutes and Kirkland replaced the phone.

'Jesus,' he muttered.

'Cutler?' King asked, grinning.

'Who else do you know who can talk non-stop for twenty minutes flat?' Kirkland said, picking up his mug of tea. He sipped it, wincing when he found that it was cold.

'What did he want?'

'The usual. "Is everything going according to schedule? Are we going to be finished on time?" I don't know why he doesn't move his fucking desk out here so he can sit and watch, at least it'd save him ringing up so often.'

Frank King chuckled and poured his colleague a hot mug of tea, repeating the action for himself.

'I don't know what he's worried about,' Kirkland said. 'We're ahead of schedule if anything.' He sipped some tea. 'Anyway, Cutler reckons he's coming out here this afternoon to have a look for himself. He said something about flattening that wood.' Kirkland tapped the map which lay on the table before him. 'He wants to build on the land, extend the project.'

King peered through the window of the portakabin, rubbing some grime away with his index finger. He could see the wood that Kirkland meant. It was a mile or so to the east of the main site, on a slight rise.

'It's more work, John,' he said. 'None of us can turn our noses up at that.'

'I'm not arguing with you, but things are going to get a bit crowded around here soon,' he said, taking a sip of his tea.

'I mean, there's that archaeological dig going on over there.' He motioned to his left, to the west. 'They've been at it for a while too. Knowing Cutler, I'm surprised he hasn't offered to build them a bloody museum.'

King laughed, his eyes drawn once more to the dark outcrop of trees which grew so thickly to the east.

The wood looked like a stain against the green of the hills.

Four

It was Kim who felt the tremor first.

She felt a slight vibration beneath her feet and for a moment she paused, looking up at Phillip Swanson, who seemed not to have noticed the movement. He was more concerned with unearthing a gold receptacle from the floor of the trench in which they both crouched. Kim waited a second longer, then began to help Swanson.

'It's gold,' he said excitedly. 'Some kind of ornamental bowl.'

They had uncovered the top half of the container when the second tremor came.

'Did you feel that?' Kim asked, pressing the palm of one hand to the earth.

Swanson nodded distractedly, apparently uninterested.

No more than ten yards away from them, a small rift opened in the earth.

Loose dirt and gravel immediately began to tumble into the crack, which was widening with alarming speed and extending lengthwise along the trench they were working in.

It was now less than six yards from them.

18

Swanson dug carefully beneath the bowl, freeing it from the last clods of earth which held it captive.

The crack in the ground was widening, yawning a full six feet across now and still lengthening.

There was another vibration, so violent it rocked Kim on her heels, causing her to overbalance. As she fell to one side she saw the rent in the earth, now only two or three feet from them.

She shouted a warning to Swanson but it was too late.

It was as if the bottom of the trench had simply fallen away. The crack opened like a hungry mouth and Kim realized with horror that she was falling.

Swanson too began slipping into the crack, which was now a gaping wound across the land.

Kim clutched frantically at the side of the trench, digging her fingers into the earth in a desperate effort not to fall. There was nothing beneath her feet and she gritted her teeth, trying to force from her mind thoughts of how deep the hole might be. Swanson also grabbed onto the ledge of hard ground and felt his feet dangling in empty air. An icy cold blast of wind erupted from below them and Kim sucked in an almost painful breath, fearing that the sudden uprush might cause her to lose her grip.

But now others were running to their aid. She saw Cooper sprinting toward the side of the trench. He dropped to his knees and thrust a hand down to her. Beside him another man, whom she didn't recognize, was shining a torch past her down into the hole, trying to see just how deep it was.

The light was swallowed up by the impenetrable blackness.

The rift which had opened was obviously much deeper than anyone could have guessed.

'Take my hand,' Cooper urged, but Kim dared not release her grip on the earth ledge for fear of falling. Her boots dug into the sides of the hole but only succeeded in dislodging some pieces of rock. From the amount of time they took to hit the bottom it was painfully obvious that the hole was deep enough to cause serious injury, if not death, should either she or Swanson fall.

'Somebody get a rope,' yelled Cooper, straining to reach Kim's hand.

She felt his powerful hand close over her wrist, and with lightning speed she gripped his forearm and clung tightly. He tried to pull her up, two of his colleagues holding onto him to prevent him from toppling head first into the black chasm.

The veins on his forehead bulged as he used all his strength to haul her up, inch by inch.

The wall of the trench started to collapse.

Just small pieces of earth at first, then great lumps of it began to fall past Kim, some of the fragments striking her as they disappeared into the gaping maw which had now opened out into an almost circular pit.

Cooper almost overbalanced, his grip on Kim's wrist loosening for an instant.

She screamed as she slipped an inch or two, but Cooper regained his grip and began once more to haul her up the crumbling wall of the trench.

Behind her, Swanson was muttering to himself, struggling to retain a hand-hold on earth that was crumbling beneath his frantic fingers.

A spade was lowered to him and someone shouted to him to grab the handle but he was afraid to release his hold on the ledge. His heart was hammering against his ribs, the perspiration running in great salty rivulets down his face. He closed his eyes tightly for a moment, screwing them up until pain began to gnaw at his forehead.

A lump of earth the size of a fist came loose and hit him on the top of the head.

He lost his grip.

A woman standing on the side of the trench screamed as the archaeologist flailed with one hand, trying desperately to regain his hold.

Kim heard his shout of terror as he sensed he was slipping away. She tightened her grip on Cooper's hand as he slowly dragged her upper body clear of the hole, aware that the trench wall would not hold out much longer.

His foot slipped and he almost overbalanced, but strong arms held him upright and he continued to drag Kim out.

Her legs finally cleared the hole and with one last surge of strength, Cooper pulled her completely clear. Both of them fell back onto the earth, which was still crumbling beneath them. They rolled away, seeking firmer footing. Kim could hardly get her breath but she clambered to her feet and looked round.

'Help me!' shrieked Swanson, now clutching at the spade which was offered to him. He closed one desperate hand over the wooden shaft and clung on, knowing that his life depended on it.

His would-be rescuers kept trying to drag him up but his full weight, now dangling helplessly over the pit, was too much for them.

'Where's that bloody rope?' shouted Cooper, running to get it from one of his colleagues. He fashioned it into a makeshift loop, then lowered it towards Swanson.

'Put your arm through the loop,' he bellowed as the other end was secured to a tree stump.

Swanson did as he was told, though he hardly needed prompting. He grabbed the rope and tried to haul himself up.

Kim watched helplessly as three of the archaeologists pulled on the rope. Slowly, inch by inch, they started dragging Swanson clear.

Picking up a torch, Kim shone it into the pit and saw that the hole was cylindrical, a tube of earth with smooth sides. She daren't guess how deep it was.

Swanson was more than half clear of the pit when the rope began to fray.

At first a handful of strands sprang from the hemp, then more.

Swanson heard a creak as it unravelled quickly.

'No!' he shrieked as the final strands came undone.

The men holding the rope tried to pull him up faster and flailing hands tried to catch him, but it was too late.

With a scream of fear he plummetted from sight into the pit, his shout reverberating inside the shaft.

Kim closed her eyes, waiting for the thud as he hit the bottom.

It never came.

Instead, everyone near the pit froze as Swanson's shout suddenly changed into a bellow of unimaginable agony. The sound, amplified by the shaft, was like a slap in the face.

'Oh, God!' murmured Kim, peering down into the darkness. But she could see nothing.

The darkness of the pit hid his body from sight.

Had he broken his back? Shattered his legs? Perhaps his skull had been pulped by the fall?

Stunned by that roar of agony, the other archaeologists, too, stood gazing helplessly into the enveloping blackness.

Now they all felt an icy breeze which seemed to rise from the pit. With it came a choking smell, a pungent odour of decay which made Kim cover her nose and mouth. She looked at Cooper, but he could only shake his head, wondering, like the others, what fate had befallen Swanson.

Had he known the truth he would have been glad that he could not see the body.

Five

The lights on the two police cars and the ambulance turned silently, casting red and blue splashes of colour onto the faces of the people gathered around the deadly pit.

No one spoke, and the whole scene reminded Kim of an extract from a silent film. She stood close to Cooper, a mug of tea cradled in her hands, but the warm fluid was doing little to drive the chill from her bones. What she was feeling was not induced by the cold wind. It was the icy embrace of fear and shock, and it gripped her tighter every time she looked at the hole into which Swanson had fallen.

A couple of policemen were busy constructing a winch beside the pit, watched by the crowd of onlookers. Kim brushed a strand of blonde hair from her face, noticing that her hand was still shaking.

Cooper placed an arm around her shoulders and pulled her close in a gesture which suggested concern rather than affection.

She took another sip of her tea and glanced across the open ground towards a grey Sierra which was bouncing awkwardly over the dips and gulleys in the earth as it approached the other vehicles. Kim watched as it came to a halt and the driver climbed out.

He was tall, dressed in a suit which was stretched almost too tightly across his broad chest and back. His dark hair was uncombed and he ran a hand through it as he slammed the car door. A uniformed man approached the car and said something which Kim couldn't hear, but he motioned in her direction and the newcomer nodded and headed towards her, casting a momentary glance past her towards the pit where the winch had been all but secured.

'Inspector Stephen Wallace,' said the man in the suit, flipping open a slim leather wallet which he took from his inside pocket.

Kim looked at the photo on the I.D. card, thinking it did the policeman scant justice. He was powerfully built, and his shirt collar looked painfully tight around his thick neck. As if reading her mind, he reached up and undid the top button, relaxing slightly as he did so. He smiled reassuringly at Kim, who despite her condition found herself returning the gesture.

'I already know what happened,' he told Cooper. 'One of my men informed me over the radio. I'm sorry about Mr Swanson.'

Cooper nodded.

Wallace moved as close to the edge of the pit as he felt prudent, staring down into a seemingly bottomless maw.

'Did you know this site was unstable?' he asked.

'Certainly not,' Cooper snapped, 'or we wouldn't have started work here.'

'Just asking,' Wallace murmured quietly.

The uniformed man beside the winch gave a thumbs-up and the inspector walked around the shaft, guessing that the hole must be at least twelve feet in diameter. He pulled off his jacket, handing it to another of the waiting constables, then turned to the ambulanceman.

'I'll go down first,' he said. 'Check it out.' He took a torch from one of his constables and held out his hand again. 'Let me have that two-way.'

The harness which dangled from the winch was a piece of rope tied into a loop at the bottom. Wallace put one foot into it, gripping the hemp securely with his free hand, and lowered himself the first few feet into the darkness. He flicked on the torch, playing the powerful beam around the walls of the shaft. The rope creaked ominously as he was lowered.

A foul stench filled his nostrils. A fusty, cloying odour which made him gasp for air. It was cold too, and the policeman shivered involuntarily, pointing the torch down every now and then in the hope of illuminating the bottom of the shaft. The beam was quickly swallowed by the gloom.

He was lowered further. Slowly, evenly.

The smell was growing worse and Wallace coughed, trying to breathe through his mouth to minimize its effects. The stench was making him light-headed.

Fifty feet and still no sign of the bottom of the shaft.

'Anything yet, guv?'

The voice on the two-way belonged to sergeant Bill Dayton and Wallace recognized it immediately.

'Nothing,' he said and coughed again.

Seventy feet.

Wallace was beginning to wonder if his men had enough rope. Just how deep *was* this bloody hole? The cold, like the smell, seemed to be intensifying, so much so that the inspector was now shivering uncontrollably. And yet there

24

was no breeze. The air was unmoving, like stagnant water in a blocked well.

Eighty feet.

He shone the torch beneath him once more and, this time, it picked something out.

A few feet below, something was glistening.

'Nearly there,' Wallace said into the two-way.

'Can you see Swanson?' asked Cooper.

'Not yet . . .' He snapped his jaws together, cutting off the sentence.

There were sounds of movement from below.

Faint rustling sounds, almost imperceptible but nevertheless present. Like . . .

Like what, Wallace thought?

He swallowed hard and shone the torch down once more.

'Oh, Jesus!' he exclaimed.

Another couple of feet and he'd reached the bottom of the shaft. Wallace stepped out of the harness and shone his torch forward, waving a hand in front of his nose to waft away the nauseating stench that filled his nostrils. He wished he could wipe away what he saw, too.

There was a wooden spike in the centre of the pit, placed with almost mathematical precision so it was in the very middle. The stake was fully fifteen feet tall, tipped by a razor-sharp point unblunted by the passage of time.

Impaled on this spike, like an insect on a board, was Phillip Swanson.

The spike had penetrated his back just above the left scapula, tearing through his body before erupting from it at the junction of his right thigh and torso. He had landed on the spike with such momentum that his body was almost touching the ground. Blood had sprayed everywhere. It had run in thick rivulets from his nose and mouth, gushed freely from his shattered groin and pumped in huge gouts from his stomach which was torn open to reveal a tangle of internal organs which looked on the point of breaking loose. Thick spurts of odorous green bile from the pulverized gall bladder had mingled with the blood which was now caked thickly all over the corpse and the base of the sharpened pole. There were fragments of broken bone scattered about, and Swanson's arms dangled limply on either side of him, one of them attached only by the merest thread of skin and ligament. Smashed bone glistened whitely amidst the pulped mess of flesh and blood.

Wallace knelt close to the dangling head, hearing that strange rustling once more. It took him a second to realize that it was wind hissing through Swanson's punctured lungs. Wallace frowned. For that to be happening the man had to be alive but surely that was impossible.

He lifted the head gently, looking at the bloodied face.

Swanson's eyes snapped open.

In that split second Wallace fell back, dropping the torch, stumbling in the darkness.

He heard a thick, throaty gurgle and realized that it was Swanson's death rattle.

'Shit,' muttered the policeman, his heart thudding madly against his ribs. He wiped his face with one shaking hand, gradually regaining his composure.

Somehow Swanson had clung to life for over an hour while skewered on the stake.

Wallace didn't even attempt to imagine the suffering he'd gone through. The inspector regained his torch and shone it on the archaeologist's face once more, seeing that the eyes were now staring wide, the pupils hugely dilated. The soft rustling sound had stopped.

'Wallace, are you all right?'

He recognized Cooper's voice and found his radio.

'Terrific,' he said, wearily. 'Dayton, can you hear me? Clear everybody away from the pit, then get a stretcher down here.'

'On its way, guv,' the sergeant told him.

Wallace shone his torch around the base of the shaft, looking at the objects which were scattered in all directions. Coins, weapons, jewellery.

And bones. So many bones.

As the beam fell on Swanson again he quickly moved it away, playing it over the walls. He reached for the two-way. his eyes fixed ahead.

26

'Cooper, you still there?' he said.

A crackle of static, then the archaeologist answered.

'What is it?'

'When the body's removed you'd better come down here,' the policeman said, the torch wavering slightly as he shone it ahead. The beam flickered for a second.

'There's something I think you should see.'

Six

He didn't time it, but Wallace guessed that it took him and the ambulanceman almost twenty minutes to remove Phillip Swanson's body from the wooden stake. As the body was finally pulled free, the left arm came loose and fell with a dull thud. The ambulanceman laid it alongside the body, then carefully wrapped the remains in a thick blanket and secured the whole grisly package to a stretcher with rope. On Wallace's order the corpse was winched up, along with the ambulanceman.

The two of them had spoken little during their vile task. The ambulanceman in particular seemed glad to be away from the cloying blackness of the pit and, as he was winched up towards the light again, he did not look down.

Now the policeman stood alone wishing he had a cigarette, partly to calm his nerves, but also to mask the rancid stench which filled the shaft. He rummaged in his trouser pockets and found half a stick of chewing gum. It would have to do for now. He shone the torch over the floor of the pit, realizing at last how many strange objects lay around him. To his untrained eye it reminded him of some ancient rubbish tip. Articles of all shapes and sizes were scattered in all directions around the base of the stake.

The roving beam illuminated a skull, the jaws open in a soundless scream. There was a large hole in it just above the crown. Another lay beside it. And another. All bore jagged cracks or hollows.

But it was beyond the mounds of bones and relics that Wallace finally allowed the torch beam to rest.

What would Cooper and the others make of this?

He chewed his gum thoughtfully and glanced up. The pit's depth prevented any natural light from reaching the bottom and it also cut out any sounds from above. The combination of deathly silence and unyielding darkness was a formidable one. And there was the ever-present smell, too. An odour of decay which clutched at Wallace's throat like an invisible spectre.

A few feet above him he heard something move. He aimed his torch up into the gloom.

Cooper was descending on the winch and with him was the young woman Wallace knew as Kim Nichols.

She had a firm hold on the rope and looked unperturbed by the sight which faced her. Even when she glanced at the bloodied wooden stake she didn't flinch. Wallace watched her for a moment, offering his hand as she stepped out of the harness. There was a warmth in her touch which contrasted sharply with the bone-numbing cold in the shaft.

'You don't need an explanation, do you?' said Wallace, motioning towards the stake.

Cooper shook his head.

Kim shuddered and looked away, thinking how easily she could have been the one to suffer Swanson's agonizing death. But that thought was pushed aside as she saw the piles of artifacts before her. Cooper too was staring in awe at the array which faced him. He bent and picked up a short sword, the blade dulled but still remarkably well preserved considering its age. Flecks of rust had formed around the tip, but apart from that the weapon looked surprisingly sturdy.

Kim found a number of large bowls, some gold, some iron. But she was more interested in the bones. Skulls,

28

femurs, tibias, pelvic bones, and here and there complete skeletons. The place was carpeted with them.

'It's a sacrificial well,' said Cooper excitedly.

Wallace continued chewing slowly, watching the two archaeologists.

'That would explain the bones,' Kim added.

'I don't get it,' Wallace said.

'This shaft and the wooden stake were put here by a Celtic tribe thousands of years ago,' explained Cooper.

'Offerings like these coins and weapons,' added Kim, 'were thrown in to please their gods. So were human beings. Prisoners of war, lunatics and sacrificial victims from the tribe were all thrown down here in the hope of gaining favour with whichever deity was being worshipped.'

'I'm sure Phillip Swanson would have been pleased to hear that,' Wallace said acidly.

'You don't understand the importance of this find, Wallace,' Cooper snapped. 'It's unfortunate that Swanson is dead but it was an accident. What do you expect us to do? Close the site as a mark of respect?' There was scorn in his voice.

Wallace turned away, pointing the torch at the far wall of the pit.

'What do you make of that?'

Cooper, who had been crouching close to the wooden stake, looked up. His jaw dropped open. He got slowly to his feet and wandered across to join the policeman, closely followed by Kim.

The three of them stood mesmerized by the sight that faced them.

Two large, almost perfectly circular stones were propped against the smooth wall of the shaft. Spreadeagled on each one was a skeleton. Iron spikes fully ten inches long had been driven through the wrists and feet of each one. The mouths were open as if the skeletons were still screaming. More of the iron spikes had been driven through the eye sockets of each one, nailing the head to the stone behind it.

'Were *they* thrown in here like that?' Wallace asked. 'Because if they weren't, then whoever nailed them up died down here with them.'

'Criminals,' said Cooper, quietly. 'To have suffered punishment like that they must have transgressed against the tribe itself.'

'These stones,' Kim said, poking one finger behind the rock closest to her. 'They're like gates. There's something behind them.' She peered through the narrow gap into the odorous gloom beyond. 'It looks like a tunnel of some kind.'

'I'm going to leave you to it,' said Wallace. 'After all, I'm a copper, not an archaeologist. I've done my bit.'

Cooper nodded perfunctorily, more interested in the finds.

'Thank you,' Kim said as Wallace gripped the harness.

'I may need a statement from you, Miss Nichols,' he said. 'When you've finished.'

She nodded and smiled.

The rope, and Wallace, began to rise.

Seven

Frank King double-checked that the handbrake of the Land Rover would hold on the sharp incline, and then he and John Kirkland clambered out.

From where they stood the building site was clearly visible away to the west.

The wood stood defiantly before them, its trees jammed tightly together as if to form a barrier to any who might wish to enter. As the two men pushed their way through the chest-high bushes which grew on the perimeter, Kirkland

30

cursed the brambles that cut his flesh. One particularly long hawthorn spike dug deeply into the back of his right hand, drawing blood, and he winced in pain.

'Why the bloody hell couldn't Cutler have come up here himself?' he snarled, wiping the crimson droplets away with his handkerchief. 'I mean, if he wants the wood levelled, fair enough. All we have to do is send a dozen blokes up here with chainsaws, then bulldoze the whole lot when they've finished.'

'It seems like such a waste, doesn't it?' said King, looking around at the ancient trees which towered over them like sentinels. 'Flattening this lot.'

'Come on, Frank, don't have a fit of environmental conscience now,' Kirkland said, tugging himself free of a clinging gorse bush.

The foreman smiled.

'There should be a few thousand quids' worth of paper here,' he said, tapping the trunk of one tree.

As the men moved deeper into the wood King noticed how dark it was becoming. Despite the scarcity of leaves on the branches, the trees still seemed to be blocking out a great deal of natural light. King wondered how any of the mosses and lichens which carpeted the floor of the wood managed to grow. He kicked a rotted tree stump aside, stepping back in revulsion as he saw dozens of wood lice spilling from the hulk like maggots from a festering wound. Two or three extremely large ground spiders also scuttled into view. Kirkland crushed one beneath his foot.

Ahead of them was a clearing, perhaps twenty or thirty yards in diameter, and here the ground was covered by a blanket of brown leaves. They crackled noisily as the two men walked over them.

King stopped in the centre of the treeless area, relieved to be free of the dark confines of the dense wood. He was beginning to feel quite claustrophobic.

High above them, the sky was the colour of wet concrete and a gathering of black clouds to the north promised rain.

Kirkland kicked away some of the dead leaves and dug the toe of his boot into the earth, kicking up a large clod.

'The foundations are going to have to be laid deep if Cutler wants us to build here,' he said, sucking at the small cut on his hand. He bent down and picked up a handful of the moist topsoil, turning it over in his hand, prodding the dark matter and then finally dropping it.

His palms were stained a deep, rusty red.

The colour of dried blood.

Kirkland rubbed his hands together, trying to wipe away the stain. He smelt a musty odour and coughed. The ground around his feet was also tinged dark red.

The trees rattled noisily in the wind as the two men turned to make their way back.

'The sooner this lot's flattened the better,' said Kirkland, rubbing his hands on his overalls.

As they left the clearing, the gloom closed around them again.

Eight

'What sort of rock is it?' Kim asked, watching as George Perry used a chisel to shave off a piece of the slab.

Perry held the lantern over it and prodded the powdery rock with one finger.

'It looks like limestone,' he said. 'It would have to be reasonably soft to take those nails.' He motioned to the circles of stone with the skeletons spreadeagled on them.

'Then they shouldn't be too difficult to move,' Cooper said excitedly.

The gas lamps cast a dull yellow glow around the base of the pit, illuminating the host of artifacts and bones that littered the sacrificial well. Many of the objects had already been removed for analysis. Three or four of the team were

32

packing them carefully into the back of the Land Rover which would transport them into Longfield.

As yet none of the bones had been touched.

Cooper stepped forward, dug his fingers into the soil behind the edge of one of the circular rocks, grasped the rock and braced his shoulder against it. George Perry added his considerable bulk to the effort and they were joined by a third man, whom Kim recognized as Ian Russell. Perry was a grey-haired individual and despite the chill inside the subterranean chamber, dark rings of sweat were visible beneath his armpits. Kim directed the beam of her powerful torch at the rock and watched as the trio of men braced themselves. At a signal from Cooper they began to tug on the stone.

Gritting his teeth, Cooper pulled as hard as he could, feeling a slight movement.

The other two men also noticed that the stone was beginning to shift and they re-doubled their efforts.

An inch.

Two inches.

The concerted effort was working.

Three inches.

Several small fragments of the rock broke off and fell to the ground, and Perry found that he was losing his handhold. He swiftly dug his hands in behind the stone once more, scraping his palms as he did so.

Six inches.

Kim stepped forward, aiming the torch beam into the blackness behind the monolith.

Eight inches.

Russell grunted in pain as his finger slipped and part of his nail was torn away as far as the cuticle. A dark globule of blood welled up and dripped from the end of the digit.

One foot and still they heaved, trying to clear a gap large enough to squeeze through.

The skeleton suspended on the rock shuddered slightly as the great stone was moved. Two of the fingers broke off and dropped to the ground.

Cooper, his face sheathed in sweat, was finding it

difficult to get his breath. The effort of moving the rock was over-exerting his strength and the cloying atmosphere inside the shaft wasn't helping.

'Stop,' he grunted and the other two men carefully released their hold on the stone.

Reaching into his pocket, Russell pulled out a handkerchief and dabbed at the blood from his injured finger, but he seemed more concerned with what lay behind the rock than with his own discomfort.

Cooper took the torch from Kim and stood by the entrance they had unblocked. The gap was large enough to admit him now but he hesitated, shining the torch beam through the blackness to what lay beyond.

It was a tunnel.

As Cooper stood there he felt the beads of perspiration on his forehead turning cold, as if the icy breeze were freezing them into dozens of crystal beads.

He didn't move.

Kim looked at him and frowned, wondering why the archaeologist did not advance into the tunnel. He had been so eager to discover its secrets that she could not understand why he should hesitate now.

She sucked in a startled breath as the muscles in her body suddenly seemed to spasm, as if some powerful electric current were being pumped through her for long seconds. The feeling passed and then she was aware of a rancid stench, much more powerful than that in the shaft, but it was carried on no breeze; it simply hung in the air like a noxious invisible blanket.

Perry coughed and covered his face with one hand.

For what seemed like an eternity no one moved. Finally, as if suddenly galvanized into action, Cooper eased his way through the gap into the waiting tunnel.

The ground was surprisingly soft beneath his feet, and clay-like in consistency. The walls, too, were porous, almost clammy to the touch.

'There must be a lot of moisture in the soil,' said Kim, following him inside, touching the wall with her fingers.

34

'It's amazing,' said Perry. 'There don't appear to be any stantions to support the tunnel roof and yet it seems solid.'

'The Celts were very skilled builders and architects,' Cooper reminded him. 'You only have to look at the broch of Midhowe to realize that.'

'The broch?' Russell said.

'It's a stone tower in the Orkneys,' Kim told him, 'said to have been built by the Celts over 2,000 years ago.'

Ahead of her, Cooper found that the tunnel was curving to the right. Less than four feet wide in places, its narrowness forced the archaeologists to walk in single file. Kim touched the wall closest to her and found that in places droplets of moisture were forming and running like dirty tears down the wall.

Cooper stopped.

There was another tunnel leading off to the left.

'Which one do we take?' asked Perry.

'We could split up,' Russell suggested.

'No,' Cooper said. 'There's no telling how deep these networks go or how complex they become. We'll stay together for the time being.'

They moved on.

Kim saw her breath clouding in the air and she shuddered as the numbing cold seemed to penetrate her bones, freezing the marrow until her whole body felt as if it were stiffening. She found it an effort to lift her feet. Ahead of her, she saw that Cooper too was slowing his pace. It was as if they were walking into a high wind, battling against the force of some powerful blast of air. But there was no movement in the air. The atmosphere remained still and as stagnant as filthy pond water. The stench and the cold closed around them like a reeking glove, squeezing more tightly until each of them was gasping for breath.

Cooper stopped and pulled a box of matches from his pocket. He lit one and held it up.

The flame did not move.

Not a flicker either way:

In seconds the match burned out, as if there wasn't

enough oxygen in the foul atmosphere to sustain it.

'Shouldn't one of us go back and tell the others what's happening?' Russell suggested.

Cooper agreed.

'We'll push on and see if we can find the end of the tunnel,' he said. 'You go back.'

Russell nodded, flicked on his torch and retreated down the narrow tunnel. Within seconds the light was enveloped by the blackness and he became invisible to his three colleagues.

'Come on,' Cooper said, noticing that the tunnel turned to the right again, more sharply this time. Kim sensed that it was also getting narrower. She put out her hands and touched both sides with ease, recoiling slightly from the clammy, moist feel of the walls.

'How much further?' Perry murmured wearily. 'We must have come five or six hundred yards already.'

'The Celts didn't usually build labyrinths like this, did they?' said Kim, not sure whether it was a question or a statement.

'Their hill-forts are very complex but I've never seen anything like this *under* the ground,' Cooper confessed.

The tunnel widened slightly, turning an almost ninety degree bend. The three archaeologists came around the corner virtually together.

The sight which met them stopped them in their tracks.

Nine

The skeletons were piled six deep in places.

The bones, blackened by the ages, lay lengthways across the tunnel like a mouldering barrier, preventing the archaeologists from moving any further.

Cooper shone his torch over the macabre find, overawed by the sheer number of ancient forms. Kim took a faltering step forward, kneeling beside the closest one. Cooper joined her, muttering to himself as the torch beam flickered once more.

'This kind of mass burial wasn't normal Celtic practice,' Kim said, quietly, as if reluctant to disturb the unnatural silence around them. Even as she spoke her voice seemed muffled. Stifled by the choking smell and the almost palpable darkness. 'There must be hundreds of them.'

'They look like children's bones,' said George Perry, noticing, like his companions, that not one of the skeletons was more than about three feet in height.

Kim prodded one with the end of a pencil, hearing the lead scrape along the bare bone like fingernails on a blackboard.

Perry looked down at the skeletons, then past them, the beam of his torch catching a larger object.

It was another barrier, this time stone covered with rancid moss, its surface mottled by the few lichens that had managed to survive in such a fetid atmosphere. Perry was about to say something when Cooper stood up and spoke, a note of urgency in his voice.

'We need to examine these bones as soon as possible,' he said. 'We also need some light down here. George, see if you can rig up a generator on the surface. We can run cables down here and fix up some lights so we can see what we're doing.'

Kim had remained silent but now she got slowly to her feet, eyes fixed on the pile of bones before her. When she spoke her voice was low, subdued.

'I think George is right. They are children's skeletons. But where are the heads?'

Ten

The dog snarled as the chain was pulled tight around its neck. It wore a heavy muzzle over its jaws and thick white saliva hung like glutinous streamers from its teeth.

The dog was a bull terrier. Small and stockily built but possessing tremendous strength, its black body was slightly more streamlined than average but it lacked none of the musculature which made the breed so powerful. As it tugged on its chain the hair at the back of its neck rose in anticipation.

'Keep still, you bastard,' snapped Rob Hardy, jerking the chain once more, almost pulling the dog over.

As he spoke, Hardy looked past the men near him to where another group of men were gathered, and amongst them he recognized Vic Regis. He was also holding a dog, another terrier, a brindle dog which was slightly smaller than Hardy's but no less ferocious in appearance. It too resembled a spring about to uncoil with tremendous ferocity. The dog was making little noise except for the low breathing which Hardy could hear. It reminded him of damaged bellows.

Another man sat on one of the hay bales which had been used to construct the makeshift arena. He was in his early thirties, tall and thin-faced with a pitted complexion and dark stubble which defied even the sharpest razor. His eyebrows were also thick and bushy and met above the bridge of his nose, giving him the appearance of perpetually frowning. He was holding a thick wad of money in his tattooed hand.

'Vic wants to lay a side-bet of fifty quid,' said Mick

Ferguson, scratching one cheek with the rolled-up cash. 'Just between you and him.'

'I'll cover it,' said Hardy without hesitation. 'I've been training this dog for three months. Even *I'm* scared of him.'

Ferguson laughed and held out his hand for the ten fivers which Hardy pulled from his pocket.

'Are you in for a slice of that too?' Hardy asked.

'What do you think?' Ferguson said. 'I set up these little shows, don't I? I reckon that entitles me to some of the proceeds.' He looked at his watch. 'Come on, let's get started.'

Ferguson got to his feet and walked to the centre of the fighting area. The old barn smelt of damp straw and neglect, mingling with the more pungent odour of sweat from both humans and animals.

He guessed that there were a dozen other men besides himself in the dilapidated barn. Its beams were seething with woodworm and the roof leaked when it rained, but the place was perfect for its present purpose. It was about three miles out of town and half a mile from the nearest road. Motorists driving to and from Longfield came nowhere near it, and anyone who thought of turning into the old dirt track was usually discouraged by the sign on the heavy gate which proclaimed PRIVATE: KEEP OUT.

Ferguson thought how lucky he had been to find this place. Up until then he hadn't dared to stage dog-fights within a twenty-mile radius of Longfield. The coppers in the area knew him well enough already. He'd done a two-year stretch in Strangeways for theft and another six months for receiving. They'd also lifted him for GBH on one occasion, but the case had been dismissed for lack of evidence.

The idea of dog-fighting had come to him after attending a coursing meet one Sunday morning. Two of the greyhounds, after killing the hare, had begun fighting between themselves and one had been blinded in the ensuing battle. It had been only a small step from getting the idea to organizing things properly. He creamed off sixty per cent of the take for himself. The rest was used to pay back bets and give the winning dog owner a few bob. Ferguson had two animals of his own, but he would not unleash them in this arena until he felt the time was right. He'd bred them himself, mating a dog with a bitch from a litter which the dog itself had fathered. This incestuous inter-breeding had spawned another litter of six, four of which had been blind or deformed. Those were useless to Ferguson and he'd taken them straight from their mother, still dripping from the womb, and drowned them in a bucket of water. The other two, though, were savage beyond belief and, as such, perfect for his needs. He kept them in cages in the cellar of his house, feeding them on the best meat he could afford. Training them. Moulding them into perfect killing machines. Soon they would be ready and then he'd clean up with side-bets.

As Ferguson stood in the middle of the barn the spectators scuttled to find the best vantage points. Hay bales not used to construct the fighting area itself were hurriedly employed as seats and a hush descended as Regis and Hardy led their dogs forward.

As they drew closer to each other, the two animals began snarling and straining in their eagerness to fight. Both men removed the restraining muzzles and a cacophony of loud barking filled the barn.

'Let them go,' said Ferguson, quietly.

As the collars were tugged free the dogs hurled themselves at each other, all their pent-up fury now finding vent.

Ferguson, Regis and Hardy vaulted to safety behind the low barrier of hay bales and turned to watch as the two animals locked jaws.

The sound of barking was replaced by a succession of snarls and growls of anger and pain.

The brindle dog gripped the black terrier's bottom jaw and pulled, tearing away a long sliver of skin from its lower lip, but the larger animal pulled loose and lunged at its opponent's head. It snapped off the end of one ear as easily as shears cutting through grass, and the taste of blood seemed to inflame it even more. Like two steam trains

40

crashing head-on the dogs smashed into one another again, and this time the smaller dog succeeded in fastening its jaws on the other's shoulder. Its powerful neck muscles tensed as it pulled the black dog down, ripping a sizeable chunk of skin and fur free. Blood burst from the wound and the larger dog drew back slightly. But the respite was short. The two dogs locked jaws once more, scrabbling with their paws to get a grip on the slippery ground. There was a loud crack as the brindle dog broke a tooth.

Ferguson rolled a cigarette as he watched, apparently oblivious to the shouts of the other men. The thick roll of notes nestled comfortably in his trouser pocket. He lit up the cigarette and drew on it.

The black terrier lunged forward and managed to bury its powerful canine teeth in the back leg of its opponent, but in so doing it exposed its own sleek side to attack and the other animal was not slow to respond. It fastened its jaws firmly into the bigger dog and began shaking its head back and forth.

Blood from both animals began to fly through the air and the ground beneath them turned crimson.

Vic Regis grunted indignantly as several hot red droplets splashed his face. He hurriedly wiped them away.

The brindle terrier drew back an inch or two and then bit down even harder, chewing into the side of its opponent, causing it to loosen its grip. But the bigger dog struck at the other animal's head. Its despairing lunge caught the brindle below an eye, one razor-sharp tooth gouging up through the eyeball, almost ripping it from the fleshy socket. Both dogs drew back and Rob Hardy cursed as he saw a gleaming fragment of bone sticking through the pulped and torn mess that was his dog's side. Each time it exhaled a dribble of thick red foam spilled from its nostrils.

Similarly, Regis saw that his brindle dog had been blinded in one eye, its face a mask of blood and sputum. The savage wound on its back leg was also bleeding profusely.

'Do you want to call it off?' Ferguson said.

'No way,' snapped Regis.

41

Hardy agreed.

Before either of them could speak again the dogs had joined in battle once more.

Caught on its blind side, the brindle dog saw the charge too late and the other terrier managed to drive its teeth into the fleshy part of its opponent's neck, shaking its head madly back and forth until its teeth sheared through the smaller animal's jugular vein. There was a bright red explosion as the vein was severed. Blood spurted high into the air and soon the smaller dog began to weaken.

The barn stank of blood. The crimson fluid was everywhere. On the floor, the hay bales, the spectators, Even on the walls in one or two places.

'Right, that's it,' shouted Regis. 'Get your fucking dog off.' He glared at Hardy, who smiled and clambered into the makeshift arena. There might have been a slight chance of saving the defeated animal's life, if anyone had been so inclined, but those watching were too busy complaining or rejoicing, depending on which dog they'd backed.

Hardy gripped the black terrier by the back of the neck and pulled it away from the stricken brindle dog, which tried to drag itself upright. But loss of blood had weakened it too much, and with a throaty gurgle it fell back onto its side, its breath coming in sporadic gasps.

'Useless fucker,' snapped Regis, looking down at the dying animal. 'I've lost over a hundred quid because of you.' With a savagery born of anger he kicked the ravaged dog in the stomach.

It raised its head weakly, as if pleading for help, but Regis was unimpressed.

Ferguson joined the two men, stepping over the fatally wounded brindle dog. He handed a bundle of notes to Hardy, who quickly pocketed them. Regis, muttering to himself, stalked off to the far side of the barn and returned a moment later carrying the pitchfork they had used to move the hay bales. He held it above the dying terrier, the twin prongs poised over its heaving chest. Regis hesitated and the dog whimpered forlornly.

Ferguson snatched the lethal implement from Regis and

steadied himself momentarily, then brought it swiftly down. The prongs punctured the dog's body and he forced them down until he felt them strike the ground beneath. A blast of foul smelling air escaped from the animal's punctured lungs and it bucked spasmodically, bloody sputum spilling from its mouth.

Ferguson continued pressing down on the fork until the animal ceased to move. He smelt the pungent stench of excrement as he wrenched the weapon free of the bloodied body. He stuck it into the ground close to Regis, a faint smile on his face.

'Never mind, Vic,' he said, grinning. 'You can't win them all.'

Eleven

It was a child, that much they knew.

Anything else they could only guess at.

The skeleton lay on a piece of plastic sheeting spread carefully over the table inside Cooper's tent.

'Judging from the size,' said Kim, 'the child couldn't have been more than five or six years old. I'll run carbon-14 and nitrogen tests on the bones when I get them back to the museum.'

'If only we knew where the skulls were,' said George Perry.

A moment later the flap of the tent was pulled back and Ian Russell walked in.

'Charles, have you got a minute?' he asked. 'Mr Cutler's here. He says he wants to speak to you.'

Cooper shrugged and got to his feet, following Russell outside. He rubbed his eyes as he stepped out into the dull grey light. He hadn't slept much the previous night; his mind had been too crammed full of the sights which he and his colleagues had seen. Now he saw two men in suits standing beside one of the excavation trenches peering in at a couple of archaeologists who were busy freeing an object from the soil.

Cooper recognized James Cutler. The land developer was tall and wiry, his slim frame topped by a pinched face and thin, bloodless lips. Approaching his fortieth birthday, he was sole owner of Cutler Developments, one of the most successful private businesses in the country. The black Jensen parked on the nearby ridge testified to his material status although it looked out of place amidst the organized chaos of the archaeological paraphenalia which surrounded it.

Beside him stood a man Cooper did not recognize. He guessed that the man was a year or two younger than Cutler although his pale-grey suit was a similar colour to his hair.

Cutler smiled at the archaeologist and the two of them shook hands.

'Mr Cooper, I'd like you to meet Stuart Lawrence,' the land developer said, introducing his companion. 'He's been working as surveyor on my project.'

Lawrence looked at Cooper with ill-disguised distaste. He disliked scruffiness of any kind and this man was positively grubby. He shook hands stiffly, checking his palm to ensure that no dirt or dust had been left on his skin.

'I hope you don't mind us having a look at your little venture,' Cutler said, smiling.

'Not at all,' Cooper told him. 'After all, if it hadn't been for you and your building project we might never have found out about this site.'

'Quite so,' Cutler added. 'By the way, I was sorry to hear about the death of your colleague. As they say, bad news travels fast.' The land developer began walking slowly, Lawrence and Cooper alongside him. 'I'm afraid that I'm a carrier of bad news today, Mr Cooper.'

The archaeologist looked vague.

'My building project is set for expansion in the next few

weeks,' Cutler explained. 'That expansion will more than likely encompass this site.'

Cooper stopped walking.

'Are you trying to say that you might have to close the site down?' he asked.

'I'm afraid so, Mr Cooper.'

'But when? We made an agreement. You said that my team and I could work here.'

'Until I needed the land for my own purposes,' Cutler reminded him.

'What we've unearthed here is one of the most important finds of its type ever. I'm not about to let it be closed down.'

'You don't have any choice,' Lawrence snapped.

'Mr Lawrence is right,' Cutler continued. 'As you yourself said, it's due to me that you and your people are here at all. It was my men who first unearthed the artifacts which led to the discovery of this site. I called you in to investigate it and we both agreed at the time that there would be a time limit on your work.'

'And you're telling me that the time's running out?' snapped Cooper.

'I gave you six weeks,' Cutler said, a note of condescension in his voice. 'When that time is up . . .' He shrugged resignedly.

'You can't do it,' Cooper said.

Cutler smiled humourlessly.

'I'm a businessman, Mr Cooper. This land belongs to me. I own it. I can do what I like with it. You would have been forced to move on eventually anyway. For the moment, you can continue with your work.'

'How very generous,' Cooper sneered.

The land developer smiled again and turned away from Cooper, ushering Lawrence along with him.

'Nice speaking to you,' Cutler said without turning.

Cooper glared at the backs of the two men as they walked to the waiting Jensen.

'Bastard,' he rasped under his breath.

'Can he really stop the dig if he wants to?' asked Perry, joining his colleague.

Cooper watched the car pull away. He sucked in an angry breath, the knot of muscles at the side of his jaw pulsing.

'God help him if he tries.'

Twelve

The dull glow from the television screen provided precious little light and Kim found that she was squinting at the notes before her, so she rose and flicked on the lamp behind her chair.

While she was on her feet she pulled the curtains closed, warding off the impending night. As she returned to her seat she glanced at the three framed photos which stood on top of the record cabinet. Two of them showed her daughter, Clare, as a baby. The other was more recent and in it, the girl was clutching a battered teddy bear, smiling happily at the camera. The picture had been taken a few months before . . .

Kim pushed the thought to one side for a moment. Was it really that painful to think about? Her ex-husband had taken the picture. Photography had always been one of his consuming passions. That and womanizing. It was true to form, Kim thought, that within ten months of becoming a professional photographer he'd run off with one of his models. Walked out on five years of marriage and memories as if he were erasing a tape. She may as well never have existed as far as he was concerned. He hadn't contested custody of Clare at the divorce proceedings, hadn't baulked at paying maintainence (a pittance anyway as far as Kim was concerned). He'd been only too glad to get the case over with and get back to his model. He hadn't even asked for visiting rights where his own child was concerned and that was one of the things which she could not understand, one of the things which made her hate him a little. The other was the blow he'd delivered to her own self-esteem. At twenty-five, Kim Nichols was a very attractive young woman with fresh, natural good looks. The soft air of sexuality she exuded was all the more potent because it was uncontrived.

She had everything that her husband's lover had, so what had made him throw away his settled family life for a fly-by-night tart? It was a question she had asked herself many times and one to which she would probably never know the answer.

She sat down, massaging the bridge of her nose between thumb and forefinger, trying to force the thoughts from her mind. They still hurt, even after two years.

'Mummy, I've finished.'

The call came from upstairs. From the bathroom.

Kim smiled and got to her feet, padding up the stairs in time to see Clare emerging onto the landing, her rabbit-motif dressing gown flapping open, her glistening blonde hair flowing behind her like a diaphanous train, reaching as far as the middle of her back.

'I cleaned my teeth,' Clare said, grinning broadly to show her handiwork.

Kim nodded approvingly and kissed the top of her daughter's head as they walked into the smaller bedroom with its brightly coloured wallpaper and mobiles hung from the ceiling. Clare clambered into bed and pulled the covers up around her neck, looking into her mother's face. Kim leant forward and kissed the child once more, but as she pulled back, Clare touched her cheek, drawing one small index finger through the single tear which had slid down from her mother's eye.

'Why are you sad, Mummy?' she asked.

'I'm not,' Kim whispered. 'People cry when they're happy, too, you know. I'm happy because I've got you and I love you.' She pulled the covers more tightly around her

47

daughter and kissed her on the forehead. 'Now, you go to sleep.'

'Were you thinking about Daddy?'

The question came so unexpectedly that Kim was momentarily speechless. She swallowed hard and then shrugged.

'No,' she lied. 'Why do you ask?'

'I think about him sometimes but I don't miss him. Not as long as you're here. You won't go away, will you, Mummy?'

Kim shook her head and hugged Clare tightly, aware of more tears trickling down her face. She hurriedly wiped them away as she stood up.

'Sleep,' she said, flicking off the bedside light. 'Love you.'

She retreated slowly from the room, pulling the door closed behind her, pausing on the landing for a moment before making her way downstairs. As she reached the hall there was a knock on the door. Kim opened it to find Inspector Wallace standing there. He smiled and reached for his I.D. card, but Kim chuckled.

'It's all right, Inspector,' she said. 'I remember who you are.'

'I did ask you if I could take a statement,' he said, almost apologetically. 'I hope I'm not interrupting anything.'

She ushered him in, through the hall to the living room. He spotted her notes lying beside the chair.

'I won't keep you a minute,' he said. 'Just a few words about what happened yesterday.'

She offered him coffee and he accepted gratefully, watching her as she walked barefoot into the kitchen. She was wearing a pair of tight-fitting jeans and a baggy jumper, the sleeves rolled up as far as the elbows. He sat down on the sofa and loosened his tie as Kim returned with the coffee and settled herself in the chair opposite, one leg drawn up beneath her.

'I'm sorry to bother you at home,' he said, 'but this won't take long.'

He had the questions prepared and as she answered them

he scribbled a few notes down. Just routine, so to speak. Tying up loose ends. All part of the job, Wallace told himself. He closed the notebook again and pocketed it as Kim went to refill the coffee mugs.

'I gather that what you found was important,' he said, sipping his drink. 'At least Mr Cooper gave that impression.'

'Yes, it is important. He thinks it's the biggest site of its kind to have been discovered this century, if you take into account the underground passages. At first we thought there were just two, but it's like a honeycomb down there. Those tunnels could stretch for miles. There's a lot of work to be done. It's a pity we won't have time to finish it.'

Wallace looked puzzled but Kim explained what Cutler had said earlier.

'Charles isn't very happy at the prospect of the dig being closed down. None of us are,' she told him, 'but there's nothing we can do if Cutler makes his mind up.'

'This is going to sound like a cliché,' he said awkwardly, 'but you're not exactly my idea of an archaeologist.'

Kim laughed and the sound seemed to brighten the room. Wallace returned her smile, his eyes held by her attractive pale blue ones.

'What would you say if I told you that you don't look like a policeman?' she said. 'You look too young. And, by the way, the photo on your I.D. card is lousy. It doesn't even look like you.'

It was his turn to laugh.

They sat in silence for a moment, then Wallace got to his feet and announced that he had to go.

'Thanks for the coffee,' he said as Kim led him to the front door. 'And the compliment.' He smiled.

'I hope that next time we talk it'll be for different reasons,' she said, her eyes sparkling in the twilight.

He nodded, thanked her again and walked out to his car.

Wallace heard the door close behind him but he didn't look round. Had he done so he might well have seen the small figure of Clare Nichols standing at one of the bedroom windows looking down at him.

Thirteen

The vein pulsed thickly, looking like a bloated worm
nestling beneath the skin. It swelled even more as the youth
tugged harder on the piece of material wrapped tightly
around the top of his arm. He opened and closed his fist,
watching as the bulging vein fattened almost to bursting
point.

It was then that he inserted the hypodermic needle.

The steel needle punctured the blood vessel and the lad
pushed it deeper, his thumb depressing the plunger of the
hypo, forcing the liquid into his body. He drained the last
dregs then pulled the needle free, ignoring the small spurt
of blood which accompanied its exit from his flesh. He
pulled off the tourniquet and clenched his fist, raising his
arm up and down from the elbow.

Gary Webb sank back on the leather sofa, his body
quivering slightly, but there was a blank smile on his face as
he handed the needle to the girl who sat beside him. She
watched him for a moment. The veins in his thick bull neck
were throbbing and his muscular chest heaved contentedly.
He looked at her, watching as she inspected the crook of
her own left arm, using her nails to pick away the three or
four scabs which had formed there. The pieces of hardened
crust came away and Laura Price slapped at the raw part of
her arm using the first two fingers of her free hand,
watching as the veins began to stand out.

Henry Dexter smiled and closed the door, leaving the
two teenagers to their own devices. Out in the corridor he
turned to face Mick Ferguson, who was taking a last drag on
his cigarette. He dropped the butt onto the polished wood
floor of the corridor and shrugged.

'That had better be good stuff,' said Dexter, eyeing the other man suspiciously.

Beside them on a table lay two small bags of white powder.

'It's the best quality heroin you're ever likely to get,' Ferguson said. 'Now, I didn't come here to pass the time of day. You owe me some money.'

Dexter picked up the bags and dropped them into the pocket of his jacket. Then he and Ferguson walked down the corridor to another room. There was an open fire burning in the grate, and the smell of woodsmoke hung in the air.

'Very cosy,' said Ferguson. 'You did well when your old man died. How much did he leave you? Two million, wasn't it? I remember reading something in the paper at the time.'

Dexter passed in front of the fire, the glowing tongues of flame momentarily illuminating his face, deepening the shadows beneath his eyes and chin. He was almost forty-five, slim and athletically built. Dressed in a well-tailored jacket and trousers, his shirt pressed and sparkling white, he looked immaculate.

'Was it two million?' Ferguson persisted.

'What difference does it make to you, Ferguson?' he said, crossing to a large wall safe hidden behind a passable copy of a Goya. It depicted a young witch having intercourse with a demon, the creature's long tongue being used to penetrate her anus. Dexter fiddled with the combination of the safe, pulled the door open and fished out some money. He also carefully placed the heroin alongside the other bags which half filled the cavity.

'It's an expensive habit,' Ferguson said, grinning.

'It is at the prices you charge,' the older man told him.

'Look, most heroin is only 55% pure by the time it hits the streets. The dealers mix it with sugar, brick dust and fucking Vim. That stuff,' he pointed to the safe, 'is 70% pure.'

Dexter nodded and held out a wad of notes.

'It's all there,' he said. 'Five hundred pounds. Count it if you like.'

51

Ferguson grinned and stuffed the money into his pocket.

'I trust you,' he replied, his attention drawn by a large dagger which hung over the fireplace, its blade glinting in the glow of the flames. He reached up and took it down, hefting it before him. On the mantelpiece there was a candlestick shaped like the head of a goat. The eyes were small rubies and the firelight made it look as if they were glowing. 'Do you really believe all this shit about witchcraft?' Ferguson wanted to know.

Dexter didn't answer, he merely fixed the other man with an unblinking stare.

'Or do you think those kids you use believe in it? Have you got one of your little ceremonies coming up again, eh? Is that why you need the heroin? To keep them interested?' He chuckled.

'Why don't you just get out of here, Ferguson?'

'How many of them are underage? Those two in the other room look pretty young'.

Dexter took a step forward but hesitated when he saw Ferguson lower the knife.

'I couldn't care less what you get up to in that wood of yours,' Ferguson said, walking past the older man. 'I don't care how many kids you turn into junkies. It's more money for me. And if that's the only way you can get them to go along with you, then fine, that's your business too.'

He stood by the French doors, gazing out into the darkness, his eyes drawn to the black smudge on the nearby hillside where the wood grew. It lay less than half a mile from the house itself. He ran his thumb slowly along the blade of the dagger, then flipped it into the air, allowing the blade and hilt to spin round before catching it safely. He handed it back to Dexter and headed for the door.

'I'll see myself out,' he said, and Dexter heard his footsteps echoing away down the corridor. He held the dagger before him, then turned and looked up at the mottled sky, where silvery clouds formed a transparent shroud over the moon.

He thought about Ferguson. Arrogant bastard!

He thought about Laura and Gary in the other room, and the others.

His followers.

He smiled crookedly. So what if they only came along for the drugs. They served their purpose. Or at any rate they would. Soon.

Henry Dexter closed and locked the wall safe. Then, replacing the dagger, he wandered off to join his two young companions in the next room.

He could already feel the erection throbbing inside his trousers.

Fourteen

The cellar was large, running beneath the entire house.

As Ferguson descended the stone steps to the lower level a musty odour of urine and straw rose to meet him. The room was empty but for what looked like a set of wall bars in one corner and, against the far wall, two steel cages. The stone floor was a strange rust-red colour. Ferguson paused by the two enclosures and smiled.

Chained inside each one was a dog.

The first was jet black, its coat thick and lustrous, but unable to disguise its powerful, brutish build. The animal was a pit bull terrier. As Ferguson knelt close to the cage it strained against its chain and began barking at him, but it was the animal in the next cage that now claimed his attention.

It was the same breed as its neighbour but much larger, more striking and more fearsome in appearance. The dog was an albino. Its thin coat was brilliant white, in stark contrast to the bloodied pink of its piercing eyes. The offspring of Ferguson's incestuous mating of its sister pup and its own father, the creature was almost insane and that madness showed in the way it launched itself at the man who had come to feed it. But Ferguson merely smiled and looked deep into those watery pink eyes, transfixed by them, still amazed at the ferocity of this particular dog. He went to a small portable fridge in one corner of the room and pulled out two metal trays, both full of raw meat.

'Those bloody dogs eat better than we do.'

He allowed himself only a perfunctory glance in the direction of the voice. Swaying uncertainly at the top of the stairs was his wife, Carol. At twenty-eight, she was four years younger than her husband, but already her face was heavily lined. What make-up she wore was clumsily applied, particularly to her lips. Heavy-breasted and a little too large around the hips, she wore a skirt that was shiny through too much wear and too tight to fasten without strain at the waist.

She watched silently as her husband laid the meat trays in front of the cages. The two dogs, aroused by the smell of food, began barking loudly.

Ferguson took a lump of the dripping raw flesh and tossed it into the albino's cage. The animal snapped it up and chewed hungrily, some of the dark juice dripping from its jaws.

Carol began a faltering journey to the cellar floor, putting out a hand to steady herself.

'What do you want?' Ferguson asked. 'Run out of booze, have you?'

She stood quietly for a moment, watching the ravenous beasts as her husband continued to feed them scraps of meat. The fetid stench of excrement and straw that filled the cellar made her cough.

'It stinks down here,' she mumbled, stepping closer to the cages, her eyes fixed on the dogs.

'Nobody asked you to come down here,' he hissed. 'Go on, piss off back to your bottle.'

'You bastard,' she rasped and tried to hit him, but

Ferguson was too quick for her. He spun round and lashed out, catching her across the face with the back of his hand. The impact of the blow sent her sprawling and, as she scrambled to her feet, she tasted blood in her mouth. The blow had loosened one of her front teeth and she prodded it tentatively with her tongue. The pain galvanized her into action, and with fists flailing she ran at Ferguson.

He grinned, as if her onslaught were some kind of challenge. He ducked under her clumsy swing and grabbed her hair, several tufts coming away in the process.

The dogs were barking madly now, making an unbearable din in the confined space of the cellar. The sound reverberated around the walls until it became deafening.

Carol screamed and struck out at her husband again but he caught her wrist, squeezing tightly, dragging her down to the floor with him. He was smiling insanely as he hauled her across the ground, and her eyes bulged in terror as she saw what he intended to do.

He guided her hand towards the bars of the albino dog's cage, laughing as the ferocious animal barked and snapped at the offered appendage.

Carol shrieked as she felt her hand touch the cold steel of the bars. She made a fist to prevent her husband from pushing the hand through but he slammed it repeatedly against the bars until her knuckles bled and her fingers went limp. The dog, already going mad in its eagerness to reach the hand, became completely frenzied at the sight of the blood which dripped from the gashed knuckles.

Carol could feel its hot breath only inches away from her, and the foul odour of it made her want to vomit.

'It'll have your fucking hand off in five seconds flat,' rasped Ferguson, keeping her pinned helplessly against the bars. 'Want me to show you?' He jerked her hand closer to the foaming jaws of the crazed dog.

Both dogs kept straining violently against their chains, and their barking seemed to grow louder and louder until Carol was aware of nothing else. She felt herself blacking out, but Ferguson pulled her head back and with his free hand tugged her away from the cage. Her blouse ripped and her large breasts were exposed. She could feel his erection pressing against her as they grappled on the floor and his hands squeezed her breasts roughly, leaving red marks around the nipples.

She tried to push him off but he was too heavy for her. She felt his other hand reaching beneath her skirt, tearing at her knickers. He ripped them off with one savage grunt and flung them aside.

'Next time I'm going to let them tear your fucking hand off,' Ferguson said, his breath coming in short gasps. He stared down at Carol and she tried one last time to slither away from him, but he pinned her beneath him with one powerful arm, releasing his bulging organ from his trousers with his free hand and then forcing her legs apart.

The black pit terrier managed to slip its chain and it slammed into the bars only inches from Carol's face, its frenzied barks ringing in her ears, its saliva spattering her.

'Looks like he wants to join us,' laughed Ferguson, and he drove into her savagely, making her shriek with the sudden sharp pain. He leant forward to kiss her and, as he did, she caught his bottom lip between her teeth and bit hard, feeling the fleshy bulge split. Blood filled her mouth and she spat it at him, but Ferguson ignored the discomfort. He pinned both her arms to the filthy floor, wet with dog urine, and pounded into her, his deep grunts of pleasure mingling in her ears with the noise of the animals.

She closed her eyes tightly as she felt him tense, then a moment later she heard his groans as he reached his climax and his thick fluid filled her, some of it spilling out to mix with the reeking mess which coated the floor.

He withdrew almost immediately, rolled off her and pushed his shrinking penis back inside his trousers.

Carol rolled onto her side, the pain from her broken tooth and the taste of blood making her feel sick. Ferguson prodded her with the toe of his boot.

'Now get out,' he chuckled. 'Go on, good dog.' He began to laugh, his raucous guffaws punctuated with threatening snarls from the two dogs.

'You're a bastard,' she grunted.
'Get out,' he rasped.
The dogs continued to bark.

Fifteen

'What is it?' Cooper wondered aloud.

'I don't know,' Perry confessed, 'but I spotted it the day we first found the skeletons.'

Kim approached the slab of stone and touched it cautiously.

'Perhaps it leads into another tunnel,' she suggested. 'Like the others.'

Most of the children's skeletons had been moved away from the slab of rock, and the three archaeologists stood within a few feet of this latest puzzle.

'We've got to move it,' Cooper said. 'At least it looks much lighter than the circular stones at the tunnel entrances.'

As he spoke, the lights in the roof of the tunnel flickered momentarily, dimming until the narrow passage was bathed in sickly yellow, and then glowed brightly once more. Kim stepped back as the two men moved forward to get a good grip on the stone. At a signal from Cooper they wedged their hands behind the rock and simply tipped it forward, surprised at the ease with which it was dislodged. Slivers broke off from the edges as it hit the floor of the tunnel.

Kim picked up one of the gas lamps lying close by and held it above her head, advancing into the yawning blackness behind the slab.

She stiffened, her body quivering almost imperceptibly as if a high voltage charge were being pumped through it. She sucked in a breath but it seemed to stick in her throat, and for terrifying seconds she found that she couldn't breathe. The skin on her face and hands puckered into goose-pimples and a numbing chill enveloped her. A small gasp escaped her as she actually felt her hair rising, standing up like a cat's hackles. She swayed uncertainly for a moment as the feeling seemed to spread through her whole body, through her very soul, and Kim clenched her teeth together, convinced that she was going to faint. On the verge of panic, she screwed up her eyes until white stars danced before her. Her throat felt constricted, as though some invisible hand were gradually tightening around it. Her head seemed to be swelling, expanding to enormous proportions until it seemed it must burst.

And somewhere, perhaps in her imagination, she thought, she heard a sound. A noise which froze her blood as it throbbed in her ears.

A distant wail of inhuman agony which rose swiftly in pitch and volume until it was transformed into something resembling malevolent laughter.

Kim felt her legs weaken and she was suddenly aware of strong arms supporting her.

The lamp fell from her grip and shattered.

Voices rushed in at her from the gloom.

' . . . Kim, can you hear me? . . .'

' . . . What happened to her? . . .'

' . . . Fainted . . .'

Everything swam before her, as if she were looking through a heat haze. Gradually, objects and faces took on a familiar clarity once more.

'Kim, are you all right?' Cooper asked, feeling the deathlike cold which seemed to have penetrated her flesh.

'I must have fainted,' she said. 'Blacked out for a second . . .' Her voice trailed off.

They sat her on the ground for a moment and she rubbed a hand over the back of her neck in an effort to massage away the dull ache which had settled there. After a moment or two it began to disappear.

'I'm sorry,' she said. 'I don't know what happened.' She smiled weakly, almost embarrassed at the little episode. Then, more sombrely, she asked, 'Did you hear that noise?'

'What noise?' asked Perry.

She opened her mouth to speak, to try to describe the keening wail, but then thought better of it. She must have imagined it, or perhaps it had been the sudden outrushing of the air inside the . . .

Inside the what?

What was this place anyway?

As she regained her senses, she, like her two companions, gazed around at their latest discovery.

'What the hell is this?' murmured Perry, playing his torch beam through the gloom.

They were standing inside a chamber of some kind. It was roughly ten feet square, resembling an underground cell. But the walls were completely covered, every square inch of them, with symbols and hieroglyphics. Many were obscured by dirt and grime but they were there nonetheless, carved into the rocks and dirt. But it wasn't the symbols which captured Kim's attention. She swallowed hard, unable to remove her gaze from the sight before her.

The entire room was littered with skulls.

Hundreds of them.

And from their size they obviously belonged to children.

'So this is where they hid them,' Cooper said, his thoughts travelling the same route as Kim's. 'The bodies in the tunnel, the heads in here.'

'It doesn't look like a burial chamber,' Perry offered. 'Besides, what is all this writing on the walls?'

As well as the skulls, the chamber contained a number of swords and spears, a few pots and some other receptacles. But it was a pile of stone tablets which now attracted Kim's attention.

Lying amongst the other relics, each one was about six

inches long, hewn from heavy rock and inscribed with a series of letters, many indistinguishable because of the dirt which caked them. There were a dozen of them.

'This place obviously belonged to the *áes dana*, the wise men of the tribe,' said Cooper. 'Maybe we'll find some answers here.'

'These stone tablets,' Kim said, 'I'd like to take them back to the museum with me, see if I can decipher what's written on them. I'll get a box and load them up.'

'Are you sure you feel OK, Kim?' Perry wanted to know.

She smiled, appreciating his concern.

'I'm fine,' she told him. 'Maybe all this excitement is getting to me.' She laughed humourlessly, rubbing a hand through her blonde hair.

As she did, she noticed that her hand was shaking.

'Charles, could you get someone to load up those tablets so I can get going?' she asked.

Cooper seemed not to hear her. He was gazing at the writing on the wall of the chamber.

'Charles,' Kim called again.

He finally managed to tear his attention from what he was reading, but as he looked at her she saw that his face was pale.

He looked vague for a moment, his thoughts elsewhere.

'Charles, the stone tablets.'

'I'll see to it. You leave now,' Cooper told her, a newly found urgency in his voice.

Kim looked puzzled as, once more, he turned his back on her, his eyes scanning the ancient words before him.

She shuddered involuntarily, feeling as if the horde of skulls were watching her with those gaping eye sockets. A wave of nausea, powerful and unexpected, hit her and she shot out a hand to support herself, her head spinning. She felt her legs weaken, and for a moment wondered if she was going to fall again. Perry put out a hand to steady her, feeling the perspiration that covered her skin. She closed her eyes tightly, fighting back the stomach contractions, gritting her teeth against this new onslaught.

Kim sucked in several shallow breaths and the feeling

began to pass. Perry released his supporting hand, alarmed by the ghostly pallor her skin had taken on, but she waved him away.

'I'm all right,' she said. 'Really.'

Cooper looked on impassively as she turned and made her way back down the tunnel, the light from her torch gradually disappearing.

As she reached the base of the rope ladder she paused again, listening.

Like a long-forgotten memory dredged up from the back of her mind, she heard again that high pitched wail of agony gradually dying away until it sounded like soft, menacing laughter.

Sixteen

There was little traffic on the road leading into Longfield. It was never a busy route, and at this early hour Kim found that she had the road virtually to herself. The clock on the dashboard showed 7:46 a.m.

Rain, which had begun as drizzle, was now pelting down in large droplets which exploded with such force on the windscreen that the wipers had difficulty keeping it clear.

Kim shivered as she drove, telling herself it was the inclement weather that was making her feel so cold. The heater was turned up high and still the chill persisted. She slowed down, reached into the pocket of her jacket and pulled on a pair of woollen gloves.

In the back of the Land Rover the wooden crates were securely tied down. Each one held a precious cargo of relics. She glanced into the rear-view mirror and looked at the two on top of the pile, one carrying some of the bones they'd found in the tunnel, the other filled with the stone tablets. Perry had indeed found twelve of them and each had been carefully packed in the box so that Kim could get them back to the museum in Longfield undamaged.

She drove past a sign which told her that the town was now less than a mile away.

Kim swung the Land Rover around a corner, stepping on the brake when she saw a tractor lumbering towards her, towing a seed distributor. The Massey-Ferguson was about a hundred yards from her, but on such a slippery road, Kim was taking no chances. She pressed down harder on the brake.

Nothing happened.

The Land Rover continued speeding along in top gear, the needle on the speedometer nudging forty-five.

Kim pumped the brake pedal repeatedly, the breath catching in her throat.

Still the vehicle did not slow down.

She was less than seventy yards away from the tractor now.

Kim looked frantically through the misted windscreen, trying to catch a glimpse of the tractor driver, trying to warn him that she was unable to stop. He was just a blur in the rain.

She drove her foot down as hard as she could, feeling the pedal touch the floor.

The Land Rover sped on.

Fifty yards away.

She banged her hooter, trying to warn the farmer to pull off the road, at the same time motioning madly with one hand.

The tractor kept coming.

Forty yards.

She reached for the gear-stick, trying to change down into first, to stop the vehicle that way, but it was useless.

Twenty yards.

If only she could guide the runaway vehicle into one of the banks on either side of the road, she thought, perhaps she could bring it to a halt. But she was travelling too fast and the banks were steep. If she didn't plough straight into one, then the momentum might well send the Land Rover flying into the air, or overturn it. Or . . .

Ten yards, and now the tractor driver was turning his own bulky vehicle, finally aware that a collision was inevitable.

Kim grabbed the handbrake and wrenched it up. Even that did nothing to halt the breakneck progress of the Land Rover. She thought about jumping, but travelling at over forty-five she stood a pretty fair chance of killing herself.

She heard the tractor's hooter blaring out a warning and she crossed her arms on the wheel, waiting for the impact, thrusting her foot one last time down on the brake.

The Land Rover skidded to a halt, its rear end spinning round and coming to rest gently against the radiator grille of the tractor.

For long seconds Kim remained hunched over the wheel, her head bowed. Slowly she straightened up, her heart thudding in her chest.

The driver of the tractor was already out of his cab, scuttling across the rain-lashed road towards her.

She opened her door and stumbled out, her face drained of colour.

'What the hell happened?' he said to her. His anger and fear largely dissipated when he saw how haggard Kim looked.

'My brakes . . .' she murmured, leaning against the bonnet of the Land Rover. A wave of nausea swept over her and her legs almost buckled under her. The tractor driver watched as she gulped down several deep lungfuls of air. 'I'm sorry,' she said, quietly.

'We'd both have been sorry if you hadn't stopped in time,' the driver said.

Kim nodded slowly and wiped some rain from her face.

'How much further have you got to go?' the driver asked. She told him.

'Will you be all right?'

She was already climbing back into the Land Rover, starting the engine. There was a roar as she stepped on the accelerator.

'I'll be OK,' Kim assured him. She let the vehicle roll forward a few yards and then stepped on the brake.

The vehicle stopped immediately.

She pulled at her bottom lip with one thumb and forefinger, looking first at the speedometer, then at the brake pedal.

'Are the brakes working now?' the farmer asked, his hair plastered to his face by the rain.

Kim nodded abstractedly.

'Yes,' she said in surprise. 'They're working.'

As the farmer watched, the Land Rover pulled away and a moment later it had disappeared around the next bend.

He looked at the dark skid marks on the road before him and shook his head. He found that he too was shaking.

Longfield Museum was a large, modern building that looked more like an office complex than a storehouse for ancient artifacts.

The smoked-glass exterior reflected a mirror-image of the Land Rover as Kim parked close to the main entrance. She switched off the engine and sat silently for a moment, breathing deeply. The rain had eased off somewhat and she had wound down both front windows to let in some fresh air. This had helped to dispel the unpleasant fusty odour inside the vehicle which irritated her throat and nose.

The chill remained.

After a moment or two she climbed out of the Land Rover and strode towards the main entrance. There was a pushbike chained to the bicycle rack with a sticker on it that read SPEED MACHINE.

Kim pushed open the double doors and walked into the almost unnatural silence of the main hall. A large plan of the museum faced her, and on each wall blue signs pointed to various galleries. She turned to the left, heading for the door marked STAFF ONLY. Her heels beat out a loud tattoo on the lino as she walked but the sound was muffled by carpet as she stepped inside the room.

It was a large room with cupboards and filing cabinets

covering the walls on three sides. At the far end was a stainless steel worktop and sink and another door.

The room was empty as Kim walked through it to the door at the other end. She turned the handle, expecting it to be locked, but it opened easily.

It led to a second, smaller room which contained three or four work benches and, in one corner, the pride of the museum, an electron microscope.

On one of the worktops Kim caught sight of a steaming mug of coffee. She'd seen Roger Kelly's bike outside, so the coffee probably belonged to him. Kelly had to be around somewhere. Kim turned and headed back through the staff room, pulling open the door which led out into the main hall.

The figure loomed before her with such suddenness that she jumped back a foot or two, her heart thumping.

'I didn't know I looked that bad first thing in the morning,' Roger Kelly said, grinning.

'I wondered where the hell you were,' Kim told him, sucking in deep breaths, trying to regain her composure.

'You look as if you've seen a ghost,' he told her, noticing how pale she was. 'Are you all right?'

She thought about mentioning the incident with the Land Rover but decided against it.

'I've got some material in the back of the Land Rover,' Kim told him. 'Help me get it inside, will you, Roger?'

He nodded and followed her out to the parked vehicle, watching as she unlocked the back and motioned to the box which contained the stone tablets.

Kelly got a firm grip on the box and lifted, surprised at the weight.

'What have you got in here?' he grunted. 'Gold bars?' Roger Kelly was a powerfully built, muscular young man yet to reach his twenty-third birthday, but the effort of carrying the box appeared to be too much for him. Kim watched anxiously as he stumbled toward the main entrance of the museum, straining under the weight. For a second it looked as though he would drop the box, but after a moment he regained his handhold and struggled on. Kim collected the box containing the skeleton and followed him.

Once inside, they placed both boxes on the worktop. Kelly stood to one side gasping for breath. Kim looked at him, noticing how pale his own face was now, as if all the colour had been sucked from it. After a few moments, she and Kelly returned to the Land Rover to retrieve the remaining boxes, which contained some other relics from the dig.

'We've got to run nitrogen tests on these,' she told him when they were back inside, motioning to the first two boxes. Crossing to the one containing the skeleton, she carefully removed the lid and peered inside.

'Where's the skull?' asked Kelly, puzzled.

Kim explained briefly about the chamber full of skulls, then set about freeing the lid on the other box. Kelly helped, pulling the nails free with a claw hammer. Kim lifted it clear and pulled back the gauze in which the stone tablets had been wrapped.

'We found these with the skulls,' she told him. 'They've got to be dated before we start to decipher this writing.' She indicated the Celtic script which covered each slab of stone.

Kelly nodded and helped her carefully remove each one, laying it on a sheet of plastic which Kim had spread out on the worktop. As he removed the last one Kelly looked down into the box, and once more Kim saw the colour drain from his face. She glanced at him, then down into the box.

The wood on the bottom and sides was scorched almost black.

As if it had been subjected to a powerful source of heat.

Seventeen

Kim sat back on the stool and glanced down at her notepad. Page after page was covered by her neat jottings, some of the phrases underlined.

She sighed and reached up to massage the back of her neck. A dull ache had settled there and threatened to develop into a painful stiffness. She got to her feet and walked up and down for a few minutes, her eyes every so often drawn back to the electron microscope as if by powerful magnets.

The tests were complete. At least those she intended finishing before leaving for home. For nearly nine hours since returning to the museum that morning, she had been working on the relics. Examining the bones, the stone tablets, the coins, the weapons and God knew how many more of the finds. The carbon-14 test had been completed, as had the nitrogen test. The bones were over 2,000 years old, and as far as she could ascertain, they came from the same period as the rest of the relics.

Then there were the tablets.

She'd chipped a tiny fragment of one of them away and ground it up with a pestle and mortar, examining the minute fragments beneath the electron microscope in a test more commonly used on fossils. The petrological microscopy had revealed something which Kim had not expected and it had been nagging at her ever since.

The tablets were much older than the rest of the relics.

All twelve were at least five hundred to a thousand years older than the other artifacts she had examined. It was as if they had been buried by another tribe generations before.

Buried or hidden?

She went to the worktop where the tablets were laid out and prodded one with a small tracer. The chisel-like implement followed a path through the groove which had been fashioned into a letter. She wondered how long it would take her to decipher the writing on the small slabs.

Why the time difference between the tablets and the other relics? she wondered.

As she sat gazing at them there was a knock on the door.

'Come in,' called Kim, turning to see who her visitor was.

Roger Kelly stepped into the room.

'Everyone else has gone home,' he told her. 'I was going to lock up if you'd finished.'

'Yes,' Kim sighed. 'I've finished for today. I don't think I'm going to get any further just staring at all this stuff.' She crossed to the sink and began washing her hands beneath the hot tap. Kelly paused beside the worktop and looked at the stone tablets.

'Have you got any idea what the writings mean?' he asked as Kim dried her hands.

'None at all,' she confessed. 'But I haven't studied them yet.'

'Maybe they're Celtic commandments,' he said, chuckling.

'You could be right,' Kim agreed, also managing a smile.

Kelly began picking up some of the relics and replacing them in a box, being careful not to damage any of the artifacts. He closed the box and carried it toward one of the wall cupboards.

Kim looked across at the tablets once more, wrinkling her nose as she detected a strange smell. Alien and yet somehow familiar. Kelly, preoccupied with putting away the box of fragile relics, seemed not to notice the odour. He reached up to open the cupboard door, but it seemed to be stuck.

The smell, growing stronger, almost made Kim cough. A pungent, nauseating odour like . . . like burnt plastic?

Plastic.

She went to the worktop for a closer look.

The sheet of transparent plastic on which the tablets lay was turning a sickly yellowish-brown.

Mouth open in amazement, Kim turned toward Kelly. As she did so, the cupboard door flew open and she saw the bottle of nitric acid topple from the upper shelf.

It hit the young man in the face and shattered.

The corrosive liquid spilled onto his head and face, some of it splashing down his chest.

He dropped the box of relics, both hands clutching at his face, a scream of agony rising from his throat.

Kim ran towards him as he dropped to his knees, wailing helplessly, the deadly fluid puddling around him. But there was nothing she could do.

The action of the liquid was terrifyingly swift. As if someone had thrust a blowtorch at him, Kelly's face was instantly stripped of skin. His eyes rapidly dissolved into seething mush as the acid went to work on them, the pupils and whites merely disappearing. As he screamed in pain the acid trickled into his mouth and ate through his tongue, even dissolving the enamel of his teeth. A purple foam dribbled over lips which were little more than bubbling blisters. All over his face sores rose, then burst as more flesh was stripped away. The lobe of one ear was seared off in the agonizing deluge and his nostrils seemed to widen as his nose was pulped by the acid. Blood burst from exposed veins which, seconds later, were themselves corroded into charcoal.

Kim watched frozen in horror as a thick white plume of smoky vapour rose from Kelly's head. He fell forward, his body jerking uncontrollably, his screams dying away to gurgles as some of the acid slid down his throat and dissolved his vocal chords.

Skin came away in slippery chunks as he clawed at his face with hands now ravaged by a dozen blisters. His clothes and part of his chest were also being attacked by the lethal fluid, but soon Kelly would feel no more pain. His movements quickly grew feeble and then ceased. He was unconscious.

Kim recoiled from the stench of corrupted flesh. She gritted her teeth as she looked at the streaming ruin which had been Kelly's face. Blood mingled with liquescent skin and melting bone to form a reeking gelatinous mask.

She spun round, racing into the other room for the phone. With a trembling hand she jabbed out three nines and managed to blurt out that she needed an ambulance.

As she was about to replace the receiver she heard a sound which froze her blood.

A high-pitched, inhuman wail which drummed in her ears for interminable seconds.

It was identical to the sound she'd heard upon entering the chamber of skulls the previous day.

Had it come across the phone line or had she imagined it?

She dropped the receiver and blundered back into the lab, almost stumbling over the prostrate form of Kelly. She prayed that the ambulance would hurry, that he was still alive.

Her eyes flickered back and forth.

To Kelly.

To the stone tablets.

And to the plastic sheet on which they lay.

Shrivelled and contracted.

As if it had been burned.

Eighteen

'I don't know why we couldn't have stayed in the car,' Sue Hagen said. 'It's freezing out here.'

'Country air is supposed to be good for you,' David Christie reminded her.

A light breeze rustled the trees of the wood, stirring the fallen leaves which already carpeted the ground.

'Anyway,' said David, 'I thought you liked it in the open air.'

'I do when it's a nice sunny day. Not in the middle of the night,' Sue said indignantly.

'Well, I like it anytime,' he told her, grabbing one of her small breasts. 'I'll soon warm you up.'

Sue giggled, then gripped his testicles, squeezing hard. 'You're supposed to be gentle,' she said, smiling.

David winced; his privates were quite sensitive enough without that kind of attention. He yelped in pain and she released her hold.

'How do you know about this place, anyway?' Sue asked as they wandered deeper into the wood.

'I've been out here a couple of times with my mates,' he informed her. 'We used to bring our air rifles here. Got a couple of rabbits once.'

'That's cruel,' she told him. muttering as she snagged her sleeve on a low branch. 'Oh, God, how much further? My clothes will be ruined.'

'How far do you want to go?' he asked, pulling her close to him and stealing a brief kiss. She tasted the warmth of his tongue and wanted more. She gripped the back of his neck and pulled him to her, kissing more deeply. As they pressed together she could feel his erection pushing against her thigh and she reached down to rub it through the material of his trousers. David responded by sliding one hand up inside her short leather skirt. his fingers first gliding over the soft material of her stockings before brushing bare skin. He probed further, eagerly stroking the crutch of her knickers, feeling the coils of pubic hair pressed tightly against the sheer fabric.

'This is far enough, Dave,' she whispered, leaning back against a tree.

They kissed long and hard, each one's tongue deeply probing the other's mouth. Sue let out a slight gasp as she felt him push her long brown hair away from her neck and nip the flesh with his teeth. He repeated the action on the other side of her neck. She slid both hands inside his shirt and massaged his chest and back with firm quick strokes, concentrating on the small of his back and the area just above his belt. After two years together they knew each other's wants and needs perfectly, at least in a physical sense. Both of them had experienced sex before during their twenty years but neither had found it so stimulating with anyone else. Both were unemployed and had plenty of time for sex, but it had not yet lost its novelty value for either of them. In fact, if anything, it was getting better.

As Sue surrendered to the feelings coursing through her, she thought briefly of what her parents would say if they knew she was with David. Neither of them liked him very much, unlike her elder sister's boyfriend. Now he was a 'nice' boy. More their type.

Their type, she thought irritably. It wasn't them who had to spend time with him. But her sister, Barbara, could do no wrong. *She* had a job, and her wonderful bloody boyfriend went to university. It was a match made in heaven as far as her parents were concerned. Barbara hadn't been arrested for smoking pot when she was seventeen. Barbara hadn't cost them three hundred pounds for an abortion when she was nineteen.

Barbara hadn't done anything, had she? It was always Sue.

The vision of her parents faded as Sue felt David's roving tongue flicking its way down between her breasts while his hands skilfully unfastened the buttons of her blouse. She wore no bra and he found her small breasts firm and eager for his touch. He flicked at the swollen nipples, drawing each one in turn between his teeth, rolling his tongue around the stiff cones of flesh.

He knelt on the damp earth, unzipping her skirt, smiling as she wriggled out of it and thrust her pelvis towards him. He nuzzled her mound through her knickers, tasting the moisture which was seeping through the flimsy silk. He pulled the gusset to one side and slipped his tongue into her moist cleft, gripping her hips as she moaned with pleasure and ground herself hard against his face.

After a moment or two he straightened up and released his own throbbing member from his trousers. Sue took it eagerly in one hand, rubbing the swollen shaft, feeling the bloated veins which ran along the top. Then, eager to feel him inside her, she guided his stiffness into her vagina, gasping loudly as he penetrated her. She clasped her hands on his buttocks, urging him into a rhythm which, within minutes, had both of them approaching orgasm.

David felt something wet touch his shoulder.

He pulled his head back slightly and saw that Sue's head was pressed back against the tree, her eyes closed, both her hands fastened around his thrusting buttocks.

He thought that it must be rain.

Sue raised one stocking-clad leg and hooked it around the small of his back, allowing him deeper penetration. Her hands slipped lower, cupping his testicles, kneading the swollen ovoids, trying to coax his semen free. It would not be long now. He felt the unmistakable warm glow beginning to spread through his lower body.

Again he felt a droplet of moisture hit his shoulder, only this time it trickled down his chest, leaving a dark stain.

It took him only a second to realize that it was blood.

Suddenly frightened, David tried to slow his pace, to pull Sue away from beneath the tree, from whatever was dripping blood onto them, but even as a dark globule landed on her left breast she seemed oblivious to his urgency, mistaking it for something else.

Once more he tried to pull away but Sue, her voice a throaty whisper, urged him on.

'Don't stop, please, Dave,' she gasped, grinding harder against him. 'I'm coming!' She threw her head back and cried out her pleasure, her eyes open wide.

At that moment she saw the remains of the goat jammed into the branches above.

Still quivering from the fury of her orgasm, Sue opened her mouth to scream. As she did so, a thick clot of congealed blood dropped from the butchered carcass and splashed between her lips.

Gagging violently, she pulled away from David and dropped to her knees, her stomach contracting until a stream of vomit erupted from her blood-filled mouth.

David too staggered away from the tree, his eyes riveted to the bloodied remains of the animal, his own revulsion now growing.

Sue tried again to scream as she saw the drops of blood on her body and on David but the sound became a gurgle as a fresh wave of sickness swept over her. She saw David overbalance and trip over something hidden beneath a pile of leaves.

His hand sank into something cold and soft and it was his turn to shriek as he withdrew his arm and lifted it into view. His hand was covered in blood and there were pieces of thick, coiled tube hanging from it. It was the intestines of the goat that lay buried beneath the fallen leaves. The blood had blackened and congealed into a treacly mush which coated David's hand. The sight of it made him gag.

Half-naked, Sue and David struggled to their feet and bolted from the clearing, crashing headlong through the tangled undergrowth in their effort to escape the fear and revulsion they felt.

In the inky blackness of the dense wood another shape stirred now. But this one moved quietly, stealthily.

Nineteen

The ground felt soft, almost bog-like, as Inspector Wallace made his way through the trees and bushes, a cigarette dangling from one corner of his mouth. It was unlit. His lighter wasn't working and he'd not been able to find anyone with so much as a match. He chewed on the filter and muttered to himself as he snagged the sleeve of his jacket on a gorse bush.

Even in the light of early morning the wood still cast long, thick shadows, and the dew-soaked leaves which coated the ground squelched beneath his feet as he walked.

Ahead of him, Constable Mark Buchanan moved sure-footedly through the trees, occasionally holding back a branch for his superior. He let go of one a little too early and it swung back and hit Wallace across the chest. The constable apologized but Wallace merely dismissed the incident, smiling when he saw the look of fear on Buchanan's face. The junior man was about twenty-eight, two years younger than Wallace. He was thin and gangling with a pale complexion which made him appear as though he were permanently ill.

'I wouldn't have called you out normally, sir,' he said, apologetically, as they approached the clearing. 'But I think this is important.'

As they reached the clearing, Wallace saw two more uniformed men standing by a gnarled oak tree. He recognized them as Greene and Denton. One of them was holding a large black dustbin bag and looking up into the branches of the tree, his face grim. The other was merely staring into space as if looking at something which only he could see. Both men snapped upright as Wallace entered the clearing.

'So what have you got?' he said to Buchanan, finally taking the unlit cigarette from his mouth.

The constable motioned to the lower branches of the tree and Wallace looked up.

The goat, at least what remained of it, looked little more than an empty husk. The stomach cavity had been slit open and the internal organs removed. Wallace saw those lying in a reeking pile close by. Flies were already feasting on the congealed mess. For a moment, Wallace wondered why the dead animal looked so sickly pink in colour, then he realized with disgust that it had been flayed. Every last piece of fur had been stripped away, exposing the wasted muscles beneath. What drew his attention most was the stump of the neck. A piece of bone shone whitely through the blackened gore.

'Where's the head?' he asked.

Greene stepped forward and opened the dustbin bag, allowing his superior to look inside. The stench which rose from within was unbelievable.

The head lay in the bottom of the bag, one horn broken, the eye sockets choked with thick clots of blood.

Both eyes had been removed.

Wallace coughed, then nodded, and Greene closed the bag.

'It's not the first time this has happened,' Buchanan told him. 'In the last two months we've had reports from two local farmers saying that they've lost livestock, mostly goats and sheep. So far six have turned up, all of them skinned and gutted. Five of those we've found in this wood.'

'Did the others have their eyes torn out like this one?' the inspector asked, hooking a thumb in the direction of the black bag.

The constable nodded.

'It's not just livestock, though,' Buchanan continued. 'A number of household pets like cats and dogs have been reported missing too, but we haven't found any of *them* yet.'

'Could it be kids, Inspector?' asked Greene.

'It's possible,' Wallace said reflectively. 'But I can't think of many kids capable of doing something like this to animals. Not animals as big as goats or sheep anyway.' He sighed. 'Well, one thing's for sure, whoever did it doesn't work for the bloody RSPCA.' He glanced up at the butchered goat once more. 'Were the other carcasses as easy to find as this one? It looks like whoever did it wanted it to be found.'

'They were all found in or around this clearing,' Buchanan told him.

Wallace stroked his chin thoughtfully.

'Bury it,' he said. 'Get rid of the carcass and the head and . . . those.' He nodded in the direction of the intestines, still partially covered with dead leaves. 'Six in two months, eh?' he said, quietly, reaching for his lighter. He tried again to light his cigarette but still could raise only sparks from the recalcitrant flint. He pocketed the lighter again, looking irritably at the unlit cigarette.

'I'm going to drive out to Dexter Grange, have a word with the bloke who owns the place,' the inspector announced. 'He might have seen something. His house is only a mile or so away.'

'Henry Dexter?' said Constable Greene. 'He lives like a hermit. Never leaves the house, I hear.'

'Well, then, a visitor will make a change for him, won't it?' Wallace said, trudging off through the trees. 'Besides,' he muttered to himself, 'he might have a light.'

The inspector put away the cigarette once more and headed for his car.

Twenty

Wallace lit the cigarette from the lighter inside the car. He pushed it between his lips and sucked hard, enjoying the hot, comforting sensation as he swallowed the smoke. He had the front windows open, allowing the breeze to circulate inside the Sierra. It went some way to dispelling the smell of Chinese food left over from the previous night. The fresh-air ball which hung from the rear-view mirror had long since ceased to function.

The trees on the right-hand side of the road gradually gave way to a high stone wall topped at regular intervals by ornate carvings, most of which carried a patina of mould. A lion. A unicorn. And, perched on either side of the main gates, two eagles. Wallace swung the Sierra across the road and guided it up the long drive which led to Dexter Grange.

The house was clearly visible as soon as he passed through the gate, built as it was on a slight rise. It was an imposing place, Wallace had to admit. It reminded him of a stately home. As he drew closer he slowed down, stubbing the cigarette out in the ashtray. There was a large gravelled area in front of the house and the policeman was surprised to see a Jensen parked there. He brought his own car to a halt and climbed out, adjusting his tie and running one hand through his dark hair before approaching the main door. He reached out and banged with the huge brass knocker three times.

He waited a moment, then lifted the intricately carved metal object once more. Before he could knock again, the door opened a fraction.

Wallace found himself facing a rather bewildered-looking young girl.

Laura Price looked him up and down slowly and smiled.

'My name's Wallace,' he said, producing his I.D. card. 'I'd like to speak to Mr Dexter if I can.'

He saw her smile fade as she stepped back into the house. She wore jeans and a voluminous grey sweatshirt with the sleeves pulled up past her elbows.

'Police?' she said, hurriedly tugging the sleeves down over her forearms.

He nodded, frowning as he caught a vague glimpse of the scars on the inside of her left arm.

'Come in,' Laura said, opening the door, careful to avoid his gaze. 'You'll have to wait, though. He's got someone with him.'

The inspector stepped inside the hall, eyeing the girl suspiciously.

The walls were oak-panelled, completely bare, not a single picture or ornament to be seen. The ceiling curved up to a great height, giving the hall the appearance of an immaculately kept mausoleum. The floor, also dark wood, was devoid of carpet. A number of doors, all closed, led off from the corridor along which Laura escorted him.

'What's your name?' he asked.

'I thought you wanted to speak to Mr Dexter,' Laura said curtly.

'I do. I also asked what your name is.'

She told him almost grudgingly, aware of his eyes on her as she led him into a room and invited him to sit down. The room was pleasantly bright, with French windows looking out onto the driveway. There was no carpet here either, but there were paintings on the wall and two or three carvings on the mantel over the marble fireplace.

'How old are you?' he wanted to know.

'Look, have I done something wrong?'

'Just tell me. How old are you?'

'Eighteen,' she lied. 'And before you ask, I've left school. I'm Mr Dexter's friend. I do jobs for him.'

'That sounds cosy,' said Wallace. 'What sort of jobs?'

'Well,' she said guardedly, 'mostly errands and things. I do his shopping. He doesn't like to go into town.'

Wallace crossed to the fireplace and examined one of the carvings there. It was a male figure, the penis erect and disproportionately large. The one next to it was of a woman bending over. There was a large hole hollowed out between the legs. The policeman guessed that both pieces were made from ivory. He didn't attempt to estimate their value.

'Very tasteful,' he said sarcastically, fitting the two figures together. 'I had to make do with Lego when I was a kid.'

'I don't think Mr Dexter would like it if he knew you'd been playing about with those pieces. They're very valuable.' She turned and headed for the door, pausing as she reached it. 'I don't know how long he'll be,' she said, and with that, she was gone.

Wallace stood beside the fireplace a moment longer, then wandered over to the huge bookcase which covered most of the wall to his right. The inspector scanned the titles of some of the volumes, noticing that many were roughly bound, as if Dexter had done the binding himself, with titles handwritten in ink:

SATANISM TODAY

DEMONOLOGY

PAGAN RITES – THE NEW RELIGION

NECROPHILIA AND BESTIALITY

Wallace paused at one in particular and lifted it down from the shelf.

SACRIFICE AND POWER was neatly inscribed on the spine. The policeman flipped open the cover and scanned the closely-written A4 sheets. The volume was at least two inches thick, the words crammed together as if space was at a premium. He wondered how long it had taken Dexter to complete so much work. Wallace glanced through a chapter headed RITUAL SLAUGHTER, then replaced the volume and walked towards the centre of the room, his shoes echoing on the hardwood floor.

He heard voices, low and muffled at first.

Wallace paused, trying to locate the direction from which they came.

He heard the voices again, louder this time, more forceful.

The inspector strode to the door, realizing that the sounds were coming from the room across the corridor. He stood motionless for a moment, then slowly turned the handle, opened the door a crack and peered out.

The corridor was empty.

The sound of raised voices was much clearer now, though. Wallace detected anger in one of them. He crossed the corridor and pressed his ear to the door opposite, trying to make sense of the conversation.

' . . . the land isn't yours, you have no right . . .'

'*You* have no right, Mr Dexter. I have the deeds with me and . . .'

'I don't care about legal documents, that land has always belonged to my family . . .'

'I'm afraid that doesn't entitle you to any claim on it now. If you'd look at these deeds . . .'

Wallace frowned, wondering who Dexter was talking to. He didn't recognize the voice, but whoever it was, he seemed to be growing as angry as Dexter himself.

' . . . the wood will be flattened, with or without your cooperation, Mr Dexter.'

The wood.

Wallace chewed his lip contemplatively. Did they mean *that* wood?

'Get out of my house, Cutler . . .'

The inspector stepped back.

Cutler. The land developer. So that was who Dexter was arguing with. The policeman heard the sounds of footsteps from inside the room. He scuttled back across the corridor, stepping into the library but leaving the door slightly ajar.

A moment later he heard the door on the other side of the corridor burst open and slam back against the wall.

'Get out and take your bloody deeds with you, Cutler.'

The policeman pressed his eye close to the door and caught sight of Cutler and Dexter facing one another.

'I came here to try and talk this situation through reasonably,' the property developer said in a quieter tone. 'It's obvious that I overestimated your ability to hold a sensible conversation.'

'Don't patronize me, Cutler. Get out of here and stay away from my wood,' snarled Dexter.

'It isn't *yours*. It never has been.'

'I'm warning you,' Dexter said, taking a step towards the other man.

Cutler was unimpressed. He merely turned and walked towards the main door, his back to Dexter.

'I'll see myself out,' he said, closing the door gently as Dexter stood glaring angrily after him.

Wallace waited a moment, then stepped out of the room.

'I hope I haven't come at a bad time,' he said, smiling.

'Who the hell are you?' Dexter exclaimed, spinning round.

Wallace introduced himself.

The older man was silent for a moment, running appraising eyes over Wallace, aware that his own face was still flushed with anger from the row with Cutler.

'I'd like a word with you, if it's not inconvenient,' Wallace continued.

Dexter, regaining his composure, ushered the policeman into his study where they sat down opposite one another.

Wallace told him about the discovery of the dead goat and the other animals that had been found in the wood.

'Is that wood part of your land, Mr Dexter?' he asked finally.

'Technically, no, but my family have owned all the other land around this house for hundreds of years, and the wood was always considered part of our property by the local people. That wood is as much mine as the ground out there, if centuries of tradition mean anything. He motioned towards a large expanse of lawn right outside the window. 'Despite what Cutler says,' he added, almost as an afterthought.

'I overheard your disagreement, but coming back to what I said about the slaughtered animals, have you any idea how the carcasses ended up in the wood?'

'You're the policeman, Wallace.'

'What about the girl who lives with you? Might she know?'

Dexter shot the inspector a wary glance.

'No,' he said flatly.

'I hope she's older than she looks, Dexter. She tells me she's eighteen. Do her parents know she's here?'

'She has no parents. I suppose you could say I'm the only family she's got.' He grinned crookedly.

'How touching.'

There was a heavy silence between the two men, finally broken by Wallace.

'Why does that wood mean so much to you?' he wanted to know.

'I don't want builders ruining land less than a mile from my house,' the older man said.

'That doesn't answer my question.'

'It's been part of the landscape for centuries. Cutler has no right to destroy it. It's as simple as that.'

Wallace got to his feet and headed for the study door.

'I hope you're right about that girl's age,' he said cryptically, then closed the door behind him. Dexter listened as the sound of his footsteps echoed down the corridor. A moment later Laura entered.

'What did he want?' she asked.

'He wanted to know if I knew anything about dead animals in the wood. He also was curious about you.'

She looked suddenly afraid.

'Don't worry,' Dexter said reassuringly. 'He doesn't know anything. Besides, it's not the police who are the problem now. It's that bastard Cutler.' He leant back in his seat, his eyes gazing ahead, full of anger.

Twenty-One

The lights flickered, then went out.

In the tunnel, George Perry looked up toward the string of light bulbs, muttering under his breath as he stood enveloped in darkness.

He waited, and a moment later the tunnel was filled with a dull yellow light once more.

'I think that generator's on the blink,' he said, lifting the sword carefully from the earth. He glanced at the hilt, which was fashioned in the shape of a man with arms and legs spread wide. The archaeologists had found many of these anthropomorphic designs on sword and dagger hilts.

Ian Russell shivered, rubbing his exposed forearms briskly.

'It's so bloody cold down here,' he said, making a note of the latest find.

Perry was forced to agree.

'Where's Charles?' he asked.

'In the chamber with the skulls,' Russell told him. 'He's hardly left it since it was discovered.'

'I don't know how he stands it down here for hours at a time,' Russell continued. 'It gets claustrophobic after a while.'

Perry looked at his colleague.

'I've noticed the same thing,' he said. 'Up until a couple of days ago enclosed spaces never bothered me, but working down here . . .' He allowed the sentence to trail off as the lights flickered once more.

This time the power was not restored immediately.

'I'm going to have a look at that blasted generator,' said

Perry, getting to his feet. He rubbed his hands together, removing the dust and dirt. He set off back towards the shaft and started clambering up the rope ladder. As he did so he felt as if his legs were made of lead. Each step up seemed a monumental effort, as if all the strength had been sucked from him. Halfway up he actually groaned aloud and stood still, sucking in lungfuls of air so cold it seared his throat and made him feel as if he were being strangled.

The lights finally came back on, and in the muted glow Perry saw that his hands had turned a vivid shade of blue, as if they were badly bruised all over.

With horror, he realized that he had little feeling left in them.

He began to climb, his progress agonizingly slow, the cold seeping through him all the time until he feared he would simply seize up. It felt as if someone had dipped his hands in iced water and held them there. He managed to hook his numb fingers around each successive rung, but the effort was almost too much.

The thought of that needle-sharp stake at the bottom of the pit made him even more fearful and he closed his eyes, trying to drive away the vision of Phillip Swanson's skewered body as it had been lifted from the shaft what seemed an eternity ago.

He was just over halfway up the ladder now.

Some fifty feet from the bottom of the shaft.

And the stake.

He continued to climb, wondering now if he might be better off going back down. At least if he fell from lower down he ran less risk of badly hurting himself. But from fifty feet, he courted serious injury.

Even death.

Rung by rung he kept on climbing, however, sensing a little more feeling in his hands now. A sudden surge of relief swept through him and he urged himself on, confident now that he would reach the top of the shaft.

Perhaps it was over-confidence which caused him to slip.

He shouted in fear as one foot slipped off a rung.

Clutching the ladder with one hand, Perry desperately

shot out searching fingers and succeeded in closing them around a length of the thick rope which had been suspended by the ladder as a safety precaution.

Above him he could see a vague circle of daylight. He guessed that he had thirty feet or less to climb.

Summoning up his last reserves of strength, he began struggling upward again, soon finding it a little easier. Nevertheless, he moved with an almost robotic rigidity, unable to escape the enveloping chill which squeezed tightly around him like a constricting snake.

Twenty feet to the surface.

His breath was coming in gasps now.

Ten feet.

Daylight washed over him as he emerged from the shaft, perspiration running down his face despite the cold.

Perry slowly straightened up, his entire body shaking. He leant against the generator for a moment, composing himself, thankful that no one asked him what was wrong. The others on the site were too busy with their own work to notice him. He pulled a handkerchief from his pocket and mopped his brow, looking around the site, his expression wrinkling into a frown.

For fifty feet all around the shaft the grass and bushes were blackened and withered, as if they had been sprayed with some deadly poison.

Twenty-Two

Clare Nichols pulled the covers more tightly around herself, trying to keep out the chill which seemed to have filled her bedroom. Each time she exhaled she expected to see her breath clouding in front of her, but this did not happen. Perhaps, she told herself, she was imagining it. Perhaps the room was really warm. Perhaps she was still dreaming.

She put her hand out from beneath the bedding just long enough to feel that the air was, indeed, cold. Clare wondered about calling her mother and asking if she could have more blankets on her bed. The added warmth might at least keep the cold away.

It wouldn't keep the nightmares away, though.

She lay on her back staring blankly at the ceiling, feeling tired but not daring to drop off to sleep again. If she slept, she feared, she would return to the nightmare which had woken her just minutes before. Not with a scream or a cry of terror but with a numbing coldness which seemed to seep through every fibre of her body. Her eyelids flickered closed but she blinked hard, trying to keep herself awake, frightened of what waited for her beyond the boundaries of sleep. Frightened of the creature which crouched in her subconscious and had appeared so unexpectedly for the first time this evening. She'd had nightmares before, although she wasn't quite sure that the dream she'd experienced less than ten minutes before could be classed as a nightmare. But a nightmare was a bad dream, wasn't it? And this had been bad.

In her dream, Clare had been with several other children, none of whom she recognized. It had been dark and they had been as frightened as she because someone or something had been following them. Chasing them through the darkness, drawing closer all the time, until finally they had been unable to run any further and had been forced to turn and face their pursuer. The dark shape had run screaming at *her*, its clawed hands outstretched towards her throat. The worst thing was, she hadn't even been able to see its face.

But despite that, Clare had sensed something horribly familiar about it.

She *knew* this creature from somewhere and it knew her. And wanted her.

Now she lay in bed, her breath coming in short gasps,

trying to keep awake so that the creature couldn't pursue her again and perhaps finally catch her this time.

She heard the sound of soft footfalls on the stairs and pulled the sheet tighter up around her face. The door of her bedroom opened a fraction, light from the landing spilling through the crack, and beyond it she saw a dark shadow.

'Clare.'

She recognized her mother's voice but she didn't relax. She kept the sheets pulled up and screwed tightly between her fists.

'Are you asleep, darling?' her mother asked, but she didn't answer, and after a second or two the door closed again. The room was dark once more. Should she call out? Tell her mother about the nightmare? She decided not to and pulled the sheets up still more, wrapping them around her head until she resembled a nun, with only her face visible.

Her eyes flickered again, and this time she could not fight the part of her mind which wanted sleep. As she drifted into oblivion she had one fleeting thought.

Would the creature come for her again?

And, if it did, would she see its face this time? The face which she felt she already knew . . .

Twenty-Three

The van was parked in the hedgerow with its lights off. So well hidden that Rob Hardy almost drove past it. He stepped on his brakes and brought the Vauxhall 1100 to a halt on the other side of the road. He switched off his lights and his engine.

He turned to see Mick Ferguson clambering out of the

van and heading across the road towards him. Hardy swung himself out from behind the wheel and greeted the other man.

'You took your fucking time,' Ferguson grunted. 'I've been freezing my bollocks off in that van for the last twenty minutes.'

Hardy shrugged.

'Have you got them?' the other man asked, smiling as he saw Hardy reach into the back of his car and grasp a well-secured sack which he dragged free. A chorus of squeals and whines came from inside and Ferguson looked at his companion approvingly. Then his eyes shifted back to the sack, which was twisting and writhing as if it were alive. The two men walked back across the deserted road, satisfied that no more traffic would come this way at such a late hour. It was well past one a.m. and they were more than three miles outside Longfield. No danger of any interference from the law this far out, Ferguson told himself.

They reached the van and he fumbled in his pocket for the keys to unlock the two rear doors, blowing on his hands in an attempt to restore some of the circulation, his breath forming gossamer clouds before him. Hardy, still gripping the sack in one hand, climbed over the nearby fence into the field beyond and trudged about fifty yards through the slippery mud, pulling a torch from his belt. He directed the beam at the sack, watching its frenzied movements and listening to the cacophony of noise from inside which now seemed to be growing to a fever pitch. He jabbed it with his torch and chuckled.

From the direction of the road he heard a loud bark, followed by Ferguson's gruff voice, snarling a command for silence which went virtually unheeded. Hardy turned the torch towards his companion, feeling his own flesh rise into goose-pimples as he caught sight of the dog which Ferguson held securely on a chain as thick as his wrist.

The albino pit bull terrier pulled against the strong links, restrained by a metal collar. The torch light reflected eerily in its pink eyes, turning them the colour of boiling blood. Its lips slid back over huge and savagely sharp teeth. It was the first time Hardy had seen the beast and he was suitably impressed.

When Ferguson was about ten yards away he stopped, flicking off his own torch when the moon emerged from behind a bank of cloud, giving them all the natural light they needed. He held onto the chain with both hands, then nodded to his companion, who untied the sack and reached in, his hand protected by a thick gardening glove.

From within he pulled a spitting, rasping tomcat. Like some malevolent magician, Hardy removed the creature from the sack, gripping it by the neck, ignoring its frenzied attempts to scratch him.

'Now let's see how good this dog really is,' Ferguson said.

Hardy hurled the cat towards him.

No sooner had the cat hit the wet earth than the dog was upon it.

Both men watched fascinated as the terrier's jaws grasped the bewildered cat's right front leg and the dog pulled with all its strength. Most of the cat's limb was torn off in the savage assault and the animal toppled over, blood spraying from the stump, its anger now transformed into terror and pain as the pit bull struck again. This time its teeth closed around the cat's head. The steel-trap jaws crushed the helpless animal's skull into pulp as the dog shook its head madly back and forth, ripping away half of the cat's head. A sticky mass of blood and brain flooded from the massive bite and the terrier, apparently unconcerned that its victim was already dead, savaged the twitching body again, tearing the stomach wall open and ripping several knotted lengths of intestine free. Blood sprayed from them, some of it spattering Hardy, but he seemed barely aware of it. He merely reached into the sack and hauled out another cat.

This one was scarcely more than a kitten and a terrier needed only one savage bite to all but tear the little animal in two.

Ferguson chuckled as he watched the destruction which his mad beast wrought, keeping a firm grip on the chain as the dog tossed one half of the dead kitten into the air.

Hardy needed both hands for the next occupant of the sack.

While the terrier tore what remained of the kitten into blood-soaked confetti, he pulled a small labrador from the mêlée inside the hessian prison. The animal had its jaws firmly bound with strong tape. Hardy seized one end of the tape and tugged mightily. There was a sound like tearing paper as the sticky-backed binding came free, ripping tufts of hair from the dog's muzzle with it. The animal yelped in pain and fear, barking loudly as Hardy kicked it hard in the side, pushing it towards the waiting terrier.

The albino launched itself at the labrador and ripped off one ear with a single bite of its powerful jaws. The stricken dog howled and tried to bite its opponent, but this only seemed to inflame the albino more and it struck upwards at the labrador's belly, its teeth shearing through fur and flesh until it reached the soft entrails. The stomach wall burst open and the terrier pulled several lengths of throbbing intestine free. Blood erupted from the hideous gash and the labrador fell forward onto its front legs, helpless now as the pit bull seized it by the throat, almost severing its head, so awesomely savage was the attack. The spurts of blood looked black in the moonlight and both men watched in awe as the albino, now drenched in the dark fluid, tore ferociously at the body of its newest victim. The smell of slaughter was strong in the air, mingling with the pungent stench of excrement.

The terrier leapt and writhed amidst the carnage it had wrought, inflamed to the point of madness by the blood, until it was exhausted. Only then did Ferguson attempt to grab it by the back of the neck and secure its muzzle. The beast almost twisted from his grasp, its body was so slippery with blood, but he held onto its collar firmly and succeeded in fixing the restrainer over the deadly jaws.

'I'll get rid of these,' said Hardy, prodding the remains of the dead pets with the toe of his shoe. He began lifting the torn remains back into the sack, blood soaking through the coarse material. 'I'll bury them somewhere.'

Ferguson grunted his approval.

'That's a hell of a dog, Mick,' Hardy said, looking at the blood-spattered albino terrier.

'Yeah, that mad fucker's going to make me a lot of money. If you've got any sense you'll have something on him when he fights.'

Hardy nodded.

'Just remember, Rob, I don't want anyone else to know about him, not yet,' Ferguson reminded his companion. He turned and headed back towards his van, dragging the dog with him.

The moon cast a weak, silvery light over the deserted landscape.

The blood which covered the ground glistened blackly in the pale glow.

Twenty-Four

The rabbit was dying.

It lay on its side with its eyes closed, only the barely perceptible movement of its chest signalling that any life still remained.

Kim watched it for a moment, then opened the cage door and lifted the animal out. It was limp in her arms, its head lolling back as if its neck had been broken. She gently drew back its eyelids, noticing how a membranous film was beginning to form over the usually glistening eyes, turning them opaque.

Moving slowly, still holding the rabbit, she walked along the row of cages which housed some of the museum's live subjects. During the summer months the animals were kept outside in a small annexe where they served as an attraction for the smaller children who visited the museum. There were a few more rabbits, some mice and two white rats. Kim noticed that the food trays in every cage were still full, the food untouched. There was an almost unnerving silence too. No squeaking or any other sound came from the animals.

The other rabbits were also lying down. As Kim poked an index finger through the bars of the cage, they glanced helplessly at it, and when one tried to rise it found the effort too great and slumped over once more.

Two of the mice were already dead. They lay in the straw at the bottom of the cage, their limbs stiffening.

Stroking the rabbit she held, as if trying to coax some warmth and movement back into it, Kim gazed into the last cage. The female rat was carrying young. Its belly was bloated and swollen but the rest of its body was disproportionately thin, so much so that the bones which were now visible under its fur looked as if they would tear through. The male wandered aimlessly back and forth, ignoring the food that had been placed there for it.

Kim watched the rodents for a moment longer and then returned the rabbit to its cage, laying it gently on its side, wondering how long it would take to die.

She returned to her seat and sighed wearily, feeling strangely isolated within the museum. With Roger Kelly in hospital, she wondered if she should advertise for a replacement. The building had few enough visitors during the week but she couldn't cope alone forever, and there was also the administrative side to deal with. Normally this was the province of Alec Blane, a retired headmaster who was nominally in charge of the museum. However, he was out of the country enjoying a holiday, so Kim was left alone. She considered her position for a moment, then returned to the work at hand.

Spread out before her on the desk were two of the stone tablets, laid carefully on thick gauze to prevent them sustaining damage. Close by, Kim had placed a bottle of diluted hydrochloric acid with which to remove any particularly stubborn pieces of debris from the small slabs of rock. She tapped her notebook with the end of her pen and studied the lettering, trying to make some sense of what she had already written down:

WANDERER. THINKER. I AM SO. WITHOUT NEED OR WILL TO BE OF ANY TUATH. ONE OF THE AES DANA. MAN OF KNOWLEDGE LET ME PASS BY THESE YEARS QUICKLY. FOR TIME IS WHAT WE ALL SEEK. AND FREEDOM BUT THAT MAY NOT COME WITHOUT THE KNOWLEDGE. I AM FEARED. SON BORN OF SON BY AEDD MAWR. NONE MAY TOUCH ME. NOT PLEBES. NOT EQUITES. I AM FEARED FOR DAY THAT MUST COME

Kim shook her head, weary from the effort of trying to transcribe what she saw on the tablets into something meaningful.

Whoever had spent so much time creating these tablets, meticulously carving words so small that up to a hundred covered each slab of stone, obviously had been a learned man. One of the *áes dana* as he himself said — the wise men of the tribe. The Celts were insular people, making contact with other tribes usually only for two purposes: trade or war. And yet this man belonged to no tribe.

'I am feared,' Kim read aloud. The Druids were revered and respected by the Celts but not feared as far as she knew. They functioned as law-givers, judges and mediators. Why had this man been feared?

FEARED FOR DAY THAT MUST COME.

Kim sucked in a weary breath, noticing how cold it was in the room. She leant over and touched one of the radiators, recoiling sharply when she found it to be red hot.

And yet the cold persisted.

Puzzled, she got to her feet and walked across to the thermometer.

The mercury was stuck at fifty-one degrees.

Kim shuddered and tapped the instrument.

As she watched, the silver thread which marked the temperature slid even lower on the scale and settled at forty-eight.

She frowned in disbelief, then shrugged and returned to her seat. She glanced over the rest of her notes, blowing on her hands in an effort to restore some warmth.

I CARRY WITH ME THAT WHICH NONE SPEAK OF YET ALL FEAR. WHEN COMES THE TIME THEY SEEK ME THOUGH I KNOW ONLY MY UNDERSTANDING IS WANTED. THEY KNOW NOTHING OF MY WAY BUT FEAR MY PRESENCE NOT KNOWING I AM THEIR ONLY HOPE. YET I ENJOY THE POWER FOR AS LONG AS I AM ITS MASTER. SHOULD HE EVER OVERCOME THESE LAWS THEN MY OWN DEATH WOULD BE THE FIRST. I AM THEIR HOPE AND THEIR FEAR AND THEY KNOW OF HIS DAY. FOR MANY YEARS IT HAS BEEN. FOR MANY YEARS IT WILL BE SO. AFTER ME IF NONE COME THEN MANY WILL FEAR AND MANY WILL DIE BY HIS HAND.

A warrior? A king? Who was *He*? Kim wondered. She was assuming that the man who had engraved the stones was a Druid but whom did he speak of in the strange text? She wondered if the other slabs of rock would give the answers.

Looking up at the clock, she saw that it was almost five-thirty. Time to close the museum. As she got to her feet and walked out into the main hallway it occurred to her that it might be wise to close the museum for a week or two, or at least until she found a replacement for Kelly. She went to the main doors and pulled them shut, then retrieved a large key from the pocket of her jeans and began to lock up. She would leave by a side exit, she decided.

It was as she was turning the key that she heard the noise.

At first she wondered if her ears were playing tricks on her, but then the noise came again.

From above her there were sounds of movement.

Kim realized that someone was still inside the building.

She crossed to the bottom of the staircase which led up to the first floor and cupped one hand around her mouth.

'I've got to lock the doors now,' she called. 'It's five-thirty.'

No answer.

Obviously someone wandering around the galleries had

lost track of time and did not realize that the place was closing, Kim told herself. She walked back over to the main entrance and unlocked it again, then returned to the staircase and made her way up about five or six steps.

'Excuse me,' she said loudly, trying to attract the attention of whoever was up there. 'I'm locking up now.'

Silence.

She thought about calling out again, but instead began climbing the stairs towards the first floor, her heels clicking noisily in the stillness. As she reached the first landing she spoke again but still there was no answer.

Kim frowned. Surely whoever was up there must have heard her by now. She continued up the stairs, aware that the sounds of movement had stopped. Kim stood at the top of the steps and looked around her. Galleries lay in all directions from where she stood. Immediately ahead of her was the one which housed objects of local interest and some specimens of local wildlife and plants. She decided to look in there first. The floor was polished wood. The sound of her footsteps echoed loudly around the building, which seemed almost unnaturally quiet.

Kim paused as she reached the entrance to the gallery, peering in to see if she could see anyone.

A beautifully mounted badger gazed fixedly at her from one of the exhibit cases, and for a moment Kim caught sight of her reflection in its lifeless glass eyes. She moved into the gallery, treading a slow and measured path between the other specimen cases, her ears and eyes alert for the slightest sound or movement.

She heard breathing and spun round, her heart thudding against her ribs.

There was nothing to be seen.

Dozens of sightless eyes bored into her as she stood looking around, wondering where the harsh breathing sound had come from.

She heard it again, and this time a knot of fear began to settle uncomfortably in her stomach.

'Who's there?' she called as she heard the soft hiss once more.

It took her only a second more to realize that the noise was not really breathing, it was the wind rushing through a ventilation duct in the wall.

Kim let out a long, relieved breath, angry with herself for being so jumpy. Satisfied that she was alone in the gallery, she moved on. Perhaps her ears really had been playing tricks.

A new sound came from somewhere up ahead, in the next gallery. Then again, louder.

Kim froze, not sure whether she should continue. She stood listening for a moment, aware that someone was indeed moving about ahead of her. She considered calling out but swiftly decided against it.

Moving much more slowly, she walked on, unconsciously clenching and unclenching her fists, feeling the moisture on the palms of her hands.

She reached the entrance to the gallery and stopped, pausing a moment before taking a step inside.

In the centre of the room was a large sculpture of a mother and baby, the features missing, the limbs long and curving in an abstract way. Although she had seen it countless times, Kim suddenly found it curiously menacing.

She moved towards it, towards the middle of the gallery.

The sculpture was a large, solid object about seven feet tall and three or four feet wide.

Kim was only inches away when she realized that the sounds were coming from the other side of the object.

For long seconds it was as if time had frozen. She tried to stop herself shaking, knowing that any second she was going to confront whoever was hiding behind the sculpture.

They stepped in front of her.

Two children. Little boys, no more than ten years old.

They looked up at her in embarrassment, wondering why she hadn't shouted at them, wondering why she looked more frightened than they were.

'We weren't trying to steal anything,' the older of the two said. 'We would have gone out of a window or something if you'd locked up.'

The other boy nodded vigorously and Kim could almost

feel the relief pouring through her as she looked at them, heads bowed, as if they were about to receive punishment from a teacher. It was all Kim could do to stop herself laughing.

'Come on,' she said. 'I'll make sure you get out. And you can use the doors, not the windows. All right?'

The boys nodded again and ran on ahead of her to the stairs. Kim walked after them, her heart gradually slowing down. She felt both stupid and relieved. It *was* time she went home, she decided; her imagination was beginning to run away with her. She wiped the beads of perspiration from her forehead and actually managed a thin smile as she saw the two boys standing by the exit doors waiting to be allowed out.

'They're open,' she told them.

They hesitated for a moment.

'Go on. Let me lock up,' she called. 'I want to get home.'

They both dashed through the exit and disappeared across the car park. Kim chuckled as she watched them, then she turned the key in the lock, pocketed it and headed back to the staff room to collect her coat and notebook. She'd had enough for one day. All she wanted was to get home, relax in a warm bath and talk to her daughter. Forget everything for the time being. Even the mysterious stone tablets.

As she stepped inside the staff room the figure loomed in front of her.

This time she screamed.

Twenty-Five

'Jesus Christ,' Kim gasped. 'I didn't hear you come in.'

Charles Cooper seemed unconcerned at the fright he'd given her. He merely stood looking around the staff room as if searching for something.

'Where are the tablets?' he asked.

Kim, who was gradually recovering her breath after the shock, held one hand to her chest and felt her heart thumping hard.

'They're in there,' she said, motioning towards the adjoining room.

Without waiting for her, Cooper turned and walked through.

'You frightened the life out of me, Charles,' Kim told him.

'What have you found out about them?' he asked, ignoring what she had said. He picked up her notes and scanned what she'd written. 'Are these accurate?'

'As accurate as possible,' she told him, resenting the harshness of his tone and the implied lack of confidence in her.

Cooper flipped through the pages, his face impassive. 'I was just about to go home,' Kim said, pulling on her jacket.

'But what about the deciphering?' Cooper wanted to know.

'I'll continue in the morning, Charles,' she told him. 'I'm not staying here any longer. My daughter will wonder what's happened to me.'

He exhaled wearily and handed her the notebook.

'How are things going at the dig?' she asked.

Cooper shrugged, as if he didn't know.

'There's still lots of work to be done,' he said vaguely. 'Particularly in the skull chamber.'

'There was writing on the walls inside there,' Kim remembered. 'Have you managed to make any sense out of that yet?'

'No,' he said sharply, turning away from her, his eyes straying back to the stone tablets laid out on the nearby worktop. Then, as if anxious to shift the emphasis of the conversation, he nodded towards her notebook. 'That man claims to be the Great Grandson of Aedd Mawr, the one who actually set up the Druid order.'

'Is that possible?'

'Why should we doubt it?'

'I can't work out who he keeps referring to, such as here,' Kim replied, pointing to her words in the notebook: ' "They know of his day", and "Many will die by his hand". I don't know who *He* is.'

Cooper did not answer.

'Could it be a religious text? Could the writer be talking about one of the Celtic deities?'

'Which one? There were over 370,' Cooper said.

Kim closed the notebook.

'I'll keep at it tomorrow,' she told him.

'How long will it take to decipher all twelve tablets?' Cooper demanded.

'That's impossible to say, Charles. You know . . .'

'How long?' he snapped, interrupting her.

Kim looked at him angrily for a moment.

'I'm not sure,' she said, slowly. 'A week or two. It's difficult to say.'

'Let me know as soon as you have anything important.'

'I'll be coming out to the site in a day or two anyway,' she said.

'Why?' said Cooper, eyeing her suspiciously.

'I need to pick up some of those skulls for carbon dating,' she explained.

'The tablets are the first consideration.'

'I realize that.'

'The skulls can wait,' he said. 'We might not have that much time.'

'What do you mean?'

'Cutler threatened to close the site. We must try to do as much work as possible before he decides to go through with his plan. He doesn't realize what he'll destroy if he builds over that site.'

'Is there nothing we can do about it?' Kim asked, quietly.

Cooper didn't answer. He merely turned and headed for the door.

'Let me know what you find,' he said as he left the room.

She heard the front door as it closed behind him, then, outside, his car revving up. A moment later he was gone.

Kim shook her head, looking across at the tablets. Gathering up her handbag, she flicked out the light above the worktop and prepared to leave, deciding to glance at the animal cages again as she went out.

Every one of the creatures was dead.

Kim's mouth dropped open in shocked surprise. She quickly inspected the cages, gaping at the bodies inside.

The mice were huddled together in one corner of their cage, their small bodies stiff and unmoving. The rats, including the pregnant female, were also stiff with rigor mortis. Kim noted with renewed revulsion that the skin of the female's belly had split, spilling the unborn rats into the bottom of the cage. Their tiny bodies were shrunken and hard, looking more like faeces. The rabbits too were dead. But it wasn't only the fact that the creatures had died so suddenly which caused Kim to shudder. It was also the appearance of their bodies.

All of them were shrunken and shrivelled, their fur patchy and discoloured. The bodies looked only half their normal size. Every one was thin, as if they'd been starved to death.

As if the life itself had been sucked from them.

Twenty-Six

Stuart Lawrence slipped the bookmark into the paperback and laid it on the coffee table. He sat back in his chair, massaging the bridge of his nose between his thumb and forefinger, listening to the wind which whistled around the house. He reached for the glass of white wine on the table and finished what was left, then went into the kitchen and rinsed the glass beneath the tap. Outside the kitchen window the lilac bushes which grew so lushly in summer were now little more than shrunken stumps buffeted by the wind.

Lawrence wasn't one for gardening, but the bushes had been there when he'd moved into the house and he'd decided to leave them. The rest of his considerable garden was laid to lawn so that all he had to do was mow it every now and then. Any garden job beyond that constituted hard work to him, and as far as the young surveyor was concerned, work should be reserved for the office.

He switched off the kitchen light and padded back into the sitting room, checking first that he'd left the porch light on. Ruth would return sometime later, and he didn't fancy having to clamber out of bed in the dead of night to let her in because she couldn't see the lock in the dark. She had been gone since seven that evening, visiting friends in the nearby town of Mossford. No doubt comparing notes on babies, Lawrence thought scornfully. His sister was six months pregnant and staying with him until her husband returned from his three-month stint on one of Shell's North Sea oil rigs. Lawrence didn't object to his sister staying temporarily. It meant that he ate a good breakfast and dinner, and she was company for him, especially in the evenings. Not that being alone bothered him that much; he rarely arrived home before eight. It made a break for Ruth as well, but her little visits would only continue until she had the child. After that, Lawrence would have to find some excuse to stop her visiting so frequently. He didn't want any whining, puking kid messing up *his* carpets. He sat down to watch the tail-end of the late news, then switched the set off and made his way upstairs, taking his book with him. He found it difficult to sleep, but he had discovered that reading seemed to do the trick. He usually nodded off after a couple of chapters. His insomnia he put down to an over-active mind. He was forever turning new projects over in his brain, and at present the Cutler development was occupying all of his working time. He and his partners had worked for the land developer before and had always been more than satisfied with the financial rewards. This time was no exception.

Lawrence tossed the paperback onto the bed, then went into the bathroom to clean his teeth. As he finished he paused and stood listening, a sound from outside having caught his attention.

It sounded like fingernails scraping on glass.

He remained motionless until the sound came again.

Lawrence opened the bathroom window to find the branches of a leafless willow scratching the pane. He decided to leave the window open rather than risk being kept awake by the perpetual tapping and scraping.

He undressed quickly and slipped between the sheets, reaching for the book. The slow, rhythmic ticking of his alarm clock was the only thing that broke the silence of the room. He glanced at it and saw that the time was approaching 11:30. Ruth was late, he thought. He hoped she hadn't missed the last bus; he didn't fancy having to get dressed and drive to Mossford to pick her up.

Just then he heard movement outside the front door and nodded to himself, satisfied that she had finally returned.

A minute passed.

Two minutes.

Perhaps she had lost her key and couldn't get in. He waited for the knock.

It didn't come.

The noise seemed to fade and Lawrence returned to his book.

For the first time that night he noticed how cold it was in the room. He lowered his book for a moment, watching his breath clouding in front of him. He shuddered and pulled the covers up higher. He hadn't noticed the chill until now. Christ, it was freezing. He put down the book and tucked both hands beneath the covers in an effort to restore some warmth to them. Perhaps he'd left a window open in one of the other rooms. The draught couldn't be coming from the bathroom because he'd shut that door. After a moment or two he climbed out of bed and padded across the landing, heading for one of the spare rooms.

He opened the door and stepped into the darkness.

Switching on the light, Lawrence saw that no windows were open and decided to try Ruth's room next. Her door was open, but as he walked in he saw that the windows were firmly closed. The surveyor stood with his hands on his hips, puzzled by the unexpected drop in temperature. He turned and headed back toward his own room.

From downstairs there was a deafening crash. A sound like glass being shattered.

Lawrence froze, his heart pounding.

Still on the landing, his skin puckering into goose-pimples, he stood waiting.

Silence.

He swallowed hard and took a step forward, peering over the edge of the balustrade down into the gloom below.

Still there was no sound, only the low hissing of the wind as it swirled around the house.

The surveyor moved to the top of the stairs, muttering under his breath as the uppermost step creaked loudly.

He stood still, wondering if there would be more noise from downstairs.

For what seemed an eternity he remained at the head of the staircase. Finally, with infinite care and slowness, he began to descend. The darkness closed around him and now another sound reached him. The rushing of blood to his ears, driven by his wildly pumping heart.

Gripping the bannister with one hand, Lawrence moved closer to the bottom of the stairs.

He was halfway down when the figure loomed up out of the darkest shadows below.

For an interminable moment the surveyor could not move. His entire body was frozen, transfixed by what he saw, but then, as the figure started up the stairs after him, he found the will to turn and run. Gasping in terror, he fled back up the steps, aware that the intruder was closing rapidly. He could hear the footfalls behind him as he stumbled on the top step and went sprawling onto the landing.

If only he could reach the phone . . .

Lawrence dragged himself upright and sprinted across the landing, hurling himself through his bedroom door, slamming it shut only an instant before the figure crashed into it with a force which almost sent the surveyor flying. But he kept his weight against the wood, his eyes closed, his breath coming in terrified gasps. He felt another crashing impact against the door, so powerful that it was all he could do to retain his balance. Then, nothing.

Quivering madly, Lawrence kept both hands on the door handle waiting for the next blow. Sweat was running from his face despite the numbing cold and his legs felt like water. He pressed his ear to the door, listening for any sounds of movement outside the room.

He heard nothing.

If he could just get to the phone . . .

It was on the bedside table. Five or six feet from the door against which he now leant. But dare he try to reach it?

If he released his grip on the door and the intruder charged it again, there would be no hope for him.

If he did manage to dial the police, would they arrive in time?

If . . .

He released his grip on the handle but kept his shoulder

104

pressed firmly to the wood, trying to control his breathing in case the figure on the other side could hear him. Only by a monumental effort of will did Lawrence manage to open his eyes and look down at the handle, now smeared with his own perspiration.

He looked across at the phone.

Down at the handle.

At the phone again.

He eased away a fraction from the door.

The handle moved down slowly and it was all Lawrence could do to prevent himself from screaming.

His eyes bulged wildly in their sockets as he watched, then the realization seemed to hit him and he threw all his weight back against the door.

The handle now jerked up and down with terrifying rapidity until it threatened to come free.

Lawrence closed his eyes again as he felt a shuddering impact against the wood. He stood with his back against it, arms spread wide, gripping the frame as his body shook under the repeated hail of blows.

He didn't know how much longer the door would hold up to such sustained punishment.

There was a loud crack and part of it splintered. A great hairline splinter which ran half the length of the door.

Lawrence whimpered in terror, praying that someone would come to his aid, but knowing that there *was* no one who could help him.

The pounding stopped and, in the silence which followed he sank to his knees against the door, fear sapping his strength as surely as physical movement.

He looked around him for something to barricade the door with. The bedroom chair could be wedged under the handle, but how long would that hold the intruder back? A mad idea sprang into his mind, one born of desperation. Perhaps he could wedge the door shut just long enough to jump from the bedroom window. Surely the fall wouldn't kill him. He would be landing on grass. Then he could reach the next house, get help.

It wasn't much of a choice but it was the only one he had.

With his back still pressed against the door he snaked out one leg and hooked his toes around the chair leg, pulling it towards him, waiting for the seemingly inevitable assault on the weakened door.

He dragged the chair nearer, closing his hand around it, then scuttled swiftly away from the door and jammed the chair under the handle.

He backed off and ran to the window, clawing wildly at it.

And now the pounding began again, much louder and more intense than before. Massive blows which shook the door and its frame.

Lawrence chanced a look over his shoulder as he struggled with the recalcitrant window catch.

'Please, God!' he whimpered, tugging at it with hands that shook insanely.

Part of the door was staved in by a thunderous blow that sent fragments of wood spraying into the room.

Another few moments and it would all be over.

He managed to free the catch, panting with renewed hope. He looked out into the night, guessing he was fifteen or twenty feet up.

There was no time to worry about the risks. If he stayed in the room he was sure to die.

He began to clamber onto the sill.

The door exploded inwards with an ear-splitting shriek, the sound mingling with Lawrence's scream of pure terror as the figure bounded across the room towards him.

He allowed himself to slip off the window sill.

A hand was thrust out after him and closed around his wrist. He felt an incredible power in that hand as, by sheer physical force, the intruder hauled him back inside, cracking his head on the window frame in the process.

Lawrence could only stare up at his assailant in disbelief, his terror now reaching an even higher pitch. He was close to madness now.

His attacker wasted little time and the surveyor felt vicelike hands close around his throat, lift him to his feet and then, with almost nonchalant ease, hurl him clear across the bed. He slammed into the dressing table, the impact making him feel sick.

The figure was upon him like lightning and now Lawrence roared in agony as he felt fingers tearing at his eyes, pushing into the bulging orbs, burrowing into the sockets themselves until blood burst from them in crimson spurts. Denied even the mercy of unconsciousness, he felt the fingers driving deep into his skull, tearing the eyes free, leaving pieces of optic nerve dangling over his cheek like bloodied tendrils, before oblivion finally came to him.

Blood pumped in thick gouts from the riven eye sockets, splashing down the dying man's cheeks to form a puddle beneath his head. One of the eyes fell into this red pool, but it was quickly retrieved.

Lawrence's body began to spasm uncontrollably but the killer took no notice.

There were other tasks to perform.

Twenty-Seven

The first thing that struck Wallace as he entered the house was the smell.

He could not help recoiling at the pungent odour as he stepped into the sitting room and looked at the shattered patio doors. Pieces of broken glass were scattered everywhere. It looked as if someone had been at the windows with a sledgehammer.

'Subtle, wasn't he?' Wallace muttered to a constable who was standing close to the doors. 'Have you found a tool he could have used to get in?'

'Not yet, sir,' the PC told him.

Wallace took one last look at the doors, then turned his back and headed for the stairs.

As he ascended the stench grew more powerful. The odour reminded him of bad meat.

On the landing he was greeted by Bill Dayton, and Wallace was surprised to see that the sergeant looked a little pale.

'What have we got, Bill?' he said.

'I'm buggered if I know, guv,' murmured Dayton, wiping the corners of his mouth with a handkerchief. 'I've never seen anything like it in my life.' He swallowed hard and apologized for his lack of composure. 'Young Buchanan was the first one in there.' He hooked a thumb in the direction of the room behind him. 'He's still in the toilet throwing up. I bloody nigh joined him.'

'Has the place been dusted?' Wallace wanted to know.

'Yes. Dr Ryan and the photographer are in there now. I didn't leave any of the men inside. I didn't think it was fair to them.'

Wallace nodded slowly and walked past the sergeant into the room.

He paused at the door, nodding a greeting to the elderly man who sat on the edge of the bed looking down at something which, as yet, Wallace could not see.

Rick Piper clicked off another photo, his flash gun momentarily bathing the room in cold white light.

'Morning, Steve,' said the photographer. 'I think you've got problems.'

He nodded towards the object sprawled at his feet.

'Jesus Christ Almighty,' whispered the inspector, struggling to retain his breakfast. His stomach lurched violently as he gazed at the body of Stuart Lawrence.

The surveyor was spreadeagled on the floor of the bedroom, the carpet all around him matted with dried blood. There was a large quantity splashed over the bed and the walls, too. His mouth was open in a soundless scream and Wallace could see the congealed blood clogged inside, as well as in the torn eye sockets. But, if anything, the ravaged face was the least offensive of the catalogue of

108

atrocities inflicted on Lawrence. Stepping closer, Wallace saw with renewed revulsion that the man's stomach had been torn open. A jagged gash fully twelve inches long had been hacked into his belly from sternum to groin. Lumps of torn intestine protruded from the hole like mushy fingers, and pieces of the entrails had also been scattered around the room like so many bloodied streamers. Clots of blood so dark they looked like tar had formed in the shredded ends of the colon, most of which had been pulled from the riven torso and now lay draped over the shrivelled groin.

Wallace shook his head, fumbling for a cigarette, his eyes compulsively returning to the body time and time again, as if to convince himself that he wasn't imagining what was possibly the worst atrocity of all.

Stuart Lawrence had been flayed as completely as a rabbit in a butcher's shop. Nearly every inch of skin had been stripped from the disembowelled body.

The inspector stuck a cigarette in his mouth and reached for his lighter, flicking it in vain, getting only sparks. He had to be content to chew on the unlit Rothmans.

'The killer must have been covered in blood,' said Ryan, scratching his head. 'There would have been massive haemorrhage from a wound like the one in the abdomen.'

'Have you found a weapon?' the inspector wanted to know.

'It's not my job to find them, Inspector,' Ryan said, smiling.

'Sorry, I meant what do you think was used on him?'

'Well, it's impossible to say for certain until the autopsy has been carried out, but from initial examination, especially of the face, I'd say that there *was* no weapon.'

Wallace shot the doctor a disbelieving glance.

'Those injuries,' Ryan continued, 'were inflicted by hand. Someone literally tore his eyes out, and judging from the appearance of the abdominal wound I'd say the same for that.'

'But who's got the strength to tear through a man's stomach with their bare hands?' Wallace said incredulously as if doubting what the physician had told him.

'You're the policeman, not me. I merely gave you a medical opinion. As for the other injuries, particularly the flaying, I can only assume that a knife or some sharp object was used. Although whoever did it was clumsy.' He pointed to a particularly deep gash on Lawrence's right thigh. 'Not only has the skin been removed but a large portion of the muscle has also been torn away.'

'Flayed,' Wallace murmured. He looked at Ryan. 'You know we found the remains of a goat up in that wood near Dexter Grange. *It* had been flayed too.'

'You think the killer's graduated from goats to human beings?' Ryan asked, cryptically, the slightest hint of sarcasm in his voice.

'It wasn't just that. There are other similarities in the mutilations.' The inspector looked down at the body once more, thoughts turning over in his mind. He shook his head slowly and then glanced up at the doctor again.

'What about the intestines?' he said, removing the unlit cigarette from his mouth and pushing it back into the packet.

'They wouldn't have been too difficult to remove once the torso was opened. Merely a case of pulling,' Ryan said, shrugging his shoulders.

'So where are the eyes?' the inspector wanted to know.

'Nobody has found any trace of them,' Piper told him. 'Nor the skin.'

'Oh, shit, that's all we need,' Wallace sighed. He turned as Dayton re-entered the room. 'Is that right, Bill? There's no trace of the eyes or the skin?'

Dayton nodded, trying not to look at the body.

'We searched every inch of the house,' he said. 'The sick bastard must have disposed of them afterwards.'

'Or kept them,' Ryan offered.

Wallace looked at the doctor for a moment, then sighed and chuckled humourlessly.

'You're a great comfort, doctor,' he said.

'He must be a total fucking nutter to do this,' Piper added.

'I couldn't agree more,' Wallace said, reaching for a

cigarette once again. 'Have any of you got a light?' he asked
hopefully.

'Don't look at me,' said Ryan, reproachfully.

Piper obliged and the inspector hungrily sucked in the
tobacco smoke. He drew a hand across his forehead and
exhaled deeply.

'Who found the body?' he asked.

'His sister,' said Dayton. 'She was the one who called us.
They took her to hospital suffering from shock.'

'I wonder why?' the inspector said, bitterly. 'Well, get on
the blower and tell the ambulance to pick this poor sod up.
Once the autopsy's been done maybe we'll have a bit more
to go on.'

'Inspector, I'm afraid there's something else you ought to
see,' Ryan told him, getting to his feet.

Wallace followed the doctor around to the other side of
the bed, where a sheet had been laid on the floor to cover
something. Blood was soaking through the material.

As the policeman watched, the doctor carefully pulled
the sheet back.

On the blood-soaked carpet was a thick length of
intestine, lying there like some bloated greyish-pink worm.

It had been carefully shaped to form the letter M.

Twenty-Eight

Wallace flipped silently through the pile of photographs,
pausing for as long as he could over each one. The fact that
they were in black and white didn't make them any easier to
look at. The subject matter remained the same. An
obscene horror that he wished he could simply expunge
from his memory.

111

There were ten photos in all. Of Stuart Lawrence. Of the room where he was killed. Wallace paused on the last of the batch.

He inhaled deeply on his cigarette and ran the tip of his pencil across the monochrome print, tracing the shape of the letter M which had been created using at least two feet of the dead surveyor's colon. The inspector knew that it was the large intestine because he also had the autopsy report on his desk. He looked once more at the photos, then put them aside and picked up the report, scanning through it to find the salient points. He still could not quite fully comprehend some of the things he read on the carefully typed sheets:

. . .EXTENSIVE DAMAGE TO BOTH ZYGOMA DOUBTLESS CAUSED BY REMOVAL OF THE EYES . . .SPHENOID BONES CRUSHED . . .SOME DAMAGE TO BOTH OCCIPITAL AND PARIETAL BONES INDICATING THAT CONSIDERABLE FORCE WAS USED TO REMOVE THE EYES.

Wallace blew out a long stream of smoke and turned the page, glancing as he did so at the photo of Stuart Lawrence's face. It was a silent affirmation of what was written in the report:

. . .X-RAY TESTS SHOW NO EVIDENCE OF WEAPON USED TO REMOVE EYES . . .

No evidence of weapon, the inspector thought, shaking his head. He looked again at the photos, noting the savage gashes on Lawrence's cheek bones, then he turned his attention to the shots of the eviscerated torso and the report's conclusions about this:

. . .LARGE PORTIONS OF BOTH THE COLON AND THE DUODENUM REMOVED WITH SUBSEQUENT DAMAGE TO THE BLADDER AND ALSO THE STOMACH . . .CAUSE OF DEATH CARDIAC ARREST PROBABLY PRECIPITATED BY LOSS OF BLOOD BUT EXTERNAL CAUSE CANNOT BE RULED OUT.

And once more:

NO EVIDENCE OF WEAPON.

Wallace looked at his own hands. They, he knew, were not powerful enough to tear open a man's stomach and rip out his entrails. What kind of man, then, was he looking for?

'A right bloody head case,' he muttered aloud, answering his own question. He picked up each of the photos of Stuart Lawrence again, studying them one at a time, his attention drawn particularly to the last one.

That obscenely fashioned letter M

An initial? If so was it the first or last name?

M.

For Maniac?

Wallace almost smiled.

He turned and looked out of his office window at the grey sky with its swollen clouds that promised rain. Somewhere out there he would find the killer but right now he just wished he knew where to start.

He was still gazing out into the gloomy afternoon when the phone rang.

Twenty-Nine

The skull was heavy, despite its small size.

Charles Cooper took the small brush from his belt and flicked some fragments of dirt from the eye sockets, studying the skull a moment longer before putting it into the small wooden crate with the others he had removed. There was still a large pile of them left, however, built in a pyramid shape which rose as high as the archaeologist's

113

waist. He felt as if they were watching him with their sightless eyes, angry that he was disturbing their final resting place.

He had been in the chamber for the last four hours, working alone, resentful of any intrusion by his colleagues. A number of them were working in the tunnels close by, but they had come to realize that Cooper was best left alone while he worked amongst the pile of skulls. And, unlike the others, he seemed not to feel the constant chill which permeated the chamber and tunnels.

It was not only the skulls which interested him.

The carvings on the walls of the chamber were beginning to show up with greater clarity as he removed more dirt. As yet, Cooper was still unable to make much sense of the drawings and the chiselled script. He wondered if it had been done by the same people or person who had been responsible for the stone tablets which had been removed to the museum. He decided to determine this as soon as possible.

The lights inside the chamber glowed with a feeble yellow tinge that belied their hundred-watt strength. They periodically flickered or went dim, but Cooper seemed unconcerned. Now they went out completely, but he merely stood silently in the darkness waiting for the restoration of power.

After a few minutes the lights came back on with a brilliant flash and he saw George Perry standing at the entrance to the chamber.

'Bloody generator must be on the blink again,' Perry said and Cooper noticed that he was shivering, his breath clouding in the dank air.

'What do you want?' Cooper asked, taking a step towards the chamber entrance.

'They've found some more relics in the other tunnels. Gold statuettes and ornaments. I thought you might like to see them.'

'I've got too much to do here,' Cooper told him.

'Charles, you've been down here for four hours,' Perry said, wearily. 'Ever since we found this chamber you've spent most of your time in here. Isn't the rest of the dig important to you any longer? We know that the skulls belonged to those bodies we found. What more can you discover by hiding yourself away in here every day?'

'I don't have to justify myself to you. This chamber could be the key to the whole site, and there's still a great deal of work to be done here. I intend to find out what these carvings on the walls mean.'

'Then let me help you,' said Perry, taking a step forward.

Cooper moved towards him, blocking the entrance to the chamber, his steely eyes boring into his companion.

'I don't need any help,' he snapped.

'What have you found?'

'Look, just leave me to get on with my work, will you?'

The two men eyed each other for long moments, then Perry shrugged and walked away. Cooper watched him disappear along the subterranean passage, making sure he was well out of sight before stepping back inside the cell-like chamber. The silence enveloped him as he returned his attention to the strange series of symbols on the wall before him. There were a number of drawings, each one hacked into the stone, he guessed, with a piece of flint. Beneath each one were letters, some of which formed recognizable words. Others he could make no sense of. As he scraped away more dirt from the stone he saw that the words were beginning to form a sentence. Cooper used a tracer to remove the last vestiges of debris and give himself a clear view of the writing. He read the sentence, mouthing the words silently to himself, his speech slowing as he reached the end.

'My God,' he whispered, his eyes riveted to what he'd read. He scanned it again. And again. More of the Celtic script was carved into other parts of the chamber and he knew that it must all be uncovered, but his eyes kept on returning to the single complete sentence he had so far revealed.

He tried to swallow but his throat felt as if it were full of chalk.

As he stepped back he found that his hands were shaking.

Thirty

'Not bloody cheese again!' groaned Mike Spencer, pulling back one edge of his sandwich and examining the contents. He bit into the bread and chewed quickly.

'Why don't you ask your wife to put something else in them?' Colin Mackay asked.

'I make them myself,' Spencer told him, grinning. 'Cheese was all we had in the fridge, except salami, and I didn't fancy any of that stuff. I'd have ended up smelling like a bloody Italian.'

The other men inside the Portakabin laughed. There were half a dozen of them, all on their lunch break. Outside, on the building site itself, earth-moving machines rumbled back and forth and the roar of powerful engines was a constant background to the men's conversation. Close by, a bulldozer was flattening some ground, the excess earth being scooped up by a JCB. The clanking of caterpillar tracks reminded Spencer of a war film he'd seen the night before. The lorry which he drove back and forth to remove the excess earth was parked on a small incline about thirty feet from the Portakabin. Usually he'd had his lunch at a cafe in Longfield, but that was proving to be expensive so he'd decided to start bringing sandwiches. He'd just come in, having retrieved them from the parcel shelf of the ten-ton Scania.

'You know, I bet the leisure centre is a wreck within six months,' Keith Riley said, gazing out of the window towards the building beyond. 'Once the bloody vandals get at those walls with their spray cans and what have you.'

'I saw a good bit of grafitti in town the other night,'

116

Spencer announced. 'It was sprayed on the bottom of a poster for abortion, and it said "*You rape 'em, we scrape 'em.*" ' He laughed throatily, almost choking on his sandwich.

'I know what Keith means, though,' Mark Little added, pouring himself a cup of tea from his thermos flask. 'I mean, we spent weeks painting that place and it's going to be ruined.'

'You don't have much faith in kids do you?' said Frank King. 'Wait until you've got a couple of your own.'

'Sod off, I'm not having kids,' Little told him. 'They tie you down.'

'Only for the first twenty-five years,' chuckled King.

'So what happens if your old lady gets pregnant, then?' Spencer asked his companion. 'You haven't got the money to pay for an abortion.'

'You can get it done on the National Health, you berk,' Little said. 'Anyway, she'd better not get pregnant. She's been on the pill long enough.'

'My wife's got the coil,' Spencer informed his colleagues. 'On a good day she can pick up Radio One on it.' He burst out laughing again. 'She was going to use the Dutch cap but we couldn't find one to fit her head.'

'How much longer are we supposed to be working on this site, Frank?' Colin Mackay asked the foreman.

'That depends on what Cutler decides to build next,' he said. 'Your guess is as good as mine.'

'I don't care how long we're here,' Spencer said. 'At least the money's good.'

'Come on, fellas,' King said, looking at his watch. 'If *Mr* Cutler decides to pay us a visit I don't think he'll be too happy to find us all lounging about in here.'

Amidst a chorus of complaints and mutterings, the men filed out of the hut. All except Spencer.

'Come on, Mike,' King said.

'Can I just finish my coffee, Frank?' he asked.

'Don't be too long about it,' the foreman said and closed the door behind him leaving Spencer alone.

Inside the Portakabin, Mike Spencer fumbled in his

jacket pocket for his cigarettes, cursing when he realized he must have left them in the lorry. Sod it, he'd wait a few more minutes. He took a sip of his coffee.

If he had been asked to swear on a stack of Bibles, Mike Spencer would have said that he had left the Scania's handbrake on when he parked it on the incline near the Portakabin.

And Frank King naturally would have expected the driver to have done so.

That perhaps was why the foreman was so taken by surprise when he saw the juggernaut move slightly, then begin to roll towards the hut, picking up speed as it did.

For a moment he stood frozen, watching the heavy Scania roll inexorably down the slope, bumping violently over the rough ground as its speed increased. By the time he was able to shout a warning, the lorry was moving at an unstoppable speed.

Still lounging in the Portakabin, Spencer took one last mouthful of coffee, then got to his feet and stretched, becoming vaguely aware of the sound of shouting from outside. He crossed to the window, trying to locate the source of the noise. He frowned in puzzlement as he saw Frank King running towards the hut. Spencer could see him mouthing words but he could not make out what they were.

A second later the lorry ploughed into the hut.

Frank King shouted one last hopeless warning, then he could only stand helplessly and watch as the Scania hit the Portakabin.

The entire structure buckled as the huge bulk of the lorry flattened it.

Others nearby turned to see what was happening, their attention caught by the noise, especially the high-pitched scream which rose from the wreckage.

The foreman started running again, joined by Keith Riley and John Kirkland, and the trio dashed stumbling and swearing across the uneven ground towards the remains of the hut.

Mike Spencer had been caught completely unawares by the collision. The truck had caved in the side wall and the roof of the small building, pinning him beneath the debris, unable to move before the massive rear wheels ran over his legs and thighs. The bones were crushed into pulp by the weight of the huge lorry. Both femurs snapped like matchwood, one jagged edge tearing into his femoral artery before bursting through the skin and muscle of his pulverized thigh. Most of his pelvis was also crushed by the giant wheels. Mercifully, he blacked out as a huge fountain of blood sprayed from the torn artery, rising in a great crimson parabola to splatter the rear end of the truck.

Seated high in the driving seat of the bulldozer, Bob Richardson saw the lorry flatten the hut and immediately jammed the great machine into neutral and switched off the engine. Using one of the caterpillar tracks as a ladder, he began climbing down to join the other men who were running towards the scene of disaster.

He actually had one foot on the ground when the bulldozer's engine roared into life.

Bob looked up in dismay and surprise as the machine rolled forward, instantly trapping his left hand between two of the tread links.

He had one brief second of terrifying realization, then the searing agony began.

As the machine rolled forward he felt an unbearable pressure on his wrist and arm as the 'dozer dragged him a few feet. It was moving slowly but not slowly enough for him to extricate his arm. He shrieked in pain as the tread crushed his wrist and hand, the snapping of bones clearly audible above the clatter of the tracks. He tried to pull himself free, to stop the unbearable wrenching at his shoulder. The entire limb was going numb, the material of his coat tearing under the prolonged tugging.

With one final despairing roar of pain, Bob felt his hand come off.

He sprawled in the mud, the bloodied stump spouting crimson while he screamed for help. His severed hand rolled free of the track as if it had been spat out and he noticed, even through his pain, that the fingers were still twitching.

The bulldozer rolled a few more yards, then stopped.

Bob Richardson continued to scream.

Frank King turned and saw the bulldozer driver sprawled on the ground, his shattered arm spewing blood, the severed hand lying close by. The foreman spun round in time to see Riley and Kirkland, who had reached the smashed hut ahead of him, trying to pull the motionless form of Mike Spencer from beneath the Scania. Apparently they were unaware that too much pressure could rip his body in two. Whether either of the injured men could survive, King didn't know. He stood, hands pressed to his temples, listening to the shouts of alarm from other men running to help, and the next voice he heard was his own, yelling frantically.

'For God's sake get an ambulance!'

Thirty-One

George Perry lifted the crate into the back of the Land Rover, grunting under the weight. He set it down as gently as he could, then stepped back, wiping the dust from his hands.

'There are twelve skulls in there,' he told her. 'That should give you plenty to work with.'

Kim smiled and raised her eyebrows.

'Have you been able to decipher anything from the tablets yet?' Perry asked.

'A little, but I'm still working on them,' she said, looking closely at her colleague, who seemed somehow distracted. 'Is anything wrong, George?' she finally asked.

Perry sighed.

'As a matter of fact there is,' he told her. 'It's Cooper. There's something wrong with him. I don't mean he's ill. It's . . . I don't know, his personality. His entire character seems to have changed in the last day or two. Ever since we discovered the chamber of skulls. He spends all his time in there. He doesn't like anyone else going near it.' The archaeologist sounded indignant. 'He's got no right to do that. I intend having a look myself, whether he likes it or not.'

'Has he found anything else?' Kim wanted to know.

'If he has, he hasn't mentioned it. He seems . . .' Perry struggled to find the right word, 'I don't know . . . obsessed with what he's doing. But it's not only that Cooper's become more aggressive. I think he's frightened as well.'

'What of?'

'I wish I knew. He's found *something* in there and whatever it is, it's scared the hell out of him.'

The two archaeologists looked at one another for a moment, as if both were lost for words.

'Let me know if anything happens,' Kim said finally, climbing behind the wheel of the Land Rover.

Perry nodded, watching as she started the engine and drove off across the field.

He felt a sudden chill sweep through him and it felt uncomfortably familiar. He turned and looked towards the gaping mouth of the shaft.

It took Kim over five hours to carbon-date the first four skulls and put a reasonably accurate fix on their age. Like the rest of the relics recovered from the site, they were at least 2,000 years old. A fluorine test, together with the petrological microscopy, confirmed that fact.

As she worked with the skulls, Kim glanced almost unconsciously at the stone tablets still laid out on the worktop. She intended to continue with them as soon as she'd finished with the skulls.

The museum was closed and she worked alone in the silence, having decided that the building was best left shut while she toiled over the finds.

As she worked, though, she was aware of the ever-present chill which filled the air like invisible freezing fog. She got up to check the radiators, deciding that if it got much colder she could not continue working in the museum.

She returned her attention to the skull before her. She had removed the lower jaw and part of one side, leaving the yawning cranial cavity gaping at her. She had used a small portion of the jaw to grind up for a nitrogen test, but it was the cheek bones and eyes which drew her attention. She studied the same features on all the skulls more closely and saw that each of the skulls bore deep, irregular striation marks. Particularly around the eyes, both above and below. As if some sharp object had been used on them at some time. A knife perhaps.

The thought sent a shudder of revulsion through her body.

It looked as if, all those centuries ago, the eyes had been gouged from their sockets.

Thirty-Two

There were twelve of them.

All naked.

The youngest barely sixteen. The eldest yet to reach twenty.

As they moved back and forth in the clearing the dead leaves rustled beneath their feet and the branches of the trees shook spidery fingers at them. The gloom of the starless night was like a black shroud which had closed over the wood as if to hide what was going on.

Henry Dexter stood slightly to one side of the crudely fashioned cross, his face impassive, his grey hair ruffled by the breeze which swept through the wood.

The cross consisted of two large pieces of wood, nailed together at the apex. They were merely particularly large tree branches which had been broken off and joined by three large masonry nails. A youth stood in front of the cross, a lad of sixteen with a smattering of acne on both his face and shoulders. He faced three girls, all of the same age. One was tall and slender, the other two a little overweight, their bellies and thighs slightly too large.

At a signal from Dexter, Gary Webb and another youth stepped forward and pulled the acne-spotted lad towards the cross, tying his arms securely to the cross-beam so that he was spreadeagled. He shuffled uncomfortably, feeling the ropes cutting into one wrist where they had been fastened a little over-zealously. He put up with the discomfort without complaint, however, because he knew what was to follow.

Led by the tallest, the trio of naked girls knelt before the boy, whose penis was already beginning to harden. As the first girl reached out and drew one finger tip along the shaft, his organ rapidly attained its full stiffness.

The second girl leant forward, took his penis into her mouth and sucked gently on it for a minute or two before the next girl did likewise, tasting her companion's saliva as well as the salty taste of the lad's erection. He strained against the ropes as the feeling of pleasure began to grow more intense.

The tall girl took her turn, this time massaging his swollen testicles while the other two ran their hands up and down his thighs.

'The Cross,' said Dexter. 'Symbol of Christ. Monument to that filthy Jew they called the Son of God.' He spat on

123

the ground in front of the cross. 'He who sent his only bastard offspring into the world via the whore Mary. He who watched his own son die on the Cross. He who denies pleasure.'

The youth tied to the cross was moaning more loudly now as the girls began to work more vigorously on his penis, sucking and rubbing until the lad tensed and prepared for release.

The movements stopped and he gasped, looking down first at his saliva-soaked erection and then at Dexter.

Gary Webb stepped forward and handed the older man a large chalice of gold, watching as he moved closer to the helpless boy. Dexter gripped the boy's penis in his powerful hand, beckoning the tallest of the three girls forward once more. His hand was replaced by hers and Dexter watched her pump it rhythmically up and down on the boy's stiff shaft until he pushed his hips forward and moaned loudly.

A thick stream of semen splattered into the chalice, followed by several more spurts until the white fluid covered the bottom of the receptacle. The boy gradually relaxed as the girl slowed her movements.

From the deep shadows around the clearing, Laura Price stepped into view. She crossed to Dexter and looked at him for a moment before dropping to the ground on all fours, her legs spread, her bottom lifted high in the air.

Dexter knelt swiftly before her and offered the chalice to her lips, watching as the liquid trickled towards her open mouth. She swallowed some of it.

'The body of Christ,' Dexter said, smiling. He got to his feet.

It was as he stepped back that Laura caught sight of the dog.

It was a short-haired collie, a sleek-bodied animal restrained by a length of rope around its throat. As she watched, it was led towards her by Gary Webb, who paused, then handed the make-shift leash to Dexter. The dog barked once but Dexter tugged hard on the rope and the animal was silent except for low panting sounds.

The older man nodded and Gary dropped to his knees behind Laura, his penis now swollen and hard.

Another of the young men stepped forward and took up a position beside Dexter.

He carried a long, double-edged knife.

Dexter began winding the rope around his hand, pulling tighter on the dog's leash, causing the animal to yelp in pain as pressure was increased on its throat. It turned and tried to bite Dexter but he merely twisted the rope tighter, listening as the animal's panting subsided into hollow gasps. Then he yanked it hard, lifting the collie off the ground until it dangled by the rope, its legs thrashing wildly. It required a surprising amount of strength to hold the dog up with one hand but the athletic Dexter found it no effort. The dog was now bucking uncontrollably, its eyes bulging wide as the rope throttled it.

The young man with the knife stepped closer, and with lightning speed drew the blade across the dog's throat.

A great fountain of blood erupted from the wound, spraying all those close by with sticky crimson fluid. Dexter kept his hold on the rope, watching as the dog's struggles gradually became less frantic. Blood continued to spurt from its gashed throat and he watched the red gouts for a moment before lifting the chalice to the wound. The blood spilled in, mixing with the semen to form a thick, coagulated mess.

Dexter dropped the dog and held the chalice above his head with both hands.

'The host,' he said, smiling.

He leant forward and tilted the receptacle so that some of the fluid dripped onto Laura's arched back. She felt the warmth of the blood and squirmed. Dexter spilled more onto her buttocks, watching intently as Gary gathered some on his fingers, rubbing it around her vagina.

Laura groaned slightly. Then she felt Gary force his penis into her vagina. He steadied himself, then began thrusting back and forth, both of them grunting like animals.

Dexter dropped the chalice and took the knife from the other boy, who looked on with the rest as Dexter gripped the dying collie by the hair at the back of its neck, yanking its head back.

Gary Webb speeded up his thrusts as he felt his orgasm beginning to build.

Dexter rolled the dog onto its back and drove the knife into its chest, tearing downwards to expose its insides. Then, using both hands, he pulled the reeking tangle of intestines from the gaping cavity, ignoring the vile stench which rose from the slippery coils. Like springs, the entrails seemed to suddenly expand and Dexter continued pulling until the animal was completely gutted, the steaming vital organs lying in a bloody pile beside him.

Laura, meeting Gary's vigorous thrusts with her own, began to shudder as the pleasure grew more intense. She saw that other couples had also begun copulating. The entire clearing was a mass of pale undulating bodies.

Even the youth tied to the cross was not forgotten. The tall willowy girl took his penis into her mouth and began sucking it while another boy drove his shaft into her from behind.

Dexter, his naked form drenched in blood, began skinning the dead dog, tearing off hunks of skin and hair with his vicious cuts. Finally, he managed to rip the complete coat free.

This he draped over Laura's back, and as she felt the warm blood from the hide covering her skin she began to climax.

Her cries of pleasure mingled with those of others in the clearing.

Dexter stood smiling amidst the wild depravity, his grin broadening as he saw the two girls approaching him. They were young, slim and small-breasted. Their nipples stuck out proudly in the chill wind. The first of them, a girl with short red hair, ran her soft hands over Dexter's body and caressed his swollen testicles while her companion kissed the head of his throbbing organ.

Both bore numerous scabs on the insides of their arms, the flesh purple where it had been bruised and punctured so often. Scar tissue had turned into a vivid crust, purple in places where it had been picked away only to grow again in a more purulent form.

Dexter smiled down at them and stroked their breasts, enjoying the mixture of pleasure and anticipation on their faces.

More eyes turned towards him now. Expectantly.

He knew what they wanted and he raised the bag of heroin into the air, displaying it like some obscene trophy.

A chorus of giggles, cheers and cries of delight rippled around the clearing. The two girls standing beside the older man clung more tightly to him, their eyes riveted to the package of white powder as if it possessed some kind of hypnotic power.

Dexter laughed aloud, the sound carried on the breeze to be lost in the dense trees all around the clearing.

'It's time,' he said, quietly.

Thirty-Three

Who the hell did Cooper think he was?

Not allowing anyone else into the chamber of skulls. Ridiculous!

George Perry was muttering to himself as he clambered down the rope ladder, descending deeper into the shaft.

During the day the hole was black enough, but now, in the darkness of the night, it was impossible to see a hand in front of him as he climbed down, bracing himself carefully on each rung, making his way slowly and cautiously into the abyss.

As he reached the bottom he pulled the powerful torch from his belt and flicked it on. The beam pushed a small funnel of light through the gloom. He moved swiftly through the opening which led on into the maze of tunnels beyond. Once inside the main tunnel, though, Perry slowed his pace, careful not to slip or twist his ankle on the dozens of hazards which littered the tunnel floor. Relics, bones and pieces of fallen rock all combined to create an uneven and treacherous surface and, more than once, the archaeologist had to steady himself against the moist walls.

He sucked in a deep breath, surprised at how taxing the walk along the stone corridor was proving to be. His body felt heavy, as if weights had been attached to his legs, slowing him to a snail's pace, preventing him reaching his goal.

His torch beam dimmed momentarily but he banged the light and it glowed more brightly again.

Perry pressed on, knowing that he must be close to the chamber of skulls. Up ahead, dimly illuminated in the light of the torch, he saw the entrance. He immediately quickened his step although the feeling of heaviness was growing almost intolerably strong now. He gritted his teeth and forged ahead, the icy chill seeping into his flesh, into the bones themselves.

George Perry was a fit man, but by the time he reached the chamber entrance he was puffing and panting as if he'd just run a marathon. He sagged against the stone portal, sucking in lungfuls of the stagnant air, waiting for his strength to return. After what seemed hours but was only minutes, he stepped inside and pulled his notebook from the pocket of his jacket. His torch beam played back and forth over the Celtic script which covered the walls of the chamber. He looked all around the small area but could see nothing that Cooper should want to protect. There didn't seem to be any secrets worth hiding.

Then he saw the words.

A large portion of one wall had been cleaned by Cooper, exposing the ancient letters and symbols carved into the stone. Perry now moved closer, a frown already beginning to crease his forehead. He read the words to himself, faltering in places, but the gist of them came through. He went back to the beginning and started again, the full impact hitting him this time.

'Jesus!' he exclaimed, his voice amplified by the

subterranean tomb. It echoed off the walls and died away slowly to a low whisper.

He spun round, listening to the soft, sibilant hiss, realizing after a second or two that it was his own voice he was hearing. Bouncing off the cold stone and reverberating around him.

Jamming the torch into the crook of one arm, Perry began to scribble down what he saw on the walls before him. He wrote quickly, anxious to be out and away from this place. Simultaneously, he was frightened to go back through the tunnel, but he finished writing and pocketed his notepad. He read the words from the wall again, mouthing them silently this time, his skin prickling.

He had wondered what Cooper had found in this underground tomb but nothing could have prepared him for this.

Perry read the words once more, as if to reassure himself that he had got the sense of them right, then turned and hurried, almost fled, from the chamber. The notebook nestled safely in his pocket.

He would re-read the words when he got home.

Then he would decide what to do.

Thirty-Four

At first she thought she was dreaming.

Kim heard the low whispering but merely sighed, rolled over and settled herself again, her eyelids growing heavier. Yes, that was it, she told herself, she was dreaming. She wasn't really hearing the soft, but insistent, whispering. The sound continued and she finally sat upright, realizing that the noises she heard were not the product of her

129

imagination. She could hear them clearly now, beyond the door of her own room, drifting through the darkness.

The sound stopped for a few moments. Kim thought about sliding back beneath the covers, but then it began once more, slightly louder if anything. She swung herself out of bed, pulling on her dressing gown, now drawn irresistibly towards the low whispering.

She paused at her bedroom door, listening, trying to detect the source of the sound. There didn't seem to be any movement, only the noise. Low and conspiratorial, occasionally rising in volume, then dying away completely for a moment or two.

Kim eased her door open, cursing as it creaked on its hinges.

The whispering stopped.

She took a step onto the landing, wishing that the light switch was beside her room instead of being on the far side of the landing. It was dark and she squinted hard in an effort to distinguish shapes in the gloom. She reached out with one hand and touched the balustrade, which felt icy cold. Kim took two more tentative steps forward, hoping that the floorboards wouldn't creak beneath her, wondering why she felt so uneasy.

She heard the hissing once more.

Close to her.

Her heart thudded harder against her ribs as she turned, realizing that the low whispering was coming from her daughter's room.

Kim crossed to the door and put one hand on the cold handle.

'Clare,' she called softly. 'Are you awake?'

No answer.

The whispering stopped again.

Kim hesitated a moment longer, then pushed the door open and stepped into the darkened room, her hand hovering over the light switch.

She heard the sound once more and a slight frown creased her forehead as she realized that it was indeed Clare who was making it. Even in the gloom she could see her daughter's lips moving as she mouthed the words. Whatever they were. The girl was obviously dreaming. She'd thrown her blankets off and lay completely uncovered. Kim stepped to the bed and pulled the blankets up around her once more, afraid that she might catch a chill.

As she bent low over her daughter she heard the words which escaped her fluttering lips and she froze.

They came only sporadically but a few of them were recognizable.

Kim crouched beside the bed, looking at Clare's face and listening.

'Help me,' the girl whispered. 'Time is coming . . . *He* is coming . . . Sa . . .'

Kim listened more closely.

'He knows . . . can't stop . . . too late now . . . He's coming . . .'

The words trailed off as Clare rolled onto her side.

For what seemed an age Kim remained crouched beside her daughter's bed, waiting to see if the girl continued whispering, but she did not. After ten minutes, Kim got to her feet and padded towards her own room, taking one last look at her daughter before closing the door behind her.

She climbed into bed, aware of how cold it had become inside the house.

Her daughter had only been dreaming, she told herself. It was nothing to be alarmed about.

But, for some reason, Kim found it difficult to drift off to sleep again. The hands of the alarm clock showed three a.m. by the time she fell into welcome oblivion.

She was still asleep an hour later when Clare pushed open the bedroom door and looked in.

The girl stood gazing almost mesmerized at her mother for a full five minutes, her eyes wide and staring. Then she turned and walked slowly back to her own room.

However, she did not sleep again that night.

Thirty-Five

Dew lay over the ground like a gossamer sheet and dripped from the roadside bushes like liquid crystal. Spiders' webs looked as if they'd been constructed from spun glass as they glistened in the first rays of dawn light.

Mick Ferguson lit up a cigarette and sucked hard on it, coughing throatily before propelling a lump of mucus into the field behind him. He dug his hands into the pockets of his jacket and leant against the wooden fence behind him, his eyes darting up and down the road which led into Longfield, although he doubted there would be much traffic about at such an unholy hour of the morning. He glanced at his watch and saw that it was not yet six-thirty a.m. He'd already been waiting for fifteen minutes, freezing his balls off. Another five minutes and he was bloody well going.

Now he saw the figure striding purposefully towards him, apparently oblivious to the early morning chill.

Ferguson waited until the newcomer was within three or four yards of him, then hawked loudly and spat into the roadside grass.

'About fucking time,' he rasped. 'I've been standing here like a right prick for the last twenty minutes.'

'It's not my fault you got here early,' Henry Dexter told him, regarding the other man with ill-disguised contempt.

'Have you got the money?'

'If you've got the stuff.'

'Yeah, I've got it. You must have used quite a bit at your little *party* last night,' Ferguson said, sarcastically. 'You'll have to invite me sometime.'

Dexter didn't answer. He followed the other man over to

132

the van which was parked by a clump of leafless trees. Ferguson unlocked it and reached inside, pulling out two small bags. He held the heroin before Dexter.

'Two hundred a bag,' he announced.

'That's fifty more than last time,' Dexter protested.

'Where else are you going to get it?' Ferguson snapped. 'Now either pay up or piss off. I'm the one who runs the fucking risks. I'm the one who takes the chances. I have to pay the dealers I get it from. When they put their prices up, so do I.' He chuckled. 'Just put it down to inflation.'

Dexter hesitated a moment then dug his hand into his pocket and pulled out a thick wad of notes. He counted out four hundred pounds in twenty-pound notes and pocketed the remainder, taking the heroin from Ferguson.

'How pure is it?' he asked, brandishing one of the bags before him.

Ferguson shrugged.

'I got it from a different dealer this time. I don't know.' He smiled. 'You'll just have to take a chance.'

Dexter slipped the bags into his pocket.

'What do you care, anyway?' Ferguson asked. 'You don't use it yourself, do you? You only give it to the kids.'

'That's my business, Ferguson, I've told you before.'

'I know that. It makes no difference to me what you do with it. But when the builders get around to flattening that wood where you hold your little parties, what are you going to do then? It looks like you might have to find something else to occupy your time.' He chuckled.

'I don't know why you think it's so funny. If I stop holding the ceremonies then those who attend will go elsewhere. You'll lose business as well. It's in both our interests to see that the wood stays untouched.'

The two men locked stares for a moment, then Dexter turned and walked away.

Ferguson stood by the van for a moment longer, watching him disappear around a bend in the road, before he started the engine, jammed the vehicle into gear and drove back into Longfield.

Thirty-Six

The light burning in the sitting room was a welcoming sight to John Kirkland as he swung his Metro into the short drive alongside his house. He clambered out of the vehicle and opened the garage door, making a mental note to oil the hinges as he heard them squealing. Then he walked back to the car, got in and drove into the dark garage.

The dashboard clock showed 8:22 p.m.

Kirkland switched off the engine and sat in the gloomy silence, stretching in his seat, feeling the stiffness in the muscles.

Christ, what a day he'd had. Checking every single piece of machinery at the building site to ensure that there were no more accidents like those of the previous day. He and Frank King had been over every one of the vehicles with a fine-tooth comb but had found nothing out of the ordinary. No electrical or mechanical faults of any kind. Just as they had found nothing wrong with the bulldozer the day before to account for it starting up and tearing Bob Richardson's hand off.

They had found no apparent fault with the handbrake of the Scania, either, but it had still managed to roll down that incline and crush Mike Spencer to death.

Kirkland rubbed the bridge of his nose between his thumb and forefinger and exhaled wearily. He was thankful that he hadn't been the one chosen to tell Spencer's wife what had happened. The constable who'd turned up at the scene of the accident had taken it upon himself to perform the task. All part of the job, thought Kirkland, clambering out of the car. He locked it and made his way to the door which led into the kitchen.

His stomach rumbled loudly as the smell of food reached him.

He winced for a moment as he stepped into the well-lit kitchen, the fluorescents presenting a glaring contrast to the darkness of the garage. As his eyes became accustomed to the brightness he noticed a couple of saucepans simmering on the stove. Steam was rising in a white cloud from the bubbling pans, creating a film of condensation on the windows and walls.

On the worktop close by there was a half-finished glass of orange juice.

Kirkland frowned and turned down the heat under the saucepans.

'Jaqui,' he called, wondering if his wife was on the phone in the hall. Yes, he decided that must be the answer. Why else would she leave the kitchen unattended so long while the meal was cooking?

He wandered through to the sitting room, glancing at the television set. The sound was turned right down, but as he approached the hall he could hear no voices. No phone conversation.

'Jaqui,' he called again.

No answer.

Only the low murmurings from the television set.

A thought struck him. One which should have been so obvious.

One which sent him bounding up the stairs two at a time.

He found her in the bedroom.

She was lying on her back, one arm resting across her forehead, her skin as white as milk.

Kirkland crossed to her, taking one of her hands in his, feeling the clamminess of her skin.

'Jaqui,' he whispered, watching as her eyes flickered open. 'Are you all right, love?'

She managed a smile, then nodded almost impercept- ibly.

'I felt faint,' she said, answering his unasked question.

135

She reached for the packet of Dextrosol tablets on the bedside table and popped one into her mouth. In moments Kirkland saw some of the colour coming back into her cheeks. She sat up and kissed him lightly on the lips.

Jaqui Kirkland had been diabetic every since she was nine, and in the twenty years since that discovery she had been forced to inject herself with insulin twice every day. The problem had been well under control until she became pregnant. Now, six months after discovering that she was carrying a child, she had undergone a series of hypogly-caemic attacks due to the fluctuation of her blood sugar level. The doctors had warned her that the level would rise because of the pregnancy but none had told her of the discomfort she would experience when the level dropped. However, the Dextrosol seemed to work for her and so far she had only been admitted to hospital once in those six months. Only occasionally did she succumb to the full fury of an attack.

'I left the saucepans on,' she said apologetically.

Kirkland brushed a strand of dark hair from her face.

'It's OK,' he said. 'We've got our own Turkish bath in the kitchen but there's no harm done.'

They both giggled.

'I'm all right now, John,' she assured him, trying to swing her legs off the bed, but he restrained her.

'Stay here,' Kirkland instructed. 'You rest for a while. I'll see to the dinner.'

'I'm all right, honestly.'

'Don't argue with me, woman,' he said with mock sternness. 'Don't you dare move off this bed until I get back. I've got to go and shut the garage door anyway.'

She nodded and squeezed his hand as he got to his feet, turning towards the bedroom door. He made his way down the stairs, through the sitting room and into the kitchen. The steam had not yet dissipated, so Kirkland opened two of the kitchen windows, watching for a moment as the condensation was sucked out into the dark night.

He fumbled in his trouser pocket for the key which would

lock the garage door, then stepped into the gloom, closing the kitchen door behind him.

There was a light switch close to his left hand and he flicked it on.

Nothing happened.

The garage remained in darkness.

He muttered something about having to change the bulb, then walked cautiously towards the door which was still letting in some faint light from the streetlamps outside. He cracked his shin on the frame of a baby's pushchair, an early present from Jaqui's parents. Cursing the object, he rubbed his leg and hobbled the remaining few feet to the garage door. Once there he reached up and pulled it down, plunging the garage into impenetrable blackness. There was another light switch nearby and he tried that one too.

For a split second the bulb flickered.

In that instant of twilight Kirkland saw a dark shape close by his car.

He stood still, his heart suddenly beating faster.

The light flickered once more, then went out.

Kirkland snapped the switch up and down frantically, and again the bulb burst into brief life.

The dark shape was gone.

He let out a long sigh and made his way back across the garage, careful to avoid the pushchair this time. He found himself putting out a hand to prevent himself tumbling over any other obstacle that might be blocking his path.

Close by him, something moved.

Kirkland spun round, trying to see in the gloom, screwing his eyes up in an effort to penetrate the darkness that surrounded him.

He heard a metallic scraping sound, then a loud crash, the sound amplified by the silence inside the garage.

For a moment he leant back against the car, his heart pounding. He fumbled in his pocket for his lighter and flicked it on, holding it high above him.

He breathed an audible sigh of relief when he saw the rake lying a few feet away. It had been that which he'd

137

dislodged, and its handle had struck some other garden tools which leaned against one wall and had toppled them like over-sized skittles.

Kirkland closed the lighter, plunging himself back into the gloom. He was now almost to the door which led through to the kitchen.

Strong hands closed suddenly round his throat, jerking upward so powerfully that he was momentarily lifted off his feet.

Eyes bulging in their sockets, blind in the blackness, he could only flail his arms uselessly against his invisible attacker.

Kirkland grunted helplessly as the incredibly powerful hands lifted him fully off the ground before hurling him towards the car.

He hit the vehicle with a sickening thud which jarred him from head to foot and made stars dance before his eyes. He opened his mouth to shout for help, but the pressure on his windpipe had been so great that he could produce only a strangled wheeze.

Head spinning, he tried to rise, clawing his way up the side of the car.

He was upright when he heard the arc of the rake.

The prongs caught him in the side of the face, splintering his cheekbone with the force of their impact. Two of the sharp points pierced his left eye and now he found voice for a scream of agony as blood spilled down his cheek, mingling with the spurts of vitreous fluid from his torn eye.

He crashed to the floor, already beginning to lose consciousness, but before merciful oblivion could claim him he felt fingers tearing at his other eye.

Sharp nails digging into the socket, gouging beneath the sensitive orb, shredding skin and muscle in the process.

Kirkland raised a hand and pushed against the garage door. A thin shaft of light suddenly illuminated his attacker.

Jaqui Kirkland heard the scream.

She hauled herself upright, her heart pounding wildly, a

sudden uncontrollable fear spreading through her.

She swung herself off the bed and scuttled towards the stairs, slowing her pace slightly as she reached them for fear of falling.

As she made her way down she spoke her husband's name over and over again. Reaching the hall, she ran through the sitting room with its television that still whispered and into the kitchen.

From the garage there was an almighty crash.

Jaqui hesitated for what seemed an eternity at the door which led to the garage. Finally, with one last surge of courage, she threw the door back, hearing it crash against the garage wall.

Light from the kitchen spilled into the blackness beyond, illuminating the scene before her.

For long seconds she stood upright, her eyes riveted to the ragged bundle which lay by the car. Then, with a moan, she sagged against the door frame, her stomach churning, her lips fluttering soundlessly.

John Kirkland lay like some bloodied, broken mannequin in the centre of a spreading pool of blood. Some of the crimson liquid had sprayed up the side of the car. Great thick smears of it covered the walls. He lay on his side, his stomach gaping open to reveal the slippery lengths of intestine which had been pulled from his belly.

His head, one side of which had been pulverized by the blow from the rake, was twisted around at an impossible angle, the empty eye sockets fixing Jaqui in a sightless stare. Clogged with congealing gore, they reminded her of ink wells filled with bright crimson.

There were deep cuts around his neck and chest, and several reaching from his throat to his pelvis.

Most of the flesh of his torso, arms and legs had been stripped away to expose the bleeding network of muscles beneath.

Jaqui retched, feeling the nausea sweeping over her. She stared, mesmerized, at her dead husband. When she finally tore her horrified gaze from his ruined corpse, her eyes only alighted on something equally vile.

139

On the windscreen of the car, lying there like some monstrous parasite, still pulsing in places, was a thick length of intestine.

It had been quickly but unmistakably shaped to form the letter S.

Thirty-Seven

'The injuries are identical to those of the first victim,' Doctor Bernard Ryan said, pulling at the end of his nose.

Wallace nodded and glanced at the photos spread out before him on the desk.

'So I see,' he murmured wearily.

In the relative silence of the office, the ticking of the wall clock sounded thunderous. The hands were just moving past twelve noon.

More than fifteen hours had passed since the first policeman had been called to the home of John Kirkland. The screams of the dead man's wife had alerted neighbours who had not been slow in summoning help. Wallace himself had arrived at the house at the same time as the ambulance, less than fifteen minutes after the corpse had been discovered.

The garage and its contents had been dusted thoroughly for fingerprints. Particularly the rake which had been used to fell Kirkland in the first place. But now Wallace looked down at the report and shook his head.

There had been indentations on the rake handle, such was the strength of the hands which had held it.

But it bore not one single print of any description.

The killer had obviously been wearing gloves, Wallace

reasoned, but why had Ryan found no trace of fibres from them on or around Kirkland's mutilated body?

Surgical gloves, the inspector speculated.

They would have left no trace.

And yet . . .

He sucked in a weary breath and flipped through the report once more as the doctor sat by silently.

It showed that the eyes had been removed by hand and that the evisceration also had been completed without the aid of any tool or weapon.

No fingerprints, and yet there were scratch marks on the dead builder's face. How could this be if the killer had worn gloves?

Wallace ran a hand through his hair and sat back in his seat, eyes glued to the set of prints before him. The ten monochrome photos only served to compound his obvious bewilderment. They lay there like silent accusations. Constant reminders of his inability to find the leads he so desperately sought.

'The killer has a grouse against the builders on Cutler's site,' he said finally, breaking the long silence. 'You don't have to be Sherlock Holmes to work that out.' He sat forward, glancing up at Ryan as he tapped the photos with the end of his pencil. 'But why go to so much bother mutilating the bodies?'

'Is that a rhetorical question?' said the doctor, 'Or are you asking my opinion?'

'Have you got one?' Wallace asked.

'The fact that the killer steals the eyes and the flayed skin could point to some motive deeper than revenge against the builders.

Wallace looked vague.

'There's something almost ritualistic about these murders,' Ryan continued.

'So you think the eyes and the skin have been taken for a reason?'

'It's a possibility. At this stage I don't think you can afford to ignore *any* angle.'

'Unfortunately it doesn't bring us any closer to

understanding what kind of person actually carried out the killings.' The policeman stroked his chin thoughtfully. He picked up the photo which showed the letter S so crudely yet effectively fashioned from a length of Kirkland's intestine.

What the hell was this bastard playing at? First an M. Now this. Wallace knew of psychopaths who felt compelled to leave evidence of their involvement in bizarre crimes, evidence which would eventually lead to their own arrest. Had he just such a psychopath on his hands now? Was this all part of a monstrous game?

He got to his feet and walked to the large picture window behind his desk. It looked out over the car park of the police station. Down below, Constable Denton, sleeves rolled up, was busy washing down one of the police cars parked on the tarmac.

'You say that the eyes and the intestines were removed by hand,' Wallace said, his back to the doctor, 'but the actual flaying was done using some kind of cutting edge?'

'A piece of broken glass was used on Lawrence,' Ryan confirmed. 'I found a trowel close to Kirkland's body. Both implements were used to remove the skin, although as I said, whoever did it was clumsy. Especially in Kirkland's case. Most of the musculature of the chest had been hacked away too.'

'How much do you know about ritual murder?' Ryan wanted to know.

Wallace shrugged.

'Not enough. I mean, it's not the sort of thing you spend your time studying, is it?'

'It seems as if someone out there disagrees with you,' the doctor said, cryptically.

Wallace picked up the autopsy report on John Kirkland, flipping through it until he found the entry he sought.

His eyes skimmed back and forth over the short sentences as if by constantly re-reading them he would make some sense of them. Perhaps they would at least lose some of their impact.

There was no such effect.

142

The most disturbing aspect of both murders still remained before him. Something which sent a shudder through the inspector each time he glanced at the neatly typed reports.

Besides the appalling injuries inflicted upon them, both Stuart Lawrence and John Kirkland had suffered massive cardiac arrests.

As if, prior to death, each had witnessed something so dreadful it had simply caused their hearts to burst.

As if they had been frightened to death.

Thirty-Eight

Banks of grey cloud were gathering in the late afternoon sky, signalling the approach of rain. They cast a dull, threatening shadow over the land.

Kim reached for the tracer and cleaned some fragments from the stone tablet she was working on, then blew the dust off and began carefully transcribing the Celtic script onto a fresh sheet of A4 paper. The job was a tortuous one, but already that day she had filled five of the sheets with her neat handwriting.

Yet even though she had now deciphered three of the stone slabs she was no closer to understanding them.

The tablets retained their secrets for the time being.

Kim reached for the mug of tea close by and took a sip, gazing down at what she'd written:

THEY COME FOR THEIR FEASTS AND THEIR DAYS OF PRAISE AND THEY SEE ME PRESENT. THEY WISH ME THERE FOR THEY KNOW I COMMAND HIM WHO THEY FEAR . . .

She tapped the paper with her pen, cradling the mug of tea in her free hand, and read on:

> BUT THERE ARE OTHERS TOO WHOM THEY FEAR AND WITH GOOD REASON FOR THERE IS MUCH POWER IN THIS WORLD BEYOND THAT I ALONE AM ABLE TO TREAD.

Kim shuddered slightly, feeling tickling fingers playing icily across the back of her neck as she read:

> I AM BOTH MASTER AND SLAVE. FEARED YET FEARFUL.

She sat unmoving on her stool, listening to the silence which seemed to close around her like a living entity.

She felt almost in a trancelike state when the car pulling up outside broke the solitude.

Kim waited a moment, feeling annoyed at the intruding noise, then got to her feet, heading out of the laboratory to the entrance hall of the museum. Her heels echoed noisily in the empty silence. The sign on the outside door said clearly enough that the museum was closed until further notice. She waited in the hall for the new arrival to see it and depart.

There was a loud knock.

'We're closed,' she called. 'There's a notice . . .'

'Police,' the voice replied. 'I'd like to come in.'

She hesitated a moment, then stepped forward, slid the bolt and opened the door.

She recognized Wallace immediately.

'Sorry to disturb you,' he said, smiling.

'Inspector Wallace!' she exclaimed, returning his smile. 'To what do I owe this pleasure?' She ushered him into the hall.

As Wallace stepped inside he drew a breath which felt as though it would freeze his lungs.

It was numbingly cold in the building and he felt as if millions of icy pins were pricking his face and hands.

'I need your expert help,' he said, raising his eyebrows. 'I've just come from the library in Longfield. They didn't

144

have what I wanted so they suggested I try this place. They said you had a considerable collection of books in the building.'

'That depends on what you're looking for,' said Kim, leading him to the right, towards the archway that led into the library.

Wallace scanned the room, which seemed full to bursting with row upon row of volumes in all shapes and sizes, new and old.

'I'm looking for information on ritual murder,' he said flatly, and Kim frowned in concentration as he eyed the shelves.

'That's not my field of expertise, Inspector,' she told him, leading him toward the closest shelf, 'but I think we have a few books here that might be helpful.'

He pulled a packet of cigarettes from his pocket and stuck one in his mouth.

'Is it OK if I smoke?' he asked, fumbling for his lighter.

She nodded, watching as he flicked at the recalcitrant object, unable to raise more than a few sparks.

'You wouldn't happen to have a light, would you?' he asked, almost apologetically.

Kim smiled and turned away, heading for the exit.

'I'll see what I can do. Would you like a cup of coffee a little later?

He winked at her.

'You're a mind reader.'

Wallace set to work.

4:56 p.m.

Wallace closed the great leather-bound tome and pushed it away from him. He stretched, hearing his joints crack. His back ached and there was a dull pain settling into the base of his skull. He was no closer to discovering the exact nature of the rituals carried out on Stuart Lawrence and John Kirkland, and that irritated him. There was one single word written on his notepad, underlined several times:

WITCHCRAFT.

He closed the pad.

'Did you find what you were looking for?'

The voice startled him momentarily and he spun round to see Kim standing in the doorway holding two mugs of coffee.

'I'm not even sure what I was looking for to begin with,' he confessed wearily, thanking her as she set down his coffee, then pulled up a chair opposite him. Wallace warmed his hands around the mug for a moment before taking a sip. He found his gaze drawn to hers and for brief, but telling, seconds they exchanged glances.

'Do you mind if I ask you some questions, Mrs Nichols?' he said finally.

'My name's Kim,' she told him. 'Unless it's *that* serious.'

Wallace smiled.

'You're aware of the fact that two men working on the building project just out of town have been murdered recently?' he asked.

'There was something in the paper, yes, but no details.'

'Did you know either of them personally? Either Stuart Lawrence or John Kirkland?' He went on to describe them.

'I'd seen Lawrence a couple of times. He came out to the dig a week or so ago with Cutler, the land developer. I didn't know the other man.'

'How did Charles Cooper get on with Lawrence?'

'He hardly knew him.'

'He can't have been too happy about the builders closing down your dig. You told me yourself that he thought it was one of the most important ever.'

'I don't understand what you're getting at, Inspector. You're not implying that Charles had something to do with those men being murdered, are you?'

'Just thinking aloud,' he told her.

'That site *is* very important. I think Charles has a right to be angry at the prospect of it being closed down. Some of the finds are priceless, both in an archaeological and a financial sense.'

'Worth killing for?' asked Wallace.

Kim eyed him irritably for a moment, then took a sip of her coffee.

'Sorry,' he said. 'But I'm only doing my job. I had to ask.'
She nodded.
'I understand,' she told him.
There was a heavy silence, broken by Wallace.
'How's your daughter?'
'She's fine. She'll be wondering where I am, though a neighbour looks after her until I get home.' Kim looked at her watch. 'I'm going to have to throw you out, Inspector,' she said, smiling.
'Steve,' he told her. 'My name is Steve.'
She coloured slightly but returned his smile.
'I need some more information,' he told her. 'I was wondering if you could give it to me. I need to know something about the Celts. I understand you're quite an authority. Only if you're closing up now, perhaps you'd like to discuss it over dinner tonight?'
Kim smiled.
'I don't know,' she said, reluctantly. 'It's not always easy to find someone to babysit for Clare, especially not at such short notice. I'm sorry.'
He felt momentarily deflated and did his best to hide it.
'It would be much easier if you came over to my house,' she suggested. 'I'll cook a meal for us. Then I don't have to worry about Clare. If that's all right with you?'
He laughed, watching as she pulled his notepad towards her and wrote down her address.
'Just in case you'd forgotten,' she said. 'About eight o'clock?'
'That's fine. Thanks, Kim.' He was already getting up. She handed him the notepad and showed him out, ensuring that the door was locked behind him.
Wallace stood in the car park grinning broadly for a moment, then he headed towards his car. However, halfway there he turned and looked back in bewilderment at the museum.
Despite the cool breeze which was blowing, it felt considerably warmer out in the car park than inside the building.

Thirty-Nine

The floor was drenched with blood.

The entire cellar reeked of the sticky crimson fluid.

Mick Ferguson spread sawdust thickly over the gore but it merely soaked through, filling his nostrils with an odour that reminded him of an abattoir. The comparison was particularly appropriate.

The remains of two cats lay scattered over the red-flecked floor. Torn lengths of intestine and lumps of bloodied flesh were strewn over most of the underground room. Ferguson kicked at the severed head of one of the dead animals and watched it roll across the floor, blood still draining from the shredded veins and arteries of its neck.

He turned and looked at the two dogs in the cages behind him, both of them smeared with blood. Rob Hardy sat on the bottom step of the stone staircase smoking a roll-up, his eyes also fixed on the dogs. Particularly the albino terrier. He was pleased that the bloody thing was locked away safely in its cage once more. It frightened the shit out of him. Even Ferguson had no real control over the demented beast. Only the thick chain it always wore prevented it from savaging the two men once it was released from its prison. But now, to Hardy's relief, the bastard was penned up again. He gazed at it, finding his stare returned by those vile pink eyes.

'Do you think he's ready for the pit?' Hardy asked, motioning towards the dog.

Ferguson nodded.

'I heard that some big shot's flying in from Belfast to see the fight,' he said. 'They go a bundle on dog-fighting over

148

there, you know. If he's interested I might sell the dog. For the right price of course.'

Hardy sucked hard on his cigarette, watching his companion scoop up the cat's head and drop it into a plastic bag as he began clearing up the bloody debris.

'You know, I'd bet my life on that dog tearing the shit out of anything sent against it,' Ferguson said, nodding in the direction of the albino. 'But there's one test I'd like to give it before it fights.'

Hardy looked vague.

'I'd like it to have a go at something that could put up a real fight.'

Inside the cage, the dog eyed both men and began barking.

Forty

The footpath stretched away before him, snaking between trees whose skeletal branches bent low as if threatening to reach down and scoop up anyone who came within reach.

Thick bushes also lined the dirt track, which even at its widest point was no more than five feet across.

Jonathan Ashton knew that he shouldn't have taken this route home. He knew because his mother had told him on numerous occasions not to walk the footpath alone. And now, as he hurried along it, he knew that there were other reasons too.

The light of early evening still filled the sky, but beneath the canopy of leafless trees it was already preternaturally dull. Crane flies, some of the last to survive the summer, skimmed through the air and occasionally bumped into

Jonathan as he walked, hands thrust deep into the pockets of his jeans.

Wraith-like swarms of gnats assaulted him every now and then and he quickened his pace, wanting to run but knowing that the extra effort was wasted.

He was over an hour late for tea as it was. His mother would be furious.

If she knew he'd used the footpath to get home she'd be even more angry. He'd be confined to the house for a fortnight, perhaps longer. Jonathan took one hand from his pocket and brushed the fine blond hair from his eyes, glancing around him as he did so. As is the nature of six-year-olds, his imagination was working overtime. He knew that he shouldn't have come this way, shouldn't have strayed from the main streets even though it cut his journey in half. His mother would rather he was even later than have him wandering along the dusk-shrouded footpath alone.

But it was too late now. He was half-way along the dark track. There was no point turning back.

As he walked he kicked with trainer-clad feet at the fallen leaves, humming to himself, noticing how even that soft sound seemed to echo in the stillness.

Only the occasional twittering of birds broke the solitude which bore down on him from all sides.

The bushes ahead of him moved, and Jonathan slowed his pace, wondering if he should turn after all and run back the way he'd come.

He kept walking.

The bushes moved again and this time he felt his heart quicken.

He was only feet away when the blackbird rose from the tangled mass of twigs and soared into the air, a dark arrow-head against the mass of gathering cloud.

Jonathan kept on walking, approaching a curve in the path which would put him on the final three hundred yards. It ended at a broken-down stile and he saw it as the winning post in some kind of race. Once he'd reached it he'd be fine. Up and over the stile then a short run home. He'd get told

150

off by his parents but at least they wouldn't find out he'd used the footpath. If they did, his dad would fetch the wooden spoon for sure. Jonathan didn't fancy three cracks across the backside with that this evening. Again he wished he hadn't decided to take the path home.

The dark trees seemed to glower down at him, but Jonathan tried to keep his gaze fixed on the path ahead.

He rounded the corner.

Another crane fly buzzed him and he knocked it aside angrily, stamping on the insect as it fell to the ground.

It was as he stood watching its last twitchings that he heard the sound.

Further up the footpath, behind him and out of sight, he heard footsteps.

Heavy rhythmic footfalls which grew steadily louder.

And closer.

Jonathan looked around frantically for somewhere to hide.

Should he try to climb a tree?

Hide behind a bush?

He decided to run instead.

Fear gripped him like a metal vice, squeezing tighter as each second passed.

He glanced behind him but could see nothing.

Whoever was behind him had yet to round the corner. But he could hear the footfalls drawing nearer.

Louder.

Jonathan ran as fast as he could, almost stumbling on the uneven surface.

Closer.

He looked round again and almost screamed.

The figure was just rounding the corner, bearing down on him.

Clad completely in black, the figure pounded along the footpath towards Jonathan, drawing closer with each stride. Until finally the figure reached him.

Jonathan stopped running as the jogger in the black track suit went puffing past him, arms flailing wearily, breath coming in short gasps.

151

The youngster watched as the jogger reached the stile about a hundred yards further on. The black-clad man hauled himself over it with what looked like a monumental effort. Then he was gone.

Jonathan was alone once more.

He felt his heart thudding madly against his ribs but he still managed to chuckle to himself, amused at his own fear, glad that he had almost reached the end of the path.

He was still laughing when two strong hands shot out from the bushes and dragged him out of sight.

Forty-One

Wallace sat back in his chair and patted his stomach approvingly.

'That was a beautiful meal,' he said, smiling.

Kim made a theatrical curtsey before carrying the plates into the kitchen. She returned a moment later with two plates of gateaux.

'I hope you've got room for it,' she said. 'It's home-made.'

'I'll make room,' Wallace said and picked up his fork.

They had spoken easily and with unexpected warmth whilst eating dinner, and both had become certain of a strong mutual attraction between them. They felt at ease in each other's company; Kim had found no difficulty explaining how her marriage had broken up, and similarly, Wallace had talked freely about his days as a constable in London and his move to Longfield as an inspector. What had surprised him most was that he had actually felt the need to tell her of his feelings when he was three and his mother had died of cancer, and when his father, years later,

152

had married a much younger woman. His respect and even his love for the man had been eroded and finally destoyed. Now his father too was dead, victim of a massive heart attack only three years earlier. He had no close family left.

With formalities over and confessions exchanged, sipping wine and eating the cake that Kim had made, both of them felt unusually relaxed.

'So, tell me about the Celts,' Wallace said. 'What kind of people were they?'

'They were strange in many ways,' Kim said. 'Great artists and builders, intelligent men, but also barbaric, violent people. But I can't see how this will help your investigation, Steve.'

'Just humour me, Kim,' he asked, pushing a forkful of cake into his mouth. 'I was reading today about the Druids and their practices. Is it right that they burned people alive and watched them die so that they could foretell the future?'

Kim nodded.

'It was a kind of divination, a way of foretelling events to come. That was only done to prisoners of war or lunatics, though. The most popular method of foretelling the future was by studying the entrails of sacrificial victims.'

Wallace looked up, chewing more slowly now, listening to every word as if frightened he'd miss something.

'The victim, or offering, was cut open and the Druid would pull out the intestines and spread them on the ground. The victim's death throes were studied first, then the entrails themselves. Patterns were made with them.'

'Like letters?' Wallace asked, his mind suddenly filled with grisly visions of what he'd seen in Lawrence's bedroom and Kirkland's garage.

'Sometimes.' Kim said.

Wallace exhaled deeply.

'What about flaying the victims, or removing the eyes?' he wanted to know.

'There were so many practices it's difficult to say which ones were most common.' Kim told him. 'Each tribe worshipped a different god or goddess, and the details of sacrificial rituals depended on which deity was involved. At least 394 have been counted.'

'But what about this business with the intestines? Was that widespread?'

'It was one of the few things that was practised by nearly all the tribes.'

Kim looked puzzled as the inspector sat back, brushing a strand of hair from his forehead.

'I don't see how this can help you,' she said.

'When we found Stuart Lawrence and John Kirkland,' he began, ' – and for God's sake keep this information to yourself – both of them had been mutilated. They'd had their eyes torn out, they'd been flayed, and also their stomachs had been torn open. The intestines had been removed and formed into letters.'

Kim swallowed hard and put down her wine glass.

'Now you see why I had to ask you about Cooper,' Wallace said. 'It looks as if the killer has some knowledge of this type of ritual murder.'

'I noticed on your notepad, earlier, you'd written 'Witchcraft'. Are you considering that too?'

He told her about the animals in the wood near Dexter Grange.

'I also read something about the Druids cutting off the heads of their enemies and eating the brains,' he said. 'Why did they do that?'

'Well, the Druids believed that different parts of the body were capable of carrying different powers. If they killed an enemy in battle they'd cut off his head and eat the brains. They felt that the head was the source of all power and knowledge so, by eating it, they'd inherit the strength and courage of the enemy they'd killed. They also thought that by doing that they would stop the soul of their victim from attacking them. They believed in the transmigration of souls. The ability of a dead person's soul to invade the body of another, someone still alive.'

'You mean like demonic possession?' Wallace said.

Kim nodded.

154

'By destroying the body in a physical form they felt they were destroying the soul too. That way it couldn't take them over. Possess them.'

Wallace laid his fork gently down on the plate.

'Why were Lawrence and Kirkland killed?' Kim wanted to know.

'I wish I could tell you,' Wallace said. 'Obviously someone doesn't want that building project finished.' He shrugged and reached for his wine glass, draining the last drops.

In the sitting room the phone rang.

Kim got up and walked through to answer it, leaving Wallace alone for a moment, gazing at his empty plate. He heard her speaking, then:

'Steve, it's for you.' There was a note of surprise in her voice.

Wallace joined her in the sitting room.

'Sorry about that,' he said. 'I'm on twenty-four hour call, so I had to leave this number with the station.' He took the receiver from her and she retreated into the dining room as he spoke. She knew from the few words he uttered that it was bad news. A moment later she heard the phone being replaced.

'Kim, I've got to go,' he said, heading for the hall, pulling on his jacket. 'There's trouble. A child has been kidnapped.'

He paused for a moment, looking at her, their eyes locked. Then both of them moved forward and embraced gently but firmly, their lips pressed together.

'I'm sorry,' he said, breaking the kiss and turning for the door.

'There'll be other times,' she said, smiling, watching as he hurried out to his car and started the engine. In a second he was gone.

Outside, the wind began to howl.

Like some kind of wailing lament.

PART TWO

'All spirits are enslaved that serve things evil.'

P. B. Shelley

Forty-Two

She had seen the scientific proof, carried out the tests herself.

She had written it down in her notes. It was there before her.

Yet still she could not believe it.

Of the three skulls which Kim had carbon-dated, two were, as expected, of Iron Age origin. Around 1,000 B.C. or earlier, she guessed.

It was the third which had caused her consternation.

She'd checked and double-checked but there was no mistake.

It was less than 500 years old.

She'd written down the approximate date as 1490.

How could it be possible?

Could she somehow have made a mistake with the dating process, she wondered? But the more she thought about it, the more she re-ran the events in her mind, the more her certainty grew. There had been no mistake. More puzzles, she thought, rubbing her eyes, noticing how heavy the lids felt. But those puzzles would have to wait until the next day. It was late and Kim could feel the stiffness in her joints. She stretched, groaning as she felt a dull ache in her back.

She glanced at her watch, muttering irritably when she saw that it had stopped at 5:15 p.m. She looked across to the wall clock.

The hands were frozen at 5:15.

Kim got to her feet and wandered out into the large hallway of the museum, heading towards the clock there.

It too showed 5:15.

She swallowed hard, aware, as ever, of the chill in the air. But it had intensified now to the point where her breath clouded before her as she exhaled.

The silence was pierced by the strident ringing of the phone.

She hesitated a moment, then lifted the receiver.

'Kim?'

She recognized Charles Cooper's voice immediately. 'Have you made any progress with the tablets?' he asked.

'Some,' she told him. 'I've been working on the skulls too, and there's something peculiar about one of them. It's much more recent.' She told him about it.

'It could be a miscalculation on your part,' he countered.

'I've checked and double-checked. The skull is less than 500 years old. I want to examine more of them, see if there are any more anomalies. There could be others from more recent periods.'

'Don't come out to the dig,' Cooper said quickly, and Kim was puzzled by the tone of his voice. 'I'll get someone to bring the skulls to you.'

She paused a moment, bewildered by his attitude.

'How are things going with the dig?' she wanted to know.

'We haven't made any more progress,' he said, a little too sharply. 'Look, I'll send the skulls to you, but I need to know what those stone tablets say.'

Before she could speak again, he replaced the receiver and all she heard was the single tone purr of a dead line. Kim put the phone down and got to her feet, moving quickly about the staff room and laboratory, closing doors and windows, flicking off lights. She didn't bother to check upstairs because no one had been up there. She finally stepped outside, pulling the museum's doors shut behind her, fumbling for the key which would lock them.

'Kim.'

The voice was close to her and its suddenness almost caused her to scream. She spun round to see George Perry standing there, his face impassive.

'You frightened the life out of me,' she said, panting, but Perry seemed unimpressed.

'I need to look at those tablets,' he said.

'Not now, George,' she said, pocketing the key, attempting to step around him.

Perry shot out an arm and grabbed her by the wrist.

She pulled away indignantly.

'What the hell are you doing?' she snapped. 'Look, George, I'm very tired and I want to get home, all right? If you want to talk to me then do it tomorrow, please.' She began to walk past him once more and this time he did not move. He merely turned slowly and watched her as she walked to the car.

In her rear-view mirror, Kim could still see him as she drove away.

Standing.

Watching.

Forty-Three

The water gurgled noisily as it swirled away down the sink, carrying grease and suds with it. Sarah Potter dried her hands on a towel and made her way through to the sitting room, examining her long fingernails, muttering to herself when she saw that another one was chipped. She'd already broken one earlier in the day while typing a letter but that, she told herself, was an occupational hazard. Sarah had been James Cutler's private secretary for the last four years, having secured the job a day before her twenty-sixth birthday. Now she was an integral part of the company, trusted and respected by Cutler himself and also the longest-serving employee on the payroll.

'The washing up's done,' she said, brushing a hand through her tousled brown hair. 'I'm going to have a shower when I've finished this.' She reached for the glass of white wine which was sitting on the dining table. 'Do you want a refill?'

Penny Allen looked up from the pile of exercise books before her and shook her head.

'Later,' she said, smiling. She sat back in her chair and allowed her head to loll back, her fine black hair cascading down her back. Sarah got to her feet and stood behind the other girl, resting both hands on her shoulders. Then, gently, she began to massage the taut flesh, easing away the tension. Penny sighed contentedly and moved her head forward, letting her chin rest on her chest. She wriggled slightly, feeling the stiffness leave her neck, as Sarah kept up her expert manipulation.

At twenty-nine, Penny was only a year younger than Sarah and her round face and the fact that she wore almost no make-up would have allowed anyone who didn't know her to take her for five or six years younger. She was the opposite in almost every way to her companion. Sarah was tall and slender, while Penny, although slim, was more rounded and scarcely five feet tall. She had been a teacher at one of Longfield's largest schools for the past five years.

Two years longer than she and Sarah had been lovers.

It had seemed so natural. They had always been close. They'd attended the same schools, belonged to the same small circle of friends and as time had passed, their friendship had blossomed almost inevitably into love of a kind neither had ever felt with a man.

There was a tenderness about their relationship which Penny had never been able to attain with her husband.

The marriage had lasted only ten months. He'd walked out on her after arriving home early one afternoon to discover Penny and Sarah locked in each other's arms. Neither of the women had attempted an explanation. It was hardly necessary. He'd packed his bags there and then, leaving Penny the house and everything in it. She hadn't heard from him since that day.

There had been no attempt on the part of either woman to hide the nature of their relationship. They still had to put

162

up with the occasional snide remark or sly look when they were out together, but as Sarah had said on numerous occasions, small towns breed small minds and Longfield was no exception.

Penny had been asked to leave her last job, supervising a play-group, as a result of the rumours and innuendo, but other than that, they had encountered little trouble and she had settled easily into her post as teacher.

She leant her head against one of Sarah's soothing hands, allowing her silky hair to flow over it, enjoying the sensations which were beginning to course through her body. Sarah moved closer, pressing herself up against the back of the chair, a familiar warmth beginning to manifest itself within her lower body. She moved to the side of the chair, sighing with anticipation as she felt Penny's left hand brush against her exposed thighs. The short house-coat she wore barely covered her buttocks and she tensed as she felt her lover's gentle fingers gliding over her flesh. Sarah kept up the massage, gradually slipping one hand around to caress Penny's throat and begin removing the blouse from her shoulders.

'Take a shower with me,' she said, softly.

Penny smiled and nodded.

The figure moved quickly but sure-footedly through the darkness, towards the house.

It had seen the silhouettes of the two women against the curtains and now it darted furtively but purposefully towards the window at the side of the building. It was masked from the house next door by a high privet hedge and the night closed around it like a welcoming ally.

It stood before the French windows.

Waiting.

Water splattered noisily from the bulbous head of the shower-spray and Sarah reached forward to adjust the temperature. The room was filled with steam which billowed like thick white mist, covering the mirror and tiles with a thin film of condensation.

Both women stood beneath the spray, enjoying the feel of the warm jet of water on their skin, laughing as they soaped each other lovingly, paying particular attention to each other's breasts.

Inside the glass cubicle they embraced, hearing only each other's voices and the constant noise of running water which masked all other sounds.

Even the noise of breaking glass from downstairs.

The figure drove its hand through the glass of the French windows and strode inside, overturning chairs in its path. It stood in the centre of the room, becoming annoyed by the bright light from the lamp on the table before it.

One powerful swipe sent the lamp hurtling against the wall, where it shattered.

The figure turned towards the door which led into the hall and wrenched it open. The sound of splashing water reached its ears.

It paused for a moment, then began to climb the stairs.

Sarah Potter closed her eyes and allowed the water to spurt over her face, forming rivulets which coursed down her neck and ran between her breasts. She felt Penny's soft touch on the back of her neck and sighed contentedly, turning to face her lover.

She opened her eyes to look at Penny, and it was then that she saw the dark figure outside the shower cubicle.

Through the frosted glass it looked hideously distorted, but Sarah was able to make out the semblance of a shape, like some kind of grotesquely hewn statue.

She opened her mouth to scream.

One side of the cubicle exploded inwards, huge jagged shards of glass erupting into the shower itself.

Penny shrieked as a particularly long shard sliced open her forearm. Blood spurted from the wound, spilling onto the white tiles of the shower, while other fragments cut her feet as she tried to move away from the terrifying intrusion.

Sarah pressed herself into a corner, her eyes bulging wide in horror, and screamed again as she felt a vice-like grip fasten around her left wrist. Bones crumbled under the powerful clamp and she felt searing pain lance up her arm. A second later she was flung effortlessly from the cubicle, as easily as if she had been a rag doll. She skidded helplessly across the slippery floor, knowing in that brief instant that she could not stop herself hitting the mirror on the opposite wall.

She struck it with devastating force, her head snapping forward, powering into the glass, splintering it.

The impact sent her reeling back and she went down in an untidy heap, blood pouring from a vicious gash just below her hair-line. Fragments of the broken mirror rained down on her, slicing her naked body, lacerating her face, arms and chest. She lay unconscious, oblivious now to the screams of her lover.

Penny tried to run, nursing her cut arm, but the figure merely gripped her by the throat, lifting her off her feet for several seconds before slamming her back against the cubicle wall. As she slumped forward again the figure took a firm hold on her hair and forced her face towards the shower-spray.

Penny felt the hot water spattering her skin and it was only that which kept her conscious. She struggled but her assailant was far too powerful to be thwarted.

As she opened her mouth to scream, the attacker pushed her head forward.

Penny's mouth closed over the bulbous head of the shower-spray. Her body bucked madly, but her head was held firm by the vice-like hand. She felt the water gushing down her throat; felt her stomach contract as it filled up. Her body twisted insanely. She gagged violently as the spray touched the back of her throat and the vomit rose, only to be swept back down by the torrent of water.

Penny felt herself blacking out but not before she saw her assailant's hand grasp the temperature control of the shower and turn it to hot.

Blistering, scalding water filled her mouth and throat and she was enveloped in unbelievable agony as the searing cascade gushed through her.

Her lips and tongue were transformed into little more than massive blisters which finally burst in a welter of pus and blood that ran down her chin to mingle with the crimson stains already splattering the shower tiles.

For interminable seconds Penny suffered this excruciating pain, and then her attacker, still using just one hand, slammed her viciously forward.

Such was the force of the movement that the shower-spray itself first gouged through the back of her throat, then burst from the base of her skull. Large fragments of bone broke away and torrents of blood gushed from the hole, washing over her shoulders and back.

She sagged against the wall, arms dangling limply at her sides, held upright by the water conduit which protruded a good six inches from the back of her head.

The figure turned away from her for a moment and moved towards Sarah.

The bathroom was transformed into a dripping slaughterhouse and steam swirled around the room, closing about the figure and its victims like a white shroud.

Forty-Four

Wallace sucked heavily on his cigarette, before stubbing it out in the ashtray. From his office window he could see a good deal of Longfield. If only, he thought, he could see an answer to the questions which now tormented him. He took a deep breath of the cool fresh air in an effort to clear his head.

Who had murdered Stuart Lawrence, John Kirkland and now Sarah Potter and the woman they knew to be her lover?

Was it the same person who had kidnapped little Jonathan Ashton?

What *kind* of person was it who had impaled Penny Allen's head on a shower spray? Who had ripped Sarah Potter's eyes from their sockets? Who had flayed almost every inch of flesh from both bodies using a piece of broken mirror?

Who had gutted them both completely, pulling their intestines from the riven torsos, and then used the slippery, steaming lengths to fashion a crude letter A on the bathroom floor. And, in the bath itself, a bloodied N?

Wallace exhaled deeply and reached for another cigarette. How come nobody ever saw or heard anything? In every case, the killer had forced entry to the homes of his victims, and the extent of the mutilations seemed to indicate that he spent at least thirty minutes, if not longer, on each corpse. Wallace knew from previous experience that people avoided getting involved in police affairs wherever possible, but even so, someone at some time must have seen events taking place before or after the killings which looked odd. This time a neighbour *had* heard something but had assumed that it was kids messing about, throwing stones at the windows of the house where the two women were. By the time he got around to phoning the police it was too late.

The inspector blew out a long stream of blue smoke and watched it disperse in the air.

Four murders and a kidnapping.

'The quiet little town of Longfield,' he murmured humourlessly, but his thoughts were cut short as he heard raised voices in the corridor outside his office.

He spun round as the door crashed open.

James Cutler strode into the room, his eyes fixed on the inspector. Wallace caught a glimpse of Sergeant Dayton trying to pull the land developer back.

'You're supposed to knock first,' said Wallace, unimpressed by the anger which contorted the older man's face into a twisted mask.

'I tried to stop him, guv,' Dayton said. 'I warned him.'

'You incompetent bastard, Wallace!' rasped Cutler, pulling away from the sergeant.

'Right, that's it,' snarled Dayton, gripping the land developer by the arm and twisting.

Cutler hissed in pain but Wallace shook his head.

'Leave him, Bill. Otherwise we'll have Mr Cutler crying police brutality.' The inspector motioned for Dayton to leave the room. Looking a little perplexed, the sergeant did so, closing the door behind him.

Cutler brushed the sleeve of his jacket and glared at Wallace.

'You know why I'm here,' he snapped.

'Telepathy isn't one of my talents,' Wallace told him.

'Another of my employees was butchered last night. When the hell are you going to find the murderer?'

'It isn't as simple as you seem to think, Cutler,' the inspector said, trying to keep his temper. 'There aren't many leads.'

'Then find some,' Cutler hissed. 'God knows who'll be next. It could be me. I initiated this building project. If the killer has a grudge against me and my workers then it's only a matter of time before he comes after *me*.'

'That had occurred to me, too. I know you're a likely target. So is everyone who works for you, but I simply haven't got the manpower to give all of you protection if that's what you're driving at.'

'Then call in some help, for Christ's sake,' the land developer shouted, anger and fear colouring his tone. 'Do your superiors know how you're handling this case? Perhaps it's time they did.'

'What's that supposed to mean?' Wallace said, his own anger now boiling up.

Cutler didn't answer; he merely glared at the policeman.

'If the building project is the cause of these killings then call it off, at least temporarily,' Wallace suggested.

'No. My men are working to schedules,' the older man said. 'To call a halt would mean losing hundreds of thousands of pounds.'

'Well, it's up to you, Cutler. You'll have to decide what

price you put on your own life. If there's any way you could stop the project . . .'

'Not a chance!' The land developer turned and headed for the office door, then glared back at the detective. 'I'm telling you Wallace, I want results. Fast!'

'Get out, Cutler,' Wallace said, watching wearily as the other man pushed open the door and strode out, almost colliding with Dayton in the process.

The sergeant hesitated for a moment, then walked in.

Wallace sat down and ground out his cigarette in the ashtray on his desk.

'What is it, Bill?' he said, massaging the bridge of his nose between thumb and forefinger.

Dayton approached the desk slowly, clutching a piece of paper in his hand.

'I just took this message, guv,' he said, quietly. 'Her name's Julie Craig. She's five years old.'

'I'm not with you,' Wallace said, frowning.

Dayton sighed and handed over the piece of paper.

'Another kid's been taken.'

Forty-Five

As Frank King watched, thick white wisps of steam rose from the tar trailer, a cylindrical tank about six feet long which carried the molten fluid. The tarmac-laying crew were careful to keep a safe distance from the blistering black mess as it spilled over the ground, covering an area which would eventually form part of a car park servicing the leisure centre.

The smells of tar and diesel fumes were strong in the air but the foreman seemed oblivious to the odours as he surveyed the building site like some kind of nineteenth-century general inspecting a battlefield.

He shuddered involuntarily as a powerful gust of wind swept past him. He'd be pleased when this bloody project was over and done with. King turned and headed towards the Portakabin, glancing up at the rain-heavy clouds above.

In the cab of the JCB, David Holmes was also watching the sky, but his attention was drawn to his watch as the alarm went off, telling him that it was one o'clock. Lunchtime, he thought with relief. It was freezing in the cab of the JCB. He couldn't wait to reach the relative warmth of the Portakabin. Holmes worked the controls of the machine expertly, guiding the great metal arm around, swinging it in a wide arc before it thudded down into the earth, ploughing deep, scooping up a mound of the dark soil. The arm rose again and Holmes manoeuvred it around so that the load could be dropped into the back of the lorry which stood alongside, its engine idling. He watched as the dirt cascaded from the bucket.

The machine's giant arm swung back into position and Holmes locked it there, twisting the key in the machine's ignition to cut off the power. The JCB stood silent and motionless in the chill wind which was sweeping over the building site.

Holmes checked once more that the vehicle was securely locked up. Then, using one of the caterpillar tracks as a step, he lowered himself to the ground.

There seemed to be fewer men working on the site today, he thought, pausing to extract a cigarette packet and matches from his pockets. He knew that because of the accidents of a few days ago and now the news filtering through of Cutler's employees being murdered, a number of men had simply refused to work on the project anymore. But Holmes was not one to be frightened easily. Besides, he needed the money. The blokes who'd chucked it in must be mad or well off, he hadn't figured out which yet.

A gust of wind blew out the match as he tried to light his cigarette. He struck another match but the wind blew it out, too.

170

The gusts seemed to increase suddenly in ferocity, drowning out the creak of the JCB's metal arm.

As Holmes struggled with a third match the great machine seemed to move an inch or two, its massive bulk like some lumbering metallic dinosaur.

The metal arm came free.

Even above the roar of the wind, Holmes finally heard the rush of air as the heavy bucket came hurtling towards him as if to scoop him up.

He did not hear it in time.

The metal edge hit him just above the waist, shearing through muscle and bone effortlessly. Slicing his body in two.

Blood and intestines erupted from the severed torso which was sent pinwheeling across the ground, spraying crimson in all directions. Fragments of pulverized spinal column mingled with a trail of viscera. Like a decapitated farmyard chicken, Holmes' lower half staggered a few yards, as if searching for the other half, then buckled and fell to the ground, blood still fountaining madly from the torn arteries. The torso, blood now running from the dead man's nose and mouth, finally came to a halt on its torn base. As the blood poured out in a wide pool around it, the body looked as if it had been buried up to the waist in a thick gore.

The bucket of the JCB swung slowly back and forth, gobbets of flesh and streamers of crimson dripping from it.

The cigarette which Holmes had been trying to light was still stuck firmly between his cold lips. Blood had soaked into the filter like ink into blotting paper.

Forty-Six

The classroom was large, holding somewhere in the region of thirty children. From that considerable group, a steady babble of excited chatter rose.

Clare Nichols seemed oblivious to any extraneous sound as she carefully considered the set of coloured crayons before her. So many colours to choose from. Where should she begin her drawing? Beside her, Amanda Fraser, Clare's best friend (at least for the past week she had been), was already busy on her own drawing. As were most of the children in the room.

Clare tapped her bottom lip with the blue crayon and decided to start with the sky, so she scribbled a blue border along the top of her paper, glancing up as Miss Tickle moved from desk to desk inspecting the work of the others.

Clare giggled. She always did when she thought of Miss Tickle. Not just her name, but those funny red tights which she always wore. It looked as if someone had painted her legs the colour of a letter box, Clare thought, reaching for the yellow crayon. She gripped it firmly, and just beneath the rim of blue she drew a large yellow sun, remembering to add spoke-like rays around it. It was going to be a nice sunny day in her drawing, she'd decided. Not like it was outside.

Rain was coursing down the window panes in torrents and Clare hoped that it would have stopped by the time she had to go home. Still, perhaps her mother would pick her up in the car. Or, if not, she could always get a lift from Amanda's mother.

Clare liked Mrs Fraser. The large wart with its three ever-present hairs growing beneath her chin never failed to mesmerize the small girl. She glanced out of the window once more, watching the rain as it ran down the glass and she felt a chill run through her.

Clare swallowed hard and looked down at the paper, wondering why her hand seemed to freeze as she reached for the green crayon which she needed to draw the grass. Her hand hovered over the wax stick for a moment longer, then she picked up the black one, and with swift strokes began to draw.

Her breath was coming in low sighs and her eyelids had partially closed, yet still her hand worked over the paper, moving in unfailing curves and lines, fashioning an image which she herself could see only in her mind's eye.

Amanda spoke and looked over at Clare and her drawing, but the girl seemed not to hear.

Her eyes were now almost completely closed and her lips fluttered rapidly as she mouthed soundless words, the crayon moving back and forth across the paper with dizzying speed.

The black crayon, then the red one, then the black again.

Clare heard a loud noise from beside her and the sound seemed to rouse her.

She looked up, like a dreamer awaking from a deep sleep, her eyes focussing on Amanda, who was backing away from her, eyes riveted to the drawing before her. Miss Tickle was making her way towards the desk, her face knitted into that familiar look of concern.

She saw how pale Clare looked. How the colour seemed to have drained from her cheeks. The child looked like death.

Miss Tickle approached her slowly, seeing that Clare was about to faint. She was swaying from side to side on her chair, one crayon still gripped in her hand, gliding across the paper.

'Clare,' the teacher said, softly. 'Clare, are you all right, dear?'

It was patently obvious that the child was not.

Miss Tickle turned to a boy near her and told him to run and fetch the nurse. All other eyes in the classroom turned towards Clare, who had now turned the colour of rancid butter.

She was still swaying back and forth, and now Miss Tickle rushed towards her, seeing the child's eyes roll up in their sockets.

From somewhere deep inside her Clare heard a sound like rolling thunder. A deafening roar which seemed to hammer at her eardrums. So loud that it hurt.

She screamed and fell forward onto the desk.

Miss Tickle reached the girl and cradled her in her arms, lifting her away from the desk. As she did so she looked down at the drawing, and she, too, felt an unearthly chill run through her.

'Oh God,' she murmured, softly.

Kim knelt beside the bed and brushed a strand of hair from her daughter's forehead, feeling the soft skin with the back of her hand.

'There's no sign of a temperature,' the school nurse told her. The woman was young, Kim's age, but painfully thin, the dark uniform she wore accentuating this feature. 'She woke up as soon as we got her in here,' the nurse continued, making a sweeping gesture with her hand to encompass the school sick room. It was small, clean and smelt of disinfectant. There were pictures of animals and toys on the walls, competing for space with cabinets and shelves.

'How do you feel, sweetheart?' Kim asked her daughter.

'I'm all right, Mummy,' Clare assured her, the colour having returned to her cheeks. She sat up quite happily and sipped the plastic beaker full of orange squash which the nurse had given her.

'I think it might be best if you took her home, Mrs Nichols,' said the thin woman and Kim agreed, fumbling in her jacket pocket for her keys. 'It's a good job we were able to reach you at the museum,' the nurse added.

Miss Tickle, who had been standing by the doorway throughout the conversation, now stepped forward and beckoned to Kim.

'Might I have a word?' she asked, almost apologetically.

Kim smiled, noticing as she approached the woman that she held a piece of paper. The two of them moved out into the corridor, while inside the room, the nurse helped Clare into her shoes and coat.

'Your daughter was drawing when she . . . passed out,' the teacher said. 'This is what she'd done.'

Kim took the paper from the other woman and looked at it, her brow furrowing.

'I didn't know what to make of it,' the teacher confessed. Kim noticed that goose-pimples had risen on the woman's flesh.

Drawn in thick black crayon, sketched with remarkable dexterity for a child so young, was a large figure. The features were smudged apart from the red eyes. At its feet Kim saw several hastily drawn small stick figures, each one surrounded by a smear of red. There were more of the small figures in the black shape's hands, too, with red dripping from them. But it was the lettering over the top of the shape which Kim found the most disturbing. In letters two inches high were scrawled four words:

HIS TIME IS COME

Forty-Seven

The loud knocking seemed to echo throughout the wood-panelled interior of Dexter Grange, bouncing off the walls and high ceilings until it faded away to a low hum. After a moment or two of silence the banging came again, louder and more insistent.

175

Laura Price hurried down the wide staircase and crossed the hall to the door, anxious to silence the knocking and also curious as to who could be calling at the house with evening approaching. The grandfather clock nearby struck six as she pulled open the door.

The figure barged past her, arms pinwheeling in an effort to remain upright.

Laura, taken by surprise, screamed and turned to look at the intruder, who was standing unsteadily in the centre of the hallway, clothes soaked by the rain which was still falling outside.

The youth was in his early twenties. His face was twisted with pain and a thick growth of stubble covered his cheeks and chin. He wore a T-shirt which had at one time probably been white, and a pair of faded jeans tucked into scuffed ankle boots.

She recognized him as Tony Evans. As he stood dripping wet before her she could see the suppurating sores on his arms, grouped around the insides of his elbows.

'Where's Dexter?' he barked, his throat sounding tight.

'What do you want?' Laura demanded.

'I want some stuff,' he snapped. 'I've got to see Dexter.' His breath was coming in gasps. 'I'm fucking strung out.'

Laura looked past him towards the two figures approaching from the corridor behind Evans. He noticed the movement of her eyes and turned, almost overbalancing.

Henry Dexter approached him slowly, running appraising eyes over the wretched youth.

'Dexter, I need some stuff,' he moaned. 'I need a fix. Now!'

'Why did you come to the house?' Dexter said. 'You were told never to come here. Any of you.'

'I fucking need it,' Evans rasped, taking a faltering step towards the older man.

Gary Webb stepped ahead of Dexter, his imposing frame stopping Evans' advance.

'You could have been followed,' Dexter said, angrily. 'Anyone could have seen you.'

Evans dug his hand deep into his jeans pocket and pulled out a handful of crumpled five pound notes.

'I've got money,' he said. 'Just give me the stuff.'

'Where did you get that?' Dexter demanded. 'Did you steal it?'

The youth was already clutching his stomach, wincing as he felt another powerful contraction.

'Please.' he whimpered, doubled up in pain. 'Take the money. I promise I'll never come here again. Just let me fix.' The money fell from his quivering hand.

'Get him out of here,' Dexter said, looking at Gary.

'You bastard,' roared Evans and ran at the older man. His reactions, however, were dulled and Gary merely stepped between them, driving one powerful fist into the other youth's face. There was a loud crack as Evans' nose broke. He toppled forward, but Gary caught him by the front of his T-shirt, held him up and drove another pile-driver blow into his face, shattering two of his front teeth, driving one of them through his upper lip. Blood ran down Evans' chin and he burbled incoherently as Gary threw him to the floor and drove a kick into the base of his spine.

'If you speak to anyone about this,' Dexter said, looking down at the injured youth, 'I'll kill you. If one policeman turns up here, I'll kill you. Do you understand?'

Grabbing Evans by the hair, Gary lifted his head a foot or two off the ground then slammed it down, hard enough to open a gash below his hairline.

'Understand?' he said.

'Yes,' Evans whimpered as he was hauled to his feet.

Laura opened the front door and Dexter watched as Gary hurled the other youth out onto the driveway. He rolled over twice and lay still, the rain lashing his exposed body. He lay on his back, one arm twitching slightly, mumbling to himself through his split lips and broken teeth, groaning every now and then as a fresh contraction knotted his stomach muscles.

The three of them stood watching, waiting for him to drag himself to his feet which, moments later, he did. He looked back once, then stumbled off down the long driveway, falling once.

Dexter closed the door.

'Do you think he will go to the police?' Laura asked, apprehensively. 'Not just about the drugs, I mean . . .' She paused, aware of Dexter's unfaltering gaze upon her. 'I . . . You know, about what we've been doing?'

'The police won't find out,' he replied, striding back down the corridor.

The two youngsters followed Dexter into the library, where he crossed to the wall safe, fiddled with the combination and opened it. He placed the notes Evans had dropped inside with the money that was stacked there beside bags of heroin, glancing at the store of cash and drugs indifferently. Gary looked at Laura then at the heroin. He took a step forward, as if the drug were some kind of magnet, drawing him. Laura, too, felt a tingle run through her. She nudged him and a knowing look passed between them, unseen by Dexter.

'If one of us was ever strung out,' Laura said, 'you wouldn't treat us like you treated Evans, would you?'

Dexter smiled and closed the safe, shaking his head almost imperceptibly.

'If anything happened to you, how would we get hold of the stuff in the safe?' Gary asked.

Dexter smiled again.

'But nothing *is* going to happen to me,' he said, brushing past them as he left the room.

Gary looked at the older man, then at the wall safe with its precious contents.

But it was on the ornamental dagger over the fireplace that his gaze finally came to rest.

Forty-Eight

The rain which had been falling all day finally disappeared soon after the onset of night. It was replaced by a chill wind which swirled and eddied around the houses of Longfield, occasionally rattling window frames like a mischievous child.

Frank King looked up from his newspaper as a particularly powerful gust howled around the house. He was the only one in the room who seemed to notice it. All around him his family were engaged in pursuits of their own.

His wife Linda was sitting on the floor studying the large jigsaw puzzle laid out on the coffee table. He saw her smile triumphantly as she slotted a piece into the maze of shapes and colours.

Behind him his youngest son, Ian, was busy trying to destroy the next Imperial walker as it lumbered across the snow. He manoeuvred his X-wing fighter expertly, pumping shot after shot into the evil agent of the Empire. The scores lit the multi-coloured screen of the TV set as he punched buttons on the computer, teeth gritted in concentration.

'Dad,' he said, not taking his eyes from the screen. 'When will you be able to finish that desk you're making for me?'

'Your father's trying to rest, Ian,' Linda reminded the lad.

'I only asked,' he muttered, narrowly avoiding a laser blast from a marauding Imperial craft.

'I was going to do some work on it tonight,' said King.

'Oh Frank, for heaven's sake,' Linda protested, fitting another piece into the jigsaw. 'It's freezing out in that workroom.'

'I don't notice it when I'm working. Besides, there's not much left to do now. I've nearly finished,' King told her.

'I don't know why you couldn't have built the shed closer to the house instead of putting it right at the bottom of the garden.'

'That, my dear,' he said, getting to his feet, 'is so I don't disturb you with hammering and banging when you're busy with your puzzles.' He picked up a piece of the jigsaw and slotted it smugly into place.

'I'll be making a cup of tea in a little while,' she told him.

'What's Simon doing?' asked King, wondering where his other son had disappeared to.

A moment later the floor above seemed to shake as the older boy switched on his record player. King stood listening to the rhythmic thud of the bass for a moment and then, smiling, he shook his head and headed for the back door. He heard Linda yelling to the boy to turn the record player down as he stepped out of the kitchen.

The darkness closed around him and he shivered as the wind jabbed icy fingers into his flesh.

Ahead of him, barely visible in the gloom, was his workshop. King had built it himself two years earlier, shortly after the family had moved into the house. Since then he'd worked in it most nights, turning his mechanical and practical skills to useful ends. He'd built them a dining room table and the six chairs which went with it, all finished in dark wood and carefully varnished.

He hurried down the path towards the workshop, fumbling in his trouser pocket for the key.

The trees which overhung the structure bowed and shook as the wind blew with renewed ferocity. King let himself in and clicked on the light.

The dark figure saw the light flash on inside the hut.

It saw Frank King illuminated in the window.

Keeping close to the trees and bushes at the bottom of the garden, the figure moved closer.

Linda was right, thought King, shivering. It was freezing inside the workshop. He rubbed his arms briskly for a moment, trying to restore some circulation before he moved over to the workbench and picked up a piece of sandpaper. He set to work on the legs of the desk.

It had taken him barely a week to complete his latest project. Copying the design of some that he'd seen in a stationer's the previous weekend, he had worked quickly but methodically to construct the article, and he was pleased with his handiwork. Ian had been going on for months about wanting a desk on which to put his computer.

The lad was fascinated by the bloody gadget, but King couldn't make head nor tail of how it worked. When he'd been eleven, no one had even heard of calculators, let alone computers, and the thought that his kids would be using them in school one day would have been beyond the bounds of imagination.

King's other son was a year older, but electronic wizardry held no such appeal for him. He was much more at home with his records and tapes. Despite the diversity of their interests, King was pleased to find that the two of them got along well together. There was little of the rivalry, even open hostility, which was usually associated with brothers. Especially two so close together in age.

Frank King was more than happy with the way his children and his marriage had turned out. Life had been kind to him, and for that he was grateful.

The wind howled mournfully around the workshop, the sound reminding King of a dog in pain.

He heard a harsh scraping sound on the roof of the hut.

Like bony fingers being drawn across the canopy.

King looked up briefly, listening to the disembodied sound. It promptly ceased and he continued with his task.

Something smacked against one of the windows and he spun round, squinting to see what it was.

He straightened up and walked over to the window, cupping one hand over his eyes so that he could see out into the wind-blown night.

Nothing moved except the trees.

181

As he stood there a sudden movement immediately in front of him caused him to step back in surprise.

A low branch from one of the trees had swung down and scraped against the glass. Clattering against the pane as if trying to gain access.

King shook his head, annoyed at his own jumpiness. Perhaps the thoughts of what had happened to Stuart Lawrence, John Kirkland and those two women were causing his mind to play tricks, he told himself. He returned to his job, trying to blot out the night sounds.

He finished sandpapering the desk and blew the wood dust away, reaching for the tin of varnish on the worktop. He stirred it thoroughly, enjoying the smell of the fluid.

The door of the workshop rattled in its frame and King looked up, watching it for long seconds, listening to the wind and the creaking wood.

He shivered slightly and frowned. His imagination *must* be playing tricks now.

It seemed to be getting colder inside the hut.

King continued stirring the varnish, his eyes still on the door.

The handle turned a fraction.

He almost dropped the tin.

The handle moved again, twisting full circle this time, and at last King put down the varnish. He stepped quickly across to the door.

He stood by it for interminable seconds, watching the handle twisting back and forth, but there seemed to be no attempt to push the door open.

Outside, the wind howled with ever-increasing force.

The rattling of the handle stopped and the puzzled man was left staring at it, as if expecting more movement at any moment.

He reached for the key in his pocket, wondering whether or not he should lock it.

But why? he asked himself. What was he locking out?

Then again, could the wind move door handles?

The key hovered close to the lock.

The handle moved again, more slowly this time.

Could it be one of the kids winding him up, he wondered?

If it was, he'd teach the little bugger a lesson.

King moved closer to the door, his hand reaching towards the knob.

'Come on,' he whispered. 'Try it again.'

He waited for the handle to move.

The wind screamed, banshee-like, shaking the small structure to its foundations.

The door shook in its frame.

Quick as a flash, King gripped the handle and wrenched open the door, taking one step out into the night.

'Right, you little sod . . .' he began, but let the sentence trail off.

There was no one out there.

From where he stood he could see the light in the kitchen of the house, nearly a hundred feet up the garden.

He could see a figure silhouetted against the lowered blinds, but apart from that, he saw nothing.

Just the darkness.

He stepped back inside the hut and closed the door.

Linda King lit the gas under the kettle, then dropped a tea bag into her husband's mug.

'Ian, take your Dad his tea when it's ready,' she called and received a belligerent affirmative from her son, who had just been hit twice by Imperial tie-fighters.

She flicked off the light and returned to the sitting room.

The scratching on the roof of the hut continued, and Frank King made a mental note to cut away the bare branches of the overhanging trees when he got a moment. The noise was irritating him.

He looked up sharply when he heard the door being rattled once more in its frame.

This time he stepped back because the movement was not caused by the wind. The powerful gusts had ceased for the time being, yet still the door of the hut rattled and shook as if it were going to explode from its hinges.

King felt ever more penetrating cold wrapping itself around him and he backed off, eyes fixed on the door, fear now gripping him tightly. It was as if all rationality and reason had left him, only his fear remained.

He stood with his back to the window, waiting for the door to open.

Waiting.

He snatched up a hammer from the workbench and hefted it before him.

If there was someone out there then the bastard would not catch him unawares.

The wind shrieked loudly. A cry of the damned which pounded shrilly in his ears.

He gripped the hammer more tightly and watched the door, which rattled furiously again.

He waited.

The window behind him exploded inwards with an earsplitting crash.

Glass sprayed into the hut, cutting the back of his neck and grazing his scalp. Before he could turn, hands had closed around his throat and were pulling him backwards.

He struck at them with the hammer but to no avail. The vice-like grip only tightened and King grunted as he was slammed back against the wall with bone-numbing force. He dropped the hammer and clutched feebly at the hands which were throttling him. His eyes bulged in their sockets and he gasped for air as the clawed fingers dug deep into the flesh of his throat.

White-hot agony lanced through him as he felt his larynx splinter under the pressure. It finally collapsed and he heaved as blood filled his mouth and ran down his throat.

His attacker now released one hand and grabbed King by the hair, spinning him round, tugging his head down towards the jagged glass which poked up in uneven peaks from the window frame.

Stars danced before his eyes and he fought in vain to prevent what was about to happen.

The powerful hands were forcing his neck onto the glass.

King tried to scream but his shattered larynx would

produce only a liquid croak which caused fresh blood to spill over his lips.

With his last reserves of strength fading rapidly, he still fought to free himself, but it was useless.

Six inches away from the glass, and he could feel incredibly cold air rushing through the broken window, bringing with it a nauseating stench which reminded him of rotting meat.

Five inches.

His attacker was exerting even more pressure in an attempt to force King down.

Four inches.

The desperate man felt his knees going weak, realized that he was losing the strength to resist.

Three inches.

As he tried to scream again an agonizing pain filled his head and neck and he tasted blood, warm and coppery in his throat.

Two inches.

The longest points of glass were actually brushing the bruised flesh of his neck.

One inch.

Frank King knew he was finished.

The hands of his attacker thrust his head down, dragging it back and forth across the jagged glass, allowing the short lethal splinters to act as a rasp. The razor-sharp slivers sliced easily through the flesh and muscle of King's neck, severing veins and arteries, carving a path through the flesh as the sawing action was speeded up.

Blood erupted from the torn neck in great jets which splattered the floor and walls of the hut, spraying from the sliced blood vessels like water from a fountain.

King's body began to spasm uncontrollably as his assailant continued to rake his throat back and forth over the glass until it seemed his head would be severed. Then, suddenly, the hands hurled King back, blood sprayed out in a wide arc as he fell, his body crashing onto the desk he had made with so much care.

He hit the floor with a thud, the massive gash in his throat opening and closing like the gills of a fish, blood still spurting from it.

King was unconscious, close to death, as his attacker entered the workshop.

The figure hauled itself in through the broken window and dropped to the floor, standing over King's prostrate form for long seconds, oblivious to the stench inside the small structure and the thick slicks of crimson which were splattered everywhere.

It knelt beside the corpse and began its work.

As she heard the shrill whistle of the kettle, Linda King got to her feet, peering for a moment longer at the jigsaw before her, then at the piece she held in her hand. As the kettle continued to squeal she muttered something to herself and put the piece back on the table.

She patted Ian on the head as she passed and he grunted. The momentary disturbance caused him to sustain slight damage to his X-wing fighter as a neutron blast from one of the walkers caught him unawares.

Linda switched off the kettle and poured boiling water onto the tea bag in Frank's mug, stirring it around briefly.

'Ian,' she called, peering through the blinds towards the hut at the bottom of the garden. 'Take this tea down to your Dad, will you, please?'

No answer.

'Ian. Did you hear me?' she repeated, puzzled by what she saw from her vantage point in the kitchen.

The light in the workshop went out and then came back on again, twice in rapid succession. She wondered if the wind was affecting the power lines. But if that was the case, why were the lights in the house all right?

She watched as the light went on and off once more, then finally came back on and stayed that way.

'Ian,' she called again. This time the boy appeared in the doorway.

'Why can't Simon take it?' he asked irritably. 'I was on my highest score ever.'

She seemed unimpressed and handed the boy the steaming mug of tea.

'I asked *you*,' she said. 'And tell your Dad to hurry up or I'll lock him out for the night.' She chuckled and opened the back door for her son.

The boy braced himself against a particularly strong gust of wind, then set off down the path towards the hut where his father was working. As he drew closer, Ian felt the flesh on his arms rising into goose-pimples. He slowed his pace somewhat, looking around him in the gloom.

'Dad,' he called, but his voice was snatched away by the wind.

He reached the door and knocked twice, calling to his father again.

No answer.

Ian pushed on the door, surprised when it wouldn't open. His dad never usually locked it. He put more force behind it, almost spilling the tea in the process.

It moved slightly, and as it did, a noxious stench filled his nostrils, drifting from inside the hut.

The boy recoiled momentarily, then began pushing again, harder this time, now ignoring the cold wind which whistled around him.

'Dad,' he called, his voice catching slightly. 'Open the door.'

The wooden partition suddenly gave, as if a weight on the other side had been removed, and Ian found himself stumbling inside, enveloped by the obscene smell which he'd first noticed outside.

He stood transfixed, his body shaking uncontrollably, as he took in the scene of carnage before him. And saw what had once been his father.

He dropped the tea, the brown liquid mingling with the thick red fluid which seemed to be everywhere inside the hut. On the walls, on the floor, even on the ceiling.

Ian gulped down huge lungfuls of the foul air, his eyes darting back and forth, to his dead father, then to the broken window, then to the blood.

He turned and tried to run, but felt as if someone had injected his legs with lead.

It was like standing in a slaughterhouse. His head was swimming, his stomach contracting violently, threatening to empty its contents onto the floor with the spilled tea and the congealing blood. Finally he found the strength to run, a strength born of horror.

Horror made absolute by the sight of what lay on his father's workbench.

Forty-Nine

The wind had, to some small extent, helped to dispel the vile stench of blood and excrement from the workshop. Even so, the odour still hung like an invisible pall, causing Wallace to cough every time he inhaled too deeply.

The inspector reached for his cigarettes and stuck one in his mouth. He patted his pockets, looking for a light. One of the ambulancemen standing close by came to his rescue and lit the cigarette for him. The inspector nodded his appreciation and sucked in the smoke gratefully, his eyes scanning the scene of slaughter before him.

Frank King lay on his side, his head twisted back savagely, the muscles severed as far as the spinal column. The killer could hardly have been more thorough if a chainsaw had been used. The head was practically severed.

The face, rent by numerous deep gashes from the broken glass, was lacerated particularly badly around the nose and cheeks.

The eyes had been ripped from their sockets.

King's shirt was open to reveal the horrendous injuries inflicted on his torso. A massive wound running from neck to navel had been opened up, and the torn edges of the stomach wrenched back to allow the killer access to the intestines. Several thick lengths lay scattered around the hut, now stiffened and covered in caked gore.

Most of the flesh had been flayed from the body with a blood-stained chisel which lay close to the corpse. But the thing which drew Wallace's closest attention was the object lying on the dead man's workbench.

Two thick lengths of entrail had been used to fashion a reeking letter A.

'I hope this bastard isn't working his way through the alphabet,' said Sergeant Dayton, who held a handkerchief to his face to prevent the worst of the smell from penetrating.

'If he is, then he's dyslexic,' Wallace said sardonically. 'He started with M.'

'Can we move the body now, Doctor?' the ambulance-man asked, looking down at Dr Ryan, who was still hunched over the dead man.

He nodded and got to his feet, careful not to step in any of the puddles of sticky crimson gore which were splattered all around.

'Did you speak to the boy?' he asked.

'The poor little bastard can't say a word,' said Wallace. 'All he does is grunt.'

'Traumatic shock syndrome,' Ryan informed the police-man.

'Your brilliant insight does surprise me, Doctor,' Wallace said, his voice heavy with sarcasm. He caught the anger in Ryan's eyes and apologized. 'Could you let me have the autopsy report as soon as possible? I know it hardly seems worth it but . . . this other business . . . about the hearts.'

'You mean you want to know if King was frightened to death, too?' said Ryan. 'I doubt it. I think he died from massive loss of blood from the wounds in the throat, but I'll check.'

'Died of fright?' said Dayton, looking puzzled. 'You mean that's what happened to the others?'

Wallace nodded.

'But not a word to anyone else, Bill. If that reaches the papers then we'll all be cleaning shit off the walls because it's going to hit the fan faster than any of us can imagine.' He took a long drag on his Rothmans.

'*Frightened* to death,' the sergeant repeated. 'What the hell happened to them? What did they see before they were cut up?'

Wallace shook his head.

'You tell me,' he said, cryptically. 'But if it was that bad, I'm not so sure I *want* to know who killed them.'

Clare Nichols swung herself out of bed, perspiration soaking through her nightdress. She padded slowly to the bedroom window and peered out into the night, the image of the dream still strong in her mind. She gazed out at the street lamp on the other side of the road, its sodium glare casting cold light around it.

She stood there for a long time, peering into the gloom as if searching for something which she knew was there but which she could not see.

Not yet.

But it was coming.

Coming soon.

Fifty

It was nine o'clock the next morning when Wallace swung the Sierra into the street which led to Longfield police station. He braked, allowing a couple of children to cross the road. The sight of them sparked thoughts of the two children who were missing. As far as he knew there had been no further word on either, despite the efforts of his men to find them. Both killer and kidnapper — if they were not one individual — were managing to keep an annoyingly low profile for a town the size of Longfield, Wallace thought.

He brought the Sierra to a halt in the police station car park, then clambered out and strode across the tarmac towards the main building.

As he walked in, Sergeant Bill Dayton looked up and nodded feebly. Wallace frowned.

'You've got a visitor, guv,' he said.

'Who is it?' Wallace wanted to know. 'Oh Christ, not Cutler again . . .'

'The Chief Inspector,' Dayton told him. 'He's in your office.'

Wallace nodded and walked on, his forehead wrinkled in surprise, and also irritation. What the hell did his superior want, dropping in like this? As he reached the door of his office he paused, wondering whether to knock or not. He hesitated a moment longer, then knocked once and walked in without waiting for an invitation.

Chief Inspector Gordon Macready looked up at the sudden intrusion, his cold grey eyes fixing Wallace in an unflinching stare. The inspector thought that his superior's features appeared to have been modelled from wax. His expression did not change as he looked up at Wallace.

Macready was in his early fifties, balding and over-weight. The buttons of his waistcoat strained to meet across his stomach and Wallace expected them to explode open at any moment. Despite the bald patch on top of his head, the older man sported thick sideburns and a bushy mane of hair at the back. Speckles of dandruff dotted the shoulders of his jacket.

Wallace noted with slight annoyance that his superior had made himself at home in the inspector's own chair. He rocked gently to and fro on the back legs, eyeing the younger man up and down.

The two of them exchanged greetings and Macready motioned to Wallace to sit down.

'I've read the files on the murders,' the older man said. 'And the kidnappings.' He folded his arms across his chest. 'You're not making any progress, Wallace. You're no closer.'

'If you've read the files then you'll realize what we're up against, sir,' Wallace said, his eyes never leaving the other man. 'The killer's a clever bastard. We've got virtually nothing to go on. He leaves no clues. Nothing.'

'What about the kidnappings? Any motive for those?'

'Not that I can find.'

'Do you think the killer and kidnapper are one and the same?'

'I'd have thought it was a pretty safe bet, yes.'

Macready made a clucking sound with his tongue and looked first at the files before him, then at Wallace.

'As from now, Inspector, I will be taking over this investigation,' he said. 'I think it's fair to say that the incidents which have occurred are somewhat beyond your capabilities.'

'You mean you're relieving me?'

'That's exactly what I mean. This case needs, shall we say, an older head.' He smiled condescendingly. 'Wouldn't you agree?'

Wallace clenched his teeth, the knot of muscles at the side of his jaw pulsing angrily.

'Yes, sir,' he muttered.

'I've already asked for more men to help with the search,' Macready told him. 'We might even need to cordon off the town eventually.'

'I'd requested extra men, sir,' the inspector said, trying to mask his annoyance.

'I'm aware of that, Wallace,' Macready said.

'Whose decision was it to replace me, sir?'

'That isn't important.'

'It's important to me,' rasped Wallace, a little too vehemently.

Macready regarded him reproachfully for a moment.

'I said it isn't important,' he muttered, keeping his voice low. 'You haven't been suspended. You're still on the case, but from now on you will report directly to me and you'll take your instructions from me. Clear?'

'Yes, sir,' Wallace said through clenched teeth.

There was a heavy silence, finally broken by the younger man.

'May I go now, sir?' he asked.

Macready nodded, watching as Wallace headed for the door. As he closed it behind him he let out an angry breath.

Inside the office the phone rang.

From the police station Wallace drove to the museum, a little puzzled to find the car park empty when he arrived. There was no sign of Kim's Land Rover. He drove up to the main doors, got out and knocked three times. He waited several minutes for an answer, but only silence greeted his arrival. He knocked once more, then walked around the building to the window which looked into the laboratory.

The blinds were down. As he stood listening, he heard no sounds of movement from inside.

Wallace strode back to his car, clambered in and drove off.

He reached Kim's house in less than fifteen minutes.

The Land Rover was parked outside, so Wallace drew up behind it. He climbed out and walked up to the front door, brushing a hand through his hair as he knocked. The door opened a moment later.

Kim smiled happily as she saw him.

'Steve! Come in,' she said, touching his hand as he entered. She felt him squeeze hers softly. They looked into each other's eyes for a moment and felt that tingle they'd experienced the other night.

'When I couldn't get hold of you at the museum I thought something might be wrong,' he told her, wandering through into the sitting room.

Clare was sitting on the floor in front of the television, one eye on 'Sesame Street', the other on the dolls which lay before her. When Wallace entered the room, she turned and looked at him. A smile which spread from her lips to her eyes lit up her whole face.

'Clare, this is Inspector Wallace,' Kim told her. 'He's a policeman.'

'Hello, gorgeous,' Wallace said, smiling at the child, struck by her radiant beauty. She looked strikingly like her mother, he thought.

'Are you friends with Mummy?' Clare asked.

Wallace grinned and looked fleetingly at Kim.

'You could say that,' he answered.

'Are you her best friend?'

It was Kim's turn to smile.

She ushered Wallace through to the kitchen where he sat down at the table, watching while she switched on the kettle.

'A very astute young lady,' the inspector said, waving to Clare through the partially-open door. She waved back. 'And very beautiful, like her mum.'

Kim coloured slightly.

'You didn't come round here just to pay me compliments,' she said. 'What's happened?'

'Another man's been killed, another of Cutler's employees. The method was exactly the same. It happened last night.'

'Oh, Christ,' she murmured as she dropped tea bags into the mugs on the draining board.

He also told her about the arrival of Macready.

'So you're really no closer to finding the killer?' she asked.

'Or the kidnapper,' he added. 'Kim, it's like looking for a bloody ghost.' He sighed, then seemed to push the questions aside momentarily. 'Why aren't *you* working? I thought you still had things to do at the museum.'

Kim crossed to the door and pushed it shut, then spoke in a lowered voice.

'It's Clare,' she said. 'She's been having nightmares for the past week or so, and she hasn't been sleeping too well. I thought it best to keep her out of school for a while.' She paused for a moment, then told him about the incident at school the previous day. From a cupboard above the sink, where it lay rolled up and held by an elastic band, Kim pulled out the drawing and unfurled it in front of Wallace.

He studied it, puzzled by the grotesque image and the scrawled words.

'Clare says she doesn't remember drawing it,' Kim told him, switching off the kettle as it began to boil. 'Or writing those words.'

Wallace picked up the drawing and held it before him as if that simple act would reveal its secrets.

'Is she ill?' he wanted to know.

'In perfect physical condition, the doctor said. I took her to see him earlier today. She's just tired. Like I said, she hasn't been sleeping very well. She says she has bad dreams but she can never remember them the following day. At least not what they were about.' Kim handed the policeman his tea, wandering round to stand beside him. They both looked down at the drawing.

'Perhaps this figure is what she's been seeing in her dreams,' Wallace offered.

'It's possible,' Kim sighed. 'Do you believe in premonitions? Second sight?'

Wallace shrugged.

Kim picked up a notepad from the worktop nearby and handed it to him. It contained more of the transcribed words from the Celtic tablets she was working on.

'I finished the transcription yesterday teatime,' Kim told him, her eyes following the words across the page:

ONCE IN EACH YEAR THE TIME COMES. TIME OF FEAR FOR THEM. TIME OF FEAST. OF TARBFEIS AND OF THE OFFERINGS. THEN I AM NO LONGER A WANDERER. THE KING IS SELECTED BY THE OFFERING OF A MARE. A WHITE MARE IS SLAUGHTERED AND IN THE HOT LIQUID THE KING DRINKS AND BATHES UNTIL HE HAS ABSORBED THE SPIRIT OF THE DEAD ANIMAL. FOR THOUGH DEATH COMES IT BRINGS LIFE TO OTHERS. DEATH THROUGH LIFE. THE DEATH OF ONE MAN MEANS POWER TO ANOTHER. AND THE DEATH OF MANY MEANS POWER TO HIM.

Wallace looked at the drawing done by Clare and then at the final phrase which Kim had written down. It was underlined three times.

'His time is come,' he read aloud.

Kim nodded.

'Clare did that drawing and wrote those words yesterday lunchtime,' she said. 'Three hours *before* I'd deciphered the writing on the tablet.'

'I'll call you later,' Wallace said as he slid behind the wheel of the Sierra. He looked up at Kim and smiled. She bent forward and kissed him on the lips, surprising him with the suddenness of her movement, but he responded, still more surprised by the passion which he felt. He felt her tongue probing against his lips, pushing past his teeth to find the warm moistness of his tongue. He gently touched her cheek as he returned the kiss with equal fervour. When they finally parted it was very reluctantly.

'Take care,' she said as he drove off.

He could see her in one wing mirror as he drove away, but his thoughts were interrupted by the harsh crackle of the two-way. He immediately snatched it up.

'Wallace.'

'It's Dayton, guv. The C.I. wants you back here straight-away.'

Wallace didn't ask why. He merely acknowledged and put his foot down.

He reached the police station in a little under ten minutes, parked his car and walked across the tarmac towards the entrance, wondering what Macready wanted.

As he entered the station he heard unfamiliar sounds.

A woman crying.

Puzzled, he glanced around, trying to find the source of the anguished sounds.

The frosted glass partition was down and locked, separating the entry-way of the police station from what lay behind it. There was no one in sight and the only sound was of the woman crying.

196

Wallace climbed the stairs to his office, knocked once and then walked in.

Macready was standing with his back to the door, gazing out of the window. He turned as the younger man entered the room and Wallace saw the worried expression on his superior's face.

The chief inspector said nothing. He reached for something on his desk and handed it to Wallace.

It was a photograph. A wallet-sized snap of a young boy, no more than six years old, the inspector guessed. Short brown hair, one front tooth missing, the gap revealed by a wide and cheeky grin.

Wallace felt an uncomfortably familiar chill creeping up his spine as he looked at the picture.

'Carl Taylor,' Macready said. 'He's not quite six years old.'

Wallace suddenly understood why the woman downstairs was crying.

Macready sighed and continued:

'He disappeared from outside his home an hour ago . . .'

Fifty-One

The huge Scania lorry rolled inexorably up the slope towards the site, the first of a massive convoy of steel vehicles. Belching diesel fumes in great bluish-grey clouds, the trucks and other metallic juggernauts made their way over the uneven ground as easily as a tank rolling over a shell-ravaged battlefield.

Alongside the lorry, looking curiously incongruous, was James Cutler's Jensen. The car bumped and bounced over

197

the ruts in the earth, but its suspension prevented the land developer from feeling the worst of the uneven ride.

Charles Cooper stood close to the entrance of the ancient shaft, watching the vehicles drawing closer, feeling the anger boiling up inside him. So, this was it. The end. The most valuable archaeological find of its type for years was to be wiped out by bulldozers and earth-movers. All in the name of profit.

'What's going on?' asked George Perry, appearing beside him, his gaze also drawn to the convoy of lorries heading towards them. Other members of the dig, alerted by the roar of engines, were also watching apprehensively.

'Cutler,' said Cooper, angrily. 'It looks as if he's finally getting around to doing what he threatened.'

The Jensen sped on ahead of the heavier vehicles and came to a halt at the top of the slope. Cutler got out, muttering to himself as he saw that the mud was sticking to his shoes. He walked towards Cooper, a thin smile on his face.

'My men won't be starting work until tomorrow,' he said. 'You and your people will have plenty of time to move your things out.'

Cooper clenched his fists, his anger preventing him from speaking.

'Come on, Cooper, you knew it would happen eventually,' Cutler said. 'You've already had longer on this dig than you originally envisaged.'

'But our work isn't finished,' Perry said.

'I'm afraid it is,' Cutler told him. 'I'm very sorry but we made an agreement when the site was first discovered. I'm sure I don't need to remind you.'

'How can you do this?' Cooper hissed. 'Still, asking you to appreciate *true* value is like asking a dog to shit in a toilet.'

Cutler waved a finger reproachfully.

'I didn't come here for a slanging match, or to be insulted. I came to tell you to move off *my* land. I hoped that it could be done amicably but I see that it can't.' The land developer's tone had hardened. 'Now I'm telling you,

Cooper, I want you and all your people away from here by tonight. Otherwise I'll call the police in and press trespass charges. Understood?'

Cooper suddenly lunged forward, hands outstretched in an effort to reach Cutler. The other man stepped back, avoiding the frantic attack. The archaeologist slipped and sprawled in the mud but he dragged himself upright immediately and went for Cutler a second time. This time he was stopped by two of his colleagues.

'Do you want assault charges added to those for trespass?' Cutler asked scornfully. 'Now, get out of here. I won't tell you again.' He walked back to his car and climbed in. 'I'll be back first thing in the morning, and I don't expect to see you here,' he said and started the engine. The wheels spun in the mud for a moment, then the Jensen roared away. Only then did Cooper's companions release him.

'You bastard,' he bellowed after the car, hurling a handful of mud in its direction.

George Perry looked on in silence.

Cooper stood for a moment longer, then turned and stalked away towards his tent.

Fifty-Two

The chink of ice against crystal sounded almost unnaturally loud in the peacefulness of the room.

James Cutler dug his hand into the ice bucket and dropped more of the frozen squares into the whiskey tumbler before pouring a generous measure of Johnny Walker.

He drank deeply, allowing the amber fluid to burn its way to his stomach. The land developer had drunk three or four scotches at the restaurant an hour or so earlier, and he wondered how he had managed to remain so stone-cold sober. He didn't even feel a hint of light-headedness. He poured himself another drink, wondering how long it would take him to get smashed.

Even though the liquor inside him was warm and the central heating was on full-blast he still felt cold. As if icy fingers were tickling the back of his neck. He took his drink and sat down facing the television set. He didn't bother to turn the set on but merely gazed at the blank screen, sipping his drink a little too hastily.

Beside him his dog, Rebel, a red setter, lay with its head raised as if listening to something in the distance.

Cutler reached down with one hand and stroked the animal's head, surprised when it growled.

'What's the matter with you?' he said, withdrawing his hand an inch or two.

The dog's ears had pricked up and it was now looking round, its head jerking from side to side. Finally it contented itself with glaring at the sitting room door.

Cutler looked at the dog a moment longer, sipping more of his drink.

'You're a temperamental so-and-so tonight,' he said, patting the dog again, more cautiously this time.

Again the animal growled, low in its throat. It got to its feet, padded across to the door, and stood facing it, its growls gradually building into barks.

Cutler frowned and rose from his chair.

'What the hell is the matter, Rebel?' he asked as if he actually expected the dog to tell him.

Once more he felt those icy fingers at the back of his neck but with more cause now. His dog wouldn't behave this way unless it had a reason.

The animal was now barking, growling and whimpering by turns. It stood unmoving by the door as Cutler approached. He pulled the door open, expecting the setter to run out, but it remained where it was, looking out into the darkened hall and the front door beyond.

He himself looked at the wood-panelled door, then back

at the large bay window with its curtains still undrawn. Cutler suddenly felt very vulnerable.

And frightened.

Couldn't dogs sense the presence of others? he thought. They could tell when there was an intruder about.

An intruder.

Or a murderer perhaps?

The thought struck Cutler like a thunderbolt and he moved away from the door towards the windows, hastily drawing the curtains across, shutting out the darkness of the night.

His house stood on the outskirts of Longfield, surrounded by two acres of grounds. He was, in short, isolated. Cut off. And, with what had been happening recently to those who worked for him, the land developer felt suddenly afraid.

The dog had now moved out into the hall slightly, still growling.

Cutler followed it, moving slowly in the gloom, his ears alert for any sound from outside the house.

He listened intently but heard nothing. Still the setter growled, its lips sliding back over its canine teeth.

Cutler glanced to his right, up the stairs, then to his left, towards the dining room. The dog seemed intent on the front door and now, as he watched, it began to bark frenziedly, the sound echoing in the stillness of the house.

The land developer crossed to the door, one hand resting on the lock.

Should he let the dog out? Let it chase whoever was out there?

But if he did open the door . . .

He swallowed hard, looking down at the setter, which was now barking loudly, its body stiff. The only part of it moving was its head.

Open the door? he asked himself.

He finally slid back the bolt and pulled it open, letting the setter scurry out into the night. He slammed the door quickly behind it and stood with his back to it, shaking. If there was a burglar or prowler out there, then Rebel would soon see them off, he thought, trying to reassure himself.

The barking ceased abruptly and silence descended once again.

Cutler listened, waiting for the noise to continue.

Nothing.

Maybe the dog had been unable to find anyone. Perhaps it was even now trotting back towards the house. Cutler glanced at the phone on the hall table and wondered if he should call the police. If he did, what would he tell them? That his dog had been barking at sounds he himself could not hear? It was scarcely a good enough reason to bring two panda cars screeching to his door. He closed his eyes for a moment, surrounded by the darkness, wondering what to do.

He heard his dog yelp wildly and his blood froze.

The cry died away on the breeze which swirled around the house.

Cutler looked across at the phone once more.

Should he phone?

What if the killer were outside?

He had a right to be protected.

Again he hesitated, peering out of the window beside the door in an effort to see where the dog had got to. The darkness was impenetrable. The light switch which controlled the porch lamp was close to his hand. If he put that on he would be able to see. He flicked the switch.

As the front path was bathed in light, Cutler sucked in a strangled breath.

His dog was lying about ten yards from the house in a spreading pool of blood.

Its head had almost been severed. It hung at an impossible angle, twisted to one side to reveal a jawbone which was shattered into crimson mush. Both eyes had been torn out, leaving only the weeping sockets, and Cutler noticed that one of the dog's long ears had also been ripped away by its killer. The ear lay discarded a couple of feet away. The body was still twitching spasmodically, one rear

202

leg quivering insanely as the last muscular movements racked it.

Cutler turned immediately, snapping off the porch light, and dived for the phone. He snatched it up and dialled three nines.

The line was dead.

Shaking uncontrollably he dialled again, not stopping to think that the lines had most likely been cut.

With a final despairing moan he threw the receiver down and blundered into the sitting room, slamming the door behind him, his breath now coming in short gasps.

He heard scratching outside the front door, the sound gradually building until a series of loud bangs rang through the house.

Cutler looked around desperately for something with which to defend himself.

The bangs became blows of sledgehammer proportions and the land developer heard the strain of cracking wood.

He ran from the sitting room, through the kitchen, and unlocked the back door.

If he could just get to his car . . .

The garage was about thirty feet from the house at the end of a long tarmac drive.

With the sound of the splintering front door still echoing through the night he plunged on towards the garage, slipping once on the grass. He rolled over and sprang to his feet, not daring to look back. The cold air rasped in his throat as he gulped down huge lungfuls. Finally, with a whimper of relief, he reached the garage. Only then did he afford himself a look back over his shoulder.

No one was following him.

He flung open the garage door and scurried around to the driver's side of the Jensen, fumbling in his pockets.

He'd left the keys in the house.

His heart seemed to accelerate to an impossible speed, hammering madly against his ribs.

He tugged on the car door in his anger and fear, knowing that he had no choice but to go back for the keys. Clenching his teeth he turned and sprinted back across the grass towards the open back door, the sound of splintering wood still loud in his ears.

Another few moments and the intruder would be inside.

Cutler crashed into the kitchen table in his haste, bruising his hip. He ignored the pain, intent only on finding his car keys, on escaping with his life.

He looked around frantically for the keys, aware that the front door could not hold out for much longer. Each hammer blow rained upon it brought his would-be killer closer.

'Oh God,' he grunted. Where had he put the bloody keys?

A huge lump of wood was torn from the door, clattering into the hall. Cutler spun round, his eyes darting back and forth.

He saw the keys on the drinks trolley and snatched them up, hurtling back out through the hall and the kitchen.

The front door finally crashed inwards and the intruder blundered into the hallway, catching sight of the fleeing land developer.

He knew without turning round that he was being pursued but that knowledge only spurred him on to greater effort and, seconds later, he was outside again, sprinting towards the garage, praying that this time he didn't slip and fall.

Behind him, his attacker followed.

Cutler reached the garage. Only then did he turn and look back.

The sight he saw nearly caused him to drop his keys.

The would-be killer was within twenty feet of him.

Cutler smelled the noxious odour, saw the blood, felt the searing cold.

He kicked open the side door of the garage, dashed through and slammed it behind him, slipping the bolt, praying that it would keep the intruder at bay long enough for him to get away.

His hands shaking madly, Cutler struggled to push the key into the lock on the car door.

There was a deafening crash as the first powerful blow landed against the garage door. It was followed by many more.

Murmuring to himself, Cutler struggled with the keys again.

They fell from his grasp but he hurriedly snatched them up and rammed the appropriate one into the lock. In an instant he was behind the steering wheel.

As he jammed in the ignition key he heard the side door of the garage beginning to give.

It would only be a matter of seconds now.

He twisted the key savagely, stepping on the accelerator simultaneously. The engine roared into life and he rammed the Jensen into gear, but his foot slipped off the clutch and the car stalled.

On the verge of hysteria now, he started the engine once more, the loud roar drowning out all other sounds.

Cutler didn't even bother opening the main doors. He merely ducked low behind the wheel and put his foot down.

The Jensen shot forward as if fired from a cannon, smashing through the double doors and out into the night, skidding on the tarmac for precious seconds as Cutler struggled to control the vehicle.

He heard and felt a tremendous thud which seemed to rock the entire car and, for a second, he thought with delight that he'd managed to run his attacker down.

It took him a second to realize that the thud had come from above.

There was someone on the roof.

He braked hard, trying to dislodge the attacker, but as he did so, a powerful hand swung down towards the driver's window.

Glass exploded inwards under the impact and Cutler shrieked as he felt the slivers cutting his skin. The scream was silenced a moment later as the hand fastened itself around his throat.

He swerved, running the car onto his front lawn, skidding to a halt, both hands now clutching at his assailant's arm and at the hand which was throttling him.

His attacker slid from the roof of the car without releasing the strangling grip on Cutler's throat.

He felt himself being pulled towards the broken window and, for one bizarre moment, he thought his assailant was going to try to pull him through the tiny opening.

Instead he saw another hand reaching in, clawing at his face, at his eyes. Sharp nails started digging into the soft flesh of his lids, curving inwards to scrape the sensitive orbs themselves.

Pain enveloped him and he struggled even more fiercely, but his frantic movements only seemed to inflame the attacker more.

Cutler felt his head being turned to an impossible angle, felt the muscles and bones creaking and popping.

Then suddenly, he was staring into the face of his attacker.

Horror such as he had never felt before overwhelmed him and he felt sharp pain stabbing at his heart.

He managed one final scream.

Gripping his head like a bottle top, the killer twisted with incredible ferocity.

The bones in Cutler's neck cracked with a strident shriek, the muscles tearing like paper as the killer continued to twist.

Cutler slumped forward, his head turned completely around, facing backwards.

Without a second's hesitation, the assailant tore open the car door and dragged the body from the confines of the vehicle, which already reeked of excrement and blood.

The killer stood over the corpse for a moment, then fell upon it.

There was much still to be done.

PART THREE

'His heart is black,
His blood is cold,
Returning to destroy our World.

Warrior

Fifty-Three

WHEN THE LEAVES DIE ON THE TREES THEN THEY FEAR
HIM. WHEN THE WIND IS COLD THEY FEAR HIM. AND
THEY KNOW THAT ONLY THE DEATHS OF OTHERS CAN
STOP HIM RISING SO THEY KILL. THEY KILL IN HIS NAME
BUT THEY KILL IN FEAR OF HIM AND HIS POWER WHICH
IS SUCH TO SPLIT THE WORLD IN TWO. NONE CAN STAND
AGAINST HIM FOR NONE POSSESS SUCH POWER AS HE.
SAVE ONE. THEY KNOW LITTLE OF THIS OTHER. OF THE
ONE WHO IS ALWAYS WITH HIM. THE ONE WHO SEEKS
LIVING BODIES NOT DEAD ONES. THE ONE WHO LIVES IN
OTHER MEN'S MINDS. I HAVE PLACED THIS KNOWLEDGE
IN MANY PLACES. HIDDEN. FOR I SERVE HIM AND I
CARRY THE SECRETS.
THE LEAVES ARE DYING ON THE TREES. THE YEAR IS AT
AN END. THEY MUST KILL AGAIN.
DAGDA COMES.

Kim sat back from the notebook and exhaled deeply.
Wallace stood beside her, looking down at the words which
she had so painstakingly transcribed from the stone tablets.

'Who the hell is Dagda?' said Wallace, glancing at the
notes once more.

'Each Celtic tribe worshipped its own individual god or
goddess,' Kim told him. 'For instance, Maponus was a
Northern God, but the lord of them all was Dagda. He was
the most powerful, the most feared. Supposedly grotesque
to look at. He's described as an immense figure with
incredible powers.'

'What about the other name?' the inspector said,

pointing to one which was underlined further down the page.

'Morrigan, the Queen of Demons, Dagda's mate in fertility rituals. She was also known as *Nemain* which means panic, or *Badb Catha*, the raven of battle. In some ways, thought to be as powerful as Dagda himself.' She looked down at her own scribblings.

WHEN COMES THE SEASON OF COLD THEN COMES
DAGDA UNLESS THEY ARE WILLING TO OFFER TO HIM
THE YOUNG OF THEIR TÚATH.

'The Celtic year was divided into two halves,' Kim said. 'The season of warmth and the season of cold, basically summer and winter. They had no concept of spring and autumn, only that there was one time of the year for growing crops and another for storing them.' She sighed. 'But don't ask me how all that ties in with the murders.'

Wallace shrugged, sipping at his coffee, looking down at the photos of the murder victims spread out on the table in front of Kim. The most recent one showed the butchered remains of James Cutler. His body had been flayed, his eyes torn from their sockets, his stomach cavity almost emptied. Beside him lay the final abomination.

Three lengths of intestine used to form a capital letter I.

The clock on the mantelpiece struck one a.m. and Wallace rubbed his face with one hand, simultaneously stifling a yawn. He had driven to Kim's house after leaving the scene of Cutler's murder, returning quickly to the police station to collect the photos. That had been three hours ago. He stretched and looked across at Kim, who was dressed only in a short house-coat, her slender legs drawn up beneath her. He did not drop his gaze when he saw her look back at him.

'You look exhausted, Steve,' she told him, brushing a stray hair from his forehead. As she withdrew her hand he held it and kissed her slender fingers. She responded by moving closer, snaking one hand around the back of his head, pulling him to her as they kissed.

210

The scream which echoed through the house caused them both to gasp aloud.

It came from upstairs.

From Clare's room.

Fifty-Four

Kim leapt to her feet and dashed for the stairs taking them two at a time in her haste. Wallace was right behind her, the scream still drumming in his ears.

They reached the landing and he followed as she pushed open the door of her daughter's room and hurried in.

'Oh God,' Kim gasped as Wallace joined her and they both stood gazing down at the girl.

Clare was lying spreadeagled on the bed, the covers thrown off in an untidy heap. Her head was moving slowly from side to side, her lips fluttering constantly, expelling a series of low mutterings. Her eyes, though, were closed tightly.

Kim moved forward but Wallace stepped in front of her.

'Don't wake her,' he said, seeing that the girl was obviously still asleep. He picked up the covers and laid them gently back on the bed, moving closer to the sleeping girl. Her entire body was quivering gently, as if a mild electric shock were passing through it. Kim crouched beside the bed, touching her daughter's hand, feeling how cold the skin was despite the thin film of perspiration which covered her face, matting her hair across her forehead and beading into minute crystal droplets on her arms.

The low whispering continued, like some kind of muted litany, the same mumblings repeated over and over again as the girl's head moved from side to side.

211

'This happened to her once before,' said Kim, anxiety etched on her face. 'It must be another nightmare.' She bent close to her daughter's face, brushing a strand of hair away. As she did so, she realized that it wasn't a string of words which Clare was mouthing. It was one single word. Kim strained her ears to pick it out.

'Can you understand what she's saying?' Wallace asked.

Kim merely raised one hand to silence him, the word now becoming more distinct.

It sounded like steam escaping as Clare mouthed that one word over and over again.

'*Samain. Samain. Samain.*'

Kim frowned, unsure at first if she had heard right, but Clare continued and there was no mistaking the word.

Wallace saw the look of concern on Kim's face.

'What is it?' he asked.

'*Samain. Samain. Samain,*' Clare breathed, more insistently now.

The sound stopped abruptly. In the silence they both heard the girl's breathing return to a semblance of normality. The rigidity in her limbs seemed to disappear and she curled up into a ball beneath the covers. Kim sat on the edge of the bed, one hand resting on her daughter's shoulder, her eyes never leaving the girl.

'I'll sit with her for a while, Steve,' she said softly.

Wallace nodded and walked slowly from the room. Kim heard his footfalls on the stairs as he descended. From the kitchen she heard the sound of the kettle being filled.

Clare continued to sleep peacefully.

Kim found that it was she who was quivering now.

'Is she all right?' Wallace asked as Kim entered the sitting room, closing the door behind her.

She nodded and sat down beside him on the sofa, gratefully accepting the mug of coffee which he handed to her. A heavy silence settled over them, finally broken by Wallace.

'What was she saying, Kim? That word, you seemed to recognize it,' he said.

212

She nodded slowly, her eyes drawn towards the photos of the murder victims before her. Kim put down her cup, her own breathing now becoming more rapid. She looked at each of the photos that showed the letters which had been formed from lengths of bleeding intestines. She pulled a notebook towards her, one eye on the grisly photos, and said, 'When the letters the killer left behind are placed in the correct order they do make a word.'

Wallace watched as she wrote down in block letters:

SAMAIN

'Samain,' she said quietly. 'It's a Celtic word. It means the end of summer. The Celts held a great festival to mark its ending.'

The inspector swallowed hard.

'Is there any way Clare would know that word?' he asked. 'Could she have seen it written in one of your notebooks?'

'It's possible, I suppose,' Kim said, her brow furrowed. 'That's what the writing on the stone tablets must refer to: "When comes the time. Time of cold. Time of Samain." Whoever carved those tablets was a very powerful Druid. He claims to have had power over Dagda. "When comes the season of cold then comes Dagda," ' she re-read.

'So what happened at Samain?' Wallace asked.

'In order to ensure that their crops would grow in the coming year, the Druids would sacrifice children to Dagda. It was like a kind of fertility rite but also a means of appeasement to prevent Dagda from rising and entering this world. It was done every year.' She pointed to a line of the transcript.

ONCE RISEN HE CANNOT BE STOPPED. ONLY THE OFFERING OF THE YOUNG WILL PREVENT HIS COMING

'Steve, don't you see? The children's skulls that we found in that underground chamber must have belonged to sacrificial victims killed in the name of Dagda, to prevent him from rising. Every one of those children had been

213

decapitated and the eyes gouged out. It was part of the ritual. Except that the carbon-dating tests I ran on the skulls showed that not all of them came from the same period. They weren't all Celtic sacrifices. One of them belonged to a child who was murdered in 1823. Other people, in the past, have found those tablets and deciphered them. The knowledge has been passed down through the ages, the superstition continued for thousands of years. Right up until 1823 when that last child was murdered.'

Wallace felt a chill envelop him.

'Children must have been sacrificed on that same spot for thousands of years. Since 1,000 B.C. that site had been used for the ritual murder of children,' Kim continued.

'Was it always children?' the inspector asked.

'Young children. They would be killed on the night of Samain. Usually three at a time because three was a mystical number to the Celts. How many children have been kidnapped from Longfield?'

Wallace stiffened.

'Three,' he said quietly. 'When was Samain? The date?'

'October 31st,' she told him.

'Christ, that's tomorrow,' said Wallace. 'October 31st. Halloween.'

'The name changed but the festival has persisted in different forms,' Kim told him. 'The early Christians called it Hallowmas. Then in the Middle Ages, November the 1st was consecrated as All Saint's Day so the night before became All Hallow Even. Over the years it was shortened to Halloween.'

'The kidnapper must have some knowledge of all this,' Wallace said, agitatedly.

'When you were at the museum you were reading up on witchcraft,' she reminded him. 'Halloween is the most important time of the witches' year too.'

Wallace nodded, remembering the butchered animals that had been found in the wood near Dexter Grange. His gaze strayed to the photos of the murder victims, slaughtered in a similar, though even more horrendous fashion. But one question plagued his mind.

214

'Why would the killer spell out the word?' he mused, looking at the pictures. There was a heavy silence.

'The three kids that have been kidnapped,' he continued, 'obviously whoever's got them is going to use them as sacrifices tomorrow night.' He looked at Kim. 'Charles Cooper would know about this ritual, wouldn't he? *And* he had it in for Cutler and the others that were killed.'

'You could say the same about anyone who was part of the archaeological team on that dig,' she told him. 'They all had a grievance against Cutler.'

'Maybe,' he said, unconvinced. 'But three kids are going to be murdered tomorrow night unless I find out who's got them. I've got to concentrate on the likeliest suspects first.'

'But what if the legends about Dagda are true?'

'Kim, you're not serious?' he snorted.

'A lot of people *have* been serious about this over the past few thousand years. Serious or frightened enough to murder children to prevent unleashing this . . . evil, whatever it is.'

'So you think I should let the kids die?'

She lowered her head.

'I've got to find them.'

Kim gripped his hand.

'Do you have to leave tonight?' she wanted to know. He heard the anxiety in her voice.

He leant forward and kissed her lightly on the lips.

'No,' he said softly, pulling her closer, but as she wrapped her arms around him he glanced at the table once more. At the sentence from the transcript which made him shudder:

WHEN COMES THE SEASON OF COLD THEN COMES DAGDA UNLESS THEY ARE WILLING TO OFFER HIM THE YOUNG . . .

215

Fifty-Five

The policeman slammed the knocker down three times and stepped back, waiting for Charles Cooper to open the door.

There was no response.

Wallace knocked again.

Still no answer.

He pushed open the letter box and peered through. It looked dark inside the hallway. He called the archaeologist's name, then wandered halfway back down the path, glancing up at the bedroom window. The curtains were open.

The inspector spotted a gate which he guessed led around to the back of the house. It was flanked on one side by the house itself, on the other by a high privet hedge, now leafless and bare. Through it, Wallace could see the woman next door peering curiously at him, a yard broom held in her hands.

'You looking for Mr Cooper?' she called.

'Yes,' Wallace replied, tersely, without looking at her. He reached the back of the house, and cupping one hand over his eyes, peered through the kitchen window.

The place certainly looked empty.

'You a friend of his?' the woman asked.

'You could say that,' Wallace told her, knocking on the back door. 'Have you seen him about today?'

'No, but then I don't see him much anyhow.'

'Terrific,' murmured Wallace and made his way back to the waiting Sierra. He picked up the handset and flicked it on.

'This is Wallace. I want a car sent to 12 Elm Street now.'

'Anything wrong, guv?' asked Dayton at the other end.

'I don't know. Yet. Look, when the car arrives I just want the blokes in it to watch the house. But if Charles Cooper shows up I want him pulled, got it?'

'What's the charge?' Dayton wanted to know.

Wallace sucked in an impatient breath.

'Indecent exposure,' he snapped. 'I don't give a toss what they use. I just want Cooper brought in for questioning. Over and out.' He replaced his handset before the sergeant had a chance to reply. Wallace sat looking at the house for a moment longer, then started his engine and drove off.

It was 10:56 a.m.

As Wallace guided the Sierra through the gateway which led up to Dexter Grange he peered through the windscreen towards the gaunt edifice as if looking for signs of movement within the house.

The gravel of the driveway crunched loudly beneath the wheels of the car as he swung it around before the imposing structure. He got out of the vehicle and stood looking up at the house for a moment before striding up to the front door. He banged loudly three times.

No answer.

Muttering to himself, Wallace walked back to the car and pressed hard on the hooter, keeping his hand there until even *he* could stand the strident wail no longer. He then hurried back to the front door and banged again.

There was still no reply.

'Shit,' he murmured, wandering past the large windows which led into the library, the study, the lounge. He reached the side of the house and a set of French doors. The inspector hesitated a moment, and then, cupping one hand over his eyes, he peered in through the glass. Nothing moved inside the room. The policeman took off his jacket and wrapped it around his fist and lower arm. With one swift punch, he stove in a panel of glass close to the door handle. The glass shattered loudly, small shards spraying into the room. Wallace snaked a hand through, careful not to cut himself, twisted the handle and let himself in.

There was still no sound or movement inside Dexter Grange. No one had heard, or else they had chosen not to hear, Wallace thought as he made his way across the room to the door which he knew led out into the corridor.

He paused for a moment, then stepped out onto the polished wood floor.

He moved quickly from room to room, pushing open doors, something at the back of his mind asking him what the hell he was going to say should Dexter appear. But the inspector swiftly administered himself a rebuke. He was searching for evidence. More to the point, three missing children. He didn't need a search warrant and if Dexter started mouthing off then *he'd* be hauled down to the station too.

But there didn't seem to be any sign of either the recluse or his young girlfriend. If, Wallace thought, that was the right word.

As he reached the front door he saw that two large bolts had been slipped into position.

Obviously Dexter didn't want any visitors.

Wallace glanced to his right, towards the broad staircase.

The steps seemed to climb precipitously up to a landing which looked strangely dark and forbidding. Wallace told himself that some curtains up there must be drawn, cutting out the daylight, and the sky was grey and overcast in any case.

He began to climb.

The stairs were uncarpeted so he trod as softly as he could.

The sound of his shoes echoed in the stillness and more than one of the steps creaked protestingly under his weight as he drew nearer the top of the flight.

He thought about calling Dexter's name but decided against it.

He reached the landing and stood still, looking around at the closed doors which faced him. The solitude was almost oppressive on this floor and Wallace, for some unaccountable reason, felt strangely apprehensive about approaching the first of the doors.

'Come on,' he whispered to himself, annoyed at his own reticence. He strode towards the door and flung it open.

There wasn't a stick of furniture in it. No carpet either. A thick film of dust covered the floor and Wallace coughed as the choking particles swirled before him, disturbed by his sudden entrance.

It was the same in the next room.

And the next.

He approached the fourth door, his initial apprehension having given way to annoyance.

He threw open the door and walked in.

The sight which met him caused him to freeze momentarily.

He frowned, his eyes drawn to what lay in the centre of the room.

Drawn on the bare boards was a huge pentagram.

At the apex of each of the five points of the star there was a small silver bowl. In the centre lay another, larger than the others.

Wallace moved closer, kneeling beside the carefully drawn shape. He touched the closest line, surprised to find that it was fresh. Chalk smudged his finger tips.

What the hell had Dexter got in mind? Wallace thought. And, more to the point, where was he?

The policeman straightened up. Taking one last look at the pentagram, he walked out of the room and headed down the stairs.

He made his way back through the house and out through the French doors, glancing towards the wood which lay about a mile or so from the building. With the dark clouds gathering above it, the sight made Wallace shudder.

'Witchcraft,' he muttered to himself.

Witchcraft. Ritual murder. Kidnapping.

A thought struck him, at once logical yet absurd.

Could both Cooper and Dexter be involved together in the killings and kidnappings? Both men had motives for wanting Cutler and those who worked for him dead. Both had knowledge of ritual murder.

219

He slid behind the wheel of the Sierra and started the engine. He threw the car into a screeching turn and drove rapidly away from Dexter Grange.

Fifty-Six

'You were in breach of regulations, Wallace.'

Chief Inspector Gordon Macready sat back in his seat, his fingers clasped across his stomach.

'You had no right to break into Dexter's house. He could prosecute you for trespassing and he'd be perfectly within his rights. You had no search warrant, no authorisation of any kind.'

'I think that reason to suspect he's holding three kidnapped children is authorisation enough, sir,' Wallace snapped, trying to light a cigarette.

'There are certain procedures to be followed in a case like this . . .'

Wallace cut him short. 'My only concern is to find those kids. They could be dead by morning.'

'Your concern should be with carrying out correct police procedure,' Macready told him, his voice taking on a menacing tone. 'You also had no business calling a car and two constables to keep watch on Charles Cooper's house.'

'How the hell else are we supposed to find him?'

Macready sat forward in his seat, his dark eyes fixing the younger man in a piercing stare.

'Look, Wallace, I came to Longfield to replace you because you weren't getting results. I also told you that you were to take your orders direct from me. Now *I* didn't order surveillance on Cooper's house, did I?'

'But you do agree that it's rather strange that the two

prime suspects in this case are . . . unobtainable?' he said, acidly.

'Strange, yes, but I don't attach the importance to it that you do.'

'Maybe it's a pity you don't, sir,' Wallace replied, sucking hard on his cigarette.

Macready studied him for a moment, the knot of muscles at the side of his jaw pulsing angrily.

'You also had no business showing the results of our investigation to that woman,' he said.

'We *had* no results until I showed her,' Wallace gasped. 'She was the one who told me what those bloody letters stood for!'

The older man was unimpressed.

'And you expect me to believe that these murders and kidnappings are being done by someone who practises witchcraft? Just because the letters happen to spell out some mythical name? What do you take me for, Wallace? It's only a coincidence that the letters spelled out a word this woman recognized. We don't know that the word is Celtic. More likely it could be a foreign word and mean something completely different. For God's sake, man, you're a policeman. You're supposed to think rationally, not believe the first piece of mystical hocus-pocus you hear.'

'How do you explain the accidents on the building site, then?'

'That's precisely what they were. Accidents. Nothing more. There's nothing sinister about them.'

'Two men died.'

'That was unfortunate. You have no proof to support any . . . occult links.'

'But the murders have a basis in ritual, you have to agree with that. A ritual which could apply equally to witchcraft or to Celtic sacrifice. And the kidnappings too. Children are or were used in both Celtic ceremonies *and* the Black Mass.'

Macready sucked in a deep breath.

'No, I'm sorry, Wallace,' he said. 'I can't accept that

there's a supernatural element involved here.'

'Well then, if you won't do anything about it, at least let me. I *do* care if those kids are killed.'

'One more word out of you and you're suspended. I mean it.' Macready pointed an angry finger.

Wallace sucked hard on his cigarette, locking stares with the older man for a moment.

'From now on you do everything by the book, got it?' Macready continued. 'You report to me, you don't do anything without my say-so. You step out of line once more and you're finished.'

The inspector took one last drag on his cigarette, then ground it out in the ashtray next to his superior.

'I'm going to drive around, if that's OK, sir,' he said sarcastically. 'Perhaps I can help the men who are looking for the children.'

'Keep away from Cooper and Dexter,' Macready warned him. 'They'll be brought in for questioning when, and if, we find enough real evidence to link them to this case. Understood?'

Wallace nodded, turned and left.

Outside the office he looked at the door, as if glaring through the wood itself at his superior beyond.

'Bastard,' he hissed.

He headed out towards his car.

It was 12:08.

Fifty-Seven

'Come on, come on.'

Mick Ferguson tapped on the wall agitatedly as he waited for the phone to be picked up at the other end. He waited a full minute, finally tiring of the persistent ringing in his ear. He slammed the receiver down, waited a moment, then tried again. This time he only had to wait a few seconds.

'Dexter?' he snapped.

'This is Henry Dexter,' the voice on the other end informed him.

'Where the fuck have you been? I've been ringing for the last half hour,' Ferguson snapped. 'Do you want this stuff I've got or not?'

'Of course I want it, but don't come to the house.'

'Bollocks,' the other man interrupted. 'I've got two kilos here, I want to unload it quick. I'm coming straight out there now.' He paused for a moment. 'And by the way, Dexter, it's going to cost you £3,000 for this little lot. You could say my supply's about to dry up. The bloke I bought it off was collared by the law yesterday.'

'Will they be able to trace his contacts?' Dexter asked, apprehensively.

'Do you think I'd have touched the stuff if I thought they could?' Ferguson added scornfully and put the phone down. He turned to see his wife standing in the sitting room doorway. 'I've got to go out,' he told her.

'More business,' she said. 'I overheard.' The anger in her voice turned to something akin to pleading as she approached Ferguson. 'Mick, just dump the heroin. If the law find you with it they'll lock us both up. What with that and those bloody dogs.'

'Get out of the way,' Ferguson snapped, trying to push past her, but she grabbed his arm.

'No, you bastard. You're not dragging me down with you. I'll ring the law myself, tell them it was you. I'll tell them what's been going on.'

Ferguson eyed her malevolently for a second.

'You wouldn't dare,' he hissed.

'Wouldn't I?'

She took a step towards the phone.

Out of the corner of her eye she saw her husband lunge forward, but before she could avoid his flailing arms, he was upon her.

223

Wallace reached for the packet of Rothmans on the parcel shelf of the car, cursing when he found that it was empty. He tossed the empty pack out of the window, startled when the radio crackled into life, the message coming across in metallic tones:

'... Respond ... We've had a call about a disturbance at number twenty-five Victoria Road ... check it out, will you ...'

He listened for a moment longer, then picked up the handset.

'Base, this is Wallace, over.'

The man at the other end sounded somewhat startled to hear his superior's voice.

'Oh, hello, guv, it's Dayton here,' he said.

'I know who it is, Bill. Look, what's this about a disturbance in Victoria Road?'

'Some woman rang up about ten minutes ago, reckons she heard screaming.'

'Who's the occupant of number twenty-five?'

'Mick Ferguson and his wife.'

'I pulled that bastard about six months ago for GBH but he got off. Have you sent a car? Well, I'll cover it too.' He replaced the handset and put his foot down.

He was less than ten minutes from Victoria Road.

Fifty-Eight

The woman was on her knees in front of the house.

As Terry Laidlaw brought the police car to a halt close to her, he could see that the blouse she wore was ripped in several places. One flap hung open to reveal her left breast. She turned briefly, and in that split second Laidlaw saw the blood which covered her face.

'Jesus,' he muttered, clambering out of the car.

Constable Roy Denton followed him toward the woman who they now knew was Carol Ferguson.

She seemed oblivious to their presence as they approached her, her eyes never leaving the house before which she knelt. The blouse she wore was also stained with blood, and as the two policemen drew nearer they could see vicious gashes on her face. One eye was swollen and surrounded by blackened, puffy flesh. It looked as if it had been pumped up. A repulsive, throbbing balloon.

Her nose had been broken; the bone was shattered and the flesh misshapen.

As the two policemen drew level with Carol they heard her muttering to herself, the words forced out through lips which were split and weeping blood.

'Bastard,' she mumbled. 'Bloody bastard.'

Denton knelt beside her, slipping one hand beneath her arm to help her up.

'Come on, love,' he said, quietly.

'Get off me,' she rasped, twisting loose. Then she suddenly seemed to find untapped reserves of strength. She dragged herself upright and bellowed towards the house.

'Some man you are. You're a fucking animal just like those bloody dogs you keep.'

'Let's get her into the car,' Denton said to his companion and they took one arm each and tried to guide her towards the waiting vehicle.

'Come on, now,' Laidlaw said, urging the defiant woman to move.

'Leave me,' she hissed, turning to face him, forcing him to look upon the hideous extent of her injuries.

Her features were little more than a crimson mask. A patchwork of cuts and bruises. The constable also noticed several angry red marks on her throat.

'I'm going to call a doctor for you,' the constable said, using all his strength to guide the injured woman towards the car as she still resisted. Denton asked if he needed help but the other man shook his head.

Both men turned as the Sierra skidded to a halt about ten yards away.

Wallace jumped out and strode over to the waiting men. He took a brief look at the battered face of Carol Ferguson and shook his head.

'Is Ferguson still inside?' he wanted to know.

Before either of the uniformed men could answer, the inspector had set off towards the front door. Denton followed him.

'You cover the back,' he told the constable. 'If Ferguson comes out, flatten him.'

The constable looked surprised.

'Lay him out,' Wallace repeated. 'Because you can be bloody sure he won't hesitate to deck you if he gets the chance. Give me five minutes. If he hasn't come out by then, *you* come in. Right?'

Denton nodded, then disappeared around the side of the house.

Wallace banged three times on the front door and waited.

There was no response.

He didn't try a second time.

Wrapping his handkerchief around one fist he smashed one of the glass panels of the front door, hurriedly fumbling for the key which would unlock it. He twisted the key and hurled the door open, stepping into the long, narrow hallway.

Ahead of him was the staircase, to his left the sitting room, to his right a white door, firmly closed.

In the momentary silence, Wallace heard frenzied barking and it took him only a second to realize that it was coming from below. From the cellar.

He tugged at the white door, surprised when it opened so easily.

The heavy bulk of Mick Ferguson came hurtling through the door, ducked low, catching Wallace in the midriff. Both men crashed into the sitting room, toppling over a coffee table and upending a standard lamp as they struggled.

Wallace, despite being taken by surprise, managed to bring his knee up hard between his attacker's legs and Ferguson groaned in pain, rolling off.

226

The inspector struggled to his feet, his hand closing around the leg of a small stool.

As Ferguson rose the policeman swung the stool like a club and caught the bigger man across the shoulder with it. It broke apart in his hand and he was left holding the one leg. Hefting it before him like a truncheon he steadied himself for his opponent's next attack. This time, the bigger man ducked beneath the swing and drove a fist into Wallace's stomach, winding him, the impact propelling him back over a chair.

Before he could react, Ferguson was upon him, both ham-hock hands grasping the policeman's throat, the thumbs pressing into the windpipe. He found himself looking up into a face which was distorted into a mask of sheer rage.

Wallace struck out with his left hand, driving two fingers into his attacker's eyes.

As Ferguson screamed in pain, Wallace tore the large hands from his neck and rolled to one side, scrambling to his feet. The bigger man struggled to rise, but the policeman kicked him hard in the side, hearing the sharp crack of breaking ribs. Ferguson went down in a sprawling heap, clutching his injured side, and Wallace saw him spit blood. A second later he was up again, lashing out wildly, catching the inspector across the face with a backhand swipe that split his bottom lip. Blood spilled down his chin, and for precious seconds white stars danced before his eyes.

The lapse was enough to give Ferguson the upper hand.

He launched himself at Wallace, knocking him back into the hall, slamming him up against the wall with a bone-jarring thud. As the policeman slid to the floor Ferguson drove the toe of his boot into his stomach twice in quick succession, then tore open the front door and prepared to flee.

He cursed as he saw Laidlaw running towards him.

Ferguson ducked back into the house, wrenched open the white door and bolted down into the cellar.

Wallace struggled upright, helped by Laidlaw, and both men hurried after their quarry, struck by the foul smell as

227

they entered the cellar.

Now they heard the barking of the dogs, echoing around the subterranean room until it was deafening.

In the gloom, Wallace saw Ferguson over by the two cages, fumbling with the lock which held the black dog firmly behind bars.

Laidlaw ran at the bigger man, apparently unaware of what was about to happen. Wallace's restraining arm wasn't enough to halt him.

The cage door swung open.

Jaws open wide, long streamers of saliva dripping from them, the pit bull terrier bounded forward, snarling madly.

As Laidlaw opened his mouth to scream, the dog launched itself at him.

Fifty-Nine

The cellar had become a madhouse.

Shouts from the men mingled with the frenzied barking and growling of the dogs in a deafening cacophony.

The black dog crashed into Laidlaw, and as he raised both arms to protect his face, it clamped its jaws over his right forearm, shaking its head back and forth frenziedly as if the arm were a rabbit. With horror the policeman felt the material of his tunic tearing, and an instant later the sharp teeth found his flesh.

The skin and muscle were shredded as easily as by a meat grinder and the taste of the blood which jetted from the wounds inflamed the ravenous dog further. It jerked its head away and struck at the policeman's unprotected stomach, tearing through his clothing until it reached his midriff. He screamed in pain and fear as he felt the sharp teeth gnawing at him and grabbed desperately at the beast's head.

Laidlaw succeeded in grasping the beast by the ears and dragging its head up by sheer force, but he knew that he wouldn't be able to hold on forever. The brute twisted and writhed in his grip, its fetid breath strong in his face as it struggled to snap at the hands which held it.

Wallace, after fighting his way past Ferguson, now dashed across and drove a powerful kick into the animal's side, almost grinning as he heard bones splinter under the impact. The dog rolled over, then came hurtling back at Laidlaw, as if sensing which was the weaker of the two men. This time he could not raise his arms in time and its snapping jaws closed over one of his ears like the sprung blades of a man-trap, severing the fleshy appendage with ease.

The dog swallowed the severed ear and came at the policeman once more.

He was moaning in pain, one hand clapped to the place where his ear had been. Now there was just a ragged hole which pumped crimson down the side of his face. Some hair had also come away, torn from the roots to leave a bloodied bald patch above the hole.

The bull terrier skidded on some blood and this time only succeeded in sinking its teeth into Laidlaw's belt.

He gripped it by the ears once again and dragged it off him, trying to hold the snapping, squirming beast at arm's length.

Wallace, meanwhile, spotted Ferguson preparing to free the other dog and made a dash for him, knocking the bigger man backwards over the second cage.

They grappled as the albino dog leapt and barked at the bars, anxious to be free of its prison, to taste blood in its mouth.

Wallace picked up one of the stainless steel trays used to store the dog's meat and swung it in a wide arc at his opponent.

There was a dull clang as it caught Ferguson full in the face, shattering his nose and causing him to stagger back, blood pouring down his face. Wallace struck again, using the side of the tray in a backhand swipe that splintered two of Ferguson's front teeth and opened a hideous gash in his upper lip.

The bigger man dropped to his knees, the barking of the dog loud in his ears. Beside the cage lay a palette knife which Ferguson used to cut up the meat and offal which he fed the beasts. In one swift movement he snatched up the weapon and lashed out at Wallace.

The broad blade caught the inspector on the thigh, slicing effortlessly through the material of his trousers and into the muscle. He winced in pain and drew back, blood running freely from the cut.

'Fucking coppers,' rasped Ferguson, moving towards the front of the cage which held the albino. His free hand fumbled for the lock while he kept the knife lowered towards Wallace.

The inspector knew he had only seconds to act.

Using the metal tray as a shield, he ran at Ferguson and managed to swing the object downwards to deflect the thrust. The knife went spinning across the floor, but Ferguson lashed out with his other hand and Wallace groaned in pain as the backhand swipe connected with his throat. He tumbled backwards, rolling close to where Laidlaw still struggled with the first dog.

The black beast had, by now, all but slipped loose of his desperate hands and it twisted its head to one side, closing its jaws on the policeman's left hand. He shrieked as the razor-sharp teeth penetrated, but fear gave him an added strength and he threw himself on top of the dog, using his free hand to rain blows down on its skull.

Still it would not release his left hand.

Wallace knew that he would never reach Ferguson before he could set the other dog free. All he could do was look around for something to defend himself with.

The bigger man slipped the lock on the albino brute's cage.

Wallace leapt to one side, his hand closing over a stout

length of wood which had been broken off from a fruit box during the struggles in the cellar.

Two long nails protruded menacingly from one end, their points rusted but razor sharp.

Ferguson threw open the door of the cage. The insane barking of the dog reached nerve-shredding heights as it flew forward as if fired from a cannon.

Wallace braced himself for the onslaught.

Ferguson gave a shout of triumph which turned suddenly into a yell of fear as the dog rounded on *him*.

The powerful beast leapt at its owner and, with one well-aimed bite, fastened its steel-trap jaws around his genitals.

Ferguson shrieked in uncontrollable agony as the white brute bit through his jeans, its teeth shearing through his scrotum and most of his penis.

With one powerful twist of its head it tore his testicles away, ripping a thick length of penis with them.

Blood erupted from the massive hole, spraying the floor beneath and also covering the dog, which merely swallowed the fleshy ovoids as if they had been boiled eggs. Blood dripped from its jaws, the smell exciting it as much as the taste.

Wallace was transfixed by the sight, watching helplessly as Ferguson screamed and dropped to his knees, both hands clutching at the torn mess between his legs, his fingers sinking into the gore-filled chasm. He was helpless as the dog attacked again, its frenzied charge knocking him onto his back.

Horrified by what he saw, Wallace reacted in the only way possible. He lashed out at the dog with the slab of wood, the two nails cutting open its right shoulder. But the animal seemed oblivious to the wound, reluctant to let go of its prey.

Its head darted forward and it snapped its jaws together around Ferguson's throat, crunching the larynx to pulp, ripping away most of the skin and muscle beneath his chin.

Huge fountains of blood burst from the severed arteries,

231

rising a full three feet into the air, some of the red liquid spattering Wallace. He struck out at the dog once more as it began to shake Ferguson, whose head rocked back and forth with such terrifying speed that Wallace feared the beast would rip it from his shoulders.

The animal was drenched with blood, looking as if it had just emerged from an abattoir.

The policeman struck at it again with the spiked wood, and this time the nails punctured the side of its head, almost gouging one of its watery pink eyes from the socket.

Snarling in pain, it turned on him.

Wallace swung the piece of wood again but the dog caught it between its teeth. The inspector gripped both ends, hearing the timber crack as the dog bit through it and, in horror, he hurled the two ends away, throwing himself to the blood-soaked floor in an effort to reach the knife.

As his fingers closed around the handle he felt agonizing pain shooting through his leg.

The dog had fastened its teeth in his calf, practically ham-stringing him with the ferocity of its bite. But he lashed out with his other foot and drove a piledriver kick into its face, forcing it to release its grip for precious seconds. Wallace rolled over as it launched itself at him again, teeth aimed for his throat.

He raised one arm to protect himself, and with the other struck upwards with the knife, using all the force he could muster.

The dog's jaws closed around his wrist, lacerating flesh and almost snapping the bone, but the pain was only momentary.

He drove the knife into its belly and, using all his strength, tore downwards, gutting the beast with one savage cut.

Its stomach opened and Wallace moaned in revulsion as its intestines spilled onto him like thick, reeking spaghetti. An evil smelling flux of bile and viscera splattered him and it was all he could manage to prevent himself from vomiting. The stench was unbelievable. But the grip around his wrist loosened and he managed to push the

232

creature off, rising unsteadily to his feet, his head swimming now, pain gnawing at his arm and leg.

Laidlaw was still struggling with the first animal, still trying to force the beast to release his left hand. It took Wallace a second or two to realize that the creature was actually dead. The blows which the constable had been raining down on its head had finally succeeded in shattering the skull. His hand was coated in a sticky greyish-red porridge which Wallace realized must be the brain.

As he staggered across to the injured constable, Wallace felt his leg starting to go numb. He stumbled, then fell, sprawling alongside the dog, the knife slipping from his hand. He felt sick, his clothes sticking to him, soaked in blood.

'Oh, my God!'

He heard the voice from the top of the cellar steps and looked up to see PC Denton scuttling down, his face draining of colour as he saw the carnage before him.

Wallace exhaled almost painfully, coughing up blood which, for a moment, he thought was his own. With disgust he realized that he must have swallowed some of the albino brute's blood. The thought made him violently and uncontrollably sick and he rolled onto his side, retching until there was nothing left in his stomach.

'The ambulance is on its way,' Denton said, struggling to retain his own self-control.

'Terrific,' murmured Wallace, using his handkerchief to staunch the flow of blood from the bite on his leg.

Laidlaw had blacked out.

Sixty

The light above the worktop flickered once then went out.

Kim looked up and muttered to herself, annoyed at being plunged into darkness for long moments until the power came back on again. Outside, the wind was roaring like an enraged animal and she wondered if it had brought down a powerline somewhere in the vicinity.

The light flickered again, and this time she decided that enough was enough. She'd been at the museum since three that afternoon, having left Clare in the capable hands of Wendy Barratt, a neighbour from across the street. Now, as the hands of the clock reached 9:45, she decided to ring her home and tell Wendy she was on her way.

Kim had spent most of her time at the museum carefully packing and labelling the stone tablets and skulls as well as the scores of other relics which she'd examined over the past couple of weeks. Now they were all secure in wooden boxes. She wondered what would become of them and the other relics found at the dig now that work there had ceased. That decision would be up to Charles Cooper, but her attempts to contact him throughout the evening had proved futile.

She gazed at the box containing the tablets, her eyes narrowing slightly. Although Kim had sealed it herself, one corner looked loose, as if it had been prised open slightly with a chisel. She picked up the hammer which lay nearby and banged each nail twice to ensure that the lid was adequately fixed on, then she returned to the staff room and picked up the phone, dialling her own number. She waited for the receiver to be picked up.

The wind shrieked around the building.

She waited.

Finally she pressed down the cradle, waited a moment, then dialled again.

The ringing tone sounded loudly once more.

Twice. Three times.

No answer.

Kim tapped on the worktop with her index finger, waiting.

Waiting.

The lights suddenly went out and, as they did, there was a tremendous hiss of static from the phone, so loud that she held the receiver away from her ear.

The line was dead.

Kim dropped it back onto the cradle, cursing the storm. She bumped her shin on the stool as she turned, waiting for the lights to come back on.

It was a full minute before brightness once more flooded the room.

She rubbed her eyes as the fluorescents flashed on, illuminating the staff room and the laboratory beyond it. Kim swallowed hard and took a step into the other room, her eyes fixed on the box which held the stone tablets.

There was a pungent odour in the air, like burnt wood, and she waved a hand before her as she moved into the lab, her breath coming in short gasps.

The lid of the box lay on the floor, the nails twisted and bent.

As if the lid had been torn free with great force.

There were dark patches on the lid and sides of the box.

Like burn marks.

235

Sixty-One

The house was in darkness.

Kim brought the car to a halt, pulling up the collar of her jacket as she climbed out, shivering as the wind swirled around her.

Perhaps some power lines actually had come down. Maybe that was why not one single light burned in her house. She approached the front door glancing to her right and left. The houses on either side were both well lit, and the street lamps too were on.

Why was it only *her* house which remained in darkness?

She fumbled in her pocket and pulled out the key, turning it quickly, walking into the hallway.

The house was as quiet as a grave. The only sound Kim heard was her own muted breathing as she pushed open the sitting room door, reaching for the light switch.

The lights came on instantly.

The television set was on too, but the sound was turned off.

On the nearby coffee table was a mug of tea. Full but cold.

'Wendy,' she called, wondering where the child-minder had got to.

Kim moved through to the kitchen, flicking on that light too. The fluorescent sputtered into life, bathing the room in a cold white glow.

'Wendy,' Kim said again, softly, her voice almost a whisper.

She felt the first twinge of fear then. As if cold hands were being placed on her back and neck.

She turned and headed through the sitting room, towards the hall and the stairs. She tried the light at the bottom but it merely flickered once, then went out.

The staircase remained in darkness.

Kim began to climb slowly, her eyes never leaving the black-shrouded landing.

'Clare,' she called, feeling a much stronger fear now.

Was her daughter alone in the house?

There was no answer.

'Clare!'

Still nothing.

She reached the landing and paused before her daughter's room.

There was a dark stain on the white paintwork of the doorframe, visible in the dull sodium glare from the street lights which penetrated the landing window.

Kim froze, her hand shaking as it hovered near the dark smear.

She touched it and almost screamed.

It was blood.

The smell was unmistakable.

From inside her daughter's room there was a thud, followed by a low moan.

Kim gritted her teeth until her jaws ached; then, bracing herself, she flung open the door, her shaking hand reaching for the light switch. She felt more of the sticky fluid on the switch. The light came on, and she saw that there was blood on the walls, too. And on the sheets, which had been ripped away from the bed.

Of her daughter there was no sign, but huddled in one corner of the room was a crumpled shape which she recognized as Wendy Barratt.

Kim rushed to the other woman who, she now saw, was bleeding badly from two savage wounds on her head. One of them, just above the right ear, seemed to be the worst of the two. The other had almost laid open her forehead, though, and blood had poured down her face and into her eyes.

'Wendy, can you hear me?' Kim said, frantically,

squatting beside the injured woman. 'Who did this to you?'

Wendy could only look at her with eyes full of fear and pain and gently shake her head.

'Did you see who it was?'

'No,' she croaked, her eyes widening as she saw the amount of blood she was losing.

'Where's Clare?' Kim demanded.

'Oh God, I'm hurt badly. Get an ambulance.'

'Where's Clare?' Kim rasped.

'I don't know.'

Kim felt her stomach contract.

'Who took her?' she demanded, her concern for the injured woman now secondary to her fear for her daughter. 'Who took her, Wendy? You have to remember, please.' Her voice had risen close to a shout. Unable to help herself, she shook Wendy. 'Who took her?'

'I didn't see who it was.'

With one despairing moan the woman blacked out.

'Oh God,' Kim gasped, scrambling to her feet, blundering down the stairs, almost stumbling at the bottom. She crashed into the sitting room, tears brimming in her eyes. Tears of desperation and fear.

She snatched up the phone, praying that it hadn't been cut off, almost crying out loud when she heard the dial tone.

With shaking hands she dialled Longfield police station.

Sixty-Two

From the time she put the phone down until the time the ambulance screeched to a halt outside her house, each minute seemed an eternity to Kim Nichols.

She'd sat with Wendy, holding the woman's hand as she

burbled incoherently, occasionally drifting off into unconsciousness. Throughout that time, Kim's only thoughts had been for her kidnapped daughter. Fear and foreboding such as she'd never experienced before filled her. When the emergency vehicle and its stricken cargo had finally left she'd begun pacing the floor.

Now, as she heard the squeal of tyres from outside, she dashed to open the front door.

Wallace hauled himself from the Sierra and sprinted up the path towards her, ignoring the pain from his injured leg.

'It's Clare,' she blurted. 'She's been taken.'

'Come on,' the policeman said, unhesitatingly, beckoning her towards the car.

She looked puzzled.

'Kim,' he said, a note of urgency in his voice as he slipped back behind the wheel and re-started the engine.

She clambered into the passenger seat and the car sped off.

As the inspector glanced across at her he could see that her eyes were puffy and red-rimmed from crying. He tried to coax some more details from her, and tears began to course down her face. He squeezed her hand tightly.

'We'll find her,' he said.

'She could already be dead,' Kim said, wiping the tears from her eyes with a sodden handkerchief.

Wallace didn't answer.

The streets of Longfield seemed strangely deserted as Wallace guided the car towards its destination. Here and there street lamps had gone out, adding further darkness to the gloom which already seemed to hang over the town like a blanket.

The lamp outside Charles Cooper's house burned brightly, though, and Kim looked up in surprise as she saw where they were. Wallace was already out of the car and heading towards the front door when Kim scuttled after him.

'Why would Charles take her?' she wanted to know, aghast at the prospect of her colleague being a kidnapper.

'He would have known about Dagda, wouldn't he?'

Wallace said. 'About the need for sacrifices.'

Kim swallowed hard and watched as the inspector banged hard on the front door.

There was no answer.

The house remained in darkness, silent and defiant.

Wallace hurried around to the back of the building, Kim following breathlessly. Without waiting he drove one foot hard again the back door, hearing wood splinter under the impact.

'What if you're wrong?' she asked.

'Then I'm wrong,' he rasped, using even more power against the barrier. It swung back on its hinges and crashed against the wall. Wallace stepped inside, moving quickly through the kitchen, flicking on lights as he went.

The smell reached him as he came to the sitting room.

A cloying odour which he thought he recognized.

He slowed his pace, moving more quietly now, listening for any sounds of movement from upstairs. Kim followed, her heart thudding against her ribs as they began to climb the stairs. This time Wallace did not turn the light on. They climbed in darkness, one of the steps creaking in protest, the sound echoing through the silent house.

The smell was getting stronger.

He paused as they reached the landing, peering into the gloom, trying to make out the dark shape ahead.

Kim stifled a gasp.

The inspector fumbled for the light switch at the top of the stairs and the sixty-watt bulb burst into life.

This time Kim screamed.

Dangling by his neck from the attic trapdoor was Charles Cooper.

The step ladder which he had used to climb up lay beneath him, kicked aside before he jumped. Wallace approached the body, reaching out to touch the cold, rigored flesh. He ran appraising eyes over the corpse, trying to ignore the smell as he stood close by.

Cooper's eyes bulged in their sockets, the flesh beneath them blackened, the skin of his cheeks as white as milk. He'd obviously been dead for some time, thought the

240

inspector. The rope was thin and poorly suited for the job. It had cut deeply into the archaeologist's neck, drawing blood which had caked hard over the hemp itself. There was no knot at the back of the neck. Cooper had probably choked to death. Dark stains at the front and back of his trousers had dried stiffly and Wallace saw a puddle of stale urine beneath the body. A swollen tongue protruded from his mouth like a bloated leech.

Wallace exhaled deeply and looked around at Kim, who was standing at the top of the stairs, her gaze lowered slightly.

It took the policeman a second or two to spot the piece of paper sticking out of Cooper's trouser pocket. He pulled it free and unrolled it. Kim looked up as he began to read the note aloud:

'I realize that suicide is the coward's way out, or so they say, but it takes more strength than anyone knows to take your own life. I know I am going to die soon. We all will.'

Wallace frowned, looked at Kim, then continued reading:

'No one would have believed me anyway if I'd told them what I had discovered in the chamber of skulls. I knew how to stop this horror, how to prevent it, but I could not bring myself to take the lives of children. Someone else may have seen the writing on the wall of the chamber. If so, then I pray that he has the strength. I am sorry for the children but there is no other way. If there is a God, let him help us all. The children in the chamber must die but I cannot do it. When the end comes I don't want to see it.'

Wallace folded the note and slipped it into his pocket.

'Jesus,' he murmured. 'Come on.' He gripped Kim's arm and together they hurried down the stairs.

'If Cooper couldn't kill the children then he might have an accomplice,' Kim said as Wallace snatched up the phone from the hall table. He dialled and waited for the receiver to be picked up at the other end.

241

It was finally answered and he recognized Sergeant Dayton's voice.

'Listen to me, Bill,' he snapped. 'This is Wallace. I want a car sent to Dexter Grange now. If the men can't find Dexter there, then tell them to search that wood nearby.'

'But guv,' the sergeant began.

'Don't argue with me,' Wallace rasped. 'Do it. I also want another car to meet me at the archaeological site in twenty minutes. Got that?'

'I can't do that. The Chief Inspector told me to disregard any orders you gave me,' Dayton protested.

Wallace gripped the receiver so tightly it seemed he would snap it in two.

'Fuck Macready. Just do it. Do what I tell you, Bill, please. *I think I know where those kids are.*'

There was a moment's silence at the other end.

'Did you hear me?' he repeated.

'The cars are on their way, guv.'

Wallace managed a small grin of triumph. He told the sergeant to send an ambulance to 12 Elm Street but didn't say why and, before Dayton could ask, Wallace had replaced the receiver.

He and Kim dashed out to the waiting Sierra.

Sixty-Three

'And don't forget, make it convincing,' said Gary Webb. 'Dexter's no fool.'

'What if something goes wrong?' Laura Price wanted to know.

'It won't,' he assured her, raising a hand for silence when he heard footsteps in the corridor outside the room. A second later Henry Dexter entered the room. He looked closely at his two young companions, particularly Laura, who was lying on the leather sofa with both legs drawn up to her chest, her face contorted.

'She's strung out,' Gary said. 'She needs some stuff now.'

Dexter eyed Gary for a moment and the youngster found that he couldn't hold the older man's gaze.

Laura moaned softly and rubbed at the crook of her left arm.

'Please, Henry,' she said, sucking in a sharp breath as she feigned a contraction that made her wince.

Like a doctor, the older man crossed to the sofa and sat down on the edge, looking at Laura impassively, brushing a strand of hair from her face. She squirmed beneath his gaze and closed her eyes in mock pain, waiting until he got up once more and crossed the room towards the wall safe where the heroin was kept. Gary edged closer to the mantelpiece, one eye on the ornamental dagger which hung above it.

'Open it,' he said, swallowing hard as Dexter turned to look at him.

The older man hesitated.

'What would you do with all this heroin?' he asked. 'Sell it? Use it yourselves? And the money? How would you spend that?'

'Just open the safe,' snapped Gary.

Dexter grinned broadly.

'Subtlety was never one of your strong points, was it, Gary?' he said, the grin fading. 'I wondered how long it would take for you to try this.'

Gary snatched the dagger from the wall and moved towards the older man.

'Open that fucking safe now. I don't want to hurt you but I will if I have to,' he rasped.

Laura sat up and looked anxiously at the two men.

'And if you kill me, who's going to open the safe?' Dexter asked, fixing the youth in a cold stare. 'Put that knife down before I use it on *you*.'

Gary took another step forward, the blade glinting wickedly.

Dexter braced his foot against the coffee table nearby and kicked out, sending the object skidding towards Gary. It slammed into his shins, the suddenness of the assault causing him to lose balance. Dexter was on him in an instant, one hand grabbing for the knife.

Laura screamed as the two of them grappled. She leapt up off the sofa, moving towards the fireplace, her hand reaching for the poker which stood beside it.

Gary, despite being at a disadvantage, managed to turn the blade on his attacker and Dexter grunted as he felt the cold steel cut into his forearm. He slammed Gary's hand down hard against the floor and the knife skidded from the youth's grip. Blood from the cut ran down Dexter's arm as he reached for the boy's throat and fastened both hands around it, squeezing hard. Gary first gripped his assailant's wrists and then, unable to relieve the pressure on his throat, struck out at Dexter's face with a punch which sent him sprawling sideways. Gary leapt to his feet, his eye on the knife, but the older man swung his left foot and kicked the youth's legs out from under him.

He fell forward heavily, cracking his head on the floor, stunned by the impact.

Dexter leapt on him, one knee pressed between the lad's shoulder blades while he slipped both hands beneath his chin and tugged his head back. Gary could feel unbelievable pressure on his neck and spine and he actually felt the muscles tearing. Another moment or two and Dexter would break his spine.

Laura, galvanized into action by this sight, lunged forward and brought the poker down with bone-crushing force onto the back of Dexter's head, opening a large gash on his scalp. The loud crack of bone filled the room and the older man sagged forward, collapsing onto Gary, who tried to roll free. Laura helped him shift the motionless form of Dexter and then supported him as he got to his feet. Gary took the poker from her and aimed a blow at the combination lock of the safe. The metal rod sang off it and vibrated in his hand, so he struck again. And again.

It wouldn't budge.

Behind them, his head throbbing from the powerful

blow, Dexter began to crawl towards the momentarily forgotten dagger.

Gary struck the safe again, desperation now aiding his efforts. Laura looked on anxiously, both of them too intent on their task to see that Dexter had reached the knife and was dragging himself upright.

Still the safe door would not give and Gary paused for a moment, his breath coming in gasps, the pain at the back of his neck growing with each movement.

It was Laura who heard the sounds from behind them.

She screamed as she saw Dexter run at Gary, his face a mask of rage.

The warning came too late and Gary turned only to take the knife-thrust in the stomach.

He felt as if he'd been punched, the wind knocked from him. Dexter dragged the blade free and drove it home with even greater ferocity, up under the boy's sternum, feeling it grate against bone as he tugged the bloodied weapon out, ripping open the upper part of Gary's torso in the process. He gripped his victim by the hair, powering more knife strokes home with ferocious strength.

Blood splattered the floor as Gary began to sag to his knees. As he fell, Dexter drove the knife forward once more. The blade tore into his open mouth, slicing through gums and tongue before bursting from the base of his skull.

Laura screamed once more and jumped at Dexter, scratching at his eyes, forcing him to drop the knife. Her desperate fingers found the hilt and, with a blow that owed more to luck than judgement, she brought the knife down with terrifying force, driving it through Dexter's left eye, pressing down on the hilt until she felt the blade puncture the floor beneath.

The dying man screamed in agony and writhed helplessly, held firm by the blade through his eye, blood shooting from the wound like crimson rain.

She collapsed, sobbing, between the two bodies, looking up at the door of the safe.

It had swung open, revealing the money and the heroin inside.

Laura smiled bitterly through her sobs, looking at the

bags of white powder, smelling the stench of death all around her.

Seconds later, she heard the loud knocking on the front door.

Sixty-Four

As Wallace swung the Sierra around the corner of the road he could see the police car already parked across the entrance to the field leading up to the archaeological site.

One of the two uniformed men was caught in the glow of the Sierra's headlamps as he stood urinating into the long grass.

Neither Kim nor Wallace paid him any heed.

The nearest of the two policemen crossed to Wallace's car and looked in at the inspector.

'How long have you been here?' the inspector asked.

'A couple of minutes, sir,' Buchanan told him.

'Right. Follow me up to the site. Get that bloody car out of the way.' He jabbed a finger at the panda car and Buchanan signalled to his colleague, Kendall, to move it. The constable reversed leaving a clear path.

'A message just came through from the other car,' Buchanan said. 'They found Dexter in his house. He'd been killed.'

Wallace chewed his lip contemplatively, listening as Buchanan recounted the details. Then the inspector nodded and pressed down on his accelerator.

'Follow me,' he instructed and the constable sprinted back to the waiting police car.

Both vehicles skidded over the uneven ground, the wheels of the Sierra spinning as they reached the crest of the rise. The headlamps cut through the darkness, illuminating the rope barrier which was around the entrance to the shaft.

Wallace swung himself out of the car, snatching a torch from the glove compartment in the process. Kim joined him along with the two uniformed men.

'Kendall, you stay up top,' Wallace said. 'If we're not back here in thirty minutes you'd better get help.'

Kim took the policeman's torch from him and looked at Wallace.

'I'm going with you,' she said determinedly.

Wallace thought about protesting but finally merely nodded his agreement. He turned towards the rope ladder which dropped away into the black abyss.

'Thirty minutes,' said Kendall, checking his watch.

Wallace nodded.

They began to descend.

It was 11:32.

Sixty-Five

The torch beam was swallowed up by the murky blackness, unable to penetrate the tenebrous depths for more than a few feet.

Wallace finally switched it off, jamming it into his belt, leaving two hands free to grip the rope ladder. He shivered as he climbed down, the icy air searing his throat, filling his chest so that it was difficult to breathe. He moved with agonizing slowness, as if unable to coax any more speed out of his legs. Already he felt as if he'd run twenty miles. His muscles were throbbing with the effort of the climb

247

although, he guessed, they couldn't have been on the ladder more than a couple of minutes.

Above him, moving just as cautiously, Kim and Buchanan clambered downward.

The inspector gritted his teeth. Trying to push through the darkness was like fighting against a solid object. He grunted loudly, the sound bouncing back off the walls of the shaft. He pulled the torch from his belt and shone it down into the depths.

The beam glinted off something metallic and he realized that they had almost reached the bottom.

He tried to move quicker but the effort was beyond him.

The air itself seemed thick and oppressive. Unclean, he thought.

As he reached the bottom a particularly noxious odour reached him for the first time, a dank, cloying stench which seemed to float about like invisible tendrils, filling his nostrils and lungs until he thought he was going to be sick.

Kim jumped down beside him. Then the two of them were joined by Buchanan who also coughed as he drew breath and smelled the rank scent.

'What the hell is that?' he croaked, dragging a handkerchief from his pocket to cover his face. But even the fabric couldn't mask the fetor, such was its intensity.

Wallace shone his torch over the floor of the shaft, the beam picking out many relics left behind by the archaeologists. Spears, swords, torcs, the odd piece of pottery.

But there was something which *didn't* belong.

On the tall pointed stake which formed the centrepiece of the pit was a piece of fabric. Clean and new.

Wallace pulled it free and turned it over in his palm.

It was brushed cotton.

The sort of fabric that might be used to make a child's dressing gown or similar garment.

Kim took the fragment from him, her hand shaking slightly.

She said nothing, merely followed Wallace as he

248

advanced towards the first tunnel entrance, his torch cutting a path through the blackness.

The smell remained as strong as ever.

They moved quickly, sure-footedly through the tunnel until they came to a fork.

The two tunnels yawned like hungry mouths and Wallace exhaled deeply, his breath forming a white fog in the freezing air.

'We should split up,' said Kim.

'No,' Wallace whispered. 'If the murderer *is* down here we're better off together.'

'But it could take all night to search these tunnels. We haven't got all night,' Kim reminded him, clutching the piece of fabric. 'I know these tunnels. Let me search that one.' She pointed to the stone corridor on the right.

Wallace shook his head.

'Buchanan. *You* search it. If you find anything, shout. If you hear me, then come running. Meet us back here in twenty minutes.'

The young constable swallowed hard, his face, already drained of colour, looked sickly yellow in the reflected beam of the torch. He hesitated a moment, then nodded uncertainly and headed for the opening. Wallace watched as his torch beam slowly disappeared, consumed by the darkness.

'Come on,' he whispered to Kim, and they too pressed on, down the left-hand tunnel.

Wallace had his right hand outstretched, feeling his way along the walls. He suddenly recoiled as his fingers slipped into something wet and slimy. The putrescent moss stuck to the policeman's fingers like noxious porridge. The stench was unbelievable. They moved on, treading carefully now over piles of bones and more relics.

There was another tunnel immediately to the left.

An icy breeze was blowing from it, further lowering the already sub-zero temperatures in the tunnels. Wallace was convinced, anyway, that it must be below freezing. His hands and face felt numb and he only forced himself to continue walking by a supreme effort of will.

He passed the tunnel entrance, the torch flickering as he reached the other side.

'Shit,' he murmured, shaking the light, cursing when the bulb failed completely, plunging them into total blackness.

'Kim,' he whispered. 'Give me your torch.'

No answer.

'Kim.'

The silence was as total as the gloom.

He reached out a hand behind him, trying to touch her. His fingers clutched only empty air.

The policeman banged his torch on the tunnel wall, and to his surprise it came back on, flooding the narrow stone passageway with light, momentarily driving back the dark. He turned and shone the torch behind him.

Kim had gone.

He was alone in the tunnel.

It was then that he heard the sound ahead of him.

Sixty-Six

For interminable seconds Wallace froze, unsure of what to do.

Should he go back and look for Kim?

The muffled sound from ahead came again, distracting him once more.

He frowned, trying to make out what the sound was. It was muted. A soft, almost asthmatic wheezing punctuated by low moans.

'Kim,' he whispered again, shining the torch into the secondary tunnel. She must have stepped down there.

She'd told him she knew the network of underground walkways. Perhaps she knew a quicker route.

But to where?

The children?

The murderer?

Wallace shuddered and moved on, the sound ahead of him growing louder, then suddenly dying away. Only the silence remained. He paused again, his heart thudding just that little bit faster, then, gripping the heavy torch like a weapon, he moved on.

Constable Mark Buchanan pressed himself close to the wall of the tunnel and advanced slowly, ears and eyes alert for the slightest sound or movement. Despite the numbing cold below ground he could feel a thin film of perspiration forming on his forehead. His breath was coming in short gasps even though he struggled to control it. The smell which had filled the tunnels from the outset seemed to be growing worse, if that was possible. Buchanan slowed his pace even more, also trying to breathe through his mouth to lessen the effect of the noxious air.

He heard movement behind him.

Buchanan turned quickly, shining the torch in the direction of the sound.

The beam quivered from the shaking of his hand as he tried to pick out the source of the noise.

The silence was thunderous, the rushing of blood in his ears like a tidal wave.

He could see nothing.

For what seemed an age he stood there, and then, very slowly, he moved on. Every few paces he would turn and point the torch over his shoulder. Just in case someone was following him. He tried to tell himself that his imagination was playing tricks but the thought did not ease his mind. Fear continued to grip him, steadily squeezing tighter.

There was movement behind him again.

This time he spun round in time to see some small rocks toppling from a ledge in the side of the tunnel. They fell to the ground with a sharp crack and Buchanan breathed a sigh of relief as he realized he must have dislodged them himself.

Or had he?

He still wasn't completely satisfied with his own explanation. It did little to calm his already tattered nerves. However, it was all he had and he clung to it as a drowning man would cling to a piece of driftwood. He *wanted* to believe that the falling stones were all he'd heard if only his mind would let him.

As he moved on he found that the tunnel was beginning to curve to the left.

He stopped and glanced over his shoulder again, then walked on.

He heard another noise.

This one came from ahead of him.

An almost imperceptible mewling sound. A stealthy murmur.

Buchanan frowned.

The sound came again.

He moved on.

Whatever was making the noise, Wallace decided, was closer than he'd first thought. What he couldn't figure out was why it was so muffled.

He shone the torch ahead of him, watching as the beam bounced off the rough stonework. Bones crunched beneath his feet, causing him to wince. If anyone was up ahead, they would hear him coming. He stood still for a moment. Listening.

The noise ahead continued. Low, beckoning.

His flesh was crawling.

The atmosphere inside the tunnel had also changed. Almost impossibly, it had become still more oppressive until he felt as if he were literally pushing against the darkness and the cold as he walked. They sucked the strength from him as surely as invisible parasites. But he fought it, battled the urge to lean back against the wall and rest. He forced himself to continue, the sound ahead acting as a guide.

Or was it bait?

Wallace suddenly had the uncomfortable feeling that he was walking into a trap, but he rapidly shook the thought away, more intent on finding the source of the strange sound.

Beneath him he heard, and felt, a low rumble.

The ground vibrated for long seconds and the policeman shot out a hand to steady himself, only to find that the walls of the tunnel were also shuddering slightly. Several fragments of stone fell from the tunnel roof and Wallace tried to shield his head as they rained down around him.

He struggled to retain his balance as the ground beneath him throbbed menacingly.

The tremor stopped as suddenly as it had started.

Wallace stood motionless, stunned by the unexpected event, waiting to see if there were any more earth movements. The tunnels were stable as far as he knew. There had been no mention of subsidence. But if the whole network should collapse . . .He let the thought trail off, not allowing himself to dwell on the idea of being buried beneath tons of rock and earth.

He wondered where Kim and Buchanan had got to.

They must have felt the tremor too.

Perhaps both had left the labyrinthine tunnels at the threat of collapse.

Perhaps they were waiting at the bottom of the shaft for him to emerge.

Perhaps the killer had found them first.

He swallowed hard and pressed on more cautiously, his torch beam picking out something ahead.

The disembodied moaning sound came again, louder. Wallace realized that he was close to its source. Very close.

He saw the stone slab.

He saw the piles of skulls inside the chamber.

He felt the cold breeze from another secondary tunnel, this time to his right, as he drew nearer the chamber, shining his torch inside, allowing the beam to move over the mounds of skulls.

Wallace took a step inside. It was clear now that the

253

muffled sound was within the chamber.

He didn't think to look over his shoulder.

Had he done so, he would have seen the figure approaching him.

Sixty-Seven

PC Kendall rubbed his hands together in an effort to restore some warmth to the freezing extremities. He blew on them, but to little effect.

The headlamps of the police car were still aimed at the entrance to the shaft, but he had heard nothing from Wallace and the others since they descended almost twenty minutes earlier. Leaning on the bonnet of the car, he glanced at his watch and shook his head, deciding that it would be warmer inside the car.

As he slid into the driver's seat the two-way crackled.

'Unit three, come in,' the metallic voice rasped and the constable frowned. It wasn't Sergeant Dayton's voice. The harsh tones belonged to Chief Inspector Macready.

'Unit three, come in,' the voice repeated.

Kendall reached for the radio, his hand shaking slightly. He told himself it was because of the cold.

'Unit three. Go ahead.'

'Where the hell are you?' Macready snapped.

'I'm at the archaeological dig, sir . . . '

Macready cut him short.

'Did Wallace order you there?' he demanded, already knowing the answer.

'Yes, sir.'

There was an angry silence, then Macready came on again.

'Let me speak to Wallace. Quickly.'

'He's not with me, sir. He and PC Buchanan and a woman . . .'

'What woman?' the older man demanded.

'She's one of the archaeologists, I think. The three of them climbed down into the tunnels. The inspector said he knew where the missing children were.'

'Jesus Christ!' snarled Macready, angrily. 'Listen to me. Don't move from there. I'll be over as quickly as I can. Wallace has some explaining to do.'

The radio went dead in his hand and Kendall replaced the handset. He groaned as he thought of Macready's reaction. What the hell, thought the constable, he was only doing what he'd been told. If Wallace got his head chewed off that was tough shit. Kendall knew that *he* hadn't done anything to merit a bollocking.

He glanced down at the dashboard clock and checked it off against his own watch.

11:51.

He wondered if they'd found anything yet.

Kendall was still wondering when he felt the ground begin to tremble.

He sat bolt upright in the car, looking out of the windows as the vehicle slid back a foot or so, shaken from its stable position by the minor tremor.

He heard an ominous rumbling which seemed to come from deep within the earth. The vibrations rapidly spread through the car until the whole vehicle seemed to be shuddering. The rumbling continued for no more than ten seconds, then ceased abruptly.

Kendall didn't move at first, Then, cautiously, he stepped out of the car, treading gently on the ground.

There was no more movement.

He sucked in a worried breath.

What the hell was going on?

Sixty-Eight

A rough estimate indicated that there were up to three hundred skulls in the chamber. For long moments, Wallace stood looking at them, their sightless sockets seeming to stare back at him. Then he raised his torch, allowing the beam to trace a pattern over the walls, across the ancient writings which covered the stone.

He never heard a sound from behind him.

He only felt the hand as it closed on his shoulder.

The inspector almost shouted aloud in fear, twisting around, pulling away from the hand, swinging the torch up like a club. He ducked down, ready to face the intruder, the heavy torch poised to strike.

PC Buchanan seemed as startled as his superior.

He stepped back, avoiding the impending swing of the torch, his face pale.

'It's me, guv,' he gasped.

Wallace let out a long breath and glared at the constable.

'Sorry if I startled you,' the constable said, apologetically.

'Startled me?' Wallace gasped. 'I nearly had a fucking heart attack. Why the hell couldn't you have warned me? Jesus.'

'I didn't find anything in that other tunnel,' Buchanan explained. 'But I heard a noise, like . . .well . . .like an animal. Like something trapped.'

'Yeah,' Wallace said. 'It's coming from in here.' He motioned around the chamber, trying to locate the exact point from which the sound was emanating.

'There,' the inspector said, pointing to a place beneath a pile of skulls.

The two men beg... [...]
in their haste.

The sound grew louder.

The last of the skulls was flung aside and Wallace saw
that they had covered an oblong stone set into the ground.

'Help me lift this,' he said, digging his fingers under the
rim.

Both of them strained for a moment, then the stone slab
began to lift with surprising ease, rising like the lid of a
coffin until they pushed it back against the wall and peered
down into the hole below.

'My God,' murmured Buchanan.

Lying in the hole, which was roughly six feet long and
four feet wide, were four children.

Each one was tightly bound. Gags had been stuffed into
their mouths. Wallace studied the faces, their eyes bulging
wide in fear.

Jonathan Ashton. Julie Craig. Carl Taylor.

And Clare Nichols.

The missing children.

Wallace and Buchanan lifted the children from their
tomb-like prison and laid them on the ground next to the
hole. Clare and one of the boys were crying, making a soft,
muted mewling sound.

The two policemen untied the children, pulling the gags
from their mouths. Immediately, Clare embraced the
inspector, who kissed her on the cheek, pulling her close to
him.

'It's all right now, sweetheart,' he said. 'All of you, it's
going to be all right. We're policemen. We're going to get
you out of here.' He felt another minor rumble from
beneath them. His breath was now coming in gasps.
'You're going to leave now. I want you to go with the
constable. Will you do that for me?'

The children agreed in a pitiful chorus of whines and
sobs.

'Take them out now,' Wallace said to the other man.
'I've got to stay and find Kim.'

Buchanan hesitated.

257

...whole place could come down around our ears in a minute.'

Buchanan, carrying Clare, nodded and gathered the other children around him. He felt one of them clutching the leg of his trousers as he tried to walk. He struggled on, out of the chamber.

The constable caught only a glimpse of his attacker as the shape emerged from the blackness.

He heard the air part as something heavy was swung at him, then suddenly he felt a bone-cracking impact against his right temple.

The flat of the sword smacked savagely into his head, splintering his skull and opening a cut which sent blood shooting into the freezing air.

He went down in an untidy heap, his slack arms losing their grip on Clare, who fell with him, her scream drumming in his ears as his blood splattered her.

Wallace pulled the nearest child to him, shielding it against the attacker, gripping his torch in a vain attempt to defend himself. He shone it at the face of the one who wielded the rusted blade.

Illuminated by the powerful beam, George Perry stood before him.

Sixty-Nine

'They have to die, Wallace,' the archaeologist said, flatly. 'I wish there was some other way but there isn't.' He glanced briefly at his watch.

It was 11:52.

'In eight minutes it will be too late,' Perry told him. 'Dagda will rise. Dagda, the Celtic God. The Lord of

Destruction. I read it here.' He gestured about him toward the walls of the chamber with their strange words and symbols. 'This creature, or power, whatever it is, exists. Perhaps it only exists in men's minds or perhaps it has a tangible form but it lies dormant in the earth for years at a time until it's disturbed, the way this dig disturbed it. And then, the only way to stop it is by sacrifice. At midnight on the day of Samain, unless three children are sacrificed on this spot, Dagda will rise.'

Wallace could see that he was shaking.

'We can't begin to understand the extent of the power we're dealing with, Wallace,' Perry told him. 'This thing . . . if it's allowed to rise, is unstoppable. Dagda will destroy us all. These children must die. Cooper knew that too. We spoke about it. He knew what had to be done but he was weak. It's my job now.'

'You'll never get away with this,' Wallace reminded him. 'Even if you kill me too.'

'It doesn't matter. What can they do to me? Lock me up for life. What are the lives of three children compared to so many? A drop in the ocean. It's a small price to pay to prevent such obscene evil entering our world. Entering and destroying.'

'You're insane!' Wallace shouted.

'I'd be insane if I did nothing,' the archaeologist countered.

'Why did you kill James Cutler and the others?' Wallace wanted to know.

Perry smiled crookedly.

'Cutler and the others were killed by Morrigan.'

Wallace frowned. The name rang a bell.

'The Queen of Demons,' Perry told him. 'A being able to take on the form of a human. A creature with incredible strength. She fed on the flesh of her victims. The Celts used to flay sacrificial offerings and lay the skin on the altars of Morrigan.'

'This is bullshit,' rasped Wallace, watching as Perry pulled one of the children to him, the sword poised at its throat.

'You still don't understand, do you?' Perry snarled. 'That was why I took *her* daughter. I had to bring *her* here tonight. I had to make sure *she* would come so that I could destroy her.'

'Who?' Wallace demanded.

'The Queen of Demons, the creature that killed Cutler and all the others. The one possessed by Morrigan.'

Wallace shook his head.

'No,' he murmured.

'She murdered them. Kim Nichols killed them all,' Perry told him. 'Or at least what once was Kim Nichols. Morrigan has found a new host body now. She was safe inside Kim until I discovered the truth in the writing on these walls. Kim is possessed. She has been since we opened this chamber. Only now I know it for sure.'

Wallace shook his head, edging closer to Perry, ready to jump him if the chance arose.

'Let the children go.'

The voice lanced through the blackness and both men turned to see Kim approaching them.

'Stay back,' Perry said, a look of absolute terror crossing his face.

'Let them go,' Kim said again, and Wallace too was shocked as he heard her voice deepen from its normal feminine pitch to a thick deep bass.

'Release them,' she said, the words now almost slurred due to the depth of tone. They boomed around the tunnel and Wallace stood transfixed as Kim moved closer, her body beginning to shudder. She stood still, only feet from him, her head tilted backwards slightly, her arms stiff by her sides. The shudders intensified and suddenly she let out a roar which froze his blood.

Her head snapped forward and Wallace found himself witnessing something plucked straight from a nightmare.

There was a sound like tearing fabric and the skin on her face split in three or four places, peeling back to reveal dark, pitted, rotted flesh beneath. It welled through the rifts like pus-filled growths, expanding and contracting as even greater convulsions racked her body. The flesh beneath Kim's own skin was sickly yellow and Wallace saw a number of liquescent boils pushing through it like fingers through wet pastry. Like a mask, her entire face seemed to peel off, hanging by a thick tendril of skin from her stubby neck.

And now he saw her chest and stomach undulating madly, the clothes she wore stretching over each fresh bulge, ripping in places to reveal the scabrous flesh beneath.

Her eyes rolled white, the pupils disappearing, and the glistening orbs then turned red as blood vessels dilated and swelled. She opened her mouth to reveal an array of sharply pointed teeth, all blackened and stained like her lips, which reminded Wallace of swollen leeches. Only they were dark blue, like two corpulent bruises framing a leering mouth which stretched wide and expelled a blast of air so rank that both men almost vomited.

Her hands and arms twitched madly as more flesh peeled back in great leprous folds, dropping away as if she were some kind of snake undergoing a sloughing process. Thick veins pulsed obscenely beneath the new, odorous skin, throbbing like blackened, animated worms.

Wallace shook his head in horrified disbelief as her fingers seemed to reshape themselves into points, not just the nails but the digits themselves, which contracted until they were like bloated needles.

He suddenly understood why they had found no fingerprints on the bodies of the murder victims. This beast had no pads to leave indentations.

Her hair turned grey, then white. In stark contrast to the colour of her putrescent skin.

The change was complete.

The thing which had once been Kim Nichols threw back its head and uttered a loud ululation which could never have come from anything human.

Wallace felt his bowels loosen, the screams of the children now also drumming in his ears.

With another inhuman roar, Morrigan launched herself at Perry.

The archaeologist screamed and went down in a heap beneath the raving monstrosity, the sword falling from his grip.

Wallace took his chance.

'Run,' he shouted at the terrified children. 'Go on, down the tunnel. Now.'

They set off in the darkness, crying in terror, stumbling over bones and other objects as they went, but they struggled on, Clare sobbing with a particularly despairing tone.

Wallace turned to look back at the writhing forms close to him. He heard Perry scream in agony as one of Morrigan's clawed hands slashed open his cheek, exposing the bone, ripping a large portion of the flesh away.

'Slaughter the children,' the archaeologist wailed. 'Stop Dagda.'

Wallace felt as if he was frozen to the ground, unable to move as he watched the creature lift Perry with one scabrous hand, dangling him as a child would dangle a puppet. Then he saw the bloodied hand dart forward towards the man's stomach. The nails pierced the flesh effortlessly and the leathery fingers closed around the archaeologist's intestines, pulling hard. Thick gouts of blood burst from the rent, followed by several sticky, bloated lengths of entrail which the abomination held before it like dripping trophies. Wallace could see that the innards were still pulsing like heavy veins. Blood sprayed everywhere, some of it splattering the policeman, who felt his stomach contract.

Blood filled Perry's mouth, his shrieks of agony gurgling through the crimson clots which filled his throat and surged upwards to cascade over his lips.

Morrigan lowered him a foot or two, his body already beginning to spasm. The monstrosity glared at him. With one lightning movement, it jabbed the needle-sharp claws into his right eye, carving through the soft flesh of the lids, scooping the bulging orb free of the socket and into the palm of its hand where it studied this new prize for a second before shoving it into the gaping maw of its mouth. As the jaws came together the eye burst, a gush of clear fluid and blood spilling down Morrigan's chin. The monster chewed for a second then swallowed the pulped orb.

Wallace could hold back no longer. He bent double and vomited violently, staggering past as the beast dug out Perry's other eye and devoured it, dragging him closer, allowing a wolfish, tumefied tongue to probe deep inside the bleeding sockets, sucking out the clotted blood and other matter which remained inside. Then, with a roar, Morrigan flung the body to one side and set off after Wallace.

He ran as he'd never run before, his head spinning, his breath drawn in great racking gasps. Aware only of the monstrous creature that chased him, moving sure-footedly in the gloom which was its home.

He slammed into a rock wall, bounced off and carried on running, not knowing how far he had to go to reach the shaft.

Or the children.

Dear Christ, the children . . .

They were just ahead of him. He could see them in the light from the torch. He flicked it behind him and Morrigan was illuminated in the beam, a vision of such monstrous corruption that Wallace began to fear for his sanity.

And she was gaining on him.

The ground before him suddenly erupted, a shower of dirt and stones spraying up into the tunnel. All around, the stonework began to crack.

The rumbling grew louder until it filled his ears.

Even the wild roars of the pursuing creature and the high-pitched screams of the children were lost to him now as more earth showered down.

The tunnel was collapsing.

Wallace threw himself forward as on his left another portion of the tunnel floor exploded upwards as if punched by some massive fist.

Was this the end? Was it to be as Perry had described it?

Wallace could see nothing but he could feel the life being sucked from him, his will draining away as the entity known as Dagda began to rise. He knew, in that split second, what he must do.

There was a child close to him, one of the two boys.

Wallace made a grab for him but, before he could seize the fleeing child, he felt strong hands tearing at his back and he knew that Morrigan was upon him.

The claws cut effortlessly through his jacket and quickly found his flesh, reducing the skin on his back to bloodied tatters. Wallace rolled over, despairingly driving one foot into the creature's face, feeling bones splinter beneath the impact. He gripped the torch and used it like a club, bringing it down with bone-crushing force on her head. Blood gushed from the wound but Morrigan did not cease her attack.

Wallace put up an arm to shield his face and felt his forearm torn open by the claws. He drove his fist towards her face but one powerful hand clutched his wrist, squeezing tighter until much worse pain shot up his arm and the bones began to splinter. Wallace roared in pain and rage and drove a powerful backhand swipe into the monster's face. To his horror, it gripped his other wrist too, lifting him into the air with a strength that belied its size.

He felt mind-numbing agony sweep through him, then Morrigan hurled him against the wall of the tunnel. His head snapped back and a sharp piece of rock sliced open his scalp. But as he slid downward he used his one good hand to clutch a lump of the stone. He used it as a bludgeon, crashing it into the face of his attacker, feeling the nose disintegrate under the impact. Morrigan picked him up and hurled him to one side. He hit the ground hard and rolled, finding that he was close to the bottom of the shaft.

The children were there, waiting for him, screaming and crying with new shock as first Wallace, then Morrigan, emerged from the tunnel.

The ground burst open again, and now the entire complex of tunnels was beginning to rumble and shake as Wallace felt the air growing colder.

He struggled to his feet, searching for a weapon, knowing that time had already run out for him.

And for those above.

He snatched up a broken sword from the floor of the shaft and hefted it before him. The pain from his broken wrist was excruciating, but he gripped the sword as tightly as he could, bracing himself as Morrigan, Queen of Demons, came hurtling towards him.

Seventy

Broken though it was, the sword was still almost two feet long and it put sufficient distance between Wallace and his attacker. As she ran at him he swung the blade in a downward arc and it sheared through her puffy skin, opening her arm from shoulder to elbow.

A mixture of blood and blackened pus spurted from the wound, bringing with it a choking stench. Wallace ignored this, almost shouting with triumph when he saw the creature stumble.

He struck again.

Morrigan raised an arm to protect herself, but Wallace was driven on now by a mixture of fear and desperation which seemed to increase his strength.

The blade scythed through her arm just below the elbow, shattered the bone and carved swiftly through the remaining muscle, severing the limb, which fell to the ground twitching wildly. Morrigan roared and leapt at Wallace, using her remaining arm to seize him by the throat. The severed stump of the other spewed reeking fluid onto the policeman as he was pushed back against the wall of the shaft, the beast's claws cutting into his neck, drawing blood in several places.

His eyes bulged and he felt as if someone were filling his

head with air. The fetid stench of the creature's breath combined with the even more noxious odour of the blood and pus almost caused Wallace to be sick again.

He found himself staring straight into the demon's blood-flecked white orbs, seeing nothing there but blind hatred and something like triumph.

The ground all around them seemed to be bubbling. Small geysers of earth rose and fell rapidly as the pressure beneath grew to an intolerable level. Wallace knew he had lost, unless . . .

With a despairing moan he managed to push the creature away, smashing it across the face with the flat of the sword.

It staggered, momentarily stunned, and in that split second Wallace struck.

Gripping the sword in both hands he swung it with all his strength.

The blade caught Morrigan just below the jaw, carving through bone and muscle with ease.

The head rose on a thick arc of blood, screaming its defiance even though it had been severed. The mouth yawned open in a last roar of rage, then the head thudded to the ground on the stump of the neck.

Wallace fell back, not prepared for what happened next.

Morrigan's body remained upright, like a beheaded chicken, staggering back and forth for interminable moments. Then it seemed to swell up, muscles bulging outwards as if pumped by air. Bloated, replete with corruption, it burst like one massive boil.

The entire body exploded in a welter of blood and pus. A great stinking eruption of it seemed to fill the shaft, showering Wallace and the children. Great twisted lengths of intestine spiralled upwards like uncoiling springs coated in glutinous red muck. Nails burst from the swollen finger tips even as they flew through the air with the other sickening debris. Wallace screamed despairingly as the vile mixture covered him, matting his hair, lathering his face with reeking red foam.

Even the severed head erupted, greyish-pink gobbets of brain propelled from the riven skull which cracked open to reveal its sticky contents. The eyes burst in their sockets, viscous fluid from the obscene spheres mingling with the blood and pus.

Wallace staggered towards the children, one of whom had fainted.

He saw that two of them had already begun to climb.

'No,' he screamed, his voice drowned as the ground near him split open, the fissure shooting close to his feet.

Beneath him something huge, something loathsome, moved.

He looked down at the little girl, tears now coursing down his cheeks, cutting a path through the gore which coated his face.

He had no choice. He had to do it.

The girl moved closer to him, as if for protection, and as he tried to push her away he noticed that she too was crying.

'Oh Jesus, God forgive me,' he roared and brought the blade down on her head.

Such was the power of the blow that her skull practically split in two. A greyish slop of brain splattered him as she fell, her body twitching slightly.

'No. No!' Wallace shrieked, looking down at the body, at the fissures which were opening up in the earth. Then he turned back towards the tunnel entrance.

'There's your fucking sacrifice,' he screamed. 'Your damned offering.'

But his voice was swallowed up by the groan of parting earth, some of which clattered down around him as the shaft itself began to cave in. Massive lumps of debris thudded down like chunks of shrapnel.

'Stop it,' he wailed. 'Stop it!'

He dragged the unconscious boy to his feet and ran the sword into the lad's throat, holding the body for a moment before letting it fall beside the girl.

'You bastard,' he roared. 'You've had your offering. How many more? How many more, you dirty fucker? Take me instead.'

He turned and grabbed the rope ladder, jamming the sword into his belt, hurrying up the rungs in pursuit of the

267

other two children. One more, he thought, one more. There had to be three sacrifices.

Just one more and it would all end.

He was close to them now, he could see the little girl ahead of him, about to swing herself out of the shaft.

He saw other figures too.

Policemen.

He drew closer, his hand reaching for the girl. He pulled her down, steadying the sword as he rolled her over.

Wallace found himself looking into the tear-stained face of Clare Nichols.

'Please don't hurt me,' she cried, and for precious seconds he hesitated. He couldn't hold onto her. She was pulled free and he found that men in uniforms were backing away from him, shielding the children from him.

Wallace hauled himself up and stood, sword in hand, his mad eyes flicking from one figure to another.

'Give the children to me,' he shouted.

The ground to his right was rippling, dirt and stones flying up in a series of tiny explosions. Elsewhere, huge rifts had scarred the earth. Men were running back and forth.

He saw a car topple into a large fissure, the driver screaming for help as the vehicle disappeared, then exploded in a sheet of flame as the earth contracted around it.

'Give them to me,' Wallace roared, his voice drowned by the shouts of his former colleagues, the roaring flames, and now, a low but growing cry which built to a terrifying crescendo. Beginning like a strong wind, it increased in ferocity until the sound was unbearable. Men nearby screamed and covered their ears, feeling blood burst from them as the onslaught grew worse, reaching an incredible pitch, forming into one monstrous obscene bellow of triumph.

Wallace looked up to see the sky turning red. Redder than a thousand sunsets, as if it had been drenched in the blood of millions. Then, against that redness, he saw a black outline. A shape so huge, so enormous that it stretched up into and beyond the clouds.

The shape was unmistakably humanoid, but grotesque beyond description. And it was still growing.

Wallace clapped his hands over his hears. Inside his head he could hear his own laughter.

The laughter of the mad?

Of the damned?

And all the time that loathsome black shape expanded, its monstrous roar filling the night as it stretched across the boiling skies. Its hideous form blotting out those blood-soaked clouds, filling the heavens.

Then there was only darkness.

Spawn

Acknowledgements

Some of the research which went into this book was difficult, to put it mildly, and I would like to thank everyone who answered my questions, however bizarre they may have seemed. Particular thanks to Nurse Anne Bozia for her help. I would also like to thank Niki, whose criticism was as hard but as helpful as always. Also thanks to everyone concerned with the production of the book, particularly Mike Bailey, my editor, who put up with my numerous phone calls and lousy spelling. And, as ever, to Bob Tanner. Indirect thanks to John Carpenter, Iron Maiden, Black Sabbath, Tobe Hooper. All worshipped from afar. And lastly and most important, to my family. My parents, who thought I was mad to write a book like this and to Belinda, who *knows* I'm mad. For suffering my obsessions these past few years I am indebted to her One day soon . . .

Shaun Hutson

FOR MIKE BRETT WITH THANKS AND ADMIRATION

PART ONE

". . . some of us are born posthumously. . ."
                                    – *Nietzsche*

". . . the foetus is conscious or aware. It
can sense and react not only to emotions
such as love and hate, but to more
complex and ambiguous feelings."
                                    – *Dr Thomas Verny*

One

The flickering wings of the crane-flies inside the jar sounded like whispers in the darkness and Harold Pierce held it to his ear, listening. He smiled and looked at the three insects struggling helplessly inside their glass prison. It was the light that attracted them, he had reasoned, as it did the moths. But Harold wasn't interested in moths, they moved too quickly. They were too hard to catch but the daddy-long-legs were easy prey. He smiled as he repeated the name. Daddy-long-legs. He stifled a giggle. His mother called them Tommies and that amused him even more. She was sleeping across the narrow hallway now, alone for once. Harold didn't remember the succession of men who she brought home, he wasn't really interested either. All he knew was that his father would not be coming back.

Jack Pierce had been killed at Dunkirk six years earlier and, since then, Harold's mother had entertained a never-ending series of men. Sometimes Harold had seen them give her money as they left but, it not being in the nature of fourteen-year-olds to question strangers, he had never asked any of them why. One night he had crept across the narrow landing and squinted through the key hole of his mother's room. She'd had two men in there with her. All of them were laughing and Harold had smelt liquor. They had been naked, all three of them, and for long moments he had watched, puzzled by the strange goings-on before him.

It was shortly after that night that his mother announced he was to have a brother or sister. The baby had duly arrived and Harold had been dragged off to church for the Christening, puzzled when there was only him and his mother present to witness the ceremony. In fact, his mother was shunned by most of the women in the neighbourhood. They spoke to her in the street but it was never anything more than a cursory 'hello'.

Harold held the jar of crane-flies up before him once more, wondering if their whispers would tell him the answers he needed to know.

He lowered the jar and looked across at the cot which held his baby brother, Gordon. The child was sleeping, lying on its back with the thick flannelette sheet pulled up around its face. Harold hated having to share a room with his brother. In the beginning, it had been all right. Gordon had slept in his cot in his mother's room but, since his first birthday, he had been put in with Harold. That meant that Harold was forced to come to bed when Gordon was tucked up for the night and that could be as early as seven in the evening. Most of the time, Harold would sit in the bedroom window watching the other kids kicking a big old leather football about in the street below. He had watched them doing that tonight, perched in his customary position until nine o'clock came around and the other kids were called indoors. Then, Harold had switched on his bedside lamp and watched as the crane-flies and moths flittered in through the open window.

Gordon was sound asleep, little gurgling noises came from his cot as he shifted position occasionally. The nylon eiderdown was crumpled at his feet where he'd kicked it off. It was covered with stitched-on rabbits. Beside the heavy wooden cot stood a pile of yellowing newspapers. Harold didn't read very well but he knew that the papers were called *The News Chronicle*. Just why his mother kept them he didn't know. There was another stack downstairs beside the coal fire, those she used to get the fire started in the mornings. Perhaps the pile in his bedroom were destined for the same purpose.

He crouched on the end of the bed for long moments, propping the jar of crane-flies on the window sill. The night was still and windless and, from somewhere nearby the strains of "String of Pearls" came drifting in with the night. Harold listened to the distant music for a moment then he swung himself off the bed and padded across to the door. The lino was cold beneath his feet and he hissed softly as he tip-toed from the bedroom, across the hall to the door of his mother's room. A framed painting of George VI watched him impassively as he gently turned the handle and popped his head round. His mother was asleep, her black hair smeared across her face in untidy patterns. Harold stood there for long seconds, watching the steady rise and fall of her chest, almost coughing as the strong odour of lavender assaulted his nostrils. Finally, satisfied that she wasn't likely to disturb him, he gently pushed the door closed and tip-toed back to his own room.

"String of Pearls" had been replaced by "Moonlight Serenade" when he got back but he ignored the music, more intent on the task at hand. He reached beneath his pillow and took out a box of Swan Vestas matches. Harold held them in his sweaty hand for a moment then he took hold of the glass jar. The crane-flies began flapping about even more frenziedly as Harold began to unscrew the top, as if sensing freedom. When it was fully loosened he held the jar before him, eyeing the insect closest to the neck of the jar. With lightning movements, he reached in and grabbed it by one membranous wing, simultaneously pushing the lid back in place.

The insect tried to escape his grasp and, quickly,

8

Harold pulled both its wings off. He did the same with three of its legs. The unfortunate creature was then dropped onto a sheet of newspaper where it tried, in vain, to scuttle away. Harold watched its helpless writhings for a moment then he picked up the box of Swan Vestas and slid the tray out, taking a match. It flared orange and the smell of sulphur filled his nostrils momentarily. He bent lower, bringing the burning match to within an inch of the crane-fly which immediately began to wriggle more frantically. Harold pressed the tiny flame to one of its legs, watching as the spindly limb seemed to retract, much like hair does when it is burned. The insect rolled onto its back, its two remaining legs thrashing wildly, its tiny head moving frenziedly. Harold burnt off another of its limbs then pressed the spent match-head against its slender abdomen. There was a slight hiss and the creature's head and remaining leg began moving even more rapidly.

Harold hurriedly lit another match.

This one he held right over the crane-fly, giggling when the stumps of its legs moved spasmodically as the flame drew closer. He dropped the match onto the insect, smiling as it was incinerated, its body rapidly consumed by the flame, charred black by the tiny plume of yellow. A whisp of grey smoke rose into the air. When the match had finished burning, Harold took another and prodded the blackened remains of the insect. It merely disintegrated.

Totally enthralled, Harold stuck his hand inside the jar and took out another of the crane-flies. This one he held by its wings, waving the match beneath it until all its legs had been burnt off. He twisted the wings so it couldn't fly away then he dropped it onto the newspaper and finished the cremation job with another match.

For the last insect, Harold had reserved something

special. His *pièce de résistance*. He took a handful of matches from the box and, with infinite care and patience, built them up until they were stacked cross-ways, on top of one another in a kind of well. Into the centre of this well, after removing its wings, he dropped the last insect. Then, quickly, he covered the top with three more matches. There must have been about twenty-five in all comprising that miniature funeral pyre and Harold sat back for a second admiring his handy-work. He could see the crane-fly inside the little stack of matches, its long legs protruding through the slits here and there as it tried to escape.

There were half a dozen matches left in the box and Harold struck one, gazing into the flame for a second before carefully applying it to the head of the match at the bottom of the pile.

It ignited with a hiss, burning for a second then setting off a chain reaction. The little structure went up in a flash of yellow and white flame and Harold grinned broadly.

He grinned until he saw that his blazing creation had set light to the paper it rested on.

The newspaper was dry and the flames devoured it hungrily. Harold felt a sudden surge of panic and he snatched up the blazing paper, scattering the burning remains of the tiny pyre as he did so. Matches which still hissed, alive with wisps of yellow, were scattered all over the room. One fell beside the pile of *News Chronicle*s and licked at the edge of the dry papers. Flames began to rise. The room was filled with the smell of charred paper and smoke wafted in the still air.

Another of the blazing matches fell into Gordon's cot. It hit the nylon eiderdown and seemed to explode, the quilt suddenly flaring as bright tongues of fire sprang from it.

Gordon woke up and began to scream as the fire touched his skin.

10

For long seconds, Harold was frozen, not knowing what to do. He took a step towards the cot, then backed off, his eyes bulging wide. Gordon's night-shirt was on fire. The baby was screaming, trying to drag itself away from the all-consuming inferno. Already, the skin on its arms and legs was a vivid scarlet.

Harold opened his mouth to scream but no sound would come out. The pile of newspapers beside the cot had ignited with a frightening vehemence and the tongues of flame rose a full three feet into the air. The whole room was ablaze. His own bed was seething, a mass of writhing fire. Smoke, thick and noxious, filled his nostrils and finally, as a piece of burning wallpaper fell and stuck to his arm, Harold found the breath for a scream. For interminable seconds, the paper clung to his arm, searing the flesh. He tore it away to see that the skin was red and blistered. His head swam and for a second he thought he was going to faint but, as he saw the cot disappear beneath a flickering haze of fire, he spun round and dashed for the door.

His mother had heard the screams and they crashed into one another on the landing. She saw the smoke billowing from the children's room, saw the leaping flames and she shook her head in disbelief. Pushing Harold aside, she ran into the room – into the furnace and flames which seared her flesh and set her clothes ablaze. Harold followed her back in, watching as she fought her way to the cot, reaching in to lift something which had once been her baby son. The body of Gordon was little more than a blackened shell. One arm had been completely burned off from the elbow down, the stump was still flaming. His mouth was open to reveal a blackened, tumefied tongue. The flesh looked as if it had been peeled away with red hot pincers. Through the charred flesh, white bone showed in places.

Harold's mother screamed and clutched the baby to her. Her own hair was now ablaze, the stench filling

11

the room. She turned, a look of agony etched on her face and she screamed something at him but he couldn't hear through the roaring flames. As he turned to open the door a particularly violent eruption of flame exploded before him. Harold shrieked and felt one side of his face sizzling. The skin rose swiftly into blisters which immediately burst, the welts hardening as the fire stripped his flesh away as surely as if someone had thrust a blow torch at him. He felt something wet dripping from his burning cheek. Things went black as his right eye swelled under the intense heat then, in a moment of mind blowing agony, the sensitive orb seemed to bulge and burst. Blood gushed freely from the ruptured eye, turning immediately to charcoal under the ferocity of the flames. Harold clapped a hand to his face and felt the oblivion of unconciousness creeping over him but the pain kept him awake and he managed to yank open the bedroom door. The hair on his arms was singed and his veins seemed to bulge as his skin contracted. He turned to see his mother, on her hands and knees, crawling towards him, the flesh of her body apparently bubbling, lumps of it falling from calcified bones. She raised an accusing finger at him and screamed:

"You're to blame!"

The empty box of matches lay close beside her. Her hair was burnt off and the stench of charred skin was overpowering. Smoke poured from the open window and those living nearby hurried out into the street to see what was happening. The fire-engine was called.

Harold reeled amongst the flames, screaming in agony as what remained of his face was stripped clean by the flames. But, shielding himself as best he could, he stumbled out onto the landing, throwing himself against the wall in an effort to put out the fire which still devoured his clothes. He stumbled and fell, crashing heavily to the floor.

12

Downstairs, someone was trying to batter down the front door.

Harold looked round.

Through the haze of pain he saw his mother, a blackened vision which seemed to have risen from the fires of hell, standing in the bedroom doorway. She had her arms outstretched, the skin like crumbling parchment. When she opened her mouth, smoke billowed forth. Her eyes were gone, they were now just black pits in a bleeding, ruined face. Bone shone through the charred skin as blisters formed then burst with rapidity. She no longer had hair just the dancing snakes of flame which topped her skull, like some kind of fiery Gorgon.

She swayed for long seconds then, as the front door was broken down, she toppled backwards into the flames.

Harold began to scream.

"Mr Pierce."

Everything was darkness, he could feel his body shaking.

"Mr Pierce." The tone was more forceful this time.

He could hear screams, close by, drumming in his ears.

"Harold. Wake up."

He realized that the screams were his and, suddenly, he opened his eye and sat up, panting for breath, his body bathed in sweat. He looked round, fixing the woman in a glassy stare.

"Harold, are you all right?" she asked him.

He exhaled deeply and rubbed his eye. His hands were shaking madly, like a junkie who needs a fix. But, finally, his breathing slowed and he felt his heart returning to its usual rhythm. He looked at the woman, at her blue and white uniform, the small triangular hat which perched precariously on her head. Gradually the realization spread over him and he smiled thinly.

13

"I was dreaming," he said apologetically.

The woman smiled and nodded.

"I know," she said. "But you frightened the life out of all of us."

He apologized once more and wiped his forehead with the back of his hand. He looked up to see two maroon-coated interns standing on the other side of his bed. He recognized one as Pat Leary, a big Irishman who bore a bottle scar just above his right eye.

"You all right, Harold?" he asked.

The older man nodded and swung himself onto the edge of the bed. His pyjama jacket was soaked with sweat, a dark stain running from the nape of his neck to the small of his back. He pulled it off and began searching in his locker for his clothes.

His audience left, the interns moving off towards the exit at the far end of the ward, Nurse Beaton ambling across to the bed next to Harold to wake its occupant. He was a man older than Harold, completely bald and with skin like the folds of a badly fitting jacket. In fact that was what his face reminded Harold of. Harold watched as Nurse Beaton woke the man and then took two red pills from a plastic container she held. She supported the bald man while he took the pills, wiping away the water from his chin when it spilled over his rubbery lips. He heard her ask the man if he'd swallowed them and he nodded slowly. The nurse gently lowered him back into bed and moved on.

Harold was dressed by this time. He picked up a small imitation leather shaving-bag from his locker and headed towards the toilets at the far end of the corridor. The place smelt of disinfectant, as usual, but it was a smell with which he was well acquainted after so long.

Harold Pierce had been a patient in Exham Mental Hospital since 1946. Apart from the first fourteen years of his life, the institution had been his only home. It had been his world. And, in all that time things hadn't

14

changed much. He'd seen scores of people, both staff and patients, come and go and now he was as much a part of the hospital as the yellow-painted walls.

He reached the toilets and selected his usual wash basin. He filled it with water and splashed his face, reaching beneath to find a towel. Slowly he straightened up, regarding the image which stared back at him from the mirror.

Harold sucked in a shaking breath. Even after all these years the sight of his own hideously scarred face repulsed him. It was a patchwork of welts and indentations, the whole thing a vivid red. The hair over his left eye was gone, as was the eye itself. A glass one now sparkled blindly in its place. His left ear was bent, minus the lobe it was in fact little more than a hole in the side of his head. One corner of his mouth was swollen, the lip turned up in a kind of obscene grin. A dark growth of flesh, what had once been a large mole, protruded from just below his left cheek bone, jutting out like the gnarled end of an incinerated tree branch. His left nostril was flared wide. What little hair remained on the left side of his head was thin and grey, a marked contrast to the thick black strands on the other side.

In fact, the right side of his face was relatively unmarked except for a slight scar on his forehead, most of the damage had been done to the left side of his body.

Harold took out his electric razor and ran it swiftly over the right cheek and beneath his chin. No stubble would grow on the left side.

He turned to see two interns carrying another patient from a wheel chair into one of the toilet cubicles. The old man was paralysed from the neck downwards, leaving one intern with the unsavoury task of cleaning him up when he'd finished. The old man was well into his eighties and suffered from Senile Dementia too. A common complaint amongst most of the patients at the institution.

One of the other patients, a man in his thirties who Harold knew as John, was cleaning the floor of the toilet with a mop, slopping the water everywhere in his haste.

"Careful, John," said Phil Coot, trying to slow him down. "You'll drown us all."

John laughed throatily and plunged the mop back into the bucket making a monumental splash. Coot, who was senior male nurse on the ward shook his head and smiled, watching the patient merrily slopping his way across the tiled floor.

"How are you this morning, Harold?" he said as he passed.

"Very well, Mr Coot, thank you."

Coot paused.

"You had some trouble last night?" he said.

Harold looked puzzled.

"The dream," Coot reminded him.

"Oh yes, that." Harold smiled thinly and raised one hand to cover the scarred side of his face but Coot reached up and gently pulled the hand away.

"The usual thing?" he asked.

Harold nodded.

"You're not on medication any more are you?" asked the male nurse.

"No, Mr Coot."

"This is the first time you've had this dream for a long time isn't it?"

"Yes, I don't know why. I'm sorry."

Coot smiled.

"No need to be sorry, Harold," he said. "Some of it is probably just tension at the thought of leaving here after so long." He patted Harold on the shoulder. "Once you get out of here you'll be OK. You'll settle into your new job and forget you've ever seen this place." He gestured around him, his tone turning reflec-

16

tive. "To tell you the truth, I shan't be sorry when we all leave here. The place is falling down around our ears it's so old."

"Where are you going then?" Harold wanted to know.

"The staff and patients are being moved to a new hospital on the other side of Exham in a couple of weeks time."

Harold nodded absently, lowering his gaze. He felt Coot touch him once more on the shoulder and then the male nurse was gone.

Harold took one last look in the mirror then pulled the plug in the sink, watching as the water swirled around the hole before disappearing. It was something which never failed to fascinate him.

Back by his bed, Harold put away his razor and smoothed out the creases in his trousers with the palms of his hands. He glanced out of the nearest window and scanned the grounds. The wind of the previous night had dropped and the leaves which had fallen from the trees now lay still on the lawns below. There were already a number of patients at work with large rakes, gathering the leaves up. Two interns stood close by, smoking.

Three nurses were walking past and they paused to speak with a doctor. Harold could see that they were laughing together and he saw the doctor kiss one of them on the cheek. They all laughed again. Laughter was something which Harold didn't hear too much of these days. He watched the little group almost enviously for long moments then turned away from the window and set about making his bed.

Finally satisfied that all was in order, he wandered off towards the staircase which would take him down a floor to the Therapy rooms.

There were already two other patients at work in the

17

large room when Harold walked in. He inhaled deeply, enjoying the odour of the oil paint. His own easel was set up close to one of the meshed windows and he crossed to it, inspecting the canvas which he had lovingly decorated these past three weeks. The picture was a series of bright colour flashes, mainly reds and yellows. What it was no one was quite sure, not even Harold, but he swiftly hunted out a brush and some paint from the wooden cupboard nearby and set to work.

Harold looked carefully at his canvas before applying the first vivid brush stroke. It was as if he saw something in those reds and yellows, something which stirred a memory inside him. His brush hovered over the place on his palette where he squeezed a blob of orange.

Flames.

He swallowed hard. Yes, they looked like flames. The memories of his nightmare came flooding back to him and he took a step back from the canvas as if he had discovered something vile and obscene about it. Perhaps, unconsciously, he was painting that nightmare scene as it had appeared to him all those years ago. Was this his punishment? To commit his crime to canvas for eternity? He bowed his head and, with his free hand, touched the scarred side of his face. A single tear blossomed in his eye corner and rolled down his unmarked cheek. Harold wiped it away angrily. He looked up and gazed at the painting once again. The bright colours *did* look like flames.

He dabbed the brush into the puddle of orange paint and tentatively applied a few strokes. For some reason, he found that his hand was shaking but he persevered. Why, in the last few weeks, had the canvas never appeared to be a canopy of dancing flames, he wondered? Was it because of the nightmare? The re-kindling of memories which he thought he had at last succeeded

18

in pushing to the back of his tortured mind? Harold could not, would not, forget that horrific night in 1946 and he had more than his scar to remind him of it.

Along the length of his arms, from elbow to wrist, long white marks showed. They were all that now remained of the near-fatal attempt he'd made to kill himself. The scars were barely visible now but he would sit and look at them sometimes remembering the day when he'd inflicted the cuts which he had hoped would bring him the welcome oblivion of death – the ultimate darkness which would rid him of the guilt that gnawed away at his mind like a hungry rat. He had locked himself in the toilet and slashed his forearms open with a piece of broken glass. He'd smashed the window in the toilet with one powerful fist and then drawn his arms back and forth across the jagged shards on the frame until his thin forearms were crimson tatters. The blood had pooled at his feet and Harold could still remember the strange feeling of serenity which had fallen over him as he'd watched his arteries and veins spewing forth their vivid red fluid. The pain had been excruciating but not as bad as the fire. The fire. That was all he could think of as he stood there that day, his arms reduced to dripping rags as he tugged them back and forth across the glass.

But two interns had battered the door down and found him. They dragged him away, one of them applying make-shift tourniquets to his arms while Harold burbled:

"I'm sorry, I'm sorry."

They tried to comfort him as he slid into unconsciousness, not understanding that his words were for his dead brother and mother.

Now Harold stood in the Therapy room, brush in hand, his eyes lowered. The thoughts tumbling over in his mind.

He had learned to live with the guilt. He knew it

19

was something he would always have to bear and he accepted that. He *had* been responsible for the death of his brother. He knew that and it was something that would haunt him forever. There was no atonement for him, no way of releasing that guilt. It grew and festered in his mind like some kind of poisonous growth, the dreams which it brought like the discharge from a rank boil.

"Good morning, Harold."

The voice startled him and he turned quickly, almost dropping his palette. The Occupational Therapist, Jenny Clark, stood beside him looking at his canvas. "What are you going to call your painting, Harold?" she asked.

"It looks like a fire to me," he told her. "Can't you see the flames?" He looked directly at her and she tried to fix her gaze on his one good eye, deliberately avoiding his burned skin. She held the questioning stare for long moments then looked back at the canvas.

Jenny smiled thinly,

"Yes, they do look like flames don't they?" she said, softly.

They stood in silence for long moments, both inhaling the cloying odour of the oil paint, then Harold spoke again.

"Have you ever done anything you're ashamed of, Miss Clark?"

The question came completely out of the blue and took her by surprise. She swallowed hard, her brow furrowing slightly.

"I suppose so, Harold. Why do you ask?"

"This painting," he told her. "I think it's like a punishment. A reminder to me never to forget what I did to my brother. I was ashamed of that. I still am. I killed my brother, Miss Clark. I think that's what I'm painting."

Jenny exhaled deeply.

She was about to say something when he spoke again.

"I think it's my way of saying sorry. Sorry for what I did."

She was silent for a moment, her eyes searching his, straying from that wretched glass orb to the real one and then back again.

His tone suddenly lightened.

"I'll call it 'Fire'," he announced. "Just 'Fire'."

More patients were arriving now and Jenny left Harold alone with his masterpiece in order to help the others. Soon the room was alive with activity and noise. Someone knocked over an easel but Harold ignored the clatter and continued with his painting. Finally, satisfied that it was complete, he picked up a tube of red paint and squeezed some of the sticky liquid onto his palette. He dipped his brush into it and, in thick letters at the top of the canvas, painted one word:

FIRE

Two

The road which led from Exham itself, to the larger town of Cornford twelve miles away, was flanked on both sides by wide expanses of fields. Some belonged to the handful of small farms which dotted the countryside round about, but others just sprouted weeds, they stood unwanted and untended.

The road was usually busy but, as the early morning mist cleared slowly, it was strangely devoid of the customary bustle of commuters who clogged it. The

Panda car passed just three other vehicles, one of which was a large lorry carrying vegetables.

Constable Bill Higgins stepped on the brake, simultaneously easing the Panda to one side of the road, its nearside wheels actually mounting the footpath at the side of the tarmac. The lorry swept past, its tail flap rattling loudly and Higgins watched it in the rear view mirror, half expecting to see it spill its load behind it. He swung the car back in lane and drove on.

Beside him, in the passenger seat, his superior gazed out of the side window, watching as the trees sped past. The window was open to allow some cool air into the stifling confines of the car. Despite the slight chill, the refreshing breeze was welcomed by both men. The Panda's heater was on the blink, jammed at maximum output it transformed the vehicle into some kind of mobile sauna.

Inspector Lou Randall fumbled in the pocket of his jacket for a packet of Rothmans and lit one, the wind blowing smoke back into his face. He coughed and waved a hand in front of him. A stronger smell reached his nostrils through the bluish haze of fumes and he winced as he realized that it was manure.

"Why does the countryside always smell like a shithouse?" he said, blowing out a disapproving breath.

"What is it about fresh air that you hate so much, guv?" asked the driver, grinning.

"I wouldn't call *that* fresh air."

Randall had been born and brought up in London, always used to its cramped confines. To the steady crush of buildings and people around him. He felt strangely exposed in the countryside, as if light and space were somehow alien to him. Apart from holidays when he was a kid, he'd never been out of London longer than two weeks at a time. He remembered how his parents always took him to the Lake District when he was a nipper, and how much he hated water too. Large

22

expanses of it always put the fear of Christ into him even though he was a good swimmer. The strange brooding silence which seemed to hang over the lakes always disturbed him just as now the perpetual solitude of endless fields brought back that youthful unease. Randall was thirty-six, stocky and heavily muscled. He usually put himself through a routine of exercises three or four times a week to keep in shape. Not that much happened in Exham to compel sudden strenuous physical activity though. In his sixteen months as head of the small force, he'd dealt with nothing more serious than a couple of rape cases.

He slumped in the seat, the plastic hot against his back, puffing on his fag, his blue eyes scanning the endless tracts of arable land. He ran a hand through his brown hair and exhaled deeply. The clock on the dashboard showed 8.09 a.m. and Randall yawned. He hadn't slept too well the previous night and his eyes felt as if someone had sewed the lids together. He took a last drag on his cigarette and tossed the butt out of the window. Grunting, he straightened up in the passenger seat. He reached over onto the back seat and picked up a manila file, which he flipped open. Inside was a report and, clipped to that, another sheet of paper which bore the signature of the county coroner. Randall yawned again and ran his eyes over the typewritten report which he'd already looked at half a dozen times that morning.

"Paul Harvey," he read aloud. "Age twenty-nine. Detained Cornford Maximum Security Prison, June 1979. No previous prison record." He closed the file, drumming on it agitatedly. "Convicted of two murders, sentenced to life."

"I can still remember when he was arrested," said Higgins, some of the colour draining from his normally ruddy complexion. "It took four of us to hold the

23

bastard down long enough to cuff him. He was a bloody maniac."

Randall raised an eyebrow.

"The reports seem to agree with you," he said. "It must have been quite a shaker for a little place like Exham."

"It was," Higgins confirmed.

"The killings were random. There was never any motive established," said the Inspector, reflectively.

"What exactly *did* he do to them?" Higgins wanted to know. "We never did find out for sure."

Randall opened the file again.

"Both victims were dismembered," he read. "Apparently there was so little of them left that identification was almost impossible. Fond of the old carving knife our Harvey," he added, sardonically.

"Most of the bits were never even found."

"Oh Jesus," murmured Higgins.

"And now he's out again," said Randall, flatly. "He escaped at five o'clock this morning."

The two men continued their journey in silence. Higgins swung the Panda off the main road and down a narrower off-shoot flanked on both sides by trees. Through the windscreen both men could make out the gaunt edifice of Cornford prison. It was built of red brick, discoloured with the ravages of time and the elements. The high wall which surrounded it was similarly scarred, a row of iron spikes and barbed wire running along the top. Two huge black-painted doors barred their way as the constable brought the Panda to a halt.

Randall straightened his tie, cursing when one of the buttons popped off. Higgins grinned.

"Get your wife to sew it. . ."

The smile and the sentence trailed off and the constable coloured as he felt Randall's eyes on him.

"Sorry, guv," he said, softly.

24

Randall found the button and dropped it into his pocket. Then, clambering out of the car he said:

"I don't know how long I'll be."

Higgins nodded and watched as his superior walked across the tarmac towards the towering black gates. On his way he passed a blue sign which proclaimed in large white letters:

HER MAJESTY'S PRISON: CORNFORD

There was an old mini parked outside the gates, its side panels rotting, the white paint peeling away to reveal the rust beneath. The decaying metal was the colour of dried blood and the peeling paint reminded the Inspector of a picked scab.

He reached the huge gates and banged on a small door set into the right hand one. After a few seconds a panel slid open and a face appeared.

Randall showed his ID and the panel closed. A moment later the door opened and the policeman stepped through to find himself in the courtyard of the prison. A uniformed warder showed him the main entrance of the building and Randall set off across the vast expanse of wet tarmac.

To his left a group of prisoners, dressed in their familiar dark blue overalls, were standing or shuffling idly about while two warders stood chatting. One or two heads turned as he made his way towards the huge main building which was still wreathed in the early morning mist, the grey fog drifting round it like some kind of ethereal shroud.

The Governor's office was enormous, fully thirty feet long and perhaps twenty wide. A huge oak table stood in the centre, an oval shaped antique which sparkled brightly. The legacy of many years polishing. It had nine chairs around it and, suppressing a smile, Randall wondered where King Arthur and his knights had got to. The thought quickly vanished however.

The walls were a sky blue colour dull with the dust

of the years, as with most of the paintwork in the prison it seemed. The ceiling rose high above him, three large banks of fluorescents set into it – the only concession to progress. The rest of the room seemed forty years out of date. Large windows looked out onto the West Wing of the prison, the office itself separated from the prisoners' quarters by a high stone wall and a large expanse of well-kept lawn. The carpet on the floor was so threadbare that Randall's footsteps echoed as he walked towards the desk at the far end of the office. As he approached, Governor George Stokes rose to greet him.

The two men introduced themselves, a sign on Stokes's desk adding a silently corroborative affirmation that he was indeed Governor. He was well into his sixties, his hair almost white, even the wisps that curled from his wide nostrils. But his handshake was strong, belying his years. He was tall, ungainly. Dressed in a two piece brown suit, the trousers of which were an inch too short, he looked like some kind of be-spectacled stick insect.

Stokes introduced the other man in the room as Doctor Kevin Hayes. He was, or had been up until his escape, Harvey's psychiatrist. A short, nervous looking man in his fifties, he was prodding one ear with the blunt end of a pin.

"You're probably wondering why I called you, Randall?" said Stokes, clasping his hands before him and leaning on his blotter.

"It had crossed my mind," said the Inspector.

"We have reason to believe that Harvey will return to Exham," Stokes told him. "We thought you should be forewarned." The older man plucked at the end of his nose. "If there's anything we can do to help you, ask."

"Well, for one thing, I'd like to know why he was having psychiatric treatment," the Inspector said.

26

"From what I've read about the case there was never any hint of mental disturbance."

"During the last six months," said Hayes, "Harvey had become very introverted. He brooded. He'd always been a loner but he seemed to become more hostile towards the other prisoners. He got into fights frequently."

"We had him in solitary most of the time," Stokes interjected. "As much for the safety of the other men as anything else."

"How dangerous is he?" Randall wanted to know.

Hayes stroked his chin thoughtfully.

"It's difficult to say," he said, evasively.

"Could he kill again?" Randall demanded. "*Would* he kill again?"

The psychiatrist exchanged a brief glance with Stokes then looked at Randall.

"It's possible," he said, almost reluctantly.

"How the hell did he manage to get out of here in the first place?" Randall snapped, just a little too forcefully.

"That, Randall, is not your concern," rasped Stokes. "Catching him again is all that matters. *That's* your job I suggest you set about doing it." The two men locked stares for long seconds and the Inspector could see the anger in the older man's eyes. The escape had hurt his pride, it might, Randall reasoned, cost him his job. He probably had every right to be angry. But there was fear there too.

Randall got to his feet.

Randall didn't speak much on the way back to Exham, his mind was too full of thoughts and questions, one in particular nagging at him.

Where and when would Paul Harvey turn up?

Three

Paul Harvey stumbled and fell, crashing heavily against a nearby tree. He lay still on the damp moss for long seconds, sucking in painful breaths, each of which seemed to sear his lungs. His calves and thighs were stiff, as if someone had clamped a vice on each leg and was slowly turning the screw. He dragged himself upright, using a low branch for support. Panting like a bloodhound, he leant against the tree and massaged the top of his legs. He licked a furred, tumefied tongue over his cracked lips. It felt as if someone had stuffed his mouth with cotton wool. He stood still for a moment longer then blundered on through the small wood.

He walked awkwardly, like a drunkard and was forced to use the trees and bushes to hold him up. He couldn't remember how long he'd been running. Four, five hours. Perhaps more. He wasn't sure of anything except the gnawing pain in his legs and the burning in his belly. He must have food, that much he *did* know. The prison was a good six miles behind him now and he afforded himself a smile as he continued his haphazard course through the woods.

A bird twittered overhead and he spun round, taken aback by this sudden sound. He raised a hand as if trying to pluck it from its perch. When that failed he attempted to shout at it but no sound would come. His throat was like parchment. He slumped against another tree, head bowed, ears alert for the slightest movement. *They* would be after him by now but they would not catch him. Not this time.

He cocked an ear expectantly but heard nothing, just the ever-present sound of the birds and. . .

A twig snapped close by and he froze, pressing himself closer to the trunk of the elm, trying to become a part of it.

28

As he watched, a small boy, no more than twelve years old, pushed his way through the bushes and picked up a football. With the object safely retrieved, he scrambled back towards the clearing beyond where two of his companions waited. Harvey could see the other children now. He relaxed slightly and moved forward with surprising agility for a man of his size. He was well over six feet two, weighing around fourteen stone. His hair was black, closely cropped and shining. Pupils like chips of emerald glittered amidst whites criss-crossed by bulging red veins.

He moved closer to the edge of the woods, keeping low, well away from the children playing beyond. There were three of them he could see, all engrossed in their game. Harvey parted a bush to peer out at them. His large fingers twitched spasmodically but a look of bewilderment crossed his face when he saw them stop kicking the orange ball around and cross to a large plastic bag which lay behind one of the make-shift goal posts.

They took out some sandwiches and began eating.

Harvey put a hand to his stomach as it rumbled loudly.

He watched the three of them eating.

The time would come.

He watched and waited.

Graham Phelps stuffed the remains of the ham sandwich into his mouth and chewed noisily.

"Let's have a drink," he said, motioning towards one of the two thermos flasks.

Colin Fulton dutifully poured him a cup of steaming hot chocolate which he swigged, burning his tongue.

"Fucking hell," he gasped. "That's hot."

Colin and his younger brother, Miles, both chuckled.

Graham, on the other hand, didn't see the joke.

"What's so fucking funny?" he demanded, angrily.

29

He swore a lot. His father and his elder brothers did it too. His eldest brother had been in Borstal for six months and Graham hero-worshipped him, as he did his father. Both of them would think nothing of smacking a woman in the teeth too, if the need arose. They were really hard. Graham's mind contained a simple equation because he was somewhat simple minded:

Swearing and hitting women = manliness.

As easy as that.

Now he rounded on Miles again. The twelve-year-old, three years younger than Graham and Colin, was an ideal target.

"I said, what's so fucking funny?" he persisted.

"You, burning your mouth," Miles told him. "You shouldn't be such a pig."

"Fuck off," rasped Graham and got to his feet, kicking the ball about, dribbling it close to the brothers, bouncing it off Miles's legs every so often. They finally took the hint and got wearily to their feet, dropping the remnants of half-eaten sandwiches back into the plastic Tesco bag.

Paul Harvey kept perfectly still amongst the trees and bushes, his breath now slowed to a rasping hiss. He watched the three boys kicking the ball about and a twisted grin spread across his face.

Graham decided to show off his shooting ability and lashed a shot in the direction of the makeshift goal but a gust of wind caught the ball and it went flying wide, hurtling into the trees beyond. Graham planted his hands on his hips and looked at his companion.

"Well, go and get the fucking thing," he shouted, watching as Miles sloped off in the direction of the trees.

Paul Harvey saw him coming.

Miles pushed his way into the bushes and onward until he was surrounded by trees. For the first time that morning he noticed just how quiet it was inside the copse. His feet hardly made a sound as he walked over the carpet of moss, glancing around in his search for the ball. It obviously must have gone further than usual. Even its bright orange colour seemed invisible in the maze of greens and browns which made up the small wood. He stepped up onto a fallen, rotting tree stump, hoping to get a better view. At his feet a large spider had succeeded in trapping a fly in its web and, for a moment, Miles watched the hairy horror devouring its prey. He shuddered and moved away, his eyes still scanning the copse for the lost ball. He stepped into some stinging nettles and yelped in pain as one of them found its way to the exposed area between his sock top and the turn-up of his jeans. He rubbed the painful spot and wandered further into the wood. Where the hell was that ball?

He stood still, hands on his hips, squinting in the dull light. Mist still hung low on the floor of the copse, like a blanket of dry ice, it covered his feet as he walked. Droplets of moisture hung like shimmering crystal from the few leaves which remained on the trees. They reminded Miles of cold tears.

Something caught his eye.

He smiled. It was the ball, about ten yards away, stuck in the top of a stunted bush. He hurried towards it, suddenly aware of the unearthly silence which seemed to have closed around him like some kind of invisible velvet glove. He shivered and scurried forward to retrieve the ball, tugging it loose from the grasping branches of the bush.

Something moved close behind him, a soft footfall on the carpet of moss. He spun round, his heart thumping hard against his ribs.

31

A sudden light breeze sprang up, whipping the mist into thin spirals.

Miles started back towards the openness of the rec, away from the stifling confines of the copse. He clutched the ball to his chest, ignoring the mud which was staining his jumper. The odour of damp wood and moss was almost asphyxiating, as palpable as the gossamer wisps of fog which swirled around him.

Something cold touched his arm and he gasped, dropping the ball, spinning round, ready to run.

It was a low branch.

As he bent to pick up the ball, Miles could see that his hands were shaking. He straightened up, a thin film of perspiration on his forehead. And it was at that moment he felt the hand grip his shoulder.

This time he screamed, trying to pull away but the hand held him back and he heard raucous laughter ringing in his ears.

"All right, don't shit yourself," said a familiar voice and Miles finally found the courage to turn. He saw Graham Phelps standing there, his hand gripping Miles's shoulder. "Just thought I'd give you a bit of a fright." He laughed again, pushing Miles towards the clearing ahead of them.

"How would you like it if someone had done that to you?" Miles bleated.

"Oh shut up and give me the ball," said Graham, snatching it from him.

The huge frame of Paul Harvey loomed ahead of them, rising from behind a fallen tree stump as if he had sprung from the very ground itself. He towered over them, huge hands bunched into fists which looked like ham hocks. Wreathed in mist, he looked like something from a nightmare and, when he took a step towards them, both boys screamed and ran. They darted in opposite directions, the football falling to the ground where it bounced three or four times. Forgotten. They ran and Harvey ran after them.

They crashed through bushes, ignoring the low branches of trees which clawed at their faces, oblivious to the thorns which scraped their flesh. They both burst into the open, running like frightened rabbits. Colin saw them, saw the terror in their eyes and he too, without knowing why, joined them in their crazed flight.

Harvey watched the children as they dashed across the clearing. He waited until they were out of sight, then, scanning the open ground ahead, anxiously emerged from the trees. He crossed to the Tesco bag and rummaged inside, finding several sandwiches, some of which he stuffed into his mouth immediately. The others he jammed into his pockets. He picked up the first thermos flask, flinging it to one side when he discovered it was empty. The second one, however, was full and he could hear the contents slopping about as he shook it. Pieces of half-eaten sandwich fell from his mouth as he tried to swallow as much as he could.

Beyond the clearing lay the rolling fields which marked the outskirts of Exham. Careful not to drop any of his food, he loped off.

In twenty minutes he had disappeared.

It was 10.05 a.m.

Four

The Exham police station was a two storey red brick building set on the perimeter of the town centre. A small construction, barely large enough to house the force of nine men and three women, Randall himself excluded.

At 2.56 p.m., the entire force was crowded into what normally passed as the rest room. There wasn't enough seats for everyone to sit down so one or two of the constables leant against the white-washed walls, their attention focused on the Inspector who stood beside a board at the far end of the room. There were several monochrome photos stuck to it and, resting precariously on the chair in front of him, Randall had a dozen or so more of them.

"Paul Harvey," he said, motioning towards the photos. "Get to know that face because we've got to find him and quick."

The Inspector lit up a cigarette and sucked hard on it.

"Exham's quite a big town," he said. "So there's plenty of places for the bastard to hide. That's if he's even got here yet." He paused. "Or even coming that is."

A murmur of sardonic laughter rippled around the room.

"I want a thorough search of the whole town. Any disused houses, places like that and ask people too. Take one of these with you." He held up the photo and waved it before him. "But just be careful with your questioning. If word gets around that Harvey is on his way back to Exham then we could have a panic on our hands. It's going to be difficult enough finding him without having people ringing up every five minutes wanting to know if we've caught him." He blew out a stream of smoke. "And if the local press ask any questions, tell them to sod off. This lot around here can't write about jumble sales without getting the facts wrong so we don't want stories about Harvey splashed all over the front page of the local rags." A lump of ash dropped

34

from the end of his fag and Randall ground it into the carpet.

"Any questions?" he asked.

"Did Harvey have any family, guv?" The question came from P C Charlton,

"Yes he did. If you can call it a family. The information's a bit vague but it seems he lived with his father up until three years ago when the old boy died. Nobody could find any trace of his mother though. The murders were committed after his father's death."

"How do you know he's coming back here?" It was Constable Reed this time.

Randall repeated his conversation with Stokes and the psychiatrist, expressing his own doubts about the killer returning to Exham. Reed seemed satisfied with the explanation.

There was an uneasy silence and Randall scanned the collection of faces before him

"Any more questions?" he asked.

There were none.

"Right," he glanced at his watch. "There's a couple of hours of daylight left. We may as well make a start."

The uniformed men and women got to their feet, filing past Randall and the board, each one picking up a couple of the black and white photos. The inspector himself waited until they had all departed and then made his way up to his office on the first floor. He lit up another cigarette and sat down at his desk, flicking on the desk lamp. Already the sky outside was overcast, heavy with rain, it hastened the onset of dusk and the watery sun which had tried to shine for most of the day had finally been swallowed up by the banks of thick cloud.

Randall held one of the photos before him, studying Harvey's chiselled features. There was a piercing intensity in those eyes which seemed to bore into the policeman even from the dull monochrome of the picture. Harvey carried two distinctive scars on his right cheek which Randall guessed were bottle scars. They were deep and the Inspector wondered how and when the escaped prisoner had sustained them. He sat back in his seat, tossing the photo onto his desk. The smoke from the cigarette drifted lazily in the air, curling into spirals around him. He closed his eyes.

The wind moaned despairingly at his window.

Five

He couldn't remember how long he'd been running, only that it had been daylight when he'd begun but now the countryside was wrapped in an almost impenetrable cloak of darkness. He wondered if he had been running in circles, chasing his own tracks round and round as he sought some vague escape route. The hills and fields all looked alike in the blackness. His legs felt like ton weights, burdened as they were by clods of mud. His heart thumped hard against his ribs and the breath rasped in his lungs as if it were being pumped by defective bellows.

He paused for a moment, atop a hill, and looked around. Below and behind him lights were shining. In some places the sodium glare of street lamps, in others the brighter glow which spilled from the windows of houses. If he had been able to calculate distance, Paul Harvey might well have guessed that he was about two miles from the centre of Exham. The town was little more than a collection of dim lights in the distance. Like a scattering of fire-flies. He panted loudly, his mouth filled with a bitter taste. He was cold, the first particles of frost now sparkling on the grass around him as the moon fumbled its way from behind a bank of thick cloud. Harvey looked up at the wreathed white orb and blinked. He put up a hand, as if trying to sweep it from the sky and, when this ploy didn't work he decided to keep on running.

The hill dipped away sharply before him and he slipped on the slick grass as he descended the slope. He lay still for what seemed like an eternity, ignoring the dampness which he felt seeping through his clothes. He merely lay on his back, gazing up at the moon, sucking in huge lungfuls of air. Every muscle in his body ached but he knew he couldn't stop. Not yet. Grunting painfully, he hauled himself upright and stumbled on. As he ran he could feel the sandwiches bumping in his coat pockets. He'd eaten one or two since taking them from the children earlier in the day and the flask was now half empty, its contents only luke-warm. He realized that he would have to eat as soon as he found shelter. Eat and drink. But what would he do when that source of food was exhausted? The question tumbled over in his mind as he ran. Yes, the food was important but so was shelter. The night was already digging icy fingers into him, he needed somewhere to hide. And not just from the elements. From *them*. *They* would be looking for him. He knew they would come soon but perhaps not for a few days. Even *they* would have difficulty finding him out here.

The moon escaped a bank of cloud once more and, in its cold white light, Harvey saw a group of buildings ahead of him.

He stopped dead in his tracks, even his breathing slowed for a moment.

Shelter.

He was sure it was a farm. There were. . .

He clenched his fists. Why was it so difficult to think?

One, two, three. There were perhaps more buildings,

arranged in a quadrangle, with a large open area at their centre – a farm house, a barn, a pig pen, another barn. He moved closer, his wide eyes ever watchful. There were no lights on in the house, perhaps whoever lived there was out, gone to bed maybe. Or perhaps *they* were in there, watching him. Just waiting for him to walk into their trap. He stood still, panting. No, there was no possible way they would find him here, they couldn't know he would find this place. Harvey smiled crookedly and licked his lips, advancing a few more yards. It was certainly quiet, there didn't appear to be anyone around.

He reached the broken fence which surrounded the entrance to the farmyard. It was rotten with damp, the wood black where at one time it had been regularly creosoted. The gate hung from one hinge, an invitation to enter which Harvey took. The yard itself was covered with weeds, some as high as his knees. He walked across to the overgrown hedge which surrounded the garden. There was no gate here, just a weather-beaten arch covered with the spidery remains of a rose plant. Harvey moved tentatively up the path towards the front door of the house, his eyes moving back and forth, waiting for the slightest sign of movement.

When nothing had happened by the time he'd reached the front door, he began to relax slightly. He went from window to window, trying to peer through the grime-encrusted panes in an effort to see what lay inside the house but he could make out no shapes in the gloom. He thought about breaking in. He could smash a window. With his tremendous strength he could even break down one of the doors.

But, what if someone came by? They would see that the farmhouse had been damaged. They would know something was wrong. He would be found. *They* would come for him again. He smiled crookedly again, pleased with his own cunning. He turned and scuttled back down the path, crossing the yard in the direction of the barn. This time, two huge wooden doors stood open and Harvey walked cautiously into the black maw which lay beyond.

The barn smelt of dampness and rotting straw. Bales of it were stacked in one corner and also up in the loft. A rickety looking ladder offered a route up to the loft and the big man put one huge foot on the first rung, testing it. It groaned under his weight but held and he began to climb.

There were about a dozen bales of damp straw in the loft, the wooden floor itself covered with a thin carpet of the fibrous stuff. The stench was almost overpowering but Harvey seemed not to notice it. The darkness inside the barn was broken only by the weak light provided by the moon, the beams creeping in through the numerous cracks in the roof. Here and there, large chunks of the slate roof were gone and Harvey shied away from these as if anxious to remain in the enveloping darkness. He settled down against a straw bale and rummaged through his coat pockets for the remaining sandwiches he'd taken from the three boys that morning. He ate ravenously, stuffing the food into his cavernous mouth until it was gone then he reached for the thermos flask. He took a large mouthful but the contents were cold and Harvey spat the liquid out angrily, hurling the empty receptacle away.

He felt tired, needed to sleep and something told him that this was the safest place to spend the night. Even *they* would not find him in this place, he was certain of that. He stretched out his arms and yawned.

Something cold touched his right hand and he almost shouted in surprise.

He spun round, crawling away but simultaneously trying to see what his hand had brushed against. He listened for sounds of movement but there was nothing, just the hammering of his heart against his ribs and, gradually, he regained his composure. The moon, spilling through one of the many cracks in the roof, fell onto the cold object and, eyes fixed on it, Harvey got slowly to his feet.

It was a sickle.

Stuck into a straw bale, it protruded from the rotted bundle, its rusty blade still wickedly sharp. Harvey reached out and grasped the handle, pulling the sickle clear. He hefted it before him, tracing the curve of the blade with his forefinger. He grinned and swung it through the air, the swish disturbing the solitude of the silent barn. Harvey chuckled throatily, excited by his discovery as a child would be with a new toy. He wiped the wooden handle on his trousers in an effort to remove the dampness which seemed to have penetrated the wood. His stomach rumbled noisily and, once more, he was reminded of the craving gnawing deep inside him. He gritted his teeth and swung the blade at a nearby bale of straw, watching as his powerful blow hacked off a large chunk of it. He rubbed his belly with his other hand and grunted irritably.

The big man turned the sickle over in his hand, his eyes drawn to the cutting edge. He rubbed it with his thumb, pressing just a little too hard and a small globule of blood welled from the cut. He cursed and sucked the wounded digit. He grunted. So sharp. His father used to have an open razor and occasionally, as a child, Harvey had watched the man shaving with it. It always remained in its wooden case at other times, on a small ledge in the bathroom. The strop hung next to it. Harvey remembered the strop well, its smell. That cloying odour of oiled leather which he had come to hate.

And he remembered how it felt.

A vision swam into his mind and it brought almost physical pain with it. The vision of a small child being

40

beaten by a raging drunken man who laughed as he brought the strop down across the boy's pale body.

Across Harvey's pale body.

He swung the sickle through the air, slicing off more of the straw bale. The memories of his childhood were burned indelibly in his mind like a brand. A festering sore which would always be there to torment him.

He was an only child. There had never been brothers or sisters for him to share his miserable world with. His mother, Elizabeth, had seen to that. Harvey had been a breech birth. The labour had been long and agonising and, after it, his mother had vowed never to go through that hell again. Eventually she came to deny Harvey's father intercourse so great was her fear of another pregnancy. But Richard Harvey was not a man to be refused. In the beginning he had sought solace in drink, turning in three years from a large muscular man to a dark, haunted, shadow. When he drank, it seemed a part of himself was sucked into the bottle.

Harvey could still remember the night he had come home, drunk as usual, but this time raving, demanding that Elizabeth allow him what he said was rightfully his. Young Harvey, then just four years old, had heard them rowing in the room next door. He had heard the words turn to shouts and finally to screams and at that point he had climbed out of bed and padded along the landing towards the sounds of the screams and curses. He had pushed the door open and stood watching as his father tried to hold Elizabeth down, forcing her legs apart with one rough hand. Attempting to guide his own puny erection towards her with the other and, when she screamed, he would butt her with his wrinkled forehead until finally, he broke her nose and they were writhing on the bed like bloodstained puppets. Their movements jerky and uncoordinated.

Young Harvey had turned to leave but his father had roared at him to stay. And he had obeyed. Quivering

41

helplessly, watching in bewilderment as his mother moved painfully beneath his father who finally achieved his climax and rolled off the bed, leaving Elizabeth almost unconscious. Richard Harvey had grabbed his son by the shoulders and rasped some whisky soaked words into his face, then he had dragged him to the bathroom and beaten him with the strop until the skin had risen in welts all the time screaming at him that *he* was to blame for what had gone wrong between his parents. If *he* had not been so difficult to bring into the world then things might have been different.

His mother had left the next day.

But for Paul Harvey, the nightmare had just begun. His father's drinking had grown worse. He would drag Paul out of bed at nights and shout and curse at him. Telling him that it was *his* fault Elizabeth had left.

And there was always the strop.

But, even as he grew older, Harvey was forced to put up with it because it became his accepted way of life. Abuse, both physical and verbal became commonplace for him and he stayed with his father in that tiny house in Exham where he had lived his life because he knew nothing else. He had no friends, no relatives he could go to and, somewhere, beneath that hatred which he felt, there was something akin to pity for this shrivelled-up piece of humanity which was his father. For perhaps Harvey had come to believe that he *was* responsible for the break-up of his parents' marriage. Maybe the punishment *was* deserved.

His father had died three years earlier and Harvey's world had collapsed around him. What remained of his self-control and esteem had died too.

Freed from the living hell in which he'd grown up, alone in a harsh world where there was no one he could turn to for solace, he had snapped.

He didn't know how to make friends. He was spurned by the people of Exham, and treated with ill-disguised scorn, for everyone had known what Richard Harvey had been like. Why should his son be any different?

Paul Harvey had taken a fearful revenge. He had killed two of them those three years ago. They had not spoken to him but he had sensed, behind their eyes, the disgust which they felt for him. And he had killed them. For that he had been locked away but now things were different. He was free once more and the people of Exham would be made to pay. *They* would not find him. Not until it was too late.

He smiled crookedly and hefted the sickle before him.

There was movement below him.

He froze, listening to the sound. A steady but cautious sound which wafted up from below on the reeking air. Harvey dropped to his knees and peered through the gaps in the beams, trying to see what was making the sound. Could *they* have found him already? He gripped the sickle tighter.

There was more movement.

He spun round, his heart pounding.

This time it was in the loft.

Harvey struggled to his feet, squinting in the gloom. He gripped the sickle tightly, ready to defend himself.

The moon was suddenly enveloped by clouds and the barn plunged into deep, impenetrable darkness. Harvey felt a strange mixture of fear and anger. He sucked in an anxious breath.

Something brushed against his leg and he shrieked.

He heard a rustling sound from behind him and turned, blind in the darkness, striking out helplessly with the sickle. Something else touched his leg and he jumped back, twisting his ankle in the gap between two beams. He fell forward and a foul smell filled his nostrils. Something rubbed against his face. Something wet.

At that precise moment, the moon broke free of the

enveloping cloud and cold light flooded the barn once more.

Harvey found himself staring into the cold black eyes of a rat. There was another one behind him. It had been their scratchings and scurryings which he'd heard. He got to his knees, grinning, watching the rat as it sat on its haunches nibbling at something it held between its forepaws. Harvey kept his eyes fixed on it, then, with a devastatingly quick movement, he brought the sickle down. Before the rat had a chance to move, the lethal point of the blade had pierced its back, the steel itself ripping through its tiny body until it thudded into the beam beneath. The rat squealed and Harvey grabbed it by the head, ignoring its feeble attempts to bite him. He pulled it free of the sickle, ignoring the blood which dripped onto his trousers. The big man held it in one huge hand, thick streamers of saliva dripping from his mouth. The rat felt so warm. So warm. The gnawing in his belly seemed to become a raging fire.

So warm. . .

He bit the creature's small head off with one powerful bite, chewed twice, feeling bones splinter and then swallowed. With his bare hands he tore the rat open, chewing on the raw flesh, tugging the matted fur away with his teeth, swallowing the jellied pulp of intestines. He even chewed on the tail before tossing the remains away. His stomach glowed, despite the fact that he thought, for a second, he was going to be sick. But, nevertheless, he wiped the rat's blood from his chin and, sickle in hand, went looking for another of the furry creatures. As he grabbed a second one he decided not to eat the head and lopped it off with the sickle. Blood spurted from the tiny arteries and Harvey giggled childishly for a second, watching the headless animal bucking spasmodically in his huge hand.

He ate that one too.

By the time the gnawing in his belly had been quelled,

44

he felt drowsy, ready for sleep. He was even more satisfied now that this place was safe. *They* would not find him here. Not yet anyway and even if they did, it didn't matter. He touched the blade of the sickle and smiled.

Besides, he had other things on his mind.

He went to sleep with the vicious blade held in one hand.

Six

Harold Pierce brushed away an imaginary speck of dust from the sleeve of his white overall and swallowed hard. He was staring at the floor of the lift as it descended, listening to the steady drone as it headed for the next floor. On the other side of the cramped enclosure stood Winston Greaves. He glanced across at Harold, his eyes straying to the disfiguring scar which covered half of his companion's face. He looked at the burn with the same hypnotic fascination as a child stares at something unusual and he felt all the more self-conscious because of this. He tried to look away but couldn't. Only when Harold raised his head to smile sheepishly did Greaves suddenly find the ability to avert his eyes.

Harold knew that the other porter was looking at him. Just as he had felt the stares and sometimes heard the jibes of others, so many times before. He could understand their fascination, even revulsion, with his own disfigurement but their prolonged stares nevertheless still made him feel awkward.

For his own part, Greaves had only succeeded by a

monumental effort of will from openly expressing his horror at the sight of Harold's face. He told himself that, in time, he would come to accept it but, at the moment, he still found his attention drawn to the red and black mess. His eyes fastened like magnets to the vision of tissue destruction. And yet, he had been a hospital porter for over fifteen years, he had seen many appalling sights during his working life. The road crash victims (one of whom, he remembered, had been brought in DOA after taking a dive through his windscreen – when Greaves and another man had lifted the body from the gurney on which it lay, the head had dropped off, so bad were the lacerations to the man's neck), the injured children, other burn victims, casualties of modern day living such as the victims of muggings. The youth who had staggered into casualty trying to push his intestines back through a knife wound which he'd sustained in a gang fight. The woman who had been so badly beaten by her husband that, not only had her skull been fractured, part of her brain had been exposed. The child with the severed hand, a legacy of playing near farm machinery. The old lady with a cut on her hip which had been left unattended for so long there were actually maggots writhing in the wound.

The list was endless.

Small wonder then that Greaves's black, wiry hair was shot through with streaks of grey. They looked all the more incongruous against his black skin. He was a small man with large forearms and huge hands which seemed quite disproportionate to the size of his body. He was a hard worker and good at his job which was probably the reason, he thought, why he'd been saddled with the task of showing Harold the ropes.

For the first week, until he became accustomed to hospital procedure and proficient in his duties, Harold was to be under almost constant supervision by

Greaves. Now he looked across at his black companion and smiled again, conscious of his scar but trying not to hide it. Greaves smiled back at him and it reminded Harold of a piano keyboard. The black man's teeth were dazzling. It looked as if someone had stuck several lumps of porcelain into his mouth. His eyes however, were rheumy and bloodshot but nevertheless there was a warmth in that smile and in those sad eyes which Harold responded to.

He had arrived at Fairvale Hospital just the day before. Phil Coot had driven him there from the asylum and helped him unpack his meagre belongings, moving them into the small hut-like dwelling which was to be his new home. The small building stood close by the perimeter fence which surrounded the hospital grounds, about 400 yards from the central block, sheltered by clumps of beech and elder.

Fairvale itself consisted of three main buildings. The central block contained most of the twelve wards and rose more than eighty feet into the air, each storey bore an A and B ward, both able to maintain over sixty patients. The children's wing was attached to the ground floor part of the hospital and connected to it by a long corridor, thus it was effectively classified as a thirteenth ward. Also separate from the main building was an occupational therapy unit where a small but dedicated staff helped the older patients, and those recovering from debilitating illnesses, to regain some of the basic skills which they had possessed before being admitted. It was here that the previously simple task of making a cup of tea now seemed like the twelfth labour of Hercules. Also attached to this wing was a small gymnasium where patients with heart complaints were encouraged to undergo mild exercise and those with broken legs or arms underwent rigorous tests to regain the proper use of their damaged limbs. Also separate from the main building, accessible only by a brief walk

47

across the car park, were the red brick buildings of the nurses' quarters.

Fairvale, standing as it did about a mile from the centre of Exham, served an area of about thirty square miles. It was the only hospital within that radius to offer emergency care and its turnover of patients was large. It also boasted a dazzling array of medical paraphernalia, including a cancer scanner and many other modern devices. Its X-Ray, EEG, ECG, and Pathology departments ensured that the turnover of out-patients matched, if not exceeded, the number of those confined. But the Pathology department which the out-patients saw was the one which took blood samples and urine samples. The real work of Fairvale's team of pathologists took place in the basement of the main building. Here, in four separate labs, each containing three stainless steel slabs and a work-top, bodies were examined and dissected. Pieces of tissue were pored over. Moles, growths, even skin-tags were examined and put through the same rigorous tests. There were no secrets to be kept in the pathology labs, detailed notes were made on each specimen be it a full scale post-mortem or the examination of a lump of benign cells. The filing cabinets which held this information stretched the full length of two of the large rooms. Each one was more than twenty feet wide, double that in length. Inside the labs, cold white light poured down from the banks of fluorescents set into the ceilings but, outside, in the wide corridor which led from the lift to the labs, it seemed to be forbiddingly dark. A perpetual twilight of dim lights which reflected a dull yellow glow off the polished floor and walls.

Harold looked up as the lift came to a halt and saw that the line of numbers and letters above the lift entrance were now dark. Just the "B" flared in the gloom. Winston Greaves ushered him out into the corridor which led towards the pathology labs and

Harold felt a curious chill run through him. He shivered.

"It's always cold down here," Greaves told him. "The labs are kept at fifty-five degrees. Otherwise, things start to smell." He smiled, his teeth looking yellow in the dim light.

Harold nodded and walked along beside him, his skin rising into goose-pimples as they neared the door of the nearest lab. A sign greeted them defiantly:

No Entry By Unauthorised Staff

"That includes you at the moment," said Greaves, smiling at Harold. He told him to wait then he himself knocked and, after a moment or two, heard a voice telling him to enter which he duly did, closing the door behind him. Harold was left alone. He stood still for long moments, wrinkling his nose at the odour which came from inside the lab. It wasn't the familiar antiseptic smell to which he'd become accustomed, it was something more pungent, more unpleasant. It was in fact, formaldehyde. He dug his hands into the pockets of his overall and began pacing up and down before the door, looking around him. The labs seemed to be silent, if anyone was working inside there, they certainly weren't making any noise. Harold walked past the door of first one then two. He came to a bend in the corridor.

Straight ahead of him, another twenty feet further down a shorter corridor, was a plain wooden door. Harold advanced towards it and stood silently before the entry way. There were no signs on this door telling him to keep out and, as he stood there, he could hear no sound coming from inside. Except. . .

He took a step closer.

There was a low rumbling sound coming from inside the room, punctuated every now and then by what sounded like extremely loud asthmatic breathing.

He put his hand on the knob and turned it.

49

The door was unlocked and Harold walked inside.

The heat hit him in a palpable wave and he recoiled. For long seconds he struggled to adjust to his new surroundings; then, as he looked around he saw just how large the room really was. It must have been a good forty feet square, the ceiling rising high above him. The paintwork which had once been white, was dirty and blackened in places and, directly ahead of him, over a bare floor, lay a huge metal boiler. A chimney thrust up from it, disappearing through the ceiling. It was the boiler that was rumbling but now Harold noticed another sound. A loud humming and, turning to his left he saw what he took to be a generator. It was covered by a profusion of dials, switches and gauges but Harold's attention was quickly diverted away from the generator back to the boiler and its adjacent furnace. The heavy iron door was firmly closed and the metal looked rusty. The wall above it was blackened and scorched and there was a faint odour of burning material in the air. Harold shuddered, felt his hands beginning to shake, his body trembling slightly. He sucked in a slow breath which rattled in his throat and when he tried to swallow he found it difficult.

There were half a dozen trolleys in one corner of the room, each piled high with linen and as Harold took a step closer towards the strange bundles he coughed at the vile stench which emanated from them. He recognized them as sheets; some soiled with excrement, some stained dark with dried blood or vomit.

A bead of perspiration formed on his forehead and he wiped it away with a shaking hand as he moved closer towards the door of the furnace, the heat growing more powerful as he did so. He saw a pair of thick gloves lying on a ledge close to the tightly sealed door, beside them a set of long tongs and a wrench. Coal was piled in countless buckets nearby, some of it having spilled over onto the floor, its black dust swirling in the hot air.

Harold was trembling uncontrollably now and, as he strained his ears, he could actually hear the sound of the roaring flames from within.

A nightmare vision of his mother flashed into his mind. She was on fire, the skin peeling from her face and arms as the flames devoured her and she was holding something in those blazing arms. It was Harold's baby brother. The child was little more than a ball of flame, one stubby, blackened arm reaching out from the searing fire-ball which consumed it.

Harold closed his eyes tight, trying to force the image from his mind. He took a step back, away from the furnace.

"Harold."

He almost shouted aloud when he heard the voice behind him. He spun round, his face flushed, his breath coming in short gasps.

Winston Greaves stood in the doorway looking at him.

"Are you all right?" he asked, seeing his companion's obvious distress.

Harold nodded.

"I'm sorry," he said. "I wandered off. I found this room."

Greaves nodded.

"The furnace," he said. "The boiler heats some parts of the hospital and that," he motioned to the generator, "that's for auxiliary power, in case we get any power failures or anything, the system is wired so that the emergency generator switches on straight away."

"What about those?" said Harold, motioning to the piles of reeking laundry.

"Some of it is kept here until the laundry department can take it away," Greaves told him. "Some of it is so bad, we just have to burn it." The black man turned

51

and motioned Harold out of the room, closing the door behind him. They made their way back down the corridor, back to the lift. "I would have showed you that room anyway," said Greaves. "That was what I came down here for in the first place. You and I have got some work to do in there this afternoon."

Harold swallowed hard but didn't speak. He gently, almost unconciously, touched the scarred side of his face and remembered the awful cloying heat inside the furnace room, the terrifying vision of his mother and brother flashing briefly into his mind once more. Greaves had told him they had work to do in there. What sort of work? His mind was spinning.

As they waited for the lift to descend, Harold felt the perspiration clinging to his back.

For some unfathomable reason he felt terribly afraid.

For the remainder of that first morning, Greaves took Harold on a conducted tour of the hospital, telling him what his duties would be, showing him where things were kept, introducing him to other members of staff all but a couple of whom managed to disguise their revulsion at the sight of Harold's scarred face. Greaves chattered good-naturedly about all sorts of things, the weather, hospital work, football, politics, and Harold listened to him. Or at least he gave the impression that he was listening. His mind was elsewhere, more specifically on just what he and Greaves had to do in the furnace room that coming afternoon.

The two of them went along to the hospital canteen at about one fifteen and ate lunch. Harold managed a couple of sausages but merely prodded the rest of his dinner with his knife and fork. Greaves, on the other hand, between mouthfuls of fish and chips continued to babble happily to his new companion. But, gradually, the extent of Harold's worry filtered through to the other porter.

"What's wrong, Harold?" he asked, sipping at a large mug of tea.

Harold shrugged and looked around him. The canteen was full of people, nurses, porters, doctors, all sitting around tables eating and chatting. The steady drone of conversation reminded him of the hum of the generator.

"Is it about the furnace?" Greaves asked, cautiously.

"I'm frightened of fire," said Harold, flatly.

Greaves studied his companion over the lip of his mug.

"I'm sorry to ask but. . ." He struggled to find the words. "Your face. Was that . . . is it a burn?"

Harold nodded.

"I've had it since I was fourteen," he said but didn't continue. The rest was knowledge for him alone. He tried to smile and, indeed, his tone lightened somewhat. "I suppose I'll get over my fear sooner or later."

Greaves nodded, benignly and took another hefty swallow of tea. The two men sat and talked and, this time Harold found himself contributing to the conversation instead of merely acting as listener. The images of the morning began to recede somewhat. He relaxed, telling himself that he was tense. After all, it was his first day at work. His first *ever* day at work. Greaves asked him, coyly, about the asylum but Harold answered his questions candidly not wishing to hide anything. He felt no shame about having spent over thirty-five years in a mental home. No, his shame was reserved for that particular subject which Greaves had touched on briefly just moments before. Fortunately the coloured porter didn't ask how Harold had come to be in a mental home since he was fourteen and he himself certainly didn't volunteer the information.

Greaves finally finished his meal and pushed the plate away from him, downing what was left in his mug as well. He patted his stomach appreciatively and smiled at Harold who returned the gesture with more assurance. He looked around him and saw a group of nurses sitting nearby. They were all in their early twenties, pretty girls tending towards plumpness as is the habit of their profession. Harold found himself captivated. One of them, the youngest of the group, her brown hair tucked up beneath her white cap, noticed his obvious interest and smiled at him. Harold smiled, lowering his gaze, one hand reaching up to cover the scarred side of his face in a gesture which had become all too familiar for him. He coloured and turn back to face Greaves who was smiling.

"Are you married?" Harold asked him.

"Yes," his colleague told him.

"What's your wife's name?"

"Linda. We've been married for twenty years."

Harold nodded. He wondered what it was like to be married. What was it like to have someone who cared for you, who needed you? To be wanted, loved – it must be a wonderful feeling. He had loved his mother but it had been so long ago he'd forgotten what the emotion felt like. All that was left inside him now was a hole. A kind of emotional dustbin filled only with guilt and want. He needed someone but was equally resigned to the fact that he would end his life alone, dying with only his memories and his shame for company. He swallowed hard.

Greaves got to his feet and tapped the table top.

"Well, we'd better get on," he said. "I think it's about time you and I did some work."

Harold nodded and followed his companion out of the canteen, leaving the sounds of joyful chatter behind, moving out once more into the hushed corridors of the hospital.

He worked hard that afternoon. On the third floor landing between Wards 3A and 3B, Harold swept and polished the lino until it shone. He muttered to himself when visitors walked over his handiwork in their muddy shoes, for it was raining outside, but no sooner had they passed than he was scrubbing away again.

It was approaching 3.15 p.m. when Winston Greaves arrived. Harold stopped what he was doing, put the cleaning materials away neatly in the cupboard indicated by Greaves then followed his coloured companion into the lift. The senior porter punched a button and the car began its descent towards the basement.

Harold felt a chill filling him, an unexplainable foreboding which seemed to intensify as they drew nearer the basement.

The lift bumped to a halt and the doors slid open. Both men walked out, immediately assailed by the cold. They walked to the end of the corridor to one of the labs, outside which stood a gurney. Whatever was on the trolley was hidden beneath a white plastic sheet. Hanging from one corner were two aprons. Greaves handed one to Harold and told him to put it on which he did, repeating the procedure with a pair of thin rubber gloves that the porter handed him. Suitably decked out for their task, the two men headed left, pushing the gurney towards the room which housed the furnace.

As he opened the door, Harold once again felt the heat, smelled the cloying stench of the coal dust. He saw the black particles swirling in the warm air. The piles of filthy linen had been disturbed, one or two of them removed.

"We'll have to burn what's left as well," said Greaves, indicating the reeking material. He pushed the trolley close to the furnace and, as Harold watched, he slipped on the pair of thick gloves which lay on the ledge before the rumbling boiler, pulling them over his rubber ones. That done, he reached for the wrench and used it to knock the latch on the furnace door up. Immediately the rusty iron door swung open. A blast of searing air swept out, causing the men to gasp for breath. Harold stood transfixed, gazing into the blazing maw. White and yellow flames danced frenziedly inside the furnace which yawned open like the mouth of a dragon. Like the entrance to hell, thought Harold.

"Fetch those sheets," said Greaves. "We'll do those first."

Harold paused before the roaring flames, seemingly hypnotized by the patterns they weaved as they fluttered before him. A low roar issued forth from the blazing hole. Even standing six feet away, the heat stung him and he took a step back.

"Harold," said Greaves, more forcefully. "The sheets."

He seemed to come out of his trance, nodded and crossed to the corner of the room, gathering up as many of the soiled sheets as he could carry. The stench was appalling and his head swam. A piece of rotted excrement squashed against his apron and he winced, trying to hold his breath as he struggled back to the waiting furnace. Greaves took them from him and began pushing them into the flames on the end of a large poker. The ferocity of the fire hardly diminished and even sheets damp with urine and blood were quickly engulfed by the furious fire. Dark smoke billowed momentarily from the gaping mouth of the furnace, bringing with it acrid fumes which made both men cough.

"I hate this job," gasped Greaves, pushing more of the filthy material into the fire.

Harold returned with the last of the faecal linen and together they shoved it into the furnace, watching as it was consumed.

"We'll clean those trolleys up later," said Greaves, motioning to the reeking gurneys in the corner of the room.

Harold nodded blankly, his eyes now turning to the trolley before them and its blanketed offerings. He watched as Greaves took hold of the blanket and pulled it free, exposing what lay beneath.

Harold moaned aloud and stepped back, eyes rivetted to the trolley. His one good eye bulged in its socket, the glass one regarded all proceedings impassively. He clenched his teeth together, felt the hot bile gushing up from his stomach, fought to control the spasms which racked his insides. The veins at either temple throbbed wildly and his body shook.

The foetus was in a receiver, dark liquid puddled around it. It was a little over six inches long, its head bulbous, its eyes black and sightless. It had been cleaned up a little after coming from pathology but not enough to disguise the damage done to it. The umbilicus was little more than a purple knot, gouts of thick yellowish fluid mingling with the blood that oozed from it. Its tiny mouth was open. There was more blood around the head which looked soft, the fontanelles not having sealed yet. The entire organism looked jellied, shrunken, threatening to dissolve when touched.

Harold backed off another step watched by Greaves. "Not a pretty sight is it?" he said, apparently unperturbed. But then why should he be? He'd done this sort of thing often enough before. Harold gagged, put both hands on the trolley to steady himself and stared down at the foetus, his heart thudding madly against his ribs. He watched as Greaves picked up a pair of forceps, large stainless steel ones, from the trolley beside the receiver. Then, he picked the occupant of the tray up by the head, having to readjust his grip when the body nearly fell out. A foul-smelling mixture of blood, pus and chemicals dripped from the tiny body and Greaves wrinkled his nose slightly. Then, almost with disgust, he cast the foetus into the furnace. Immediately the body was consumed and there were a series of loud pops and hisses as the tiny shape was devoured by the flames.

Harold watched, mesmerized.

"Gordon," he whispered, watching the tiny foetus disappear, reduced in seconds to ashes.

He thought of his brother.

"Gordon," he whimpered again.

But, this time there was no screaming. His mother didn't dash in and try to drag the small creature from the roaring inferno. There was nothing this time. Just the terrible feeling inside himself. A cold shiver, as if someone had gently run a carving knife into his genitals and torn it upward to his breastbone. He felt as if he'd been gutted.

Greaves pushed the furnace door shut and hammered the latch back into place with the wrench then he turned to look at Harold who was still swaying uncertainly. For a moment, the senior porter thought his companion was going to faint.

"Are you all right?" he said.

Harold gripped the edge of the gurney and nodded almost imperceptibly.

"You'll get used to it," Greaves told him, trying to inject some compassion into his voice.

Harold was confused. He looked imploringly at Greaves as if wanting him to elaborate on the statement.

"That's how all the abortions are disposed of," the coloured porter told him. "We get through above five a month."

"Will I have to do this?" said Harold.

"Eventually."

The two of them stood there for long moments, neither one speaking, only the roaring of the flames from inside the furnace and the persistent hum of the generator interrupting the silence.

Harold drew a shaking hand through his hair. His face was bathed in perspiration and he was finding it

58

difficult to swallow, as if the furnace had sucked in all the air from the room. He was suddenly anxious to be out of this place, back into the chill of the corridors. Away from the furnace. Away from the dragon's mouth that devoured children. Away from the memories. But he knew that they were one thing that would always pursue him. No matter where he ran or hid they would always find him because they were always inside him and now, as he thought about that tiny body being incinerated, his mind flashed back to another body burning, to another time. To 1946. To Gordon.

He turned and blundered out of the room, leaning against the wall, panting as he waited for Greaves to join him. The black man closed the door behind them, sealing off the sounds of the generator and the furnace.

He touched Harold gently on the shoulder, urging him to follow.

"Come on," he said, softly and Harold walked beside him, brushing one solitary tear from the corner of his eye.

And Greaves's words echoed in his mind:

"You'll get used to it."

Seven

One of the barn doors creaked loudly in the wind and the high pitched whine made Paul Harvey sit up. He gripped the sickle tightly in his hand, trying to control his breathing. The creak came once more and he realized that it was the door. Exhaling wearily, he lay down on the bed of straw again, gazing up through the hole in the roof immediately above him. Clouds skudded past, buffeted by the wind, passing swiftly before the moon until it resembled some kind of celestial stroboscope. The unrelenting glare reminded Harvey of an unshaded light bulb.

There are many things which stick in the memory, some of them inconsequential, and one of the things which now came to the big man's mind was the fact that, in the house where he grew up, not one single light possessed a shade. The rooms downstairs were bright but those upstairs were lit by dim sixty watt bulbs. His own bedroom included. He could still see it in his mind's eye. The unshaded bulb, the large bed with its rusty legs, the dusty floorboards. After his mother had left, the house had become steadily filthy. His father was never there to clean it and, even when he was, the dirt and grime didn't seem to bother him. During summer, the kitchen became a playground for all kinds of insects. Flies would feast on the congealed grease and rotting food which coated plates and saucepans. They were tossed, unwashed, into the chipped sink. Perhaps once a week, Harvey's father would force him to wash them and Harvey would obey because he feared his father. Fear was a stronger emotion even than hatred, over the years Harvey had come to learn that much. He had, even as a teenager, been a big lad, powerfully built. It would have been relatively easy to snap his father's frail neck with one strong hand. But, the spectre of fear, ingrained within him for so long, always seemed to be there, preventing him from harming his father who was, after all, the only person he had to share his worthless existence with. He cooked for him, he cleaned as best he could. Sometimes forced to launder sheets which his drunken father had fouled the night before. Harvey had done it all because, along with the fear was a perverted sense of duty. He owed this shrunken, sadistic little bastard his existence and that was what hurt most of all.

He wondered what it would have been like if he had left home with his mother. Would it have been different? Perhaps there wouldn't have been the beatings and the abuse but words sometimes hurt more than actions and his mother did not easily let him forget the pain she had gone through to give him life.

Harvey pressed both his hands to his temples as if the thoughts hurt him. He screwed his eyes up until white stars danced behind the lids. The knot of muscles at the side of his jaw throbbed angrily and he kept his teeth clenched until his head began to ache. Only then did the images begin to recede somewhat. He sat up rubbing his face with both huge hands, head bowed. And he remained in that position for some time.

The wind howled around the barn.

Eight

Harold watched the milk bubbling in the battered pan and listened to the powerful wind outside. At times, the gusts grew to such awesome proportions it seemed they would demolish the little hut. Built only of wood, it shook with each fresh onslaught of the gale.

The solitary dwelling was about 300 yards from the main building, which was itself visible through the window in the other room. There were no windows in the kitchen and Harold now stood in the yellowish light provided by an unshaded fifty watt bulb which dangled from the ceiling by a worn flex. The kitchen contained a hotplate, an old enamel sink and some cupboards which had been hastily nailed to the wooden wall at some time. The rusted heads of the nails were still visible in places. The tiny room was less than twelve feet square and it smelt of damp. There was mould on the west wall but at least, thought Harold, the place didn't leak. It had been cleaned up somewhat before his arrival but still showed the signs that it had been uninhabited for more than six years. There was a deep layer of dust and grime on nearly everything and Harold decided that he must clean the place up on his day off. It was, after all, to be his home from this point onwards.

He switched off the gas and removed the saucepan of milk, carefully pouring the contents into a mug which stood nearby. He then dropped the pan into the sink where it landed with a clang. Harold shuffled into the other room. It was slightly larger than the kitchen, boasting a single bed, a table and two battered chairs and more cupboards which looked as if they'd been assembled by a group of unenthusiastic woodwork students. The room was heated by a parafin stove which stood close to the bed and Harold warmed himself beside it before crossing to the window and peering out. He scraped away some of the accumulated muck from the window pane and squinted through the darkness. The lights of the hospital blazed in the night.

Harold lowered his head, the memory of what he'd seen that afternoon suddenly filling his mind. He turned his back on the hospital as if, by doing so, he would be able to blot out the visions of what he'd witnessed there earlier. He crossed to the bed and sat on the edge of it, sipping at the milk. It was hot. It burned.

He exhaled deeply, the thought of that tiny foetus consumed by the hungry furnace causing him to shudder. My God, that sight brought so many unwanted memories with it. He had thought that when he took this job it might help him to forget or at least come to terms with what had happened all those years ago. But now he had learned that it was to be his duty to burn things. Things. Were they human? he asked himself. The one in the tray had looked like something from Outer Space but it was still human. It was still a child. They were asking him to burn children. Asking him to relive his nightmare day in, day out.

Asking him to burn Gordon, to burn his brother, over and over again.

Harold walked slowly towards the door of the furnace room. Even ten feet away he could hear the steady hum of the generator. His footsteps echoed in the dimly lit corridor and his breath formed small vapour clouds in the heavy air. For some reason it seemed colder in the basement than usual. Behind him, the pathology lab doors were closed, retaining their secrets. Harold put his hand on the furnace room door and pushed it open. He stepped inside, immediately recoiling from the all too familiar smell of soiled linen. He walked across to the furnace itself, the generator humming noisily nearby. He could hear the muffled roar of the flames as he picked up the thick gloves which lay on the ledge before the furnace door. He pulled them on then reached for the wrench, giving the lock a hefty whack.

It sprang open.

Flames, white and orange, danced madly before him and Harold felt their searing heat on his face. The air seemed to be sucked into the blazing hole and he struggled to get his breath. He took a step back, wincing at the intensity of the heat.

The door behind him swung shut with a loud bang and Harold spun round, heart thumping hard against his ribs. For long seconds he watched the door, expecting someone to walk in – Winston Greaves or maybe one of the other porters. The door remained firmly closed. Harold turned slowly back to look into the roaring furnace. As he stared into the raging inferno his one good eye began to pick out shapes in the blazing hell which was the furnace. Much as children watch the dancing flames of a coal fire. A vision slowly formed before Harold.

He wanted to move away but it was as if his feet were nailed to the ground and, all he could do was stare into the fire.

A single tear blossomed in the corner of his eye and rolled down his cheek. They were in there, the charred remnants of countless children like the one he had seen Greaves burn.

He had felt so powerless as he had watched the tiny body consumed. Just as he had felt powerless that night in 1946 when he had seen his mother and Gordon burned to death in the fire.

The fire which *he* had started.

The leaping flames seemed to alter shape, reform until Harold found himself looking into the face of his dead brother and, all at once, he realized that he must pluck Gordon from the flames.

He plunged both hands into the firebox.

Mind shattering pain enveloped his arms, the gloves which he wore disintegrating in seconds as the flames devoured them. Harold found that he could not move and, as the agonizing pain began to spread through his entire body he actually saw the flesh of his arms turning black, huge blisters growing and bursting like flowering plants which spilled their fluid in thick gouts. Bone showed white through the charred stumps and finally Harold found the breath to scream.

He was still screaming when he woke up, propelled from the dream with a force he could almost feel. For long seconds he continued to scream but then, as he realized where he was, he quietened down and his screams turned first to whimpers and then to tears.

Curling up beneath the covers he sobbed uncontrollably.

Nine

Judith Myers stood before the bedroom mirror and studied her reflection in the glass. She ran a hand over the small, almost imperceptible bulge below her sternum then turned sideways for a better view. She touched the shape gently, allowing her eyes to stray momentarily from it, studying the rest of her naked body. Her hair was still wet from the shower she'd just taken and it hung in dark dripping strands, the droplets of water making brief circlets on the beige carpet. Her make-up had been washed off but her face was all the more striking for that. It seemed to glow in the half-light cast by the bedside lamp, her cheeks seeming sunken and hollow in the twilight. She ran an appraising eye over the rest of her body – the taut breasts, the unwanted bulge of her belly, the dark nest of pubic hair at its base. She'd put on some weight around her bottom and that fact made her even more irritable. Finally, after taking one last look at her slightly distended stomach, she turned away from the mirror and reached for the large fluffy towel which lay on the bottom of the large double bed. She began to dry her hair.

"You still intend to go through with it then?" said Andy Parker. He was stretched out beneath the sheets, watching her. He took a last drag on his cigarette and ground it out in the ash-tray on the bedside table.

"I thought I asked you not to smoke up here," said Judith, still rubbing frenziedly at her hair.

"Don't evade the question," he said.

She paused for a second and looked at him.

"Yes, I am still going through with it."

Parker held her gaze for a moment then he shook his head resignedly.

"Look, Andy," she said, irritably. "We've been over

65

this time and time again. Now I don't want to keep talking about it."

"I wonder sometimes if you've given it enough thought," he said.

"Christ," she threw the towel down. "I've done nothing *but* think about it ever since I found out I was pregnant." There was a long silence then Judith retrieved the towel and set about drying her hair once more. Her tone was more subdued when she spoke again. "Look, I can understand the way *you* feel, but try and understand how *I* feel. A baby at this time just wouldn't be. . ." She struggled to find the word.

"Convenient?" said Parker.

She nodded.

"I don't know why you're so worried, Judith. I mean, if it's the money that's bothering you, my wage is plenty for the two of us. We don't *need* the money you bring in."

"The money's got nothing to do with it and you know that," she told him, folding the towel. She shook her head, her shoulder-length hair flowing tantalizingly as she got up and crossed to the linen basket in the corner of the bedroom. He watched her, still naked, as she tossed the towel in amongst the other dirty washing. She stooped to pick up one of his handkerchiefs which was lying nearby. She glanced at it, saw that it was clean so proceeded to fold it neatly and push it into the drawer with the others. She was a stickler for neatness, everything must be in its place. It was one of the many little things which Parker had noticed about her during their six years together. She was twenty-five, eight years younger than him and they had shared each other's lives for the past six years, four of which they had spent living together in a house on the edge of Exham town centre. There had never been any mention of marriage, in truth it was an unspoken fact that they would probably live out their days together without the intrusion of matrimony. It was something which suited them both. But the subject of children was another matter. At thirty-three, Parker was keen, almost anxious, to be a father. He had everything else he wanted. He owned a highly successful restaurant in Exham, he had gone through his hell-raising days and enjoyed every minute of it but now he was ready to set the seal on his success, their relationship and his own newly-found passivity by drawing the cosy cocoon of a family around himself.

Judith, apparently, had other ideas. She worked for one of Exham's biggest firms as a graphic designer and she took her job very seriously. She was in with the chance of promotion, the opportunity to take charge of her own department and she certainly didn't want to jeopardize the impending promotion by the unwelcome intrusion of a child.

She crossed to the dressing table and picked up a brush, sitting before the mirror to sweep the bristles through her hair. She glanced at Parker's reflection as she removed the knots and tangles from her hair, brushing away enthusiastically until it sprang up to its usual lustrous fullness. She dug fingers into it then crossed to the bed and slid in beside him.

"Is this bloody promotion *so* important?" Parker demanded, scarcely concealing his annoyance.

"To me it is," she told him. "I want that department."

"You could go back after you'd had the baby," he suggested.

She snorted.

"And start at the bottom again? No thanks."

She put one hand on his chest, curling the thick hair with her index finger, tracing the outline of his muscles with her long nail, allowing it to glide down towards his navel. The muscles of his stomach tightened slightly as she drew patterns across his belly, working lower until she was at the forest of his pubic hair. The head of his erection nudged against the probing digit and she enveloped it with her whole hand, feeling its hardness. With her free hand, she reached up and touched his face, curious at his apparent lack of response.

"You realize the moral implications of what you intend to do?" he asked, unexpectedly.

She looked puzzled.

"You're over four months pregnant."

She released his penis immediately, rolling onto her back. Judith let out a long, angry breath then propped herself up on one elbow, glaring at him. "You never give up do you?" she said. Her voice took on a hard edge. "Just drop it, Andy. Once and for all. Drop it."

"Judith, it's a human life," he insisted.

"For God's sake, shut up about the bloody child." She sat up, looking down at him. "For the last time, I'm having the abortion. Don't start this philosophical crap about taking a human life because, apart from being about the lowest trick you've pulled so far to try and stop me, it doesn't make the slightest bit of difference to the way I feel. Nothing you can say or do will make me change my mind." Her face was flushed with anger and it was reflected in her voice. "I don't *need* this baby. I don't *want* this baby."

She suddenly sucked in a tortured breath as a violent stab of pain lanced through her.

"Oh God," she gasped and rolled onto her back again.

Parker threw back the sheets, seeing that her hands had gone to her belly, were pressing the slight distension. She winced again. It felt as if someone were jabbing her stomach wall with a red hot knife, just below the navel. She inhaled deeply and the movement brought a renewed wave of pain. As a child she had been bitten by the family cat once, and the pain which she now felt inside her abdomen reminded her of that pain.

She allowed her hands to slide away from her belly and both she and Parker watched as the flesh rose slightly, first above the navel and then to one side of it. Her stomach undulated slowly for long seconds then was still. The pain ceased as abruptly as it had come.

She lay still for what seemed like an eternity, afraid to move in case the agonizing torment returned. Her forehead was greasy with perspiration and her breath came in shallow gasps. Eventually she touched her stomach. There was no discomfort.

"What the hell happened?" Parker asked, anxiously.

Judith smiled thinly, her face pale.

"I don't know. I think it must have been a muscle spasm," she said. But, even as she spoke, she looked down at her stomach, remembering the undulations.

She turned, trembling, to face Parker, who took her in his arms.

It was a long time before either of them slept.

Ten

Randall got out of the car and walked across the pavement towards the front of the cinema. A few red letters still hung from the track which ran around its canopy, others had been displaced long ago by the wind. He looked up and read:

TH P LA E

"I can remember when the Palace used to be the best cinema in Exham," P C Higgins told him, scanning the front of the building.

"Well, it's been empty for two years," said Randall. "It's as good a place as any to hide."

"You don't really think he'd pick somewhere in the middle of town do you, guv?" asked the constable.

"I doubt it," Randall confessed, "but we'd better check it anyway." He pulled a large key from his jacket pocket, one which they'd picked up from the owner of the building earlier that morning. He owned both The Palace and The Gaumont further up the road and had asked why the police should be showing so much interest in the deserted cinema. Randall had told him there'd been a spate of arson recently and they wanted to check the building out in case the fire-raiser should strike there next. The owner had not asked any more questions.

"You stop in the car," Randall told his driver. "Just in case anything comes over on the two-way."

Higgins hesitated for a moment.

"I'll be OK," the Inspector reassured him. He waited until the constable had retreated to the car then inserted the key in one of the padlocks which hung from the four sets of double doors. The Inspector threw his weight against the doors and they swung open reluctantly. He coughed at the smell of damp and decay inside.

A door to his left led into the stalls, to his right, a staircase which would take him up to the circle. He checked the stalls, the beam of his torch scarcely able to penetrate the gloom. Dust, at least a couple of inches thick, swirled up and around him, the particles drifting lazily in the glow of the torch.

The circle was worse.

Seats had been torn up and piled at both sides of the balcony and Randall had to put a handkerchief across his face so foul was the odour of decay. He checked everywhere, including the projection box, but all he found up there were a couple of yellowed copies of *Men*

Only. He glanced through one, smiling thinly to himself then dropped it back into the dustbin. Rusted spool cans lay discarded on the stone floor.

Satisfied that the cinema was, indeed, deserted, Randall made his way back outside and across to the waiting Panda car.

"Not a bloody trace," he said, dropping the torch on the parcel shelf.

It had been the same story all day, not just in the places where Randall had searched but from the other members of the force. The Inspector had ordered hourly reports from each car but, as yet, with the time now approaching noon, no sign had been found of Harvey. There was no hint that he was anywhere near, let alone in, Exham. As Higgins moved the Panda gently out into traffic, Randall looked at the people who thronged the streets of the town. Some were shopping, some stood talking. There were children with their mothers, youngsters standing in groups smoking. The Inspector exhaled deeply wondering what any of them would think or say if they knew that there was a psychopath heading for their quiet little town. If that fact was correct of course. Randall hated trusting other people and he felt especially reluctant to trust the opinions of a prison psychiatrist and a jumped-up bastard like George Stokes.

As yet another report came in, again drawing a blank, Randall began to think that he and all of his force were on one big wild goose chase.

Paul Harvey slept until almost one o'clock in the afternoon, a fitful, dreamless sleep which he awoke from abruptly. He tasted something bitter in his mouth and he spat as he clambered to his feet. He stretched, the joints in his arms cracking loudly. He bent and picked up the sickle, gripping it tight in one huge hand. From his perch inside the barn, he could see the farmhouse.

His stomach rumbled noisily and he belched loudly. Perhaps there was food in the house.

Either way, he decided to find out.

Eleven

Harold Pierce worked unsupervised now and, freed from the watchful but helpful eyes of Greaves, he became more confident. Now, as he mopped the floor, he hummed a tune merrily to himself.

Harold was still humming his tuneless ditty when the lift nearby opened and Brian Cayton stepped out. He too was dressed in a porter's overall, a small blue name badge attached to his lapel. Cayton was a young man, yet to reach his thirties, with a shock of red hair and a smattering of freckles, Harold had seen him about the hospital many times.

"Harold, do me a favour will you?" he said.

Harold put down his mop.

"What is it?" he asked, smiling, noticing that Cayton made a point of not looking at him. He was one of the few members of staff who had not yet become accustomed to the sight of the vile scar.

"There's some work to be done down in bloody pathology," said Cayton. "I would help you only there's an emergency op. about to go ahead on nine and I'm supposed to be there. So, if you wouldn't mind helping them out down in pathology."

Harold's smile faded quickly and he swallowed hard.

"What do they want?" he asked, warily.

"I'm not sure," said Cayton, stepping back into the lift and punching the button marked nine.

72

The doors slid shut and there was a loud burring as the lift rose.

Harold stood still for long moments, gazing at the floor, staring at his own distorted image on the wet surface. Then, leaving the mop and bucket in the middle of the floor, he headed for the steps which would take him down to the basement.

Harold found that, by the time he reached the door of Pathology One, his body was sheathed in a fine film of perspiration. He knocked tentatively and stood waiting, listening to the sound of footsteps approaching from inside. The door opened and a middle-aged man in a white plastic apron peered out. He looked at Harold over the rims of his thick spectacles, brushing a loose strand of hair from his forehead. He glanced briefly at the scar then ran an appraising eye over the nervous porter.

"Wait there," said the man, attempting a smile but not quite managing it.

Harold peered through the half-open door, at the stainless steel slab nearest the door which, he noted, bore an occupant. The other men in white overalls were poring over it. There was a type of scale suspended over the slab and, as Harold watched, one of the men lifted a crimson lump from the slab and laid it in the bowl which registered a weight on the metric scale it bore. The man ran a blood-soaked finger along the scale, recording the weight to the last gramme. He then said something about the liver and Harold saw his companion jot the weight down on a clipboard which he held. The crimson lump was removed and placed on a trolley nearby, some congealed blood spilling in blackened gouts from the organ. Harold blenched and turned away, his stomach somersaulting.

"Here you are."

The voice startled him and he turned to see the

73

bespectacled man standing in the doorway, leaning on a trolley covered with a white sheet.

"Just some specimens to dispose of," he said and pushed the trolley out.

Harold took a firm grip on the gurney and began to push it in the direction of the furnace room, hearing the door close behind him as the pathologist retreated back inside the lab. One of the wheels squeaked and it offered a discordant accompaniment to the rhythmic tattoo beaten out by Harold's shoes which echoed through the chill, silent corridor. He looked down at the trolley as he walked, running a suspicious eye over the sheeted exhibits hidden from view. He could detect that familiar smell, the cloying, pungent odour of chemicals which made his eyes water. Harold tried to swallow but found that his throat was parchment dry, his tongue felt like a piece of sun-baked meat. He paused at the door of the furnace room and opened it, feeling the familiar blast of warm air as it greeted him. The generator hummed unceasingly as he dragged the gurney in beside him and closed the door. Unable to contain his curiosity any longer he pulled back the sheet, uncovering the objects which lay on the trolley.

He moaned as if in pain. His one good eye riveted to the foetus which lay in the tray. For long seconds, Harold stared at it, tears brimming in his eye. He didn't know at what stage the thing had been aborted but it was slightly larger than the one he'd seen Greaves incinerate on the first day. Its eyes were sealed shut by membranous skin. The head once more looked swollen and liquescent but this time it had a thin, almost invisible covering of fine hair. The whole body was covered by the langou and Harold reached out a shaking hand to touch the silken fibres. But the body was cold and dripping with chemicals and it felt so obscenely soft that he hastily withdrew his hand. The forceps lay beside the

74

receiver and they glinted in the cold white light cast by the overhead banks of fluorescents.

Harold pushed the trolley closer to the furnace, using the wrench and gloves to open it as he had seen Greaves do. The door swung open and a blistering wave of heat gushed forth, sweeping over Harold like a burning tide. He took a step back, recoiling from the sudden intense temperature. He pulled on a pair of thin rubber gloves and looked down at the foetus, then at the forceps. The furnace yawned invitingly. Harold picked up the metallic clamp and prepared to pick up the tiny body. His breath was coming in gasps, a single tear now rolling down his unscarred cheek.

He reached for the foetus.

"No."

He threw the forceps down and gripped the side of the trolley to steady himself.

"No," he said again, his voice cracking. "No."

He looked at the body, lying in its pool of rancid fluid, the arms and legs drawn up stiffly in a pose which reminded him of some kind of vile, hairless cat waiting to have its belly stroked. He sucked in huge lungfuls of stagnant air, his head bowed. When he finally managed to straighten up he looked into the furnace until the roaring flames burned yellow and white patterns on his retina. He could not, *would* not, put the foetus into that hungry mouth. His anxious gaze strayed back to the liquid-covered body and he shook convulsively.

"Gordon," he whispered, softly.

His head was beginning to throb, his nostrils and eye stinging from the odorous substances which lay in the tray with the abortion. He looked around him, at the generator, at the filthy trolleys which stood in one corner of the room, at the piles of fouled linen. There was something else too, something which he hadn't noticed the first time. It was like a large plastic dustbin

75

standing near to the piles of filthy laundry. Harold crossed hastily to it and lifted the lid, immediately gagging at the disgusting stench which rose from it. He looked down and saw that it was full of old dressings. Some were stiff with dried blood, others still crimson and fresh. There were gauze pads soaked with yellowish fluid, bandages that had pieces of skin sticking to them. Harold backed away, his mind churning with ideas. He crossed to the gurney and, with infinite care, as if he were lifting a sleeping child, picked up the foetus with both gloved hands. A drop of fluid burst from the umbilicus and splashed Harold's overall but he ignored it, carrying the tiny creature towards the bandage filled dustbin. There, he gently layed it on the ground and dug deep into the mass of bloodied dressings, making room at the bottom. This done, he once more lifted the foetus and placed it in the dustbin, covering it with the used bandages and pads, hiding it from view. He wiped some pus from his glove and then hastily put back the lid of the dustbin.

The furnace room door opened and Winston Greaves walked in.

Harold spun round, heart hammering against his ribs. Greaves looked at him for a moment, at the dustbin, at Harold's bloodstained hands. Then he smiled thinly.

"I thought I'd see how you were getting on," said the senior porter.

Harold walked back to the furnace, satisfied that Greaves suspected nothing. After all, he reasoned, what *could* he suspect? Together they disposed of the remaining things on the gurney, consigning them to the blazing fire then returning the trolley to pathology.

As they left the furnace room, Greaves leading the way, Harold took one last look across at the dustbin. The foetus would remain hidden in there, free from prying eyes. As far as anyone else was concerned, it

76

had been incinerated along with everything else. He had told Greaves that he'd burned the contents of the dustbin along with the pathology specimens and the coloured porter nodded his approval. Harold smiled to himself and pulled the furnace room door closed.

The foetus would be safe in its hiding place until he could return.

Night came without bringing the rain which had threatened earlier. Instead, the air was filled with a numbing frost which glittered on the grass and trees, reflecting the light from the hospital like millions of tiny diamonds. Harold stood at his window, watching as more and more lights were extinguished in the huge building as the hour grew late. He watched with almost inhuman patience, his mind a blank; the only thing scratching the surface of his consciousness being the persistent ticking of his alarm clock. He stood in the hut in darkness, not having bothered to turn on the light and, when he glanced behind him, the phosphorescent arms of the clock radiated their greenish glow revealing that it was almost 12.36 a.m.

Harold didn't feel tired, despite the fact that he'd been up since six that morning. His mind was too full of ideas for him to notice any fatigue. In another twenty-five minutes or so he would slip out of the hut, cross the few hundred yards of open ground which separated his own dwelling from the main building and go through the entrance which faced him.

It led past the mortuary to a flight of steps and a lift which would take him down to the basement and, eventually, to the furnace room.

The hands of the clock crawled slowly to one o'clock and Harold decided that it was time to leave. He slipped silently out of the door and locked it behind him, hurriedly making his way across the large expanse of grass between his hut and the nearest entrance. The frost crunched beneath his feet but, despite its severity, it had done little to harden up the ground and Harold twice nearly slipped in the mud. His breath came in short gasps, each of which was signalled by a small cloud of misty condensation. As he drew closer he realized just how dark the hospital was. There seemed to be only a couple of lights burning on each floor and that was not enough to illuminate his dark shape in the blackness.

He paused, ducking behind a nearby bush when he heard a clicking sound. Looking up he saw that it was two of the nurses returning to their quarters. They were laughing happily, the sounds of merriment drifting through the chill, silent night. Harold watched them until they disappeared out of sight then he continued forward, almost running the last few yards to the entrance.

A blue sign to his right proclaimed:

Mortuary

He pushed open one of the swing doors and moved as quietly as he could into a short corridor which led to a staircase. He blinked hard in the darkness, for no light had been left on. Indeed, as he reached the top of the stairs, he grabbed the handrail to guide himself, so impenetrable was the darkness.

It seemed even colder inside the building than out and Harold shuddered as he made his way tentatively down the stairs. How he wished he had a torch. He was completely and utterly blind, unable to see a hand in front of him and this sensation made him feel all the more uneasy. He could feel his body trembling and, as he put his foot down to find the next step, he stumbled. Harold gasped in shocked surprise and fell hard on the base of his spine. The impact sent a pain right through his body and, for long seconds, he sat where he was, moaning softly, one hand still gripping the handrail, the other massaging his back. He slowed his breathing, afraid that someone might hear him, worried that his little venture would be halted because some conscientious pathology assistant had decided to stay late and finish some work in the labs. His trepidation grew stronger when he noticed that there was a light burning at the bottom of the staircase. He had to round a corner to reach the base and that was still a dozen or more steps down. As yet the light was indistinct but, hauling himself up, Harold moved on, drawn towards the light like a moth to a flame.

He reached the bottom of the stairs, emerging in the area before the lift. The doors to all the labs were closed. Perhaps, he reasoned, someone had left and forgotten to turn out the light. But another part of his mind told him that the men who worked down here were too thorough to let such a minor thing as a light escape their notice. Heart pounding against his ribs, he walked to the door of the first lab and pressed his ear to it.

There was no sound coming from inside.

He twisted the handle and found that the door was locked. The same procedure was repeated with the other three labs and Harold was finally satisfied that the light had simply been overlooked. For that, to some degree, he was grateful. Although it lit only the area near the lift, it did provide at least some light for him as he made his way up the corridor.

In the furnace room the heat was as powerful as ever, but this time he welcomed it for it drove some of the chill from his bones. The generator kept up its ceaseless humming. Harold crossed quickly to the plastic dustbin and lifted the lid, pulling the used dressings aside, ignoring the blood and other discharge which sometimes stuck to his flesh. He finally felt something soft and jellied beneath his hands.

Very carefully, he lifted the foetus out, holding the tiny body before him for long seconds. Even in the half-light, he could see that the skin was already turning blue. He turned and laid it on one of the soiled sheets which were stacked on the gurneys behind him, then, as if he were wrapping a fragile Christmas present, he carefully pulled the dirty linen around the foetus. A rank odour filled his nostrils but he tried to ignore it and, with his "prize" secured, he made his way back towards the door, holding the small thing as a mother would hold her baby.

Harold ran across the open ground towards his hut finally slowing down when he reached the flimsy dwelling. He leant against the wall, trying to catch his breath, his one good eye squinting through the gloom to the doors he'd come through. No one had heard or seen him. There was no one following. Harold smiled thinly and closed his eyes. He took great gulps of cold air, trying to ignore the rancid stench which rose from the sheet and its dead occupant but that didn't seem to matter any longer. He had completed the first and most hazardous part of his venture, the second step was merely a formality.

The hut in which Harold lived stood about ten yards from a low barbed wire fence which marked the perimeter of the hospital beyond it lay large expanses of open fields, some of the ground was owned by the hospital but it was fenced off nevertheless. In the far distance, Harold could see the lights of Exham and, occasionally, the headlamps of a vehicle travelling along the dual-carriageway which led into the town. He headed towards the fence and cautiously stepped over it, catching his trousers on one of the vicious barbs. The material ripped slightly and Harold pulled himself free.

The ground sloped away before him slightly, leading down towards a deep cleft in the field which looked like an open black mouth in the darkness of the night. Harold steadied himself and made his way towards the depression. Above him tall electricity pylons rose high into the sky, their metal legs straddling the field, the high voltage cables they carried invisible in the gloom. There was a smell of ozone in the air, rather like the aftermath of a thunderstorm and Harold could hear a distant crackling sound from overhead.

He reached the foot of the small hill and stood close by the foot of a pylon. He was exhausted, both mentally and physically drained. His eye felt gritty and his throat was dry but he walked on, finally finding what he thought looked like a suitable spot. There was enough natural light for him to see what he was doing. He paused and laid the bundle of dirty sheet on the frosty grass, then he knelt and began scraping at the earth with his bare hands. He found that it was soft enough for him to achieve the necessary depth. Like a dog who's found a good spot to hide a bone, Harold pawed the earth away until it began to form a sizeable mound behind him. By the time he'd finished he estimated that the hole must be about two feet deep and twice that in length. He was panting loudly, his hands caked in mud, his clothes already reeking from the foul smell of the soiled linen. With the hole prepared, he unrolled the sheet, exposing the foetus inside. He lifted it gently from the cover and laid it in the hole.

For long seconds he stared down at it, tears brimming in his eye. He lowered his head, his body shaking.

"Gordon," he whispered. "Forgive me."

He felt a strange contradiction inside himself, a great sadness but also something akin to relief. Had he at last found a means of atonement? He began pushing the wet earth back into place, covering the tiny body.

"Mother," he said, as he continued to pile earth back into the grave. "It's different this time. This time I won't let it happen again. There'll be no more burnings."

He looked up, as if expecting to see someone standing

over him. Expecting to hear voices. There was only the far-off whistle of the wind in the pylons.

Harold finished piling in the earth and stood up, flattening it down with his shoe. He wiped his hands on the piece of soiled sheet then balled it up and hid it beneath a nearby bush. That done, he returned to the small grave. At first, when he tried to speak, no sound would come and his lips fluttered noiselessly but he swallowed hard and clasped his dirty hands before him.

He didn't know anything religious. No prayers. No hymns. He lowered his head, his eyes closed.

"Now I lay me down to sleep," he began, falteringly. "I pray the Lord. . ." He struggled to remember. "I pray the Lord my soul to keep." A long silence. "If . . . If I would . . . should," he corrected himself. "If I should die before I wake. I pray the Lord my soul to take." Tears were coursing freely down his cheek by now.

"Amen."

He turned and headed back to his hut.

It was not to be the last time he performed the cathartic ritual.

Twelve

Lynn Tyler prodded the bacon with a fork, turning it over in the hot fat. She hated fried food and the small kitchen already smelt strongly of it, the odour making her feel queasy. How the hell anyone could ever eat a cooked breakfast she didn't know but, in about five minutes, Chris would come downstairs and devour his usual four rashes of bacon, two eggs and a couple of slices of fried bread. He was sleeping upstairs at the moment, undisturbed by the sounds coming from the room below him. The radio competed with the frying bacon for supremacy in the cramped area.

Lynn jumped back as the fat spat at her, some of it catching the arm of the sweatshirt which she wore. At least three sizes too big for her and with "Judas Priest" printed across it, the garment came to just below her bottom. She wore nothing else and the lino in the kitchen felt cold beneath her bare feet. She ran a hand through her uncombed black hair and exhaled deeply, looking down at the pan but also at herself. She was almost shapeless beneath the thick folds of the sweat-shirt but even that wasn't enough to disguise some painfully obvious facts about her body. Her breasts, for so long unfettered by a bra, were beginning to droop – legacy of all those years she had spent enticing men. Ever since she'd reached her fourteenth birthday, just over five years ago, she had flaunted herself in every flimsy blouse and T-shirt she could find. There had been dozens of men in the intervening years, too many for her to count, attracted not just by her sizeable bust but by her easy manner – and easy was the operative word. She knew that some called her a tart, a slag, someone had even called her a whore once, but to Lynn Tyler the moral double-standard which governed the sex lives of men and women was ludicrous. And unfair. If a man slept around he was patted on the back and admired, earning the name of stud with each new conquest. If a woman chose to take different men to bed for her own private pleasure, she was sneered at, insulted and, in Lynn's case, thrown out of the house. Her parents had kicked her out when she was seven-teen after coming home to find her locked in a torrid embrace on the floor of their sitting room with her boyfriend of the time. Since then she had shared a three-bedroomed house near the centre of Exham with her best friend, Jill Wallace. Jill worked in nearby Camford and her job often took her away from the house for days at a time. It was during these respites that Lynn invited Chris to stay. She herself was unemployed and had been for over a year. Chris worked in Exham's largest engineering firm. They had been together for over nine months. It was something of a record for Lynn and, during that span of time, something had happened to her which she had always consciously avoided before. She had fallen in love. All the countless other men, they had been for *her* private gratification although more often than not it had not turned out that way. But it was different with Chris. She had never had any intention of falling in love, in fact the emotion had proved so alien to her that at first she hadn't been sure what she was feeling, but she knew it was ten times stronger than anything she'd felt in her life before. And she knew she wanted Chris on a more permanent basis than meetings three times a week and the odd weekend together. She wanted to marry him.

That was why she had stopped taking her pill. For the last three months she had left it untouched in its green packet. And, finally, she was sure. She was pregnant. She'd missed two periods, and a trip to the doctor last week had confirmed her suspicions. Surely with a baby on the way Chris would marry her? But she had yet to tell him her news.

She finished cooking his breakfast and while the kettle boiled for coffee she lit a cigarette, went to the bottom of the stairs and called him. She waited until she heard the creak of the bedsprings, signalling that he was up then she padded back into the kitchen and sat down to her own breakfast – a cup of Nescafé and a Marlboro.

He was down in a matter of moments, chest bare to expose his hard lean body with its tangled growth of light hair on the chest and stomach. He wore a faded pair of jeans, held up by a studded leather belt. Around one wrist was a leather band, similarly dotted with studs. He rubbed his stomach and sat down in front of the plateful of food.

"Don't you ever wash in the mornings?" she asked him, smiling. She watched as he started hacking away at the bacon.

"Well, I didn't have time this morning," he told her, chewing furiously. "I felt hungry."

She shuddered.

"I don't know how the hell you can eat *that* first thing in the morning." She took a drag on her cigarette, blowing out a long stream of smoke. She crossed her legs beneath the table, tapping her feet together agitatedly. Should she tell him now? Excuse me Chris but you're going to be a father? She took a sip of her coffee instead.

The DJ on the radio was babbling some hip bullshit which neither of them seemed to hear. Chris because he was too engrossed in his breakfast and Lynn because she was too wrapped up in her own thoughts. She watched him as he set about the first egg, slicing it in two, dipping his fried bread in the runny yolk. He looked up at her and smiled that warm, welcoming smile she had come to know so well these past nine months. She wondered if there was room for love in that smile.

"What's on your mind?" he said.

She looked surprised.

"Not a lot," she lied. "Why do you ask?"

"You're not usually this quiet," he told her.

Lynn smiled weakly, taking mock offence.

"Thanks a lot."

He smiled again, pushing half the egg into his mouth. She sucked hard on her cigarette, held the smoke in her mouth for long seconds then blew it out in a long blue stream.

"Chris, I'm pregnant."

The words came out as easily as that but, once she'd said them, it felt as if a hole had opened up inside her. Well, there it was. She'd told him, flat out. She sipped at her coffee and eyed him warily over the rim of the mug.

He slowed the pace of his chewing, looking down at his plate, not, as she'd expected, at her. He didn't speak.

"I said. . ."

He cut her short.

"Yeah, I heard you." There was an edge to his voice, almost imperceptible but nevertheless present. Like a knife blade in the darkness, invisible but razor sharp.

She ground out the fag in a nearby saucer, the plume of smoke rising mournfully, disappearing above her like a forgotten dream.

"Haven't you got anything to say?" she wanted to know.

"Are you sure?" he asked, still looking at his plate.

She told him about the visit to the doctors, the missed periods. He nodded.

They sat in silence for an eternity then he dropped his knife and fork onto the plate where they clattered noisily. Finally, he looked her in the eye.

"I thought you were on the bloody pill," he said, exasperatedly.

"I was," she told him. "I just didn't take it for a few weeks."

With the deception now revealed, it was she who dropped her gaze, unable to meet the unrelenting stare from his green eyes.

"Jesus Christ," he murmured, then his voice gradually grew in volume. "You bloody tricked me didn't you?"

86

"I didn't," she countered although the accusation bore weight and she was crumbling beneath that weight.

"You had me thinking it was safe and all the time you weren't taking your pill. You made a fucking mug out of me for all that time?" He was struggling to keep his anger in check and he wasn't making much of a job of it.

"It was just two months, Chris," she said.

"Two months. Two *years*. What's the difference? It's still me who ends up looking the twat, isn't it?"

She could feel the tears building but she fought them back, angry with herself now. They sat in silence for a long time. A silence finally broken by Chris.

"So what are you going to do?" he demanded.

"What do you mean?"

"About the kid."

"I'm going to have it."

He shook his head.

"Well, it's your business I suppose but I think you're stupid," he told her.

Her brow furrowed.

"It's not just *my* business," she said, defiantly. "It's yours too. You are the father after all."

"Are you sure?"

The remark was barbed and it cut deeply.

"You bastard," she growled. "Yes, I'm sure it's yours. If anyone else had been fucking me in the last nine months I think you might have found out about it."

"So, what are you going to do about it?" he asked again.

"I've told you once. I'm going to have it. I wanted the child. It's *our* child."

The realization gradually swept over him and a bitter smile creased his face.

"You know, Lynn, you've got more brains than I gave you credit for," he said.

"What's that supposed to mean?" she said.

"The baby. Not taking the pill. You planned it all didn't you?"

She reached for his hand, almost surprised when he didn't pull away. When she spoke again her tone was low, almost pleading.

"Chris, it was the only way I knew of keeping you," she said. "I love you. I've never loved anyone else in my life before. I didn't want to lose you."

"So you thought you'd trick me into becoming a daddy?" His voice was heavy with sarcasm.

She pulled her hand away.

"I hoped you'd marry me when you heard about the kid," she confessed. "You are its father after all."

"Only because you didn't take your fucking pill," he rasped. She watched as he got to his feet. "I'm sorry, Lynn but I'm not ready for this." He swallowed hard, not sure whether to pity her or punch her in the teeth. She too got to her feet.

"I love you, I want your baby. I want *you*," she said, the first salty tear sliding down her cheek.

"I'm sorry," he said. "Look, I think a lot of you, you're a good kid, fun to be with. . ."

She cut him short, her own anger now overriding his.

"And an easy fuck," she growled.

"I just don't love you," he told her, almost reluctantly.

She stood quivering for a moment, trying to hold back the flood of tears which she knew would come any minute. Her voice was cracking.

"So what's *your* answer then?" she demanded.

He stepped away from the table.

"I think it'd be simpler if we just didn't see each other again," he said.

"As easy as that? Forget the relationship. Nine months down the drain. Is that all it meant to you? Is it?" She was shouting now, the tears flooding down her cheeks. "A good screw when you wanted it? What was I, just a convenient piece of equipment when you got fed up with wanking?"

"I think I'd better go," he said, quietly.

"Yes, go on. Go. Fuck off." She started to tug the sweatshirt off, despite his pleas for her to stop. Eventually she pulled it free and threw it at him, standing there naked in that smoke filled kitchen, the odour of fried food heavy in the air.

"I'm sorry, Lynn," he said.

"Get out," she screamed at him, hurling the sauce bottle in his direction. It hit the wall close by him and exploded, splattering the sticky red liquid all over the place. Lumps of glass skittered across the lino.

She sat down at the table, sobbing, her head resting on her arms and she heard the front door close behind him as he left.

Naked, she sat alone in the kitchen her tears falling onto the paper table cloth and spreading out like transparent ink on blotting paper.

She remained like that for at least thirty minutes before wiping her face and shuffling upstairs to dress. She pulled on a pair of drain-pipe jeans and hauled a khaki coloured T-shirt over her head. She went back downstairs and cleaned up the mess in the kitchen.

At 10.03 a.m. she phoned her doctor and made an appointment to see about getting an abortion.

Thirteen

"Well, this is better than standing under a fucking tree isn't it?" said Keith Todd, adjusting the volume control on the Dolomite's cassette.

Penny Walsh giggled and moved closer to him, gazing out through the windscreen at the rain clouds which were gathering ominously. It was already dark but the impending storm seemed to bring a heaviness to the air, gripping the small car in a black velvet fist. The headlamps were off and the only light came from the sodium lamp about ten yards behind then down the lane. Flanked on both sides by trees and high bushes, it had wide grass verges on either side and it was on one of these that Keith had parked the car.

"And you're really going to buy this off your dad?" Penny said, patting the passenger seat.

"Once I get a job, yeah," Keith reassured her. "He doesn't mind me borrowing it until then."

Neither of them had jobs, both Keith and Penny had left school at sixteen, just two years earlier. The ritual of signing on had become, as it had to hundreds of thousands more of their generation, a way of life. But Keith was an eternal optimist and, tonight, in particular, he felt lucky. That feeling proved to have foundation as he felt Penny slide one hand onto his thigh. He responded by pulling her towards him, their mouths locking, tongues darting feverishly back and forth, each anxious to taste the other.

Keith felt her hand clawing its way up to the growing bulge in his jeans. He responded by squeezing her left breast feeling the nipple stiffen through the thin material of her blouse.

She turned in her seat, one leg now drawn up beneath her. His rough hand found the buttons on her blouse and undid them, moving more urgently now as he massaged her plump breasts. For her own part she managed to undo the zip of his jeans, coaxing his stiffness free, running one finger along the shaft from tip to base before enveloping it with her warm hand.

Keith grunted and reached beneath her short skirt. As her hand began to move rhythmically up and down, he felt her part her legs slightly and his probing digits pulled the slinky material of her panties aside in an effort to reach the moist warmth beyond. He slid two fingers into her eager cleft and she stiffened in response.

Paul Harvey was less than ten yards from the car.

He crouched in the bushes, the sickle held firmly in his hand, watching the young couple inside the vehicle, his expression a mixture of disgust and bewilderment. The first spots of rain began to fall but Harvey ignored them, his attention riveted to the car. The windows were steaming up and it was becoming difficult to see inside from his present vantage point. The two young-sters inside were merely indistinct blurs before him. He gripped the sickle tighter.

During his own teenage years he had never known the pleasure of a companion, male or female. He had tried to make friends, when his father had allowed it but Harvey's self-consciousness and naivety had let him down until at last, he resigned himself to being a loner. Not that the people of Exham did anything to help him overcome those shortcomings. Fate, and the towns-people, seemed to be conspiring against him, trying to ensure that he would never know what it was like to be a part of society. And, in truth, perhaps Harvey didn't want to be a part of it.

He moved slowly towards the car.

Penny bent her head and closed her mouth over the bulging purple head of Keith's penis, flicking some drops of clear liquid from its tip. He gasped as he felt her warm tongue curling around his erection, the sensations which he felt becoming stronger by the second. He, himself, continued to move his fingers within her, using his thumb to tease the hardened bud of her clitoris. Keith allowed his head to loll back onto the head-rest, closing his eyes as he felt her pushing more urgently against his hand. He could hear her rasping breath, feel its hotness on his slippery shaft.

There was a thunderous roar as the first rumble of thunder broke like a wave on a rock and the sound make Keith open his eyes.

He almost screamed.

Glaring in at him through the side window, his face distorted by the swiftly flowing rain, was Harvey.

Keith, pulling Penny upright, withdrew his fingers and reached frantically for the ignition key. The girl sat back, dazed and confused.

"Keith, what. . ."

The engine roared into life and the young lad looked once more out of the side window.

The face had gone. Of Harvey there was no sign.

Keith slumped back, shaking uncontrollably and, high above them, a powerful fork of lightning tore open the clouds.

Fourteen

The eighth foetus had been buried, its tiny body now lying beneath the slippery mud with the others. Harold dried his hair with a towel and checked on the milk bubbling in the pan on the hot-plate.

Eight of them in that shallow grave. He yawned and glanced across at the alarm clock. It was 1.45 a.m. It hadn't taken him so long to bury the last one. The constant rain had transformed the earth into a quagmire. Indeed, it had been raining for the past two days on and off and that, at least, made his task easier. The clods came away easily.

He lifted the saucepan just in time to prevent it boiling over, poured the milk into a mug and tossed the pan into the sink.

Outside, there was a particularly loud growl of thunder which seemed to roll across the land like an unfurling blanket. The little hut shook and Harold stood still for a moment, wondering if the entire flimsy structure was going to collapse around his head. The rumbling died away to be replaced by a whiplash crack of lightning which seared across the bloated, mottled sky and, for brief seconds, left a brilliant white afterburn on Harold's retina as he watched it. Mesmerized by the sight of nature's fury at its most potent, he crossed to the tiny window and stood looking out as the storm gathered for its furious onslaught on Exham and the countryside round about. Black cloud, buffeted by the wind, came rolling in to empty its load while lightning split the heavens with blazing white forks of pure energy. The thunder grew to a crescendo, like a thousand cannons being fired at once. The little hut shook once more as the storm intensified. Harold watched in awe, recoiling every now and then from the particularly violent flashes of lightning or the seemingly endless volleys of thunder. And, through it all, came the persistent pounding of the rain as it hammered against buildings and turned the ground into sticky slime. On the tarmac around the hospital entrance, the water puddled in pools ankle deep, each droplet exploding on the black, saturated surface. Even inside the hut, Harold could detect the strong smell of ozone as the sky was torn open by the powerful fingers of light which rent the thick black clouds like hands through wet tissue paper. Thunder roared menacingly and, in one or two places in the hospital, windows rattled in their frames. For those patients still awake, the world outside became a blur as they squinted through the rain-drenched windows. There was no steady trickle of tear-like droplets this time but a massive deluge which seemed to strike the windows and cascade down in one liquid flow, as if there were many men standing out there throwing buckets of the stuff at the panes. The few lights that burned outside were diffused into mere blurs through the rain-battered windows.

Harold sipped at his milk and watched the celestial fireworks, drawing back slightly as each blinding burst of forked or sheet lightning exploded across the sky, to be followed by a deafening blast of thunder. It sounded like some gigantic animal roaring in pain, the lowing of a massive steer lashed by a whip of ferociously undiluted force.

In the field behind Harold's hut, the pylons swayed ominously in the high wind, their normally stable structures looking suddenly vulnerable. They crackled loudly and the thick power lines hummed as they were rocked back and forth by the onslaught. The metal groaned as it was bent and blasted by the wind and, beneath one of the pylons, less than fifty feet from its base, the shallow grave which Harold had dug was saturated to the extent that some of the top soil began to wash away.

There was a crack of lightning which screamed across the black heavens for a full five seconds, a blast of energy so powerful that for long moments even the thunder seemed to cease. The crackling fork hit the pylon nearest to the hospital fence, striking it at the very point where the huge power lines were attached. There was a blinding flash of blue and white sparks and an angry sputtering as the thick cable, twice as thick as a man's torso was wrenched free of its housing by the fury of the impact. Then, it simply fell to earth, the other end of it still attached to the preceding pylon. But the severed end twisted and writhed on the wet earth like some kind of gigantic snake, showering the sodden mud with sparks and pumping hundreds of thousands of volts into the sticky ooze. The pylon itself shook violently as the cable twisted at its base, contorting madly like an eel on a hot skillet as it poured its immense reservoir of energy into the earth. The grass nearby was immediately blackened by the furious discharge, the mud even bubbling in places as the endless supply of electricity continued to gush into the ground. The cable twisted and whiplashed for what seemed like an eternity as it unleashed its pent-up power in a display which even overshadowed the mighty forks of lightning still flashing across the sky. The power line poured seemingly endless stores of crackling volts into the wet earth which, itself, acted as a conductor, further aiding the explosive exhibition.

Fifteen

The picture on the TV broke up into a maze of static and Judith Myers looked up as she heard Andy Parker curse.

"I knew we should have got a different set," he grunted, thumping the TV with the flat of his hand.

"It's the storm," said Judith, gazing out of the bedroom window at the forks of lightning that rattled across the sky. She lowered her book and ran an appraising eye over Parker who stood naked before the television as if daring it to start playing up again. The picture gradually gained clarity and he nodded appreciatively, but still waited defiantly. Judith giggled.

"What's so funny?" he asked, without turning to look at her.

"You," she said. "Get back into bed or at least draw the curtains. Someone will be calling the police. They'll lock you up for indecent exposure." She chuckled again. Parker remained where he was.

Slowly, almost reluctantly, she slid the sheets down a little way to uncover her stomach, stroking a hand over its firm flatness. Gone was the bulge she had hated so much. The abortion had been successful and she had been out of Fairvale for more than a week now and had even been into work for a couple of hours.

A particularly thunderous crack of lightning tore across the sky as the storm reached ever greater heights and Judith winced as she felt sudden, unexpected pain just below her navel. She pressed the area gingerly, as Parker shouted and cursed at the TV which was again hissing at the onslaught of so much static in the air.

Judith sucked in a painful breath, eyes fixed on her abdomen. The flesh seemed to stretch across her pelvic bone, becoming shiny, then, as she watched, a single drop of blood welled inside her navel. It spread outwards until it overflowed and trickled down her side like a solitary crimson tear.

"Oh my God," she gasped, her eyes bulging.

"What's wrong?" asked Parker, still more concerned with the recalcitrant TV. He had his back to Judith.

She opened her mouth to speak but no words would come. The single drop of blood dripped onto the sheet beside her, blossoming on the material. The pain below her navel grew stronger and it felt as if someone had punched her. The flesh suddenly contracted then rose an inch or two, rising and falling almost rhythmically.

She threw back the covers and finally, Parker *did* turn round.

He saw the blood, saw the skin on Judith's abdomen stretching and contracting, saw her naked body trembling.

She tensed for immeasurable seconds, her entire body stiff then, with a gasp, she crumpled. He dashed for the phone but she stopped him.

"Judith, for Christ's sake. . ." he said, fear in his voice.

"The pain's stopped," she told him, her voice quivering.

She reached for a tissue and wiped away the blood from her belly. "I'm all right."

He slammed the receiver down.

"All right," he shouted. "It's that fucking abortion. I told you not to have it. I'm getting a doctor, now." He reached for the receiver once more and dialled.

She pressed her abdomen once more but there was no pain. Parker was speaking to someone now, telling them that it was urgent but his words didn't seem to register with her. The blood in her navel had congealed into a sticky red syrup which she wiped away. Parker slammed the phone down and told her that the doctor was on his way.

Outside, another shaft of lightning ripped across the sky, followed a second later by a clap of thunder which threatened to bring the house down around their heads.

They both sat in stunned silence, waiting.

Sixteen

Even in the deep gloom inside the hut, Harold could make out his mother's features. Her skin was peeling away, mottled green in places where it had turned gangrenous. Her hair hung in loose, flame-seared strands, blackened wisps against the pale pink of her scalp. When she opened her mouth no sound came forth, just a swollen blackened tongue which dripped dark fluid over her scorched lips. She moved towards him, her own putrefying odour almost palpable, wrapping itself around his throat like obscene tentacles.

As her stench filled his nostrils, Harold screamed and screamed. . .

He awoke beating at his pillow, the covers thrown off. His body was soaked in sweat and his throat felt raw from screaming. Gradually he realized that it had been yet another dream.

Someone was pounding on the door of his hut.

Harold uttered a small moan of fear then, as he saw the murky daylight flooding through the window, he found the courage to get to his feet. He padded across to the door.

"Who is it?" he called.

"Harold are you all right?" the voice from the other side asked and, after a moment or two, he recognised it. Harold unlocked the door and pulled it open to find Winston Greaves standing there. The senior porter was spattered with rain which was still falling from the banks of grey cloud overhead. He looked Harold up and down, noticing how pale the unscarred side of his face looked. There were deep pits beneath both his eyes and his hair was plastered to his head with sweat.

"Are you OK?" asked Greaves, stepping inside.

Harold nodded.

"Do you know what the time is?" Greaves asked him.

He shook his head, sitting down on the edge of the bed.

"It's after nine o'clock," the coloured porter told him. "You should have been on duty over an hour ago. I thought you were ill or something."

"I'm sorry," said Harold, apologetically. "I didn't sleep very well last night." He got to his feet. "If you give me a minute, I'll get ready."

"If you don't feel well, I can get one of the doctors to come over and have a look at you. You. . ."

Harold cut him short.

"No. I'll be all right. I'm just tired," he explained.

Greaves nodded and sat down on one of the rickety old wooden chairs while Harold padded into the small room which housed the chemical toilet. He emerged a moment later and, after splashing his face with water from the cold tap in the kitchen, he began dressing. The muddy clothes which he'd worn the previous night to bury the foetus were pushed out of sight beneath the bed. Finally, he pulled on his overall and together he and Greaves began the walk across the open ground towards the main building. Harold looked up at the sky which still promised rain but now was falling in small droplets, quite different from the downpour of the previous night.

"I hear there was a blackout last night," said Greaves.

Harold nodded.

"It's the worst storm I can remember," Greaves confessed. "Still, the electricity company should have everything fixed by this afternoon. I heard that one of the cables was brought down." He stopped and looked behind him towards the field where the damaged pylon was. "They're trying to fix it up now."

Harold spun round and his eye bulged. There were indeed men moving about in the field near to the pylon, some climbing on it, others using ladders to reach inac-

99

cessible areas. There was even a small crane crawling through the mud.

"Oh my God," he murmured, softly.

The men were all around the pylon. They were working in *that* field.

Near to the grave.

Harold swallowed hard. If they should find it. . .

Greaves walked on but Harold remained where he was, his gaze fixed worriedly on the men in dark blue overalls who swarmed over the pylon in their efforts to repair it. He saw the crane, the large white and blue van parked nearby and he began to tremble. They would find it. They must do. But, it was at least fifty yards from the base of the pylon he told himself. It should be relatively safe. His ready-made assurances did not have the desired effect and he wondered if the rain might have washed the shallow covering of soil right off exposing the bodies beneath. He hurried on to join Greaves, his mind in a turmoil.

He spent most of the day thinking about the men in that field, expecting at any time one of them to walk into the hospital and tell of the grave that they'd discovered. Then his secret would be there for all to see. His crime would be exposed. For that was what they would call it. A crime. Not understanding, they would punish him, they would not want to listen to his reasons. They would not be able to comprehend the thought behind his actions.

Every chance he got, he stole a look at them, to see how far their work was progressing. To see if they had stumbled on the grave. He could eat no lunch, so knotted with fear was his stomach. He spent his entire break standing in the rain outside watching the blue-clad men repairing the damage to the pylon.

When, at three fifteen that afternoon, they finally left, Harold breathed an audible sigh of relief.

100

Seventeen

Harold pulled on his shirt, wincing when he felt the damp material touch his skin. He hadn't had time to wash the garment since the previous night and it was still stiff with dried mud. So were the trousers which he put on but, after a moment or two, he grew to accept the cloying feel of the odorous cloth against his skin. He pulled on his coat and tucked the torch into one pocket – he'd taken it from a store-room in the hospital earlier in the day. The fifty watt bulb hung above him. He hadn't put it on since returning to the hut over four hours ago and the hands on his alarm clock had crawled around to 12.26 a.m. Harold knew that he was taking a small risk leaving the hut earlier than usual but, he reasoned, his business in the muddy quagmire was more important than usual and, besides, if someone did see him it would be easy enough to explain away the fact that he was out that late. Also, he was carrying nothing with him tonight. Nothing, that was, except his fear. He realized that the men from the electricity company who had repaired the downed power line could not have discovered the grave of foetuses, he would have known about it by now. However, he was worried that the driving rain might have disturbed the top soil which covered the grave.

He folded the blanket up as small as he could and tucked it inside his coat. It was to be used as an extra covering on the grave. He would drape it over the eight bodies interred there and then build more layers of earth over the blanket, ensuring once and for all that they were hidden from prying eyes. It was cold but, despite that, Harold could feel the beads of perspiration on his forehead and between his shoulder blades. He swallowed hard, checked everything one final time and then headed for the door of the hut.

Harold peered out, making sure that there was no one about, then he slipped around the side of the small building and was swallowed up in the shadows which formed so thickly at its rear. He walked to the low barbed wire fence and clambered over it, nearly slipping on some damp grass at the top of the ridge. It had stopped raining and the night air smelt crisp, filled with the aroma of wet grass. His hot breath formed small white clouds every time he exhaled and Harold was pleased when he finally reached the bottom of the ridge, almost slipping half way down. He walked across to the pylon and felt his feet sinking into the mud at its base – a testament to the comings and goings of men and machinery earlier in the day. He flicked on the torch and shone it over the ground, seeing the outline of heavy footprints in the soft soil.

There was not enough natural light for him to find his way so he kept the torch on.

Above him, the sky was a patchwork of clouds and stars. It looked like a canopy of soggy black velvet that someone had thrown a handful of sequins onto. There was a slight breeze, cold and just strong enough to send the clouds rolling across the dark backdrop.

Harold shone the torch down once more and saw where the fallen power cable had scorched the earth over a wide area. He didn't know how many volts each of those massive overhead wires carried but it certainly had done some damage. The blackened grass and mud seemed to extend as far as thirty yards, perhaps more. He could pick out the tracks of the crane in the mud too and, close by, someone had dropped an empty cigarette packet. He kicked it aimlessly with the toe of his shoe and walked on, the breath now rasping in his throat. He was very close to the grave.

The boot marks and crane tracks ended abruptly and Harold realized that the men had not gone anywhere near to the hole. He moved on, slowing his pace somewhat. He sucked in a shaking breath, the frosty air making his mouth and the back of his throat even drier. He tried to swallow but couldn't. It felt as if his heart was trying to smash its way through his ribcage. He played the powerful torch beam over the area ahead of him, his boots creaking on the soft mud as he advanced.

Something pale gleamed in the shaft of light and Harold held the torch on it, moving forward with even more deliberate steps until he was at the spot which he knew so well.

"Oh God," he croaked.

The bulbous head of one of the foetuses had been exposed when the constant rain had washed away the covering of earth. As Harold had feared, the top soil had been almost completely eroded and, as he shone the torch over the length of the grave, he saw that more of the tiny creatures lay virtually in the open, only the tiniest covering of mud hid them from view. He scratched his head in puzzlement. Even if the men from the electricity company hadn't actually come as far as this, surely, he reasoned, they could not have avoided seeing the exposed bodies? The grass round about, what remained of it, was blackened so the cable had discharged its power into this part of the field too. How could they have missed the small grave? However, the important thing was that he was still undiscovered. He knelt, and scooped up a handful of wet earth, ready to cover the corpses once again.

But, looking down at the vile array of abortions which lay before him, something nagged at the back of his mind. He dropped the handful of soggy muck and frowned. It was something about the position of the creatures. Harold had buried them in a straight line and yet, three, perhaps more, were lying sideways now. One even lay spread-eagled across one of its unfortunate companions. The driving rain would have been enough to wash away the top soil but not to move the

103

position of the foetuses. Had the men from the electricity board found them? Had he been reported? His mind suddenly began to race, his heart beat even faster. It would take maybe a day or two for the people at the hospital to discover that *he* was responsible. He would not know immediately that he had been found out. He began to shudder with cold and fear. What would they do to him? He clenched his fists, his confused mind searching for some other answer. *Any* other answer. Perhaps animals had disturbed the grave. A fox? A badger perhaps? He picked up his torch and shone it over the nearest foetus, inspecting the small body for damage. The arms, the legs, the body were all untouched. Harold leaned closer, casting furtive eyes over the head. It looked swollen, mottled red and black in places, it appeared like a huge festering sore. The tiny mouth was open, pieces of mud clogging it. Harold reached forward with one shaking finger and brushed the muck away. The body looked so limp, not rigored as would be expected, but soft and malleable. Harold shone the torch close to it, prodding the skin with his fingers, mildly disgusted by its slimy softness. He was breathing hard now but his fear had been replaced, to some degree, by an appalling kind of curiosity. He prodded the tiny body with his fingers, even touching the torn, putrescent umbilicus for a second before returning his attention to its face. The stench which rose from the grave was almost overpowering, a cloying odour of decay which couldn't even be driven away by the fresh breeze which sprang up but Harold didn't seem to notice it. He shone the torch over the other bodies, some of which were in an advanced state of decomposition. Harold looked on them with a feeling akin to pity and, for long moments, he crouched in the mud gazing at the bodies, then, he took the blanket from his coat and laid it beside him. He decided to lay the foetuses back in their original position before completing the burial so he lifted the one nearest to him and placed it gently between two smaller specimens, one of which had already had its sightless eyes devoured by worms. Harold shuddered and hurried to complete his task. The smell, which he had not noticed before, suddenly seemed to be unbearable to him, filling his nostrils and making his head ache.

Each foetus he touched felt similarly cold and soft, the touch of their flesh on his fingers making him quiver violently. But, nevertheless, he completed his task, finally reaching for the body which he had first inspected. Puzzled once more by its position in the grave, Harold lifted it gently in order to replace it in the original space he had made for it. It seemed heavier than the rest and he guessed that it must have been aborted at a much later stage than the others. He lowered it gently into place and shone his torch over it one last time.

The foetus opened its eyes.

Harold's body stiffened, his hand almost crushing the torch. It was as if thousands of volts of electricity were being pumped through him, the shock making him rigid. His single good eye bulged madly in the socket, he shook his head gently from side to side.

The foetus moved one arm, raising it slowly, as if soliciting help and Harold heard a low sucking sound as its mouth opened. A blob of black fluid appeared on its lip and trickled down its chin. The tiny chest heaved once then settled into a more rhythmic motion.

He kept the torch aimed at the thing, his entire body shaking uncontrollably.

To his left there was another low, liquid, noise which reminded him of asthmatic breathing only it was thicker, more mucoid and Harold swung the torch beam around. He began to mouth silent words as he saw a second foetus slithering awkwardly in the sticky ooze.

105

It was smaller than the first one, its umbilicus moving tentacle-like, as it struggled in the slime.

Harold felt his heart beginning to pound. He felt as though his head were swelling. The execrable stench filled his nostrils, hanging in the air like an almost palpable cloud of corruption. He dropped the torch but it fell to the ground with its light pointing into the grave and, in that light, Harold saw a third creature begin to move. It rolled onto its side, yellowish fluid so viscous it was almost jellied, oozing from the hole in its belly where the umbilicus should have been. Part of its body was blackened and rotted, one arm mottled, two of the tiny stubby fingers missing. It clambered up and fixed Harold in a hypnotic gaze, the twin black orbs which were its eyes holding him immobile.

He pressed both hands to his head and screamed but no sound would come. His mouth was stretched open as far as it would go, the shriek of terror and revulsion waiting to be released but he could not summon it. That ultimate exclamation of disgust remained deep within him. He tried to stand, to get away but his knees buckled and he fell face down in the mud, close to the edge of the grave, watching helplessly as the three living foetuses crawled towards him. He felt as if someone had laid a huge weight on his body, for when he tried to rise again he felt an intolerable pressure pinning him down as surely as if he'd been skewered to the mud with a long knife. He could only watch, mesmerized, as the trio of abominations drew closer to him. He was babbling incoherently now, his words unintelligible even to himself. His mind struggled to accept what his eye saw but could not, *would* not. He fought against the pressure above him and managed to rise, dragging himself to his knees, eyes still locked on the monstrosities before him.

"No," he murmured, his entire body trembling.

The leading foetus had reached the edge of the grave and was trying to crawl up the side.

Harold shook his head violently. He heard voices.

Was there someone else with him?

He spun round, searching for the source of the voice. Had someone discovered him?

"Who's there?" he gasped, his gaze still riveted to the trio of creatures beneath him.

Again the voice came only this time it was joined by another, and another. Soft, hissing words which he could barely understand seemed to flicker inside his head like a dying candle flame. He stopped trying to back away and watched the three foetuses writhing in the grave. He tried to tell himself that he would awake in a moment, safe, in his hut. He would leave this nightmare behind him, wake up to find that it had all been a figment of his imagination.

He bowed his head and tears began to flood down his cheek. Kneeling like some kind of penitent, he remained where he was, his body racked by sobs, his vision blurring as he cried like a child. Gradually, the spasms subsided and he stared down at the three creatures which lay in the sticky mud, pinned in their collective gaze. Then, very slowly, he unrolled the blanket and lifted the first of them out, putting it gently onto the soft material. He repeated the procedure with the other two. They lay before him, grotesque parodies of human babies – living nightmares. The third moved slightly and Harold reached forward and wiped some of the thick yellow discharge from its belly, rubbing his hand clean on the wet earth.

"Yes, the grave," he said, nodding blankly, as if speaking to some invisible companion. He began scraping huge clods of reeking soil onto the other five bodies in the grave, sweating with the exertion. It took him nearly half an hour to fill it in then he turned back to the three creatures who lay on the blanket.

"I will find you shelter," he said. He smiled crookedly. "Gordon." He looked down at them.

"Gordon."

The word echoed inside his head, swirling around in a fog of confusion that seemed to be thickening by the second. A mist made of nightmares from which there was to be no escape.

Harold sat on the edge of his bed, looking down at the three foetuses on the blanket before him. He had left the light off in the hut and, in the darkness, the hands of his clock glowed dully. Harold noted that it was approaching 2.23 a.m. His head was throbbing and his body felt stiff, every muscle crying out for rest but he could only sit. Sit and stare at these. . .

He didn't even know what they were. He realized that they were abortions but, more than that. . . The thought trailed off once more.

Words. Soft, sibilant, came hissing inside his head once more and Harold wondered if he was imagining them. Were they really his own thoughts? He swallowed hard. The voices seemed more distinct now, as if they were speaking directly to him.

He nodded in response to the silent question.

"Yes," he said, softly. "I am afraid of you."

A pause.

"Because I don't know what you are." If not for the fact that he was constantly pulling at the flesh on the back of his right hand, he might still have thought that this was some horrendous nightmare from which he would be hurled screaming at any second, to wake up sweating and trembling in his bed with the daylight streaming in through his window. As it was, all he heard were the voices again, echoing, resonating like whispers in a cave.

He gave answers to unspoken questions.

"Food? What can I do?"

Hissing inside his head.

Harold shook his head and stood up.

"I can't."

The whispers became louder.

"No." He backed off until suddenly he felt a searing pain explode inside his head. White light danced before his eyes and he felt something warm and wet trickle from his nostril. He put a finger to the orifice, withdrawing it to see dark fluid on the tip. The blood looked black in the darkness. Harold swayed drunkenly. It felt as if someone had clamped a vice on his skull and were twisting the screw as tightly as possible.

"All right," he yelled and the pain receded. He leant against the nearest wall, panting. "Tell me how," he sobbed.

The words came slowly and, at first he recoiled again but remembrance of the awful pain when he disobeyed forced him to listen. Tears streaming down his face, he sat motionless, hands clasped together, head bowed until finally he got to his feet and walked into the tiny kitchen. He pulled open one of the rotting wooden drawers and rummaged through until he found a butcher's knife. It was a heavy bladed implement, rusty in places, its black handle missing a screw but, as Harold pressed his thumb to the cutting edge he found that it was still wickedly sharp. He shambled back into the other room and sat down on the bed, the knife held in one unsteady hand. The ghostly voices spoke to him once more and he put down the vicious blade in order to undo his shirt. As each successive button was unfastened, he could hear the soft sucking sounds which the foetuses made echoing around the room. They moved only occasionally on the blanket but, all the while, their black glistening eyes were fixed upon him. One of them, the smallest of the trio was gurgling thickly, a stream of fluid spilling from its mouth which it kept opening and closing rather like a goldfish. Harold looked at it and then across at the knife.

Perhaps he should kill them now, destroy these foul things. Cut. . .

He groaned once more as a white hot burst of agony seared his brain. He imagined his head swelling then exploding into a thousand sticky pieces. He undid the final button and pulled his shirt off then, with shaking hands, he reached for the long bladed knife. His own body looked pale in the gloom and his skin was puckered into goose-pimples. He held the knife before him, looking at the wicked weapon then, with infinite care, almost without looking, he pressed the sharp edge to his chest. It felt cold and he held it there for what seemed like an eternity then, with one swift movement, he drew it across his pectoral muscle, opening the flesh, slicing through veins. He moaned in pain, felt the hot bile bubbling up in his throat but he fought it back, hacking at himself once more until a bright stream of blood gushed from the torn breast. His second cut was more random and he was fortunate not to carve his left nipple off. His chest felt as if it were on fire and he swayed for a second, some of his blood splashing the bedclothes and, all the time, the voices inside his head urged him on.

He bent forward and lifted the first of the foetuses, cradling it in his arms for long seconds, allowing some of his blood to drip onto the tiny body, then he raised it to his torn chest. He felt its jellied, putrescent flesh in his hands, he smelt the stench which it gave off and he allowed it to press its bulbous head against his wounds. Harold was shaking uncontrollably as he felt the thing's lips on his chest, probing the ragged edges of the twin gashes, burying its small mouth inside the bleeding maw as it swallowed his life fluid. It bucked violently in his hands and he felt that familiar wave of sickness sweeping over him again but the pain in his

110

chest kept him conscious. Tears streamed down his face, dripping from his chin to mingle with his blood and the odorous fluid which the foetus itself seemed to exude.

He heard the voice deep within the darkest recesses of his mind and he laid the creature back on the cover where it lay still, its face slick with blood, its body bloated and immobile.

He repeated the procedure with the second monstrosity, opening a third wound on the other breast to satiate it. He moaned once more, feeling the thing grip his flesh with stubby fingers as it pressed itself tightly to the weeping wound. It too signalled its satisfaction and Harold completed the vile ritual by lifting the third foetus to his torn pectoral.

When the task was over, Harold got to his feet, unhindered, and staggered into the kitchen. He hung over the sink and vomited violently, remaining there for a long time afterwards, finally spinning both taps and washing the foul mess down the plug-hole. Then he sponged down his chest wounds with a wet towel, pressing it hard against the wounds in an effort to seal them. When he withdrew it, the material was stained orange and red. He was bruised black in some places where the creatures had fed. Harold held the towel in place until he was satisfied that the bleeding had stopped then he dried himself and sought out some adhesive strip which he had in the bedside cabinet. He carefully cut some lengths of it and placed it delicately over the wounds. It still felt as if someone were using a blow torch on his chest but the pain was diminishing somewhat.

Bleary eyed, he looked down at the three abortions.

Where the hell was he going to hide them?

He inhaled deeply, wincing as his torso began to throb once more, looking around for a suitable place. There seemed to be just one.

There was a large cupboard beneath the sink which appeared to be ideal. He carried them, one by one into the kitchen and knelt before the cupboard door, a sliding effort with a metal handle.

"I have to hide you," he said. "Someone might come here."

Silent questions.

He nodded, pulling open the door. A strong odour of mildew wafted out, taking Harold's breath away momentarily. He looked inside and saw that, but for a couple of old saucepans and a plastic bucket, the cupboard was empty. He hastily removed the offending articles, pushing them to one side. A silver-fish scurried from the dark confines of the enclosure and Harold crushed it beneath his foot, gazing down at the shapeless mess for a second before lifting the blanket into the cupboard. This done, he carefully laid the foetus' onto it, finally pulling it over them. He gazed into the darkness, heard the vile mewling sounds which they made, the soft mucoid snortings and gurglings and he closed his eyes. Then, the voices came to him again, soft but full of menace. Full of power. He slid the cupboard door shut and stumbled back into the other room where he collapsed on the bed. Immediately, he was overcome with the welcome oblivion of unconsciousness but whether it was sleep or a blackout he was never to know. Either way, he sprawled on the blood-speckled bed, the odour of the creatures still strong in the air.

Outside, the rain had begun to fall again, pattering against the window, thrown by the wind which rattled the glass in its frame. Inside, the steady ticking of the clock was the only sound.

It was 3.17 a.m.

Part Two

"... death could drop from the dark
As easily as song."

— Isaac Rosenberg

Eighteen

Inspector Lou Randall pushed two coins into the vending machine at the end of the corridor and pressed one of the buttons. A plastic cup dropped down but no tea followed it. Randall muttered something to himself and pressed the reject button but the machine had swallowed his money and obviously didn't intend parting with it. The Inspector swore and kicked the recalcitrant contraption, smiling when he saw a stream of tea suddenly gush forth into the waiting cup. Grinning, he retrieved the tea and retreated back to his office, closing the door behind him.

He crossed to his desk and sat down, lighting up a cigarette before flipping open the first of half a dozen files spread on the work-top.

They were statements from four residents of Exham, all of whom claimed to have seen Paul Harvey in the past two days. Randall read each one slowly, shaking his head every now and then. Every one gave a different description and at least two of the sightings had happened at exactly the same time but on different sides of town. He closed the file and dropped it amongst the others. He sat back in his chair, the plastic beaker in one hand, the cigarette in the other. His office was already full of smoke and an empty packet of Rothmans lay at his elbow. He put down his tea and massaged the bridge of his nose between thumb and forefinger, trying to assess what little he knew of the investigation so far.

He ticked the items off mentally, as if striking them from some kind of psychological shopping list.

1. Harvey escaped six weeks ago.
2. Four sightings so far, all unsubstantiated.
3. All possible hiding places searched.

Randall sat forward in his chair. If the escaped prisoner *was* in or around Exham then where the hell was he hiding? He reached for a green file and opened it. It was a psychiatric report on Harvey, something which the Inspector had read before but now scanned yet again in an effort to glean some insight into the man he was hunting.

Harvey was dangerous – there was no doubt about that – but, as far as he could tell, the man was no idiot. A number of tests had been carried out on him by the prison psychiatrist. The results showed that he was prone to bouts of manic depression. His IQ was below average, his faculties not quite spot on but he wasn't crazy. That was what made him more dangerous, thought Randall. Harvey was unpredictable.

Randall shut the file and closed his eyes for a moment. So far no one had been harmed and the Inspector was becoming more and more convinced that the prisoner was nowhere near the town. Nevertheless, somewhere, nagging at the back of his mind was the conviction that eventually he would meet Paul Harvey face to face and it was a prospect he did not relish.

Lynn Tyler hauled herself out of bed, wincing slightly at the pain from her abdomen. She straightened up and the pain receded. The doctors had told her to expect a little discomfort after the abortion and, after all, she had only been home for a week. She stood up and looked down at her pale body, noticing how her stomach had begun to fill out. She was surprised at this, expecting

115

that it would flatten after the operation. She drew in a breath and held it, pulling in her belly for a moment. It didn't flop forward when she exhaled, the skin remained taut across her pelvis and stomach and she ran both hands over it. It felt hot, as if she had been standing next to a radiator and Lynn pressed the tight skin cautiously, puzzled by its feel. There was no pain, just the peculiar sensation of heat. She sat down on the edge of the bed once more, one leg hooked beneath her, both hands still pressed to her belly. She lay back, letting her hands slip to her sides and, gradually, the burning seemed to disappear. When she replaced her hands she felt only the familiar coolness of her skin. She gazed at the ceiling, tracing the many cracks, her thoughts rerunning the events of the last couple of weeks, as if she were rewinding a piece of cine-film – with each frame a memory.

She thought of how happy she'd been when she first discovered she was pregnant but of her fear at telling Chris. And how well that fear had been founded. She could still remember that morning he walked out on her, the morning she had decided to have the abortion.

As she lay there, a feeling of bitterness swept through her. Not only had she lost Chris, the one man she had ever loved, she had also lost the child she wanted. She had been forced out of necessity to have the abortion, knowing she would never be able to bring up a child alone.

The tears came suddenly and unexpectedly and she rolled onto her stomach in an effort to stifle them in the pillow. She wanted to forget him, tell him to fuck off, that she didn't need him. She wanted to yell it in his face. Tell him that there were plenty more men around. Her mind was in a turmoil and, as she rolled back onto her side, the tears dripped onto the sheets and soaked into the material. She wiped them away, smearing her mascara, wincing slightly when she felt the peculiar

116

burning sensation return, the skin stretching across her stomach and pelvis until it seemed it would tear.

She gasped at the stab of pain below her navel.

But, as quickly as it had come, it vanished and, tentatively, Lynn Tyler got to her feet, her hands gently stroking her belly.

There was no more discomfort.

She crossed to the wardrobe and began to dress.

Nineteen

Harold leant on the edge of the sink and gazed at the pale, ghost-like image which stared back at him from the mirror. There were deep, dark pits beneath both his eyes, his eyelids looked crusted and heavy and, when he exhaled, it came out as a deep sigh. There was no one else in the hospital toilet to see him and, for that, Harold was thankful.

God, how the day had dragged. It seemed more like eight years not eight hours since he'd started work. He'd been in on time and had done his best to disguise the fact that he felt so wretched. The three vicious cuts on his chest ached beneath the plaster and his joints seemed to groan in protest every time he moved.

His efforts to disguise how he *felt* might have been successful but there was no hiding his appearance. He looked, in the tradition of that time-honoured phrase, like death warmed up. He'd only eaten a small lunch and a couple of chocolate biscuits and even they had made him feel sick. His stomach rebelled at each new intrusion and, at one point, he had thought he was going to vomit.

117

He pulled the plug in the sink and shuffled over to the towel-roll, tugging hard on it to find a clean piece. Then he dried his face and hands, took one last look at his drawn visage and walked out into the corridor.

The wall clock opposite him showed 7.30 p.m. He still had another two hours before he was finished for the day. Harold sighed, thankful, at least, that it was time for a break. He made his way to the lifts and found an empty one. He punched the five button and leant back against the rear wall as the car rose swiftly. He would have preferred to have spent his break alone but Winston Greaves had insisted that he come to the office so that the two of them could talk. As the lift reached five and the doors slid open, Harold decided that talk was the last thing he needed but, nevertheless, he had to keep up appearances as best he could. As he walked towards the door of Greaves's office he felt his legs go weak and, for long seconds, he thought he was going to faint. Thankful that no one was around, he stood still for a moment, supporting himself against a wall. His head was spinning, the floor swimming before him. That ever-present pulse of pain at the back of his neck had now developed into a series of hammer blows to his skull and, once again, he fought back the urge to be sick. Sucking in deep breaths of stale, antiseptic air, he walked on.

Greaves had the kettle on when Harold entered the small office. The coloured porter looked up and smiled and Harold managed a thin grin in return. He sat down heavily, leaning back in the plastic chair. Greaves eyed him appraisingly. He too noticed the pallor, the milkiness of Harold's unscarred skin. The dark rings beneath his eyes looked as if they had been made by soot. The one good eye was bloodshot, the glass one sparkled with its customary unsettling brilliance. It looked all the more incongruous set against the drawn quality of the rest of his face.

Greaves waited for the kettle to boil then made the tea, handing Harold a mug. He watched as his companion struggled to remove the tea bag, scalding his fingers in the hot liquid. Greaves handed him a spoon and Harold finally succeeded in lifting the tiny bag out. He dropped it into a nearby ashtray and sat gazing down into his mug.

"Are you all right, Harold?" asked Greaves, sitting down opposite him.

"Yes."

The answer came a little too quickly, full of mock assurance.

"You look a bit under the weather," Greaves told him. Actually, Harold, he thought, you look half-dead.

"I'm OK," Harold told him, sipping at his tea.

"The job isn't getting you down is it?" Greaves asked. "I mean, I know it can be depressing sometimes."

Harold ran a hand through his hair again.

"I didn't sleep well last night," he confessed.

"That's not the first time is it? Why don't you ask one of the doctors for some sleeping pills?"

Harold shook his head.

"I'll be all right. I've just got a bit of a headache."

"There's nothing worrying you is there?"

Harold looked up.

"Why?" His voice was heavy with suspicion, perhaps a little over-cautious.

Greaves caught the inflection.

"I just asked," he said, smiling, trying to sound calm.

When Harold raised his mug to drink again, his hands were shaking, something which did not go unnoticed by his companion. Greaves regarded him warily over the rim of his own mug. Harold certainly looked rough, he thought, and he was unusually jumpy. Still, if he hadn't had any sleep. . .

He sat up as Harold swayed uncertainly in the chair. The coloured porter was on his feet in an instant,

119

moving around the desk towards his companion. Harold put one hand to his head and leant forward, taking the weight on his other elbow.

"Harold," said Greaves.

The older man waved him back.

"I'll be all right," he said. "I just felt faint."

Harold was shaking all over and a fine film of perspiration had greased his skin. He sucked in deep lungfuls of air and gradually straightened up but Greaves remained where he was.

"I think it might be best if you went back to your hut for half an hour or so, just for a lay down," the coloured porter said. "And while you're there, get something to eat. That's half of your trouble, you don't eat enough." He put out a hand which Harold grasped, allowing himself to be helped up.

"Come on," said Greaves. "I'll help you."

Together, the two of them made their way to the lift, descending to the ground floor. They headed for the main entrance without Harold speaking a solitary word. He stopped twice, worried that he was going to pass out but Greaves supported him. The senior porter suggested they see a doctor but Harold resisted the offer with a determination bordering on panic. So, slowly, they made their way out of the main building and towards the stretch of grass which led to Harold's hut. As they drew closer, perhaps a hundred yards from the flimsy structure, the older man pulled away and stood, swaying uncertainly, his good eye looking as glazed as the false one.

"I'm all right now," he said.

Greaves looked puzzled.

"I'll just see you inside," he said. "Make sure –"

Harold cut him short.

"No."

There was a note of near pleading in the word and Greaves wrinkled his brow.

"Don't come inside," said Harold, then he managed a weak smile. "I'm OK. Really."

Greaves did not move but he remained unconvinced.

"I'll be back on the ward at quarter past eight," Harold promised, nodding vigorously. "Quarter past eight."

He turned and headed for the hut, tottering drunkenly until he finally reached the hut. Greaves watched him through the darkness his eyes fixed to the small dwelling, waiting for the light to be put on inside. The hut remained in darkness. The coloured porter stroked his chin thoughtfully. Perhaps he should go and check on Harold anyway.

He began walking towards the hut.

Less than ten yards further on, he slowed his pace then finally stopped. No, he told himself, Harold must be allowed some privacy and, after all, he had promised to be back at work in less than forty-five minutes. Greaves stood a moment longer, his eyes riveted to the hut. Still no light came on. The senior porter sucked in a deep breath then turned and headed back towards the main entrance. His mind was full of unanswered questions the main one being, why would Harold not let him inside the hut? What was he hiding? Greaves administered a mental rebuke for himself. Harold probably had nothing to hide. He was probably just ashamed of the fact that the hut was a bit of a shambles. Nevertheless, as he reached the main entrance to the hospital, Greaves looked round once more, expecting to see a light coming from the hut and he was mildly disturbed when he saw nothing.

His curiosity was aroused and, as he made his way back up to his office, he became more and more convinced that Harold was hiding something. Perhaps he'd been stealing? Greaves swiftly dismissed that particular notion. For one thing there was nothing worth nicking in the hospital and, secondly, Harold probably wouldn't have the intelligence to pass for a thief. It was probably a quite innocent reason, Greaves told himself as he reached his office. He sat down and sipped his tea which was now stone cold. He put the kettle on to make a fresh cup, glancing at his watch.

It was 7.46. Harold would be back in half an hour.

Greaves waited for the kettle to boil.

Harold stood in the darkness, his back to the door of the hut, his eyes closed. He finally crept across to the window and, squinting out, he could see Greaves as he stood and watched and then finally turned and left. Harold had breathed an audible sigh of relief at that point. He didn't reach for the light switch but moved furtively in the gloom, making his way into the kitchen. He stood staring at the cupboard door for long seconds, the cupboard beneath the sink with its sliding door. With a shaking hand he reached out to open it then swiftly withdrew, the breath catching in his throat. The cuts on his chest began to throb and he took a step backward.

The hissing began.

He placed both hands to his temples as his headache seemed to intensify, the voices fluttering inside his mind like dialogue from a half remembered dream.

He moved towards the door.

Harold knelt and opened it, sliding the cupboard opening back an inch at a time, recoiling from the rancid odour of mildew and something stronger. Something more pungent and cloying. The stench of decay. It wafted out of the cupboard in an almost visible cloud making Harold cough.

He had covered the three foetuses with the blanket and now he could see their dark shapes moving slowly beneath the material.

Words came into his head, words which he had heard before. Mutterings and commands which he knew he must obey and which, now, he found himself wanting to obey.

The kitchen knife was still lying beside the sink, its blade dull with rust and dried blood and Harold's groping hands closed around the handle. He swallowed hard, listening to the words which whirled around inside his head, making him dizzy. His ears were buzzing and he was finding it difficult to focus on the three writhing shapes beneath the blanket but, finally, the feeling diminished somewhat and he reached for the loose corner of the material, pulling it back to expose the trio of creatures beneath.

Harold gaped at them, the breath rasping louding in his throat as he inhaled the rank air. At first he thought he was mistaken but, on closer inspection he realized that his first reaction had been correct. There was *no* mistake.

All three of the foetuses were growing.

Twenty

Winston Greaves glanced at his watch, drumming on his desk top with his free hand. It was almost 8.35 p.m. Where the hell was Harold? He had promised to be back on the ward by quarter past eight. Greaves chewed his bottom lip contemplatively. Perhaps the other porter had just returned and gone back to work without letting him know. Greaves pushed the thought to one side. No. Harold would have come up to the office first, to let him know that everything was all right. Greaves stared at the bottom of his own empty mug. Perhaps everything *wasn't* all right. Harold had looked ill, maybe he'd been unable to return to work. He might even need medical attention of some kind.

Greaves sat for five more anxious minutes then he got to his feet and headed out of his office towards the lifts. He reached the ground floor asking a number of other staff members if any of them had seen Harold. None had. Greaves exhaled deeply. Obviously he had not returned to the main building. Not sure whether to be angry or anxious, Greaves headed for the main doors, intent on finding Harold. He must still be in his hut after all. Perhaps he'd just fallen asleep. Was he really ill? These and other thoughts passed through the coloured porter's mind as he crossed the expanse of grass which led to the small dwelling where his companion lived.

There was still no light on in there.

Greaves wondered how Harold would react to his appearing at the hut this way. Would he refuse him entry as he had done earlier? Maybe he *did* have something to hide. If that was the case, Greaves told himself, he would find out what it was.

As he drew nearer the hut he became aware of how quiet it was. The darkness seemed to envelope the tiny hut like a black velvet glove, shutting out all sounds too. Greaves slowed his pace as he approached the door, straining his ears to pick up the slightest hint of movement from inside. It remained as quiet and forbidding as a tomb. For the first time, Greaves became aware of the cold, not just the ever-present chill in the air but a deeper more numbing cold which seemed to seep into his bones. He shuddered and glanced around him. Trees nearby swayed gently in the breeze, the beginnings of a mist swirled in the hollows of the field beyond the hospital grounds.

Greaves knocked hard on the door of the hut.

No response.

He knocked again, tapping his thigh with the flat of his other hand.

Nothing. Just silence. And the cold.

"Harold," he called, knocking again.

This time he knelt and tried to see through the key-hole but it was too dark inside the hut. He clambered to his feet and moved across to the window, cupping both hands over his eyes as he pressed his face to the soiled pane. He narrowed his eyes and could just make out a dark form on the bed. He banged the window but the shape on the bed remained immobile. He returned to the door and twisted the handle.

It was locked.

Perhaps he should go back and get help. For a moment he considered the idea but then decided that he should deal with it himself if possible. He didn't want to get Harold into trouble unnecessarily. Greaves put his hand on the door knob and twisted it again, this time throwing his weight against it. The lock was old and rusted and it came away with relative ease. The subsequent momentum sent Greaves stumbling into the hut itself. He almost fell, only retaining his balance by hanging onto the door. Then he gently pushed it shut behind him, immediately aware of the appalling stench which filled the hut – a pungent, nauseating odour which made him gag. It seemed to have no source but to be permeating the entire hut, oozing from the woodwork like sweat from pores.

He flicked the light switch. The bulb flickered, buzzed irritably then blew out. Greaves fumbled in his overall pocket for his lighter. He flicked it on and held the small flame above his head. It cast a pool of weak orange light and, in that sparse illumination, the porter saw the shape on the bed was Harold.

Greaves crossed to the prone body, his mouth drop-ping open.

Harold lay on his back, one leg drawn up foot resting

on the bed, the other stretched out so that the heel of his shoe was touching the floor. One arm lay across his stomach whilst the other hung limply at his side. Greaves stepped closer, seeing the dark stains on the floor, on the bedclothes. He realized that it was blood and, as he leant over the older man his foot brushed against Harold's outstretched arm. The knife fell with a dull clatter and Greaves almost shouted aloud. The blade was slick with blood too. There were pieces of plaster lying on the bedside cabinet and some soaking cotton wool. The crimson gore on it looked black in the darkness. But it was Harold himself who gave Greaves the biggest shock. The coloured porter leant as close as he could, staring at the vicious cuts on his companion's chest, one of them still weeping blood. The others were in the process of sealing, their ragged edges held together by congealing gore.

"Oh God," murmured the porter and he reached out to touch Harold's shoulder. He could see the man's torn chest rising and falling but he could solicit no reaction from him. Greaves prised open the unconscious man's eyelids and held the lighter close. Its flame sparkled in the glass orb. The pupil of the good eye contracted. Greaves pressed a tentative index finger to the older man's jugular vein and felt it pumping.

I've got to get help, he thought. He flicked off the lighter and headed towards the door.

Something fell with a crash in the kitchen and Greaves spun round.

"Who's there?" he said.

Silence.

He moved towards the other room, once more flicking the lighter on, using its meagre light as a guide. His own footsteps sounded heavy and conspicuous on the wooden floor as he advanced.

He heard breathing. Faint, mucoid breathing which seemed to grow louder as he paused in the doorway of

126

the kitchen. He held the lighter higher. It was beginning to get hot and he changed hands as his eyes scanned the tiny room. A plate lay shattered close by. There were drops of dark fluid on the enamel of the sink. Greaves crossed to it, his nostrils once more filled with an unbearable carrion stench. He dipped a finger in the dark fluid and sniffed it.

It was blood.

There was more of it on the door of the sliding cupboard opening beneath and Greaves knelt, pulling the door back as far as it would go. A blast of almost palpably rancid air gushed out and he had to fight hard to prevent himself from vomiting. He saw the blanket inside the cupboard, the dried blood caked on it. He reached out to touch it.

The first foetus seemed to roll into view from a darkened corner of the cupboard.

Greaves opened his mouth to scream, his eyes bulging as he saw the monstrosity. It pinned him in a hypnotic stare, its own black eyes glinting with a vile lustre. There was blood around its mouth and on its chest – even on the minute, shrunken genitals.

Greaves tried to back away, the lighter falling from his grasp, but he was unable to tear his horrified gaze away from the foetus's twin black orbs. He saw the second one drag itself into view, its own eyes focusing on him too. He reached back to grip the door jamb in an effort to pull himself away but his hand closed over something soft and jellied. He shrieked and looked down to see the third of the creatures. Greaves had grabbed its arm. He hurriedly pulled his hand away, noticing the trail of blood which the thing had left behind when it had dragged itself from beneath Harold's bed.

He was trapped. Pinned by their gaze, he was a prisoner of his own crippling terror. Now he felt the pain begin to build behind his eyes and at the base of his skull as the three abominations concentrated their fearful powers on him. It felt as if their eyes were burning into his head, like black laser beams they bored through his skull to his brain. He moaned and put both hands to his head in an effort to stop the pain which was growing more intense by the second. He tried to shut his eyes and blot out the insane vision before him but he couldn't and now he felt blood running from his nostrils. Filling his ears. Even his tear ducts seemed to swell and burst until he was weeping crimson. The pain in his head reached unbearable heights. He felt his legs go numb. He opened his mouth to scream but his tongue felt thick and useless, as if it had been injected with novocaine. Blood gurgled in his throat. His hands dropped from his head as he lost the use of them and finally he could only sit and watch, through a haze of red as the three creatures made one more concerted effort against him. Both his temporal arteries seemed to swell, pulsing madly for agonising seconds. His eyes seemed to swell and protrude as if pushed from the inside. But, somehow, Greaves managed to roll onto his belly and, using his legs as a means of propulsion, he pushed himself away from these nameless monstrosities. Into the other room he crawled, past the still motionless form of Harold, until he reached the door, the pain now reaching heights beyond endurance. Greaves managed to haul himself upright and, with a despairing moan, he flung the door open and staggered out, tottering drunkenly towards the beckoning lights of the main building.

He was almost there when, in a blinding moment of incredible agony, the veins and arteries inside his brain ruptured with so much force that most of the frontal and temporal lobes were destroyed. Winston Greaves collapsed but his body continued to jerk spasmodically for a few moments even after his death.

128

His body was found the next morning by an ambulance driver and the autopsy revealed that Greaves had died as the result of a massive cerebral haemorrhage.

Harold took the news of his friend's death badly. So badly that he spent his day off lying in bed but he did not sleep because, all the time, inside his head, the voices whispered.

It was to be a long time before he recovered from the news of Winston's death and the loneliness which he had thought banished now returned with numbing intensity.

Twenty-one

The onset of night brought about contradictory feelings within Paul Harvey. He welcomed it because it hid him and cloaked his furtive excursions from the farm. But he feared it too because it brought memories. Night had, in the past, always been a time of fear for him. The time when his father and mother would fight or when, in later years, he would be dragged from his bed and beaten, forced to bear that reeking stench of stale whisky and tobacco in his face as his father shouted at him.

Harvey hated to be shut in. It was another legacy of his childhood. His bedroom door was always locked from the outside, and this practice continued right up until his father died. There was no chamber pot in his room and, more often than not, he would be forced to urinate out of the window if he awoke during the night. Before he understood that trick he would simply wet the bed or do it into one of the drawers. Consequently, the clothes inside stank most of the time. However, whichever course of action Harvey had taken it had brought savage retribution from his father. During his troubled years at school, Harvey had been quizzed by teachers and taunted by his fellow pupils about the cuts and bruises which he bore almost all the time but, of course, he never dared to divulge the truth of how he sustained them.

His hatred of enclosed places had intensified during his stay in Cornford prison. The fact that he was kept in solitary, for the sake of the other prisoners, made things worse. But now, to a certain extent, he was free to wander the open fields and hillsides of Exham for the first time in his life and, with night now draped across the countryside like a shroud, he did just that.

As he stood at the top of a hill, the lights of the town glittered invitingly below him and Harvey gripped the sickle tightly as he made his way down the incline. An owl hooted close by but Harvey ignored its cry.

The town beckoned and Harvey did not refuse its call. He felt no fear, just a peculiar feeling that was something like exhilaration.

The woods on the outskirts of town swallowed him up.

Twenty-two

Ian Logan pulled up the zip on his leather jacket and shivered. He stood beneath the swaying sign of "The Black Swan", fumbling in his pocket for the packet of Marlboro and a box of matches. Thanks to the gusting wind, it took him three attempts to light the fag but finally he succeeded and, hands dug deep into his pockets, he started walking.

Other staff members, another barman included, were also leaving and Logan muttered cursory farewells to them. They all seemed to have cars except him and nearly all of them were going in the opposite direction. Even the one vehicle that was going his way sped past without offering him a lift. Logan exhaled deeply, his breath clouding in the night air.

He glanced at his watch and saw that it was approaching 12.15 a.m. He was usually home by half past eleven at the latest. He could imagine Sally's reaction now, almost hear her whinings as he walked in the front door. Moaning that his supper was spoiled, asking him where he'd been. He worked six nights a week, the only other day he spent at home listening to Sally moaning about how he should get a better job so that they could move into a *decent* house.

He decided to take a short-cut. There was bound to be an argument when he got in anyway so he might as well get it over and done with.

He cut down the lane to his left, knowing that he could be home in ten minutes. He quickened his step, the cigarette bouncing up and down between his lips as he walked.

The lane was dimly lit at the best of times but now, with the witching hour twenty minutes old, all but three of the lamps had been extinguished. There was the odd porch light on outside one or two of the cottages but, apart from that, the lane was wreathed in a heavy gloom. Visibility was made all the worse by a writhing mist which seemed to have settled over the fields. Blown by the wind, it seemed to ooze over the hedges like some kind of ethereal sea whose waves moved in slow motion.

Logan glanced at the white-washed cottages as he walked. Each one had its own drive and there was hardly one which did not boast two cars. These private dwellings stood out in marked contrast to the estate on which he lived. It lay a mere few hundred yards down the lane and the staid uniformity of the council houses offered a marked contrast to the gleaming individuality of these expensive properties. Perhaps Sally was right, he thought, it would be nice to live in a place like that. He was contemplating that thought when something moved away to his right.

He glanced round, slowing down only slightly, squinting into the blackness in an attempt to see what had made the sound. He heard a shuffling, scratching noise and, a moment later, a hedgehog scuttled out from beneath one of the hedges and trundled across the lane. Logan smiled to himself as he watched it disappear into one of the gardens opposite. A few yards further on another of the tiny creatures was splattered across the road. Cars sometimes drove down the lane and, obviously, this one had squashed the unfortunate hedgehog. It had been there a long time for, even in the gloom, Logan could see that its flattened remains were stiff, giving it the appearance of a spiky frisbee. He smiled at his analogy and walked on.

There was a farmhouse on the right. Painted black, it was almost invisible in the darkness but, from inside, he could hear the barking of a dog. The bloody thing had gone for him a couple of times in the past and he passed by hurriedly despite the fact that the animal was safely penned in the building. He walked another few yards and came to a rotting wooden stile. Beside it a bent and battered sign declared:

FOOTPATH

The so-called footpath led across a field and came out right opposite his own house. He decided to risk the many cow-pats which littered the field and cross it in an effort to get home quicker. He put his foot on the bottom plank of the stile and hoisted himself up. It creaked ominously under his weight and for a second he thought it was going to collapse but, as nimbly as possible, he swung himself over and landed with a loud plop in the mud on the other side.

"Sod it," he said, aloud, scraping some of the glutinous muck off on the bottom plank. That done, he set off across the field.

The light from the lane diminished to a point where his only guide was the odd light burning in the houses which backed on to the field. It was virtually impossible to see more than fifteen or twenty feet ahead. The crispness of the night air made the smells around him seem all the more prominent and he winced at the strong odour of cow dung. The ground was soft despite the frost and he almost slipped over twice, the second time shooting out a hand to grasp the fence which ran alongside him. He yelped in pain as his groping fingers closed over some barbed wire. Logan stopped dead, fumbling in his trouser pocket for a handkerchief, dabbing at the small cuts and muttering irritably to himself. He reached into his coat pocket for his fags and lit one up, puffing at it for a second before moving on.

The field was separated from the nearest house by a double row of trees, the ground in between each one thick with underbrush. Gorse and blackberry bushes grew in rampant abundance, in many places reaching shoulder height. There was a powerful smell of rotted vegetation in the air and Logan muttered to himself as he walked.

A twig snapped close by and, instinctively, he stepped back, the noise sounding thunderous in the stillness of the night.

His foot sank into something soft and he realized that it wasn't mud.

"Bloody cows," he groaned, shaking his foot.

However, his complaints were cut short when he heard another sound – the low rustling of bushes being parted. Logan squinted into the thick underbrush but he could see nothing. There was a moment's silence then the sound came again, closer this time.

A fox perhaps? Probably another hedgehog.

He swallowed hard and walked on, quickening his step for reasons he himself was not sure of. The other stile which marked the far end of the footpath was less than a hundred yards away and Logan could see the light from a nearby house beckoning him. His feet made squelching sounds in the mud and, as he walked, he glanced towards the trees nearby.

There was a loud scratching sound in the bushes less than two feet from him and he opened his mouth, allowing a small gasp to escape his lips. A sibilant rasping sounded so loud in the stillness and, at last, Logan broke into a run. He kept his eyes firmly fixed on the light ahead of him but it seemed to be a million miles away.

Beside him, the snapping of twigs seemed to grow to deafening proportions and he realized with horror that whatever was in the bushes was keeping pace with him.

His mind sought an explanation. It wanted to find a logical answer but all he could think of was getting to that bloody stile and clambering out of the field.

It was fifty yards away and he was still running, the bushes actually moving beside him now, some pushed over by his invisible companion. He could not bring himself to look for fear of what he might see.

Thirty yards.

The light ahead gleamed brighter and Logan found renewed strength in his legs as, beside him, he heard a low whining sound.

His breath was rasping in his lungs, his mouth dry.

Ten yards and he could see that stile. It was broken

134

in two places and for that he was grateful, because it meant he wouldn't have to waste time clambering over it.

Five yards.

He almost fell, slipping in another cow-pat. His arms pinwheeled wildly for a moment but he retained his balance. The perspiration was now heavy on his face, his breath harsh and almost painful. His legs ached from running and he could feel his heart hammering against his ribs.

There was a loud screech and a snapping of wood to his right, so close it seemed that it was coming from inside his own head. Something burst from the underbush and flew at him. He tried to scream but couldn't find the breath. He went down, face first into the mud, rolling over quickly, his eyes bulging and terror winding icy tendrils around his throat.

The cat which had leapt out of the bushes at him was already scampering off into the darkness, a mouse held firmly in its jaws.

"Jesus Christ," he gasped, wiping his face and dragging himself to his feet. For long seconds he stood there, trying to regain his composure. He closed his eyes and sucked in a deep breath, holding it for a second before exhaling in an audible sigh of relief. His clothes were splattered with mud and cow dung and he tried to brush it off with his hands. What the hell would Sally say about this? He suddenly found that he could smile and, as he watched the cat loping off across the field, he began to laugh.

"Bloody idiot," he said to himself and, still chuckling, he clambered over the stile.

The dark shape which loomed behind him seemed to grow from the blackness itself. Where gloom and night air had swirled around, there was suddenly something tangible.

Ian Logan thought he had heard a gust of wind but

what he did hear, *all* he heard, was the arc of metal as the weapon descended. The scream was locked in his throat. His eyes bulged wildly as he saw something metallic glinting above him. The dark outline of. . .

Before he had time to discern the shape, his throat was slashed open.

Darkness became eternal night.

Twenty-three

Despite the fact that the sun was shining, there was a harsh chill in the air and Randall shivered involuntarily as he stepped out of the Panda car. He yawned and rubbed a hand across his face. Behind him, the radio crackled and Constable Higgins reached for it; Randall didn't hear what he said because he was already making his way up the small incline that led to the footpath. A piece of rope had been tied across the entrance to the footpath and another uniformed constable stood there. The Inspector recognized him as Chris Fowler, the youngest man on the force. Yet to reach his twenty-sixth birthday, the constable looked fresh-faced and alert and seemed to remind Randall of his own weariness.

"Morning, sir," said Fowler.

Randall smiled thinly. The youngster was still nervous, only having been on the force for six months and he was still somewhat in awe of his superior. The Inspector patted the younger man on the shoulder as he passed. He swung his leg over the piece of rope and started up the narrow path. There were houses on either side of it, both separated from it by high hedges and a welter of rampant wild plants which seemed still

136

to be flourishing despite the onset of the cold weather. Clumps of stinging nettles grew thickly on either side, spilling over onto and into the cracks in the broken concrete in places. Long fingers of blackberry bush clutched at the policeman's jacket as he passed. Muttering irritably to himself, Randall tugged the jacket free and walked on. The heady aroma of wet grass and damp wood filled his nostrils and he reached for a cigarette, lighting it hurriedly as if trying to dispel the fresh natural odour of the countryside. He sucked hard on the filter and walked on.

Ahead of him, tall trees were dotted with black clumps which signalled the presence of crows' nests. Most of them were abandoned by the look of it. Just one solitary bird hovered in the crisp blue sky, as if casting an eye over the proceedings beneath it. Randall glanced at the houses on either side of the path. They were all simple red-brick buildings, with neatly kept gardens and suitably gleaming windows. Nothing seemed out of place on the estate, for every building appeared similarly immaculate.

Opposite him at the moment, in the house across the street, Sally Logan was being comforted by her mother while a perplexed police-woman tried to make some sense out of her hysterical blubberings.

Yes, everything was in its place on the estate. Even the corpse in the field just ahead.

Randall clambered over the wooden stile at the end of the footpath and eased himself down, trying to avoid the glutinous pools of mud. There was a powerful smell of rancid muck and, Randall suspected, cow shit. His suspicions were well founded when he nearly stepped in a pat. He glanced around, at the trees and undergrowth which ran alongside the barbed wire fence marking the boundaries of the field to his right. To his left ran another fence which separated the back gardens of nearby houses from the expanse of field and, straight ahead, he saw a group of three men standing around a blanketed shape. All three turned to face him as he drew nearer.

Two were on his force, Constable Roy Charlton and Sergeant Norman Willis. The third man looked like a midget placed beside the two burly policemen. He nodded a greeting to Randall and the Inspector returned the gesture. Dr Richard Higham stepped back from the shape at his feet and took off his glasses, polishing them enthusiastically with the monogrammed handkerchief he took from his trouser pocket. Randall exhaled deeply, looking down at the grey blanket. All around it, the mud was stained a deep rust colour, the dried blood mingling with the thick, oozing slime. The Inspector sucked hard on his cigarette and blew the smoke out in a long thin stream.

"What have we got?" he asked, his question addressed to no one in particular, his gaze riveted to the shapeless form at his feet. A hand protruded from beneath the blanket, the fingers curled and rigored.

Sergeant Willis handed the inspector a wallet and watched as his superior flipped it open. It contained about twenty pounds, mostly in pound notes, an Access card which bore the embossed name Ian J Logan and a couple of small photos. The photos showed a young woman, the man's wife Randall reasoned, and the other had her smiling out at the camera, a dark-haired man beside her. Randall held the photo before him and then looked down at the shape beneath the blanket.

"We haven't been able to make positive identification yet, guv," said Willis. "But we're pretty sure it's him."

Randall looked puzzled and handed the wallet back to his sergeant.

"What's the problem with identification then?" Randall wanted to know. He looked at Higham who knelt down and took hold of one corner of the blanket.

"The bloke under there is the one in the picture, isn't it?" He took a final drag on his fag.

"You tell me," said the doctor and pulled the material away to expose the corpse.

"Jesus Christ Almighty," murmured Randall, quickly clenching his teeth together, fighting to control the somersaults which his stomach was performing.

Willis lowered his head, Charlton looked away. Only Higham glanced first at Randall and then at the corpse.

The head was missing.

Randall wiped a hand across his face and sucked in several lungfuls of air. His stomach was still churning and he could almost feel the colour drain from his cheeks. Yet, somehow, he managed to keep his gaze fixed on the decapitated body. Blood was caked thickly all down the front of Logan's coat and for many yards around the body. The dark stains were everywhere. Randall felt a bead of perspiration burst onto his forehead as he studied the hacked and torn stump of the neck, a portion of spinal cord visible through the pulped mess. The head had been severed very close to the shoulders and apparently with some difficulty because there were a dozen or more other equally savage gashes at the base of the neck and even on the shoulders themselves. At first sight however, the damage seemed to be confined to that particular area, the blood which covered the body having come from the severed veins and arteries of the neck rather than from any wounds in the torso.

"Put it back," said Randall, motioning to the blanket and Higham duly obliged. The Inspector reached for his cigarettes and hurriedly lit another.

"The ambulance is on its way," Willis told him. "They'll take the body to the hospital."

"How long has he been dead?" asked Randall, looking at the doctor.

"It's difficult to say without the benefit of a thorough

139

post-mortem," Higham told him. "The pathologist at Fairvale will be able to tell you that more precisely than I can."

"Try guessing," said Randall, taking a puff on his cigarette.

Higham shrugged.

"There's very little surface lividity," he pulled back the blanket once more and indicated the pale hand with its clawed fingers. "Although the massive loss of blood may well be a cause of that." He sighed. "I'd say he'd been dead about eight or nine hours."

Randall looked at his watch. The hands showed 9.06 a.m. He nodded.

"Who found him?" he asked.

"A couple of kids," Willis said. "On their way to school."

"Christ," muttered Randall. "Where are they now?"

Willis explained that both children were being treated for shock at their homes close by.

The Inspector walked around the corpse and ambled over towards the thick bushes close by. A portion of the fence had been broken down and some of the underbrush crushed flat.

"Have you checked this out?" he asked, indicating the overgrown area.

Willis joined him.

"We found footprints in there and in the field over here," he motioned for Randall to follow him. He motioned to the single set of deep indentations in the mud. The Inspector knelt and examined the imprints more closely.

"Looks as if he was running," he said, blowing out another stream of smoke. "But why the hell are there only one set of tracks? It doesn't look as if anyone was chasing him."

"Whoever did it must be a right fucking maniac,"

140

said Willis. "I mean, who the hell cuts off a bloke's head and. . ."

Randall cut him short.

"By the way, where is the head?" he asked.

"It was taken, guv." The words came out slowly. "We can't find it anywhere."

Randall raised one eyebrow questioningly, his mind suddenly preoccupied with another thought.

"Paul Harvey," he said. "How long is it since he escaped?"

Willis shrugged.

"It must be going on for eight weeks, maybe longer," the sergeant said. "We haven't been able to find hide nor hair of him. He's probably in another part of the country by now, guv." The two men looked at each other for long seconds, the gravity and drift of Randall's suspicions gradually dawning on the older man.

"Get all the cars out. I want this bloody town searched again," Randall said.

"But guvnor, we hunted high and low for him for over a month," Willis protested. "There's no way he can still be in or around Exham."

"I want that search initiated, sergeant." The Inspector paused. "Look, there's been two murders in the history of this town, both committed by Paul Harvey. In the last two days, four people reckon to have seen him. Now we've got this," he pointed to the covered remains of Ian Logan. "Doesn't it seem just a little *too* coincidental?"

Willis shrugged.

"So you reckon Harvey killed Logan?"

"I'd lay money on it and, once the pathologist's report is in, then I'll have an ever clearer picture." The Inspector walked over to the fence. "The footprints you found in the bushes, can you get casts from them?"

Willis shook his head.

"There's too many and, what with the rain last night. . ." He allowed the sentence to trail off.

"Shit," muttered Randall. He turned to see a couple of uniformed men clambering over the stile, one of them carrying a furled stretcher. They made their way across to the body and, under the careful supervision of Higham, lifted the corpse onto the stretcher. Randall watched them as they carried the headless body away, struggling to get back over the stile with their recumbent load.

"I want that coroner's report as soon as it's completed," he said to Willis. "Send one of the men over to the hospital to pick it up as soon as it's ready."

The sergeant nodded. The two men walked back towards the waiting figure of Higham and Charlton, then the four of them made their way back down the footpath behind the two stretcher bearers. The ambulance itself was parked behind one of the Pandas, two of its wheels up on the grass verge to allow cars easy passage in the narrow street. Randall watched as the body was loaded into the back of the vehicle and he could see people peering from their front windows to see what was happening. Some had even opened their front doors and were standing there quite unconcerned in their efforts to get a better view of the proceedings. A handful of people already knew that something sinister had happened in the field. By lunch-time probably the entire street and half the estate would know what was going on, such was people's fascination with the macabre, Randall had found. Anything even slightly out of the ordinary was a source of endless curiosity to them and, in a way, he felt a curious kind of pity for these people whose hum-drum existences were only brightened up by the occasional death or break-in on the estate. A murder would no doubt fuel their coffee time chats for months to come as they speculated and fabricated, each teller adding his or her own particular

142

brand of exaggeration until the tale would eventually become local folk-lore. It was something to be mulled over in years to come – and perhaps even laughed about.

As he climbed wearily into the waiting Panda, the last thing Lou Randall felt like doing was laughing.

The afternoon grew dark early and, at four o'clock, Randall found that he had to switch on the lights in his office at Exham's police station. The building itself was a two storey, red brick edifice about five minutes walk from the centre of the town. Its ground floor comprised an entrance hall, the complaints desk (where Willis now stood doing a crossword) and, beyond that, a type of rest room which doubled as a briefing base for the small force. A flight of steps led down to the basement and its six cells whilst the upper floor was made up of offices and store-rooms. There was a vending machine at the head of the stairs and Randall had managed to coax a cup of luke-warm coffee from it by the simple expedient of kicking it. The bloody machine was playing up and force seemed to be the only thing it responded to. Usually, one of the men popped in his twenty pence and the machine swallowed it gratefully without offering a drink in return. There'd been numerous complaints about it and Randall had decided it was time to get in touch with the manufacturers to see about getting it replaced. However, his thoughts lay on matters other than vending machines as he sat at his desk tapping his blotter with the end of a pencil.

Thoughts raced through his mind at break-neck speed, not allowing him to focus on them.

The murder of Ian Logan. The hunt for Paul Harvey. Even now, men were out searching for him, retracing ground which *he* knew they had already covered in the first early days when the maniac escaped. Randall sipped his coffee but found that it was cold. He winced

143

and put the cup down. Harvey. Harvey. Harvey. The name rolled around in his mind like a loose marble. He thumped his desk irritably and got to his feet. There *had* to be a link between Logan's murder and the escaped maniac. He walked to the window of his office and gazed out. From his vantage point he could see the small railway station which served Exham. A train was just pulling out, heading for London. The people of Exham were lucky in so far as they were able to reach the capital direct. Just a few stops up the line, in Conninford, lay Regional HQ and Randall's superiors. They had already been on to him about his failure to find Harvey, once they discovered that the wanted man had committed a murder they would probably try and nail Randall to their office wall.

He sighed and ran a hand through his hair. He felt so helpless, so frustrated. He looked out over the town.

"Where are you, Harvey?" he muttered, aloud.

He knew he would return home that night, the problem still on his mind. It was always like that now. He had many sleepless nights sifting through problems, unable to divorce work from home any longer. Home. He smiled bitterly at the irony of the word. It wasn't a home any longer, not without Fiona and Lisa to welcome him. The house was still and lifeless without them and had been for the past five years. There was no warmth any more, just the harsh white greeting of the walls and their glass smiles beaming out at him from behind carefully framed photos. When it had happened, Randall had wondered whether or not he would ever recover. It had felt as if something had been torn from inside him, as if a part of his being had ceased to exist, robbed of their love and companionship. He had seen the change in himself over the past few years. He had his work and that was something but it was precious little substitute for a wife and daughter. He had become, against his own will, a cynical and embittered man. To a certain extent the cynicism had always been present – it went with the job someone had once told him. The bitterness, however, and the feeling of desolation which sometimes bordered on anger, was something which he had only recently learned to live with and even, in his worst moments, to nurture. He had allowed the seeds of resentment to blossom into blooms of hatred and fury. He closed his eyes, feeling as lost and lonely as he had ever done in his life.

The knock on the office door brought him back into the real world so fast that the thoughts vanished from his mind.

It was Constable Stuart Reed, a tall, gangling individual with a heavily pitted complexion. He was in his mid-thirties, perhaps two or three years younger than Randall himself. The constable was carrying a thin file.

"Coroner's report on Ian Logan, guv," he announced, waving the file in the air.

"Thanks," said Randall, taking it from him.

The PC turned to leave but the Inspector called to him.

"See if Norman's got any coffee or tea on the go will you?" he asked. "The stuff out of that bloody machine tastes like cat's piss."

Stuart nodded and, smiling, left his superior alone. Randall flipped open the file and found that it contained just three pieces of paper. The coroner's report, another report on the possible murder weapon and a carbon headed:

FAIRVALE HOSPITAL/NOTICE OF DECEASE

All three were signed with the same sweeping signature – *Ronald Potter.*

Potter was chief pathologist at Fairvale, a fact born out by the legend below his name stating that in block letters.

Randall ran a close eye over each of the three docu-

145

ments in turn, pausing here and there to reread certain sections. He fumbled in his jacket pocket for his cigarettes and took out the packet muttering irritably to himself when he found it was empty. He picked up his biro and chewed on the end of that instead. The initial report ran for four pages much of which was comprised of medical jargon but, by the time he put it down, Randall understood how, if not why, Ian Logan had died.

"Eight lateral wounds on the shoulders and neck," he read aloud. "The head was severed by a single edged weapon. Depth of wounds ranges from a quarter of an inch to two and a half inches. No other external damage."

Randall dropped the report onto his desk and leant forward in his seat, glancing at the second sheet. It was a short piece on the possible nature of the murder weapon. Once more he read aloud.

"Traces of rust found in all but one of the wounds." The Inspector drummed softly on the desk top with his fingers.

"Rust," he murmured. He pulled a notepad towards him and scribbled on it:

1. Rusty knife?
2. Strong man (depth of cuts)?
3. No motive?

He pulled at one eyebrow as he considered his own scribblings. It would take someone of extraordinary strength and savagery to sever a man's head without the aid of a serrated tool. The implement appeared to be straight-edged. He checked back over the first report. No, there was no mention of any straight blade. A single edge, yes. He ringed the word knife and drew three question marks beside it. An axe maybe. He quickly dismissed the thought. The wounds would be much deeper if an axe had been used. Even so, the deepest had penetrated two and a half inches. To Randall, that implied the weapon had been used in a swatting not stabbing action. Ian Logan's head had been hacked off, not sliced off. He glanced back over the report and noted that portions of chipped spinal cord had been found, something which further indicated that the head had been cut off by repeated powerful blows. Where the severed appendage was now remained to be seen.

Randall exhaled deeply and sank back in his chair. He tapped on the arm agitatedly, wondering if any of his men had found Paul Harvey yet. It had to be Harvey, he reasoned. Everything pointed to that. The bastard was still in or around Exham somewhere. The Inspector gritted his teeth. He had to be found, even if it meant tearing every house and building down brick by brick. He glanced at the pathologist's report a last time and felt the hairs prickle on the back of his neck. He had the unshakeable feeling that it would not be the last such report he read.

Twenty-four

The staff canteen at Fairvale seemed more than usually crowded and Harold Pierce found that he had to move carefully with his tray of lunch. The mug of tea lurched violently and threatened to spill and, twice, the plate which bore his beans on toast slid dangerously near to the edge of the laminated board. Harold eventually found a seat alone and set his lunch down, almost grateful to have reached the haven of a chair. He sat, exhaling heavily. His stomach was rumbling and he felt

147

hungry but the sight of the food made him feel nauseous. He picked up the knife and fork and held them before him, gazing down at his steaming food but, after a moment or two, he put the cutlery down and contented himself with sipping at his tea.

His head ached, something not helped by the constant hum of conversation which filled the canteen.

All around him, groups of nurses, doctors, porters and other hospital staff chatted and laughed, complained and swore. Harold sat alone, the sea of sound washing over him like an unstoppable current. It had seemed like a loud buzzing at first but, as the day wore on, the buzzing had diminished until it became words. Admittedly they were fuzzy and indistinct, but they were words nevertheless. Harold could not make out what the voices said but they persisted. He closed his eyes and put one hand to his ear as if he thought it possible to pluck these ever-present sounds from inside his head with his finger-tips. But the noises continued, mingling with the cacophony of sound in the canteen.

Harold sipped his tea, wincing as he picked up the mug. He raised it to his lips with effort, almost as if it were made of lead instead of porcelain. The brown liquid tasted bland on his furred tongue.

Someone asked him to move his chair and Harold turned to see a very attractive woman standing behind him. She was dressed in a white coat, open to reveal the full swell of her breasts beneath the blouse she wore. The skirt hugged her slender waist and hips and as Harold looked into her face he found himself captivated by a pair of the brightest blue eyes he'd ever seen. Her thin face was framed by short, brown hair. She was smiling.

For long seconds, Harold gazed at her, realizing from her attire that she was a lady doctor. He woke up to the fact that he was blocking her way and hurriedly pulled his chair in, allowing her through. She smiled again and thanked him, and he watched her as she made her way up to the food counter and began picking things out, talking happily to the women there. Harold touched the scarred side of his face with a shaking hand, his one good eye still riveted to the woman in the white coat. All the other sounds in the canteen seemed to fade as his attention focused exclusively on the doctor. She had carried her tray of food to a table where a number of other doctors sat and he could see her laughing and joking with them. He lowered his head again, once more aware of the pain which gnawed at the back of his neck and head. The voices in his mind continued to mutter and mumble their incomprehensible dialogue and Harold gritted his teeth until his jaw ached.

Finally, he got to his feet but as he did so he felt his knees buckle and he shot out a hand to steady himself. His flailing hand caught the edge of the plate and, before he realized what was happening, it had fallen from the table and smashed on the floor. Those nearby turned to see what had happened and Harold coloured beneath their curious gaze. He looked down at the mess of broken porcelain and baked beans and shrugged apologetically as a large woman in a green overall waddled across the canteen carrying a mop and bucket.

"I'm sorry," mumbled Harold.

"That's all right, love," said the woman. "It happens all the time. But if you didn't like our cooking you could have told us. You didn't have to chuck it all over the floor." She looked up at him, laughing loudly.

Harold swallowed hard, his body trembling.

"I'm sorry," he repeated, not seeing the joke. He hesitated for a moment then turned briskly and made for the exit door, imagining all eyes were on him.

"Who is that man?" asked Dr Maggie Ford, running a hand through her short brown hair. She watched

Harold's rushed departure with a feeling akin to pity. "I don't remember seeing him around the hospital before."

Frederick Parkin drained what was left in his coffee cup and dabbed at the corner of his mouth with a handkerchief, paying particular attention to the thick white moustache that overhung his top lip.

"His name is Pierce as far as I know," he told Maggie. "He was a patient at the old mental hospital until recently."

Maggie nodded slowly.

"I wonder how he got that terrible scar? Poor devil."

"No one seems to know too much about him," Parkin told her. "A fire I would think, looking at it." His tone brightened and he smiled broadly at Maggie. "Why the sudden interest?"

"You know me, Fred," she said. She pointed to her nose and winked. Both of them laughed. "I just feel sorry for him," she added finally. "It must be an awful burden going through life like that. He's got guts to walk about in that state."

"Your compassion is overwhelming, Maggie," said Parkin, good-naturedly. "Sometimes I think you're in the wrong job. You should have been a social worker."

"There's nothing wrong with taking an interest in people," she said, defensively. "After all that's what we're all paid for isn't it?"

Parkin smiled.

"I bow to your superior logic," he said. He got to his feet, said a few words to another man at the end of the table and then made his way out. Maggie sipped her coffee, her mind still unaccountably fixed on Pierce.

She was thirty-two and had been a consultant gynaecologist at Fairvale for the last four years during which time she'd built up an enviable reputation for herself. She had not, as might have been expected, encountered any resentment from her male colleagues – rather the opposite in fact. They had welcomed her eagerly into their midst, impressed by her abilities and also, she thought with a smile, by her female assets. She was the sort of woman who exuded that peculiarly ambiguous demeanour that combined sensuality with innocence; although, with a handful of lovers behind her, Maggie could scarcely claim the word innocent in its literal sense. She was a dedicated woman, single-minded to the point of obsession about her work, something which had caused conflict in many of her relationships but it was not a matter on which she was prepared to compromise. Her mother was always telling her that she should be married but, for Maggie, a career was the only thing which mattered. Men, when she found the time for them, were little more than a brief interlude. At the moment, she lived alone in a small flat about twenty minutes drive from the hospital and she went back to an empty home every night. She said this did not bother her and, on the surface, it appeared that she was telling the truth. However, somewhere inside her was a need which had to be fulfilled and fulfilled by far more than the occasional brief relationship or one night stand. Maggie harboured a brooding fear of loneliness. Some nights, lying alone in her bed she would contemplate the idea of sharing the rest of her years with a partner who cared for *her* above all else. But that thought was always tempered by the fear that she would not be able to reciprocate that bond no matter how hard she wanted to. If many people struggled with the problem of wanting to *be* loved, Maggie Ford was trying to come to terms with the fact that she wanted *to* love. It seemed as if that pleasure were to be denied.

She sat in the canteen and finished her coffee then, finally, she got to her feet. Glancing at her watch she remembered she had a patient to see in ten minutes.

It was almost 1.55 p.m.

Harold pushed the trolley out of the lift into the eerie twilight of the basement. He guided it over the polished floor, past the pathology labs, towards the furnace room. His head felt as if it were swelling and then contracting like some bulbous extension of his pulse. The voices inside his head continued to hiss but they were gaining a startling clarity now. Harold listened to his own footsteps echoing in the corridor as he approached the furnace room, surprised to see that the door was open.

He hesitated, his hands suddenly trembling and he gripped the handrail of the trolley until his knuckles turned white. The noise inside his head grew to a fresh crescendo and it sounded as if someone were holding two gigantic sea-shells against his head such was the roaring in his ears.

He could see the furnace through the open door, its great metal door yawning open to reveal the blistering flames within, competing with the ever-present hum of the generator. Harold's world had become one of noises and he closed his eyes momentarily before walking on towards the room. He could already feel the heat from inside. He bumped the door open with one end of the trolley.

Brian Cayton turned as the door opened. He recognized Harold and smiled.

"Hello, Harold," he said, reaching for a pair of forceps which lay on the trolley which he himself stood next to.

As Harold watched, he saw Cayton grip the forceps and clamp them around the limp and dripping form of a foetus which he took from a receiver. Its head lolled back as if the neck had been snapped and Harold saw blood running from its tiny mouth.

"What are you doing?" he demanded, stepping towards the other porter who was still holding the tiny body before him, trying not to inhale the rank odour which it gave off.

"You know what I'm doing," said Cayton, a little impatiently. "I've just come from pathology."

He held the foetus closer to the hungry mouth of the furnace.

"You're going to burn that child," said Harold, flatly.

The smile faded from Cayton's face.

"Yes. Of course I'm going to burn it." He paused, fixing his gaze on Harold's good eye. "Besides, it isn't a child."

The words inside Harold's tortured mind finally burst through the fog of indecision like diamond bullets.

"Stop it," he said, moving closer.

Cayton raised a hand to ward him off.

"Look, Harold, I know it's not very pleasant but it's got to be done," he said, forcefully. "Christ, you've done it yourself, what's the big deal?"

Harold felt searing pain inside his head and he blundered towards the other porter who stepped back, bewildered. Then, suddenly, he turned and tossed the foetus into the flames.

Harold screamed. A high keening wail torn raw from his throat, the wild ululation of a creature in pain. He crashed to the ground heavily, pulling the trolley over with him. His last conscious thought and sight, one of the foetuses being devoured by the ravenous fire. He rolled onto his back, vaguely aware that Cayton was heading for the door.

"I tried to stop him."

Words pounded in his ears, low guttural raspings, thick with power.

"I tried, I. . ."

Pain. Agonizing, white hot pain, filled his head for interminable seconds. Mercifully, Harold Pierce blacked out.

153

Maggie Ford yawned and reached up to massage her neck, allowing her head to rest against the rear wall of the lift. There was no one else in it and Maggie slipped one foot out of her shoe, flexing her toes. Her feet were killing her. Come to think of it, she ached all over.

"A good hot bath when you get home," she said aloud, suddenly embarrassed with herself when the lift doors slid open, the car having bumped to a stop without her even noticing.

She saw Brian Cayton standing there, his face flushed, a thin film of perspiration on his face.

"Doctor," he gasped, jumping into the lift. "Can you come down to the basement straight away? One of the other porters has collapsed."

She was going to protest but the concern on the young porter's face was such that she decided to remain silent. He jabbed the basement button and the lift dropped the remaining floors. When it came to a halt at its appointed place, Maggie found herself running behind Cayton, so infectious was his anxiety. She followed him to the furnace room, immediately struck by the foul odour of soiled linen and the blistering heat which poured forth from the still open metal door. She saw Harold lying prone beside the overturned trolley, arms outstretched.

"Go and get help," she told Cayton. "Get someone to help you, we've got to get him up." Even as she spoke, she slid back the lid of one eye and shone her penlight on it mildly repelled by the feel of the cracked skin beneath her fingers but she administered a swift mental rebuke to herself at her reactions, now more concerned when she realized that Harold's pupil didn't react to the light. She tried again, feeling mildly foolish when she realized that it was the glass eye she was gazing into. She repeated the procedure with the good eye, relieved to see that this time there was pupilary contraction. Even as she pocketed the penlight, he began to stir. He tried to sit up but Maggie restrained him.

"Just take it easy," she said, softly and the initial look of fear on Harold's face was replaced by one of pained bewilderment.

He found himself looking into the face which he'd seen earlier. That beautiful thin face framed with the brown hair. *Her* soft hands were touching his wrist, feeling for his pulse.

"Why do they do it?" he croaked.

"Do what?" she wanted to know, checking his pulse against the second hand of her watch.

"Burn the children."

She looked puzzled.

"They burn babies in there," Harold said, tearfully, motioning towards the furnace.

Maggie understood and was thankful that, at that precise moment, Cayton arrived with another porter. On her instructions, they helped Harold to his feet and supported him to the lift.

"Shall we take him to casualty?" asked Cayton.

Maggie shook her head.

"No. Take him to my room on the fourth floor. I think it's time someone examined him."

All four of them climbed into the lift and, in seconds, it was rising.

Twenty-five

Harold sat on the edge of the couch, fidgeting uncomfortably. He watched Maggie as she crossed to her desk and selected a number of implements with which she obviously intended to perform the examination. He didn't know what the things were although he had seen one or two of them many times during his spell in the hospital.

It was warm in the office, the gentle hum of the radiator reminding him of the furnace room. The walls were a brilliant white, the snowy expanse broken only by one large picture window to his right which looked out over much of the hospital below. The room itself was sparsely decked out, containing three hard chairs, a large desk and the couch upon which he now sat. There were filing cabinets against the far wall, each drawer marked with red labels bearing letters. On the desk itself there was a small pile of books, a pencil holder and a clock. The ticking seemed unnaturally loud in the silence.

"When was the last time you had an examination, Mr Pierce?" Maggie asked him, turning back to the couch.

Harold smiled weakly.

"I don't remember," he said. "You can call me Harold if you want to," he added, falteringly.

Maggie smiled and asked him to take off his overall which he did. Beneath it he wore a slightly off-white shirt, the cuffs fraying and worn. She asked him to undo his sleeve which he also did, being careful not to pull the material any further than an inch or two from his wrist, ensuring that his forearm was still covered. Maggie took his pulse once again and scribbled something down on a piece of paper.

"How long have you been working here, Harold?" she asked him, reaching for the opthalmoscope, flicking it on and testing the tiny beam of light against the palm of her hand. Satisfied, she peered into his one good eye, adjusting the implement until she found the correct magnification.

"About eight or nine weeks," he told her.

156

As she leant close to him he could smell her perfume. Just a vague hint but nevertheless detectable. She smelt so clean and fresh and, as she peered through the opthalmoscope, her silky hair brushed the unscarred side of his face. He felt a peculiar tingle run through him and his breathing quickened slightly.

"Have you ever had blackouts before?" she wanted to know.

Harold shrugged.

"I don't think so."

She asked him to take off his shirt.

A look of panic flashed across his face, as if she had just asked him to jump from the fourth storey window. He quivered, the breath catching in his throat.

"Why?" he asked, agitatedly.

She smiled, surprised by his reaction.

"I want to check your heart and lungs." She was already reaching for the stethoscope.

Still he hesitated, dropping his gaze momentarily then looking up at her with something akin to pleading sparkling in his eye.

"I'm all right," he told her, his voice cracking.

"Please, Harold," she persisted.

His mind was racing. What would she say when he took it off? Should he leave now, run out of the room? But then, he knew that they would come for him and when that happened. . . He pushed the thought to one side.

"Harold, please take off your shirt."

With shaking hands, he began to undo the buttons, pulling the bottom free of his trousers. Maggie took the sphygmomanometer from its metal case, preparing to test his blood pressure when she'd finished the chest examination. She tugged the cuff open, the velcro rasping noisily in the silence of the room.

Harold pulled his shirt free, balled it up and held it on his lap, his body trembling.

Maggie turned to look at him.

She swallowed hard, trying hard to disguise her horror at what she saw. Harold sat impassively, his eyes closed as if ashamed of the sight of his body.

His chest and arms were covered by numerous raw, angry cuts. Some had scabbed over, others were purple knots where the scar tissue had formed, only to be picked or cut away later. Dark, vicious welts covered his arms from the wrist to the elbow and the parts of his torso and limbs not disfigured by the multitude of sores and wounds were milk white. He had obviously lost a lot of blood from the cuts. One or two were festering, a large one just below his left elbow was a suppurating cleft in the mottled flesh. The most striking thing about the wounds, however, was their positioning. Each seemed to be a measured distance from the next, almost like carefully carved tribal scars. His chest was a patchwork of crusted flesh and dried blood, one nipple having been sliced in two. It was so badly bruised it was black. And that was the curious thing about all the cuts. Around each one was a dark area which, if anything reminded Maggie of a love-bite. It was as if the skin on Harold's body had been drawn between someone's lips, the suction causing the resultant discoloration of the flesh.

"Where did you get these cuts?" she asked him, her voice low and full of muted fear. Fear? Yes, Maggie told herself. Spidery fingers were playing a symphony along the nape of her neck and she felt the hairs rise in response.

Harold didn't answer, he just continued gazing down at the floor.

She moved closer, taking hold of his left wrist, anxious to get a closer look at the numerous gashes. He pulled away from her, his breath coming in gasps.

"Did you cut yourself like this for a reason?" she wanted to know.

158

He opened his mouth to speak, thoughts still whirling around inside his head and now, he began to hear the familiar voices growing in volume as he fought to find some kind of explanation for the shocking appearance of his upper body.

"I think I should call Dr Parkin, let him. . ."

"No." He practically shouted at her. "No."

"Something has got to be done about these cuts, Harold," she said. "Now, will you please tell me how you got them?"

"I . . . I dream," he mumbled.

"About what?" she asked him, taking his left arm in her hand and, this time, she encountered no opposition. She probed the edges of the nearest gash with a wooden spatula, withdrawing it when Harold winced.

"I dream about different things," he said, vaguely, gazing ahead as if he were addressing someone on the other side of the room.

"What do you see in these dreams, Harold?" she asked him. She was using the conversation as a means of distraction while she got a better look at the cuts on his body. The one below his elbow was undoubtedly fresh. She wiped some sticky liquid from it with a piece of gauze and prodded the torn flesh but, this time, Harold didn't react.

"Fire," he said, flatly. "I see fire."

"Can you tell me more about the dreams?" she asked.

"I killed my brother and my mother," he said, almost as if it were a confession. "That was why they put me away." The smile that he flashed at her caused her flesh to rise into goose-pimples. Maggie wondered just how deeply Harold's apparent obsession with the disposal of abortions, and his insistence on calling them "children", went. It made her wonder just how much more he could cope with. The wounds on his body were obviously self-inflicted, perhaps, she thought, as some kind of bizarre revenge against himself for the crime which he felt he'd committed.

"How did your mother and brother die?" she asked.

He told her, and the significance of the fire, the destruction of the embryonic creatures, immediately fell into place.

"I dream about them sometimes," he said. "I dreamt about the furnace room once, I. . ."

He felt a stab of pain inside his head and the voices were there, loud and commanding.

"Tell me about the dream," Maggie said. He swallowed hard, his tone lightening somewhat.

"I don't think I remember now," he told her. "It's best if I don't talk about it. I don't like to think about it."

Maggie nodded, pressing the stethoscope to his chest. His heartbeat was slow. When she took his blood pressure she found it was a fraction lower than normal. Harold may have appeared to be anxious and disturbed but none of his bodily signs showed anything to back that up. She told him to put his shirt back on, dressing the worst of the cuts first.

"Can I go now?" he asked.

"If you're sure you're all right," she said. "But I'd still feel better if you'd let me call Dr Parkin in to have a look at you."

He refused, tucking his shirt back into his trousers and pulling on his overall.

"I'd like you to come back and see me in a couple of days, Harold," Maggie told him.

He nodded, still eager to leave.

"Why don't you go and lie down for a while."

"I feel much better, thank you."

Maggie shrugged. They said brief goodbyes and Harold left, closing the door behind him. He walked slowly down the corridor, the voices inside his head buzzing agitatedly.

"I didn't say anything. I kept the secret," Harold whispered to empty air.

"Will you hurt her?" he wanted to know.

The voices continued to speak and Harold listened intently.

Maggie sat down at her desk and ran a hand through her hair. Outside, grey rain clouds were gathering and the first fine particles of drizzle were beginning to coat the window like early morning dew on a spider's web. It was gloomy in the office but she did not switch the lights on, merely sat in the deepening shadows, lost in her own thoughts, the vision of Harold's savaged body still vivid in her mind. What could drive a man to inflict such damage on himself, she wondered? She looked at the phone on her desk for a long time, pondering on whether or not to ring Harold's old psychiatrist. Perhaps if she knew more about his background she would better understand why he had done what he'd done. She drummed restlessly on the desk top, her eyes still fixed on the phone then, finally, she got to her feet and crossed to the window, gazing out at the approaching banks of grey cloud.

If he had dreams, nightmares, she reasoned, then maybe the cuts had been inflicted whilst he was in the dream-state. She had heard of people lifting objects in their sleep which they would never be able to move while awake. Perhaps the same principle applied in Harold's case. What he could not bring himself to do in his waking state, he found the subconscious strength to do during his dreams. Namely the self-mutilation. She exhaled deeply. It was too simple an explanation. The cuts seemed *too* carefully spaced, there was nothing random about them. Unlike other psychotics who, given a sharp instrument, would carve themselves up just for the hell of it, Harold seemed to have chosen the spots where he inflicted the damage. It was almost as if he had been guided.

Maggie shook her head, trying to dismiss the thought. For one thing, Harold, as far as she knew, lived alone. He had few friends and certainly no enemies. And, as for the theory of him inflicting the wounds in a psychotic orgy of masochism – well, that didn't tie up because, although he may be mildly disturbed, Harold was certainly not psychotic.

She crossed back to her desk and glanced at the clock. 4.11 p.m.

What really puzzled her was the dark, bruised area around each cut. If Harold was a haematophile and thereby obsessed with the drinking of his own blood then the bruises on his arms could be easily explained but, she thought, that seemed unlikely.

Besides, it still wouldn't explain how his chest came to be in the same state.

Maggie chewed her bottom lip thoughtfully, already determined that if she had not heard from Harold in two days' time, she would personally go to his home and find out just what was happening to him.

Twenty-six

Judith Myers got up from her desk, smiling happily at the other people in the room, anxious to disguise the pain which was gnawing at her stomach and groin. She tried to tell herself that it was muscle strain. She'd been away from work for too long and now bending over a drawing board all day. . .

The idea quickly vanished as she felt a searing jab of

agony in her side. She stood still in the corridor for a moment, leaning against the wall, feeling as if someone had kicked her in the side. She put one hand to the throbbing area and felt it gently, the pain seemed to recede somewhat and she hurried down the short flight of steps which would take her to the toilets.

Once inside, she was relieved to discover that she was alone. She locked herself in one of the cubicles and sat down on the toilet seat, rubbing both sides now, taking short breaths. The pain seemed to be moving deeper into her groin so she stood up and slipped her tights and panties down to her knees, probing gently at the lips of her vagina with her index finger. She withdrew the digit after a couple of minutes, her hand shaking, her eyes half expecting to see it stained with blood. The incident the other night had frightened her but the doctor had told her that slight bleeding was not uncommon so soon after an abortion. Bleeding from the navel however, *was* uncommon but a trip to her own GP had revealed no complications and, despite Andy Parker's protestations, she had returned to work as soon as possible.

Now she pulled up her underclothes and unlocked the cubicle aware still of the pain which seemed to be spreading throughout her abdomen. She felt a sudden wave of nausea sweep over her and just made it to one of the sinks. Bent double over it, she retched until there was nothing left in her stomach. The pain, curiously, seemed to vanish. Judith spun both taps to wash away the mess, cupping some water in one palm and swilling it around her mouth. She looked up, studying her reflection in the mirror. Her face was the colour of rancid butter, the dark brown of her eye-shadow giving her the appearance of a skull. She pulled some paper towels from the dispenser and wiped her mouth, tossing the used articles into a nearby bin. Then, once again, she pressed both hands to her stomach.

163

"Judith, are you all right?"

The voice startled her and she turned to see Theresa Holmes standing just inside the door.

"It's OK, Terri," she said.

"You look awful," Theresa told her. "Do you want me to fetch the first aid bloke?"

"No, I'll be all right. I just felt sick."

Terri crossed to the sink and stood beside her, the ruddiness of her own complexion a marked contrast to the palour of Judith's. She was two years older and the women had been friends ever since Judith joined the firm.

"A friend of mine, she had an abortion," Terri said. "She had stomach trouble for months afterwards."

Judith smiled sardonically.

"Thanks, Terri, you're a great comfort."

"Sorry, I didn't mean it like that. All I'm saying is, I think it's common to feel bad soon after one."

Judith shrugged.

"It's been over three weeks now," she said.

She went on to describe the incident the other night.

Terri frowned but could offer no helpful information or advice. She asked Judith once more if she felt fit enough to come back to work and the younger woman nodded.

At two o'clock that afternoon, Judith Myers collapsed and was taken home, a slight swelling in her stomach noticed by no one.

Twenty-seven

The doors of the cellar bulkhead rattled in the powerful wind and Paul Harvey grunted irritably, awoken by the sound. He sat, screwing his eyes up in an effort to re-orientate himself with his surroundings. It was dark in the cellar, the only light coming through the slight gap where the two bulkhead doors met. Outside, the moon hung high in the sky, a solitary cold white beam finding its way down into the subterranean gloom. The cellar was large, stretching far away from him on three sides. It ran all the way beneath the farmhouse but he had not ventured far from his present hiding place for some time now. Not during daylight at least.

They had come, as he had expected. Two of them in one of their cars but, he had seen them and he had hidden. Pleased with his own cunning, he had gained entry to the house by breaking one of the small glass panels in the front door and simply wrenching the lock off with one huge hand. He had blundered around inside the empty, dust-choked dwelling until he finally found the cellar door. The rusty key still in the lock. He had unlocked the door and taken the key in with him. *They* had searched the house, he had heard them moving about inside, one of them had even mentioned something about a break-in but, when they had tried the door to the cellar and found it locked, they had gone away. Harvey had remained silent all the time they searched, the sickle held tightly in his grasp just in case. When one of them had tugged at the rusty iron chain on the bulkhead doors, Harvey had thought that they would discover him but his luck had persisted. Through the gap in the doors he had been able to see one of them in his blue uniform, speaking into the box which he carried and which seemed to answer him back. But, after what seemed like an eternity, Harvey had heard them return to their car and drive off. However, determined not to fall into one of *their* traps, he had remained in his hiding place. They would not catch him out again.

The cellar had proved to be far more than somewhere to hole up. Harvey had found that it was full of wooden shelves, each stocked with dusty jars of home-made preserves, pickles and even some bottles of amateur wine. The previous owners of the farm had obviously gone in for that kind of thing and Harvey had been glad to find a seemingly endless supply of food. He'd scooped jam from jars with his bare hands, drunk dandelion wine until his head ached, devoured entire jars full of pickled onions, upturning the receptacle to swallow the vinegar when all the other contents were gone. But his ravenous appetite had proved his undoing. He didn't know how long it was since he'd eaten – three, maybe four days. He'd lost track of time down there in that dank hole. The cellar smelt like an open sewer, splattered as it was with excrement and rat droppings. In the beginning the rodents had competed for the pieces of food which Harvey had dropped but now, as his hunger reached new heights, the rats themselves, as in the barn, had become the prey.

Broken jars littered the floor, their contents now rotting and moulding. Lumps of glass lay everywhere, two of the wooden shelves had been torn down during one of Harvey's frenzied moments. He had tried to eat some rotting marmalade which he scraped up off the floor but it had made him vomit and he sat in one corner now, his trousers damp and reeking of urine. Surrounded by his own excrement, the gnawing in his stomach seemed to fuel the anger which was growing within him. He had left the cellar just once, two nights ago, breathing clean fresh air instead of the fetid cloying odour of putrescence he had come to know so well. He had wandered over the fields, the lights of Exham acting like beacons, attracting him as surely as a candle would attract a moth. He had carried the sickle with him, its rusty blade tucked into his belt.

Now he hefted it before him, running one finger over the cutting edge, pieces of dried blood flaking off along with some minute fragments of rust. He stood up, reaching for the key in his pocket, realizing that he would have to leave this place again. But, the night was his friend, it hid him. Allowed him to move freely. He began climbing the cellar steps towards the door, the gnawing in his belly growing stronger by the second.

Liz Maynard held the book close to her face, peering through her glasses at the print before her. She was holding the paperback in one hand, the other she had balled into a fist beneath the sheet. As she read she would murmur aloud at each fresh development in the chapter, turning the pages with trepidation as the huge flesh-eating creature drew nearer to the hero and heroine who were trapped in a deserted house. She shuddered, lowering the book for a moment when a particularly powerful gust of wind rattled the bedroom window in its frame. After a moment she returned to the book, reading more quickly than usual now. The creature was stalking the young couple and Liz began to tug on the sheet in the anxiousness. The dull glow of the bedside lamp added even more atmosphere to the proceedings and she was completely caught up in her horrifying read. So caught up that she didn't notice she was pulling all of the sheets and covers to her side of the bed.

The creature in the book had found the young couple and was now chasing them.

A hand reached up and grabbed her wrist.

Liz yelped and dropped the book, looking down to

see her husband glaring up at her, trying to claw back some of the covers which she had pulled off him.

She let out a sigh of relief and glared down at Jack.

"You frightened me to death," she said.

"You were pulling all the bloody clothes off," he protested. Then he smiled, picking up the book which she'd dropped. He glanced at the cover. It showed a creature with glowing red eyes and huge teeth, dripping blood. "How the hell can you read this sort of rubbish?" he asked, grinning.

She snatched back the book indignantly and placed it on the bedside table with half a dozen others like it.

"It's very good actually," she said, defensively. "Besides, reading this sort of book is good for you. It's a medical fact, and so is watching horror films. It does you good to have a fright every now and then."

Jack nodded.

"Well, the bloody tax man frightens me, without having to read about monsters from hell and things with two heads." He exhaled deeply. "You know I don't know what's more disturbing, the fact that people part with good money to buy the damn things or that there's someone somewhere who dreams them up. I mean, what sort of mentality must a bloke have to write a book like that?"

"You've got no imagination, Jack, that's your trouble," she told him. "You should let yourself go every once in a while. Try reading one of these."

He snorted indignantly.

"I should think so. There's enough horrors in the real world without having to make them up."

She blew a raspberry at him and they both laughed. Married for twenty-eight years, they ran a small shop on the outskirts of Exham selling everything from fresh vegetables to newspapers. They were a rare and welcome commodity in the age of the supermarket and had a large and loyal clientele to prove it.

Liz leant over flicked off the bedside lamp, pulling the covers up around her neck as she settled down.

She was in the process of adjusting her pillows when she heard a distant crash. It sounded distinctly like breaking glass. She sat up, ears straining to pick up any other noise. The window rattled frenziedly in the frame for a second then the powerful gust seemed to ease and silence descended once more. Liz lay down again, ears pricked, heart thumping just that bit faster. She closed her eyes. Jack was already snoring softly beside her, he took a short course in death when he went to bed.

The noise came again and this time she was sure it was breaking glass. Liz sat up, simultaneously shaking her husband. He grunted and opened his eyes.

"What's wrong?" he said, thickly.

"Listen," she said. "I heard something."

Jack Maynard hauled himself up the bed and propped his head against the board at the top.

"I know I heard something," she repeated.

"What was it?"

She told him.

"Probably the wind, love." He smiled. "Or your imagination running away with you after reading that bloody book."

She was just about to agree with him when they both heard a much louder crash. This time it was Jack who reacted. He swung himself out of bed and walked to the bedroom door, opening it as quietly as he could. There was no light on in the landing and it was like looking out into a wall of blackness. A couple of yards ahead lay the staircase which led down into their sitting room. Beyond that, lay the shop itself. As he stood there, he heard unmistakable sounds of movement from below him. Hurriedly, he closed the door and padded back towards the bed.

"I think there's someone in the shop," he said, quietly.

169

"Oh God," Liz murmured. "We'll have to call the police."

Jack nodded.

"I know," he said, cryptically. "But just in case you'd forgotten, the bloody phone is in the living room. I'll have to go downstairs anyway." Even as he spoke he knelt, reaching beneath the bed and pulling out a long leather case. He lifted it up onto the bed and unzipped it, pulling back the cover to reveal a gleaming double-barrelled shotgun which he hurriedly loaded.

Liz reached across and flicked the lamp switch.

Nothing happened.

She got out of bed and crossed to the main point, flicking it on. The room, however, remained in darkness.

"Oh Christ," muttered Jack. "The wind must have brought a power line down."

"Or someone's been at the fuse box," Liz said, ominously.

He nodded, touching her cheek with his free hand, noticing how cold it was.

"Jack, please be careful," she whispered.

"It's probably just somebody larking about," he said, reassuring neither Liz or himself. "I'll give them a bit of a fright." He hefted the shotgun in front of him. "You close this door behind me."

She nodded, watching as he moved cautiously out onto the landing, immediately enveloped by the inky blackness. He motioned to her to close the door which she did, resting her forehead against it for long moments, her heart hammering against her ribs.

The wind swept around the shop, growling at the windows like some beast of prey.

Jack Maynard could hear it too as he padded stealthily across the landing, moving with surprising agility for a man of his size. He paused at the top step and peered down into the gloom. The darkness was like a thick,

170

clinging blanket wrapping itself around him as he stood there, breathing softly. He gripped the shotgun tighter but, he reasoned, with it being so dark he wouldn't even be able to see the intruder if he decided to come at him. The bloody gun was useless in such impenetrable gloom. It was like trying to teach a blind man to shoot bottles.

Cursing the power failure, Jack began to descend the stairs.

The third one creaked beneath him and he stood still, a thin film of perspiration greasing his face. He could still hear some distant scrabblings from beyond, now certain that the intruder was in the shop. He moved more quickly down the stairs, the shotgun held across his chest, ready to swing up to his shoulder at the slightest hint of movement. As he reached the bottom of the stairs he flicked the light switch there.

The room remained in darkness.

Jack swallowed hard and moved cautiously through the living room, narrowing his eyes in an effort to make out the dark shapes before him. Some light was coming in through a window but most of that was masked by the large tree which towered outside. To his left lay the door to the kitchen. Straight ahead the door which would take him through into the shop.

He banged his shin against the coffee table and almost overbalanced, stifling a yelp of surprise as he struggled to remain upright. He cursed silently and rubbed his injured leg, ears still alert for any sounds. Other than the howling of the wind, he could hear nothing. His heart jumped a beat and he strained his ears for the noises which he'd heard just moments earlier.

Something cracked against the window pane and Jack swung round, bringing the shotgun up, his thumb instinctively jerking one of the twin hammers back. He saw that it was a tree branch which had struck the glass, the bony fingers of low branches clawing at the window

171

as if seeking entry. He breathed an audible sigh of relief then, turning, decided to check the kitchen before progessing into the shop itself.

It too was empty.

As Jack stepped back into the sitting room the lights flashed on momentarily but the welcome illumination was all too brief and, seconds later, the house was plunged back into darkness.

He reached the door which would take him through into the shop, his hand quivering as he reached for the key. He glimpsed the phone out of the corner of his eye. Should he call the police now? He inhaled deeply. Sod it, he'd have a look for himself.

The lights flickered once more as he reached for the key and turned it.

Paul Harvey heard the door open slightly as Jack Maynard entered the shop. He had heard the other man moving about in the sitting room moments earlier and so he had ducked down behind one of the three counters inside the main room. The one behind which he sought shelter was topped by tin cans and through those Harvey could see the man edge his way cautiously forwards, towards the front door. A small pane in the door had been broken and, as Jack touched it, the wooden partition was blown open by a particularly violent gust of wind.

The shopkeeper jumped back, the gun at hip height.

Harvey saw the weapon and touched his chin thoughtfully. He looked up and saw the door through which the other man had come. Moving as swiftly and silently as he could, he scuttled towards it and disappeared inside the sitting room.

Liz Maynard paced back and forth beside the bed listening for any sounds of movement from beneath her. She looked at the clock on the bedside table, then checked it against her own watch. Jack seemed to have been gone an eternity. The lights flickered on briefly yet again and she gasped aloud at the suddenness of it. What the hell was he doing down there? She hadn't heard his voice. Why wasn't he phoning the police? Perhaps whoever it was that had broken in had attacked him down there in the dark, he could be lying there now with his throat cut. Thoughts tumbled wildly through her mind. She sat on the edge of the bed but her entire body was trembling so she took to her pacings once more. Another glance at the clock. She would give him one more minute then, warning or not, she would go down after him. Her own anxiety about Jack had to a certain extent overcome her fear. She watched as the second hand swept round, marking off the minute.

"Bastards," muttered Jack Maynard.

He was standing before one of the shelves in the shop. The jars had been taken down, the tops wrenched off and some of the contents spread over the floor of the shop. Remnants of half eaten fruit also littered the dusty floor. A can of soup had been gashed open with something sharp, the cold contents now gone. Jack frowned, whoever had broken in must have been *really* hungry if they were prepared to drink cold soup. He hefted the riven can before him, the shotgun cradled over his other arm. Other cans and jars had been taken, one of the shelves all but empty. Sweets, kept on the counter to his right with the newspapers, had also been taken by the handful. Kids? He shook his head. Kids wouldn't do this. He put the can down wondering just who the hell would?

Liz Maynard could wait no longer. She opened the bedroom door and peered out onto the landing, her heart pounding. It was still pitch black out there and she moved somewhat nervously towards the hand-rail.

There was no sound from the sitting room below or the shop itself, only the ever-present roaring of the wind. She placed one hand against the wall and took the stairs tentatively, one at a time. As she reached the third one, the lights flashed on and continued to fill the house with their glow for a full minute and a half.

Liz Maynard screamed.

Harvey was already half way up the stairs, the sickle gripped in his fist.

She turned and ran back to the bedroom, hearing the heavy footsteps thudding up the stairs behind her. She screamed again as she threw the door shut and pressed her pitiful weight against it, expecting at any second for him to launch his huge bulk against it. Instead, she heard the loud thud and the splintering of wood as he buried the sickle's vicious curved blade in the door. The point protruded a few inches through it and, as Harvey tore it free, a panel was ripped loose.

She screamed again.

Jack heard her and dashed into the sitting room, looking up to see the large figure of Harvey poised before the bedroom door, the sickle swinging back and forth as it made matchwood of the partition. Jack raised the shotgun to his shoulder simultaneously yelling something at the madman who turned to face him. Harvey moved with lightning speed and, slobbering like a rabid animal, threw himself to the ground.

There was a thunderous roar as the shotgun barrel exploded in an orgasm of fire and lead, the sound amplified by the enclosed space. The deadly load struck the wall just above Harvey's head. Paint and lumps of plaster were blasted away by the impact and Jack cursed aloud when he saw Harvey scramble to his feet, running across the landing towards the solitary window there.

He hit it with the force of a steam train, crashing through the glass and wood, heedless of what lay below. Shards of crystal sprayed out in all directions as Harvey hurtled through. He clutched at empty air for a second before plummeting to earth. He crashed into a privet hedge, the wind knocked from him, but, other than that, he was unharmed. He rolled clear and got to his feet.

Jack Maynard ran to the window and looked out in time to see Harvey loping off into the darkness. Then, the shotgun still gripped tight in his hand, he dashed into the bedroom where he found Liz on her knees beside the bed sobbing uncontrollably. It took him fully fifteen minutes to calm her down then, that done, he made his way downstairs and dialled three nines.

Twenty-eight

Inspector Lou Randall skimmed the file once more then threw it down onto his desk.

"Jesus Christ," he growled. "Doesn't anybody ever see this bastard? What is he a man or a fucking ghost?" He leant back in his chair and rubbed his face with both hands, feeling the stubble on his cheeks and chin as he did so. He'd been called out at six that morning and had driven to the police station without shaving or eating. His stomach rumbled disapprovingly and his mouth felt like the bottom of a birdcage.

"Who found this one?" he asked, wearily.

"A milkman," Norman Willis told him. "He said the body was lying in the road. No attempt to hide it." The sergeant studied his superior's worried face. "He wasn't making much sense when Charlton took the statement from him." He paused. "He's still badly shaken up."

175

Randall grunted.

"I'm not surprised," he said. "Finding a headless body at half past five in the morning lying in the middle of the street is enough to give anyone the bloody shakes." He glanced at the report again. "Same murder weapon?" It came out more as a confirmation than a question.

Willis nodded.

"Everything about it is the same as Ian Logan's murder. Rust in the wounds, a single-bladed weapon and the head was taken."

Randall fumbled in his pocket for his cigarettes, finding them with some difficulty. There was only one in the packet and he tossed the empty receptacle away, not really bothering whether it reached the waste-bin or not. He lit the fag and drew hard on it.

"What about this other incident?" he said, picking up Jack Maynard's statement regarding Harvey's attack and break-in. Willis told his superior about it while Randall quickly read the statement himself.

"The break-in happened at half past one," said Randall. He flipped open the file in front of him. "The pathologist's report puts the time of death at around two." He tapped on the desk top with his index finger as if seeking some kind of magical inspiration, a clue to what the hell he was going to do next. "He didn't kill anyone at the shop where he broke in, maybe he lost his rag and decided he owed himself one anyway. This poor sod just happened to be the first one he came across." He took another drag on his cigarette. "Where was the body found? Which side of town?"

"Going out towards the main road into Mayford. There's lots of fields out that way," Willis explained.

"Is it being checked?" Randall wanted to know.

"Not yet, we're spread a bit thin at the moment trying to find him but as soon as a car calls in I'll send them out that way."

The Inspector nodded.

"I just don't get it," he said, wearily. "How the hell can Harvey just keep disappearing like he does? He must be hiding somewhere around Exham and yet we've already checked it over once." The Inspector smiled sardonically. "Perhaps he's not as mad as everyone seems to think he is."

"They always say that it's the brains who are locked up and the lunatics who are free," added Willis, shrugging.

"I'm beginning to agree," said Randall. He ground out his cigarette, watching the plume of grey smoke rise mournfully into the air.

"We'll get him, guv," said Willis.

Randall raised an eyebrow, questioningly.

"Can I have that in writing?" he said, humourlessly. The phone rang and, as he picked it up, Willis turned to leave. Randall picked up the receiver, quickly cupping his hand over the mouthpiece. "Hey, Norman, a cup of tea would go down a treat."

Willis smiled and left.

Randall pressed the phone to his ear.

"Inspector Randall speaking."

"I'm not going to beat about the bush, Randall," said the voice at the other end, one which the Inspector immediately recognized as belonging to Chief Inspector Frank Allen. There was a harsh, cold quality to the CI's voice which made it unmistakable. The younger man stiffened in his chair.

"Yes, sir," he said, wondering what his superior wanted. He glanced across at the wall clock opposite him and saw that it was almost 9.05 a.m. Whatever the miserable old sod wanted must be important, Randall mused.

"I understand you're having some problems down there," said Allen. "This escaped maniac, Harvey isn't it? How long has he been free now?"

177

Randall swallowed hard.

"Just over nine weeks, sir. Everything possible is being done to apprehend him. My men. . ."

"And how many has he killed. One or two?"

Randall paled.

"Two, sir." It came out almost as a confession.

Allen exhaled deeply, his voice taking on an even harder edge.

"I see," he said. "Well, look Randall, you don't need me to tell you how serious this whole business is. Your inability to find the man in the beginning was bad enough but now this. For Christ's sake put the lid on it and find Harvey quickly." There was a pause, during which time the CI's mood seemed to lighten a little. "Do you need any help?"

"A couple of bloodhounds I think, sir," he japed.

"Don't be facetious, Randall," Allen snapped. "This series of events is not going to look very good on your record. Now, I asked if you needed any help."

The Inspector clenched his fists until the knuckles were bloodless, trying hard to control his anger.

"Some extra men wouldn't go amiss, sir," he said, brusquely.

"Very well. But catch this bastard. Quick."

"Yes, sir."

Allen hung up.

Randall held the receiver in his hand for a second, listening to the persistent drone then, angrily, he slammed it down onto the cradle. He had the uncomfortable suspicion that someone was keeping tabs on him. Christ, he wanted a cigarette but, as he peered at the empty packet nearby he could only mutter irritably to himself. "Catch Harvey". He shook his head. Any ideas where we should start, big head? He thought, glaring at the phone, the anger still boiling inside him. He got to his feet and looked at the map of the town on his office wall. It bore two red crosses, each marking the scene of the murders. Both were in different parts of Exham. At least two miles separated the scene of each crime. Randall stood gazing helplessly at the map.

"Come out, come out wherever you are, you bastard," murmured the Inspector.

Twenty-nine

The windscreen wipers of the Audi swept slowly back and forth across the glass, brushing away the rain which had been falling steadily for the past three hours.

"I need a new set of blades," muttered Mick Calvin, jabbing a finger at the area on the windscreen which was still rainsoaked.

"You always need something, Mick," said his wife, Diane, firmly belted into the passenger seat beside him. "I think it's about time we had a new car."

Calvin snorted.

"Well, my darling," he said, sarcastically. "As soon as we get home you write me a cheque for six thousand and I'll nip out and get us one."

"You know what I mean," she said, irritably. "*You've* been saying the same yourself for months."

"I just wish your bloody mother didn't live so far away," he added.

Diane studied his profile for a second.

"I suppose it's her fault that the car's falling to bits?" she said, acidly.

"Did I say that? I just said that it's a long drive to where she lives."

Diane smiled impishly.

"She could always come and live with us, that would save the journey."

She laughed aloud at the expression which crossed her husband's face.

"I could get to like long journeys," he said, smiling.

"She wouldn't be any trouble."

"That's what they said about Hitler."

Diane punched him playfully on the arm.

"Dad, can we stop?"

The voice came from the back seat where Richie, their eldest son at eleven, was dressed in a pair of freshly pressed jeans and a Spiderman sweatshirt. He was on his knees, pulling at his crutch agitatedly. Beside him sat his brother, Wayne, two years younger, his face round and red as if he'd been holding his breath for a long time.

"Dad."

"What?" said Calvin.

"Can't we stop? Wayne and me both want to go for a wee," he protested.

"Can't you hold it? We're nearly home now," said Calvin. "And it's Wayne and *I*," he added as an afterthought.

The oldest lad was bouncing up and down now.

"Dad," he persisted, clutching his groin with both hands, as if letting go would release a flood tide.

"Oh, pull over, Mick," Diane said. "They can nip behind a hedge."

"It's wet out there you know," said Calvin, as if trying to deter his two sons.

Diane looked at Wayne who was going ever redder in a monumental effort of self-control which he was obviously going to lose at any minute.

"It's going to be wet in here if you don't pull over," she said.

Calvin nodded and glanced ahead for a suitable place to stop. There were fields all around them but few seemed to be blessed with bushes. He saw the massive edifice of Fairvale hospital towering above a row of trees and remembered that there was a lay-by just beyond. The fields that backed onto the hospital itself would offer plenty of cover for the two kids. He could see the electricity pylons towering over the field, their cables swaying in the breeze. Checking his rear-view mirror, he swung the Audi across the road and into the lay-by. Immediately, the two kids were fumbling for the door locks in their efforts to get out and Calvin couldn't resist a smile as he watched them both scramble out of the car.

"Go behind those bushes over there," he said, pointing towards some bare gorse bushes which masked a sizeable hollow in the field. The hollow ran from the base of one of the towering pylons.

He and Diane watched as the kids clambered over the low fence which separated the lay-by from the field, then both of the boys were racing towards the bushes. They disappeared behind the bushes and Calvin grinned broadly.

"Do you want to go as well?" he asked Diane. "There's plenty more bushes in the field." He laughed.

"No," she whispered, leaning closer. "But I'll tell you what I do want." She pulled him to her and their mouths met eagerly. She spoke something into his ear, kissing the lobe as she did so, one hand straying to his thigh.

"Now that *will* have to wait until we get home," he said.

They both laughed.

The screams which they heard made them both sit bolt upright, but it was a matter of seconds before Calvin was unhooking his seat belt, pushing open the car door. He slipped as he leapt out onto the wet tarmac but regained his balance and hurried towards the fence. Diane was close behind him, her high heels sinking into

181

the mud as she reached the low wooden fence. She struggled over it, seeing that her husband was already racing towards the bushes where the screams were coming from.

He was panting madly, the high pitched screams of his sons ringing in his ears as he ran. The rain plastered hair to his face but he ignored it and ran on, his only concern to reach his children. As he drew closer, he saw Richie staggering from behind the bushes, his face colourless, his mouth open. Behind him came Wayne, his jeans wet around the crutch, his flies still open. By now, Diane could see them. She called their names but no sound seemed to come, she was mouthing the words but only silence escaped her.

Calvin reached his eldest son and held him by the shoulders, gazing into his eyes that were bulging wide and red-rimmed. He was motioning behind him, his breath coming out in deep, racking sobs. Wayne merely stood where he was, apparently oblivious to the rain. Calvin hurried across and lifted the boy into his arms. He seemed limp, like a puppet with its wires cut and, but for the fact that his eyes were open and blinking, he had the appearance of a waxwork model.

"What's wrong?"

It was Diane's voice, trembling and full of fear.

"Wayne, Richie, what is it?" she repeated.

Calvin himself held the eldest boy close to his chest while Diane took over the responsibility for Wayne.

"There," gasped Richie, once more motioning behind him.

"Take them both back to the car," said Calvin but Diane hesitated, watching as he walked behind the bushes and along the depression in the field, stopping at one point. He turned to face Diane, her hair now hanging in dripping coils.

"Take them back," said Calvin, waving Diane away.

"What is it, Mick?" she demanded.

182

"Take them back to the car," he shouted and the vehemence in his voice startled her. She turned and led the two children back across the field towards the shelter of the Audi.

Calvin watched them, waiting until he saw them reach the vehicle before returning his attention to what he had found. He bent, squatting on his haunches, peering at the rain-sodden earth. The grass had been dug over in an area he guessed measuring about twelve feet by six. The mud was sticky and oozing, like reeking gravy and, through this thin film of muck, he could see a face. It was the face of a baby although the definition was questionable. The head, uncovered by the torrential rain, was bulbous with two large growths over the holes where the eyes should have been. In the black pits of sockets worms writhed, one of them disappearing into the open mouth of the putrescing body and it was all Calvin could do to stop himself from vomiting. One rotted, mottled arm protruded from the earth nearby, the fingers stubby, two of them missing. Close to that an entire tiny corpse had been uncovered by the elements. What remained of it had been gnawed in places, maybe by rats or a badger. The stomach had been torn open to reveal a seething mess of mouldering viscera. The stench rising from the grave was overpowering and Calvin took a handkerchief from his pocket to cover his nose, his head swimming. He counted at least half a dozen pieces of human debris and one complete corpse. What lay deeper he could only guess at. He stood up, swaying slightly, the realization that he was indeed standing beside some kind of grave, sweeping over him as surely as the choking stench which wafted from it on invisible clouds. He stood there for long seconds, his eyes fixed on the worm-eaten, ravaged body of one of the foetuses then, as he saw one of the slimy creatures wriggle from a hole in the

183

corpse's stomach like some kind of animated umbilical cord, he finally lost control and vomited violently.

Diane, watching from the back seat of the car, where she was doing her best to comfort the two boys, saw her husband tottering drunkenly back across the field. He finally reached the wooden fence and swung himself over it, supporting himself against the Audi before pulling the driver's side door open. He flopped heavily into the seat and sat motionless, gazing ahead. Diane could hear his laboured breathing.

"We've got to report this," he said, falteringly, reaching for the ignition key and turning it.

"What did you find, Mick?" she demanded. "For God's sake tell me."

He lowered his head momentarily.

"There's . . . something buried." He coughed and, for a moment, thought he was going to be sick again. He gritted his teeth and the feeling diminished somewhat. "Something . . . embryos. There's a grave in that field." He sucked in a deep breath. "We've got to report it, now."

He started the car, swung it round and headed back towards Fairvale's main entrance.

Within an hour he had made a full report to a senior doctor and, thirty minutes later, Mick Calvin led that same doctor and three porters, Harold Pierce amongst them, to the spot where he'd found the grave. And there, under the watchful eyes of both men, five aborted foetuses were uncovered. The bodies were put into a sack and carried back to the hospital where they were disposed of in the usual way. Cast into the mouth of the furnace as they should have been weeks before.

Harold watched as the tiny bodies were born away for disposal his body shaking.

The voices inside his head had begun to chatter once more.

Thirty

Harold sat nervously in the outer office, his hands clasped on his knees. The room was large, a white-walled enclosure which he shared with just three leather chairs and a secretary who sat across from him hammering away at the keys of an old Imperial type-writer. The constant clacking sounded like dozens of tiny explosions. The secretary herself was a woman in her forties, a plump lady with greying hair swept back from a face coated with far too much make-up. It seemed to shine beneath the banks of fluorescents set into the ceiling. There was a mug on her desk with a slogan written on it in large red letters. Harold wondered if it was her name as he saw the word June on it. She glanced up at him every now and then and when she did, he would self-consciously touch the scarred side of his face as if trying to shield it from her gaze. She smiled at him warmly and he returned the gesture sheepishly. He shifted uncomfortably in his seat which made a sound like someone breaking wind, as is the wont of leather chairs. Harold tried to sit still but it was a difficult task. He glanced up at the wall clock above the secretary's head. It showed 4.26 p.m. Below it was a painting which Harold could not make out. It was just squares, all painted different colours, forming no pattern or shape. Not unlike the paintings Harold himself had done in occupational therapy.

The memory of those days seemed so distant now. Then he had felt as if he belonged at the hospital. He had friends and, more importantly, he was not burd-ened with responsibility as he was now. It seemed like a million years ago. Now he sat in the outer office, waiting, remembering back to just a few hours ago when he had helped to disinter the foetuses which he had spent so much care saving in the first place. Saving was the word to describe his actions but now he feared that they would punish him for it. He closed his eyes and allowed his head to rest against the wall. Immediately, the buzzing in his ears became the rasping voices which he had come to know so well.

Harold sat up, his eyelids jerking open. He looked around, as if expecting to see someone sitting next to him but then he realized that the voices were inside his head.

He swallowed hard.

There was a loud bleep and a green light flared on the console beside the secretary. She flipped a switch and Harold heard her say something into the inter-com. When she'd finished speaking she looked up at Harold, smiled and told him to go in. He nodded, got to his feet and made for the varnished door to his right. It bore a nameplate:

Dr Kenneth McManus, R.C.S.

Harold knocked and received the instruction to enter. He walked in to find Brian Cayton in there as well as McManus who was shielded behind a huge mahogany desk. He motioned for Harold to sit down and brief pleasantries were exchanged. McManus was a big man, tall but muscular with sunken cheeks and lustrous black hair which was brushed back, accentuating the widow's peak he had. His eyes were set close together, rather like fog lamps on the front of a car, only these particular lights glowed with a pale grey hue as Harold found himself pinned beneath their gaze.

"Pierce, isn't it," said McManus, smiling thinly.

Harold nodded.

"How long have you been with us?"

"Two months, sir," said Harold, lowering his head slightly. "Perhaps a bit longer."

"And you were entrusted with the disposal of aborted foetuses on a number of occasions during this time

186

Correct?" The words had a harsh, almost accusatory ring to them.

Harold nodded.

"Did you in fact complete the disposal procedure?" McManus wanted to know.

"I did as I was told, sir," Harold insisted, a slight pain gnawing at the back of his neck.

McManus nodded in the direction of Cayton who was sitting to Harold's left.

"Mr Cayton tells me that you tried to prevent him from disposing of a dead foetus," said the doctor. "Is this true?"

"I didn't feel well that day," Harold said, blankly, his one good eye staring right through McManus. He appeared to be in a dazed condition, his mouth forming words which his mind had not formulated.

"How many other times have you tried to interfere with the disposal procedure?"

"I haven't done . . . I didn't try to stop anyone else." The words were coming slowly, monosyllabically. As if each one were an effort. Something not unnoticed by either the doctor or Cayton.

"Are you all right, Pierce?" asked McManus.

"Yes, sir," Harold insisted.

Doctor and porter exchanged puzzled looks.

"Did *you* bury those bodies in the field, Pierce?" McManus wanted to know.

Harold hesitated, closing his eyes for a moment.

He shook his head.

"Why do the children have to be burned?" he asked, looking straight at the doctor with a stare which made the other man recoil.

McManus sucked in a troubled breath.

"Could you wait outside for a while please, Pierce?" he said, watching as the porter got unsteadily to his feet and walked to the door, closing it gently behind him.

"Pierce was the only one who could have prevented the disposal of the five foetuses we found in the field. Correct?" said McManus.

Cayton nodded.

"Yes, sir, but God knows how he did it," the porter confessed.

"I think it's more to the point, *why* he did it? Although his past would go some way to explaining that I suppose." The doctor exhaled deeply. "I don't see that we have any alternative other than to dismiss him. It's unfortunate but I'm just grateful the papers didn't find out about it."

"Wasn't there a similar case in Germany a few years ago?" said Cayton. "Only there, they'd been making soap out of the remains."

McManus raised one eyebrow.

"He lives on the grounds doesn't he?"

"Yes," Cayton told him. "In that old hut."

"Well, I'm afraid he'll have to leave there too."

"What if he's got nowhere to go, sir?"

"That's not our problem, Cayton. The man is obviously unbalanced in some way. He'll probably end up back in an institution. Probably the best place for him. I just don't want him in *my* hospital." The doctor was already reaching for a switch on the console before him. He flipped it up.

"Send Pierce back in will you, please," he said, settling back in his chair, hands clasped across his lap.

Harold re-entered and sat down, listening unconcernedly as McManus explained that he was to lose his job. It wasn't until the doctor mentioned leaving the hut that the older porter showed any trace of reaction. His one good eye seemed to bulge momentarily but the moment passed and he sat in silence as the reasons for his dismissal were reeled off. But Harold wasn' listening to McManus, his attention was focused on the voices which spoke to him from within. The docto

188

finally finished and leant forward in his chair, glancing first at Cayton and then at Harold.

"I'm sorry things turned out like this, Pierce," he said. "I realize your problems. Perhaps you would be better off. . ." he was struggling to find the words, rummaging amidst the welter of bluntness for a few morsels of tact. "It might be best if you returned to the institution. I can contact doctor Vincent, I'm sure, if you have nowhere else to go, he would understand."

"Thank you," said Harold, blankly, absently touching the scarred side of his face. It felt dry beneath his fingers.

"Do you have somewhere to go, Harold?" asked Cayton.

"Yes." The word came out almost angrily. "I have somewhere to go." He got to his feet, a new found strength filling him. "I have somewhere to go."

A hissing, sibilant command sounded so loud inside his head that he almost winced but he turned and walked towards the door, moving as if each step were an effort.

"Goodbye," he said and left them.

It was a long time before either McManus or Cayton spoke.

As Harold stepped into the lift he looked straight through Maggie Ford. She smiled at him but the gesture provoked no response. His one good eye looked as glassy as the false one, his skin was the colour of rancid butter.

"Harold." Maggie put out her hand to touch his shoulder.

He looked at her again, some of the mistiness vanishing from that blank stare. He touched his face and swallowed hard.

"Harold, are you all right?" she asked him, as the lift doors slid shut.

189

He opened his mouth to speak, his lips fluttering noiselessly.

The words inside his head became warnings.

Harold looked squarely at Maggie, his brow furrowing slightly. She released her grip on his shoulder, much as someone would let go of a dog when they'd just discovered it was liable to bite them at any minute. The doctor regarded Harold warily, somewhat relieved when his expression changed to its customary calm blankness.

"I'm leaving here," he said, softly.

Maggie looked puzzled.

"Leaving? Why?"

"They told me to leave. Because of the children."

"What children, Harold?" she demanded. "And who asked you to leave?"

"Doctor McManus told me to leave." He gazed at her with that seething vehemence once more, his face darkening.

"They kill the children," he hissed.

Maggie was almost relieved when the lift reached its appointed floor and she could step out and away from Harold. She glanced back at him, watching as the doors slid shut on his disfigured visage. She waited a moment then took the stairs up to the fourth floor and Doctor McManus's office.

Maggie didn't time how long she was in the senior consultant's office but she guessed later that it couldn't have been more than five minutes. She tried to persuade her superior that Harold was in a bad way both physically and mentally.

"He's ill," she insisted. "He should be taken into care, not thrown out onto the streets."

McManus was unimpressed.

"He committed a breach of hospital regulations," the

190

older man said. "He's lucky he's not being prosecuted never mind dismissed."

When she asked what he meant, he explained about the foetuses, the grave in the field, how Harold had hidden the bodies and then interred them in secret rather than incinerating them.

"Oh God," murmured Maggie.

"*Now* do you understand why he has to go?" said McManus, irritably. "The man's disturbed. I should never have taken him on in the first place."

"Well then that's all the more reason to take him into care," Maggie insisted.

"He needs psychiatric help, not medical help."

She told him about the cuts on Harold's body but McManus was obviously tiring of the conversation and it showed in the sharp edge which his words acquired.

"As far as I'm concerned, Miss Ford, the matter is closed. Pierce will be out of the grounds by tomorrow morning." He looked at his watch, tapping the glass. "Now I suggest you return to *your* duties. I presume you have patients to attend to?"

"Yes, doctor," she said, her face flushed.

She left the office, closing the door just a little too firmly behind her. There was something badly wrong with Harold and she was determined to find out what it was. She glanced at her watch. It was 5.30 p.m., in another two hours she would be off duty. When that time came, she decided she would go to Harold's hut and speak to him.

Thirty-one

Harold moved slowly about the hut collecting what few possessions he had, bundling them into the battered old suitcase he'd been lent. Every now and then he would stop still and glance towards the kitchen, as if trying to catch sight of something. The voices whispered insistently inside his head, like the wind rustling paper.

He heard scuffling sounds coming from the cupboard in the kitchen. There was hessian laid out before it and, when the last item was dropped into the suitcase, Harold passed into the other room and knelt before the door, his hand quivering slightly as he slid it open.

A vile, cloying stench billowed from the hiding place and Harold recoiled at the ferocity of the odour. He gazed into the cupboard, mesmerized.

All three of the foetuses had doubled in size.

Maggie Ford glanced at the clock on the wall of her office and noted that it was approaching 7.40 p.m. She sat back in her seat, slipping the cap back onto her pen. Her neck and shoulders ached and she reached up with both hands to perform some swift massage. Outside, the sky was mottled with rain clouds and a thin film of drizzle covered the office window like a gossamer shroud. Maggie yawned and got to her feet, remembering that she'd promised herself a visit to Harold's hut before she went home that night. She took off her white coat and hung it up on the hook, pulling on a lightweight mac in its place. She glanced at a chart on the office wall and noticed that she was due in surgery at eight-thirty the following morning. Maggie took one final look around the office then flicked off the light and left.

She took the lift down to the ground floor, mumbling

a few hasty "goodnights" on her way to the main entrance. When she reached it she paused, pulling up her collar to protect herself from the worst ravages of the icy wind. The chill in the air was turning the drizzle into particles of sleet and Maggie shivered, turning to her left, heading towards the open stretch of ground which would take her to Harold's hut. Almost invisible in the gloom, she could see that no lights burned inside and she wondered if perhaps he'd gone to bed. As far as she knew he didn't go out at nights so it was more than likely that he was in the small dwelling. She muttered to herself as her heels sank into the soft earth but she struggled on towards the still and black shrouded hut.

She found herself shivering but the movements were not merely a product of the cold weather. She felt an unaccountable fear rising within her as she drew nearer to the building. Perhaps it had been Harold's reactions in the lift which had unsettled her, she thought, angry with herself for feeling the trepidation she now experienced. It was pity she should be feeling for Harold, not fear.

Maggie found that the door of the hut was slightly ajar. She knocked all the same, simultaneously calling the older man's name. When she received no answer, she cautiously pushed the wooden door which swung back on its hinges with a high pitched shriek. Maggie called Harold's name once more then stepped inside.

The smell of damp was almost overpowering but mingled with it was a more pungent odour which she had difficulty identifying. She looked around the interior of the place. The bed had been stripped, the sheets and blankets gone but, on the mattress she noticed a dark stain. Now dried and powdery, the substance seemed to crumble beneath her probing fingers. She wet the tip of her index finger and on withdrawing it from the mysterious patch she found

193

that it was congealed blood. Maggie swallowed hard and looked around. The door to her right, the one which led through to the kitchen, was closed.

"Harold," she called, moving towards the door.

The hut greeted her with silence.

She pushed the door but found that it was stuck.

Maggie tried again and, this time, it budged a few inches. She put her weight against it, realizing that the door was a fraction of an inch too large and was sticking. Eventually, she succeeded in opening it and found herself standing in the tiny kitchen.

The door of the cupboard beneath the sink was open, the handle splashed with blood.

Maggie squatted before it and squinted through the gloom at the crimson liquid. It glistened in the half-light and she could see that it was fresh. There was a fetid stench coming from the cupboard and Maggie paused for long seconds before deciding to look inside. She gripped the handle, trying to avoid the blood, and pulled it open.

There was something inside the cupboard, something which she couldn't see in the blackness. Something moving.

She could hear a faint scratching too, an agitated skittering which stopped abruptly. The cupboard was large, large enough for a fully grown man to climb into but Maggie certainly had no intentions of crawling inside to see what was making the noise. She coughed, her eye suddenly caught by something which lay on the wooden floor beside her. She picked up the matted strands, turning them over in her fingers.

There was a sudden movement from within the cupboard and Maggie screamed as something soft and furry brushed against her leg. She dropped the stiff fur, almost overbalancing.

The mouse scampered away, past her and disappeared through a hole in the wall.

Maggie sucked in a deep breath, held it for a second then exhaled.

"God," she murmured and got to her feet.

She ran both hands through her hair and blew out a troubled breath. Harold Pierce was gone, no doubt about that. But exactly where, she had no idea.

The old Exham Mental Hospital now stood deserted and already dust had begun to accumulate in thick layers on the floors and window-ledges. Some of the windows had been broken, the dirty glass lying in the wards which were now empty of beds. It was as black as pitch in the empty building and Harold blinked his one good eye repeatedly, as if the action would somehow give him the power to see through the darkness. But he had lived at the hospital for so long he knew every inch of it and he moved with assurance through the long corridors, his tired footsteps echoing loudly in the silence. He was aware of nothing but the musty smell of the place and the aching in his legs where he had walked for so long. He had no idea what the time was but, outside, a large watery moon gave him some light and illuminated his stumbling progess somewhat.

He had left the three foetuses in a room on the first floor while he himself explored the remains of the deserted asylum. For the first time in months he actually felt happy. It was like a homecoming for him. He belonged here in this place, in this empty Victorian shell which smelt of damp and was thick with dust. It had been his home for so many years before and now it would be his home again.

He paused at the foot of the staircase which would take him up to the first floor, the voices hissing in his ears again. They were calling him and Harold made his way almost eagerly to his room where they waited.

Thirty-two

Lynn Tyler grunted as she felt the weight of the man's body on top of her. She sucked in a deep breath but it slowly subsided into a groan of pleasure as she felt his swollen penis slide into her. He bent his head forward, his unshaven cheek scraping her.

"Don't you ever shave?" she murmured, her complaint dissolving away into another exclamation of pleasure as he began thrusting into her with firm strokes.

She couldn't remember his name. Barry or Gary. Something like that. It didn't matter much to her either way. She'd picked him up at a disco about two hours earlier and was now enjoying the consummation of what, for her, was to be yet another notch on the bedstead.

She ran a hand through his thick black hair, wincing slightly as she felt the slick greasiness of it. His breath smelt of beer and, when he kissed her, it was a clumsy slobbering action, rather like being accosted by a Saint Bernard. However, she weathered his attentions, enjoying the sensations he was creating within her. One of his rough hands went to her breast and squeezed hard. So hard that she yelped in pain but all he did was grin and squeeze the other one with equal force. Her nipples rose to meet his strong advances, her hips now beginning to rotate in time to his thrusts.

She felt a glow around her groin which spread slowly to her belly but it was not the pleasant warmth that signals the approach of orgasm. It was an uncomfortably familiar burning sensation which she had experienced two or three times since returning from hospital. Lynn sucked in a sharp breath as a stab of pain jolted her. Her lover took it to be a sign of her excitement and grunted something but she didn't hear him, her mind was now occupied with the growing pain in her lower region which seemed to be intensifying. The weight on top of her seemed almost unbearable but she gritted her teeth, whispering words of encouragement in his ear, trying by any means she could to drive the thoughts of the searing pain from her mind.

Barry or Gary or whatever his name was, suddenly withdrew his organ, leaving her panting in frustration but that feeling of frustration did not remain long as, a moment later, she felt his hot breath on her left breast then the right. His tongue flicked against her swollen nipples and he drew them between his teeth making them even harder and more erect.

The pain in her abdomen grew more acute. The skin across her belly seemed first to contract and then to stretch, rising in two places in the form of almost imperceptible bumps. Lynn swallowed hard, the burning sensation now even stronger. It felt as if someone had poured a kettle full of boiling water all over her abdomen.

A particularly prominent bulge rose just to the right of her navel, strained against the flesh defiantly for long seconds then vanished.

The man was up on his knees now, looking down at her vagina and she almost screamed aloud as she saw the blood.

Lynn Tyler thrust a shaking hand between her legs and withdrew it slowly to see crimson staining her fingertips. She felt the burning inside her, stared at the blood as it trickled down her quivering digits and, finally, she did scream.

Thirty-three

It was cold inside the pathology lab and Randall dug both hands deep inside his trouser pockets. The smell of chemicals was strong and the inspector wrinkled his nose, peering around the large room with its green painted, white tiled walls. There were three stainless steel slabs set side by side, the last of which bore a sheet covered occupant. There was a small tag attached to the big toe of the left foot. It bore a name and a three digit number. The number coincided with one of the many lockers that ran the full length of the far wall. A storecase for sightless eyes.

Above the slab dangled a scale, beside it there was a tray littered with surgical instruments, one of which, Randall noticed with revulsion, was a saw. He glanced across at PC Fowler who looked even paler than usual beneath the glare of the fluorescents. The young constable was gazing at the covered body on the far slab. He was shivering and, he told himself, it was not solely the product of the chill air.

In one corner of the lab there was a sink and it was there that the hospital's chief pathologist stood. He washed his hands then pulled on a pair of rubber gloves, pressing his fingers together to ensure that they fitted like a second skin. Ronald Potter turned and headed for the slab. He was in his forties, his bald dome hidden by the toupée which he wore. It was a bad fit because flecks of what little hair he retained showed beneath it at the rear but Randall was concerned with more important things than ill-fitting hair pieces at the moment. Both he and Fowler moved forward as Potter reached the slab and pulled back the sheet.

The pathologist eyed the corpse indifferently, leaning over it, inspecting the preliminary damage. He stroked his chin thoughtfully, considering the object before him with the same concentration which a child would apply to selecting a sweet from a chocolate box.

Randall looked at the body for a moment then diverted his gaze towards the pathologist.

Fowler gritted his teeth and looked away, trying to retain his breakfast.

The body was badly mutilated about the shoulders and was, once again, headless. Blood had trickled into the gutter which ran around the rim of the slab, most of it from the torn stump of the neck. The head had been severed much higher up this time, just below the bottom jaw as far as Randall could see. Indeed, fragments of bone and even a tooth also lay on the slab where the head should have been.

Potter reached for a metal probe and began poking about in one of the many gashes that criss-crossed the remains of the neck.

"This is becoming something of a habit isn't it, Inspector?" he asked, plucking a pair of tweezers from the trolley.

"What?" asked Randall, puzzled, his attention riveted to the stomach-turning sight before him.

"Finding headless corpses." The pathologist looked up and smiled, humorlessly. "How many is this now? Three isn't it?"

Randall clenched his fists at his side and glared at the older man.

"Someone somewhere must have quite a collection. I didn't know we had head-hunters in Exham."

"What are you a pathologist or a fucking comedian?" snapped the Inspector, irritably. "I want to know what he was killed with. I don't want Sunday Night at the London Palladium."

It was Potter's turn to glare. The two men locked stares for a moment then the pathologist returned to his work. He laboured in silence for a good ten minutes

199

then straightened up, wiping some blood off on his apron.

"As far as I can see, the head was severed with the same weapon as the one used on the two previous victims." He paused. "A single-edged blade of some kind. There's rust in two or three of the wounds as well." The older man pulled the sheet further back and regarded the remains of the body. "No other external damage. The pattern's the same."

"With the other two you said that there was a lot of blood in the lungs," Randall reminded him. "What about this one?"

Potter smiled thinly and reached for a new tool. He held it before him and Randall saw that it was a tiny buzz-saw, its steel blade glinting beneath the lights.

"Let's have a look, shall we?" said Potter and checked to see if the instrument was plugged in. It was. He stepped on a pedal near his left foot and the buzz-saw whirred into action with a sound that reminded Randall of a dentist's drill. As he watched, the pathologist lowered the spinning blade to a point just below the sternum of the corpse, then, with one expert movement, he buried it in the flesh, allowing the screaming blade to carve a path through dead flesh and bone, opening the rib cage until the lungs were exposed. A foul stench rose from the open chest cavity and both Randall and Fowler backed away.

The high-pitched whine ceased abruptly, to be replaced by a sickening crack as the older man prized open the sawn-through rib cage exposing the vital organs beneath. He picked up a pair of scissors and carefully snipped away at the lining of the chest, finally cutting into the left lung just below the trachea. As the expertly-wielded scissors sliced through the pleura, a clear fluid spilled out to be followed, a second later, by the first dark, almost black, clots of congealed blood. Seemingly oblivious to the thick red cascade, Potter opened the lung from top to bottom finally pulling open the organ with his gloved hands. Randall swallowed hard.

"Exactly the same as the other two," said Potter.

"What exactly does that mean?" the Inspector asked, trying to look anywhere but at the ruined torso of the corpse before him. He wanted a smoke and his fingers anxiously toyed with the packet of Rothmans in his pocket but he kept his composure as best he could and waited for an answer.

Potter shrugged.

"The killer attacked from behind. That's easy enough to see from these wounds here," he pointed to three particularly large gashes on the lower part of the neck. "The blade was used in a type of swatting action. These are cuts, not punctures. The fact that there are no defence cuts on the hands or arms would seem to indicate that the victim was dead after the first or second blow."

"Could the head have been severed with one stroke?" Randall wanted to know. "By a very strong man for instance."

Potter shook his head.

"No,"

"You sound very sure."

"Well, Inspector, for one thing, strength has nothing to do with it." He smiled thinly. "It's technique. When beheading was the accepted form of execution during the Middle Ages, right up to the sixteenth century, there was a certain art to it. The headsmen were trained for their job and even then it was common for them to take two or three blows to sever the head completely. And they used axes or large swords. These wounds were inflicted with a small weapon."

Randall nodded.

"Thanks for the history lesson," he said.

"Besides, in this case," he motioned towards the

corpse, "As with the previous two, the head was removed by a series of blows. Chopped not sliced off."

Fowler blenched and decided he needed some fresh air. Randall told him to wait in the car outside. The young constable left, gratefully, his footsteps echoing around the large cold room. The other two men waited until the PC had departed then they spoke briskly, Randall watching as the pathologist completed the autopsy. His mind was brimming over with ideas and thoughts. Harvey. The murder weapon. But, something which Potter had said troubled him, something about strength having nothing to do with it. He turned the thought over in his mind finally dismissing it. The incident at the grocer's shop the other night had confirmed his suspicions once and for all. Paul Harvey was responsible for these killings. It was just a matter of finding him. Randall chewed his bottom lip contemplatively. Find Harvey. That was what he'd been trying to do for nearly three months now and he was still no closer. As he stood in this cold room his men were out searching Exham and the surrounding countryside, covering ground which they'd already searched months before in a vain effort to find the maniac. Randall exhaled deeply and looked at his watch. It was 10.34 a.m. He'd been at the hospital for over three hours, ever since the corpse had been discovered in the front garden of a house on the south side of town. The Inspector had driven to the scene of the crime and then ridden the ambulance to the hospital to await the autopsy report. He had not intended to stay for the actual event but, he had reasoned, there was nothing for him to do back at his office except twiddle his thumbs and lose his temper trying to figure out just where the hell Harvey was. So he had stayed.

Potter completed his work and pulled the sheet back over the body, calling in one of the lab technicians to complete the task of sewing the corpse up again.

202

Randall watched as the older man washed his hands at the sink, humming happily to himself as he did so. When he'd finished he turned to face the policeman.

"Is there anything else I can do for you, Inspector?" he said, sardonically.

Randall shook his head.

"I do have other work to do," the pathologist reminded him, motioning towards the door.

The policeman shot him an acid glance and headed towards the exit, glad to leave this foul place. He slammed the door behind him and headed for the lift, jabbing the button which would take him up to the ground floor. He closed his eyes as the car rose the short distance to the upper level. It smelt of plastic and perspiration in there and Randall was pleased when he could step out. He fumbled in his jacket pocket and retrieved his cigarettes, hurriedly lighting one up. He'd taken two drags on it when a voice called to him and he turned to see an attractive woman walking towards him. She wore a long white coat, open to reveal a green blouse and grey skirt. But, as she drew closer, Randall found himself captivated by a pair of piercing blue eyes. They gleamed like chips of sapphire but there was a warmth to them.

She pointed to a sign on the wall to his left which said "NO SMOKING" in large red letters. He took the cigarette from his mouth and dropped it, grinding it out beneath his foot.

She had seen him emerge from the lift and, immediately, her curiosity had been aroused.

"You're not a member of staff are you?" It was a statement, not a question.

"No." He smiled, still gazing into those gleaming blue eyes. "You could say I was here on business."

She looked puzzled but Randall fumbled in his pocket for his ID. He flipped the slim wallet open and showed it to her.

"Police," she said.

He nodded.

"It's not a very good photo," she said, indicating the small snap in the wallet. Their eyes locked for brief seconds and Randall detected the hint of a smile on her lips.

"Is it about the murders?"

He snapped the wallet shut, his expression hardening.

"What makes you think that?" he asked, sharply.

"Because we don't have too many policemen calling here at this time in the morning." She studied his face, hard and lined, puffy beneath the eyes from lack of sleep. He still had some stubble on his chin from his hasty shave. "Don't look so alarmed," she told him. "Word does travel you know. Three murders in less than a week is bound to be news."

Randall nodded.

"So who are you?" he wanted to know.

She introduced herself and, as he held her hand he found his gaze drawn once more to those blue orbs. She was, indeed, a very attractive woman. He looked for the wedding ring on her left hand but didn't see one, something which surprised him. They exchanged brief pleasantries then Randall announced that he should be going.

She called him back.

"Have you got any idea who you're looking for?" she asked.

Randall eyed her suspiciously.

"That's police information, Miss Ford," he said. "Why do you ask?"

"Well, it's probably nothing. . ." She allowed the sentence to trail off but Randall's curiosity was suddenly and unexpectedly aroused.

"What is it? If you've heard anything, tell me." There was a note of urgency in his voice now.

She explained about Harold. Falteringly, not sure whether she was making a fool of herself or not, she told Randall about the ex-porter's background, about the examination she had carried out, and about Harold's apparent regression. Randall listened but was unimpressed. She mentioned her search of the hut, the discovery of the blood and finally, almost reluctantly, the incident with the foetuses' grave.

"Jesus Christ," muttered Randall. "Where is he now?"

"No one knows," said Maggie.

The Inspector ran a hand through his hair.

"Everybody seems to be disappearing," he said, wearily.

"Maybe it's just my imagination but, well, he was disturbed," she said.

Randall nodded.

"I don't think this. . ." He asked the porter's name again and she told him. "I don't think Pierce is tied up with these killings. The severed heads, they're like Harvey's trade-mark. I can't see that it's anyone but him." He hesitated. "But I'll check out this Pierce anyway." He turned to leave but paused. "Thanks, Miss Ford."

"Maggie," she said.

"Thanks, Maggie," he said, smiling. "You know, if every doctor looked like you the Health Service would have an even longer waiting list." He winked and headed for the exit.

She watched him go, wondering if she had done the right thing. She doubted that Harold was connected in any way with the killings but if Randall could find out where he was she would feel a little easier. She took the lift to her office, the vision of Randall's hard but appealing face still strong in her mind. It was a vision that would not fade easily.

205

Randall slid into the passenger seat beside Fowler and nodded for the constable to start the car. He told the young PC to drive out to the new psychiatric hospital on the outskirts of Exham and the journey was completed in less than twenty minutes. Neither of the men spoke, each wrapped up in his own thoughts. Fowler still felt queasy at the thought of the autopsy and Randall's mind was trying to digest the information which Maggie had given him. However, there was something else on the Inspector's mind, something not directly linked with police business. It was the doctor herself and, as he allowed his head to loll back against the head-rest he thought about those sparkling blue eyes and that soft brown hair. He even afforded himself a smile.

Messages came through over the two-way as they travelled as other cars reported in. The news was the same every time – not a trace of Harvey. Randall hooked the receiver back into place and looked up as Fowler swung the Panda into the driveway which led up to the new psychiatric hospital. What a contrast to the old place, thought Randall as he got out. Where there had been granite there was now glass. Where there'd been barred windows there was now double glazing. The entire structure looked light and airy, a marked contrast to the forbidding monolithic bearing of the old asylum.

Randall got out of the car, telling Fowler he wasn't sure how long he'd be. The Inspector discovered that Doctor Vincent was with a patient so Randall paced up and down a spacious outer office until the head of the hospital found time to see him. He smoked six cigarettes in the thirty minutes he was forced to wait, gleefully ignoring the sign which asked visitors to refrain from the habit. He ground out the final butt just as the doctor's door opened to admit him.

Randall declined the offer of a cup of coffee, more interested to know what Vincent could tell him about

Harold Pierce. The psychiatrist seemed puzzled at first but then produced a file which included a photo. Randall looked at it, struck immediately by the appalling disfiguring scar which covered half of Harold's face. He asked how the man came to bear it and Vincent told him the whole story.

"Have you seen anything of Pierce since he left the old asylum?" Randall wanted to know.

Vincent shook his head.

"He hasn't been readmitted?"

The psychiatrist looked puzzled.

"Is Harold in some sort of trouble, Inspector?" he asked.

Randall shook his head and asked, "Have you any idea where he might go? Did he have any relatives around here?"

"Look, Inspector Randall, is there something I should know? What exactly *is* going on?"

"Nothing as far as I know," said the policeman. "It's just that Pierce has gone missing. I wondered if you might know of his whereabouts. That's all."

Vincent stroked his chin thoughtfully, looking hurt, as if Harold's aberrations were some kind of personal slight against *him*.

"I haven't a clue where he might be," said Vincent.

The two men sat in silence for long moments then Randall coughed preemptively.

"While Pierce was under your care did he ever display any violent tendencies towards other patients?" he asked.

"Absolutely not," said Vincent, emphatically.

"What about against himself? Self-mutilation, that type of thing?"

Vincent looked shocked.

"No."

Randall nodded, took one last look at the photo of Harold Pierce then got to his feet. He thanked the

207

psychiatrist for his time and walked back out to the waiting Panda.

Fowler was dozing behind the wheel, the unrepaired heater still blasting out its full fury. The PC jerked upright when Randall knocked on the window. The Inspector climbed in and, after rubbing his face with both hands, Fowler started the engine, swinging the car round in the direction of Exham. They were back at the police station in less than thirty minutes.

Randall pulled off his coat and stuck it on the hanger on the back of his office door. He took the cigarettes from the pocket and crossed to his desk, lighting one up as he did so. He slumped into his chair and blew out a mouthful of smoke in a long blue stream. It swirled before him, writhing gently in the still air, forming patterns then dissipating. He sat forward and pulled a pencil and notepad towards him then, with rough strokes, he sketched a passing likeness of Harold Pierce's face somewhat over-emphasising the scarred side. Tiring of his attempts at art he wrote down two names beneath the sketch.

Paul Harvey

Harold Pierce

He considered them both for a moment then crossed out the bottom one, tapping on the pad with the end of the pencil.

Both men had disappeared, apparently without trace. Was there some bizarre link which he hadn't yet thought of? Randall scribbled across the rough sketch, tore the leaf from the pad and tossed it into the waste-bin. He pushed the thought from his mind. There was no link between the two men, he was searching for answers where there were none. Clutching at straws had become something of a hobby for him just lately.

The phone rang.

"Randall speaking."

"Inspector, it's me," the voice was immediately recognizable. "Maggie Ford."

Randall smiled to himself.

"What can I do for you, Miss. . ." He corrected himself. "Maggie?" He heard her laugh at the other end.

"It's about what I said earlier, about Harold Pierce. I didn't think at the time but I remember now, when he was dismissed, apparently he said that he *did* have somewhere to go."

"You wouldn't happen to know where that was?" Randall enquired.

She didn't.

"Well, not to worry. I've got some news for you too. After I left the hospital this morning, I went out to the new psychiatric place and did some checking up on your friend Harold. I think you can stop worrying. I spoke to the Chief Consultant psychiatrist there and he assured me that Pierce had never shown any signs of violence. If I had a list of suspects I'd cross him off it right now." He laughed, humourlessly.

"So you're convinced it's Harvey?" she said.

"No doubt about it."

There was silence at the other end for a moment. Randall frowned.

"Maggie."

"Yes," she said. "I'm still here." The pause was a nervous one, both anxious to prolong the conversation but not sure how to progress. Randall felt like a schoolkid and noticed, with amusement, that his hand was trembling slightly.

"What time do you finish work tonight?" he asked.

"I'm off at ten," she said, almost apologetically.

"I know a nice little restaurant that stays open until late. I can pick you up outside the hospital."

Maggie laughed.

"If you're asking me to dinner the answer is no."

Randall felt suddenly deflated, almost shocked at her refusal but his mood rapidly lightened as she continued speaking.

"I know the restaurant you're talking about," she said. "It's too expensive. Besides, I'm a better cook anyway and, my flat's nearer. You wouldn't have so far to drive."

It was Randall's turn to laugh.

She gave him her address.

"Be there at about quarter to eleven."

They exchanged farewells and Randall put the phone down, feeling happier than he'd felt for a long time.

There was a knock on the office door and Randall shouted for the visitor to enter. It was Sergeant Willis.

"Thought you might have brought me a cuppa, Norman," said the Inspector.

"Sorry, guv," said Willis. "Just the pathologist's full report and this." He handed another piece of paper to his superior. It bore the numbers of all the Panda cars belonging to the Exham force. Each number had the driver's name next to it.

"They've all just checked in," said Willis. "The East side of the town is clear. There's still no sign of Harvey."

The smile faded rapidly from Randall's face and the familiar feeling of angry frustration swiftly drove away the fleeting twinge of elation he'd experienced moments before.

"I suppose we just keep looking then?" said Willis.

Randall nodded.

"Yes," he muttered, his voice low. "We just keep looking."

Outside, it was beginning to get dark.

Thirty-four

"Well, I don't think the bus is coming," said Debbie Snell pushing another stick of Juicy Fruit into her mouth.

"If we hadn't been mucking about in maths we wouldn't have got detention and we wouldn't have missed the bloody bus would we?" Colette Hill told her irritably.

"Well we *were* mucking about and we *did* get detention," Debbie said, leaning against the bus stop.

"Why don't you ring your precious Tony up," Belinda Vernon told her. "If you hadn't been going on about him we wouldn't have got told off in the beginning."

"Oh piss off," Debbie said, defiantly. "Anyway, if the bus isn't here soon I might just do that."

All three girls were from Exham Comprehensive School, the largest of the town's three schools and they wore its distinctive maroon blazer. Which, in Debbie's case refused to do up because of her mountainous breasts. All three girls were fifteen but Debbie was a taller, more mature-looking youngster than her two companions. They stood forlornly at the stop glancing agitatedly at their watches or periodically glancing up the road in the hope that a bus would appear from around the corner. The bus stop itself, complete with its glass shelter, backed onto a thick outcrop of trees which, in turn, masked some of the rolling fields that formed Exham's boundaries.

It was from these trees that Paul Harvey watched the three girls.

As a teenager he had always found girls impossible to cope with. Their jokes, their jibes, their little tricks. He had not known how to react and, on one occasion, when one of them had made exaggerated advances towards him, he had been left humiliated – standing alone amidst the jeers and laughter trying to hide an uncontrollable erection. The memory, as did so many of the others, still hurt.

Now he watched the girls from the shelter of the trees, close enough to hear what they were saying. The sickle was gripped tightly in his hand.

Debbie took one more look at her watch.

"Well, I'm not waiting around any longer," she proclaimed. "I'm going to phone Tony."

She rummaged through her pocket for a coin and, with a haughty "Goodbye" set off down the hill towards the phone box. The other girls watched her go until finally she turned a corner and disappeared from view.

Harvey moved swiftly but stealthily through the trees, tracing a parallel path with the lone girl. The dusk was deepening into darkness now, further adding to his concealment and he was content to remain within the confines of the woods, his eyes constantly on Debbie.

She reached the phone box and pulled open the door.

Harvey watched as she dialled. He could see her speaking into the mouthpiece and, a few minutes later, she put the receiver down and stepped back outside.

He watched her for a full five minutes as she paced back and forth then, slowly, he rose to his full height and moved through the trees towards her.

Debbie had her back to him and the growing wind masked the sound of breaking twigs and the big man emerged from the woods.

He was within ten yards of her now, almost clear of the trees.

She looked at her watch, oblivious to his approach.

The black Capri came speeding round the corner headlamps blazing. Debbie ran across the road to meet it, jumping in happily. The driver a young man in hi early twenties, spun the wheel and the vehicle turned full circle, heading back to Exham.

Harvey melted back into the woods, merging with the darkness as if he were a shadow.

Thirty-five

Harold sat up, the nightmare fading rapidly as consciousness swept over him. He blinked in the darkness, rubbed his eyes and, as he did so, he felt the perspiration on his face.

It was almost pitch black in the deserted asylum. He had a hurricane lamp in the room but he dare not light it. He sat shivering in the darkness, listening to the high mournful wailing of the wind as it whistled through the countless broken windows on the lower floor, stirring the dust which coated the floors so thickly.

The foetuses were in one corner of the room, covered by a blanket to protect them from the cold. Harold squinted through the gloom, his ears picking up the sounds of their low guttural raspings. He could see the blanket rising and falling intermittently. For what seemed like an eternity he sat cross-legged on the dirty floor then, slowly, he reached for the hurricane lamp and the box of matches nearby. He struck a match, lifted the housing on the lamp and watched as the wick began to glow yellow then he dropped the housing back into place, the dull light gradually filling the room, spreading out like an ink blot around him, driving back the darkness. Holding the lamp in one hand, Harold crawled towards the dormant foetuses.

His hand hovered over the blanket for what seemed like an eternity, then he slowly pulled it back.

The creatures appeared to be sleeping, their eyes closed, sealed only by the thin membrane of skin through which the gleaming blackness of those magnetic orbs still showed. Harold ran an appraising eye over them, swallowing hard.

One of them moved and its arm flopped limply against his knee. Harold let out a low moan and held the hurricane lamp closer to the outstretched limb. The breath caught in his throat and his one good eye bulged in its socket.

As if pulled by invisible wires, the stubby fingers of the nearest foetus slowly elongated, lengthened into spidery tendrils. The flesh looked soft but leathery. Harold pulled the cover back a little more and watched in fascination as the same thing happened with the creature's other hand.

He backed off, heart pounding hard against his ribs.

They were developing at a faster rate than even *he* had first imagined.

Harold sat gazing at them, his mind in a turmoil. Torn between fear and fascination. There was no revulsion any longer, just foreboding.

He wondered how long it would be before the foetuses completed their growth.

Thirty-six

Randall parked his car and walked across to the sma group of flats on the other side of the street. Beneath th sodium glare of the street-lamp he checked his watc

10.43 p.m.

"Spot on," he said to himself, pushing open the double doors which led into the hallway. There was a staircase ahead of him and a lift to his right. He chose the stairs, walking up slowly, feeling somewhat self-conscious carrying the spray of red carnations. Two kids, about fifteen, bundled their way past him laughing raucously and, minutes later, Randall heard the roar of motor-bike engines as the two of them sped off. They'll probably be wrapped round a tree by midnight, he thought. He'd always wanted a motor-bike when he was a kid but his parents had resolutely forbidden it. Death traps, his father had called them. Over the years, with the number of accidents he'd seen, Randall had come to agree.

He reached the landing and found that it was bright and clean-looking with paintings hung on two of the walls. There was an enormous rubber plant outside one of the flat doors which looked like something out of "The Day of the Triffids". The building consisted of just three storeys, six flats on each floor and it bore a marked contrast to the flats on the larger estates on the other side of Exham. No grafitti here, he thought. No dog shit in the hallway or cat's piss on the landings. Sweetness and light he mused, somewhat sardonically. The small block was quiet, everyone either went to bed early or Maggie was the only one on this floor he thought as he found her number. He pressed the bell and a two tone chime answered him. He held the carnations beside him, finally producing them when Maggie herself opened the door.

She smiled broadly, her face lighting up and, once more, Randall was struck by her extraordinarily sparking eyes. It was like looking at a June sky – two pieces of heaven captured within those glittering orbs. She was dressed in a crisply laundered grey dress and a pair of high-heeled gold shoes which seemed to accen-

215

tuate the smooth curve of her calves. Maggie was a small woman, about five-three Randall guessed, but the graceful suppleness of her legs made her appear taller. He ran a quick, appreciative eye over her, thinking how different she looked from when he'd first seen her that morning.

She ushered him in, taking the flowers gratefully.

"I didn't know what sort of chocolates you liked," he said, somewhat self-consciously. "So I thought I'd play safe."

"They're beautiful," she said and went off to find a vase. "Sit down."

He sank into the welcoming luxuriance of the sofa and looked around him. The room was quite large but sparsely furnished with just the three piece suite, a sideboard and a coffee table. A gas fire blazed before him, one of those with mock flames. There was a portable TV perched on a high table in the far corner of the room, a small music centre to his left. Two doors led out of the room, the one which Maggie had disappeared through led into the kitchen, the other one, closed at the moment, led to the bedroom and bathroom.

Behind the sofa on which he sat there was a small dining table set for two and the policeman could smell food cooking. The lights were dimmed and the whole room had a cosy feel to it. Immediately Randall felt relaxed.

Maggie returned a moment later carrying the flowers in a white vase. She set it down on the coffee table. He smelt her perfume as she leant over, a subtle aroma which lingered after her.

She poured him a drink and they talked gaily for a while until Maggie got up, announcing that the supper was ready. Randall got to his feet and wandered across to the table, watching her as she carried the meal in.

Randall savoured the meal. It was indeed a treat to eat something prepared by a woman's hands, especially when she was as attractive as Maggie. He looked up at her and for long seconds he imagined he was sitting opposite his dead wife but the vision hastily vanished.

"I'm not used to cooking for two," she said.

He reached for the wine bottle and poured them both a glass.

"That surprises me," he said.

"Why?"

"You're an attractive woman. It's not usual to find women like you on their own."

"Men don't seem interested in women who can compete with them on the same level," she said. "I mean, as far as a career goes. It seems to frighten them off. A woman anywhere else but the kitchen sink is a threat to their egos."

Randall raised his glass in salute.

"Come back Germaine Greer, all is forgiven," he said, smiling. "Where did you dig that speech up from?"

"I'm sorry," she said.

"It's ok, but, like I said, I'm still surprised you're single."

"I could say the same about you," she said, smiling.

Randall grinned.

"I think there's a compliment in there somewhere but I can't quite find it."

"You do live alone though?" she asked.

His smile faded somewhat. He nodded and sipped at his wine.

"Yeah, I have done for the last five years," he told her.

He returned to his food, aware that her eyes were upon him.

"I *was* married. I had a little girl: Lisa. She was two when it happened." He chewed his food slowly, finally sitting back in his chair, running the tip of his index finger around the rim of his glass. Maggie watched him silently.

217

"My wife, Fiona," he began, "she asked me to drive her and Lisa to her mother's. Well, I was just about to set off when I got a call through, could I come down to the station? They'd hauled a suspect in, wanted me to talk to him. I forget what it was about. Anyway, I told her that she'd have to drive herself, that the case was important." He sipped his wine, the voice which he heard sounded alien, distant, as if it didn't belong to him and he realized that he was speaking about the event for the first time since it had happened all those years ago. It seemed like an eternity.

"She'd only passed her test a few weeks earlier." He smiled thinly. "I remember how pleased she was when she *did* pass. But she didn't fancy driving at night, that was why she asked me to take her and Lisa." He paused again. "A lorry hit the car. Big bastard it was, sixteen wheeler. It took the fire brigade four hours to cut them loose from the wreckage. Of course they were both dead by that time anyway." He took a long swallow from his glass.

"Oh God, I'm sorry, Lou," she said.

He nodded.

"If *I'd* have been driving, it probably wouldn't have happened."

"You can't know that," she said.

"Sometimes I wish I'd have died with them," he confessed.

"You shouldn't blame yourself," she said.

He smiled, humourlessly.

"People used to say that to me all the time after it happened. All except Fiona's mother who seemed to agree that it *was* my fault. She hasn't spoken to me since the day it happened."

There was a long silence finally broken by Randall.

"Well, things are getting a bit morbid, aren't they? Shall we change the subject?"

He suggested they clear the table, offering to help

218

with the washing up. They carried the plates into the kitchen where she washed and he dried. They talked unceasingly, as if each had finally found some kind of confessor. Someone to whom their life's secrets could be revealed without the risk of scorn or judgement. And, in their openness they discovered just how desolate and empty their lives really were, but the discovery of that fact seemed only to pull them closer until, by midnight when they moved back into the sitting room with a cup of coffee each, they felt as if they'd known one another all their lives.

Randall sat down on the sofa, Maggie kicked off her shoes and sat beside him on the floor, legs tucked beneath her. She rested her coffee cup on the cushion next to him and ran a hand through her hair.

Randall watched her, realizing that he wanted her badly. Maggie felt a similar yearning but there was something nagging at the back of her mind. Something which she had not experienced with the other men she'd known. She wanted him, that much she knew but, for some unknown reason, she was afraid of rejection. She knew that he felt something for her, even if it was only physical, but she could not shake the feeling that she would be betraying the memory of his wife and child if she gave herself up to her feelings. But those feelings were powerful and, even as she sat talking to him, she felt compelled to take his heavy hand in hers, gently stroking the back, tracing the outline of his thick veins, stirring the hair which grew thickly on his hand and wrist.

Randall too was thinking about Fiona, wondering if he should be sitting here with this very attractive young woman wanting so badly to feel his body pressing against hers, to feel her hands on him and his on her. He had lost more than his family when Fiona and Lisa had been killed, he had lost a part of himself. The part that once knew happiness, compassion and optimism, but, in Maggie, maybe he had found someone who might help him to rediscover what he had lost. He gazed down at her as she bent forward to kiss the back of his hand and he could not resist the urge to lay one hand on the back of her neck, kneading the flesh there with his strong fingers. She felt so soft, so pliant and a tingle ran through him. You only met her this morning, he told himself, but that didn't seem to matter anymore. They were together and it seemed so right. As if they belonged with one another. He felt a single tear burst from his eye corner. There was fear there too. It had been so long. So long since he'd allowed himself to share any feelings he wondered if, when the time came, he would be able to.

Maggie climbed up onto the sofa beside him. She brushed the tear from his cheek with her index finger but she did not speak.

She thought of all those men before. Was this one going to be different? Could she actually find someone to love? She felt his arms pull her closer and she rested her head on his shoulder. For long seconds they remained still then she twisted around to face him and, tenderly at first, leant forward and kissed him on the lips. Randall responded and suddenly their kisses were deep and probing, making them both shudder. Almost reluctantly, Maggie broke away, her eyes wide, searching his.

"Does it bother you that I've been to bed with men in the past just because *I* wanted to?" she asked.

"Why should it?" he said. "It's your business, Maggie and, besides, the past doesn't matter."

"I think I've been very naive," she confessed. "I was confusing want with need. I wanted physical relationships but I needed something more."

Randall slid his arm around her, shuddering as he felt her hand touch his thigh.

"Do you always get philosophical at this time of night?" he asked, smiling.

"It depends on who I'm with," she said, grinning. "You're a good listener."

They lay down together on the floor and made love in the heat from the fire.

For long seconds afterwards, both of them gasped and shuddered with the intensity of their passion. Coupled together and breathless, they held each other tightly.

She bit his shoulder, drawing the skin between her teeth for brief moments until, when she withdrew her head, there was a small red mark there.

"Ouch," he said and nipped her ear lobe.

Maggie laughed, one hand stroking his hair, her finger finally tracing the outline of his eyebrows and, above those, the deep furrows which creased his forehead. She propped herself up on one elbow, looking down at him. She seemed fascinated by his hard face with its many lines and creases, each of which she seemed to follow with her nail.

"You must worry a lot," she said.

He looked vague.

"Wrinkles," she said, kissing him gently on the end of his nose. He frowned and she giggled.

"Do you know it takes forty-five facial muscles to frown but only fifteen to smile?" she asked.

"Thank you, doctor," he said, gripping her soft hand in his. "I don't usually have much to smile about."

She nodded, her expression softening.

"Will I still be smiling tomorrow, Maggie?" he asked.

"What do you mean?"

"This," he said. "Was this just another one night stand?"

She kissed him softly on the lips.

"I hope not," she whispered.

"The lonely doctor and the cynical, embittered copper

221

eh?" he said and, for a moment, she thought she heard a note of sarcasm in his voice. "Sounds like a perfect match."

She smiled as his tone lightened somewhat. He reached up and pulled her to him, holding her tightly. They gazed into each other's eyes, he, once more captivated by those glittering blue jewels with which she stared back at him.

"Would it surprise you to know that you are the first woman I've had since Fiona died?" he said.

Maggie looked a little shocked.

"Lou, I'm sorry if I've made you feel guilty. I. . ."

He put a finger to her lips to silence her.

"I suppose I can't live in the past forever," he said softly. "Nothing is going to bring her or Lisa back. I've got my memories and I'm grateful for them. I loved Fiona more than I thought it was possible to love anyone, and even more so when Lisa was born. When they were killed, something inside me died with them." He paused, swallowed hard and she could see his eyes misting over.

"Don't talk about it," she said, stroking his face.

"No, it's all right," he reassured her. "For the first time since it happened, I *want* to talk about it. For five years it's been bottled up. Because, until now there's been no one who I wanted to tell."

Maggie felt something stirring deep inside her. A feeling almost of pity for Randall.

Her voice took on a reflective tone.

"You know, all these years I've been calling myself liberated," she said, bitterly, "when all I've really been is a slag."

"Don't say that," he said.

She shook her head.

"It's true. I can't remember how many men I've had or maybe I've been fooling myself there too. Perhaps they've been having me." She kissed him on the cheek.

"And do you know what I've missed more than anything?"

He shook his head.

"Kids," she told him. "I've always loved kids but my bloody career came first where they were concerned too. Maybe that's why I work with kids. I'm a frustrated mother. Parent by proxy." She smiled humourlessly. "What I wouldn't give for my own child. . ." She allowed the sentence to trail off.

"I think that's enough soul-searching for one night, don't you?" said Randall, touching her face. He pulled her close to him once again and kissed her. She responded fiercely for a moment then broke away and got to her feet. For precious seconds, she stood, naked, before him and Randall gazed almost wonderingly at the smooth outlines of her glowing body.

"Let's go to bed," she said, flicking off the light.

Once in bed they found their passions roused once again and this time they were joined with an abandoned intensity.

Finally, exhausted, they fell asleep, clutching one another feeling that a shared demon was in the process of being exorcised.

PART THREE

". . . Evil, what is evil? There is only one evil,
to deny life."

– D. H. Lawrence

". . . And after the fire a still small voice. . ."

– Kings 19:12

Thirty-seven

Harold was shaking, his entire body racked by uncontrollable shudders. He knelt over the three foetuses and tentatively reached out a hand to touch the one closest to him. Its skin felt soft and puffy, like the swollen flesh on a blister. It moved only slightly as his probing fingers pressed against its chest. The creature made a low gurgling sound and Harold recoiled slightly as some yellowish fluid oozed slowly from one corner of its mouth. The foetus had its eyes closed, the thin membranes of skin scarcely concealing the dark pits beneath.

Close by, the other two creatures dragged themselves towards it, black eyes shining malevolently. Harold looked round, heard the sounds as they approached, shook his head as if to dispel the sibilant hissing within. The voices gradually took on a sharp clarity. It was like the static clearing from a radio transmitter. First there would be just rasping sounds then the words would come through.

"What's wrong with him?" asked Harold, gazing down at the barely moving foetus before him. The thing lay completely motionless by this time, just its thin lips fluttering, the thick pus-like liquid dripping from its mouth.

"Please tell me," Harold said, almost pleadingly.

Hissing, more loudly now.

Harold shook his head.

"No."

They were more insistent.

"What should I do?"

Commands, which he knew must be obeyed.

Harold looked at the ailing foetus and then at its stronger companions. He hesitated for a moment realizing what must be done. But, his reluctance was momentary. He got to his feet and crossed the room to the blanket where he himself slept. Beneath the rolled up coat which passed as a pillow lay the kitchen knife. Harold picked it up, glancing at the dull blade for a second before hurrying back to the trio of creatures. He could feel a slight gnawing pain at the back of his neck and, when he knelt beside the first foetus again, he found that the other two were glaring at him. They fixed him in that formidable stare, watching as he rolled up one sleeve exposing a forearm already criss-crossed with purple scabs and welts. Taking the knife in his right hand, he extended his left arm, flexing his fingers until the veins stood out. He swallowed hard, the razor sharp blade hovering over his own flesh.

Harold drew the knife swiftly across his arm, wincing in pain as the cold metal cut easily through his skin, opening the bulging veins. Blood spurted from the wound and Harold gripped the top of his left arm, dropping the blade beside him. The gash seemed to burn for long seconds and his arm felt as if it were going numb but he fought back the nausea and slowly lowered the slashed appendage, allowing the crimson liquid to run down. It oozed over his hand and dripped from his fingers and Harold carefully dangled the limb above the mouth of the dying foetus, watching as the blood formed red droplets on his fingertips before falling into the open mouth of the creature. Its lips moved slightly but some of the blood splashed onto its face and chest. It made a low mewling sound as it tried to swallow the blood which was mingling with the yellowish secretion already pumping from its mouth. Harold was shaking, the pain now consuming his entire arm. He held the limb steady, watching as the crimson fluid dripped onto the foetus. A swollen tongue lapped at it hungrily. Harold reached out to touch it with his free hand.

"I did as you said," he croaked, looking at the other two creatures. God, they were much larger now, he thought, and he recoiled slightly, whimpering. He gripped the rent in his arm, his fingers brushing against the hardened skin of the freshly healed scabs elsewhere on his forearm. Blood from the most recent cut was seeping through his fingers.

The voices were chattering once more, accusatory this time.

"I didn't kill Gordon," Harold gasped. "I didn't kill my brother."

The voices grew louder until finally, Harold shrieked. It was a cry which came from deep within him. As he looked down at the foetus, it seemed to metamorphosise, its shape changing, its features altering until it was his baby brother lying beside him. After all those years, Gordon was here in this dank, dark place. Harold began to sob uncontrollably as he reached out to pick up the small body. It felt so soft and jellied, as if his rough fingers would go right through the skin, but he lifted it nonetheless, holding the body to his chest, gazing into its face.

"Gordon," he whispered, tears rolling down his cheeks.

The accusations were there once again, whispered words of contempt from inside his head.

"I didn't kill him," he screamed. "It was an accident." Harold lifted its head, feeling how slack the neck was. Its chest was moving but only slightly and he could no longer hear the rasping, guttural breathing. Harold bent forward to kiss the thin lips and, as he did so, the face

228

seemed, in his mind's eye, to alter shape again until it was no longer his baby brother he held but the familiar form of the bloated foetus. He found his lips pressed to cold, wet flesh. He felt and tasted the blood, his blood. The pus stuck to his lips in oozing gobs and Harold shrieked once more, trying to wipe the vile substance from his mouth. He fell backwards, the body of the creature falling from his arms. Harold gagged as the obscene mixture of blood and pus clogged on his tongue. He rolled onto his side and retched until there was nothing left in his stomach.

When the spasms had finally passed, he hauled himself up on one elbow, his head spinning. He wiped the tears from his cheeks and gazed down at the dying foetus, the bitter aftertaste of his vomit still strong in his mouth.

"Oh God," he murmured.

He felt weak, barely able to support himself as he tried to stand. He managed it with effort, reaching for a filthy handkerchief which he pulled from his trouser pocket. He pressed it to the wound on his arm and held it firmly until the worst of the bleeding had stopped.

"I'll always do my best," he gasped, looking down at the foetal monstrosities. "I promise."

Harold took a step backwards. In the darkness of the room he almost stumbled over some of the other debris. The floor was smeared with excrement and dried blood. It smelt like an open sewer. The pungent odour of decaying, putrescent flesh was also noticeable. He dropped to his knees, exhausted by his sleepless night and also by the mental strain which he had been under for so long. He lay on the blanket but he dare not sleep. If he did, the dreams would come and he could not stand that. How he wished he had the tablets they used to give him, with those he never dreamed. There were no spectres waiting in his subconscious then, nothing to crawl out during sleeping hours to torment his mind.

But the dreams *had* returned now. So vividly at times that it was almost impossible to separate imagination from reality. He glanced across at the foetuses and shivered, pulling the blanket tighter around him.

The voices, now that little bit quieter, still hissed inside his head.

Thirty-eight

Maggie Ford washed her hands quickly and dried them on the sterilized towel before pulling on the surgical gloves. With her hair pinned up beneath her white cap she made her way hurriedly into the operating room where the unconscious body of a young woman lay on the table. Around her stood nurses and the anaesthetist who was checking his equipment. He already had his mask on and Maggie followed suit a moment later, crossing to her patient.

"What have we got?" said Maggie, looking down at the young woman whose smock had been opened to reveal her body. Her pubic hair had been hurriedly shaved and the area looked raw and angry but it was the blood seeping from the woman's vagina which disturbed Maggie most of all. There was a prominent bulge around the left hand side of the patient's abdomen, the skin shining beneath the lights of the operating theatre. It looked as if it were being stretched from inside.

"Suspected ectopic pregnancy," Maggie was told by a nurse standing close by. "The woman's name is Judith Myers, they rushed her in about ten minutes ago. She collapsed at work."

Maggie frowned. She inhaled and took a closer look at the bulge in Judith Myer's abdomen. It seemed to be pulsating.

The doctor wasted no time, realizing that the woman's life could be lost or saved in a matter of minutes. She set to work, something nagging at the back of her mind. She had heard the name Myers before, recently too.

The initial incision was made and Maggie worked as fast as she was able until she finally exposed the bulging Fallopian tube. There were audible gasps about the theatre.

"My God," she muttered. "It's a long way advanced isn't it?" She took the instruments that were handed to her, a bead of perspiration popping onto her forehead. The bulge was very large and, impossibly seemed to be moving even as she watched it. The blip on the nearby oscilloscope dipped violently, the rhythmic high-pitched sound fluctuating alarmingly once or twice. A nurse checked Judith Myers's blood pressure.

"Her blood pressure is falling," she said, anxiously.

Maggie held the scalpel in one hand, realizing what she must do but her hands suddenly seemed leaden, her gaze riveted to that pulsing protruberance which was stretching her patient's Fallopian tube practically to bursting point.

Harold huddled in one corner of the room watching the foetuses. They lay still, only the almost imperceptible rise and fall of their chests signalling that they were still alive. But, as he watched, he saw the veins on their bulbous heads swell and throb and their eyes gradually darken until they seemed to be glowing with some mysterious black light that filled the room, drifting like smoke all around them. Their bodies began to shake.

The blip on the oscilloscope was still diving wildly, the

231

sound occasionally shutting down for brief seconds. Maggie swallowed hard, noting that the membranous covering of the bulging Fallopian tube was actually beginning to tear. She heard muttered words around her as she worked to cut the tube free. She called for a swab, alarmed at the amount of blood which seemed to be forming in the abdominal cavity. It was lifted, dripping crimson, from the danger area to be replaced a second later by another. Then another.

A second split appeared in the thin wall of the Fallopian tube, the membrane tearing like overstretched fabric.

"We're losing her, doctor," someone called and Maggie looked up to see that the oscilloscope pattern had almost levelled out.

Harold opened his mouth in a silent scream as the entire room seemed to fill with a deafening roar. He clapped both hands to his ears but the sound continued. It was inside his head, it was all around him, filling the room until it seemed the walls must explode outwards. The foetuses continued to shudder violently, the veins on their bodies now turning purple, their eyes glowing red like pools of boiling blood.

Maggie recoiled as the large bulge in Judith Myers's Fallopian tube seemed first to contract and then erupt. There was a fountain of blood, pus and pieces of human tissue as the internal organ literally exploded showering those nearby with viscera. A young nurse fainted. The anaesthetist leapt from his seat and dashed across to Maggie's side. Both of them turned to see that the oscilloscope blip had stopped bobbing and bouncing, it just ran in an uninterrupted straight line now, its mournful note filling the operating room. Maggie worked to remove the ruptured tube, trying in vain to save her patient's life. There was blood everywhere, even on the

232

large light above the operating table. Maggie herself wiped some from her face, gazing down almost in disbelief at the damage before her. The young nurse was being helped to her feet and supported out of the theatre.

While another nurse checked the patient's blood pressure for one last time, Maggie herself listened for any sign of heartbeat. There was none. She pulled a penlight from her smock pocket and shone it into the woman's eyes. There was no pupillary reaction.

Judith Myers was dead.

Maggie untied her mask and turned to the nearest nurse.

"Fetch a porter," she said. "I want an autopsy done immediately."

Maggie, her smock and face spattered with blood, made her way back to the wash-room, her movements almost mechanical. She knew what she had just seen but she did not believe it. The ectopic pregnancy had been too far advanced. If her guess was correct, Judith Myers would have had to have been at least five months pregnant for her Fallopian tube to be in that condition. Myers. Judith Myers. Again she felt that nagging at the back of her mind. She knew that name from somewhere.

She pulled off her blood-stained gloves and tossed them into the bin, washing her hands beneath the swiftly flowing water from the tap.

The realization hit her with the force of a steamhammer and, for long seconds she stood still. Thoughts tumbled through her mind and she exhaled deeply. She finished washing and pulled her white coat back on, heading out into the corridor. Before she took a trip down to the pathology lab, she intended visiting the records department. She had just remembered where she'd heard the name Judith Myers.

It took the clerk in the records office less than five minutes to find the file on Judith Myers. Maggie took the file gratefully and walked across to the desk on the other side of the room. There she sat down and flipped the folder open.

NAME: Judith Myers. DATE OF BIRTH: 14/3/57. REASON FOR ADMISSION: Clinical Abortion

Maggie scanned the rest of the sheet, her eyes straying to the date of admission. She looked at it again. Could there have been some mistake? She doubted it. She herself had performed the abortion. She looked yet again at the admission date. Finally, clutching the file to her chest she got to her feet. She asked the clerk if she could take the file with her, promising to return it in an hour or so. Maggie left the records office and headed towards the pathology labs.

It took Ronald Potter less than an hour to complete the autopsy on Judith Myers. Maggie sat in his office drinking coffee until the chief pathologist finally joined her. He sat down heavily in his chair and ran a hand through his false hair, careful not to dislodge the toupée.

"Well?" Maggie said.

Potter sniffed.

"Well, Doctor Ford, I'm sure you don't need me to tell you that it was an ectopic pregnancy. She died of massive internal bleeding."

"Did you examine the Fallopian tube itself?" Maggie wanted to know.

Potter stroked his chin thoughtfully.

"Yes I did." His tone was heavy, troubled even.

"What caused the rupture to be so. . ." she struggled for the word, "so violent?"

"Well, the curious thing is, I don't know," said the pathologist, colouring slightly. "The size and nature

234

of the Fallopian rupture would indicate that she was carrying a foetus of over six months which as we both know is clinically impossible. But there's something else puzzling." He paused. "My examination showed no sign of a foetus, any embryonic life or even an egg. There was nothing in her Fallopian tube to cause a rupture of that size. In fact there was nothing in there, full stop."

"So you're saying that she died of a condition that was not pathological," said Maggie.

"That's correct. There was no evidence of any fertilized life-form in the Fallopian tube. It's almost as if the swelling and the subsequent rupture were. . ." He grinned humourlessly.

"Were what?" Maggie demanded.

"It's as if they were psychosomatically induced. There is *no* trace of foetus, embryo or egg in that woman's Fallopian tube." The pathologist exhaled deeply and traced a line across his forehead with one index finger.

"Well, I found something too," said Maggie, holding up the file. "How old did you say the foetus would have to be to cause a Fallopian rupture of that size?"

"Six months, at least," said Potter.

"Judith Myers underwent a clinical abortion in this hospital less than six weeks ago."

"That's impossible," said the pathologist, reaching for the file as if he doubted the truth of Maggie's words. He scanned the admission sheet, his brow wrinkling. "There must be some mistake."

"That's what I thought," she confessed. "But, as you can see from the notes, I did the operation myself."

Potter sat back in his chair and shook his head almost imperceptibly.

"A woman has an abortion six weeks ago," said Maggie. "Then dies of a Fallopian rupture that could only have been caused by the lodging of a foetus at least six months old in her tube and yet you find no trace of any foetus. Not even an egg."

Both of them stared at each other not knowing what to say. The silence in the office was heavy, like a weight pressing down on them and Maggie was not the only one to feel spidery fingers of fear plucking at the back of her neck.

Thirty-nine

PC Stuart Reed brought the Panda car to a halt outside the gate which led into the farmyard. The gate, like the fence it was attached to, was rotting. Pieces of broken, splintered wood jutting out like a series of compound fractures from the untended surround.

The farm buildings themselves looked dark and dirty in the mid-morning sunshine and the slight breeze moved the weather vane atop the barn, causing it to squeak loudly like a trapped mouse.

"Why the bloody hell do we have to check this place again?" groaned Constable Charlton. "I mean we've already been out here twice and there was no sign of Harvey."

Reed shrugged.

"Sergeant Willis said we had to go over everything with a fine toothcomb," said the younger man, glancing out at the collection of buildings. "I'd better check in." He reached for the two-way and relayed their position to the station. Willis's voice acknowledged the call.

"Do you want to toss for it?" said Ray Charlton.

Reed looked blank.

"For the privilege of looking around," Charlton clarified.

"Perhaps we should both go," said the younger man.

"And leave the car? Sod off, if the Sergeant calls through and finds out we've both gone for a walk he'll string us up by the bollocks." Charlton studied his companion's face for a moment then he reached for a walkie-talkie, taking it from the parcel shelf. "I'll go," he muttered, pushing open the door. He stepped out into a pool of muddy water and it was all Reed could do to suppress a grin.

"Shit," grunted Charlton and slammed the door behind him. The younger man watched as his companion trudged across the muddy ground, having to lift the farmyard gate out of the sticky muck before he could open it enough to squeeze through. Reed picked up his own walkie-talkie and flicked it on.

"Why didn't you jump it?" he asked, chuckling.

Charlton turned and raised two fingers in a familiar gesture. He walked on, finding, thankfully, that the ground was becoming firmer. The sun wasn't strong enough to dry it out but the chill wind probably helped to toughen up the top soil. He stood still in the centre of the yard and looked around. It was as quiet as a grave. To his right lay two barns, to his left the farm-house itself. All the buildings had been searched before. When Harvey first escaped he and Reed had been ordered to scout the deserted farm and, as Charlton had expected, they had found nothing. That had been nearly three months ago and now they expected the bloody maniac to be still holed up here when, in reality, he was probably long gone and had been since the first day of his escape. However, Charlton's cynicism did not take into account the three murders and he, as well as everyone on the Exham force, realized that the decapitations were Harvey's trade mark. The bastard was still in or around Exham somewhere but he doubted if it was here.

He decided to check the barns initially and made his way across the yard to the first of the large buildings. The door was open so the constable walked straight in, coughing as the smell of damp and rotting straw hit him. He peered up towards the loft and, glancing across at the ladder which led to the higher level, decided to check it. He reached for the walkie-talkie and switched it on.

"Stuart, come in."

Reed's voice sounded metallic as he replied.

"Have you found something?" the younger man wanted to know.

"No," Charlton snapped. "And not likely to. I'm just checking the first barn."

He switched off the two-way and clipped it to his belt as he began to climb the ladder which would take him up into the loft. The floorboards creaked menacingly beneath his weight and the policeman stood still for long seconds wondering if the entire floor were going to collapse beneath him but then, cautiously, he made a quick inspection of the upper level. A couple of dead rats and some small bones were all he found. He knelt and picked up one of the bones. It looked like a tiny femur and he surmised that one of the rodents that inhabited the barn had served as a midnight meal for an owl. He tossed the tiny bone away and headed back towards the ladder, pausing long enough to tell Reed that the first barn was clear.

It was the same story in the second of the buildings. It held just a couple of pieces of rusty farm machinery, otherwise the place was empty.

"I'm going to check the house now," Charlton said and started across the yard towards the last building.

Reed, still watching from the Panda, saw his companion approach the farmhouse and was puzzled

238

when he hesitated before it. The walkie-talkie crackled into life.

"The door's open," said Charlton, a vague note of surprise in his voice. "Probably the wind."

"Do you want any help?" Reed asked.

Charlton didn't. He slowed his pace as he drew closer to the house, nudging the door back the last few inches with the toe of his boot. The hinges screeched protestingly and, as the constable advanced, he was enveloped by the overpowering odour of damp once again. The house smelt musty, closing around him like an invisible hand. He coughed and moved further into the room. It was a hallway. Straight ahead was a flight of stairs, now devoid of carpet, some of the steps were already eaten through by woodworm or rising damp. To his right lay a door, to his left another, this one slightly ajar. He hesitated, not sure which way to go first. He decided to look upstairs so, negotiating the rickety steps, he climbed to the higher level. The curtains had been left drawn up there and it was difficult to see in the almost impenetrable gloom.

Three closed doors confronted him.

Pulling the torch from his belt with one hand, Charlton reached for the handle of the first door and rammed it down, pushing the door open simultaneously. It swung back against the wall and he immediately brought the torch beam to bear on the contents of the room. There was an old chest of drawers, obviously too big to be moved when the owners' left but, apart from that, there was nothing. The floor was thick with dust and a quick inspection told the PC that it was undisturbed.

He moved to the second door.

Once more the door opened with no trouble, this time into a cramped toilet cum bathroom. The taps were mottled and rusty, the bath itself crusted with mould.

He closed that door behind him and moved across to the last.

The door knob twisted in his grasp but would not turn. Charlton tried again, this time throwing his weight against it but still the door wouldn't budge. He flicked off the torch and slipped it back into his belt then, taking a step back, he aimed a powerful kick at the handle which promptly dropped off.

The door opened a few inches.

Charlton, feeling unaccountably nervous, pushed the door open and stood motionless in the frame, eyes alert for any movement. As with the other two rooms, things were untouched and, almost gratefully, he reached for the two-way.

"The upstairs is clear," he said. "I'm just going to check the lower floor."

"Any sign of life?" Reed wanted to know.

"There's more life in a bloody graveyard," said the older man and flicked off the set. Feeling somewhat more relaxed, he made his way back down the stairs, his heavy boots clumping on the damp wood.

He looked into the sitting room and found it to be empty then he passed into the last room in the house, the kitchen.

He paused at the cellar door, his hand hovering over the knob. Last time he and Reed had been out here, they had left without checking the cellar but, this time, Charlton knew the job must be done. The lock was old and rusty but nevertheless strong and, at first, resisted even his most powerful kicks as he attempted to break it off. Finally, the recalcitrant lump of rusted metal dropped to the floor with a clang and the door opened outwards a fraction. The constable reached for his torch once more and edged inside the doorway until he was standing on the top step of the flight of stone stairs that led down into the all-enveloping gloom of the cellar.

The smell which met him was almost palpable in its

intensity and he raised one hand to his face in an effort to keep the fetid stench away. He shone his torch down, the beam scarcely penetrating the blackness. Cautiously, careful not to slip in any of the puddles of moisture on the steps, he descended, breathing through his mouth in an effort to counteract the appalling stench.

He reached the bottom and shone the torch around, playing its beam over the floor, picking out the broken bottles, the shattered lumps of wood where some of the shelves had been overturned. His heart was beating just that little bit faster as he moved further into the dark recesses of the subterranean hole, the torch lancing through the blackness like some kind of laser beam.

He stepped in something soft and cursed, looking down to see what it was.

"Oh Christ," he murmured.

It was excrement.

He winced and tried to wipe the worst of it off, realizing that it was of human origin. A sudden cold chill nipped at the back of his neck and he stood still, sure that he'd heard something. A low rasping sound came from close by. He spun round, his torch beam searching the darkness.

There was nothing.

A loud crackle ripped through the silence and Charlton almost shouted aloud in fear, his mind taking precious seconds to adjust to the fact that it was the two-way. He snatched it from his belt angrily.

"Found anything?" Reed wanted to know

"For fuck's sake don't do that again," rasped Charlton, his hand shaking.

"What's wrong?" his companion wanted to know.

The other constable recovered his breath, angry with himself too for letting the situation get a hold of him.

"I'm down in the cellar of the house," he said. "We didn't check it out last time we were here."

"And?"

"Someone's been here. Whether it's Harvey or not I can't say but, by the look of the place whoever it was was holed up here for quite a time. The cellar's been wrecked." He described the scene of devastation and filth before him. "Call the station," he added as a post-script. "You'd better get them to send another car out here." He flicked off the two-way. Charlton shone the torch beam around the reeking confines of the cellar one last time then he turned back towards the stairs.

The massive bulk of Paul Harvey loomed before him, silhouetted in the dim light which filtered in from the kitchen and, in that half-light, Charlton caught sight of the sickle as it swept down.

Paralysed, momentarily, by the sight of the figure before him, Charlton was unable to move as quickly as he would usually have done. He tried to avoid the vicious blade but it caught him on the left arm, tearing through the fabric of his uniform and slicing open skin and muscle from the shoulder to the elbow. Blood burst from the ragged wound and, with a shriek, Charlton fell backwards, the two-way skidding from his grasp. He tried to scramble to his feet, blood pumping thickly from the hideous rent in his arm.

Harvey advanced quickly, swinging the curved blade down once more. This time the policeman managed to roll clear and the wicked point embedded itself in a broken shelf. Harvey grunted and tore it free, noticing that Charlton was making for the stairs.

"Ray, are you all right?"

Reed's disembodied voice floated up from the discarded walkie-talkie.

Charlton reached the bottom step and, clutching his torn arm, raced up the slippery steps but Harvey moved with surprising agility for a man of his size. He swiped wildly at the fleeing policeman, the sickle blade slicing through the man's thigh, hamstringing him. Charlton crashed down onto the stone steps, white hot pain gnawing at his leg.

"Ray. Come in. What's happening?"

Dazed by his fall and weak from loss of blood, Charlton rolled onto his back to see Harvey towering over him. The sickle swept down once again, this time to its appointed mark. It pierced the policeman's chest just below the sternum, then, using his enormous stength, Harvey ripped it downwards, gutting Charlton with one stroke. A tangled mess of intestines spilled from the riven torso and the policeman's scream was lost as his mouth filled with blood. His head sagged forward as he plunged both hands into the steaming maze of his own entrails, trying to push them back in.

"Ray, for Christ's sake."

Harvey looked around for the source of the voice but realized that it was the two-way. He headed up the stairs towards the kitchen, stepping over the eviscerated body of the dead policeman.

Reed actually heard the sirens in the distance as he looked up towards the farmhouse and, as he opened the door to clamber out, he heard a familiar voice rasping over the two way in the car.

"Alpha one come in," said Randall.

"Reed here," he answered. "I think we've found Harvey."

"Stop the bastard," Randall ordered. "I don't care if you have to kill him. Just stop him."

The sirens were growing louder as the other two Pandas drew closer but, when Reed looked up he saw Harvey emerge into the daylight, his clothes splashed with blood. The young PC shouted to him to stop but the desperate convict merely slowed his pace, as if waiting for Reed to come closer and, as he drew nearer, the policeman saw the sickle. Blood was dripping from its curved blade.

Reed ran across the muddy yard, tripping on something as he did so. He scrambled to his feet to see that it was a rake. He picked it up, hefting the rusty metal head before him like some kind of ancient quarter-staff.

Harvey remained motionless, even when the first of the Pandas skidded to a halt in the yard. Randall leapt out and moved towards the big man.

It was at that moment Harvey chose to strike.

He lunged towards Reed who managed to bring the rake up to shield himself. The sickle struck the wooden shaft and cut through it easily. Reed fell backwards, trying to crawl away through the mud as the big man came for him.

Randall, who had moved closer by this time, picked up a handful of mud and hurled it into the man's face, momentarily blinding him. Harvey raised a hand to wipe the oozing muck away and Randall took his chance. He launched himself at his opponent, smashing into him just above the pelvis. Both of them went sprawling, the sickle flying from Harvey's grasp. Randall reacted first and, with a vicious grunt, drove two fingers into the big man's left eye. Harvey shrieked in pain and rage and scrambled to his feet as Randall backed off, looking for something to defend himself with. Harvey roared and charged at him, catching the Inspector by the shoulder, pulling him down. Randall gasped as he felt strong hands encircle his throat. White light flashed before his eyes. His face began to turn the colour of dark grapes and it was as if his head were going to burst. Then, through a haze of pain, he saw Reed retrieve the metal topped end of the rake.

With a blow combining demonic force and terrified desperation, the young PC brought the rusty metal down on the back of Harvey's head. There was a dull clang, combined with the strident snapping of bone and Randall suddenly felt the pressure on his throat ease.

The big man tottered, then tumbled forward into the mud, groaning. Randall rolled clear, helped to his feet by PC Higgins. Both of them watched, almost in awe, as Harvey raised himself up on one elbow and tried to get up. Randall stepped forward and, with all the power he could muster, drove his foot into the big man's face. The impact shattered his nose, blood and small fragments of bone flying into the air.

"Bastard," muttered Randall, massaging his throat. He prodded the prone body with his foot then turned to Higgins.

"Get an ambulance for him," snapped the Inspector. "But put the cuffs on the bastard first."

Higgins scuttled off to call an emergency vehicle while Fowler cuffed the unconscious convict.

"He killed PC Charlton," said Reed, motioning towards the house. Randall walked slowly towards the deserted dwelling. He did, indeed, find Charlton in the house, his stomach somersaulting as he gazed at the mutilated corpse. He lingered in the reeking cellar for a moment then walked back out into the yard sucking in huge lungfuls of clean air.

An ambulance was approaching, its blue light spinning frenziedly and Randall watched as Harvey was lifted into the back of it by the dark uniformed men. The vehicle turned full circle and sped off in the direction of Fairvale, its siren gradually dying on the wind as it got further away.

"Thank Christ we found him, guv," said Higgins.

Randall nodded.

"Yeah," he said acidly. "But we were three months too late, weren't we?"

Forty

Randall lit up another cigarette and blew out a stream of smoke which diffused in the warm air. It drifted lazily in the lounge bar of "The Gamekeeper". The pub was quieter than usual but, nevertheless, Ralph the landlord busied himself behind the bar, serving and chatting, dispensing booze and gossip in equal proportions. He was a big man, about four years older than Randall and he carried a bad limp (beneath his trousers he wore callipers). He'd been landlord of the pub for the past eight years, prior to which he'd been in the Scots Guards. The limp was a legacy from one of his spells in Northern Ireland.

Every so often he would look across and nod agreeably at the Inspector who was sitting on the other side of the room beside the blazing log fire which roared in the grate. The hiss and pop of burning wood seemed unnaturally loud in the relative calm of the lounge. From the public bar, the far off sound of a juke-box cut through the subdued nattering. The pub was old but the juke-box was its concession to a livelier, more hectic age, one which was lived out in the public bar, frequented mostly by youngsters. The older regulars were content to down their pints and to play dominoes in the snug. Cocooned within that cosy environment, they were oblivious to all around them.

"Penny for them," said Maggie, studying Randall's expression.

He looked up and smiled.

"Sorry, Maggie," he said. "I was miles away."

"I noticed. What's wrong, Lou? You've been quiet ever since we got here."

"Be thankful for small mercies," he grinned.

"*Is* there something on your mind?" she persisted.

He reached for his pint and took a hefty swallow.

246

"I was thinking about Harvey," he confessed. "I rang my superior, Frank Allen, to tell him we'd got Harvey. Do you know what he said? 'About time'." He paused. "Bastard."

"What happens to him now?" Maggie wanted to know.

"They'll stick him in Rampton or Broadmoor I suppose. He'll be taken back to Cornford prison in the meantime. Though to be honest, I couldn't give a toss where they put him as long as he's out of the way. I just wish I could have got hold of him sooner than I did. Four people are dead now who might still be alive if I had."

"Come on, Lou, you can't carry the blame for those deaths too." There was a note of irritation in her voice. "Stop shouldering the responsibilities for everything that goes wrong. You did your job. What more could you do?"

He raised his glass to her and smiled.

"Point taken." He wiped some froth from his top lip. "What sort of day have *you* had?"

She considered telling him about Judith Myers but decided against it.

"Routine," she lied. "You wouldn't want to hear about it." She sipped her drink, changing the subject swiftly. "It's my day off tomorrow, can you get away a little earlier?"

Randall smiled.

"Well, with Harvey out of the way, there's just the paperwork to be written up." He reached out and touched her hand. "I should think I can sneak out around five."

Maggie smiled.

"What do you usually do on your day off?" he asked.

"Lie in bed," she began.

He cut her short.

247

"Now that sounds like a perfect way of spending a day."

They both laughed.

"I clean the flat, watch TV, read. Go shopping." She raised an eyebrow. "Really exciting isn't it?"

He smiled thinly, gazing into the bottom of his glass for a moment.

"Maggie, I hope you don't mind me asking but, well, these other men that you had relationships with –"

It was her turn to interrupt.

"I'd hardly call them relationships."

"Well, you know what I mean. Haven't you ever felt anything for any of them?"

"Why does it matter, Lou?" she wanted to know.

He shrugged.

"I'm a copper aren't I? Asking questions is second nature. I'm curious that's all."

She took another sip of her drink.

"No, there hasn't been anyone serious before. As I said to you the other night, I envy you your memories. All I've got is notches on the headboard." She smiled, bitterly. "And I'm sure that to most of the men I've slept with that's all I've been. Just another name in the little black book." She paused. "There was one man who wanted to marry me."

"What happened?" he asked.

She smiled.

"He worked for an oil company. They wanted him to move out to Bahrain for six months, he asked me to go with him. I said no. It was as simple as that. I'd just got the job at Fairvale and I didn't intend letting it go. He said that I wouldn't need to work, that we'd have plenty of money anyway but that wasn't the point. He didn't understand how important it was for me to feel needed. I enjoy the responsibilities I've got at the hospital. It makes me feel. . ." She struggled to find the word. "Accepted." She looked at him. "Anyway, I didn't love him." She drained what was left in her glass and put it down.

Ralph appeared at the table, collecting empty glasses.

"Hello, Lou," he said. "You'd better make sure one of your boys doesn't catch you boozing, you might get breathalized." The Scotsman laughed. He looked at Maggie and smiled.

"Mrs Randall," he said. "How are you?"

Maggie swallowed hard and looked at the policeman, then at the landlord. She smiled thinly in response, colouring slightly as the Scotsman made his way back to the bar.

"I'm sorry, Lou," she said, softly.

"For what?" he asked, smiling.

"The barman . . . he thought I was your wife."

"Nothing to worry about. It's not your fault and Ralph doesn't know about Fiona anyway." He took a hefty swallow from his glass. "Perhaps we look married," he said.

"Who *does* know about your wife?" asked Maggie. "About what happened to her?"

"I think most of the men on the Exham force know," he said. "Word travels fast. Coppers like to rabbit as much as anyone else. But, other than them and you," he glanced up at her, "no one here knows I was ever married or that I had a child." He lit up a cigarette. "That was one of the reasons I came to Exham. After it happened, I put in for a transfer. I thought if I got away from London and the places that reminded me of the accident, then it might help me to forget it. So, they shunted me around for a couple of years until I ended up here."

She touched his hand.

"You still miss them?" she asked.

"Naturally." He touched her hand with his own. "But not as much as I used to."

He squeezed her hand, as if afraid that she was going

to somehow disappear and she felt the urgency in his touch.

Forty-one

Sergeant Norman Willis checked that Paul Harvey was securely strapped down in the back of the ambulance before making his way back to the waiting Panda close by. He slid into the passenger seat, watching as the rear doors of the emergency vehicle were pulled shut. The blue light was spinning but the siren was turned off. Willis looked at his watch and saw that it was approaching 10.08 p.m. The ambulance pulled away, behind it PC Fowler started the engine of the police car and both vehicles pulled out into traffic.

Willis and Fowler had both been ordered by Randall to remain at Fairvale while Harvey was treated for his injuries (a hair-line fracture of the skull and a broken nose) and then to ensure that the captured prisoner reached Cornford prison.

Willis yawned and rubbed his eyes, blowing out his cheeks.

"It's bloody hot in here, isn't it?" he said.

"The heater's up the creek, Sarge," Fowler told him, without taking his eyes off the ambulance which was travelling at a steady thirty about forty yards ahead of them.

"I think you'd better wake me up when we get to Cornford," said the sergeant, smiling.

Inside the ambulance itself a uniformed attendant sat on the seat opposite the stretcher where Harvey lay. He was reading an old copy of "Reader's Digest", alter-

250

nately looking up to see if Harvey was OK. The big man moved occasionally, once even moaning softly and the attendant got to his feet and looked down at the patient. Harvey's head was heavily bandaged and a large dressing covered his nose and most of his cheeks. His mouth, however, was open and there was a dribble of thick saliva coming from one corner. The attendant, identified as Peter Smart by the small blue badge on his jacket, looked at the restraining straps and stroked his chin thoughtfully. Harvey was making even louder gurgling sounds now and Smart was worried in case the big man should choke on his own spittle. He hesitated a second longer then began to undo the first of the straps, intending to roll Harvey over onto his side.

The first strap came loose and Smart set to work on the second, the one which secured Harvey's feet.

With his back to the prisoner, Smart didn't see Harvey's eyes flicker open.

For long moments he tried to reorientate himself with his surroundings, with what was going on. There was a dull ache in his head and it felt as if someone were standing on his face but, as he saw the uniformed man undoing the strap on his legs, Harvey realized what was happening.

As the strap came free, he lashed out with his large foot, catching Smart in the solar plexus. The impact of the blow sent the ambulanceman flying backward and he thumped his head hard against the far wall of the vehicle.

Harvey, meantime, was sitting up, tugging wildly at the third and final strap which was across his midsection.

Smart reached for the small box close by, trying to get to the syringe, desperate to inject the prisoner with the 25mg of Promazine before it was too late. He scrambled towards Harvey who, by this time, had managed

251

to free himself and was in the process of getting to his feet.

Smart brought the needle down in a stabbing action, aiming for the big man's chest but Harvey was too fast for him and he clamped one huge hand around Smart's wrist, squeezing it like a vice until the appendage went white. With a despairing groan, Smart dropped the syringe. Harvey drove a powerful fist into the uniformed man's face, feeling bone splinter under the impact. He held his victim by the wrist for a second longer then, using both hands, hurled him against the other wall of the ambulance.

The driver felt the thump and slowed down.

Fowler, following close behind, saw the ambulance brake lights flare and nudged Willis.

"Sarge," he said, anxiously. "They're stopping."

Willis yawned.

"One of them probably wants to have a piss," he said.

By this time the emergency vehicle had indeed stopped. Fowler brought the Panda to a halt about twenty yards behind, watching as the driver got out and walked to the back of the vehicle. He fumbled with the doors, finally turning the handle.

Harvey came crashing out of the ambulance like a tank through a wall. The door slammed into the driver, knocking him flat and, before anyone could react, he was dashing off into the darkened woods to the left, disappearing like a fading nightmare.

Both Willis and Fowler leapt out of the car, the sergeant dashing after Harvey but it was useless. He saw the big man crashing through the undergrowth in his wild flight but the sergeant knew that he could never catch him. He ran back across the road to check on the injured ambulancemen. The driver was bleeding from a cut on the forehead, his companion inside lay unconscious.

"Get on the two-way, quick," Willis told Fowler. "Alert all cars. Tell them what's happened."

Fowler ran back to the car and snatched up the radio.

Within minutes, every man on the Exham force was picking up his frantic message.

Outside the pub, Maggie pulled up the collar of her coat and waited as Randall fumbled in his pocket for the car keys. A slight fog had come down during the evening and Maggie noticed how halos seemed to have formed around the sodium street lamps. Objects looked blurred and indistinct through the thin film of mist.

Randall finally found the keys and unlocked the car. Both of them climbed in. He was about to start the engine when the two-way hissed into life. Randall picked it up.

"Randall here, what is it?" he asked.

"It's Harvey," the voice at the other end said.

Maggie saw Randall's expression darken.

"Harvey's loose," the voice said.

Forty-two

Harold paced the corridors of the deserted asylum agitatedly. The wind was whispering through the many broken windows and it seemed to add an accompaniment to his apparently aimless wanderings. He moved with assurance through the dark avenues, through rooms which he had come to know only too well in the past and with which he was now becoming reacquainted. He could not sleep. It wasn't that he dare

253

not but, for the first time in many years, the welcome oblivion of unconsciousness eluded him.

He pushed open a door and walked into what had once been a dormitory. One or two beds, considered too old to be moved to the new psychiatric hospital, still stood in their familiar places. The iron work was rusted, the old mattresses damp and torn. Harold walked across to one and looked down at it. In his mind's eye he could see himself lying there, sleeping peacefully.

Crossing to one of the windows, he stared out into the night. It seemed a million years since he had been here, the memories now like fading photographs, the images becoming more and more indistinct.

He remained at the window for a long time then finally turned and walked back towards the door of the dormitory, pushing it shut behind him. He made his way slowly along the corridor, one hand absent-mindedly touching the scarred side of his face. Harold reached the foot of the staircase which would take him up to the first floor and the room where the foetuses lay. He paused for a moment, gazing up, as if expecting to see someone standing at the top, then, wearily, he began to climb. His legs and head ached and, as he drew nearer to the room, the stench which he had come to know so well wrapped itself around him like invisible tentacles.

He stumbled into the room and froze, both hands gripping the door frame until his knuckles turned white.

The first, and largest, of the three creatures was standing up.

It wavered uncertainly at first, those black pits of eyes pinning Harold in a hypnotic stare. Then, as if moving in slow motion, it began to walk.

Forty-three

Paul Harvey tore the last of the dressing from his nose
and cheeks and tossed it aside. He had already removed
the bandages around his head. Now he moved slowly
down the lane, sucking in lungfuls of early morning
air. He still found it difficult to breathe through his nose
and his breathing was harsh and guttural. A persistent
pain gnawed at the back of his head where he'd
sustained the fracture and, periodically, he would press
tentative fingers to it.

Exham had yet to come to life. The town seemed to
be sleeping as dawn broke but Harvey knew that, soon,
there would be people on the streets, in their gardens,
walking their dogs. He had to find shelter. He'd spent
the night in a shed at the bottom of a large garden. It
was from there he'd picked up the shears which he
now held in one huge hand but, as the daylight began
to creep inexorably across the heavens, he knew he
must find somewhere to hide.

The church stood on a hill, on the very edge of one
of Exham's many estates. It was old, its stone-work
worn and chipped, the colours in its stained-glass
windows now faded somewhat. A weather vane
squeaked mournfully in the light breeze and Harvey
ran appraising eyes over the building as he approached
it. Many of the gravestones were coloured with moss
and a good number of the plots were overgrown. Here
and there, dead flowers lay like discarded confetti, their
petals now brown and wrinkled.

He reached the main door but found it locked. He

slammed a powerful fist against it twice, angry that he could not gain entry. Muttering to himself, he made his way around the building until he found another door. This one was old too, the woodwork the colour of dried blood. It was splintered in many places and the chain which held it shut looked brittle. Harvey tugged hard on it, gritting his teeth as he felt the rusty links give. It snapped with a dull clang and he tossed the pieces away, wedging his fingers in the gap between door and frame in an effort to get it open.

The hinges screamed alarmingly but Harvey persevered, finally opening it far enough to give himself access. He slipped inside. The stench and the impenetrable darkness nearly made him change his mind but, fortunately, due to his broken nose he could not detect too much of the fetid odour and he soon found that there was some light coming into the subterranean room. He descended the stone steps cautiously only realizing when he reached the bottom that he was in a crypt.

Nevertheless, it was shelter. He sat down, the shears across his lap.

He waited for the darkness.

Forty-four

Maggie stood still at the top of the stairs, trying to catch her breath. She considered herself a fit woman but climbing up a long flight of stairs with two armfuls of shopping had all but exhausted her. She walked across towards the door of her flat, wishing that she'd put some lower shoes on. Her feet were throbbing and she decided to run a bath as soon as she got inside. She put down her bags and fumbled in the pocket of her jeans for the key.

The phone was ringing inside and Maggie muttered irritably to herself as she struggled to unlock the door; she pushed it open, snatched up the bag and hurried in, one eye on the phone, convinced that it would stop ringing the moment she picked it up. She made a dash for it and lifted the receiver.

"Hello," she said.

"Doctor Ford?"

She recognized the voice at the other end of the line but could not identify it immediately.

"It's Ronald Potter here."

Maggie wrinkled her brow.

"What can I do for you?" she wanted to know.

Potter sounded anxious, distraught even.

"I've been trying to get hold of you for the last three hours," he said, speaking quickly, not giving her time to ask why. She glanced across at the clock on the mantlepiece which showed 4.35 p.m. "There's been another death. The symptoms are identical to those of that woman the other day." Maggie heard rustling of paper on the other end of the line. "The ectopic pregnancy, Judith Myers."

"I remember," she said.

"There was another one this afternoon and the results of the autopsy are exactly the same. No foetus, no embryo, not even an egg and yet she died of a Fallopian rupture."

Maggie let out a long, slow breath, gripping the receiver until her knuckles turned white.

"Doctor Ford."

Potter's voice seemed to shake her out of her trance.

"Yes, I'm still here," she told him. "Look, I'm coming over to the hospital now. I'll be there in about ten minutes." She put the phone down and, without chan-

257

ging, she rushed out once more. The shopping was left discarded on the sitting room floor.

Maggie sipped at the cup of luke-warm coffee and winced. On the desk before her lay half a dozen different files, including those on Judith Myers but the thing which was holding her attention was the neatly typed sheet headed:

FAIRVALE HOSPITAL: NOTICE OF DECEASE.

The name entered in the appropriate box was one which she recognized:

Lynn Tyler.

Maggie exhaled deeply and ran her eyes over the sheet for the fourth time. She had read the autopsy report countless times too, glancing at that of Judith Myers as well. From the wording, it might have been a duplicate of the same woman's autopsy. *Everything* was the same about the two cases. Both young women, apparently healthy, had died from internal haemorrhage due to the rupturing of a Fallopian tube. But it was not just a rupture, it was the complete destruction of that particular internal organ. There were no warning signs, just the rapid onset of symptoms so virulent they had caused death in a matter of hours.

"No evidence of any embryonic or foetal development," Maggie read aloud. The words were the same on both reports. It wasn't a virus of any kind, that she was sure of. Could it be coincidence? The chances must be astronomical. Lynn Tyler had suffered a Fallopian rupture which would have corresponded to her carrying a foetus of over six months. Even the size of the bursts was the same, thought Maggie, and there was one more thing which made her uneasy.

Lynn Tyler, like Judith Myers, had undergone a clinical abortion just seven weeks earlier.

She swept her hair back and tried to find some kind

of explanation for the two deaths in the facts and figures laid out before her. There seemed to be no answers, just the unnervingly exact similarities between the two deaths.

There was another file on her desk, one which she now picked up and glanced through. It was a report by the senior porter on the discovery of the foetuses which Harold Pierce had buried in the field beyond the hospital grounds. She read it once, then twice, this time more slowly. It told of how the grave had been discovered, the remains disinterred and disposed of and ended with a note about Harold's dismissal because of his part in the action. Five foetuses had been dug up and incinerated. Maggie frowned and glanced across at another piece of paper to her left. It was a record of all clinical abortions carried out between the beginning of August and the end of September. There had been eight. The porter assigned to dispose of each one had been Harold Pierce.

Eight abortions but only five foetuses found in the grave.

Perhaps he just missed three Maggie reasoned. She chewed her bottom lip, contemplatively. Harold's obsession with the "burning of children", as he put it, was something which had surprised her but now, as she sat alone in her office, she began to wonder just how deep that obsession went.

"Eight abortions carried out," she muttered. "Five bodies exhumed." She drummed on the desk top with her fingers.

There was a knock on the door.

"Come in," Maggie called and was surprised to see Randall standing there.

"I went to your flat," he said. "There was no answer so I thought I'd try here."

"I'm sorry," she said, "something came up." Then, remembering he had problems of his own she added:

"Any sign of Harvey yet?"

He shook his head, producing a newspaper from behind his back. He held it before him.

"I could have done without this too," he muttered, handing her the paper.

She opened it and read the headline:

Maniac Harvey Eludes Police Again

"Oh Christ," said Maggie, quickly scanning the story that accompanied the headline. " 'Mass murderer, Paul Harvey, already thought to be responsible for four deaths in Exham recently, escaped from the police for the second time in as many days. . .' " She allowed the sentence to trail off. "What are you going to do?" she asked him.

Randall was gazing out of the window into the darkening evening sky. The first droplets of rain were coursing down the pane like silent tears.

"About what?" he demanded. "Harvey, or that fucking article?"

"Both."

"Bloody local papers," rasped Randall. "They're all the same. A bunch of two-bit scribblers. They might as well write on toilet paper because the stuff they write is only fit for wiping your arse on." He banged the window frame angrily.

"And Harvey?" she said.

Randall sucked in a troubled breath.

"My men are out there now looking for him, they've got orders to call me the minute they find anything." He turned, scanning the piles of paper and files on her desk. "What's *your* problem?" He sat down opposite her and Maggie began speaking. She explained everything. About the two deaths, about the autopsy reports, the abortions, even the discovery of the foetuses' grave.

"Christ," murmured Randall when she'd finally finished. "How do you explain it?"

260

"I can't," she told him.

"And the pathologist has no answer either?"

She shook her head.

He asked if it could be a virus.

"Any infection would have shown up in the examination," she told him.

He reached forward and picked up one of the files, flipping through it.

"In both cases," she said, "there was no *physical* cause for the Fallopian ruptures, that's the most puzzling thing. It's as if they were, well. . ." she struggled to find the words, "induced."

Randall looked up.

"I don't get you," he said.

"Every woman reacts differently to an abortion," Maggie explained. "For some it's a great relief but even the ones who want abortions and realize how necessary they are still feel guilty. It might only be in their subconcious but the guilt is still there."

"So you're trying to say that these two women induced the symptoms of ectopic pregnancy in themselves to compensate for the kids they'd had aborted?" he said.

Maggie raised an eyebrow.

"Does it sound crazy?"

Randall dropped the file back onto the desk.

"It sounds bloody ridiculous, Maggie," he said.

"Well then what the hell do you think happened?" she asked.

"Look, you're the doctor not me but you must admit that theory is stretching things a bit."

"Do you know anything about the power of the mind, Lou?"

"About as much as the average man in the street. What kind of power?"

"Thought projection, auto-suggestion, self-hypnosis. That kind of thing."

261

He sighed.

"Come on, Lou," she muttered, "I know it's clutching at straws but it's all I've got. Both women aborted for non-medical reasons."

"Meaning what?" he demanded.

"Usually abortions are carried out if the baby is found to be malformed, retarded or sometimes even dead. Both Judith Myers and Lynn Tyler would have given birth to perfectly healthy children. There was nothing clinically wrong with the babies they were carrying. They had abortions for convenience not necessity."

"You said there were three bodies missing from the grave," he said. "What about the mother of the third aborted child?"

Maggie flicked through one of the files.

"That abortion was a medical necessity," she told him. "The scan showed that the child would have been malformed."

Randall nodded.

"If your theory about the ectopic pregnancies is right," the Inspector said, "then you realize you're trying to tell me they committed suicide."

Maggie sighed.

"I know it sounds ridiculous, you're right." There was a long pause. "Lou, it's almost as if they'd both still had the foetuses gestating inside their Fallopian tubes despite the fact that they'd undergone abortions just weeks before. I don't know what to think."

"What about this business with the grave?" he asked. "Were the three missing bodies ever found?"

"Not to my knowledge."

Randall frowned, aware that what he was about to say was going to sound idiotic. He coughed.

"Is there any way a foetus could continue to grow once it had been removed from the womb?" he asked.

"No. Even in laboratory conditions it would be difficult. Not impossible but extremely unlikely."

262

He exhaled deeply.

"Now I'm not sure what *I'm* trying to say," he confessed. "But I know one thing, I'd like to talk to Harold Pierce."

"How could he be linked with this?" she wanted to know.

"Maybe he knows what happened to those other three bodies."

Maggie closed the files and stacked them on one corner of the desk. She got to her feet, switching off the lamp. The room was momentarily plunged into darkness.

"Perhaps we'll both think straighter on a full stomach," said Randall, opening the office door for her.

They walked out into the corridor, heading for the lift. Maggie looked worried and, as they reached the ground floor, she took his hand and held it tightly. The two of them walked out to the car park where Randall's Chevette waited. As he opened the passenger door to let her in, Maggie seemed reluctant to let go of his hand. He touched her cheek gently and kissed her softly on the lips.

Inside the car, despite the warmth from the heater, both of them shivered.

They were back at Randall's place in less than twenty minutes.

Neither of them ate much. They spoke quietly, as if afraid that their conversation would be overheard by someone. Again and again they discussed what had transpired at the hospital, as if repeated examination of the bizarre events would somehow lead to a solution. There was no need for either of them to suspect anything out of the ordinary but nevertheless an atmosphere of foreboding seemed to descend over them as they spoke. In the sitting room, Maggie sat close to

Randall, glad to feel his arm around her shoulder. Still they talked and still they could find no answers.

"We could go on like this all night," said Maggie, "and it still wouldn't get us anywhere." She smiled humourlessly. "Now I know what you feel like trying to find Paul Harvey."

"There seems to be more than one needle in *this* haystack, though," he said, taking a drag on the cigarette he'd just lit up. He got to his feet and crossed to a drinks cabinet where he poured them both a large measure of brandy.

Maggie glanced around the room. It was small and tidy. Randall obviously took care of the place. There was a pleasing smell of lemon in the room (from a carpet cleaner, she guessed) which further attested to its cleanliness. On the mantelpiece above the glowing gas fire there were three photos. The first was of Randall and his wife and daughter, the second and third of Fiona and Lisa alone. Maggie was struck by how attractive the dead woman had been. The little girl too, smiling out from behind the glass in the frame, sported two dimples which only added to the cheeky playfulness mirrored in her eyes.

"Your wife was very pretty," said Maggie.

Randall smiled.

"I know," he said, handing her a drink. "Lisa looked a lot like her." He crossed to the mantelpiece and lifted the photo of his daughter. "My little lady," he said, smiling. He replaced the photo almost reluctantly and turned back to face Maggie.

"She would have thought the same about you." He smiled and raised his glass.

He took a long swallow, allowing the amber fluid to burn its way down to his stomach. Maggie sipped at hers.

"So," said Randall. "What else can you do about

these deaths? Is there anything more the pathologist can tell you?"

Maggie shook her head.

"I don't know, Lou," she confessed. She gazed into the bottom of her glass and then up at him. "The only thing that bothers me is, if there's no explanation for these two deaths, what's to stop it happening to other women? Maybe even women who aren't pregnant?"

"Why should it affect them?"

"If there was no foetus or embryo in the Fallopian tubes then, theoretically, it could happen to any woman of child-bearing age."

"You can't say that until you know the cause," he protested.

"That's the whole problem isn't it? We don't know the cause."

They both lapsed into silence, a solitude broken by the strident ringing of the phone. Randall crossed to it and lifted the receiver to his ear.

"Randall."

Maggie looked at him and could only guess at what the caller was saying but, from the expression on Randall's face, it obviously wasn't good news. She got to her feet and walked across to him.

"Yeah. When? Whereabouts?" He pulled a pad towards him and wrote something on it. As he listened, the policeman was drawing small circles on the pad with his pencil.

"What's wrong?" Maggie whispered.

"A murder," he told her, handing her the note which bore the location. "But we've got a witness."

She swallowed hard, watching him as he listened, the pencil still performing its spyrographic rotations on the pad.

"Willis," said Randall. "Did the victim have any ID on him?"

"No, guv." The sergeant's voice sounded strained.

265

"We did some finger-print tests just to be sure. We double-checked. Triple-checked."

"Checked what for Christ's sake?" Randall demanded.

Willis sighed.

"The victim was decapitated."

Randall's pencil snapped with a loud crunch.

"What's that got to do with bloody fingerprints?" he demanded.

"The victim was Paul Harvey."

Forty-five

Randall brought the Chevette to a screeching halt, the tyres spinning for a second on the wet tarmac. Across the street he could see an ambulance, its blue light spinning noiselessly, and two Panda cars. Uniformed men moved around in the darkness and, as he pushed open the door, the Inspector saw that much of the far side of the road was lined with trees. Beyond them was a narrow pathway which led between two houses. The pathway was masked by high hedges on both sides. There were lights on in both of the houses and also in some further down the street. Indeed, some people had even braved the rain to stand at their gates in an effort to see what was going on.

Maggie got out too, slamming her door behind her. Together they crossed to the scene of feverish activity. Randall caught sight of PC Higgins and called him over.

"Where's the body?" he said.

"This way, guv," he said. "We didn't move anything until you arrived." He led them a little way down the narrow path to a sheet shrouded object. Randall knelt and pulled back one corner of the covering, wincing as he did so.

"Shit," he muttered.

Maggie too looked at the headless body, letting out a long, slow breath.

"Where's the witness?" the inspector wanted to know.

"He's in the ambulance. Some old girl from the house next door gave him a cup of tea. The poor sod's in quite a state. He's only a kid."

Randall and Maggie followed Higgins to the ambulance, the Inspector hauling himself up into the back of the vehicle. The youth, no more than fifteen, was milk white and shaking like a leaf. He held a mug of tea in both hands as if not quite sure what to do with it.

He looked up anxiously as Randall joined him in the back of the ambulance. Maggie climbed in behind him.

"What's your name, son?" Randall asked him.

The lad picked nervously at one of the spots on his chin and swallowed hard.

"M-Mark Rawlings," he stammered.

"I just want to know what you saw," said Randall, softly.

The youth tried to stop himself shaking but found it an impossible task. Some of the tea slopped over the lip of the mug and burned his hand. Maggie took it from him.

"Well," he began. "I was coming home from the pictures, I'd just left my girlfriend. She only lives round the corner see. So I thought I'd take a short-cut up the lane. I saw this bloke with a knife."

"In the alley?" Randall asked.

"Yeah. He was bending over something. I just saw him lifting the knife. Then I saw that there was a body there. He cut the fucking head off." The youth turned even paler and clenched his teeth together. "I saw him pick it up. He put it in a sack or bag or something. He didn't see me."

"But you got a look at *his* face? The man with the knife?" Randall said.

"Yeah. I know it was dark but, well he had this great big scar or something all down one side of his face."

Randall shot Maggie an anxious glance, the same thought registering in their minds.

"He looked like something out of a fucking horror film," Rawlings continued. "Like he'd been burned or something."

Randall got to his feet, patted the youth on the shoulder and jumped down from the ambulance, helping Maggie down after him. Neither of them spoke. They didn't have to. Randall had a quick word with Sergeant Willis then led Maggie back to the Chevette. They both climbed in, sitting there for a moment, the Inspector breathing heavily.

"When Pierce left the hospital," he said. "Where did he go?"

"I told you before, Lou, nobody knew," Maggie told him.

Randall banged the steering wheel angrily but then, his initial anger subsided. He looked at her.

"He was locked up in that asylum for more than thirty years, wasn't he?"

She nodded.

"I don't get you."

"It's the only home he's ever known." Randall started the engine.

She suddenly understood.

He put the car in gear and swung it round in the wide road. In a few minutes, they were heading out towards the road which would take them to the deserted asylum.

Forty-six

"How can you be sure he's here?" said Maggie as Randall stepped on the brake and brought the Chevette to a halt.

"I can't," he said, opening his door. "Let's just hope this is one hunch that's right." The policeman clambered out from behind the wheel and walked across to the metal gates which barred the way to the asylum. In the darkness he could just discern three words on the stone archway above him.

EXHAM MENTAL HOSPITAL

There was a padlock on the gates and Randall tugged on it. The rusty gates creaked protestingly but didn't budge. The Inspector looked round. The driveway was the only means of getting a car into the grounds but a man could slip through one of the many gaps in the hedge. Randall scanned the ground around him and finally spotted a large stone. He retrieved it and set about the padlock, striking it with all his strength. It eventually came free with a dull clang and dropped to the ground. The Inspector put his shoulder to one of the gates and pushed. It was heavier than it looked and the exertion made him sweat but he finally succeeded in opening it as far as it would go. He repeated the procedure with the other one then hurried back to the car. Starting the engine he guided the Chevette through the archway and along the drive towards the asylum itself.

Flanked on both sides by leafless trees, he estimated

that the driveway must be at least half a mile long. He drove slowly, eyes alert for the slightest movement in the darkness.

"What are you going to do if Harold is here?" Maggie wanted to know.

"I'll tell you that when I find him," Randall told her, cryptically.

He brought the vehicle to a halt before the main entrance and both of them peered out at the building itself. It was an awesome sight, a Victorian edifice which, in the darkness, looked not as if it had been built with separate bricks but hewn from one enormous lump of granite. Five storeys high, it was built in the shape of an "E", the apex of which rose like a church spire. The figure of the weather vane on the top surveyed the bleak and ghostly scene with indifference.

The policeman climbed out of the car. Maggie also pushed open her door but Randall held up a hand to stop her.

"You stay here," he told her.

"But Lou, you don't know for certain that he's here," she protested. "And, even if he is, at least *I* know him. I could talk to him."

"The man's a bloody maniac," he rasped. "Now get back in the car, lock both doors and don't move until I get back. If I'm not here in an hour use this." He grabbed the two-way and held it up. "Contact the station and tell them where we are. Right?"

She didn't speak.

"Right?" he said, more forcefully.

"All right. Lou, be careful."

He nodded, slammed the door behind him and waited until he heard both locks drop then he made his way slowly towards what had once been the main entrance. As he'd suspected, the doors were locked so he moved along, peering at all the windows, eyes alert for any sign of a break-in, any tell-tale evidence of

270

Pierce's whereabouts. He rounded a corner and disappeared from Maggie's view. She sat impatiently, hands clenched on her thighs.

Randall moved cautiously, noticing how many of the asylum windows had been broken but he could tell which had been smashed by kids. Just round holes in the panes showed where stones had been hurled. As yet, there was no sign of forced entry. He sucked in an impatient breath wondering if his hunch had been wrong. He rested his hand on one of the sills and felt something wet beneath his fingers. The Inspector turned and looked down. There was a dark stain on the peeling paint. Tentatively he raised his fingers to his nose, sniffing the substance. There was no mistaking the distinctive coppery odour of blood.

He looked up and saw that the dark liquid was puddled beneath a set of double windows, one of which had been broken about half-way up, near the handle. The policeman gripped both sides of the frame and hauled himself up onto the sill, perching there for a second before pushing the two windows. They swung open invitingly and he jumped down into the building itself.

The smell of damp was almost overpowering and the Inspector blinked hard in an effort to combat the cloying darkness. There was some natural light spilling through the windows, enough to reveal to him that he was in what had once been an office. Dust swirled around him, the particles irritating his nose and throat but he fought back the urge to cough, anxious not to alert anyone who might be hiding inside.

There was more blood on the floor just ahead of him – a large splash and then droplets of the thick crimson fluid which was in the process of congealing. The trail led to the door and Randall paused before it a moment, listening. The asylum greeted him with silence and a kind of conspiratorial solitude which made him feel uneasy.

He slowly opened the door.

Corridors faced him and, after a moment's hesitation, he chose the one straight ahead.

Harold heard the noise from downstairs.

He snatched up the long kitchen knife, its blade still wet with blood, and scuttled out into the corridor his own ears now attuned to the sounds within the asylum. There was a crooked grin on his face. Someone was inside *his* home. They would not escape. His mind suddenly seemed clearer than it had done for months and he hurried through the darkened corridors as if drawn by some huge magnet, bearing down on the intruder.

It would only be a matter of time before he found the unwanted guest.

Maggie looked at her watch. The hands had crawled round to 11.49 p.m. Randall had been gone for nearly fifteen minutes. She sighed, shifting impatiently in her seat. There was a torch on the parcel shelf before her and she eyed it with a look akin to temptation. She closed her eyes for a second, trying to think about what had happened. The thought of Harold Pierce as a killer was still one she found hard to accept but it seemed clear enough. Nevertheless, if only she could speak to him, reason with him. . .

From where she sat she could see that many of the windows had been broken. It should be relatively easy to slip the catch on one and get in. She looked at the torch once again, this time picking it up. She unlocked her door and closed it behind her then she scuttled across to the nearest window, slipped her hand through a break in the pane and undid the latch. It opened and Maggie dragged herself up onto the sill. She steadied

272

herself for a moment then jumped down into the room beyond. As she switched on the torch she saw that the door ahead of her was already open. The powerful beam shone through the darkness, lighting her way. She swallowed hard and moved quietly out into the corridor.

Randall pushed open the door of a room, surprised that so many of the asylum's places had been left unlocked but then, he reasoned, no one could have foreseen anyone returning here. Why bother? He edged cautiously into what he guessed had once been the dining room. There were a number of long tables stacked at one side and, at the far end of the vast room, a long counter. It was fronted by a corrugated metal sheet which had been pulled down and padlocked. The Inspector walked across to it, his footsteps clacking on the stone floor. Large picture windows, meshed, gave him some added light but already his eyes were beginning to ache from the effort of squinting in the gloom. He stood still for long moments, listening, trying to catch even the slightest hint of movement.

Silence.

He exhaled deeply and turned towards a door nearby which was also unlocked. It was as he passed through it that the Inspector realized he had nothing to defend himself with should he come upon Pierce. He swallowed hard and moved on, finding himself in another corridor. There were rooms every fifteen yards and each one would have to be checked.

He pushed open the first door.

Harold paused at the bottom of the stairs, looking round. He could see no sign of the intruder but he knew that his quarry was here somewhere. A surge of adrenalin swept through him and he gripped the knife tighter, his breath now coming in short, excited gasps.

He touched the scarred side of his face, feeling the crusted flesh beneath his fingertips. He moved slowly along the corridor to his right, stopping dead when he heard movement ahead of him. His knife gripped firmly in his fist, he ducked into a nearby room.

Maggie put her hand on the bannister of the staircase and hurriedly withdrew it as she felt something sticky on her fingers.

It was blood.

There was more on the bannister, even some on the steps themselves. She shone the torch on the crimson liquid and, slowly began to climb. She wiped the blood off on her jeans her heart now beating just that little bit faster. The staircase rose precipitously until, at last, it levelled out onto a landing. Faced by two corridors, Maggie took the one on her left, tip-toeing in an effort to diminish the clicking of her heels on the stone floor.

She recoiled from a sudden, nauseating stench which seemed to drift around her like an invisible cloud. She put a hand to her mouth and stifled a cough. As she moved further down the corridor the smell became almost unbearable. Her head began to swim and she was forced to lean momentarily against the wall for support. She played the torch beam before her in an effort to discover the source of the rank odour and, as she moved on, she found that the end door in the corridor was open. Maggie pressed herself against the wall once again, listening. From inside the room she could hear soft, liquid sounds – a series of rasping gurgles. She closed her eyes for a second, at once revolted by the sounds and desperate to discover their source. A part of her was wishing she had stayed in the car.

She held the torch beam up and peered round the door.

For brief seconds, Maggie had to use all her self-control to prevent herself from vomiting. She swayed slightly, supporting herself against the door frame, then, almost drawn to the sight before her, she walked slowly into the room.

Maggie shook her head, unable to believe what she saw, convinced that, any second she was going to wake up to discover that this was a nightmare. But no nightmare could be as vile as what she now saw before her.

She shone the torch on the first foetus and the creature recoiled slightly from the piercing beam, its dark eyes glinting menacingly. It was standing, something wet and sticky gripped in its fingers. The other two were on the floor, the second one pawing at something before it.

It was a few more seconds before Maggie realized that the object was a human head.

And now, as she stepped back, her foot brushed something else. Something which rolled when she made contact. She swung the torch beam round, the gruesome discovery pinned in the beam.

The second head was partially decomposed, the skin around the neck and eyes mottled green in places. The skull had been split open with a heavy object, exposing the brain and, as Maggie turned the torch back onto the abominations before her, she realized just what the sticky grey substance was which the larger creature held. As she watched, it raised the jellied matter to its mouth and clumsily pushed some in.

Maggie closed her eyes momentarily.

The foetuses seemed unconcerned at her presence. They were more interested in the severed head they were toying with. There was blood everywhere, mingling on the floor with slicks of excrement and pieces of hair. Greyish brain matter seemed to sparkle in the light.

Suddenly, everything seemed to take on a horrendous clarity: the headless murder victims that the police had found, Harold's obsession with the incineration of foetuses and, worst of all, she now understood why only five babies instead of eight had been disinterred from the grave near Fairvale.

She stood still, frozen by the sight before her, trying to find either the will to move or the power to scream but she could do neither. She felt faint, her stomach finally beginning to churn uncontrollably and she felt the vomit begin its journey up her throat. She turned away, retching violently, the foul stench of her vomit mingling with the choking odours already filling the room. But, the action seemed to shake her out of her trance and she moved for the door.

(*STOP*)

Maggie clapped both hands to her head, the torch dropping to the ground.

(*You will not leave*)

It's my imagination, she told herself.

(*No, it is not your imagination*)

She turned back to face the creatures.

Could it be telepathy? she wondered, hurriedly dismissing the thought. Her mind was over-reacting to the situation.

(*Your thoughts are open to us*)

She gazed at them, her face twisted into an expression which combined revulsion and fascination.

"What are you?" she said.

(*Nothing. We are nothing*)

"How do you know what I'm thinking?"

A soft chuckling and Maggie felt the hairs on the back of her neck prickle.

(*There can be no secrets. We know your thoughts and your fears*)

She thought about Randall. If only she could alert him to the danger.

In the blinking of an eye he was standing before her, smiling.

276

"Lou," she said and stepped forward to touch him but, even as she did so, the vision faded and she was alone once more.

The soft chuckling filled her ears.

(*Thoughts. Fears. There are no secrets*)

Thought projection, Maggie wondered? Auto-suggestion? The very things which she had mentioned to Randall and now she began to realize how Judith Myers and Lynn Tyler had come to die. The foetuses were the exact size which they would needed to have been to cause the Fallopian ruptures.

"You killed two women," she said.

(*They had to die*)

"Why?"

(*THEY WOULD HAVE KILLED US*)

Despite herself, Maggie moved closer to the largest of the creatures, kneeling before it, running expert eyes over its body. It was perfectly formed, as if it had grown within the mother's womb, reaching maturity as originally intended. The most frightening thing about it was its eyes. Black pits devoid of emotion, they pinned her in an hypnotic stare.

Randall heard the sounds of movement from upstairs and he ran towards the foot of the staircase, pausing momentarily when he reached it.

Harold came hurtling out of the room behind him, the knife held high above his head.

Randall heard the vicious arc of the steel and tried to turn but Harold was too quick for him. The blade powered down, catching the policeman in the shoulder. It tore through the flesh and actually scraped the clavical as it finally burst through his pectoral muscle, the point dripping blood. Harold pressed his advantage, wrenched the knife free and drove it down again but this time Randall managed to get his hand up in time. He deflected the blow, the knife striking concrete as the two men fell to the ground. The Inspector was surprised at his assailant's strength; despite Harold's age he seemed to possess an energy which belied his years. Randall struck out with his right fist, his left arm already numb from the knife wound. The blow caught Harold squarely in the side of the head but the impact only staggered him for a minute. However, that minute was enough to allow Randall the chance to wriggle free. He hauled himself upright and, as Harold tried to follow him, he drove a foot hard into the older man's side. There was a strident snapping of bone as one brittle rib splintered under the impact.

Harold went down in a heap, the knife held in one outstretched hand. Randall dropped to his knees, grabbing for it but Harold struck out again, the wild blow slicing open the policeman's palm. He yelped in pain but closed his injured hand around Harold's wrist, banging the hand on the ground repeatedly in an effort to make him drop the knife.

The older man clawed at Randall's face, gripping him by the hair, yanking his head to one side and both of them went sprawling again. This time Harold was first on his feet and Randall saw the scarred attacker advancing on him. The Inspector waited until his opponent was mere inches away then lashed out, catching Harold in the crutch with a powerful kick. He doubled up and Randall hastily scrambled to his feet. He grabbed Harold's hair and, in one skilful movement, brought his knee up to meet Harold's down-rushing head. The older man's nose seemed to explode, splattering the policeman's trousers with blood. Randall wrenched his attacker upright, hitting him hard in the stomach, his hand still gripping Harold's hair. The knife finally fell to the ground and Randall drove another powerful kick into the other man's stomach, watching as he crashed heavily to the ground.

"Lou!" – the scream came from upstairs. It was Maggie's voice.

Randall snatched up the knife and started up the stairs.

"No," Harold shouted and staggered after him.

He caught the Inspector half way up but, the older man was weak and, as Randall spun round he drove the knife forward. It caught Harold just above the right hip, deflected off the pelvis and ripped into his intestines. The policeman tore it free, watching as Harold tottered drunkenly on the stairs, blood pouring through his fingers as he tried to hold the ragged edges of the wound together. Then, with a final despairing moan he toppled backwards, crashing head-over-heels until he lay still at the foot of the stairs.

Randall's breath was coming in gasps. His left shoulder and most of his left arm felt numb and the slashed palm of his right hand felt as if it were on fire. He turned wearily and climbed the last few steps to the landing casting a perfunctory look back at Harold when he reached the top. The older man lay still, face down in the dust which covered the floor, a dark pool spreading out around him.

The Inspector turned and walked on towards the junction of the two corridors before him, not sure which one to check out first. Then he noticed the vile stench and moved cautiously along the left hand one, the knife gripped tightly in his throbbing hand.

He reached the last door and slumped against the frame, his mind reeling from the pain of his wounds and the sight before him.

"Oh my God," he croaked, his eyes scanning the scene of horror which confronted him. The heads, the blood, the excrement and. . .

He stared at the foetuses, shaking his head slowly from side to side. Then he took a step into the room, noticing Maggie for the first time.

"Get out," he told her, gripping the knife tighter.

The foetuses turned their black eyes on him and Randall felt the first gnawings of pain at the back of his neck. He advanced slowly on them, taking in each monstrous detail.

"Lou, don't touch them," said Maggie, her voice low.

Randall seemed not to hear, he just kept moving closer. So slowly, so feebly, as if someone had attached lead weights to his limbs.

"Don't touch them," Maggie implored.

"What are they?" he croaked.

"The grave of abortions that Pierce dug up, these are the three that were missing. They've grown."

"Oh Jesus," murmured the policeman.

(*GET BACK*)

He felt as if he'd been struck with an iron bar. He reeled, almost fell and a thin trickle of blood dribbled from one nostril.

"Lou," Maggie shouted. "Stay away, they'll kill you."

Randall gritted his teeth, raised the knife in his bloodied hand. It seemed as if someone were inflating his head with a high-pressure pump. His eyes bulged in their sockets, a small crimson orb burst from one tear duct and ran down his cheek. Still he advanced on them, the pain in his head growing.

He was less than ten yards away from them.

"Lou."

His legs gave out and he dropped to his knees but still he crawled onward. The veins in his arms and neck bulged menacingly, the wounds in his hand and shoulder bleeding freely. It was like pushing open a thousand ton door, pressing against it, moving a fraction of an inch at a time. He clenched his teeth until his jaws ached, the knife clanking on the concrete as he dropped to all fours.

He almost screamed aloud as he found himself staring into the sightless eyes of Paul Harvey.

The dead man's head lay in a pool of congealing blood, inches from the policeman's face. Thick crimson streamers still dripped from the nostrils and ears. The tongue protruded over white lips. The skull had been smashed in just above the right ear and Randall could still see fragments of brain matter sticking to the hair. The cavity had been emptied, the soft tissue devoured by the monstrosities before him, torn out with their eager hands.

As Randall crawled on, he bumped the head and it rolled over to reveal the severed stump of the neck, the slashed veins and arteries hanging like dripping bloodied tendrils.

The foetuses concentrated their mind power with greater accuracy, focusing it on Randall like some kind of invisible laser beam.

Blood burst from his ears and he went deaf for precious seconds.

"Lou," Maggie shrieked. "Stop."

He was just feet away from them now, their rancid stench filling his nostrils, mingling with the coppery smell of his own blood which was flowing from his nose and dripping onto the floor. He groaned more loudly now as his efforts to reach the creatures became greater.

He raised the knife to strike.

Randall almost screamed aloud as he found himself gazing into the eyes of his daughter.

(*No*)

"Lisa," he croaked, the knife hovering above her head.

(*Don't kill me*)

He swayed, thought he was going to pass out then, slowly, he lowered the knife, eyes fixed on the vision of his daughter.

(*Put the knife down*)

He dropped it in front of him, staring at her. God,

281

she was beautiful. She lay before him, her body unblemished. He reached out his arms to touch her smooth
skin but, as he felt her body, he gagged. The flesh was
soft and jellied. As cold as ice. The vision faded
instantly and he found himself staring once more at the
foetuses.

"No," he screamed and snatched up the knife, plunging it into the one closest to him.

A huge gout of blood erupted from the wound splattering Randall who was sobbing now as he brought
the knife down again, the second blow hacking off the
foetus's right arm. The tiny limb fell to one side twitching spasmodically, blood gushing from the severed
arteries. He struck again and again until the knife was
slippery with his blood and that of the creature. The
other one tried to crawl away but Randall was upon it
in a flash, driving the blade down between its shoulder
blades, tearing downwards to rip through its kidneys
and liver. He held it by the back of the head and drove
the knife into the hollow at the nape of its neck, ignoring the blood which spurted up into his face. He
hacked off an ear, part of its nose, buried the blade in
one of those dark pits of eyes.

The third creature didn't even move as he gutted it,
ripping the small tangle of intestines free with his bare
hands.

Finally, he toppled over onto his back, eyes staring
blankly at the ceiling. Maggie rushed across to him,
wiping some of the blood from his face with her handkerchief. There was so much of the sticky crimson gore
on him it was difficult to tell which was from his
wounds and which was from the creatures. She helped
him to his feet, supporting him out of the room and
out into the corridor.

"Got to get back to the car," he whispered, almost
collapsing.

She held him, ignoring the blood which dripped from his hands and arms and stained her own clothes.

They reached the landing and began, cautiously, to descend the stairs.

"Harold?" asked Maggie.

"I killed him," said Randall.

But, as they reached the bottom of the stairs, the policeman saw only the pool of blood there. Of Harold there was no sign.

"Come on, hurry," the Inspector said, leading her back through the maze of corridors. "He can't have got far, we've got to get help."

Harold emerged from the door opposite like a vision from hell. Mouth agape, blood spread darkly around his stomach and crutch, he was on them in a second, hurling Maggie to one side. Randall tried to strike out with the knife but Harold was too fast. The older man, wounded though he was, had the element of surprise in his favour. He swung a lump of wood which looked like a chair leg and the blow caught Randall in the side of the face, felling him like a tree-trunk.

Maggie screamed and ran, looking back in time to see Harold snatch up the knife and set off in pursuit of her.

She barged through a door and found herself in the old canteen. Maggie slammed the door behind her and ran for the window, reaching it just as Harold sent the door crashing inwards. He came after her, the bloodied knife raised above his head. Maggie turned to see him gaining and, gritting her teeth, she broke the window with her hand. Crystal shards sliced open her flesh and she screamed, but she managed to push the window open and scramble out, falling heavily onto the grass below. Harold clambered after her, seeing that she was running for the car parked nearby.

Maggie reached it and tore open the door, locking it quickly behind her as Harold advanced. He struck at the windscreen with the knife and, as Maggie recoiled from the expected explosion of glass she saw that the passenger side door was still unlocked. She flung herself across in an effort to reach the lock but Harold saw her and slid off the bonnet, grabbing for the door which he managed to pull open a fraction. Maggie screamed as she tugged with all her strength on the handle but he was slowly forcing it open an inch at a time.

He snaked one hand inside, the knife driving down, missing her by inches as it buried itself in the seat.

Maggie tugged hard on the handle and smashed his arm between door and frame, almost smiling when she heard his yelp of pain. Harold withdrew his hand and she was able to lock the door. He rushed round to the front of the car again and leapt up onto the bonnet, pounding on the glass with his hands.

Maggie snatched up the two-way radio and flicked it on, babbling into the set, not waiting for an answer.

The first hair-line splinters appeared in the windscreen as Harold continued his relentless pounding.

"Help me," Maggie screamed into the two-way. "The old asylum. Inspector Randall is here too. Help."

There was a garbled answer then the set went dead.

The cracks in the glass were spreading, spider-webbing until the driver's side resembled nothing more than crushed ice. Maggie turned the key in the ignition and the engine roared into life. She stuck it in gear but her foot slipped off the clutch and the vehicle stalled.

Almost in tears, she twisted the key again.

Glass sprayed inwards as Harold's fist crashed through the windscreen, groping around blindly as he searched for her, the jagged edges cutting his wrist, trapping him. Maggie stepped on the accelerator and the car shot forward. She heard Harold's shouts of alarm for he could see the wall which Maggie couldn't.

The Chevette hit it doing about twenty-five. The impact sent Harold hurtling into the brickwork with a sickening thud. He staggered, watching helplessly as Maggie reversed. As the car ploughed into Harold, Maggie threw herself clear.

There was a blood-chilling scream of pain followed a second later by a high pitched thump as the car exploded. Pinned between car and wall, Harold could only scream in anguish as the flames licked around him eagerly devouring his flesh. He clapped both hands to his face as he burned, his false eye falling from its socket to reveal the dark mess beneath. His hair went up in wisps of smoke and the flesh peeled from his body like a snake shedding its skin. He let out one final caterwaul of agony then the roaring flames drowned everything out. The heat rolled over Maggie, bringing with it the sickly sweet stench of charred flesh.

She dragged herself upright, the pain in her hand from the cuts keeping her conscious. Mesmerized, she gazed at the burning car and, before her eyes, Harold Pierce seemed to melt away beneath the roaring inferno.

Maggie sucked in huge lungfuls of air, suddenly remembering Randall.

It was as she was heading back towards the asylum that the first of the police cars arrived.

Forty-seven

Randall had regained consciousness by the time they lifted him into the ambulance. He even managed a smile before they closed the doors on him. Maggie had kissed him softly on the lips and then watched as the ambulance sped away.

The firemen, called to the scene by Sergeant Willis, put out the blazing Chevette and then cut the remains of Harold Pierce loose. What was left of him was put into another ambulance and taken away, then Maggie led the police up into the room where the dead foetuses were. PC Fowler threw up at the sight of so much carnage and even Willis found it difficult to retain his dinner. But, nevertheless, the room was eventually cleared, each mutilated body and severed head wrapped in a separate blanket and taken away. Maggie asked for the foetuses to be taken to Fairvale for examination.

All that had happened fifteen minutes ago; now she stood alone in the corridor looking into the room, the vile stench still strong in the air. The room, for what it was worth, was to be inspected by forensic men and then hosed down. Willis himself was coming back to take Maggie home as soon as he'd dropped the specimens off at Fairvale.

She had plenty of time.

She went to the door of another room across the corridor and pushed it open.

The surviving foetus lay in the centre of the room.

No one had thought to check any of the other rooms in the building – why should they? The power of the foetuses' thought projection had been stronger than even she had imagined. So powerful in fact that Randall could not have realized that the third foetus he had killed was merely a projection of his own subconscious.

She herself had hidden the creature in this other room before the Inspector had even reached the first floor. While he had been struggling with Harold Pierce she had lifted the foetus and carried it across the corridor to its new hiding place.

Maggie crossed to it and knelt beside the body.

It *was* rather beautiful she had decided. A perfectly formed child. *Her* child. She lifted it, surprised at its weight and it looked at her, those twin black eyes glinting malevolently.

She pulled it close to her, kissing its bulbous head, allowing it to nuzzle against her. Its lips moved slowly.

The words echoed loudly, not inside her head this time but booming off the walls, all the more incongruous because of the tiny body they came from. The words filled the small room. Deep bass, thick and full of power.

"Hold me."

Shadows

For Niki
with thanks
I'll slow down after the next one
maybe . . .

Acknowledgements

I would particularly like to thank Miss Eleanor O'Keefe of the Society for Psychical Research, whose help and kindness were invaluable during the research for this book. I am greatly indebted to her. Also, thanks, as ever, to everyone at W. H. Allen. Special thanks to Mike Bailey ('If there had been an Institute in Germany, the director's name would have been Beckenbauer'). To Bob Tanner ('Blood, guts and Rock and Roll, what a combination'). To Ray, Peter and Tony ('Enjoy your breakfast'). Indirect thanks to Iron Maiden, Liverpool F.C., John Carpenter, Tobe Hooper and Sam Peckinpah. And, finally, thankyou to my Mum and Dad, for everything. And to Belinda who really saw this one through from beginning to end. For listening to me blow up buildings, murder babies and slaughter people, this one is for you, with love.

Shaun Hutson

'Hence, horrible shadow.
Unreal mockery, hence.'
— *Macbeth, Act III, Scene IV*

PART ONE

'Dreams are true while they last, and do
we not live in dreams?'
— *Alfred Lord Tennyson*

'We're running with the Shadows of
the night. . .'
— *Pat Benatar*

1

New York

She had never seen eyes like his before.

She shuddered slightly as the piercing orbs bore into her like lasers. As if they were staring at her soul, searching for something elusive.

His eyes sparkled like chips of sapphire, the whites surrounding them unblemished but for the tiniest red veins which dared to intrude from his eye corners.

His gaze was unbroken even by the movement of his eyelids and, as he extended a hand to guide her backwards, she felt as if she were drowning in those eyes. As she lay on the couch she finally closed her own eyes, aware now only of his presence beside her.

The room was dark.

There was little sound.

An occasional cough, muted and self-conscious. And there was his breathing. It became more laboured as he stood over her and he spoke something softly to her.

Without opening her eyes, she raised her hands and began unbuttoning her dress, exposing her stomach. As she touched the flesh of her abdomen she winced and sucked in a painful breath. She almost screamed aloud as she felt his hands touch her flesh. His fingers stroked and probed the area around her navel, pausing every so often over one particular place.

Lucy West lay perfectly still, aware only of the hands which roamed her lower body with swift urgent movements but conscious of the three large intestinal growths which nestled like bloated parasites within her.

The first doctor had suspected ulcers. Nothing more. Tests had shown them to be steadily growing abscesses but a second opinion had revealed what she herself had always suspected.

The growths were tumours. Malignant and deadly.

She had been told that they were too far advanced for surgery to make any difference. At the most she might gain a six month reprieve. But of that there was no guarantee.

She felt the hands on her stomach, moving gently.

This man was her last hope.

Jonathan Mathias looked down at the woman on the couch, his brow furrowed. She was, he guessed, forty-five — five years older than himself but the ravages of pain and her disease had carved lines into her face which had no right to be there. She looked twice her age.

Mathias wore a dark shirt, the sleeves of which were rolled up displaying thick, hairy forearms. As he continued to play his fingers over the woman's abdomen, the muscles of his arms began to bulge, as if he were holding some great weight. His eyes rolled upward slightly so that she was only in the periphery of his vision. He began to breathe more deeply, less regularly. A bead of perspiration popped onto his forehead and trickled slowly past his left eye.

He sucked in a long breath and held it, raising his hands over the woman.

For what seemed like an eternity, neither moved nor made a sound.

Mathias' eyes twisted in the sockets, then he suddenly plunged his hands down, as if to drive them through Lucy West's body.

He grunted loudly, his palms pressed flat to her stomach. His fingers were splayed, quivering wildly. Then, with infinite slowness, he raised his hands an inch or two.

Beneath his palms, the flesh of her abdomen began to undulate in small, almost imperceptible, movements at first but then stronger, more urgent motions.

A bulge appeared just below her navel, the skin stretching to accommodate the pressure from within.

Mathias was shaking now, his hands still positioned mere inches from the woman's stomach. Perspiration sheathed his forehead and face, glistening in clear droplets on the light hair of his arms.

There was another movement, another undulation, this time an inch or two above her pubic mound.

Lucy West made no sound. No movement.

9

Mathias grunted something unintelligible, his fingers curling inward slightly as the third bulge began to stretch the flesh until it was shiny. And finally, his eyes swivelled in the sockets until they were glaring down at his own hands.

At the movement beneath those hands.

His entire body jerked spasmodically, as if someone were pumping thousands of volts of electricity through him. His eyes narrowed to steely slits, his teeth clenched together until his jaw began to ache.

The skin just below Lucy West's navel began to split open.

Like tearing fabric, it began as a tiny hole then gradually lengthened into a rent about five inches long.

Mathias began to breathe rapidly, his cheeks puffing with each sharp exhalation. He noticed a pungent odour as a second tear began to form beneath the first.

There was no blood. Only the smell. A rancid stench of pus which rose like an invisible cloud to envelop him.

He watched as the third razor-thin cut began to open.

Still Lucy West did not move.

Mathias drew in a deep, almost agonised breath and held it, his face contorted unnaturally for interminable seconds. The sensation of heat which he felt in his fingertips began to spread until it seemed to fill his entire body. He felt as if he were on fire. More sweat dripped in salty beads from his face. He glared down at his hands.

At her stomach.

At the three long thin splits in her flesh.

'Yes,' he grunted, his fingers twisting inward like hooked claws.

Something began to move in the cut above her pelvis. Something thick and solid. It was ovoid in shape, a reeking egg-shaped lump which nudged through the cleft of flesh as if coaxed by Mathias. His eyes bulged madly in their sockets as he saw the growth and his body began to shake with increased intensity.

From the cut below her navel another bloodied clot of dark brown matter began to rise.

The three narrow tears drew back like obscene lips, expelling their foul contents, and Mathias reached feverishly for the three rotting growths, scooping them into his hands like so many putrescent eggs.

10

His fingers closed around the lumps and a single droplet of pus dribbled through and ran down his arm as he raised both hands into the air above the unmoving body of Lucy West.

Mathias kept his eyes fastened on the trio of wounds, now slightly reddened at the edges. He closed his eyes tightly, body still shaking, the growths held aloft like grisly trophies. A vile stench surrounded him, almost palpable in its intensity, yet he seemed not to notice it. As he snapped his eyes open once more he looked down to see that the three rents had closed. The skin looked as smooth and unblemished as before he had begun.

For a moment he stood sentinel over her motionless form.

Another man, younger than Mathias, came forward carrying a shallow stainless steel bowl. He held it before Mathias who slowly lowered his arms, opening his hands to allow the growths to tumble into the bowl with a liquid plop. The man handed Mathias a towel, then retreated back into the shadows.

'Sit up,' Mathias said to the woman, his voice a low whisper.

Lucy West struggled upright, aided by Mathias' outstretched hand, and once more she found herself gazing into those hypnotic twin orbs of blazing blue.

'It is done,' he told her.

Lucy coloured slightly, aware that her dress was still open. With shaking fingers she began to button it once more. Mathias noticed her slight hesitation as she reached her stomach, the flicker of anxiety behind her eyes as she reached her navel.

He beckoned to his assistant and the younger man returned, carrying the bowl. Mathias took it from him and held it before Lucy.

She looked in at the growths. They reminded her of rotten plums but for their pale colour. The dark tinge which they'd had earlier seemed to have drained from them, creating the small amount of blood which was puddled in the bottom of the bowl.

She touched her stomach tentatively, both relieved and surprised to find that there was no pain. She pressed harder.

No pain.

It was at that point she broke down.

11

Tears flooded down her cheeks and she gripped Mathias' hand, as if threatening to wrench it off. He smiled thinly at her, those brilliant blue eyes twinkling with an almost blinding iridescence.

Another man, also dressed in a dark suit, approached from the other side and placed his hands on Lucy's shoulders, guiding her away from Mathias who walked forward towards the swelling cacophony of shouts and applause which filled the hall. As the lights inside the building were flicked on once more he gazed out at the dozens of people who stood watching him. Dozens? Hundreds? He wasn't sure how many. Some could nôt stand because they were in wheel-chairs. Some could not clap because they had withered limbs. Some could not see him because they were blind.

He raised his arms once more, a gesture designed to encompass them all.

The applause and shouting did not diminish for some time, not in fact, until Mathias turned and walked off the stage, the cries still ringing in his ears.

And some of them were cries of pain.

2

Mathias entered his dressing room and slammed the door behind him, as if eager to be away from any more prying eyes. He leant against the door, wiping the sweat from his face with one blood-smeared hand.

He crossed to the washbasin on the far side of the small room and turned the cold tap, splashing his face with water. As he straightened up he gazed at his own reflection in the mirror above.

Jonathan Mathias was a powerfully built man, his jaw square and heavy. Clean shaven and carefully groomed, he looked younger than his forty years, particularly when his eyes sparkled as they did now. Nevertheless, his forehead was heavily lined and his thick eyebrows, which strained to

12

meet above the bridge of his nose, gave him a perpetual frown. He dried his face and sat down at his dressing table. Even now he could hear the persistent applause generated by those who had yet to leave the hall.

It was like this every time. At every meeting.

He held three a week. The one today had been conducted in a large red-brick building on New York's West Side. Next time it might be in Manhattan, Queens or the Bronx. Or maybe somewhere in one of the city's more affluent areas. Over the years he had found that the rich needed his attentions as badly as anyone else.

Those he didn't reach in person could see him twice a week on CBS, his hour-long television show attracting an audience in excess of 58,000,000. He was known throughout the country and most of Europe for his abilities as a psychic but, of the man himself, little had ever been revealed. He spoke with a New York accent but the harder edges had been smoothed off and he came across as a cultured man, though he was respected and ridiculed in roughly equal proportions. There were those who still branded him a fraud and a charlatan. With an annual income of 20,000,000 dollars, the barbs seemed to cut less deeply than they might otherwise have done.

He smiled at his own reflection and began wiping his face with a paper cloth.

There was a light rap on the door and Mathias turned in his seat as if he were expecting to see through the partition.

'Who is it?' he asked.

'Blake,' a distinctively English voice told him.

'Come in,' he called, his smile broadening.

As David Blake entered the room, Mathias studied the newcomer warmly.

He was twenty-eight, about five-ten, dressed in a pair of faded jeans and a sweatshirt which, despite the folds of material, could not disguise the powerful frame beneath it. A packet of cigarettes bulged from one of his pockets and, as the young man sat down, he took one out and lit it up.

'Very impressive,' he said, re-adjusting the tinted glasses on his nose.

'It isn't intended to create an impression, David,' said the psychic. 'You know that.'

13

'Well,' Blake told him, smiling, 'That's exactly what it does. Like it or not. I should know, I was in that audience tonight. It's remarkable.' He drew hard on his cigarette. 'I've seen scores of faith-healers, most are just elaborate con men. But not you. There's something more.'

'Thanks for the compliment.'

'I saw you cure a terminally ill woman tonight, without even touching her, without using any tools or implements.'

'Is it really that important to you, David?' the psychic asked. 'Must you discover how I perform my ...'

'Miracles?' Blake interrupted.

Mathias smiled.

'I was going to say "work".'

'Yes, it is important. I don't like mysteries.' the Englishman admitted. 'Besides, if I do find out, there's a lot of potential there.'

'For a new book you mean?'

Blake was almost reluctant to admit it.

'Yes,' he said, shrugging his shoulders. He took a last puff on his cigarette and ground out the butt in an empty matchbox.

'Have you ever heard of a man called José Arrigo?' the psychic asked.

Blake nodded.

'He was killed in a car crash in Brazil in 1971. He was a psychic too. They called him the Phantom Surgeon. He performed nearly half a million operations between 1950 and 1960, all done with scissors and penknives and without anaesthetic. He removed a vaginal tumour the size of a grapefruit from a woman using only a kitchen knife. He was locked up a couple of times for practising medicine unlawfully.

'But people always went back to him. They went to him for the same reasons they come to me. Desperation and fear. When conventional methods won't work, people seek help elsewhere.'

'Arrigo claimed his powers came from Christ,' Blake protested. 'I've never heard you mention religion. You're a faith healer without any faith.'

'Power,' said Mathias, flatly. 'A strange choice of word, David.'

14

'Why? The abilities which you possess are a power of some description,' Blake said. 'I'd like to know where that power comes from.'

'It comes from here,' said Mathias, jabbing his own chest. 'From inside *me*.'

The two men regarded one another in silence for a while. Blake rubbed his chin thoughtfully. In the past five years he had written five world-wide best-sellers, all concerned with different aspects of the paranormal (supernatural was a word he disliked for it implied something which defied logical or reasoned explanation and Blake was concerned only with facts). But, in that time, he had never encountered anyone like Mathias. The man was an enigma, exuding a mixture of menace and benevolence.

Then there was his power.

Blake had seen it at close quarters during the five days he had been with the psychic and so far had collected reams and reams of questions but no answers — a wealth of research material with no discernible potential. He felt frustrated, almost angry with himself and he harboured the nagging conviction that the key to Mathias' power was something simple, so simple it could be easily overlooked. Mass hypnosis? Thought projection? He wondered if such tricks of the mind could work on the massive scale required for Mathias to retain credibility. Was it possible for someone to hypnotise an audience of 58,000,000 viewers so that they believed everything they saw? Blake doubted it.

He took a paper tissue from his pocket and began cleaning his glasses.

'Inside all of us there is another person,' Mathias continued, quietly. 'An inner being. Some psychics and probably you yourself know it as the Astral body. Jung called it "the other within". In ancient times it was thought to be the soul.'

Blake listened intently as the other man continued.

'To someone with the knowledge, the power, the Astral body can be projected and manipulated.'

'But lots of people are able to project themselves astrally,' Blake insisted. 'The sensation of leaving your own body is a skill which can be learned.'

'I agree.'

'Then I don't see what this has to do with your *powers*.'

'I can control other people's Astral bodies.'

Blake frowned, taken aback by the psychic's words.

Mathias returned his gaze, unblinking. There was a twinkle in his blue eyes which Blake mistrusted. He studied the American as if he were an exhibit in a museum, trying to muster his own thoughts.

'It's impossible,' he said, softly.

'Nothing is impossible, David,' the psychic told him.

Blake shook his head.

'Look, I know plenty about Out of the Body experiences,' he countered. 'I've met dozens of people who've had them but the idea of being able to manipulate someone else's Astral body ...' The sentence trailed off as he felt his body stiffen. It was as if every muscle in his body had suddenly contracted and the sensation forced a gasp from him.

Overwhelming, numbing cold enveloped him until he felt as if his blood were freezing in his veins. He shuddered, the flesh on his forearms rising into goose-pimples. He caught sight of his own reflection in Mathias' dressing room mirror and his skin was white. As if the colour had been sucked from him.

Mathias sat unmoved, his eyes never leaving the writer who was quivering violently.

He felt light-headed, a curiously unpleasant sensation of vagueness which made him grip the chair as if anxious to assure himself he were not going to faint.

Mathias lowered his gaze and Blake felt the feeling subside as quickly as it had come. He sucked in a deep breath, the warmth returning to his body. He shook his head and blinked hard.

'Are you OK?' Mathias asked.

The writer nodded.

'Very clever, Jonathan,' he said, rubbing his arms briskly.

'*Now* do you believe me?' the psychic wanted to know. 'Can you deny what you felt?'

'If you have this ability, how does it tie-in with the faith-

16

healing?'

'I can reach inside people. Inside their minds. Their bodies.'

'Then it would have to be a form of hypnosis, to make the subject believe you could cure them.'

'I can't give you all the answers, David,' Mathias answered. 'It doesn't matter. You can't alter the facts, you can't deny what you saw on that stage tonight or what you yourself felt here in this room.'

Blake chewed his bottom lip contemplatively.

'Think about what I've said,' the psychic added.

Blake got to his feet and announced that he had to get back to his hotel. The two men shook hands and the writer left the building via a side entrance. The sun outside was hot and the pavement felt warm beneath his shoes in a marked contrast to the coolness of Mathias' dressing room.

He spotted a cab and sprinted across the street, clambering into the vehicle. As the cab pulled away, Blake glanced over his shoulder at the red brick building, watching as it gradually disappeared from view.

Jonathan Mathias sat before the mirror in his dressing room contemplating his own features. He rubbed his cheeks and blinked hard. His eyes felt as if they had grit in them but, as he sat there, he allowed his hands to drop to his thighs, one hand curling into a loose fist. He inhaled and looked down, his fist opening as he did so.

Cradled there, now shrunken and withered like rotten, foul smelling prunes, were the three growths he'd taken from the body of Lucy West.

3

As the yellow cab threaded its way through the tapestry of traffic which clogged the streets Blake looked abstractedly out of the side window. On all sides of him buildings poked upward at the sky like accusatory fingers, probing towards the occasional banks of white cloud which passed overhead. Apart from the odd smattering of cloud and the vapour trails of aircraft, the sky was a deep blue and the sun continued to bathe the city in its warm rays. But, for David Blake, there was nothing pleasant about the warmth because with it came humidity. He could feel the perspiration on his back and face despite the fact that the air conditioning was on. The driver was a fat negro who looked as if he'd been wedged behind the steering column. As he drove his chubby fingers tapped out an accompaniment on the wheel to the music which screamed from the radio. It partially covered the insistent roar of engines, the blare of hooters and the shouts and curses of other motorists.

Blake allowed his head to loll back onto the seat. He could feel the beginnings of a headache gnawing at the base of his skull. A condition which wasn't helped when the driver slammed on his brakes to avoid colliding with a bus which had stopped abruptly in front of him.

'Motherfucker,' growled the driver and swung the cab out and around the bus, giving the other driver the finger as he drove by.

Up ahead, Blake saw his hotel and he fumbled in his pocket for his wallet, pulling out a ten dollar bill. The taxi came to a halt and Blake got out.

'How much?' he asked.

'Call it an even five,' said the driver, pushing down the arm on the meter.

'I haven't got anything smaller,' Blake said, offering the ten. 'Keep it.'

The hotel doorman nodded politely as he passed but Blake didn't return the gesture. He walked across to the reception desk and got his key.

He rode the lift to the thirty-second floor, casting a cursory glance at his fellow passenger — a porter who was cleaning his ears out with the corner of a tissue.

On reaching his room he closed the door and locked it, glad to be away from things for a few hours. The room was large, comfortable without being extravagant. The writer crossed to the window and stood gazing out for a moment or two, looking over the vast expanse of greenery which was Central Park. It looked particularly inviting amidst the grey concrete and glass of the city.

He turned and walked into the bathroom where he turned both taps. As the water splattered noisily against the enamel he undressed and lay on the bed, eyes closed. He lay there for a moment or two, massaging the back of his neck in an effort to dispel some of the tightness there, then he got to his feet and wandered back into the bathroom where he switched off the taps. Steam swirled around the room like hot fog and Blake retreated, deciding to allow the water to cool off slowly. He remembered that he hadn't eaten since breakfast so he called room service.

As he sat waiting for the snack to arrive he thought back to the incident with Mathias earlier on. Had the psychic actually managed to summon Blake's own Astral body? Was it some form of mind control? He pulled a pad towards him and scribbled:

1. Hypnosis
2. Mind control
3. Astral Body

Beside the last of the three he drew a large question mark and underlined it. Mathias obviously had more weapons in his psychological arsenal than Blake had first thought. But, manipulation of someone else's Astral body? He shook his head, his thoughts interrupted by a rap on the door. Blake got to his feet and was about to open it when he realized he was still naked. He grabbed a towel and hurriedly wrapped it around his lower body. The maid swept in, deposited the order on the table near the window then swept out again.

Blake devoured two of the sandwiches then headed

19

towards the bathroom once more.

The steam still swirled around and Blake almost slipped over on the tiles. He lifted the toilet seat and urinated noisily; then, discarding the towel, he turned towards the bath.

There was a body floating in the water.

Blake took a step back, nearly overbalancing, his eyes glued to the naked body before him. The entire corpse was bloated, the skin tinged a vivid blue, mottled from what appeared to be a long time in the water. The mouth was open, lips wrinkled and cracked. A swollen tongue protruded from one corner.

Blake shook his head, studying the face more closely.

He may as well have been looking in a mirror.

The corpse in the bath was identical, in every detail, to himself. He felt as if he were staring at his own dead body.

The writer clamped his eyes shut, screwing up the lids until white stars danced in the blackness. He raised both hands to his head and sucked in a deep breath.

'No,' he rasped.

When he opened his eyes again the corpse was gone. Nothing remained in the bath but the water. No bloated body. No deceased look-alike. Just water.

Blake swallowed hard and reached out a hand tentatively towards the surface of the water, staring intently at it as if he expected the apparition to appear again.

He heard soft chuckling and snapped his head around.

It was coming from the bedroom.

The writer felt peculiarly vulnerable and he found his breath coming in low, irregular gasps. He edged towards the bathroom door gripped by a hand of fear which tightened its hold as he drew closer.

Again he heard chuckling.

By this time, his fear had gradually become anger and he stepped into the room without hesitation.

It was empty.

He walked across to the bed. Checked the wardrobes. Passed through into the other part of the room which served as a sitting room.

Empty.

Blake looked around him, wiping perspiration from his

face. He was alone in the apartment. He headed back towards the bathroom but, as he reached the door he slowed his pace, his eyes scanning the bath anxiously.

There was no corpse floating there.

The writer licked his lips, finding that his mouth was dry and chalky. He crossed to the sink and spun the tap swallowing large gulps of cold water, then he turned towards the steaming tub once more.

The water looked inviting enough but it was a long time before he would step into it.

4

Oxford

'There was so much blood. It was everywhere. All over the floor and the bed. There was even some on the wall. It wasn't at all like you see on films or the television. When I shot her in the face her head just seemed to cave in and then the blood started spurting everywhere. I suppose that's how it got on the wall over the bed, it was like a fountain, especially from her neck. I suppose that's where the pellets hit her jugular vein. That is the big vein isn't it? The jugular? You see when you fire a shotgun at someone from close range there isn't time for the shot to spread. A shotgun cartridge is full of thousands of little lead pellets but, when you fire from close range, well, it all comes out in one lump. And I was standing very close to her. I had the barrel about an inch from her face.

'There was some thick, sticky looking stuff on the pillow. It was sort of greyish pink. I think it must have been her brain. I'd seen sheeps' brains in butchers' shops and it looked a bit like that so I suppose it must have been her brain. Anyway, when I went to move the body this sticky stuff got on my hands. It felt like … like porridge. I left her on the bed in the end.

'The baby had woken up, I suppose it was the noise of the

gun. It was crying, not loudly, just the way it does when it wants feeding. I went into the nursery and picked him up but he wouldn't stop crying. Perhaps he was frightened of the blood and the smell. That's another thing they never tell you on the TV. Blood smells. It smells like copper. When there's lots of it.

'Well, I just dropped the baby on its head. It didn't move after that so I thought it was dead. I picked it up again and took it back to the bedroom and put it on the bed beside my wife.

'I'd left the hacksaw under the bed earlier so I ... I only had to decide which one to start with. I cut up the baby first. The left arm to start with. I cut it off just below the shoulder but as I started cutting it screamed. I think the bang on the head only stunned it. The arm was almost off when it started to scream but it didn't move again after that. I cut off its right leg at the hip. It was easy, I suppose it's because the bones are still soft with babies. It wasn't even a year old you see. There was more blood, more than I'd expected. Especially when I cut the head off. It's funny isn't it? You wouldn't think a body that small could hold that much blood.

'I left the pieces on the bed then I started on my wife. It was harder cutting her leg off, sawing through the bone was like cutting wood but the noise was different, a kind of squeaking and all this brown stuff dribbled out of the bone. Was that the marrow? I suppose it was. Well, it took me nearly an hour to cut them both up and I was sweating when I'd finished. Butchers must be really fit, I mean, they cut up meat every day don't they? I was tired when I'd finished and I noticed that there was some ... mess ... well excrement. You know ... faeces on the bed. I didn't know that happened when someone died. That they sh— that they messed themselves.

'I cut one of my wife's breasts off. I don't know why. Just to see what it was like I suppose. I expected it to puncture like a balloon, you would wouldn't you? But it didn't. I just cut most of it away and left it with the other pieces. So much blood though. So much blood. Funny really.'

Kelly Hunt reached forward and switched off the tape recorder.

She had heard that particular tape half a dozen times in the last week. This had been the first time she'd managed to sit through it without feeling sick. She pressed the 'rewind' button and the recorder squealed as the spools spun in reverse. She stopped it, pressed 'play'.

'... So much blood. Funny really.'

She heard her own voice.

'And the dream is always the same?'

'Always. It never varies. Every detail's the same.'

She switched it off again and ran a hand through her shoulder length brown hair.

Beside the tape recorder on the desk in front of her there was a manilla file and Kelly flicked it open. It contained details of the voice which she'd been hearing on the recording, facts and figures which made that voice a human being. To be precise, Maurice Grant, aged thirty-two. An unemployed lathe operator by trade. Married for ten years to a woman four years younger than himself named Julie. They had a ten-month-old baby, Mark.

Kelly had been working with Grant, or rather studying him, for the last seven days. The recording was one of many which she and her colleagues had made.

She scanned the rest of the file which contained further personal details about Grant.

He'd been unemployed for the last six months and, during that time, relations both with Julie and their baby had become somewhat strained. Kelly tapped the file with the end of her pencil. And now the dreams. Grant always described them as dreams — never nightmares — though God alone knew that what he experienced during sleep was the stuff of nightmares. His detached attitude was unnerving. The tape recordings were made while Grant slept. By a combination of drugs, he could be unconscious and yet able to speak and to relay what he saw in his dreams. Dreams had been studied and monitored in the past, Kelly was well aware of that, but never before had the subject actually been able to speak whilst in that dream state, to describe the events as dispassionately as if he had been a mere observer.

In order to achieve this state, Grant was given a shot of Tubarine, a muscle relaxant usually used in medicine with a general anaesthetic, which would induce sleep. Prior to that, he would receive 45mg of methylphenidate orally. The drug

23

was a derivative of amphetamine, designed to stimulate the brain. By this combination, Grant could be *forced* to dream. His observations would then be recorded as *he* saw them in his mind's eye.

Kelly knew, from what she had read in the file, that Grant and his wife had rowed constantly during the months leading up to his arrival at the Institute. Their marriage was virtually in ruins and Grant sometimes spoke of her with ill-disguised anger. An attitude mirrored, subconsciously, in his dreams.

Kelly looked at the tape recorder once more, wondering whether to run the tape again. Instead she got to her feet and crossed to one of the filing cabinets propped against the far wall. Above it was a photograph of her and several of her colleagues. It had been taken just after she joined the Institute fifteen months ago, two weeks after her twenty-fourth birthday.

The Institute of Psychical Study was a Victorian building set in six acres of its own grounds. The weather-beaten walls were the colour of dried blood, crumbling in places. The entire structure, covered by a clinging network of ivy, looked as though it would collapse but for the tangled tendrils which snaked over it like so much flexible scaffolding. Repair work had been done to the west wing of the building, the renovated brickwork and the large plate glass windows looking strangely innocuous set against the latticed panes which dotted the remainder of the structure. The building was being dragged, albeit reluctantly, into the twentieth century. Telephone wires ran from the pole on the roof, suspended above what had once been belching chimney stacks but were now sealed holes. The gravel driveway snaked away through the grounds until it joined the main road which led into Oxford itself. Cedars and poplars lined the drive like sentinels.

However, if the outside of the building belonged to a more sedate age then the interior was modern, almost futuristic.

The old rooms had, over the years, been converted into fully equipped offices and laboratories, the latter providing every means possible for Kelly and her companions to pursue their very specialized work.

Since its inception in 1861, the Institute had devoted itself to the investigation and recording of all manner of psychic phenomena ranging from hauntings to telekinesis. Within the vast library beneath the building was housed the accumulated knowledge of over a century. But, during that time, progress had intervened and investigators now used word processors in place of quill pens and electronic surveillance equipment instead of eye-witness accounts and hear-say.

Kelly had plenty of eye-witness information about Maurice Grant including the file which she now slid from the drawer and glanced at.

It held an EEG read-out, one of the many taken from Grant while he slept. She studied it and shook her head. The puzzle was there before her.

The reading comprised five lines, four of which were flat, each representing an area of the brain.

It was the fifth line which interested her.

The tracer had drawn huge, irregular strokes across the read-out, indicating an incredible amount of activity in one particular part of the brain.

Kelly was convinced that it was the portion which controlled the dream response.

And yet she knew that there should have been movement shown on *all* the lines.

But for that one area of activity, the reading may as well have been taken from a corpse.

The office door opened.

'Excuse me barging in, Kelly,' the familiar voice apologised. The man smiled curtly, almost as an afterthought. 'I wanted to speak to you.'

Dr Stephen Vernon smiled again; a twitchy, perfunctory smile which never touched his eyes. He was what people euphemistically call portly. In other words he was fat. The buttons of his grey suit strained against his belly as if threatening to fly off at any moment. He kept his jacket fastened but, like his trousers, it was immaculately pressed. His trousers bore creases sharp enough to cut your hand on, even if the legs of the garment were two inches too short. For a man of fifty-five, Vernon had thick, almost lustrous hair which glistened beneath the fluorescent lights. His moustache, by comparison, resembled the type sprayed on advertising posters by paint-happy kids. He had narrow, hawkish features and eyes the colour of slate nestled between his puffy eyelids. Grey suit. Grey hair. Grey eyes. Vernon resembled an overcast day. But, there was a darting energy in those eyes and in that overweight frame. Vernon was as thirsty for knowledge now as he had been when he'd first joined the Institute nearly twenty-five years ago. He'd spent the last twelve years as its President. He was respected by all his investigators, both for his knowledge and also for his dedication. He would sit, most nights, in his office on the second floor, reading reports. Staying there until the small hours sometimes, when he would wander the empty corridors and deserted labs, enjoying the silence. He felt secure within the confines of the Institute walls.

He lived eight or nine miles away but it was almost with reluctance that he returned home at the end of the day.

Home.

Could he still call it a home when he was afraid to return there?

As Kelly passed him she caught the familiar smell which seemed to follow Vernon everywhere. It surrounded him like an invisible cloud. The scent of menthol. He was forever sucking cough sweets although Kelly had never known him to have so much as a cold. He carried a packet in his breast pocket as if it were a pen. As she sat down he popped another one into his mouth.

'Have you made any progress with this fellow Grant?' Vernon asked her.

Kelly told him about the tape recordings, the recurring nightmares.

'Yes, yes, I know about those,' he said, tersely. 'I heard something about an EEG.'

Kelly's green eyes met his slate grey ones and they held each other's stare for a moment.

'May I see it?' he asked.

Kelly handed the read-out to Vernon who shifted the menthol sweet to the other side of his mouth and ran an expert eye over the series of lines.

'His brain was stimulated?' Vernon asked.

'Yes,' Kelly told him. 'We're still using amphetamines.'

Vernon nodded slowly. As a qualified doctor he realized that the read-out should show much more activity. He was

26

one of four physicians at the Institute. At least one had to be present to administer the drugs to subjects and to check that there were no adverse effects on them.

'Then why is only one area of the brain affected?' he mused aloud.

'It certainly looks as if it's the area which controls unconscious thought,' said Kelly. 'The reading taken when Grant was awake showed only minimal movement in that region.' She pointed to the jagged line.

The older man sucked hard on his sweet then folded the read-out and laid it on her desk.

'Run another EEG while he's awake,' Vernon instructed. 'Then another while he's asleep — but not a drug induced sleep. I want to see the normal readings.'

Kelly nodded.

Vernon crossed to the window and peered out at the rapidly falling rain.

'This is very important to me, Kelly,' he said, clasping his hands behind his back. He reminded her of a headmaster about to admonish an unruly pupil.

'The reading from the EEG would certainly seem to indicate that the subconscious mind is capable of functioning independently,' he said. 'We have to find a way to unlock that hidden area.'

She detected a note of something akin to desperation in his voice. It seemed only a matter of time before they discovered what they sought but time was one thing Vernon didn't seem to have. Not a day passed without him visiting Kelly in the lab or her office, and it had been that way ever since the research began. There was an urgency about his interest which eclipsed his usual involvement. He was becoming obsessive. And Kelly couldn't help but wonder why.

She studied his broad back as he stood by the window, his fingers knotted together like fleshy hemp.

'I'll see about running the EEG now,' she said.

Vernon turned, nodded and swept towards the door.

'I'll be in my office,' he told her. 'Let me know as soon as you have the results.'

She smelt the menthol as he passed her, closing the door behind him. Kelly heard his footsteps echo away down the corridor.

She slipped the file back into its drawer, then she herself left the room, walking briskly towards the stairs which would take her down to the laboratories.

Stephen Vernon slumped into the leather chair behind his oak desk and closed his eyes, massaging the bridge of his nose between thumb and forefinger. In the outer office he could hear the clacking of his secretary's typewriter. An accompaniment to the tattoo which the rain was beating on his window.

His office was large, as befitted a man of his seniority. It was one of the few rooms in the building which acknowledged a debt to the past. The wood panelling of the wall smelt as if it had been newly waxed, as did his desk. Opposite him, above the empty fireplace, was a very passable copy of Gericault's *'Brigadier Gerard'*. Vernon regarded the painting blankly, his mind occupied with other thoughts.

Could the EEG of Grant's brain truly have exposed an area of the mind previously hidden? The key to the subconscious. After all these years, could he dare to hope for a breakthrough?

He sat forward in his chair and glanced at the phone.

The call might come in five minutes. Five hours. Five weeks.

But he knew it would come and he had been waiting a long time for it.

5

Paris

'Keep your eye on the watch.'

Jean Décard focused on the gently twisting gold object, watching as it spun gently around. His breathing had slowed to low rasping inhalations punctuated by small gasps as the air escaped his lungs once more. His right arm was propped up on the arm of the chair, his left lay across his lap.

'Clear your mind of all other thoughts,' the voice told him. 'See nothing but the watch. Think about nothing other than what I tell you.'

The voice seemed to be coming from a hundred miles away.

It was, in fact, coming from Alain Joubert who was kneeling less than a foot or two from him. It was he who was holding the watch, allowing it to turn gently back and forth at the end of its chain.

Beside him, Michel Lasalle watched the proceedings with a pen gripped firmly in his hand, prepared to write down whatever might happen. At thirty-eight, Lasalle was two years older than Joubert but his full features and ruddied complex-ion did not testify to that fact. They had worked together for the past two years and, during that time, had become close friends. Now Lasalle watched intently as Joubert leaned closer to Décard whose eyelids were beginning to sag.

'You are asleep but you will still hear my voice, you will still answer my questions,' said Joubert. 'Do you understand?'

Décard nodded slowly.

'Do you understand? Say so.'

'Yes.'

'What is your name?'

'Jean Décard.'

'Where do you live?'

'Sixteen Rue St Germain.'

'How old are you?'

'Forty-one.'

Lasalle scribbled something on his pad then watched as Joubert pulled a pen light from his breast pocket and shone it into Décard's eyes.

'He's well under,' Joubert said, noting the vastly dilated pupils of his subject. 'But, let's just make sure.' He reached back to the table nearby and retrieved two long, thick needles each one about six inches in length. Then, he pinched the skin together on the back of Décard's right hand and, slowly, pushed the first needle through.

There was no reaction from the subject.

'Can you feel any pain, Jean?' asked Joubert.

'No.'

He took the second needle and, opening the loose fist which Décard had made, Joubert pushed the second needle under the nail of the man's index finger until only the eye showed. There was no blood.

'Do you feel anything?'

'No.'

Joubert nodded to his companion then hastily tugged the wicked points free.

Lasalle pulled a pack of playing cards from his pocket and handed them to Joubert, standing behind his friend so that he himself could see the slim plastic sheets. The first one was the seven of spades.

'Which card am I holding, Jean?' Joubert wanted to know.

Décard told him.

'And this one?'

'Queen of Diamonds.'

Correct.

'Next?'

'Ten of Clubs.'

Correct.

They went through thirty cards and Décard was accurate every time.

'Amazing,' said Lasalle. 'Are you going to bring him out of it now?'

'In a moment,' Joubert assured him. Then to Décard;

'Jean, I am going to think of some words, I want you to tell me what they are. Do you understand?'

'Yes.'

Joubert scribbled them down on a piece of paper and showed it to his companion. Décard recited the words almost rhythmically.

Joubert smiled. Lasalle could only shake his head in amazement.

'There will be a bus crash in the Rue De Bologne.'

The words came from Décard with the same monosyllabic drone as before. Both Joubert and Lasalle looked at him aghast.

'Repeat what you said,' Joubert urged.

Décard obliged.

'When? How do you know?'

'I can see the ... the dead.' He was staring blankly ahead as if looking beyond the walls to something which neither of the other men could see.

'When is this crash going to happen?' Joubert asked.

'At 3.49 today.'

Lasalle shot an anxious glance at his watch.

'It's 3.46,' he told Joubert.

'How do you know this is going to happen?' demanded Joubert.

'I can see it now.'

'How many will die?'

'Four.'

'Is it possible?' Lasalle said, his brow furrowed. 'Can he really be seeing it?'

Joubert didn't answer, he merely looked at his own watch and saw that it was 3.48.

Jean Décard was silent for a moment then his mouth opened wide in a soundless scream, his face contorted into an attitude of fear and pain so profound that Lasalle took a step back. Then, with a low grunt, Décard blacked out.

It took the two men ten minutes to revive him and, when he finally regained consciousness, he still seemed to be in a trance. He tried to rise but fell, knocking a table over in his wake. After another thirty minutes he was coherent. His face was ashen with dark smudges beneath his eyes.

Joubert gripped his arm.

'Jean, can you remember anything of what you said earlier?'

Décard shook his head.

'I feel sick,' was all he could say.

Lasalle fetched him a glass of water.

As the three men sat in the room there was a loud knock on the door and, a moment later, a thick-set man in the uniform of a gendarme entered.

'Which one of you is Jean Décard?' the uniformed man asked.

'I am,' Décard told him.

'And you two?' the gendarme wanted to know.

'We both work here at the Metapsychic Centre,' said Lasalle.

'Step outside, please,' the gendarme said.

31

'No,' said Décard. 'It's all right, what have I done wrong?'

'Nothing, Monsieur,' said the gendarme almost apologetically. 'I must tell you that I have some bad news.'

Lasalle and Joubert exchanged glances then directed their gaze back at the uniformed man. He had lowered his voice slightly, an air of expectant solemnity having fallen over the room.

At approximately 3.49 that afternoon, Jean Décard's twelve-year-old daughter had been killed when a lorry smashed into the bus which was carrying her and her schoolfriends home. There had been three other deaths besides hers.

'Where did it happen?' Décard wanted to know, tears filling his eyes.

The gendarme cleared his throat.

'The Rue De Bologne.'

6

Michel Lasalle scooped some cool water into his hand and then swallowed it. He felt the tranquilizer stick in his throat for a moment so he swallowed more water, finally wiping his hands on the towel beneath the sink. He exhaled deeply and replaced the bottle of pills in his trouser pocket. He probably didn't need them any longer but, over the past eighteen months since the death of his wife, the pills had become more than a mere psychological crutch for him. Lasalle was dependent on them, not daring to see what life was like without the temporary relief which they brought him. He did not look like a man who had suffered a nervous breakdown, but then again his wife had not looked like the kind of woman who would die suddenly of heart failure aged thirty-five. Lasalle had retreated within himself after her death. Like a snail inside its shell he refused to be coaxed out again by work or friends. He became hermit-like in his existence.

He and his wife had been childless. She had been infertile

— her Fallopian tubes blocked. Lasalle's parents had been dead for five years so he had no one to turn to for help. His breakdown had begun slowly, gradually building up like some festering growth within his mind until, finally, his sense of reason seemed to collapse in on itself like a crumbling house.

He turned away from the sink and looked across the room at Joubert who was sitting with his eyes closed, a cigarette held delicately between his fingers. The ash looked as if it were about to drop off and Lasalle watched as smoke rose lazily from the butt. When Joubert finally moved his hand, the ash dropped on to the carpet. Lasalle quickly trod it in.

Lasalle had worked at the Metapsychic Centre for the past twelve years. The building itself stood on the outskirts of Paris, a large modern looking edifice constructed in the shape of a gigantic 'E'. Its smooth unbroken lines gave it the appearance of having been hewn from one single lump of rock instead of constructed piece by piece. Lasalle lived less than a mile from the building, near the church yard where his wife was buried.

As he stood looking absently around the room he tried to drive thoughts of her from his mind but every time he heard of more death, as he had with Jean Décard's daughter, the memories came flooding back.

His companion, Joubert, had no such ties. He was single once more after the break-up of his marriage but then again he had always found the attractions of work infinitely more exciting than those of domesticity. Despite being two years younger than Lasalle, he was possibly better informed on the subject of the paranormal, having worked at the Laboratory of Parapsychology in Utrecht for six years where he completed his Ph.D in Human Science. He had then moved on to the University of Frieburg in West Germany prior to joining the Centre in Paris.

Joubert was every bit as different psychologically from his colleague as he was physically. There was a certain detached coldness about Joubert. He saw everyone and everything as potential sources of information and study. The human volunteers with whom he worked might as well have been laboratory rats. He showed as much feeling towards them. To Joubert, work was everything and knowledge was the pinnacle. He would never rest until he had solved a problem. And, at the moment, he and Lasalle had a problem.

'Precognition.'

Lasalle looked at his companion.

'The business with Décard,' he continued. 'The telepathy and then seeing the accident. It had to be precognition.'

'Do you think he was able to see the vision because it involved his own daughter?' Lasalle asked.

'Décard didn't know that his daughter was going to be one of the victoms, only that there was going to be a crash and that four people would die. The fact that he was close to one of the victims isn't necessarily relevant.'

'What are you getting at, Michel?'

'We've tested three people, the same way we tested Décard. The results were the same in each case. Each one showed varying forms of telepathy while hypnotised but, with the other subjects, we brought them out of their trances earlier, quicker. If they had been under longer then they too may have been able to predict future events.'

Joubert got to his feet, crossed to the pot of coffee on the table nearby and poured himself a cup. He took a sip, wincing slightly as it burned the end of his tongue.

'Depending upon the susceptibility of the subject,' he continued, 'there's no limit to what future events we can learn of.' A brief smile flickered across his face. Not only could disasters be averted but foreknowledge of events could have its more lucrative side as well. Could a subject foresee the outcome when a roulette wheel was spun? Joubert took another sip of his coffee, this time ignoring the fact that it was so hot.

'But Décard was only able to foresee the future while in a hypnotic trance,' Lasalle interjected.

'Which points to the fact that there is an area of the mind which *only* responds when the subject is unconscious. An area previously unexplored, with the capacity for prophecy.'

There was a long silence finally broken by Lasalle.

'I'd better phone the Institute in England,' he said. 'They should know about this.'

'No,' said Joubert. 'I'll do it.'

He stepped in front of his colleague and closed the door behind him, leaving Lasalle somewhat bemused. Joubert

34

went to his office and sat down behind his desk, pulling the phone towards him. He lifted the receiver but hesitated before dialling.

'An area of the brain previously unexplored,' he thought. His features hardened slightly. The discovery, once announced, would undoubtedly bring fame to himself.

It was not a secret he wanted to share.

He tapped agitatedly on the desk top, cradling the receiver in his hand a moment longer before finally dialling.

Kelly picked up the phone and pressed it to her ear.

'Kelly Hunt speaking,' she said.

'Miss Hunt, this is the Metapsychic Centre.'

She did not recognise the voice.

'Lasalle?' she asked.

'No. My name is Joubert. Alain Joubert. We have not spoken before.'

Kelly disliked the coldness in his voice. She was, however, relieved that he spoke excellent English, just as Lasalle did. Her French was no more than passable.

'Did you receive the copy of the tape recording I sent?' Kelly asked.

'We did,' he told her.

'Have you made any progress with your subjects?'

There was a hiss of static. A moment's hesitation.

'None,' Joubert said, flatly. 'That is why I am phoning. I feel that it is unproductive for our two Institutes to continue exchanging information on this subject.'

Kelly frowned.

'But it was agreed from the beginning that the research would be undertaken jointly,' she protested. 'You would use hypnosis, we would use drugs.'

There was a long silence.

'The subject we tested today was unreceptive,' the Frenchman lied.

Kelly sensed the hostility in the man's voice and it puzzled her.

'Lasalle told me that your use of hypnosis seemed to be showing results,' she said, irritably. 'He was very happy with the way the research was going.'

'My colleague has a tendency to exaggerate,' Joubert said,

stiffly.

'Where is Lasalle? May I speak to him?'

'He is working. I don't want to interrupt him.'

'So you have nothing at all for me?'

'No.' The answer came back rapidly. A little too rapidly. Kelly moved the receiver an inch or two from her ear, looking at it as if she expected to see Joubert magically appear from the mouthpiece. His abrupt tone was a marked contrast to that of Lasalle who she was used to conversing with.

Kelly thought about mentioning the EEG on Maurice Grant but, before she could speak, Joubert continued.

'I have nothing to tell you, Miss Hunt,' he said, his tone unequivocal.

'I'll have to tell Dr Vernon ...'

Joubert cut her short.

'Do as you wish, Miss Hunt.'

He hung up.

Kelly found herself gazing once again at the receiver. She slowly replaced it, her initial bewilderment at the Frenchman's unco-operative attitude subsiding into anger. Joubert had come close to being downright rude. Why, she wondered?

Was he hiding something?

If so, what reasons would he have?

She shook her head, annoyed both with Joubert and also with her own over-active imagination. Nevertheless, he had no right to sever contacts between the two Institutes. Perhaps she should speak to Lasalle, she had his home phone number.

Maybe *he* would contact her tomorrow.

She sighed and sat back in her chair, listening to the rain beating against the window behind her. On the desk before her lay the newest EEG read-out taken only an hour earlier from Maurice Grant. It looked normal, in marked contrast to the one taken when he'd been in the drug-induced state. She ran an appraising eye over the lines but could see nothing out of the ordinary. There was another polygraph scheduled for later, while Grant was asleep. Perhaps there would be discrepancies on that one, some kind of clue to the tricks his mind was playing.

She thought about his description of the nightmare. The ritualistic slaughter of his wife and child.

She wondered what it all meant.

7

Oxford

It was well past midnight when the powerful lights of the Audi cut through the gloom of the driveway which led up to Stephen Vernon's house. The rain which had been falling all day had stopped, to be replaced by an icy wind which battered at the windows of the car as if trying to gain access. Vernon brought the vehicle to a halt and switched off the engine, sitting for a moment in the darkness.

The moon was fighting in vain to escape from behind a bank of thick cloud and what little light it gave turned Vernon's house into some kind of dark cameo, silhouetted against the mottled sky. He sat there for a few more seconds then pushed open his door and clambered out. The wind dug freezing points into him, nipping at his face and hands. He ran towards the front door and fumbled for his key, his breath clouding around him as he exhaled. He finally found the key and opened the door, snapping on a light as he did so. The hall and porch were suddenly illuminated, driving back the shadows from the front of the house.

The building was surrounded by a high wooden fence which creaked menacingly in the high wind, so Vernon was effectively shut off from his closest neighbours. The house was tastefully decorated throughout, walls and carpets in soft pastel colours combining to form a welcoming warmth as he stepped inside and shut the door behind him, forcing out the wind.

There was a large envelope on the doormat. Vernon saw the postmark and hesitated a second before stooping to retrieve it. He carried it into the sitting room and dropped it on the antique writing bureau which nestled in one corner of the spacious room. Then he crossed to the walnut drinks cabinet, took out a tumbler and a bottle of Haig and poured himself a generous measure. As he drank he looked across at the letter on the bureau. When he put his glass down he found that his hand was shaking.

He passed into the kitchen, the fluorescents buzzing into life as he touched the switch. He hunted through the freezer and found a frozen chicken casserole. It took fifteen minutes according to the packet. Vernon decided that that was all he wanted to eat. He hadn't much of an appetite. He left the polythene-wrapped casserole in a pan of water and wandered back into the living room, ignoring the letter on the bureau which he still had not opened.

The stairs creaked mournfully as he made his way to the first floor. From the window on the landing he could see the two houses on either side. Both were in darkness, the occupants obviously having retired to bed. Vernon resolved to do the same thing as soon as he'd eaten.

Five doors led off from the landing: the door to his own bedroom, that of the spare room, then the bathroom and another bedroom which had once belonged to his son who had long since departed.

The fifth door remained firmly locked.

Vernon paused before it for a moment, swallowing hard. He extended a hand towards the knob.

A window rattled loudly in its frame, startling him. He glanced at the door one last time then walked across the landing to his bedroom. Once inside he removed his suit, hung it up carefully and changed into a sweater and a pair of grey slacks. Without the restraint of a shirt, his stomach was even more prominent and it sagged sorrowfully over his waist-band. He tried to draw it in but lost the battle and allowed the fat to flow forward once more. Vernon glanced at the clock on the bedside table and decided that his supper would soon be ready so he flicked off the bedroom light and headed back across the landing once again.

As he approached the locked door he slowed his pace.

His breathing subsided into low, almost pained exhalations as he stood staring at the white partition. He felt his heart beating that little bit faster.

There was a loud crack and Vernon gasped aloud.

He spun round in the gloom, searching for the source of the noise.

The wind howled frenziedly for a second, its banshee wail drowning out his own laboured breathing.

The sound came again and he realized it came from inside the locked room. But it was muffled.

He took a step towards the door, freezing momentarily as he heard the sound once more — harsh scratching, like fingernails on glass.

On glass.

He realized that there was a tree directly beside the window of the locked room, it must be the wind blowing the branches against it. Nothing more.

Vernon felt angry with himself for having reacted the way he did. He glared at the door for a moment longer then turned and padded down the stairs. He walked through the sitting room, unable to avoid looking at the envelope which still lay on the bureau like an accusation. He would open it after supper he promised himself.

He sat in the kitchen and ate his supper, discovering that he wasn't as hungry as he thought. He prodded the food indifferently, left the plate on the table and went into the sitting room. There he poured himself another scotch and slumped in one of the high-backed armchairs near the fire. It was cold in the room and Vernon pulled his chair closer to the heat, watching as the mock flames danced before him. He downed most of the whisky, cradling the glass in his hand, gazing into its depths.

Above him, a floorboard creaked.

Merely the house settling down, he thought, smiling humourlessly.

He got to his feet and filled his glass once again, finally finding the courage to retrieve the letter. He slid his index finger beneath the flap of the envelope and started to open it.

The strident ringing of the phone pierced the silence and nearly caused him to drop the letter.

He picked up the receiver hurriedly.

'Stephen Vernon speaking,' he said.

'I tried to ring earlier but there was no answer.' The voice had a strong accent and Vernon recognized it immediately.

'What have you got for me, Joubert?' he said. The

Frenchman told him about Décard's prophecy.

'Does anyone else know?' Vernon asked.

'Only Lasalle,' the Frenchman told him.

'You haven't told Kelly?'

'No, you told me not to give her any information other than that which you authorised.'

'What about Lasalle?'

'He knows nothing of what is going on, he ...'

Vernon cut him short.

'I mean, what has he told Kelly?'

'She doesn't know anything about what happened today and from now on *I* will deal with her.'

Vernon nodded.

'Vernon? Vernon, are you there?'

He seemed to recover his senses.

'Yes, I'm sorry. Look, Joubert, when will you know for sure if the experiments have been successful?'

The Frenchman hesitated.

'That's difficult to say. I feel we *are* very close to a breakthrough though.'

'How long before you know?'

'You are asking for too much, Vernon. I cannot say for certain.'

'Then guess. I have waited too long for this.'

'You are not the only one.'

There was a long silence finally broken by Joubert.

'Two days, perhaps a little longer, but I can't promise.'

Vernon sighed.

'Remember, Kelly is to know nothing.'

'And if she becomes suspicious?'

'I'll take care of that.'

Joubert seemed satisfied by the answer. The two men exchanged cursory farewells then the Frenchman hung up. Vernon stood motionless for a moment then replaced the receiver, returning to his fireside chair. And his drink.

And the letter.

He opened it and pulled out the piece of paper inside. Vernon took another gulp from his glass before unfolding it.

Before he started reading he glanced, as he always did, at the heading on the paper:

FAIRHAM SANATORIUM

8

New York

Blake studied his reflection in the bathroom mirror. He shook his head. It was no use. The bloody bow-tie wasn't straight. As if he were grappling with some kind of angry moth, he pulled it from his throat and tried to fix it once again. He'd been trying for the best part of fifteen minutes but, so far, the bow-tie had resisted all attempts to remain in place and Blake was beginning to lose his temper. He looked at his watch and saw that it was 8.00 p.m., a fact confirmed by the announcer on the TV in his room who was in the process of introducing another re-run of *Magnum*.

Mathias had said he would pick the writer up at his hotel at 8.15. The drive to Toni Landers' house would take twenty or thirty minutes depending on New York's night time traffic.

Toni Landers was well known, by reputation anyway, to Blake. A stunningly beautiful woman who had, two nights ago, been presented with an Emmy for her performance in one of the year's biggest television spectaculars. At present, she was packing them in on Broadway in a production of Joe Orton's *Entertaining Mr Sloane*. Tonight she was giving a party to celebrate her triumph. Mathias had been invited and had cajoled Blake into joining him. The writer had been to showbusiness parties before and they usually bored him stiff, self-congratulatory affairs with clashes of ego which ranked alongside the collision of Mack trucks. In Los Angeles they were intolerable, the acting fraternity turning out in force to every one. Parties in L.A. were given for any reason, usually not good ones. Has-beens, no hopers, and would-be starlets thronged these almost masochistic gatherings where egos were flayed unmercifully. He had met writers who had yet to find a publisher but spoke as if they were the natural successor to Hemingway, encountered actors and actresses

41

who spoke of the promised part they had in some forthcoming epic but who would more than likely end their days doing what they did between bit parts — either waitressing or cleaning cars.

New York parties were a little different. They had their share of bores, as did any party, but Blake found he could tolerate them slightly more easily because there didn't seem to be quite such a wealth of pretension in New York as there was on the West Coast. Nevertheless, he still did not relish the prospect of the party but Mathias had asked him, so what the hell?

He was still struggling with his bow-tie when his phone rang. Blake left the recalcitrant thing in its slightly lop-sided position and picked up the receiver.

'Yes.'

'There's someone for you in reception, Mr Blake,' the voice told him.

He looked at his watch. It was 8.15, on the nose.

'I'll be straight down,' he said and, flicking off the lights in his room, he closed the door behind him and made for the elevator.

Blake recognised Mathias' chauffeur standing by the reception desk. He was taking a few hurried puffs on a cigarette which he reluctantly extinguished when he saw the Englishman step out of the lift. Blake approached him, by-passing a red faced man who was complaining about the soap in his room being dirty. The chauffeur smiled.

'Mr Blake,' he said, 'Mr Mathias is waiting for you in the car.'

The two of them headed out of the hotel lobby with its uncreasing drone of Muzak, into the symphony of car hooters, shouts and roaring engines which was 59th Street. A police car, its sirens blaring, swept past adding its own noise to the cacophony which already filled the air.

The chauffeur motioned Blake towards a waiting black cadillac and, as he drew close, the door was pushed open for him. The writer felt like some kind of cheap gangster about to be taken for a ride. The grinning face of the chauffeur behind him and the inscrutable look of Mathias, who was seated in the back, added to that feeling.

42

The psychic was dressed completely in white. White suit. White shoes. White shirt. The only thing which broke up the pure expanse was a red tie. It looked as though Mathias was bleeding.

'Good evening, David,' Mathias said.

Blake returned the greeting. He wondered whether he should mention what had happened the previous afternoon. The voice in his room. The body floating in his bath. He eventually decided against it. He glanced across at Mathias, affording himself a swift appraising glance. The white suit seemed to make the psychic's feature's even darker, the areas around his eyes and neck almost invisible. His hands were clasped gently on his lap and Blake saw that he wore two rings, each one gold set with a large pearl.

'What sort of day have you had?' Mathias asked him.

'Considering I spent most of it in a library, not very inspiring,' the writer told him.

'More research?'

Blake nodded.

'Still trying to unlock the secrets of the mind?' the psychic chuckled.

Blake ignored the remark.

'Why did you ask me to come to this party with you tonight?' he enquired.

Mathias shrugged.

'You and I have become friends over the past six days and I thought you might enjoy it.' He smiled. 'You might, you know.'

'Are any of the guests clients of yours?' Blake wanted to know.

'Some of them have, from time to time, sought my help if that's what you mean.'

'In what ways?'

'Is it important?'

'I'm just curious.'

'You're curious about a lot of things, David,' the psychic said and looked out of the side window. Blake studied his profile for a moment then he too turned his attention to the busy street. On either side of them skyscrapers rose like concrete geysers spewed forth from the ground, black shapes surrounded by the dark sky. Many were invisible but for the odd lights which shone in some of their windows. It looked as if someone had taken hundreds of stars and hurled them at the gloomy monoliths. Multi-coloured neon signs burned above shops and cinemas, theatres and clubs, as if millions of glow worms had been sealed inside the glass prison of a bulb. The city that never slept was preparing for another night of insomnia.

'I asked you before why it was so important to you to discover the extent of my powers,' Mathias said, interrupting the relative silence which had descended.

'And I told you it was because I don't like mysteries,' Blake told him. 'I've never yet run into anything that's beaten me.' There was a firm, almost harsh, resolution in the writer's voice.

Even in the gloom of the cadillac's interior the psychic's icy blue eyes sparkled challengingly.

'There are some things ...'

Blake cut him short.

'... which it's better *not* to know.'

Both men laughed.

'Well, reeling off the world's worst clichés isn't going to stop me either,' the Englishman chuckled. A minute or two passed, then, his tone more sombre, Blake continued:

'This power, this manipulation of another person's Astral personality, if you do possess such abilities would you ever consider using them as a weapon?'

Mathias looked genuinely puzzled.

'I don't follow,' he said.

'If you can control someone else's mind and actions then there's no limit to what you can do. To what *you* can make others do.'

The cadillac was beginning to slow up. Ahead Toni Landers' house was a blaze of light.

'Do you think I haven't thought of that?' said Mathias, smiling.

The chauffeur brought the cadillac to a halt behind a bright red Porsche then clambered out and held open the door for Mathias. Blake didn't wait for the same treatment, he stepped out of the other side, tugging once again at his bow-tie as he did so.

The tarmac driveway which swung in a crescent before

Toni Landers' house looked more like a car showroom. Blake counted five cadillacs, a couple of Transams, the Porsche and a silver Plymouth Fury as he and the psychic walked towards the porch.

The house itself was a three storey affair, flanked on two sides by trees, beneath which were carefully tended flower beds. Strings of light bulbs had been hung from the house to the tree branches and it seemed as if a light glowed in every single window of the building. The house looked like a beacon amidst the darkness. It was set slightly on a hill, the nearest neighbour being about five hundred yards away. Even from outside Blake could hear music and, as the door was opened, it seemed to sweep over him like a wave, mingling with the sea of conversation.

A maid took Mathias and Blake through into a spacious sitting room which looked slightly smaller than a ballroom. A staircase rose in a spiral from the centre of the room, leading up to the first floor landing where Blake could see people standing in groups or in couples chatting amiably. Two huge chandeliers hung from the ceiling like clusters of diamonds. But, for all the apparent pomp and grandeur, the house had a homely feel to it. There was a piano in one corner of the room and five or six people were gathered around it. Blake noticed that one of them, a man about his own age, was playing softly, quite oblivious to the sound coming from the Hi-Fi. The writer recognized him as the lead singer with the band currently topping the American charts. He spotted three or four well-known actors and actresses, and a film director he'd seen once or twice on TV.

Toni Landers was standing by the large open fireplace, a glass of champagne cradled in her hand. She was talking to a distinguished looking grey-haired man in his fifties who was perpetually pulling at the end of his nose, doubtless in an effort to disguise the fact he was trying to see even further down the front of her dress than the plunging neckline allowed.

Blake had seen her before but never this close and she was even more beautiful than he had first thought. She was not a tall woman, barely five-six with the benefit of long stiletto heels. She wore a black dress slashed to the thigh which, each time she moved, allowed him a glimpse of her smoothly

45

curved legs. A shock of red hair cascaded over her shoulders, catching the light every so often to glisten like rust-coloured silk. She wore a black choker around her throat, a single diamond set in its centre.

'Our hostess,' said Mathias, nodding in her direction. He took a glass of champagne from the tray offered to him by a tubby waitress and Blake did likewise.

It was as he sipped his drink that Blake noticed eyes were beginning to turn in the direction of Mathias. In his white suit, the psychic was even more prominent, but Blake had the feeling that if he'd turned up in a worn-out sports jacket the effect would have been the same. A young woman approached him.

'You're Jonathan Mathias aren't you?' she said, the words sounding more like a statement than a question.

'Yes,' he answered, shaking her hand gently.

He introduced Blake who noticed that the girl seemed somewhat preoccupied. She smiled perfunctorily at the writer then turned back to Mathias, pausing to look at him as if he were a piece of precious metal before returning to the group from which she had emerged.

A man approached and shook hands with the psychic. Blake observed that same look of reverence on his face as had been on the girl's. He too smiled thinly at the writer then wandered away as if in some kind of daze. Blake looked on with mild amusement as this happened half a dozen times. With people constantly approaching Mathias, Blake felt rather like a dog waiting at its master's table for any scraps to fall. When a girl in a royal blue trouser suit spoke to him he was so surprised he hadn't time to answer before she walked away.

Blake took another glass of champagne when the tray came round. It wasn't that he particularly liked the bloody stuff, but at least it was better than standing there with his hands in his pockets looking like Mathias' bodyguard instead of a guest.

'They obviously know you,' he said to the psychic as the last of his admirers left them. Blake drained what was left in his glass and put the empty receptacle down on a nearby table. God, what he wouldn't give for a pint. Even a can of luke-warm lager would have been respite enough from the endless flow of champagne.

'I've never met any of those people before, David,' said Mathias, sipping at his own drink.

'They know you by reputation then,' Blake insisted.

'People are fascinated by what they don't understand.' Those ice-blue eyes sparkled. 'And they can never hope to understand me.'

'Is that the way you want it?' Blake asked.

'That's *exactly* the way I want it.'

The two men regarded one another coolly for a second, eyes locked together like magnets.

'Jonathan.'

Both of them turned to see Toni Landers standing there. She was smiling broadly, displaying a set of teeth which testified to her dentist's expertise.

'I'm so glad you could come,' she said and kissed the psychic on the cheek.

'You look beautiful, Toni,' Mathias told her. 'It's a long time since we spoke.'

She turned to face Blake who returned her smile when he was introduced.

'Congratulations on winning the Emmy, Miss Landers,' he said, motioning to the statuette behind them on the mantelpiece.

'Thank you, please call me Toni,' she said. There was a soft lilt to her voice which made Blake feel immediately at ease. She was, indeed, a very beautiful woman combining a radiant innocence with that of uncultivated sexuality.

'What do you do, David?' she asked him.

'I'm a writer.'

'What sort of books?'

'Non-fiction, about the paranormal, the occult. That kind of thing.'

'No wonder Jonathan brought you along,' she said, slipping her arm through that of the psychic. 'Are you writing about him?'

'I'm trying.'

Toni chuckled and reached for her drink which was still on the mantelpiece. A ten by eight colour photo in a gilt frame perched there. It was of a young boy, no older than eight, Blake guessed. The lad was smiling, his blond hair brushed back behind ears which were a little too large. Freckles dotted his nose and cheeks in an irregular pattern and, even beneath the glass of the frame, his eyes seemed to twinkle with some kind of untold mischief.

'That's my son, Rick,' she told him. 'He's staying with a friend for the night.'

Blake cast a quick glance at Toni's hands and saw no wedding ring. He wondered who the father of the child was.

'Do you have any family, David?' she wanted to know.

'I can hardly look after myself let alone anyone else,' Blake said, smiling.

'Rick means everything to me. If you had a child of your own you'd understand that,' Toni said, her tone changing slightly. She looked longingly at the picture. At her son. It had been an unwanted pregnancy and she had been through a difficult delivery. She still saw Rick's father now and again. He was one of the top publicity men at Twentieth Century Fox. He still lived in the house they had bought together those nine years earlier. It had been his idea that they live together. He was nearly ten years older than Toni so she listened to what he said. In those early days she would have done anything for him. She had worshipped him and he had adored her. The young, in-demand actress who had played two leading roles within six months of moving to L.A. from her home in Virginia. She was already commanding fees of half a million a picture and things seemed to be running smoothly until she became pregnant. At first he had accused her of sleeping with other men but, when he finally came to his senses, the decision he made had been swift and, she realized with the benefit of hindsight, almost inevitable.

Get an abortion or get out of the house.

A child, he had told her, would wreck her career. Besides, *he* wasn't ready to be a father. For the first time in their relationship, Toni had followed her own instincts. There would be no abortion and if it meant the end of the relationship then so be it. She had gone to stay with a friend, working for as long as she could, finally doing voice-overs for commercials when she was too far advanced.

The combination of the break-up and the difficult birth, (a Caesarean delivery after sixteen agonising hours of labour) had brought her close to a breakdown. For three months she languished in the throes of such deep post-natal depression that her close family sometimes feared for her sanity but slowly she began to drag herself out of it. She decided that she had to go on for her baby's sake. It had been a monumental effort but somehow she had managed it. She began work five months later, helping out an old friend who was with the script department of MGM. Another month and she had, after rigorous exercise and dieting, regained her shapely figure and, another two months after that, she was offered a leading role in a highly successful ABC series. It had been a small step from there back to films and now, to the stage.

'How is Rick?' Mathias asked her, also studying the photo.

'He's fine,' she beamed, the very mention of the boy's name causing her to perk up. 'Jonathan was a great help to me when I started work again after having Rick,' she explained to Blake.

The writer nodded.

'So, what are you working on next?' he asked her.

Her smile faded slightly.

'Well, I have a slight problem there.'

'I'm sorry,' Blake said.

'No, what I mean is, I have a decision to make and it's difficult.'

'What kind of decision?' Mathias asked.

She drained what was left in her glass and placed it alongside the Emmy on the mantelpiece.

'I've been offered a part in the next *Star Wars* movie but it means being away from home for three or four months. I don't think I want that. I don't want to be away from Rick that long.'

'But you've been on location before and left him,' said Mathias.

Toni shook her head.

'Only for days at a time, like I said, here we're talking about months.'

'So what are you going to do?' Blake asked.

'I guess I'll have to refuse the part.' She sighed. 'Shit, my agent won't be very pleased, he busted his ass to get it for me.'

'But your son won't be alone. He'll have people to look

after him won't he?' said the writer.

Toni turned to Mathias.

'Will he be OK, Jonathan? You can tell me. You can ... *see*.'

Mathias sighed.

'I hope you didn't invite me here tonight to perform some kind of fairground trick,' said the psychic.

'Please,. Jonathan.' There was a note of pleading in her voice.

'What do you want to know?' he said, quietly.

A look of relief passed across her face.

'I want to know if Rick will be all right if I decide to leave him for a few months,' she said.

Mathias nodded. He sat down in one of the chairs beside the fireplace while Toni turned and scuttled off towards a door on the far side of the room. Blake watched with interest. He had an idea what Mathias was going to do, his suspicions confirmed when he saw Toni return moments later with a pack of cards. He could see immediately from their size that this wasn't an ordinary pack and, as she placed them on the coffee table before the psychic, he saw that they were Tarot cards.

An expectant hush seemed to fall over the room. The Hi-Fi was silent, only the steady click-click of the needle in the run-off grooves came from the speakers. Someone eventually removed it.

The group gathered around the piano stopped singing and turned towards Mathias who was gazing down at the cards, his brow knitted into deep furrows.

Blake took a step backward, his eyes straying alternately from Mathias to the cards and then across the table to Toni Landers. She, for her own part, settled in the chair opposite the psychic. He reached for the pack and shuffled it thoroughly.

'Now you,' he said to her, passing over the cards.

She followed his example and handed them back. Some of the other guests moved closer, anxious to see what was happening.

A large breasted girl with straw-coloured hair giggled.

Mathias shot her a withering glance, his eyes homing in on her like radar-guided rapiers. The colour drained from her

50

face and she clutched the arm of the man she was with, as if seeking protection from those piercing orbs.

Satisfied that he would not be forced to endure any further interruptions, Mathias proceeded to divide the cards into ten packs of seven. This done, he held the first pack, face down, before him.

'Pack one,' he said, his voice low and resonant in the silent room. 'That which is divine.' He laid it on the table.

'Pack two. Fatherhood.' That too he placed on the table, above and to the right of the first. 'Three. Motherhood.'

Blake and the others watched as he laid that one above the first pack, this time to the left.

'Four. Compassion. Five. Strength. Six. Sacrifice.'

Blake felt a slight tingle run up his spine and wondered if he were the only one.

'Seven. Love,' Mathias continued. 'Eight. The Arts. Nine. Health.'

Toni Landers shifted uncomfortably in her chair.

'Ten. Worldly matters.' Mathias sat back slightly. 'The Tree is complete,' he announced.

'Tree?' said someone behind him.

'The Tree of the Cabala,' Mathias answered without taking his eyes from the cards. He reached for the first pack and turned the card, repeating the process until all ten showed their faces.

Blake watched with interest; he had seen numerous Tarot readings over the years, all symbols usually carrying variant interpretations. He wondered how Mathias would read them? The psychic held one up.

'Number eight,' he said. 'A decision.'

Toni Landers kept her eyes on the cards, hands clasped on her knees.

The psychic reached for another card.

'Number seven. Travel.'

Blake noticed that Mathias' hand was shaking slightly as he reached for the next card. The older man swallowed hard and flipped it over for all to see.

'Sixteen. Change.'

'What kind of change?' Toni wanted to know.

Mathias fixed her in those powerful blue twin-points and shook his head almost imperceptibly.

'I don't know yet,' he said, turning over another card. It was a card of the Minor Arcana. The dagger.

There were eight cards lying away from the cabbalistic pattern made up by the remainder of the pack. Mathias chose one of these but he hesitated before he turned it over, his hand shaking more violently now.

'What's wrong?' Toni asked, her voice full of concern. 'What can you see? Tell me what you see.'

Blake, like most other people in the room was watching the psychic's quivering hand. He felt the chill begin to wrap itself around him more tightly, as if someone had clamped him in a freezing vice and was slowly turning the screw.

On the mantelpiece, the photograph of Rick Landers began to shudder, as if blown by some invisible breeze. 'Turn it over,' said Toni Landers, exasperatedly. Her breath was coming in short gasps now. 'I want to see the card. Tell me what *you* can see.'

The picture of Rick continued to vibrate, its movement unnoticed by all except the girl with the straw-coloured hair. She could not speak, all she could do was raise one finger in the direction of the photo.

'Jesus Christ,' said the man beside her, noticing the movement.

Mathias turned over the final card.

'Danger,' he said, breathlessly.

'What kind of danger?' Toni demanded, staring down at the card. 'Tell me.'

'Your son ...' Mathias began, falteringly.

There was a loud crash as the glass in the photo frame exploded outward as if there were a charge behind it. Slivers of crystal showered the guests nearby and Blake found himself stepping back to avoid the cascade.

A girl near him screamed.

The photo toppled from the mantelpiece and clattered to the ground. Toni Landers tore her gaze from the Tarot cards and saw the remains of the picture lying close by.

As she reached out to pick it up something red and shiny appeared on the photo, welling up from a cut in the paper.

It was blood.

Toni froze, watching as more of the crimson fluid dribbled over the slashed picture.

Blake looked on, mesmerised by the incident.

It was Mathias who finally snatched up the frame and its contents. He laid it gently on the table before him.

There was no more blood. The photo was unmarked.

Blake glanced at the psychic and then at the pieces of broken glass which littered the carpet beneath the mantelpiece.

'What happened?' Toni Landers wanted to know. 'What does this mean?'

Mathias hesitated.

'Is something going to happen to my son?' Toni asked. 'Jonathan, tell me, please.'

He nodded.

'Is he going to die?' she demanded.

'I saw danger, I didn't say he was going to die,' the psychic said in an effort at consolation but it didn't work.

Toni cradled the picture frame in her hands and stared down at the face of her son. Tears formed at her eye corners but she fought them back.

'I'm not leaving him,' she said. 'Not now.'

Mathias swallowed hard then looked up to see that Blake was watching him. The writer seemed relatively unmoved by what had happened. The other guests slowly began to disperse, their conversation now kept to a discreet whisper. The psychic got to his feet and put a hand on Toni Landers' shoulder.

'Perhaps it would have been better if I hadn't done the reading,' he said.

'No,' she whispered, shaking her head. 'I'm pleased you did. Thank you.'

'Will you be all right?' Blake asked her.

Another woman joined them, slightly older than Toni. She smelt of expensive perfume. The woman crouched beside her and gripped her hand. Blake and Mathias wandered across the room towards the open French windows, leading out into the garden. A cool breeze had sprung up and it washed over the two men as they walked out on to the patio.

'What *did* you see?' asked Blake, when they were out of earshot of the other guests.

'You know how to read Tarot cards, David,' said Mathias. 'You saw what I saw.'

'You know what I mean,' the Englishman challenged.

'Her son is going to die,' said Mathias, flatly. 'Is that what you wanted to hear?' He walked across the lawn towards a large ornamental fish pond which lay beneath the drooping arms of a willow. Leaves had fallen from the branches and were floating on the surface of the water. The liquid gleam caught the bright lights of the house in the background.

'You didn't read that in the cards did you?' said Blake, not sure whether it was intended as a question or a statement.

'No.'

'Then how did you know the boy was going to die?'

'You want to know all the secrets, David.'

'Yes I do.'

'I can't give you the answers.'

'You mean you *won't*.' Blake said, challengingly. 'What made the photo frame break? That glass looked as if it had been hit with a hammer.'

'The windows were open,' Mathias suggested. 'The breeze could have blown it off.'

'Come on, Jonathan,' said the writer, wearily. 'What the hell do you take me for?'

'What do *you* think made it break?' Mathias snarled, his brilliant blue eyes looking luminous in the darkness. 'This ... *power* of mine?' The psychic turned and headed back towards the house, leaving Blake alone beside the pond. The writer walked slowly around the pool, catching sight of a fish once in a while. He let out a tired breath. The broken frame. The prophecy. Were they more of Mathias' tricks? A mind-fuck — as he'd heard it put by an American psychologist? He was beginning to doubt if tricks was the right word. He had seen too much of the man over the past five or six days to dismiss him as a charlatan or fraud.

Blake shook his head and gazed into the pond, as if seeking his answers there. He caught sight of his own reflection.

Blake froze momentarily, gaping at the vision which stared back at him from the water.

It was his reflection but the features were contorted into a mask of sheer terror. The mouth open in a soundless scream, eyes bulging wide in the sockets.

He took a step back, eyes still riveted to the image, his feet

54

crunching on the hundreds of tiny stones which surrounded the pool. One of them bounced into the water, breaking the surface as it sent out endless ripples.

The reflection disappeared and, as the water slowly regained its stillness, Blake found that his image had also returned to normal. For long moments he looked down, as if expecting that terror-stricken visage to appear once more, but it didn't. A particularly cold breeze ruffled his hair and he shivered slightly, deciding that it was time he returned to the house.

Whistling through the branches of the nearby tree, the wind sounded like soft, malevolent laughter.

9

3.04 a.m.

Blake pushed back the covers and clambered out of bed. He had been tossing and turning for the past hour and still sleep eluded him.

Mathias' chauffeur had dropped him back at his hotel just after 1.30. By the time they had left Toni Landers' house only a handful of people remained and the atmosphere retained the air of solemnity which seemed to have descended after the incident with the cards.

Upon returning to the hotel, Blake had downed a couple of much-needed bottles of beer in the bar then retreated to his room but he had found the oblivion of sleep elusive. Now he stood at his window looking out on the dark mass that was Central Park. Trees bowed and shuddered silently in the wake of the wind and the writer thought how forbidding the place looked once the cloak of night had fallen over it.

He switched on the TV, flicking from channel to channel until he found an old black and white film. Audie Murphy was busy winning the war single-handed for the USA. Blake gazed at the screen for a while then changed channels once more. There was a programme about Chinese cookery so he left it on, turning the sound down. After five minutes he tired of that as well and switched the set off altogether, seeking comfort from the radio instead. He twisted the dial until he found the rock station, adjusting the volume as Y&T thundered out the opening chords of 'Mean Streak'.

Outside, the wind crept around the building as if seeking some means of entry, wailing mournfully every so often.

Blake padded into the bathroom and filled one of the tumblers with water which he gulped down thirstily. Then he returned to the bedroom, seating himself at the writing table where his notes were spread out. He had already filled three large pads with information, random jottings, hard facts and a lot of speculation. All that would have to be filtered and sifted through before he could begin preparing his next book. Blake disliked research at the best of times but, in this case, the dislike had intensified. The subject of Astral travel, Astral projection and its related phenomena, he had discovered, was even vaster than he had first thought. The paradox being that the more he learned the less he knew. He had the pieces but could not fit the jigsaw together.

As the author of five world-wide bestsellers he could afford to live comfortably, one of the few writers who ever succeeded in making a decent living from such a precarious profession. The money and the attention had been welcome if somewhat unexpected. Blake had never intended to earn his living from writing books about the paranormal, it had all come about rather suddenly.

He'd left home at twenty, hoping to make his mark as a journalist but working for the local paper covering events like school fetes, or interviewing people who were complaining because their sewers were bunged up, did not hold his interest for long. He began writing fiction in his spare time. Tucked away in his miniscule bed-sit above a laundrette in Bayswater he would return from the office and set to work at his own typewriter. He had left the paper for a job in a West End cinema but the financial rewards were small. He eked out his meagre earnings by supplying pornographic stories to a magazine called *Exclusive* who paid him fifty pounds for each 5000 word opus he delivered. He had a couple of articles published by *Cosmopolitan* then he decided to write a novel. It took him just three weeks and was subsequently rejected by eight publishers before finally gaining acceptance from a small, independent house. It went the way of most first novels, sinking into obscurity within a month. But, he had never been one to give up easily. He turned to non-fiction and, after six months of careful research and another two actually writing, he produced his first book about the paranormal.

After four rejections it finally found favour with a prominent hardback publisher.

A Light in the Black had been published two weeks before his twenty-second birthday.

Blake had used the advance to take a holiday. A luxury he had not been able to afford for three years. He returned to find that his book had not only been bought by Nova, a large paperback house, but the American rights had also been sold' for a substantial sum. Blake suddenly found that he could afford to leave his bed-sit and rent a flat in Holland Park.

Two years and two more books later he bought the place and now, with five world-wide successes behind him, he had, only five months earlier, bought a large house off Sloane Square.

He no longer needed to rush his work either. He now took up to eight or nine months on research and the rest of the time completing the mechanics of the book — the actual typing. Blake was at his happiest shut away in his study working. He was not a solitary man however, quite the contrary in fact. He was well liked by most people. An easy smile always at the ready, he was comfortable around people and yet at times still preferred his own company. Someone had once told him that the key to popularity was hypocrisy. If it was possible to be all things to all men at all times — do it. Blake had cultivated an easy-going image over the years which even those closest to him found hard to penetrate. He *was* all things to all men. Those he hated he spoke to with the same apparent warmth which he reserved for those who *were* allowed to pierce his facade.

Women were drawn to his practised charm, each one made to feel that *she* was the only girl in his life. The numerous encounters he had enjoyed since leaving home (that number increased once he became well-known) had only ever been superficial. To Blake at any rate. He smiled as he remembered something he'd read, attributed to Saul Bellow. He couldn't remember the words exactly but the gist of it was there.

'Telling a woman you're a writer is like an aphrodisiac. She can't wait to go to bed with you.'

He chuckled now as he flipped open his pad and reached for a pen.

Outside the hotel bedroom window the wind continued to blow strongly, hammering soundlessly at the panes as if threatening to break in. On the radio The Scorpions were roaring through 'Coming Home' and Blake decided he'd better turn the radio down.

That done he returned to his chair and scribbled a brief account of what had happened at Toni Landers' house that evening, including the incident with the picture frame and also of seeing his own twisted reflection in the pond.

As he wrote he found that his eyelids were growing heavy, as if someone had attached minute lead weights to them. He yawned and sat back for a moment, stretching. It was good that he felt tired, perhaps at last he'd be able to sleep. He scanned what he'd written and sat forward once more, allowing his eyes to close tightly.

The lamp flickered.

It was probably the wind disturbing the power lines, he thought but then remembered that he was in New York where cables ran underground, and not in the English countryside where they were suspended from pylons.

It flickered again, this time plunging the room into darkness for a second or two.

Blake muttered something to himself and peered at the bulb. The bloody thing was loose, no wonder it kept going on and off. He picked up his pen once more, now scarcely able to keep his eyes open. He turned to a fresh page but, before he could start writing, he had slumped forward in his seat and, within seconds, he was sound asleep.

The bathroom was full of steam,

Like a swirling white fog it curled and twisted in the air, condensation covering the mirror like a shroud so that when Blake looked into it, his reflection was smudged and unclear. He could still hear taps running, water splashing noisily into what was obviously an overfilled tub. Rivulets of water were running down the side of the bath which, for some reason, was hidden by the shower curtain which had been pulled around it. Blake shrugged, he didn't remember doing that.

He reached over and turned off the hot tap, cursing when he felt the heat in the metal. The condensation was on the shower curtain too, pouring down to puddle on the tiles beneath his feet.

Blake pulled back the flimsy plastic.

He shrieked aloud at the sight which met him.

Sitting up in the scalding water, skin covered by hideous welts from the blistering temperature, was a man.

The man was smiling broadly, his lips little more than ragged puffed up sores still leaking clear fluid. His head had obviously been immersed in the searing water because his face was red like a boiled lobster, the skin having risen to form innumerable liquescent blisters, some of which had burst and were spilling their contents down his cheeks. His entire body was scarlet and, such was the intensity of the water's heat, Blake noticed that three of the man's fingernails had been scalded free. They hung by thin tendrils of skin from the ends of the raw digits.

Blake stood rooted to the spot, his eyes gaping wide. But, it was not the appearance of the man which terrified him. It was his features.

Scalded and burnt though they were, they were unmistakably those of Blake himself.

He screamed again.

The scream woke him.

Blake sat bolt upright in his seat, perspiration beaded on his forehead. The lamp had stopped flickering, the room was bathed in a comforting yellowish glow. The sound of heavy rock music had been replaced by the sound of voices as the DJ interviewed his guest.

It took the writer a moment to realize that he'd been dreaming.

He swallowed hard and looked behind him to where the bathroom door was ajar. It was dark in there. No running water. No light. No steam.

Blake wiped his forehead with the back of his hand and released a sigh of relief.

'That's what you get for trying to work at this time in the

59

morning,' he told himself, reaching forward to close the notepad.

The page which had been blank before he dozed off had several sentences written on it.

The letters were large and untidy but the handwriting was unmistakably his.

Blake rubbed his eyes and turned back a page. He must have written the words before dozing off. But, as he re-read them, he realized that the words were new. He scanned the spidery writing:

The power does exist I have seen it
I have seen the Secrets

The writer swallowed hard as he scanned the words. His own words. Blake had heard of this kind of thing before, of so-called 'automatic writing' but it usually only occurred when the subject was in a trance. Was what he saw before him an example of automatic writing?

He sucked in a deep breath and held the paper before him. This time, he did *not* intend keeping things to himself. He would tell Mathias about what had happened and about the nightmare. Blake tore the piece of paper from the pad, wincing suddenly as he did so. He felt pain in his right hand and, as he turned it over he saw that his palm and wrist were bright red and swollen slightly.

As if they'd been scalded in very hot water.

10

Oxford

'How many days is it since you last slept?' Kelly asked Maurice Grant who was drumming agitatedly on the table at which they sat. Between them was a tape recorder, its twin spools turning slowly, the microphone pointed towards Grant.

'Two,' Grant snapped. 'Why the hell are you asking? You ought to know, you're the ones who keep pumping me full off fucking drugs.' He got to his feet and walked away from the table towards the large plate glass window in the far wall. Outside the sun was shining.

'Look out there,' said Grant. 'It's a beautiful day and I'm stuck in here with you two bastards asking me stupid questions.'

The man seated to Kelly's right leant closer.

'What are you giving him?' asked John Fraser, quietly.

'Thirty mg of Methadrine,' said Kelly. 'But without the Tubarine to put him out at nights.'

Fraser nodded and scribbled something down on the note pad before him.

The room they were in was light and airy, mainly due to the large window at the far end. Two or three bright paintings decorated the white walls, adding a touch of colour, but the room was dominated by the bulk of an EEG machine. The Eléma Schonander Mingograf was the most up to date of its kind and was one of four which the Institute owned. Readings had already been taken earlier that morning from Maurice Grant, over an hour ago according to the large wall clock which hung over the machine. But, at present, Kelly and her colleague were more concerned with Grant's verbal reactions than those culled from an electroencephalogrammatic scan of his brain. He had been deliberately deprived of sleep for the last two nights, unable to live out, subconsciously, the nightmare which he usually experienced.

Both investigators watched him as he paced agitatedly back and forth before the window.

'Why don't you come and sit down again?' said Fraser.

Kelly had worked with John Fraser on a number of occasions. He was ten years older than her but looked closer to fifty than thirty-five. His face had a mottled appearance to it as if he'd been out in the sun too long. His bulbous nose was shiny and reminded Kelly of a bald head. His eyes were rheumy and heavy-lidded like those of a man about to doze off. But he had a lean muscular body which looked as though it had somehow acquired the wrong head. The youthful frame and the haggard features seemed at odds.

61

'I said, why don't you ...'

Grant cut him short.

'Yeah, I heard you,' he rasped, hesitating a moment before stomping back to the table where he sat down heavily. 'Why the hell do you have to keep asking me so many questions? I just want to sleep.'

'Why do you want to sleep?' Fraser asked.

'Because I'm fucking shattered,' snapped Grant. 'Do I need a better reason?'

He glared at the two investigators with eyes full of rage. A razor hadn't touched his face for three or four days now and his cheeks and chin were carpeted by coarse bristles which rasped as he rubbed them.

'You knew that things might get a little uncomfortable when you first agreed to help us,' Kelly reminded him.

Maurice Grant didn't answer. He merely looked from Kelly to Fraser then back again.

'Are you ready to answer some questions?' she asked him.

'If I do, does that mean I can get some sleep?' he demanded.

She nodded.

'All right, ask your questions,' he said, picking at the skin around his fingernails, chewing it occasionally.

'When you can't dream, what do you think about?' she wanted to know, pushing the microphone closer to him.

'Things, I ...'

'What kind of things?' Fraser interrupted.

'Things,' Grant hissed. 'All kinds of things, thoughts.'

'Can you remember any of them?' Kelly enquired.

'No,' he said, flatly.

'Then try,' Fraser insisted.

Grant clenched his teeth, his malevolent gaze swinging round to focus on the investigator.

'I told you, I can't remember,' he said, the anger seething in his voice.

'Are any of the thoughts to do with your wife and son?' Kelly enquired.

Grant looked momentarily puzzled.

'Why should they be?'

'Look, if you keep answering a question with a question,' said Fraser, 'we're going to be here all day.'

Kelly shot her colleague an irritable glance while Grant rounded on him once more.

'What is this, some kind of fucking interrogation?' he snapped. 'You asked me to answer some questions, I'm trying to do that but you keep interrupting me.' His voice had risen in volume.

'Are any of the thoughts to do with your family?' Kelly asked him again.

Grant shook his head.

'Do you ever think about your wife and son when you can't sleep?' Kelly persisted.

'I just told you, no.'

'Come on, that's not natural. You mean to say you've wiped them from your memory?' said Fraser, a hint of sarcasm in his voice.

Grant brought his fist crashing down on the table top, his voice rising to a shout.

'I DON'T THINK ABOUT THEM.'

Fraser regarded the man warily. He was becoming a little nervous of Grant's aggression.

'Have you ever wanted to kill your wife and son?' Kelly asked.

'Kill them? Why?' Grant demanded.

'That's what we'd like to know,' said Fraser.

'Why should I want to kill them?'

'Because there may be a part of your mind which wants you to,' Kelly informed him. 'You've had a series of nightmares, in each one you kill your wife and son.'

'So what?' Grant snapped. 'What's so fucking important about a nightmare? Everyone has them.'

'You and your wife had experienced some problems hadn't you?' Kelly said. 'Marital problems.'

'What if we had? What's that got to do with this shit about nightmares?' demanded Grant, angrily.

'Would you like to kill your wife and son?' Fraser wanted to know.

Grant got to his feet.

'This is some kind of fucking game you're playing with me,' he growled, pointing an accusing finger at the investigators, both of whom moved back slightly from the table.

'Tell us the truth,' said Fraser. 'You want to kill them,

63

don't you?'

'No, you bastard.'

'You've told us.'

'No.'

'You want to murder them,' Fraser said, a little too forcefully.

'No. NO.' The shout became a scream of rage and Grant suddenly grabbed the heavy tape-recorder, lifting it from the desk, raising it above his head. The plug was torn from the wall, the spools falling uselessly from the machine. Kelly and Fraser jumped back hurriedly as Grant spun round and, with demonic strength, hurled the recorder at the large window. There was an ear-splitting crash as the glass exploded, huge thick shards flying out like crystal javelins.

'Get help, quick,' Fraser snapped as Grant turned on him.

As Kelly bolted for the door, Grant flung himself at Fraser. He hit the table on the way and the two men crashed to the ground amidst the shriek of snapping wood. Fraser tried to roll to one side but Grant fastened both hands around his neck and began throttling him. Fraser felt his assailant's finger-tips gouging into his flesh and he struck out with one hand, catching Grant a stinging blow across the temple. This only seemed to inflame him more for he straddled the investigator and began slamming his head against the floor.

Fraser looked up into the face of his attacker, the eyes blazing wildly, spittle dotted on his lips as he continued to bang his victim's head against the ground with gleeful force. Fraser gripped Grant's wrists and tried to prise open the vice-like grip but the relief was only momentary. He felt himself losing consciousness.

Then suddenly, the pressure on his throat eased and through pain-clouded eyes he saw two men grab Grant and pull him to his feet. Kelly was there too, so was Dr Vernon. He held a hypodermic needle in his hand.

Things seemed to swim before him as he rolled to one side, massaging his throat, the hot bile clawing its way up from his stomach.

'Strap him down,' Vernon urged, watching as the other two men dragged Grant towards the EEG. They forced him on to the trolley and swiftly fastened thick leather bonds around his wrists and ankles securing them. Grant had, however, begun to calm down somewhat and as the electrodes were attached to his head he seemed to stop thrashing about, content instead to eye his opponents with fury. His teeth were clenched, a thin, silvery trail of saliva dribbling from one corner of his mouth.

Kelly crossed to Fraser who was lying amongst the wreckage of the broken table, trying to clamber upright. She knelt beside him and offered a hand but he refused her help, struggling precariously to his feet, one hand still on his throat. He coughed and tasted blood. Vernon gave him a cursory glance then turned his attention back to Grant. The electrodes were in place on his forehead and temples, he was motionless but for the heaving of his chest.

One of the other investigators, a man with a button missing from one shirt cuff, stood beside the machine waiting. Kelly recognized him as Frank Anderson, a powerfully built man in his early forties.

Vernon nodded and Anderson flicked a switch which set the EEG in motion.

The five pencils swept back and forth across the paper as it left the machine, each one an indication of the brain waves picked up from Grant.

The fifth pencil, however, barely moved. Anderson noticed this and directed Vernon's attention to it. The older man looked puzzled.

'What the hell does that mean?' said Anderson but Vernon did not answer.

Kelly joined them, leaving Fraser to stagger over to the broken window where he gulped down lungfuls of air, still wincing in pain each time he swallowed.

'Could it be the area controlled by the subconscious?' Kelly said, directing her question towards Vernon but gazing at the virtually dormant line on the read-out.

Vernon didn't answer.

'Surely it must be,' she insisted. 'Theoretically, there should only be activity in that part of the brain when he's asleep. Put him out. This could be our chance to find out.'

Vernon did not hesitate. He rolled up Grant's sleeve, found a vein and ran the needle into it, keeping his thumb on the plunger until the last drop of Tubarine had left the slender receptacle.

Then, they waited.

They waited.

For ten minutes they waited. The only sounds in the room were the ticking of the wall clock and Grant's increasingly laboured breathing. Kelly stood over his immobile form and lifted one eye-lid, noticing how the pupil was dilated.

'He's asleep,' she said, softly, as if standing over a child she did not wish to wake.

Another five minutes and she noticed movement beneath the closed lids. The unmistakable motions of REM.

'He's dreaming,' she said, almost excitedly.

Vernon seemed not to hear, his eyes were riveted to the EEG read-out.

Four of the tracer lines were barely moving but the fifth was hurtling across the paper with frightening speed. He called Kelly to look at it.

'It certainly looks as if that fifth line denotes the area of the brain which controls the subconscious mind,' she said. 'It only registers activity when the subject is dreaming.'

All eyes turned to Grant.

'If only we knew *what* he was dreaming,' said Vernon. 'My God, this is incredible.' He was still watching the wildly swinging tracer. 'It looks as if the area is in the occipital lobe.' He lowered his voice slightly. 'The area of the brain concerned with vision.'

'Then he *is* seeing something,' said Frank Anderson.

Vernon nodded.

The knock on the lab door startled all of them.

At first no one moved but the knock came again, harder and more insistent.

Vernon muttered something under his breath and opened the door, surprised to find his secretary standing there.

'There's a phone call for you, Dr Vernon,' she said. 'It's ...'

He cut her short.

'Can't it wait? I'm very busy here.' he snapped.

'It's the police.'

Vernon nodded, aware of the interest now generated by his colleagues.

66

'I'll take it here,' he announced, indicating the wall phone. He crossed to it and lifted the receiver to his ear.

'Dr Vernon speaking. Yes, that's correct.'

Kelly watched him, noticing that his forehead was slowly beginning to crease into a frown.

'When did this happen?' he asked. There was a moment's silence. 'I see. Yes, I understand.'

'Look,' said Anderson, tugging on Kelly's sleeve.

She glanced down.

The fifth tracer had ceased its frenzied movement and was now drawing lazy parabolas on the read-out.

Kelly crossed to Grant and felt for his pulse, noticing how cold his flesh was to the touch.

Vernon, meanwhile, had replaced the receiver and re-joined his companions.

He sighed, scraping one thumb across his forehead.

'What's wrong?' Kelly asked.

'The police wanted to know if Maurice Grant had left the Institute during the last hour or so,' he told her.

Kelly looked puzzled.

'A neighbour called round to his house,' Vernon continued. 'She swears that she saw Grant there.'

'But that's impossible,' Anderson interjected.

'The neighbour was adamant.'

'I don't see why the police are so concerned about where Grant was or is,' Kelly said.

Vernon sucked in a deep breath.

'Less than twenty minutes ago his wife and child were attacked and killed in their house. Dismembered the police said.'

'Jesus,' murmured Anderson.

Kelly did not speak, her eyes were fixed on the restraining straps which secured Grant firmly to the table.

11

To Kelly, passing through the door of Dr Vernon's office was like crossing the threshold into a bygone age. The room, with its panelled walls and huge bookcases bearing endless leather bound volumes, was like something from a museum. It was a room to be looked at and appraised, one to be treated with reverence, much the same as an aged person. It did not seem like a room where anything constructive could be accomplished. It reminded her of the reading room in some gentleman's club, a place where cigars were smoked and glasses of port sipped. She even felt slightly out of place in it, dressed as she was in a khaki blouse, beige skirt and tan shoes. She felt as if she were intruding on the solemnity of the place, that she would have looked more at home in a crinoline.

Besidè her, John Fraser was still massaging his neck, complaining about the pain despite having refused the attentions of a doctor. Vernon himself stood facing the window, looking out over the sun-drenched lawns, enjoying the heat on his face. Despite the warmth in the room he had not undone a single button of his jacket. He popped another cough sweet into his mouth and the smell of menthol seemed to intensify.

Fraser sipped at the cup of tea which Vernon's secretary had brought five minutes earlier and found that it was cold. He replaced the cup and returned to the more urgent task of rubbing his throat. His head was beginning to ache as well where Grant had slammed it against the floor. All in all he looked, and felt, fed up with the whole situation. Since he had joined the Institute five years earlier, Fraser had gained something of a reputation as a moaner but today he felt he was justified in his complaints.

His grumblings, however, were not reserved for his work. He'd been married for twelve years and, during that time, his wife had been forced to endure a continual barrage of bleating and criticism. Indeed, Fraser only seemed to be truly content when he had a drink in his hand.

He was a heavy drinker and had been since he was eighteen. Fraser was walking the tightrope between social drinking and alchoholism and, just lately, he seemed to be losing his footing.

'I don't see that you have any choice, Dr Vernon,' he said. 'Stop the research before any more accidents happen like the one today.'

Kelly looked at him angrily.

'We can't stop the research now,' she said. 'There's still too much we have to learn.'

'That man could have killed me. It would be madness to continue. He's dangerous.'

'For God's sake, John. He was in that state for a reason. He attacked you for a reason,' Vernon interjected. 'And Kelly's right, there's no question of stopping the research.'

'You didn't exactly help matters, John,' Kelly said. 'You provoked him to a certain extent.'

'Provoked him?' Fraser gaped, incredulously. 'Jesus Christ. I asked him some questions that was all.'

Vernon turned to face the investigators.

'If you don't like the risks, John, there is an alternative,' he said, his voice low but full of authority. 'If you don't wish to work on the project any longer you can be re-assigned.'

Fraser shook his head.

'No, I don't want that,' he said. 'I just think we should move away from the drugs if we can ...'

Vernon cut him short.

'It was agreed between the Investigators at the Metapsychic Centre and ourselves that *we* would use drugs, *they* would use hypnosis. It is important that we continue with our own methods. Today's incident was an isolated one.'

'How can you be so sure it won't happen again?'

Vernon fixed Fraser in an angry stare.

'It's a chance we will have to take,' he rasped. 'The work we are doing is very necessary. It will benefit a lot of people if we can find some of the answers we seek.'

'And it will benefit one person in particular won't it, Dr Vernon?' Fraser said.

The older man glared at him, his jaw set, the knot of muscles at the side pulsing angrily. His eyes looked like wet concrete.

Kelly looked puzzled.

'That's enough, Fraser,' the Institute Director said and Kelly heard the anger in his voice, well-disguised but nevertheless potent. 'The research will continue. If you don't wish to be a part of it then get out of my office now and stop wasting my time.'

Kelly was surprised at the vehemence in Vernon's tone, at the naked fury burning in his eyes. She saw Fraser visibly blench beneath the verbal onslaught. He slumped back in his chair, trying to hold the Director's stare but finding himself unable to do so. He lowered his head slightly and began picking at his nails.

Vernon sat down and folded his hands across his stomach, his eyes never leaving Fraser.

'It will benefit one person in particular.' Kelly looked at her fellow investigator, wondering what he had meant by the statement.

'I think it would be best if you left now, John,' Vernon said, quietly. 'There's nothing more to discuss.'

Fraser let out a deep breath and got to his feet. He glanced at Kelly then at Vernon before turning and heading for the door.

'And the next time?' said Fraser, challengingly. 'Will you take responsibility for what happens, Dr Vernon?'

The older man didn't look up.

'Get out, John,' he said, quietly.

As Fraser slammed the door behind him, Kelly, too, rose. She was anxious to speak with Fraser.

'Wait a moment, Kelly,' Vernon said.

She sat down again, brushing an imaginary speck of dust from her skirt.

'Do you want me to replace Fraser?' Vernon asked.

'I don't think it's up to me,' Kelly told him.

'You're the one who has to work with him.'

She opened her mouth to speak but the words remained locked inside and it was Vernon who broke the silence again.

'This project is too important to be jeopardised by one man.'

70

Kelly saw that the steel had returned to his eyes.

'I hope you agree with me?'

She nodded.

'Dr Vernon, don't you think that the murder of his wife and child might have some effect on Grant?'

'In what way?'

She shrugged, not sure whether or not what she was about to say would sound ridiculous.

'The catalyst, the object of his subconscious fantasies no longer exists,' she said. 'We assumed that his nightmares were unconscious manifestations of actual desires, but now his wife and son are dead he has nothing to direct that hostility towards.'

Vernon stroked his chin thoughtfully.

'You mean his wife was the object of his fury, the cause of the nightmares?' he suggested. 'So, theoretically, the nightmares should stop.'

Kelly nodded.

'It's strange though,' she said. 'She was murdered while Grant was under a drug-induced trance, in more or less the same manner as he had previously described. Almost as if the dreams had been warnings. Perhaps that's the key we're looking for. Maybe Grant's nightmares weren't unconscious desires, they were visions of the future.'

Vernon shifted the cough sweet around inside his cheek where it bulged like a gum boil.

'Possibly,' he murmured.

Kelly sat a moment longer then got to her feet.

'If there's nothing else, Dr Vernon.'

He shook his head.

Kelly walked to the door, watched by the Institute Director. He coughed and, as Kelly turned the handle, Vernon spoke once more.

'Remember what I said, Kelly. This project means too much. There's a lot at stake. If Fraser causes any trouble I want to know about it.'

She nodded and left him alone in the office.

Vernon dropped his pen, his fingers bunching into a fist.

Fraser.

The last thing they needed now was opposition.

Fraser.

71

Vernon's breath came in short, angry gasps. No, Fraser must not be allowed to disrupt the research programme.

No matter what it took to stop him.

Kelly checked in John Fraser's office, in the labs, in the library.

He was nowhere to be found.

As she made her way back across the polished wooden floor of the Institute's reception area she spotted him outside, clambering into his familiar red Datsun.

Kelly ran out on to the gravel drive-way and across to the other investigator who had already started his engine and was in the process of pulling out.

He saw Kelly but did not slow up until she had reached the side of the car and banged on the window. He rolled it down.

'What do you want?' he said, sharply.

'Where are you going?' she wanted to know.

'I'm taking the rest of the day off,' Fraser said, sarcastically. 'I'm going to find the nearest pub and have a few beers. Maybe some shorts to wash them down.' He jammed the car into first, the gearbox groaned in protest.

'What you said in Vernon's office,' said Kelly. 'What did you mean?'

The roar of the revving engine almost drowned out her words.

'I don't know what you're talking about,' said Fraser.

'About the research,' she said. 'You said it would benefit one person in particular. Who did you mean?'

Fraser stepped on the accelerator, the back wheels spiining madly. A flurry of pebbles from the driveway flew into the air.

'Did you mean Vernon?' she persisted.

'Ask him,' hissed Fraser and drove off.

Kelly watched as the Datsun disappeared from view along the tree-lined drive. She stood silently for a moment then made her way back towards the main building.

She was not the only one who saw Fraser drive away.

From the solitude of his office on the second floor, Vernon had watched the entire tableau.

He stepped back out of sight.

12

Dr Stephen Vernon poured himself another scotch and
returned to his chair beside the fire-place. The gentle strains
of the New World Symphony issued forth from the record
player and Vernon closed his eyes for a moment, allowing
the soothing sound to wash over him. It did little to relax him
and he jerked his eyes open almost immediately, seeking
comfort instead in the whisky which he downed almost in one
gulp, allowing the amber liquid to burn its way to his
stomach.

Outside, the wind stirred the branches of the trees and
clouds gathered menacingly in the night sky, like dense
formations of black clad soldiers.

Inside the house the fire was warm, the room bathed in the
comforting glow from the flames and the two lamps which
burned, one behind him and the other on the table nearby.
But, despite the warmth, Vernon felt uncomfortable. As if
the heat refused to penetrate his pores. He swallowed some
more of the scotch, regarding warily the A4 size envelope
which lay on the table nearby. Only when he had downed the
last dregs of the fiery liquid did he find the courage to open
the envelope.

Inside was a file, a ring binder, and there was a letter
paper-clipped to it.

Vernon read it hastily then balled it up and tossed it into
the waste-bin beside him. His grey eyes narrowed to steely
slits as he opened the file. The first page, neatly typed, had
the familiar notepaper headed:

FAIRHAM SANATORIUM

It also bore a photo. A ten by eight, glossy black and white of
a woman in her middle forties, a warm smile etched across
her face. Even given the monochrome of the photo there was
a welcoming radiance about the eyes and Vernon found
himself gazing deep into them. The photo had been taken six

years earlier.

He turned the page and there was another picture, smaller this time, more recent.

If he hadn't known he would have sworn it was a different woman.

The welcoming glow in her eyes and the warm smile had been replaced by a vision from a mortuary. A gaze devoid of understanding stared back at him from sockets which looked as though they'd been hollowed out of the skull with a trowel. The mouth was thin-lipped, little more than a gash across the face. Hair which had once been lustrous and shiny now hung in unkept hunks, unbrushed and lifeless like kelp. Set side by side the most recent picture seemed to exist almost as a mockery to remind him of what once had been.

Vernon swallowed hard and read the report:

SUBJECT NAME: VERNON. JANET
KATHERINE. NEÉ HAMPTON.
AGE: 50
MARITAL STATUS: MARRIED.
DATE OF COMMITTAL: 14/5/78
TRUSTEE: VERNON. STEPHEN PHILLIP.
RELATIONSHIP TO SUBJECT: HUSBAND.
DIAGNOSIS: DEMENTIA. PARAESTHESIA.
CHRONIC PARANOID DEMENTIA, SERIOUS
IMPAIRMENT OF SENSORY-MOTOR
FUNCTION.
CAUSE:

Vernon closed the file and slammed it down onto the table, almost knocking over his glass. He snatched it up but found, to his annoyance, that it was empty. He looked across at the half-empty bottle of Haig and contemplated re-filling his glass once more but, eventually, decided against it. The file lay where he'd put it, a memory as painful as a needle in soft flesh.

Six years.

Dear God was it that long since he had been forced to commit his wife? That long since ...

The thought trailed away but he knew that he could never erase the memory of what had happened.

74

What had sent her to the verge of insanity.

Vernon got to his feet, turned off the fire and extinguished the lights, then, carrying the file, he trudged upstairs not bothering to put on the landing light. He moved slowly but easily through the darkness until he came to the locked door.

The wind had increased in strength and was howling now, like a dog in pain.

Vernon paused before the door, a cold chill enveloping him like some icy invisible glove which squeezed tighter the longer he stood there.

From the pocket of his cardigan he produced a key and, steadying his hand, inserted it in the lock.

There was a sharp crack from beyond the door, like bony fingers on glass, skeletal digits playing a symphony of torment in the gloom.

He turned the key.

The lock was well-oiled and opened without difficulty.

Vernon stepped into the room, shuddering as he did so. He felt like an intruder in this room. Like a thief in a church.

He heard the harsh clacking of the tree branch against the window and it startled him momentarily but, recovering his composure, he reached over and turned on the light.

The room smelt slightly of neglect, a faint odour of damp mingling with the more pungent smell of mothballs. There was a thin film of dust on everything. On the bedspread, the side-board, the chairs, even the photos. He crossed to the wardrobe and opened it. Her clothes still hung there, the smell of naptha more powerful now.

He had kept her in this room for three months before finally committing her. For three months after it happened he had brought her food and tried to feed her as a parent would feed a helpless child. For that was what she had become.

His Janet. His wife. The woman he had loved so much.

The woman who had been reduced to the mental status of a cabbage by what she had witnessed those six years ago.

He had tried to cope as best he could, he had tried to help her but she had withdrawn deeper inside herself until Vernon had felt as through he were nursing a corpse. Only the movement of her eyes, bulging wide constantly, gave any indication that she was even alive. He had used all his

75

expertise to try and salvage what was left of her sanity but finally he had lost the battle and had her committed to Fairham. The doctors there had made no progress though perhaps it was not surprising when he considered the events which had sent her into this death-like state of catatonia. It would, he decided, have been enough to send anyone insane.

So far, he had been able to keep his secret.

In the beginning he had thought that he could handle the problem. But, word had spread around the neighbourhood — rumours, speculation and guess-work until finally, he had found that there was no other solution but to lock her up. No one knew why Janet Vernon was in a sanatorium and he knew that, for all their do-it-yourself detective work, none of the neighbours could ever imagine anything as horrific as that which had caused her to lose her mind.

Now he stood in the room, looking around, listening to the wind outside.

He had left the room just as it had always been. For six years, only he had been inside. It contained too many memories, too much pain.

Vernon flicked off the light and retreated back on to the landing, locking the door behind him. He stood looking at it for long seconds then turned and headed for his own bedroom.

Six years.

He had searched for answers for so long and now, he felt that he might be close. The research was furnishing him with what he'd always sought. A way to cure his wife. A way to unlock her thoughts. No one must be allowed to stand in his way.

But, as he undressed, a thought passed through his mind.

What effect would it have on her? The horror of what she had witnessed that day had festered in her thoughts for so long.

Dare he release those memories?

13

New York

'It sure beats the shit out of *E.T.*,' said Rick Landers, gleefully.

Beside him, Andy Wallace was similarly impressed.

'You bet,' he murmured, watching as *The Thing* devoured another victim, ripping off both his arms below the elbow before exploding from his stomach cavity. The two boys watched mesmerised as the alien head detached itself and then dragged itself across the floor using a tentacle.

'Rewind it,' said Andy. 'Let's see it again.'

Rick nodded and scuttled across to the video, his finger seeking out the appropriate button.

'Yeah, *E.T.* was OK for kids,' Andy continued.

'My mum met the guy who made this picture,' said Rick, smugly.

'John Carpenter? Wow, when was that?'

'At some party I think.'

He pressed the 'play' button on the video recorder and pictures once more began to fill the wide screen. The two boys settled down again.

They were both nine years old, Andy perhaps a month or two senior. Both attended the same school about three blocks away. Rick knew that his mother didn't like him watching too many horror movies. She'd turned the video off halfway through his fifth viewing of *The Evil Dead* but, today, she was out filming a commercial until six o'clock so that gave him and Andy another two hours.

Andy lived about three houses down from the Landers place. His father, Gordon, wrote scripts for one of ABC's most successful comedy series and his mother, Nina, was a theatrical agent, so Andy was no stranger to the crazy world of showbusiness.

The Thing had just sprouted spider's legs and was about to scuttle away when the picture on the TV broke up into a network of lines and dots.

The two boys groaned and Rick leapt towards the video.

From the kitchen, the sound of the vacuum mingled with that of the waste-disposal unit in the sink.

The noise stopped, at any rate the grinding of the disposal unit did, the vacuum seemed to roar even louder.

'Mrs Garcia,' yelled Rick.

No answer.

'Mrs Garcia,' he bellowed louder and the vacuum was switched off.

'What you want, Rick?' Elita Garcia asked, appearing from the kitchen like a blimp emerging from a hangar. She was a huge Mexican woman who always reminded Rick of an extra in a spaghetti western.

'The vacuum is screwing up the picture on the video,' Rick told her. 'Couldn't you do it later?'

'Your mother ask me to have this finish before she come home,' Mrs Garcia informed him.

'Yeah, but the video ...'

'I no help that. I do my job, Rick. Sorry.' And the vacuum started up again.

The two boys exchanged disconsolate glances and surrendered to Mrs Garcia and her cleaner. Rick switched off the video and the TV and suggested they go into the garden for a while.

'You no be long,' Mrs Garcia called above the roar of the vacuum. 'Your dinner ready soon.'

The two boys had been outside only minutes when Rick heard the approaching tones of an ice-cream van. He guessed it was less than a block away.

Lee Jacobs spun the wheel of the station-wagon, the tyres screaming as they tried to grip the road. The vehicle's back end skidded and slammed into a parked Ford.

'Jesus Christ, man,' snapped Tony Sollozzo, who was kneeling on the station-wagon's passenger seat. 'Look where you're fucking going will you.'

'You wanna drive, motherfucker?' shouted Jacobs, sweat pouring down his black face. It beaded in his short frizzy hair like dew. 'Are the cops still behind us?'

The sound of a siren answered his question for him and he glanced in the rear-view mirror to see the black and white speeding along in pursuit, lights flashing.

'Step on it, will you,' Sollozzo urged. 'The bastards are gaining.'

'If you'd stolen a car with somethin' under the hood maybe we could outrun those lousy fucks,' Jacobs protested. 'Why the hell did you have to steal a fucking station-wagon?'

'Maybe I shoulda' walked around some showroom first, picked out somethin' you liked, huh?' Sollozzo countered.

'We shoulda' just turned ourselves in like I said,' Jacobs said, swerving to miss a bus.

'With nearly a kilo of smack in the glove compartment? Are you kiddin' me?'

'Stealing a station-wagon,' Jacobs grunted, trying to coax more speed from the vehicle. 'Dumb fuckin' wop.'

'Who're you callin' a wop you nigger son of a bitch. Now drive, man, they're gettin' closer.'

The blaring of horns greeted them as they sped through a red light.

The police car followed.

'What time does Mrs Garcia leave?' Andy Wallace asked, picking up the frisbee and throwing it back.

Rick Landers watched it carefully, jumping to catch it with one hand.

'She stays until my mum gets home,' he said.

'How come? She never used to did she?'

'Mum's been acting kind of weird for the last couple of days,' Rick disclosed. 'She says she doesn't like to leave me on my own too much.' He threw the frisbee back.

'*My* parents are as bad,' Andy confided. 'I mean, they must think we're kids.'

Rick nodded then he cocked his head on one side as he heard the chimes of the ice-cream van once more. It was closer now. Just turning into the street he guessed.

'You want to get an ice-cream?' he asked Andy, noticing the look of delight on his friend's face.

'You bet,' he said.

The frisbee was forgotten as they both hurried around to the front of the house.

Lee Jacobs banged his hooter as the station-wagon narrowly missed a woman crossing the road. He yelled something and turned the vehicle into another street. Beside him, Tony Sollozzo slid a Smith and Wesson .38 from his jacket pocket. He flipped out the cylinder, checking that each chamber carried a round.

'What you doin', man?' asked Jacobs, glancing down at the gun.

'Just in case,' murmured Sollozzo, hefting the pistol before him.

'You crazy fuck, I didn't know you was packed,' Jacobs gaped. 'What you gonna' do?'

The police car drew closer, its bonnet little more than ten feet from the rear of the station wagon. Sollozzo could see the two uniformed men inside as he turned. He wound down his window, pulling back the hammer on the .38.

Up ahead, Jacobs caught sight of an ice-cream van parked in their way. It was blocking the route. To by-pass it he would have to drive up on to the wide pavement.

Sollozzo steadied himself, bringing the gun up to a firing position.

Rick Landers and Andy Wallace ran towards the ice-cream van, unaware of the two speeding cars hurtling down the road. Andy suddenly stopped as his money spilled out on to the ground. He had a hole in his trouser pocket. Rick chuckled and watched as Andy stooped in the driveway of the house to retrieve his coins. He, himself, reached the waiting white van and asked for a chocolate sundae with lots of nuts. He hoped Mrs Garcia wasn't watching.

As he turned to see where Andy had got to, Rick saw the two speeding cars.

Sollozzo took aim and fired twice, the pistol bucking in his fist. The first shot blasted off the wing mirror of the police car, the second punched a hole in its windscreen.

The station-wagon swerved violently as Jacobs momentarily took his eye off the road and glared at his companion.

'Stop it,' he shouted, reaching for the gun.

'Fuck you,' roared Sollozzo, firing again, a twisted grin across his face.

Jacobs looked ahead of him and screamed aloud as the white bulk of the ice-cream van loomed before him.

The station-wagon hit it doing about sixty, the impact catapulting Sollozzo through the windscreen. The steering column came back at Jacobs as if fired from a cannon, the wheel cracking, the column itself shattering his sternum and tearing through him as the two vehicles were pulped by the crash. Almost instantaneously, the petrol tank of the white van exploded with an ear-splitting shriek and both vehicles disappeared beneath a blinding ball of red and white flame.

Rick Landers, standing less than ten feet from the van, was lifted into the air as if by an invisible hand, his body catapulted a full twenty feet on to the pavement by the force of the explosion. His mangled body crashed to the ground, his clothes ablaze.

The patrolman driving the police car twisted the wheel to avoid the blazing inferno, the black and white mounting the sidewalk.

Too late the driver saw Rick's body lying ahead of him.

He slammed on his brakes but the car was travelling much too fast.

The front offside wheel ran across the boy's neck, crushing his spine and nearly severing his head. Blood burst from the shattered corpse, spreading out in a wide pool around it.

Watching from the driveway, Andy Wallace felt something warm and soft in the seat of his pants as he gazed at the carnage before him. A second later he fainted.

Tony Sollozzo lay on the grass nearby, his face and neck shredded by the glass of the windscreen. Flames from the wreckage licked hungrily at his outstretched hand. Above it all a black pall of smoke hung like a shroud.

The two policemen stumbled from their car, the first of them running towards the burning vehicles but unable to get close because of the blistering heat from the leaping flames. The driver knelt and saw the body of Rick Landers lying beneath the car.

'Oh Jesus God,' he murmured and straightened up, reaching inside the car for his radio.

He called for an ambulance and some back-up, trying to explain briefly what had happened.

As he walked away he saw that he left sticky footprints

behind him where he'd been standing in the pool of Rick's blood. He dropped to his knees on the grass verge and threw up.

14

David Blake dropped his pen and yawned. He blinked myopically and scanned the pages which lay before him.

He'd been working flat out since ten that morning, pausing briefly at one o'clock to devour half a cheeseburger and some fries. Most of that now lay neglected on the table behind him.

His stomach growled noisily and he patted it gently. It was time he ate something more substantial.

Blake got to his feet and walked to the bathroom, turning the television on as he passed. A glance at his watch told him it was 5.58 p.m. The news would be on in a minute or two. He smiled to himself. It was time to find out what had been going on in the 'real' world. He'd been so immersed in his work for the past eight hours that New York could have disappeared and he wouldn't have noticed. Once safely locked away, pen in hand, Blake was oblivious to all else.

He entered the bathroom, crossing to the wash basin where he splashed his face with cold water. As he wandered back into his room, a towel pressed to his face, the news was just beginning. Blake decided to hear the headlines then get something to eat. He dried his face off, the water mingling with the perspiration on his forehead.

'... has promised a crackdown on some of the city's illegal gambling establishments ...'

The voice of the newsreader droned on as Blake opened his wardrobe and took out a clean shirt.

'... and, as reported in our earlier bulletin, the son of Toni Landers, the actress who plays ...'

Blake spun round to face the set.

'... whose son, Rick, was tragically killed today when he

82

was involved in a car accident.'

'Jesus Christ,' muttered Blake as a photo of first Rick and then Toni Landers was flashed on to the screen. The writer sat down on the edge of the bed, eyes riveted to the set as the newsreader continued.

'Miss Landers, who was filming elsewhere in the city was unavailable for comment and it is believed that she is now at her home under sedation. Her son, Rick, is believed to have been killed at approximately 4.15 this afternoon after a stolen car crashed into an ice cream van outside his home. Both passengers in the car and also the van driver were killed but, as yet, the other three victims have not been named. Police ...'

Blake shook his head slowly, his eyes and ears focused on the TV but his mind back-tracking to the party at Toni Landers' house.

To Mathias.

To the prophecy.

'Her son is going to die.' The psychic's words echoed inside his mind.

'Her son is going to die.'

Blake sat for a moment longer, then pulled on his shirt and hastily buttoned it up, tucking it into his jeans. He pulled on a pair of boots and, leaving the television set on, he left the room and scuttled across to the elevator at the end of the corridor. He rode it to the ground floor and ran through reception, out of the main doors and past the doorman who was enjoying a sly drag on a Marlboro.

The writer turned to his left and headed for the newsstand on the corner of the street. He fumbled in his pocket for change with one hand as he retrieved a late edition with the other. Half-way down the page was a photo of Rick Landers and, above it:

SON OF ACTRESS DIES IN ACCIDENT

Blake handed the vendor some coins, not waiting for his change, then he turned and made his way back to the hotel.

Once inside his room, Blake read the full story. The details didn't matter. The child was dead. That was enough. The writer folded the paper and dropped it on to the bed. He suddenly didn't feel so hungry. For what seemed like an eternity he sat there, gazing at the TV screen and then at the photo of Rick Landers.

'Her son is going to die.' He spoke the words aloud.

Blake got to his feet and switched off the TV. He snatched up the leather jacket which was draped over the back of a nearby chair, pulling it on as he made for the door of his room.

Outside, the storm clouds which had been gathering for the past hour or so were split by the first soundless flash of lightning.

Blake paid the taxi driver, peered out through the rain splashed window then pushed open the door of the cab.

The deluge hit him like a palpable wave, the heavens continuing to dump their load without hint of a respite. The storm was raging, whiplash cracks of lightning punctuating the almost continual growl of thunder. It sounded as if somewhere, deep below the surface of the earth, a gigantic creature was clawing its way up. Rain hammered against the roads and buildings, bouncing off like tiny explosions. Even as Blake left the cab he felt the hair being plastered to the side of his face, the hot droplets penetrating the material of his shirt. He knew that the storm would not clear the air, it would merely make the humidity more acute. Beads of perspiration formed on the writer's forehead, only to be washed away instantly by the driving rain.

The house of Jonathan Mathias stood before him, a large forbidding three storey building fronted by well-kept lawn and ringed by a high stone wall. Blake noticed as he approached the wrought iron gates that there were closed-circuit television cameras mounted on each side of the gates. They watched him with their Cyclopean eyes as he walked up the short driveway towards the house itself.

The building was a curious mixture of the old and new. The main structure looked as if it had been built in mock Edwardian style whilst an extension made up of glass and concrete seemed to have been grafted on to the wrong house.

The windows were unlit and the glass reflected the lightning back at Blake, they lowered over him like some kind of malevolent spectre.

There were more closed-circuit cameras above the front door. He rang the bell, pressing it twice and, a moment later, the door was opened by a man who Blake immediately recognised as Mathias' chauffeur.

'Mr Blake isn't it?' said the man, eyeing the writer who looked a sorry state with his brown hair dripping and his clothes soaked.

'I'd like to see Mr Mathias if that's possible,' the writer said.

'He doesn't like to be disturbed when he's at home,' the chauffeur began. 'I'll ...'

'Let him in, Harvey.'

Blake recognised the voice immediately and, a moment later, Mathias himself stepped into view.

'Come in, David,' he said, smiling. 'You look as if you swam here.'

Blake stepped into the hallway.

'Come through into the study,' said the psychic.

Once inside the room, he poured himself a brandy and offered one to Blake who gratefully accepted, his eyes roving around the spacious room. He noted with bewilderment that there were no windows. The only light came from a desk lamp and two floor-standing spotlamps near the drink cabinet. On one wall there was a framed original sketch by Aleister Crowley depicting the Whore of Babylon. Blake looked closely at it.

'You knew Crowley?' he asked.

'We met once or twice,' said Mathias.

'The Great Beast himself eh?' murmured Blake, sipping his brandy. 'A self-confessed Black Magician.'

Mathias didn't answer.

Blake allowed his gaze to shift to a photograph. It showed Mathias and another man who looked familiar to him.

'Anton Le Vey,' said the psychic.

'Another friend?' asked Blake.

Mathias nodded.

'Another Black Magician,' the writer commented.

The psychic seated himself behind his desk and cradled his brandy glass in one hand, warming the dark fluid.

'What can I do for you, David?' he wanted to know. 'It must be important to bring you out in weather like this.' He downed most of his brandy in one swallow.

Blake seated himself on the closest chair.

'It is,' he informed Mathias. 'Have you seen a newspaper today, or watched television?'

'No, why?'

Mathias finished his brandy and got to his feet, walking past the writer who turned until he was gazing at the psychic's back.

'Toni Landers' son was killed earlier today,' he said.

Mathias filled his glass once again then turned round, the bottle still in his hand.

'He was killed in an accident,' the writer persisted.

'Do you want another drink?' Mathias asked, apparently uninterested in what Blake had to say.

'Did you hear what I said?' the writer asked, irritably. 'Toni Landers' son is dead. Haven't you got anything to say?'

Mathias regarded him indifferently then shrugged his shoulders.

'I'm very sorry,' he said, softly. 'He was only a young boy.'

'You knew he was going to die,' Blake said, flatly. 'You told me at the party the other night, after the Tarot reading. Only you didn't learn of his death through the cards did you?'

'The cards act as a guide,' said Mathias, sipping his drink. 'They point me toward the truth.'

'Come on, Jonathan,' Blake muttered, exasperatedly. 'You're not talking to one of your bloody "flock" now.'

The two men regarded one another coolly for a moment, a heavy silence descending upon them. It was broken by Mathias.

'I told you that the Astral body can be controlled,' he said. 'Well, it can also be projected forward in time. I "saw" that Toni Landers' son was going to die because I felt no Astral presence from him.' He sipped at his brandy once again. 'The Astral body is like the life-line on a hand, someone with the knowledge can "see" it.'

'Tell *my* future,' said Blake, reaching for a pack of Tarot cards which lay on the desk near to Mathias. 'Do it now.'

He had already begun shuffling the cards.

'No,' said Mathias.

Blake divided the cards into ten packs and laid them out in the correct pattern.

'Do it, Jonathan,' he urged.

'I told you, I'm not a fairground showman,' muttered the psychic, irritably. He regarded the cards without emotion, his gaze slowly rising until his brilliant blue eyes were fixed on Blake. 'I'd appreciate it if you would leave now, David,' he said, quietly.

The two men locked stares for a moment then Blake took a step backward, brushing one strand of hair from his face.

'Are you afraid of what you might see?' he asked.

Mathias didn't answer. His face was impassive, registering no emotion at all. Finally, he exhaled, his features softening slightly.

'You asked me about my power,' he said. 'This force inside me, it's the power of the shadow.'

Blake looked puzzled.

'Not the shadow cast by sunlight or reflected in a mirror,' Mathias continued. 'The shadow of the inner self. The alter ego if you like. The Ancients called it the shadow because it represented the darker side of man, the side which only appeared in times of anger or fear. The side which could drive a man to commit acts of which he was not normally capable. Acts which went against his nature. Human nature.'

'Like a split personality?' said Blake.

'No,' Mathias corrected him. 'In cases of split personality the victim retains *some* traces of good within himself. The shadow is wholly evil.'

'Then your power is evil,' Blake said.

'Who is to say what is good and what is evil, David?'

There was another long pause then Blake turned and headed towards the door.

'I've told you as much as I can,' Mathias said. 'What more do you need to know?'

'A lot more,' he said, opening the door. Then, he was gone.

The psychic sat alone in his study, the Tarot cards still laid out in their cabbalistic pattern before him. He paused for a moment then reached towards the seventh pack. To Love. He turned the card slowly.

Thirteen.

La Mort.

Death.

Mathias stared at the sythe-carrying skeleton depicted on the card for a moment then he reached for the top card on the ninth pack. To Health.

Fifteen.

Le Diable.

The Devil.

But he knew that the cards carried much more than their face value. The card marked XV also meant The Great Secret. Mathias smiled to himself. It seemed most appropriate in Blake's case.

He turned the card on the final pack, the breath catching in his throat as he did so.

Twelve.

Le Pendu.

The Hanged Man.

Mathias dropped the card as if it had been red hot; he swallowed hard and studied the image on the card.

The Hanged Man.

Catastrophe.

He wiped his brow, finding that he was perspiring slightly. It had another interpretation.

Saint or Sinner?

Outside the thunder rumbled loudly and Mathias sat still in his seat for a moment. He finally gathered up the cards, sorting them into some kind of uniformity.

As he reached for the one which bore The Hanged Man he wondered why his hand was shaking.

15

Oxford

As she approached the door which led into Maurice Grant's quarters, Kelly looked at her watch.

It was approaching 5.09 p.m.

She slowed her pace, conscious of the sound which her heels made in the solitude of the corridor. She felt strangely ill-at-ease, like a child who has performed, or is about to perform, an act for which it knows it will be punished. Kelly brushed one hand through her brown hair and attempted to control her accelerated breathing. This was ridiculous, she told herself. She had no reason to be nervous.

Over her skirt and blouse she wore a lab coat and in one of the pockets nestled a hypodermic syringe.

She had taken it, along with its contents, from the pharmacy on the first floor. Ordinarily, it was a place only frequented by the four doctors who worked for the Institute, although the other investigators were free to come and go as they wished amongst the rows and rows of bottles and medical equipment. Kelly had found what she sought without difficulty, then she had recovered a disposable syringe from the drawer which was so carefully marked. Everything in the pharmacy was maintained by a woman in her forties known to Kelly only as Mrs King. She was responsible for ensuring that everything was in its correct place and it was a job which she did very efficiently.

Kelly knew that Mrs King usually left for home at around 4.30 so she had waited until nearly 4.50 before venturing into the pharmacy.

To her relief it had been deserted but still she had felt the compulsion to hurry, wondering what explanation she was going to use if someone should discover her poring over the chemicals which were the domain of the physicians.

She had drawn off 10ml of atropine sulphate and then placed the syringe in her pocket.

Now, as she approached Maurice Grant's quarters thoughts began to tumble through her mind with increased rapidity. But one in particular seemed to flash like neon in her consciousness. The incident the day before last when Grant had finally persuaded her to undertake this new experiment without either the knowledge or authorization of Dr Vernon. Deprived of sleep for forty-eight hours, Grant had become violent and Kelly remembered how the subsequent tests on him had revealed activity in an area of the brain normally dormant. The question of what would happen to him if he were not allowed to sleep and dream for longer than two days had tortured her ever since. She had wondered what he'd be like after a week but Kelly didn't have a week.

She would not, could not, wait that long.

The injection of atropine would have more or less the same results.

She knew that, given in overdose, the drug caused stimulation of the brain and autonomic nervous system. The usual dosage was 2ml.

She planned to give Grant three times that amount.

Kelly knocked on the door and waited, casting one furtive glance up the corridor as she did so. The Institute was silent.

'Come in,' Grant called and Kelly did so.

He was sitting at a table finishing a plate of fish and chips which had been brought to him ten minutes earlier.

'Sorry if I'm interrupting your tea, Mr Grant,' Kelly said.

He smiled and shook his head.

'I was just finishing,' he told her. 'That's one good thing about this place, the food's terrific.' He belched loudly, excused himself and pushed the plate away.

Kelly thought how different he looked from the last time she'd seen him. In place of the demonic, violent and unkempt would-be killer there was a calm, clean-shaven even handsome man. Grant wore only a white shirt and grey trousers, both of which looked neat and fresh.

'What can I do for you now?' he asked.

'I'm afraid we need your help with something else,' Kelly told him.

'Which is your polite way of saying "Excuse me Mr Human Guinea Pig, we want you back on the slab," right?'

Kelly smiled thinly.

'Yes it is,' she said.

Grant chuckled.

'No need to sound so apologetic. After all, I was the bloody fool who volunteered for all this,' he remarked, good-humouredly.

Kelly had one hand dug deep in the pocket of her lab coat, fingers toying with the syringe.

'What exactly is it that you want me to do?' Grant enquired.

'Do you remember anything about the incident the day before last?' she wanted to know. 'When you attacked one of my colleagues?'

He shrugged.

'Not much. I remember trying to ...' The words trailed off, almost as if he were ashamed of the recollection. 'I didn't hurt anyone badly did I?'

Kelly shook her head.

'You'd been kept awake for over forty-eight hours,' she told him. 'People become aggressive when they're forced to go without sleep for too long.'

'Why?' Grant wanted to know.

'If we knew that for sure, Mr Grant, you wouldn't still be here.' She thought about mentioning the dream theory then decided not to. There was a long silence broken eventually by Kelly. 'For the last two nights have you dreamed?'

'Yes,' he said.

'The dream about killing your wife and son?'

He nodded.

'But it wasn't as vivid. In fact, last night it was different. I woke up before I killed them.'

'That was probably because you weren't given any drugs,' Kelly told him. 'The amphetamines we'd been giving you had been intensifying the dreams up until that point.'

'So, what happens now?' he asked.

Kelly felt the hypodermic in her pocket.

'We try a different approach,' she said.

On the table beside Grant's bed was a new tape-recorder and Kelly checked that it was working properly. Satisfied, she asked Grant to lie down. There were restraining straps which could be fastened around his wrists and ankles but, as yet, Kelly did not touch them. She ensured that Grant was comfortable then asked him to roll up the sleeve of his shirt which he did. The vein bulged invitingly in the crook of his arm and Kelly carefully pushed the needle into it, one thumb on the plunger of the syringe.

She began to push, the atropine flooding into Grant's bloodstream.

She watched the markers on the syringe as she forced the liquid into his vein.

0.25ml.

0.75ml.

1ml.

Grant still had his eyes open, wincing slightly as Kelly pushed a little too hard on the syringe. She could see the needle-point beneath his flesh as she pressed on the plunger again.

1.5ml.

2ml.

2.5ml.

She was trying to stop herself from shaking, worried that too much movement would tear the vein open. Grant sucked in a painful breath and Kelly apologised but kept the pressure on the plunger, watching as more of the liquid was transferred to the man's body.

3ml.

3.5ml.

4ml.

Grant closed his eyes, his chest beginning to heave as his respiration became more laboured. Kelly looked at his face then at the needle embedded in his arm and finally at the markers on the slim receptacle itself.

4.5ml.

5ml.

5.5ml.

Kelly knew that the atropine would not take long to work and, with the increased dosage she was administering, that time should be curtailed further.

6ml.

She hesitated. Grant had closed his eyes tightly now. His mouth also was clamped shut, his lips bloodless.

Kelly, the needle still clutched in her hand, the point buried in Grant's vein, looked at the man. He was visibly turning pale. Had she given him enough?

'Mr Grant,' she said.

He didn't answer.

'Mr Grant.'

A weary grunt was the only reply she received this time.

Kelly pushed harder on the plunger.

6.5ml.

7ml.

Perspiration formed in salty droplets on his face, some running together to trickle in rivulets across his flesh. On his arms too there was moisture, glistening like beads. The skin around the needle was beginning to turn a dark crimson, the blue veins pulsing more strongly.

7.5ml.

8ml.

Grant moaned, his mouth dropping open. Thick sputum oozed over his lips and onto the sheet beneath. His tongue lolled uselessly from one corner and he grunted again, coughed. Particles of spittle flew into the air and, as he moved slightly, the needle came free.

Cursing, Kelly pushed it back into the vein, ignoring the single tiny droplet of blood which had welled up through the first miniscule hole. She looked at his face which was now grey, streaked with perspiration. She knew she was taking a chance but this had to work.

9ml.

9.5ml.

10ml.

Kelly withdrew the needle and stepped back, dropping the syringe into her pocket once more. She switched on the tape recorder and moved the microphone as close as she dared to Grant. His body began to undergo almost imperceptible movements, tiny muscle contractions which made it look as if he were being pumped full of mild electrical current.

'Mr Grant,' she said. 'Can you hear me?'

He muttered something which she couldn't hear so she took a step closer, bringing the microphone nearer to his mouth.

'Mr Grant.'

His eyes were shut, the lids sealed as tightly as if they'd been stitched.

'Can you hear what I'm saying?'

Grant suddenly grabbed her wrist in a grip which threatened to snap the bones.

Simultaneously, his eyes shot open like shutters and she found herself looking down into two glazed, rheumy orbs which seemed to be staring right through her.

Kelly suppressed a scream and tried to pull away from the vice-like grip but it was useless.

'Help me,' murmured Grant, refusing to release Kelly. 'Oh God they're everywhere.'

He suddenly let her go, his hands clutching at his face.

'What can you see?' she demanded.

Grant suddenly sat up, his face contorted in a mask of rage

and hatred.

'Fucking bastard,' he snarled, his blank eyes turning to face her. 'You stinking cunt.' His lips slid back in a vulpine grin and more saliva dribbled down his chin. 'She betrayed me. She thought I didn't know. *She* thought she could fool *me*.'

Kelly edged away slightly.

'Who thought she could fool you?' asked the investigator, moving to the end of the bed.

'*Her*. My wife,' Grant rasped. 'Fucking whore. She made me think the child was mine when it was *his* all along.'

'Is that why you wanted to kill her?' asked Kelly, moving towards the restraining straps, waiting for her chance to slip them over Grant's ankles although she didn't give much for her chances.

And what if she failed ...?

'Yes, I wanted to kill her. Her and the child. *His* fucking child,' Grant raved.

But, his anger seemed to subside with alarming speed and he was cowering once more from some unseen menace. Shielding his face and eyes with shaking hands.

'Get them off me,' he shrieked.

'What can you see?' demanded Kelly, deciding that it was time to fasten the straps.

'Spiders,' he told her. 'Thousands of them. All over me. Oh God, no.'

Kelly managed to fasten the two ankle straps, securing Grant to the bed, at least for the time being. The leather looked thick and stout. She hoped that it would hold.

Maurice Grant wondered why she could not see the eight-legged horrors seething over the floor of the room and onto the bed. Over his body, inside his clothes. He could feel their hairy legs on his flesh as they crawled onto his stomach, up his trouser legs, across his chest, up his neck to his face. And there they tried to force their way into his mouth. He felt one on his tongue and he plunged two fingers into his mouth to pull the creature out. The probing digits touched the back of his throat and he heaved violently.

Above him, the spiders were coming through the ceiling. They were emerging from the stone-work itself and they were getting bigger. One the size of his fist dropped from the ceiling on to his face, its thick legs probing at his eyes and nose. One of the smaller creatures scuttled up his left nostril, trying to pull the swollen bulk of its abdomen inside the orifice.

From the wall beside him, a spider the size of a football emerged and clamped itself on his arm, pinning it to the bed. Another did the same with his right arm.

Kelly watched mesmerised as Grant wriggled beneath the imaginary host of arachnids but she was not too engrossed to by-pass the opportunity to secure his wrists to the bed.

'They're inside my head,' screamed Grant as he felt more and more of the spiders dragging themselves up his nostrils, into his ears.

'I know where they're coming from,' he screeched. '*She* sent them.'

'Your wife?' asked Kelly, watching as Grant continued to squirm.

'Fucking cunt. Fucking slut.'

His fear had been replaced once more by rage.

'I'm glad I killed her,' he roared. 'She deserved to die.'

The veins on his forehead bulged angrily as he strained against the straps. 'I don't care if anyone saw me. I had no choice. I saw them together', he said, his body jerking wildly. 'I saw her with him. He stuck it between her legs, in her mouth. AND SHE FUCKING WANTED IT. I don't want to see it anymore.'

'Can you see it now?' Kelly asked.

'Yes.'

'What can you see? Tell me exactly.'

Grant was using all his strength to tug himself free and Kelly noticed with horror that one of the wrist straps was beginning to creak under the pressure.

'I can see her on the floor of the bedroom. *Our* bedroom. She's naked and so is he,' Grant snarled.

'Who is *he*?' Kelly wanted to know.

'She's sucking his cock. He's using his tongue on her.'

The right hand strap creaked ominously as Grant continued to thrash around.

'I don't want to see it anymore. Never again.'

Kelly wondered if she should get help. Grant was hallucinating madly it appeared but he was largely coherent.

And, at last, she knew why he had wanted to kill his wife and son.

'She's rolled over on to her stomach and he's putting his cock into her. The filthy fucking whore. She wants him.'

'Who is he?' Kelly demanded.

'My brother,' roared Grant and, with that, made one last monumental effort to break free.

The right hand strap split first, then came free.

'I don't want to see it. I DON'T WANT TO SEE IT,' Grant bellowed, tugging himself out of the ankle restraints and the other wrist strap. He staggered to his feet, his chest expanding until it threatened to rip his shirt. 'I don't want to see it,' he said again and lurched towards the table in the middle of the room. There, his searching hands found the greasy fork.

'I NEVER WANT TO SEE IT AGAIN,' he shrieked and raised the pronged implement.

Kelly knew that she could never reach the door. Grant blocked her way but, as she looked at him anxiously, she saw that his anger was not directed at her.

'I won't watch,' he said, quietly, studying the fork which he held only inches from his face.

With quivering hand, he pushed the fork through his lower lid and into his eye. With infinite slowness he moved it in a digging action, the prongs gouging muscle and flesh as Grant shoved it further until the eye itself began to thrust forward. The prongs raked his skull as he prised the bursting orb from its socket. Blood gushed down his cheek, mingling with the vitreous liquid as the eye itself punctured. It did not come free but hung, suspended by the shredded remains of the optic nerve.

Mind numbing pain enveloped him but he managed to remain upright, guiding the fork towards his other eye.

Kelly gagged as she saw the prongs burrow through the upper lid this time, the curve of the fork enabling Grant to reach the retina itself. With a final despairing scream he managed to scoop the bloodied eye free of his skull.

There was a muffled, liquid plop as the orb left the socket, a vile sucking sound which was soon drowned out by Grant's agonised shriek.

The eye itself dropped to the floor and lay there intact

until Grant dropped to his knees, squashing it beneath him as if it had been an oversized grape.

Kelly found herself transfixed by those oozing sockets from which crimson was pumping in thick spurts, dribbling into the man's open mouth.

She finally tore her gaze away and bolted for the door, wrenching it open and dashing out into the corridor.

The room was soundproofed. Until Kelly opened the door, the building had remained quiet but now the agonised shrieks of the blinded Grant echoed along every inch of the building. So great was the dose of atropine he'd received, so powerful the boost to his nervous system, Grant was even denied the merciful oblivion of unconsciousness. He merely slumped to the floor of the room moaning, the remains of one eye still dangling uselessly by a strand of nerve.

Inside the room, the tape recorder obediently captured the sounds of agony. Preserving them forever.

16

'How much did you say you gave him?' Dr Vernon asked Kelly, reaching for the syringe.

'10ml, perhaps a little more,' she said, quietly.

Vernon nodded and held the hypodermic between his fingers for a moment before setting it down on the table again. He laid it beside the bloodstained fork, allowing his gaze to ponder on the implement for a few seconds. He exhaled and looked around the room. The floor was spattered with blood, droplets of it had splashed a wide area, puddling into bigger pools in one or two places. There was a purplish smudge close to his foot where the eye had been squashed and Vernon moved to one side.

The remains of the restraining straps lay on or near the bed and, he noticed that there were even a few speckles of crimson on the sheets.

Maurice Grant had been removed about fifteen minutes

earlier.

Now Vernon stood amidst the carnage, flanked by Kelly and John Fraser.

Fraser looked distinctly queasy and could not seem to tear his gaze from the blood-stained fork on the table. The mere thought of what it had been used for made him feel sick.

'Is he going to die?' asked Kelly, anxiously.

'The ambulancemen didn't seem to know one way or the other,' Vernon told her. 'Once the effects of the atropine wear off he'll go into shock. After that ...' He allowed the sentence to trail off.

'So, first he nearly kills me,' said Fraser. 'Now he more or less succeeds in killing himself. Surely this is enough for you, doctor?'

'What do you mean?' Vernon wanted to know.

'There will have to be a full-scale enquiry into what happened today. There's no way that you can continue with this research now.'

'As Director of the Institute *I* will decide if an enquiry is necessary or not,' Vernon told him.

'Do you seriously think that the outside authorities are going to let something like this drop without investigating it?'

'I couldn't give a damn about the outside authorities,' snapped Vernon. 'What goes on inside these walls is *my* concern.'

'And the fact that a man could have died today doesn't bother you?' Fraser said, challengingly.

'Grant knew that he might be taking risks when he agreed to participate in the experiments.'

'Acceptable risks, yes, but ...'

Vernon cut him short.

'Risks,' he said, forcefully.

Fraser now turned his attention to Kelly.

'With all due respect, Kelly, you are responsible for this,' he said.

'I realize that,' she said. Then, to Vernon:

'I'm prepared to resign.'

'No,' he said, without hesitation. 'That wouldn't solve anything.'

Kelly could not conceal the look of surprise which flickered across her face.

98

'She broke every rule of this bloody Institution,' growled Fraser. 'She nearly killed a man as well and you ...'

It was Kelly's turn to interrupt.

'Don't talk about me as if I'm not here,' she snarled. 'I know I was in the wrong. God knows I wish I could repair the damage I've done.'

'The research had to be taken to its logical conclusion,' Vernon said, supportively.

'That conclusion presumably being the death of the subject,' said Fraser, sarcastically.

'There was no way of knowing exactly how the atropine would affect Mr Grant,' said Vernon, as if he were defending himself instead of Kelly. She looked on dumbfounded as he came to her rescue.

'A dose of 5ml is considered dangerous. We all know the effects of the drugs we use. Kelly should have known that injecting Grant with twice that amount would have serious side-effects.'

'Did Grant actually say anything of use while he was drugged?' Vernon wanted to know.

'Is that important now?' Fraser said, angrily.

Vernon turned on him, his grey eyes blazing.

'Yes, it is important. The only thing that matters is that this project is successful. If certain sacrifices have to be made then that's unfortunate but unavoidable.'

'You're insane,' said Fraser, his tone a little more controlled now. 'This isn't research to you anymore, it's an obsession. How many more people are going to be injured or killed before you're satisfied? Before you have the answers you want?'

'That's enough, Fraser,' Vernon warned him.

'Do you honestly think that any of this is going to help *you*?' the investigator said, cryptically.

Kelly looked at him, wondering what he meant.

'Fraser.' There was more than a hint of anger in Vernon's voice.

'What *are* you looking for, doctor?' the investigator demanded. 'Or more importantly, why are you looking?'

'This isn't the time or the place to ...'

'Perhaps if we knew about whatever it is you've managed to hide for so long then ...'

Fraser's words were choked back as Vernon lunged forward and grabbed him by the lapels. The older man's face was flushed and there was a thin film of perspiration on his forehead. He fixed the investigator in his steely grey stare and held him there. Kelly looked on with concern and interest, wondering whether or not she should intervene.

'This time, Fraser, you've gone too far,' hissed the doctor. He pushed the investigator away, watching as he fell against the table. 'Now get out of here. Out of this room. Out of this Institute. You're finished here.'

Fraser dragged himself upright and steadied himself against the table.

'Perhaps the police might be interested in what happened here today,' he said, threateningly.

'The police will be informed, when I think it's necessary,' Vernon told him. 'Now, get out.'

Fraser looked at Vernon a moment longer, then at Kelly.

'I'm sorry, Kelly,' he said apologetically and made for the door. They both heard his footsteps echo away down the corridor.

Vernon pulled a handkerchief from his trouser pocket and wiped his face. He pulled a chair out from beneath the table and sat down, ignoring the bloodied fork which lay before him. Kelly watched as he popped a menthol sweet into his mouth and sucked it. His face was still tinged red with anger and he shuffled his fingers impatiently before him.

Kelly licked her lips, finding them dry, like her mouth. She wanted to ask Vernon what Fraser had meant, just as she had when he'd made the other cryptic remark two days before.

'... whatever it is you've managed to hide for so long.' Fraser's words stood out clearly in her mind. Why had Vernon reacted so angrily?

'Dr Vernon, Grant said that he'd killed his wife. It was like a confession,' she said. 'It's all on the tape, every word.'

Vernon didn't speak.

'What could he have meant?' she persisted.

'It must have been the effects of the drug, you said he was hallucinating.'

'Yes, but no one mentioned to him that a neighbour had identified a man like him the day his wife and son were butchered. Why should he say that?'

100

'Look, Kelly, I think we have enough to worry about with what happened today,' Vernon said, evasively. 'And it would be best if you left here. I'll call you in a fortnight or so, the research can't continue until after the enquiry anyway.'

'Can the authorities close the Institute?' she wanted to know.

Vernon shook his head.

'No. And don't worry, your job will still be here when you come back.'

'Why didn't you accept my resignation?' she asked.

'Because what you did was based on sound theory. It was a chance which had to be taken eventually.'

Kelly nodded although it was not an explanation which wholly satisfied her. Vernon appeared to have more than a scientific interest in the outcome of the research. The question was, why?

Finally, she slipped off her lab coat and decided it was time to leave. She and Vernon exchanged brief farewells and he repeated his promise to contact her in two weeks.

Vernon waited until she had left the room then he walked slowly around it, his eyes drawn occasionally to the spots and splashes of congealing blood, now slowly turning rusty as it solidified. There was a slight smell of copper in the air. He eventually reached the tape recorder. He pressed the re-wind button and watched as the twin spools spun in reverse. When the process was completed he took the full one and dropped it into his pocket, deciding to listen to it in the privacy of his office. As he made his way out of the room, two cleaners were entering armed with mops and dusters. They set about removing all traces of the horrors which had occurred in there.

Vernon crunched his cough sweet up and replaced it with another as he walked up the stairs towards his office. His secretary had gone home an hour earlier so he had the place to himself.

Nonetheless, he locked his office door before settling down to listen to the tape.

Twice he played it through, his face impassive, even when Maurice Grant's shrieks of agony began to erupt from the speaker. Half-way through the third play Vernon switched it off. He sat for what seemed like an eternity, his chair facing the window, then he swung round and reached for the phone. He hurriedly dialled the number he wanted and tapped agitatedly on the desk top with his stubby fingers as he waited for the receiver to be picked up. He heard the click as it finally was.

'The Metapsychic Centre?' he asked. 'This is Dr Stephen Vernon. I want to speak to Alain Joubert. Tell him it's important.'

10.06 p.m.

Kelly folded the last of her clothes and laid the skirt gently on top of the other things. The only light in the bedroom came from a bedside lamp which cast a warm golden glow over the room. Kelly decided that she had packed enough clothes and lifted the case from the bed onto the floor. She felt stiff all over, her neck and shoulders in particular ached. She resolved to take a shower and have an early night.

She intended leaving early in the morning.

The day had been an exhausting one both mentally and physically and she felt the need to relax more than she usually did upon returning home in the evenings. She'd only half-eaten her dinner, washing it down with two or three Martinis. The effect of the drink was beginning to make her feel pleasantly drowsy. She unbuttoned her blouse, laying it over a chair before slipping out of her jeans and folding them carefully. Standing before the full length mirror on the wardrobe she unhooked her bra, her breasts remaining taut even when the garment was removed. Kelly skimmed off her panties and tossed them to one side, glancing at herself in the mirror. The reflection which stared back at her was a pleasing one.

Despite the fact that she was only five feet two inches tall, her slender frame gave her an appearance of striking elegance which was normally reserved for taller women. She had small but plump breasts, her lower body tapering in to form a tiny waist and smooth lean hips. Her legs were slim, usually appearing longer when she wore the high heels she favoured.

Kelly walked through into the bathroom and turned on the shower, stepping beneath its cleansing jets when it was at a suitable temperature. She stood motionless, allowing the water to run over her face, washing away what little make-up she used. She began soaping herself.

As she stood beneath the spray she allowed her mind to back-track to the events of earlier in the day. To Vernon.

Why was he protecting her? It didn't make sense. Unless, as Fraser had intimated, he *did* have something to hide. Vernon obviously saw Kelly as a useful tool.

As she closed her eyes, the vision of Maurice Grant, his eyes ripped from the sockets, flashed before her and she jerked her eyes open again.

She thought of his confession.

Had it been the drugs which had caused his outburst, she wondered? Instinct told her that there was more to it than that. And yet, how could he have killed his wife and son? She and three other people had seen him strapped down at the time the killings supposedly took place.

She stood beneath the shower a moment longer then flicked it off, dried herself and padded back into the bedroom. She sat on the edge of the bed and reached for the phone.

It was a recorded message, which suited her because she didn't feel much like talking. She scribbled down a few details as the metallic voice droned on then, finally, she replaced the receiver, glancing down at what she had written.

She would catch the 9.30 flight to Paris in the morning.

17

Paris

The restaurant in the Place de Wagram was crowded, more so than usual because many had sought shelter inside from the rain which was pelting down. Waiters threaded their way through the maze of tables balancing trays and plates precariously on their arms. A wine glass was dropped and shattered loudly on the wooden floor.

Lasalle spun round in his seat, startled by the sound. He

103

saw a waiter picking up the pieces of broken glass while a customer complained loudly.

'Did you hear me?'

The voice brought Lasalle back to his senses.

'What did you say?' he asked, blankly, turning back to face Joubert who was chewing hungrily on a piece of meat.

'I said, I don't like the idea of her working with us,' Joubert repeated.

'Come now, Alain, when these experiments first began it was agreed that there would be co-operation between the two Institutes. I don't understand your objections.'

'The experiments carried out in England have not been as successful as ours,' Joubert complained.

'How do you know that?' Lasalle asked, sipping at his wine.

His companion paused for a moment, swallowing the piece of food he'd been chewing.

'Because we'd have heard more,' he said, quickly.

Lasalle looked up and saw a familiar figure making her way back towards the table. He tapped Joubert's arm and motioned for him to be quiet but the other Frenchman merely muttered something under his breath.

Kelly sat down and smiled across the table at Lasalle. Joubert did not look up from his meal. She picked up her knife and fork and set about her salad once more.

She had arrived in Paris over three hours earlier and, after booking into a hotel, she had taken a taxi to the Metapsychic Centre. Once there she had introduced herself to the Director and asked if she could see Lasalle. The two investigators had been friends for some time and he was happy to allow her to work with him.

The reaction of Joubert could not have been more different. Upon hearing that Kelly was to assist them in their experiments he had barely been able to restrain his anger, managing only by a monumental effort of will to disguise his open dislike of her presence.

She had explained, briefly, what had happened with Maurice Grant and why she had been forced to come to France. Joubert had been unimpressed and, when she had asked to look at the notes which the two men had compiled, he had been openly hostile, guarding the files jealously. She wondered why he should have taken such a dislike to her.

'If you'd let me know you were coming,' said Lasalle, 'I could have made up the bed in my spare room. It would have saved you paying for a hotel.'

'I'm fine where I am thankyou,' Kelly assured him, smiling.

'When were you thinking of going back?' Joubert asked without looking up.

'Not for a while yet,' Kelly told him.

'What exactly do you think you can learn here?' Joubert continued, still not paying her the courtesy of a glance.

'It's not so much a case of learning,' Kelly began. 'I ...'

He cut her short, his dark eyes finally pinning her in a malevolent stare.

'Then what do you want here?' he hissed.

Kelly met his stare, her own anger now boiling up. Who the hell did Joubert think he was anyway? she thought.

'I told you why I came here,' she said. 'I couldn't carry on working at the Institute in England, not while the enquiry was being conducted. I thought I might be of some help to you.'

'Don't you think we're capable then?' he said, challengingly.

'Are you this rude to everyone or have *I* been singled out for that honour?' she said, angrily.

Joubert stopped eating and looked at her warily.

'Can't we all just finish our food in peace?' said Lasalle, looking at his two companions.

Joubert put down his knife and fork and wiped his mouth with a napkin.

'I've finished anyway,' he said. 'It's about time I went back to the Centre. There's a lot to do this afternoon.' He balled up his napkin and dropped it on to the table, getting to his feet. He looked down at Lasalle. 'I trust I'll see you later?'

Lasalle nodded.

'And no doubt you too, Miss Hunt,' Joubert added, scornfully. With that he pushed past some people who were waiting for a table and headed for the door. Lasalle watched him go.

'I must apologise for my colleague,' he said.

'I'm sorry if I've caused any trouble between the two of

105

you,' said Kelly.

'Joubert is a good man but, sometimes, he lets our work get to him.'

'I noticed,' Kelly told him, spearing a piece of tomato with her fork. 'Speaking of work, have you made much progress?'

'There is so much to discover,' said Lasalle. 'The unconscious mind is a vast area.' He took a sip of his wine. 'We did have some success three or four days ago. A subject named Décard. Whilst in a trance he was able to see the future.'

'Precognition?' she said, excitedly.

'But only while hypnotised. When he was brought out of the trance he could remember nothing of what he had seen.' The Frenchman paused. 'It was all rather unfortunate. He foretold the death of his own daughter.'

Kelly sat bolt upright, as if she had just been nudged with a cattle prod.

'I wasn't told about this,' she said.

Lasalle frowned.

'Joubert was supposed to have relayed the information to you.'

'I heard nothing,' Kelly assured him.

The Frenchman looked puzzled and a heavy silence descended momentarily.

Kelly wondered if she should mention the murder of Maurice Grant's family but she decided against it, content to let the thoughts and ideas tumble over inside her head.

'What I said about you staying with me,' Lasalle said. 'I hope you weren't offended by it.'

Kelly smiled.

'Of course not,' she said.

'I didn't mean anything by it but, since Madelaine died, the house has seemed ... bigger than it used to.' He smiled humourlessly.

'I understand,' Kelly told him. 'How are you managing on your own?'

'I get by,' he said, reaching inside his jacket for the bottle of tranquilizers. 'With a little help.' He held one of the capsules before him, swallowing it with some water.

Kelly studied his face, noticing how much he had changed since the last time she had seen him. His dark hair was streaked with patches of grey, particularly around his temples. Deep lines cut swathes across his forehead and around his eyes and his cheeks appeared bloodless. He had lost weight too she suspected. But, for all that his eyes retained a glint of passion and energy which seemed to have deserted the rest of his body.

'Probably if we had had children then it wouldn't have been so bad,' he said. 'As it is, there is no one else left for me.' He gazed at his wine glass for a moment longer then seemed to shake off the cloak of melancholy. A smile spread across his face. 'Enough of this,' he said. 'How are you, Kelly? Have you any plans to marry?'

She looked at him aghast.

'Definitely not,' she said.

'You mean there is no man waiting to sweep you off your feet?' He chuckled.

'If there is he's keeping himself well hidden,' Kelly replied.

Lasalle laughed, an infectious sound which cut through the babble in the restaurant and caused a couple of heads to turn.

Her tone changed slightly.

'Michel, about this man who had the precognitive vision. Décard you say his name was?'

Lasalle nodded.

'What exactly did he see?'

The Frenchman told her.

'And was Joubert present when this happened?' Kelly asked.

'Yes, he seemed quite excited by it all.'

Kelly brushed a hand through her hair, stroking the back of it with her palm. Why hadn't Joubert told her about the incident? Why the secrecy? When the two Institutes were supposed to be working together it seemed only natural that information as important as that should be available.

She wondered what else the Frenchman had neglected to tell her.

Lasalle looked at his watch.

'I suppose we should be getting back,' he said.

Kelly got to her feet and the two of them made their way towards the exit. Outside it was still raining, the banks of dark cloud overhead showing no promise of respite.

As they ran towards Lasalle's car, Kelly wondered if

Joubert's attitude might change as the afternoon wore on.

Somehow she doubted it.

18

Using a small wooden spatula Lasalle gently applied the sticky conductant to three places on Joubert's face. One at each temple and another just above the bridge of his nose.

Kelly attached the electrodes carefully and Joubert himself re-adjusted them, lifting his head slightly as Lasalle pressed the last two against the back of his head.

That done, Joubert lay back on the couch, hands clasped across his chest. The Frenchman lay motionless, his eyes peering at some point on the ceiling. Lasalle reached for his hand. He fumbled along the wrist and located the pulse which he took and noted on a clipboard. Then, like a doctor examining a patient, he took a penlight from his pocket and shone it in his companion's eyes, checking the pupillary reactions.

'Ready?' he asked.

Joubert nodded gently.

Lasalle turned to Kelly who flicked a switch on the EEG and, immediately, the five tracers began to move back and forth gently across the paper.

The Frenchman reached into his pocket and pulled out the pocket watch. He dangled it before Joubert, the golden time-piece twisting round slowly.

'Now, keep your eyes on the watch,' he said, seeing that his colleague's gaze had drifted to the spinning object. Lasalle began rolling the chain between his thumb and index finger.

'You can hear only my voice,' he said. Then, to Kelly:

'Turn off the lights will you?'

She left the EEG and scuttled across to the light switch, flicking it off. The room was immersed in darkness, lit only by a spot-lamp near the foot of the couch. The single beam occasionally glinted on the watch making it look as if it were glowing.

'You can see nothing but the watch,' said Lasalle. 'You can hear nothing but my voice. Do you understand?'

'Yes,' said Joubert, throatily.

'I am going to count to five and, as I do, you will become increasingly more tired. Do you understand?'

'Yes.'

'By the time I reach five you will be asleep but you will still be able to hear me. Do you understand?'

'Yes.'

Kelly moved slowly and quietly back towards the EEG, glancing down at the read-out. The lines made by the tracers were still relatively level. None showed too much movement. Just a gentle sweep back and forth.

Lasalle began counting.

He saw his companion's eyelids begin to droop but he kept spinning the watch even after Joubert had finally closed his eyes.

Kelly looked on with interest.

'You are now in a deep sleep,' said Lasalle. 'But, you are able to hear everything I say. Do you understand?'

'Yes.'

'What is your name?'

'Alain Joubert.'

'How old are you?'

'Thirty-six.'

Kelly glanced at the EEG read-out once again, noticing that the five tracers had begun to slow their movements until they were practically running in straight lines, only the occasional movement interrupting their unerring course.

'What is *my* name?' Lasalle asked.

Joubert told him.

'Can you tell me if there is anyone else present in the room?'

'A woman. I can see her.'

Lasalle frowned and inspected his colleague's eyelids more closely. They were firmly shut. He reached back to the trolley behind him and picked up a stack of cards, each bearing a word.

'Tell me what this word is,' he said, running his eyes over

the card marked DOG.

Joubert told him.

'And this one?'

'Cat.'

'Again.'

'Pig.'

Kelly noticed some slight movement from the fifth of the tracers.

Lasalle went through another ten cards and each time Joubert was correct.

'I feel cold,' Joubert said, unasked. Indeed, his body was quivering slightly and, when Lasalle gripped his hand the flesh was ice cold.

The movement from the fifth tracer became more pronounced. The other four, however, did not deviate from their almost arrow-straight course. Kelly swallowed hard. There was something distinctly familiar about this type of read-out. The vision of Maurice Grant flashed into her mind as the fifth tracer began to trace a jerky, erratic path on the paper. Whilst in a drugged, subdued state, it had been the same area of Grant's brain which had shown activity. Now it was happening with Joubert.

'I can see ...' Joubert words trailed away.

'What can you see?' Lasalle asked him, urgently.

'A room. Like this one but there is a woman working in it. She's sitting at a typewriter with her back to me,' Joubert said. 'She doesn't know I'm behind her, she didn't hear me open the door.'

Kelly saw that the fifth tracer was now hurtling back and forth with such speed it threatened to carve a hole in the paper.

'Who is this woman?' Lasalle asked. 'Do you know her?'

'Yes, I've seen her many times before.'

'What is her name?'

'Danielle Bouchard.'

Lasalle swallowed hard.

'Describe her,' he snapped. 'Now.'

'She is in her thirties, long, curly hair. It's auburn, dyed I think. Her skin is dark, not negroid but coffee-coloured. She's wearing blue eye make-up, some lipstick.'

'Do you know her?' whispered Kelly to Lasalle.

110

The Frenchman nodded.

'She's part Algerian, a beautiful girl, she works in an office just down the corridor,' he said, quietly, one eye on Joubert who was now flexing his fingers spasmodically. In fact, his whole body was jerking involuntarily.

'What sort of response is showing on the EEG?' asked Lasalle.

'There's no activity in any part of the brain except for the area around the occipital lobe,' she told him. 'Exactly the same as the subject we had.' She paused, mesmerised by the rapid movements of the tracer.

Joubert spoke again.

'She is wearing jeans, a red top. There is a slight tear near the seam of the top, beneath her arm.'

'Is she still typing?' asked Lasalle.

'Yes, she hasn't noticed me yet.'

Lasalle chewed his bottom lip contemplatively.

'This doesn't prove anything,' he said to Kelly. 'Joubert could have seen this woman earlier today.'

Kelly looked once more at the EEG read-out. The fifth tracer continued its rapid movement.

'I'm walking towards her,' Joubert said. 'She has stopped typing now, she is taking the paper from the machine. She still has her back to me.' He was silent for a moment then the tone of his voice seemed to change, it became harsher, as if his mouth were full of phlegm. 'I want her.'

'Tell me what is happening,' Lasalle ordered.

'I grab her hair with one hand and put my other hand over her mouth to stop her screaming. She falls off the chair and I climb on top of her, I must hold her arms down. She is stunned by the fall, she has banged her head. I think she is dazed. I pull up her top to reach her breasts and I am squeezing them, making red marks on them.'

Kelly looked in awe at the fifth tracer which was moving so fast it was little more than a blur.

'I try to keep my hand over her mouth to stop her screaming but she seems to be recovering. I must stop her. I am putting my hands around her throat. It feels so good, my thumbs are on her windpipe, pressing harder. Her eyes are bulging. I am going to kill her. I want to kill her.'

Kelly looked at Lasalle then back at the EEG with its

wildly careering tracer.

'I WANT TO KILL HER,' bellowed Joubert.

There was a loud scream from outside the room, long and piercing. A moment's silence and it was followed by another.

'Bring him out of it,' snapped Kelly.

'Listen to me,' said Lasalle. 'When I count to one from five you will wake up. Do you understand?'

No answer.

From down the corridor there was the sound of a slamming door then another scream.

'Do you understand?' Lasalle said, loudly.

'Hurry,' Kelly urged.

Joubert did not respond.

'I can't bring him out of it,' Lasalle said, frantically.

He thought about shaking his colleague but he knew it would do no good. He swallowed hard and looked at Kelly who was already moving towards the door. 'See what's happening,' Lasalle told her.

Kelly hurried out into the corridor and saw that, about thirty yards further down, there were four or five people standing outside one of the doors. A tall man with blond hair was banging on it, twisting the handle impotently. He put his shoulder to it as he heard another scream from inside.

'Joubert, listen to me,' said Lasalle. 'I'm going to begin counting. Five ...'

'There's something happening,' Kelly told him.

'Four ...'

The tall blond man was taking a step back to gain more impetus as he tried to shoulder charge the door of the other room.

'Three ...'

Joubert stirred slightly.

'Two ...'

Down the corridor, the blond man gritted his teeth and prepared for one final assault on the locked door.

'One ...'

Joubert opened his eyes and blinked myopically.

He too looked round as he heard the shriek of splintering wood. The blond man crashed into the door, nearly ripping it from its hinges. It slammed back against the wall and he stumbled into the room, followed by the others who had waited.

'What's happening?' asked Joubert, pulling the electrodes from his head.

Kelly walked back into the room, a look of concern on her face. She switched off the EEG and pulled the read-out clear.

'What's going on?' Joubert demanded, getting to his feet. He crossed to the door and looked out in time to see the blond man supporting a dusky skinned girl in jeans and a red top from a room further down the corridor. Even from where he stood, Joubert could see that her top was torn, part of one breast exposed. The girl was bleeding from a gash on her bottom lip and there were several angry red marks around her throat.

Lasalle and Kelly joined him in the corridor as the others approached them.

'What happened?' asked Lasalle.

'Danielle was attacked,' the blond man told him.

'Who by?' Lasalle wanted to know.

As he spoke, the dark-skinned girl lifted her head, brushing her auburn hair from her eyes. She looked at Joubert and screamed, one accusing finger pointing at him. With her other hand she touched her throat.

The girl babbled something in French which Kelly did not understand. She asked Lasalle to translate.

'She said that it was Joubert who attacked her,' the Frenchman said.

'That's impossible,' Joubert snorted, indignantly. 'Anyway, why would I do such a thing?' He looked at Danielle. 'She's hysterical.'

'Well,' said the blond man. 'Someone attacked her. She didn't make these marks herself.' He indicated the angry welts on the girl's neck. 'But I don't see how he got out. The door was locked from the inside.'

Lasalle and Kelly exchanged puzzled glances as the little procession moved past them, heading for the infirmary on the second floor. Danielle looked around, her eyes filled with fear as she gazed at Joubert.

'How could I have attached her?' he said, irritably, walking back into the room and sitting on the couch.

Kelly and Lasalle followed him.

'Can you remember anything of the last five or ten minutes?' Lasalle asked him.

Joubert shook his head, wiping his forehead with the back of his hand.

Kelly was the first to spot it.

'Joubert,' she said, quietly. 'Look at your nails.'

Beneath the finger nails of both hands were numerous tiny pieces of red cloth.

Exactly the same colour as the blouse worn by Danielle Bouchard. There were also several auburn hairs.

19

'Astral travel.'

Kelly's words echoed around the laboratory.

She looked at the pieces of cloth and hair which Joubert had scraped from beneath his fingernails and deposited in a Petri dish.

'You said you felt cold, just before it all began to happen,' she continued. 'That feeling of coldness is usually associated with Astral projection.'

'An Out of the Body Experience?' said Joubert, incredulously.

'Danielle Bouchard said she was attacked by you. I think she was right. You described her, you described how you tried to strangle her.' She held up the EEG read-out. 'There was a tremendous amount of activity in the occipital area of your brain at that time. That's exactly what happened with Maurice Grant.'

'But it isn't usual for the Astral body, once projected, to appear in tangible form,' Joubert countered. 'Danielle Bouchard doesn't just say she saw me, she says I touched her. Injured her.'

'Have you ever felt any feelings of anger or antagonism towards her?' Kelly asked.

'Not that I've been aware of,' Joubert told her.

'But, *subconsciously*, you may harbour some feelings such as those, for her. The hypnosis released those feelings, just as the drugs unlocked the violent side of Maurice Grant.'

'I don't understand what this has to do with the Astral body,' Lasalle interjected.

'The EEG read-outs seem to point to the fact that the area which controls the subconscious is housed in the occipital lobe,' Kelly said. 'The Astral body is controlled by the subconscious. It functions independently of the rest of the mind. That hidden area we've been looking for, this is it.' She jabbed the read-out with her index finger, indicating the fifth line.

'The subconscious mind controls the Astral body,' Joubert repeated, quietly.

'It looks that way,' Kelly said. 'You performed an act, while in the Astral state, which you could not have carried out while conscious.'

'Are you saying that the Astral body is the evil side of man?' said Lasalle. 'The violent, cruel part of us.'

'It's possible. And hypnosis or drugs can release that other identity,' she told him.

'The other identity knows nothing of right or wrong,' Joubert said. 'It's identical in appearance but not hampered by conscience, remorse or delusions of morality. A being which is completely free of the ethical restraints imposed upon it by society.'

Kelly caught the slight gleam in his eye.

'The Mr Hyde in all of us,' he said.

'What?' Lasalle asked, puzzled.

'Jekyll and Hyde. One side good, one side evil. The conscious mind is Jekyll, the unconscious is Hyde only it may be possible for that evil side to function independently of its host.'

'Think how this discovery will help the treatment of schizophrenia and other mental disorders,' Kelly said.

'But no one is to know of it yet,' Joubert snapped.

'Why?' Lasalle wanted to know. 'It is important, as Kelly says. People ...'

Joubert cut him short.

'It's too early to reveal our findings,' he rasped.

There was a long silence, finally broken by Lasalle.

'Kelly,' he began. 'How do we know that everyone, every man, woman and child, doesn't possess this inner force of evil?'

'I think it's safe to assume they do,' she said, cryptically. 'Only as far as we know, it can only be released by using drugs or hypnosis.'

'As far as we know,' he repeated, his words hanging ominously in the air.

Kelly looked at the dish full of hair and fabric and shuddered.

20

The clock on the wall above him struck one and Lasalle sat back, rubbing his eyes. He checked the time against his own watch and yawned.

He'd been hard at work since seven o'clock that evening, since returning from the Metapsychic Centre. Before him on the polished wood desk lay a 6000 word article which he had been slaving over for the past six hours. He'd stopped only once for a cup of coffee and a sandwich at about 9.30 but most of the sandwich lay uneaten on the plate beside the typewriter. He looked up and found himself caught in the gaze of a woman with flowing blonde hair whose crisp green eyes he seemed to drown in.

The photo of his wife stood in its familiar place on his desk at home. Each time he looked at it he felt the contradictory feelings which had plagued him ever since her death. To look at her brought back all the agony which he had suffered when she'd been taken from him so suddenly, but he also found comfort in those green eyes — as if a part of her lived on and remained with him. He reached for the photo and studied her finely-shaped features. He, himself had taken the picture three years earlier. It was all that remained of her. That and the memories.

He replaced the photo and shook his head, trying to dispel the drowsiness which was creeping over him like a blanket. He knew that he must go to bed soon but there was just one more thing left to do.

He picked up his pen, pulled the writing paper towards him and began writing:

To the Editor,

You will find enclosed an article which contains details of a discovery as important as it is fascinating. Having worked at the Metapsychic Centre in Paris for the past twelve years I have encountered many strange phenomena but nothing of this nature has ever presented itself to me until now.

I realize that the subject of Astral Travel/Projection etc. is one which has fascinated people for many years but never before have facts been so far reaching in their importance as in the case I have recounted in my article.

I hope that you will see fit to publish this article as I feel it has far-reaching implications for all of us.

Yours sincerely,

Lasalle signed it, re-read it then pushed it into the envelope with the article. He sealed it and left it on the desk, deciding to post it in the morning on his way to the centre.

He wandered into the kitchen and poured himself a glass of milk, standing at the sink while he drank it.

What they had discovered that afternoon was far too important to withhold. Besides, Lasalle felt unaccountably ill at ease. The incident with Danielle Bouchard had worried him. Even as he thought about it he felt the hairs on the back of his neck rise slightly.

Others had a right to know the truth.

Whether Joubert liked it or not.

21

New York

Blake picked up a copy of *Time* then decided to wander across to the paperbacks to see if there was anything to pass the time on the flight home. He ran his eyes swiftly over the magazine shelves once more before turning to the books.

He could have been forgiven for not noticing the slim volume.

The cover bore the title: *Journal of Parapsychology*.

Blake reached for it, one of the cover stories catching his eye: *Astral Projection: The Truth*. He flipped open the magazine, found the table of contents and traced the article he sought.

He read the first three paragraphs standing there then he paid for the magazine and left the airport newsstand.

The voice of the flight controller told him that he should go through to the departure gate. Blake hurried to the washroom.

He had flown many times before but he still felt the same twinge of nerves each time. Nerves? Who was he trying to kid? Flying scared him shitless, it was as simple as that. Already his stomach was beginning to turn gentle somersaults. He found that he was alone in the room. He crossed to a sink and filled it with cold water, laying his magazines on one side.

He splashed his face with water, wiping off the excess with his hands when he could find no towel. Blake straightened up and gazed at his reflection in the mirror. He looked pale, his eyes red-rimmed and as he glanced at his watch he saw that his hand was shaking slightly. He had ten minutes before his flight left. He scooped more water into his hands and onto his face, blinking as it stung his eyes. Blake peered into the mirror again.

The image of Mathias stared back at him.

Blake retreated a step, his eyes fixed on the vision in the mirror. The face of the psychic was immobile, only the eyes moved, those brilliant blue orbs pinning him in that hypnotic stare.

The writer tried to swallow but found that his throat was constricted. He raised both hands to cover his eyes.

He lowered them again slowly, peering into the mirror once more.

The image of Mathias was gone, only his own distraught face was reflected in the glass. Blake let out a relieved gasp and wiped the excess moisture from his face as he moved back to the sink. He peered down into the water.

This time it was his own reflection but the mouth was open in a silent scream, the eyes bulging wide in their sockets. The entire countenance was appallingly bloated and tinged blue.

'No,' rasped Blake and plunged his hands into the sink.

The apparition vanished and he stood there, immersed up to his elbows in water.

Indeed, the two men who walked into the washroom looked at him in bewilderment as he stood motionless, gazing into the sink, as if waiting for the screaming vision to re-appear.

'Hey, fella, are you OK?' one of the men asked, moving cautiously towards Blake.

He tapped the writer on the shoulder.

'I said ...'

Blake spun round suddenly, his expression blank. He looked like a man who had been woken from a nightmare.

'Are you feeling OK?' the man asked him again.

Blake closed his eyes tightly for a moment and nodded.

'Yes,' he said. 'I'm all right.' Then, fumbling for his dark glasses he put them on, snatched up his magazines and left the washroom.

'Probably freaked out,' said the first man.

'Yeah, he looks like a goddam pot-head.'

'And would you believe that?' the first man said, pointing at the mirror above the sink where Blake had been standing.

Five jagged cracks criss-crossed the glass.

22

It sounded as if someone were trying to pound a hole in the door.

Lasalle hurried from the kitchen, leaving his dinner on the table. The banging continued, loud and insistent. He turned the handle and opened it.

Joubert barged past him, his features set in an attitude of anger.

For a moment Lasalle was bewildered but he closed the door and followed his colleague through into the sitting room where he stood, splay-legged, in front of the open fire-place. He was gripping something in his right fist. A thin film of perspiration sheathed his face, the veins at his temples throbbing angrily.

'What's wrong?' asked Lasalle. 'It must be important for you to come barging into my house like this.'

'It *is* important,' rasped Joubert.

'Couldn't it have waited until tomorrow?' Lasalle said, a note of irritation in his own voice. He glanced at his watch. 'It is seven o'clock.'

'I know what time it is,' Joubert snapped.

'So what do you want?'

'I want to talk about *this*.' Joubert brandished the object in his right hand like a weapon for a moment before slamming it down on the coffee table nearby. 'What the hell do you mean by it?'

The copy of the *Journal of Parapsychology* lay before him on the table, bent open at the article written by Lasalle.

'What the hell did you hope to achieve by writing this ... garbage?' Joubert demanded.

'I felt that the discovery was too important to be hidden away,' Lasalle explained.

'It was my ...' He quickly qualified his words. 'It was *our* discovery. We agreed not to share it with anyone until the research was fully completed.'

'No we didn't. *You* decided that you wanted it kept secret,' Lasalle reminded him. 'I felt that other people had a right to know what happened.'

'So you took it upon yourself to write this article? And your ... friend. Does she know about it?'

'Kelly? No. She didn't know that I intended writing the article.' He paused for a moment. 'And even if she did, I don't see that any of this is your business. I am not answerable to you, Alain.'

'If news of this spreads we'll have the press swarming all over the Centre. Is that what you want?'

'Our discoveries on Astral projection are some of the most important ever made. Not just for our own profession but for others too. Many will benefit from our work. Hospitals, psychiatric institutions ...'

Joubert cut him short.

'And who will be credited with the discovery?' he asked, eyeing his colleague malevolently.

'Both of us of course. We ...'

Joubert interrupted again.

'No. Not both of us. *You.*' He pointed at Lasalle. 'You wrote the article.'

'But I mentioned your name, how we worked together.'

'That doesn't matter, it's you who will take the credit.' He picked up the magazine. 'What did they pay you for this?' he asked, scornfully.

'Ten thousand francs. Why?'

Joubert shook his head.

'They bought weeks of work for ten thousand francs!'

'The money isn't important,' said Lasalle.

'And the recognition?' Joubert wanted to know. 'Will you want that? Will you be able to cope with that?' His voice took on a sneering, superior tone. 'Still, you have your little tablets to help you.'

'Get out of here, Alain,' Lasalle snapped. 'Get out of my house.'

Joubert stuffed the magazine into his pocket and, with one last scornful glance at his colleague, he headed for the front door. Lasalle heard it slam behind him as he left.

Joubert brought the Fiat to a halt outside his house and switched off the engine. He closed his eyes for a moment, sitting in the shell-like confines of the vehicle, almost reluctant to leave it. He let out a long, almost painful breath and banged the steering wheel angrily. Damn Lasalle, he thought. He glanced down at the magazine which was on the passenger seat. It lay there as if taunting him and he snatched it up and pushed open the car door, locking it behind him.

As he reached the bottom of his path he heard the phone ringing inside his house. The Frenchman didn't hurry himself. He found his front door key and unlocked the door, glancing down at the phone on the hall table as he entered. It continued to ring but he hung up his jacket before finally lifting the receiver.

'Hello,' he said, wearily.

'Joubert? About time.'

He recognised the voice immediately.

'Dr Vernon, what do you want?' he asked.

'I want to know what's going on.'

'I don't know what you're talking about.'

'Let me read you something then.' There was a slight pause and Joubert heard the rustling of paper at the other end of the phone:

' "*The discovery of this form of Astral projection is the culmination of many weeks of work and many years of study,*" ' Vernon quoted.

'Lasalle's article,' said Joubert.

'You were supposed to report any findings directly to me and now I read this plastered all over the magazine. What do you think you're playing at?'

'Don't lecture me, Vernon. That article was nothing to do with me. Perhaps you should ask the girl who works for you what she knows about it,' the Frenchman hissed.

'Who are you talking about?' Vernon wanted to know.

'Kelly Hunt. She's here. She's been with us for a week or more.'

There was a shocked silence, interrupted only by the occasional hiss of static.

'Vernon.'

'Yes.'

'I said she's been with us for more than a week,' Joubert hissed.

'I had no idea where she was,' Vernon said, irritably. 'I gave her some time off while the enquiry took place here. I didn't know she was going to work with you.'

'Well, she knows everything. You won't be able to hide anything from her any longer, Vernon.'

The Institute Director sighed.

'Anyway, that's your problem. I have my own with Lasalle,' Joubert continued.

'We cannot afford any more disclosures similar to the one in this magazine,' Vernon said, cryptically. 'As it is, this might alter our plans slightly.'

'You take care of the girl. I'll handle Lasalle. And I tell you this, Vernon, there will be no more disclosures. I will see to that.' He hung up and wiped his hands on his trousers. 'No more.'

There was a malevolent determination in his voice.

23

London

As the 747 touched down, Blake breathed his customary sigh of relief. The plane slowed down and he allowed himself a glance out of the window. Heathrow was covered by a film of drizzle which undulated and writhed like a living thing. The writer had tried to sleep on the flight back but had been constantly interrupted by the woman next to him who insisted that he should 'look at the wonderful view'. Blake had made the fatal error of telling her that he wrote books about the paranormal and had been regaled by her tales of tea-leaf reading and contacts with the spirit world. She had, she assured him, been blessed with this gift of second sight as compensation for the death of her smallest child five years earlier and the subsequent departure of her husband with another woman. Blake had nodded politely and smiled a lot during the verbal barrage, as was his habit. She had apologised for not having read any of his books but promised she would. Blake had smiled even more broadly at that point. He wondered if it was a general thing with writers, that anyone they spoke to immediately swore they would rush out and buy every book that writer had written.

Despite the distractions he had managed to snatch an hour or so of sleep but it had been troubled and he had woken, it seemed, every ten minutes.

At one point he had jerked bolt upright in his seat, his body bathed in sweat, the last vestiges of a nightmare fading from his mind. The plane had crashed into the sea but he had survived the impact only to be drowned in the wreckage.

Now, as the plane came to a halt he got to his feet and stretched, trying to banish some of the stiffness from his joints. He checked his watch and noticed that he'd forgotten to adjust it according to the time difference. The clock on the plane showed 6.07 p.m.

After Blake had recovered his baggage he made his way through the terminal to the waiting taxis outside.

The drive took longer than he'd expected but, as the vehicle drew closer to his home he shook off some of his tiredness.

'Where do you want to get out?' the driver asked.

Blake directed him.

'Nice gaff,' said the driver, admiring Blake's house. 'Must have cost a fair old screw, eh?'

The man was obviously fishing for a tip and Blake didn't disappoint him. He gave him fifteen pounds and told him to keep the change.

'A reasonable screw,' he said as he walked away from the cab, suitcase in hand.

His house was set back from the road and was surrounded by a sufficient expanse of garden to protect him from the neighbours on either side. A privet hedge, which needed trimming, fronted the property and waist-high wooden fencing formed a perimeter elsewhere. There was also a garage built onto one side of the building. It housed a second-hand Jaguar XJS which he'd bought from a friend

124

three years earlier.

As Blake made his way up the short path he fumbled for his front door key and inserted it in the lock. The door opened, and the familiar cloying scent of paint greeted him. He'd had the place redecorated prior to leaving for the States and the aroma hung thickly in the air. Blake flicked on the hall light and the porch light. He smiled to himself. When his porch light was on it always reminded him of running up the Standard at Buckingham Palace. It was his mark that *he* was now in residence.

He stepped over two weeks worth of mail which lay on the mat, closed the front door behind him then scooped it up. There were circulars, four or five letters (most of which he could identify by their postmarks) and a couple of bills. The writer dropped his suitcase in the hall deciding that he would unpack later. Right now all he wanted was to pour himself a drink and flop down in a chair.

He passed into the sitting room, pulling off his shirt as he did so. It was warm in the room despite the fact that it had been empty for a fortnight. He drew back the curtains and the dull twilight dragged itself into the room. Blake switched on the lamp which perched on top of the TV. He poured himself a large measure of brandy, topped it up with soda and took a hefty gulp, then he selected a record from his massive collection, dropped it on to the turntable and switched on the Hi-Fi. While Elton John warbled away in the background, Blake skimmed through his mail. The bills he noted and then stuck in a bulldog clip on the shelf near the fire-place, the circulars he balled up and tossed into the nearby bin. Then he opened his letters. There was one from his accountant, one from a group calling itself 'The Literary Co-operative' (a bunch of struggling local writers to whom Blake had spoken before) and what looked like a couple of fan letters. Blake was always happy to receive mail from the public and he read them both with delight.

He finished his drink, re-filled his glass and wandered into the kitchen. Peering out of the back window he saw several lumps of dark matter on his patio.

'Cat shit,' he muttered, irritably. 'I'll buy a cork for that bloody thing.' He was referring to the overfed Manx cat which belonged to the family next door. It had taken to using his garden as a toilet whenever it could and, obviously, while he'd been away, had taken full advantage and dotted its calling cards about in abundance.

The writer opened his freezer and took out a pizza which he stuck under the grill. He didn't feel particularly hungry and, being basically lazy anyway, frozen food was heaven sent for his purposes. He left the pizza beneath the glow of the grill and returned to the sitting room.

It was large but comfortable and 'lived in' like the rest of the house. On the walls, framed carefully, were a number of film posters. *Taxi Driver* hung near the hall door whilst the wall nearest the kitchen bore an American print of *The Wild Bunch*. Beside it was *Halloween*.

But, pride of place went to a yellowed poster which hung over the fire-place. It was *Psycho*, and it bore Hitchcock's signature. Blake had been given it as a gift from a friend in the film business last time he had visited L.A.

The writer was not a man to overindulge in luxuries but, when he did, three things occupied him more than most. Films, books and music. His bookcase bulged, not with learned tomes and priceless first editions but with pulp creations. He read for entertainment, nothing more. Alongside the books, each one in its individual case, were video cassettes of his favourite films. Up to 300 in all.

His study, however, was a different matter.

Blake had been pleased, when he had bought the house, to discover that it not only possessed an attic but also a double cellar which ran beneath the entire building. He had converted the subterranean room into his study. Every day he retreated down the steps to work, free of the noises and distractions of everyday life.

Buried beneath the ground as it was, it reminded him of working in a giant coffin.

He kept the door locked at all times. The cellar was his private domain and his alone.

The smell of pizza began to waft from the kitchen. He ate it from the foil wrapper, saving himself any washing up. Then, still clutching his glass, he headed through the sitting room into the hall where he unlocked his case.

His notes were on top and Blake lifted them out carefully, hefting them before him. They had a satisfying heavy feel.

The fruits of so much research. The hard part was almost over. Another week or so of note-taking and preparation and he could get down to the serious business of writing.

As it was, there was one more thing he had to do.

Blake opened the cellar door, peering down into the blackness below. He smiled broadly to himself and flicked on the light.

'Welcome home,' he murmured and walked in.

Before he descended the steps he was careful to lock the cellar door behind him.

The silence greeted him like an old friend.

24

New York

Across the untarnished brilliance of the azure blue sky the only blemish was the thin vapour trail left by a solitary aircraft.

There wasn't a cloud in the sky. The sun, even so early in the morning, was a shimmering core of radiance throwing out its burning rays to blanket the city in a cocoon of heat.

The heavens did not weep for Rick Landers but there were others who did.

There were a handful of people at the graveside as the small coffin was lowered into the hole. Toni Landers herself stood immobile, eyes fixed on the wooden casket as it slowly disappeared from view. The only part of her which moved was her eyes and, from those red-rimmed, blood-shot orbs, tears pumped freely, coursing down her cheeks and occasionally dripping on to her black gloved hands. There was a photograph of Rick on the marble headstone but she could not bring herself to look at it. Every now and then, the rays of sunlight would glint on the marble and Toni would squeeze her eyes tightly together but, each time she did so, the vision of Rick flashed into her mind — memories of that day a week or more earlier when she had been forced to identify his remains. She had gazed on the mangled body of her child, stared at the face so badly pulped that the bottom jaw had been ground to splinters. The skull had been shattered in four or five places so that portions of the brain actually bulged through the rents. One eye had been almost forced from its socket. The head was almost severed.

It would have taken a magician not a mortician to restore some semblance of normality to a body so badly smashed.

Toni sucked in a breath, the memory still too painful for her. She shuffled uncomfortably where she stood and the two people on either side of her moved closer, fearing that she was going to faint. But the moment passed and she returned her attention to the gaping grave which had just swallowed up her dead child. The priest was speaking but Toni did not hear what he said. She had a handkerchief in her handbag yet she refused to wipe the tears away, allowing the salty droplets to soak her face and gloves.

Against the explosion of colours formed by countless wreaths and bouquets the dozen or so mourners looked curiously out of place in their sombre apparel.

Toni had deliberately kept the number of mourners to a minimum. She had phoned Rick's father in L.A. and told him but he had not condescended to put in an appearance. Amidst her grief, Toni had found room for a little hatred too. But now as she watched the ribbons which supported the coffin being pulled clear she felt a cold hand clutch her heart, as if the appalling finality of what she was witnessing had suddenly registered. Her son was gone forever and that thought brought fresh floods of tears from the seemingly inexhaustible reservoir of her pain.

This time her knees buckled slightly and her two companions moved to support her.

One of them, Maggie Straker, her co-star in her last film, slipped an arm around Toni's waist and held her upright. She could hear the other woman whimpering softly, repeating Rick's name over and over again as if it were a litany.

It was Maggie who first noticed that there was a newcomer amongst them.

The grave stood on a slight rise so his approach had been masked by the mourners on the far side of the grave.

Jonathan Mathias stood alone, a gigantic wreath of white roses held in his hand. He looked down at the final resting place of Rick Landers then across at Toni.

She saw him and abruptly stopped sobbing.

Mathias laid the floral tribute near the headstone, glancing at the photograph of Rick as he did so. He straightened up, listening as the priest finished what he was saying. He paused for a moment then asked those gathered to join him in reciting the Lord's Prayer.

Mathias stood by silently.

When the ritual was complete the mourners slowly moved away, back down the slight slope towards the black limousines which stood glinting in the sunlight like so many predatory insects. They too looked alien and intrusive amidst the green grass of the cemetery.

Mathias did not move, he stood at the head of the grave, gazing down into its depths at the small wooden casket. And it was towards him that Toni Landers now made her way, shaking loose of Maggie's supportive arm.

'I hope I'm not intruding,' the psychic said, softly.

'I'm glad you came,' Toni told him. She glanced down at the wreath he'd brought. 'Thank you.'

Maggie Straker approached cautiously.

'Toni, do you want me to wait I ...'

'It's OK, Maggie.'

The other woman nodded, smiled politely at Mathias then made her way down the slope behind the other mourners. Toni and the psychic stood alone by the grave.

'What will you do now?' he asked her. 'What are your plans?'

She sniffed.

'I'm going to spend some time in England with friends,' Toni informed him. 'I can't bear to be around here. Not now.' She wiped some of the moisture from her cheeks with a handkerchief which Mathias handed her. Toni turned the linen square over in her hands.

'You knew he was going to die didn't you?' she said, without looking at him.

'Yes,' Mathias told her.

'Why didn't you tell me?'

'It wouldn't have made any difference. There was nothing

129

you could have done about it.'

'Was there anything *you* could have done about it?'

'I wish there had been.'

He took her hand and, together, they made their way down the slope towards the waiting cars. But Toni hesitated momentarily, looking back over her shoulder towards the grave.

Towards her son.

It was over.

He was gone.

All that remained now were the memories.

She felt more tears streaming down her cheeks and Mathias put his arm around her shoulder, leading her away. She felt a strength and power in that arm and, as she looked up at him, a thought entered her mind. She looked back once more towards the grave of her son but this time there were no more tears.

A slight smile flickered briefly at the corners of her mouth.

Again she looked at Mathias.

25

Oxford

The smell of menthol was strong in the air.

Dr Vernon made loud sucking sounds as he devoured another of the cough sweets. The office smelt more like a pharmacy now.

Kelly crossed her legs, slipping one shoe off, dangling it by her toes as she waited for Vernon to finish reading the report.

It was her first day back at the Institute since she had returned from France barely thirty-six hours ago. In many ways she had been happy to return. The relationship between Joubert and Lasalle had deteriorated seriously since the appearance of the latter's article. The atmosphere had not been a pleasant one to work in and Kelly had decided that it was time to leave them to it. Armed with what she had learnt in France she was more confident about her own research, enjoying a newly-found enthusiasm which came only with a measure of success. However, she was worried about Lasalle. During the past week she had seen him wilt visibly beneath the open hostility displayed by Joubert. Loathe to intervene, Kelly had been a helpless spectator at their confrontations, each more vehement than before. She found it difficult to understand how so many years of friendship could, for Joubert, have been ruined so quickly and for what seemed a relatively minor aberration on Lasalle's part.

But, the question had plagued her for a while.

Kelly could still not understand why he had reacted so violently to Lasalle's article. People *did* have a right to know the facts, there was no disputing that. Joubert seemed not to agree. Despite her desire to return to England, Kelly had been somewhat reluctant about leaving Lasalle having seen his psychological deterioration over the past seven or eight days. The tranquilizers seemed to be of little help to him, despite the fact that he had upped the dosage from 45mg to 75mg a day. He was in a perpetual daze, a condition doubtless helped by the effect of the drugs. Kelly had felt something akin to pity for him. She hoped he wasn't becoming unbalanced again.

Nevertheless, she had decided to leave the Metapsychic Centre and had arrived home at around noon nearly two days ago.

Vernon's call had come within one hour of her return.

It was as if somehow he had been watching her, waiting for the right moment before calling.

She had not been surprised by the call itself, only by the urgency in the Institute Director's voice as he had asked her to return to work as soon as possible and to present him with a full report on what she had witnessed while working at the Metapsychic Centre.

Not until she had replaced the receiver did she begin to wonder how Vernon had known of her whereabouts.

She had certainly not mentioned her intentions when she left the Institute two weeks earlier.

Now, she sat impatiently, watching him as he leafed through her report. Kelly wondered if she should say something to him. Ask him how he knew where she had been? She bit her tongue for the time being.

There was probably a perfectly reasonable explanation, she told herself, although she wasn't altogether convinced.

She administered a swift mental rebuke. She was allowing her imagination to run away with her. She was becoming paranoid.

Wasn't she?

'Presumably you've noted everything which took place at the Metapsychic Centre during your time there?' Vernon asked, waving the report before him. 'There's nothing you could have left out or forgotten?'

'I wrote down everything which I felt was relevant to the investigation,' she told him, a slight trace of anger in her voice. She was becoming annoyed at his patronising tone.

Vernon shifted the menthol sweet to the other side of his mouth and tapped the report with his index finger. He was gazing into empty air.

'The area of the brain which controls the Astral body also controls emotions and desires,' he said, abstractedly.

'Yes,' Kelly said. 'But emotions and desires not present in the conscious mind. The Astral body appears to be the alterego and, from the material I collected on Grant and Joubert, it *can* become a tangible force.'

Vernon nodded.

'It sounded like a form of bi-location at first,' said Kelly. 'But I've never heard of a bi-locative presence becoming tangible before.'

'There was an American named Paul Twitchell,' Vernon explained. 'In the early sixties he began to teach what he called the Eckankar doctrine. A number of his pupils claimed to have seen him, in solid Astral form, while he was actually miles away.' Vernon sighed. 'But, Twitchell was one on his own. This ...' he picked up the report. 'This is more unusual.' He paused once again. 'It would explain many of the problems we have concerning the inner self, even some mental disorders.' He chewed his bottom lip contemplatively. 'Are you absolutely sure you've left nothing out?'

'I'm positive,' Kelly said in exasperation.

'Kelly, you don't need me to tell you how important this information is to our work, to ...'

She cut him short, infuriated by his treatment of her.

'I'm not a fool, Doctor Vernon,' she said. 'Everything that I saw is noted down in my report, some of the conversations are verbatim.'

He nodded, placatingly, as if trying to calm her down.

'But there is one thing *I'd* like to know,' she told him.

Vernon eyed her warily.

'How did you know I was at the Metapsychic Centre?'

'I was in contact with them,' Vernon said. 'One of the investigators told me.'

Kelly wasn't altogether satisfied but she didn't press the matter. A heavy silence descended, finally broken by the woman.

'Have you seen anything of John Fraser since he left here?' she asked.

Vernon shrugged.

'He came back about a week ago to collect some things.' His tone abruptly changed, his eyes narrowing. 'Why do you ask?'

She detected the defensive note in his voice.

'I was just curious,' Kelly told him.

'Fraser has no more business here,' Vernon said, acidly.

Another long silence punctuated the conversation, the only sound being made by the Institute Director as he crunched up his cough sweet. Kelly eyed him suspiciously. Vernon was usually a calm, unflappable man but, in the last twenty minutes or so, he had revealed another side of his character — one which she had not seen before. His calmness had been replaced by a tetchy impatience, the unflappability giving away to an anxious and defensive demeanour. When he finally spoke again, however, some of the urgency had left his voice.

'Could what happened to Joubert be duplicated outside laboratory conditions?' he asked. 'I mean the Astral projection which he underwent.'

'I don't see why not,' Kelly told him. 'He was hypnotised, it was as simple as that. It should be perfectly possible to recreate the condition in another subject.'

Vernon nodded slowly, his grey eyes fixed on a point to

133

one side of Kelly. She did not move. He didn't speak.

Finally, she rose.

'If that's all, Doctor ...' She allowed the sentence to trail off.

'Yes,' he said. 'There's nothing else.'

'Could I have my report please?'

Vernon put his hand on the file.

'I'll keep it for now,' he said, his eyes fixing her in an uncompromising stare.

She hesitated a moment then nodded, turned and headed for the office door.

Vernon watched her leave.

He slumped back in his seat as she closed the door, his eyes falling to the report which lay before him. Long moments passed then he picked it up and dropped it into the black attaché case which stood beside his desk.

Before replacing it, he locked the case.

Kelly nodded politely to Dr Vernon's secretary as she walked out but she barely succeeded in masking her anger.

What the hell was Vernon playing at? she wondered. Since she'd returned he'd been like some kind of Grand Inquisitor, wanting to know every last detail of what happened in France. And why should he want to keep the report she'd made? He'd already perused it half a dozen times while she'd sat before him. That, apparently, was not sufficient for him.

She walked briskly down the corridor towards the stairs, her heels clicking loudly on the polished tile floor. Down one flight of steps to the first floor then along another corridor she walked until she came to Frank Anderson's office. Kelly tapped lightly on the door then walked in.

The room was empty.

She cursed silently and turned to leave but, before she did, she crossed to his desk and found a piece of paper and a pen. Kelly scrawled a quick note and left it where Anderson would see it.

A thought crossed her mind.

If Anderson could find it easily then so too could Vernon. The Institute Director had a habit of wandering, uninvited, into his investigators' offices and this was one note which she did not want him to read. She stood still for a moment, wondering what she should do.

'Need any help?'

The voice startled her but she spun round to see Anderson in the doorway. A smile of relief creased her lips.

'Frank. I was looking for you,' she said, balling up the note and stuffing it into the pocket of her shirt.

'I gathered that,' he said, pulling at one frayed shirt cuff. 'What can I do for you, Kelly?'

'You were a friend of John Fraser's weren't you?' she said, lowering her voice.

Anderson looked puzzled.

'Yes.'

'I need to speak to him.'

'I haven't seen him since he left here. He hasn't been in touch.'

Kelly frowned.

'But you know where he lives?' she asked.

Anderson nodded.

'And where he spends most of his time,' he said, smiling. 'The first is his home address, the second one is the pub he uses most often.'

Kelly turned to leave, scanning the piece of paper.

'Is something wrong?' Anderson called after her.

'That's what I want to find out,' Kelly told him and left him alone.

Anderson heard her footsteps echoing away and frowned. What did she want with John Fraser?

26

The hands of the dashboard clock glowed green in the gloom.

9.36 p.m.

Kelly parked the Mini in the gravelled area beside the pub and sat behind the wheel for a moment. High above her, rain clouds spat erratic droplets on to the land. It was warm inside the car — muggy and uncomfortable. Kelly felt her tee-shirt sticking to her back as she leant forward and she squirmed. It felt as if someone had wrapped her upper body in a damp towel. She clambered out of the car, relieved to find that there was a slight breeze. Rain spots momentarily stained her jeans as she walked towards the building, ignoring the dirty water from puddles which splashed her ankle boots.

'The Huntsman' was a large pub about a mile outside Oxford. It wasn't pretty and it wasn't quaint but it was functional. There was a cheap and, consequently, popular restaurant attached to it which did not, on this particular night, appear to be too busy, hence her ease of parking. Normally the area was jammed with vehicles. Not so tonight. Kelly tried to see Fraser's car but, in the darkness, identification was almost impossible.

She decided to try the lounge bar first.

It was crowded with people. In groups, in couples, on their own. One corner was occupied by seven or eight men who were playing cards around a large oblong table. Kelly scanned their faces, accidentally catching the eye of a ginger-haired youth in his late teens. He winked at her then directed his companion's attention to this slim newcomer. A chorus of subdued whistling and cheering rose from the men. Kelly turned away from them, searching the bustling bar for Fraser.

There was no sign of him.

She decided to try the Public bar.

If the noise inside the Lounge bar had been loud then in the Public bar it bordered on seismic proportions. A juke-box which was obviously set at full volume spewed forth an endless stream of the latest chart hits as if trying to drown out the clack of pool balls or the thud of darts as they hit the board. To add to the unholy cacophony, in one corner of the large room an electronic motor-racing game occasionally punctuated the din with the simulated explosion of a crashed car. Whilst, beside it, the ever hungry Pac-Man noisily devoured everything before it.

Kelly scanned the bar but could not see Fraser. She decided to sit and wait for him. There was a table near the door but it was occupied by a young couple who looked as though they were about to breach the Indecent Exposure act.

The youth had his hand buried beneath his girlfriend's miniscule skirt while she was rubbing his crotch with a speed which looked likely to cause friction burns.

The bar seemed to be populated almost exclusively by youngsters, most of whom were teenagers. She drew several admiring glances as she perched on a bar stool. When she'd finally managed to attract the barman's attention, she ordered a shandy and fumbled in her purse for some money. As he set her drink down she deliberately took her time counting out the change.

'Do you know John Fraser?' she asked him.

The barman nodded, wiping perspiration from his face.

'Yeah, why?'

'Has he been in here tonight?'

'Not yet, but he will.' The barman smiled.

'You sound very sure,' Kelly said.

'He hasn't missed a night since I've worked here and that's two years.' A call from the other end of the bar took the man away.

Kelly sipped at her drink and turned slightly on the stool so that she could see the door through which Fraser must enter.

'Hello, stranger.'

She spun round again to see that the voice came from a tall, black-haired youth who was leaning on the bar beside her. He was dressed in a grey sweater and maroon slacks. His companion, like himself, was in his early twenties, his hair cut short and shaped so that it appeared as if his head was flat. Spots and blackheads dotted his face liberally. He smiled, his gaze drawn to Kelly's breasts.

'Do I know you?' she said, trying to suppress a grin.

'No,' said the black-haired youth. 'But we can soon put that right, can't we?'

He introduced himself as Neville. His friend as Baz.

Kelly nodded politely, forced to sip at her drink again to prevent herself laughing. This was the last thing she needed.

'I haven't seen you in here before,' said Neville. 'I would have remembered if I had.'

Kelly smiled, aware that Baz was still gazing at her breasts as if he'd never seen a woman at close-quarters before. She had little trouble convincing herself that might well be the case.

'It's a bit noisy in here,' Neville said, as if telling her something she didn't know. 'Fancy a walk?'

'I'm waiting for someone,' she told him. 'Thanks all the same.'

'What's his name?' asked Neville, looking quite hurt.

'I'm waiting for a girlfriend actually,' Kelly lied.

Neville seemed to perk up. He nudged Baz in the ribs, momentarily interrupting his appraisal of Kelly's shapely body.

'That's even better. We can make it a foursome when she gets here.'

Kelly smiled again.

'You don't understand,' she said, flashing her green eyes at him. 'She's more than just a friend.'

Neville looked blank.

Baz looked even blanker.

'We're *very* close,' Kelly continued, barely able to keep a straight face.

It was Baz who spoke the revelatory words.

'She's a fucking lesbian,' he gaped, already pulling his colleague away as if Kelly had just announced she had bubonic plague. She chuckled as she saw them leave, casting anxious glances at her as if they thought she was going to follow them. Kelly took another sip of her drink and checked her watch.

9.58.

Where the hell was Fraser?

Another ten minutes, she decided, and she would drive to his house.

She finished her shandy and ordered an orange juice instead.

She had her back to the door when Fraser walked in.

He strode to the far end of the bar where he was engulfed by his usual drinking companions. Kelly turned her attention back to the door, occasionally checking the faces in the bar.

Almost by accident she spotted who she sought.

She slid down off the stool and walked across to him, tugging at his arm.

'Fraser.'

He turned and saw her, a mixture of surprise and distaste in his expression.

138

'Who's your friend, John?' one of the other men asked, admiringly.

Fraser ignored the remark, addressing himself to Kelly.

'How did you know where to find me?' he wanted to know.

Kelly told him.

'I need to talk to you,' she added. 'It's important.'

'I'm not sure I've got anything to say to you, Kelly. You or anyone else concerned with the bloody Institute.'

'I need your help.'

'How can *I* help you? Is Vernon looking for more human guinea pigs?'

'It's Vernon I want to talk to you about.'

Fraser relaxed slightly, more intrigued now than annoyed. He picked up his glass and motioned to an empty table close by. They sat down, watched by the group of men standing at the bar.

'So what's suddenly important about the good doctor?' he said, sarcastically.

'Listen,' said Kelly, leaning close to him to make herself heard over the blare of the juke-box. 'When Vernon dismissed you, it wasn't because you protested about the research was it?'

Fraser sipped at his drink.

'You tell me.'

'I'm not playing games, Fraser,' snapped Kelly, angrily. 'I came here tonight because I thought you could help me.'

He raised a hand in supplication.

'OK, what are you talking about?' he asked.

'You mentioned something to Vernon about the research, about it being of benefit to one person in particular.'

Fraser shook his head slowly.

'Did you mean Vernon himself?' she continued.

He didn't answer.

'And there was something else,' she persisted. 'About what Vernon was hiding that he'd been hiding for a time. What did you mean?'

Fraser downed what was left in his glass.

'Have you ever heard Vernon talk about his wife?' he asked.

'I didn't even know he was married.'

'It's not something he likes to broadcast, at least not any more.'

Kelly leaned closer as the juke-box launched another high decibel assault.

'For all I know, his wife could be dead now,' Fraser continued. 'Something happened to her about six years ago. No one knows what it was and, so far, no one's found out. Vernon's too clever for that. But, whatever it was his wife disappeared and nobody knows where she is now.'

'How do you know this?' Kelly demanded.

'Vernon's quite a respected figure in our little community. When the wife of a prominent man goes missing there's always the odd rumour floating about.'

'Could he have killed her?' asked Kelly, warily.

'I doubt it. Perhaps she left him. Upped and walked out. The intriguing thing is, what made her leave? Whatever happened to her he's certainly managed to keep it quiet.'

Kelly ran her index finger around the rim of her glass, gazing reflectively into the orange fluid.

'And you think he's using the research to help his wife. Indirectly?' she said, finally.

'It's a possibility.'

'But how is our work on the unconscious mind going to help his wife?' she mused aloud.

'You won't know that until you know what's wrong with *her*. Or what happened to her anyway.'

Kelly sipped at her drink, thoughts tumbling through her mind. The sounds of the juke-box, the pool table and the electronic games seemed to diminish as she considered what she had heard.

'What could have happened that was so bad Vernon would keep it secret for six years?' she pondered.

Fraser could only shrug his shoulders. He started to rise.

'Where are you going?' she wanted to know.

'To get another,' he said, indicating his empty glass. 'What about you?'

'No thanks. I'd better get going. Look, thanks for the help. I appreciate it.'

He nodded.

'You can contact me at home if you want to,' he began. 'My address ...'

140

She smiled.

'Anderson gave me that too,' she confessed.

'Frank always was thorough.'

They exchanged brief farewells and Kelly left.

As she emerged from the pub she found that the rain which had merely been spotting earlier had now been transformed into a fully-fledged downpour. She ran to her car, fumbling for her keys as the warm rain drenched her. She slid behind the wheel and sat there, gazing out through the rivulets of water which coursed down the windscreen. Kelly ran a hand through her hair and then wiped her palm on her jeans. Through the cascade of rain she could see Fraser's Datsun.

Fraser.

Could he be right about Vernon's wife? Kelly wondered.

She started her engine and guided the Mini out onto the road.

High above her, a soundless flash of lightning split the clouds, reaching earthward as it lit the heavens with cold white light.

Kelly felt an unexpected chill creeping around her.

It was almost 11.05 by the time John Fraser left the Public bar of 'The Huntsman'.

He had not consumed as much booze as he normally did and he felt almost abnormally clear-headed. Fraser rarely got drunk no matter how much he had and tonight, especially, he felt only a pleasing calmness. He climbed into his car and, at the third attempt, started the engine. He made a mental note to get his battery checked.

The rain continued to pelt down and the storm which had been building all night had finally broken. Thunder shook the sky while the lightning etched erratic lines across the tenebrous heavens.

As he pulled out of the pub car park, a lorry roared past and Fraser stepped on his brakes.

The pedal sank mournfully to the floor beneath the pressure of his foot.

The car continued to roll.

The lorry swerved slightly to avoid the Datsun and Fraser gripped the wheel in terror, as if awaiting the impact, but the larger vehicle swept on, disappearing around a bend in the road.

'Jesus,' murmured Fraser, stamping on the brake pedal. This time the car stopped dead.

He tried it once more.

No problems.

He shook his head and drove on. Bloody brakes. He'd only had them checked the day before.

27

She had not slept much the previous night. Her mind had been too active, all too ready to present her with snap answers to questions for which she so badly sought concrete solutions.

Kelly glanced down at the piece of paper on the parcel shelf and re-checked Fraser's address. A sign post at the corner of the street confirmed that she had found the right place. She turned the Mini into the street and slowed down, scanning the doors for the number she sought.

The storm of the night before had cleared the air and the sun shone brightly over the carefully maintained houses with their neat gardens. Kelly saw an old man mowing his front lawn. On the other side of the street a youth was busy washing his car.

'Number fifty-nine,' she murmured to herself, squinting at the houses. 'Number fifty-nine.'

She saw it and pulled the Mini into a convenient parking space, switching off the engine. Kelly sat behind the wheel for a moment gazing at the house. She was reasonably sure that Fraser had told her everything he knew about Vernon but she had spent half the night wondering if there might just be something else which he might have neglected to mention. Perhaps in his own home, away from the noisy distractions of the pub, he might be able to give her some more information. Exactly what she was going to do with it she wasn't yet sure.

Confront Vernon?

Why should she need to confront him?

Kelly shook her head, as if trying to force the thoughts to one side, then she pushed open the door and climbed out.

There was a pleasing smell of blossom in the air, as if someone had opened a gigantic air freshener. The sun, broken up by the branches of the trees which flanked the road, forced its way through the canopy of leaves and blossom to brush warming rays against her skin. The blossom itself, stirred by a gentle breeze, fell from the trees like pink tears.

Kelly walked up the path to the front door of number fifty-nine and rang the bell. As she stood there she noticed that the garage door was closed. There was no sign of Fraser's Datsun. She hoped that he was at home.

A minute passed and no one answered the door. Kelly rang again, this time keeping her finger on the bell button for a time.

At last she heard movement from inside.

The door swung open and she found herself confronted by a rotund, middle-aged woman in a dark blue dress. Her greying hair was swept back from her forehead, giving her round face a severity which it perhaps did not merit.

'Mrs Fraser?' Kelly asked.

'No. I'm her sister,' the woman said, eyeing Kelly up and down. 'Who are you?'

Kelly introduced herself.

'I used to work with John Fraser,' she explained. 'It was him that I wanted to see really.'

The woman didn't speak at first then, slowly, she lowered her gaze and her voice softened.

'My sister is upstairs sleeping,' she said, quietly.

Kelly didn't have to be a detective to realize that something was wrong.

'And Mr Fraser?' she asked.

'He was killed in an accident last night. His car hit a tree. He was dead before they got him to hospital.'

28

There were two of them waiting outside the house.

One was smoking a cigarette and pacing agitatedly up and down while the other squatted on the pavement and adjusted his camera. Both of them would occasionally stop what they were doing and peer in the direction of the building.

Toni Landers replaced the curtain, wondering if the newsmen had seen her.

She had not seen these two before although, since her son's death, so many had thrust themselves at her with notepads and microphones that she doubted if she would remember faces. The actress walked across the room to the drinks cabinet and poured herself a large measure of J&B which she downed virtually in one swallow, coughing as the fiery liquid burned its way to her stomach.

The house was deathly silent. She had given Mrs Garcia some time off, promising to ring her when her services were required again. Exactly how long that would be even Toni herself was uncertain of. On the sofa before her the copy of *Variety* was folded open at an appointed spot and she glanced at it briefly before returning to her vigil at the window.

As she stood gazing out at the two newsmen, she thought how odd it had been that she should discover the story in such a journal. She had read with interest that Jonathan Mathias was to visit England to appear on a TV special. She had seen him as her last hope. The only one she knew who possessed the kind of abilities she had need of. Toni didn't intend to allow him to slip away.

She had need of his services.

There was a loud beeping sound and she looked out to see that the Ford Sedan had pulled up outside her house. The driver was banging the horn.

Toni drained what was left in her glass then scuttled for the front door, re-adjusting the dark glasses as she did so. She waited a second then walked out.

Immediately, the two newsmen approached her and she winced as the flash bulb momentarily hurt her eyes.

'I have nothing to say,' she told them.

'How soon will you be returning to the stage?' the first man asked, ignoring her declaration.

She swept on towards the waiting car.

'How will your son's death affect your career?'

The flash bulb exploded again, closer to her this time.

Toni struck out angrily, knocking the camera from the photographer's hands. It crashed to the ground, the lens splintering.

'Hey lady,' he shouted. 'That's an expensive fucking camera.'

She pulled open the rear door of the Ford and glanced at the driver.

'It ain't my fault your fucking kid is dead,' the photographer roared as the car pulled away.

'Where to, Miss Landers?' the driver asked.

She checked her watch. She had enough time.

'Kennedy,' she told him.

29

Paris

The occasional gusts of wind stirred the bells in the church tower, whistling through and around them to form a discordant, ghostly melody.

Michel Lasalle stood by the grave-side and read the inscription on the headstone.

Madelaine Lasalle; 1947-1982
Loved More Than Life Itself.

The wind stirred the flowers which adorned the grave, their

145

white petals standing out in dark contrast to the darkness of the night. Lasalle bent and removed them, laying them on one side.

He reached for the shovel.

Putting all his weight behind it he drove the pointed implement into the ground, pressing down on it with his foot, levering a huge clod of dark earth from the top of the grave. He tossed it to one side and continued digging. He could feel the perspiration soaking through his shirt as he toiled, gradually creating a mound of mud beside the grave. When he had excavated half of the plot he paused and pulled his shirt off, fastening it around his waist by the sleeves as if it were some kind of apron. Then he continued digging.

It took him nearly thirty minutes to reach the coffin.

He heard the sound of metal on wood and stood back triumphantly, jamming the shovel into the damp earth at the bottom of the hole. Lasalle dropped to his knees and began clawing the final covering of dirt from the casket. He split two finger nails as he did so, scrabbling there like a dog trying to find a bone. Blood oozed from the torn digits but Lasalle paid it no heed. Only when the last fragments of earth had been pulled free did he straighten up, reaching once more for the shovel. He slid the pointed end beneath one corner of the coffin and weighed down on it.

The screw which held it in place was rusted and he had little difficulty removing it. In fact, none of them presented too much of an obstacle and, with a grunt of satisfaction, he succeeded in prising the lid free. It came away with a shriek of splintering wood and he flung it aside.

A cloying stench of decay rose from the body of his dead wife.

Lasalle stared down at the corpse, his gaze travelling inquisitively up and down it. The skin on the face and neck was dry, drawn taught over the bones. The eye sockets were gaping, empty caverns filled only with a gelatinous substance which, from the left eye, had dribbled down the remains of the cheek. A thick yellowish fluid resembling pus was seeping from both nostrils. The mouth was open to reveal several missing teeth. The gums had dissolved and the tongue resembled little more than a strand of withered brown string. One hand lay across the chest, the skin having split and peeled back to reveal brittle bone beneath. The bottom of the coffin was stained with a rusty substance which looked black in the darkness.

Lasalle stepped into the coffin and knelt on the legs of his dead wife, wondering if the bones would snap beneath him. He was sweating profusely and his breath came in short gasps. As he wiped a hand across his forehead, blood from his torn fingers left a crimson smudge on his skin.

Madelaine had been buried in a black dress and Lasalle now bent forward and lifted it, pushing the fusty material up until it covered her putrescing features and exposed her festering pelvic region. Lasalle felt the erection bulging in his trousers and he tugged them down. He fell upon the body and spoke her name as he thrust, the stink of his own perspiration mingling with the vile stench which rose from her corpse.

A shadow fell across him.

Lasalle looked up and his grunts turned to screams.

Joubert stood at the grave-side, loking down at the obscenity before him, a smile etched on his face.

Lasalle screamed again and again.

Joubert continued to smile.

As he was catapulted from the nightmare, Lasalle gripped his head as if he were afraid it was about to explode. He could still hear screams and it was a second or two before he realized they were his own.

He sat up in bed, his body drenched and aching. As he swung himself round he discovered that he was shaking madly. His eyes bulged wildly in the sockets, the images from the dream still vivid in his mind.

He suddenly got to his feet and rushed to the bathroom, barely making it as the cascade of hot bile fought its way up from his stomach, gushing into his mouth. He bent double over the toilet and retched.

He staggered back, head spinning, and swilled out his mouth with water. Then, he staggered slowly back into the bedroom and sat down in the chair beside the window.

He did not sleep for the remainder of that night.

30

Oxford

It was a familiar drive for Blake. Although he hadn't visited the Institute of Psychical Study for over a year he had not needed to consult a map in order to find the place. He'd left London early, avoiding much of the worst traffic. The sun was shining with just enough power to make driving pleasant. Dressed in a pair of jeans and an open-necked white shirt, Blake felt comfortable and he whistled happily in accompaniment to the cassette as he swung the XJS into the driveway which led up to the Institute.

He found a parking space and turned off the engine, waiting until the track he'd been listening to had finished before getting out of the car. He slipped on a light jacket and made his way towards the main entrance of the building. There was a notepad stuffed into his pocket and the usual array of pens too. Blake chuckled to himself, remembering back to his days as a journalist when he'd dashed enthusiastically to each pissant little assignment armed with his trusty pad.

The entrance hall of the Institute was pleasantly cool and Blake paused, slowing his pace, trying to remember where he had to go.

He spotted someone emerging from a room ahead of him.

The writer was immediately struck by her shapely figure, the way her lab coat hugged her taut buttocks, the small slit at the back allowing him brief, tantalising glimpses of her slim calves. She walked easily and elegantly on her high heels and he realized that she hadn't noticed him.

'Excuse me,' he called, approaching her.

She turned and Blake found himself looking deep into her welcoming eyes. She smiled and the gesture seemed to light up her whole face. He chanced an approving glance at her upper body, her breasts pertly pressing against the material of her electric blue blouse.

'You're David Blake aren't you?' she said but it was more of a statement than a question.

He smiled broadly.

'Fame at last,' he beamed. 'How do you know me?'

'We have your books in our library, I recognize you from your photo on the jacket. It's the dark glasses,' she told him. 'They're quite distinctive.'

'Well, they hide the bags under my eyes,' he said, pleased when she chuckled. 'You seem to have me at a disadvantage, you know me but I don't know you.'

'Kelly Hunt,' she told him. 'I work here.'

Blake shook her small hand gently.

'You don't fit the image,' he said. 'I thought all investigators were crusty middle-aged men.'

'Not *all* of them,' Kelly said.

'So I see.'

They looked at each other for long moments, both liking what they saw.

'Is Dr Vernon in his office?' Blake said, finally breaking the silence.

Kelly frowned slightly.

'Are you here to see him then?' she asked.

Blake explained that he was. Kelly told him how to reach the Institute Director.

'Well, it's nice to have met you, Miss Hunt,' he said, heading for the stairs which led up to Vernon's office.

'You too,' Kelly said, watching as he disappeared out of sight.

She wondered exactly how friendly he was with Vernon.

Vernon was already on his feet, right hand extended, when Blake entered the office.

The men exchanged pleasant greetings and the writer sat down, accepting the drink he was offered.

'Sorry to call on you at such short notice,' he apologised. 'But I've written about two-thirds of the book and I need to check some details before I can finish it.'

Vernon produced Blake's letter from his desk drawer.

'I got it yesterday,' he said, smiling. 'So, how are things in the book business?'

Blake shrugged.

'It could be better I suppose but then again, it always could.'

'And how's your new book coming along?'

'Fine, as far as I can tell. But then who am I to judge?' He smiled.

Vernon's mood darkened slightly. He looked at Blake and then at the letter he'd received from the writer.

'You say your new book is about the unconscious mind?' he asked.

'The unconscious, dreams, Astral travel, that kind of thing. I've just got back from America, I spent some time with a man called Jonathan Mathias. You might have heard of him.'

Vernon nodded.

'He's a remarkable man,' Blake said. 'Powerful.' The writer's voice took on a reflective note.

'How do you mean, powerful?' Vernon wanted to know.

'It's difficult to explain. He performs acts of faith-healing and yet he's an atheist.' Blake paused. 'But, most important of all, he claims he can control the subconscious minds of other people. Their Astral bodies.'

'How?' Vernon demanded, sitting forward in his chair.

Blake regarded the older man over the top of his glass.

'It's some form of hypnosis,' he said. 'I'm sure of that.'

Vernon eyed the writer suspiciously.

'It's an extravagant claim,' he said.

Blake shrugged.

'Like I said, he's a remarkable man.'

The Institute Director reached forward and flicked a switch on his intercom.

'Could you send Miss Hunt up, please,' he said, then sat back in his chair once more.

'Do you believe what Mathias says about being able to control other people's subconscious minds?' he wanted to know.

Blake was about to answer when there was a knock on the door, and, a moment later, Kelly entered.

She looked at Blake but, this time, he was surprised to find that she didn't smile. He got to his feet.

'David Blake,' began Vernon. 'This is Kelly Hunt, one of our ...'

Kelly cut him short.

'We've met,' she said, curtly. 'Hello again, Mr Blake.'

The writer was puzzled by the coldness of her voice. All the earlier warmth seemed to have been drained from it.

'Mr Blake will be conducting some research here for his new book, I'd like you to help him with whatever he needs.'

'But my work ...' she protested.

'His work ties in with your own,' Vernon said, sharply.

'I hope I'm not causing anyone any inconvenience,' the writer said, aware of a newly found hostility in the air.

'It's no trouble,' Kelly said, sounding none too convincing. He smiled thinly.

'Well, I suppose I'd better get started.' He thanked Vernon, then followed Kelly out of the office.

The Institute Director sat down at his desk and re-read the letter which Blake had posted two days earlier. He held it before him a moment longer then carefully, almost gleefully, tore it up.

'Did I do something to annoy you?' Blake asked Kelly as they headed down the stairs towards her office.

'What gives you that impression, Mr Blake?' she said.

'Your attitude,' he told her. 'And stop calling me *Mr* Blake will you? My name's David.'

'What sort of research are you interested in?' Kelly asked him, dutifully.

He repeated what he'd told Vernon.

'The old boy seemed very interested,' Blake said.

'How long have you been friends?' asked Kelly.

'Well, I wouldn't exactly call us friends. Acquaintances might be more to the point. I've been to the Institute a few times in the past while I've been working on other books.'

'How close are you?' she asked.

Blake stopped walking.

'What is this? Twenty questions?' he asked, irritably.

Kelly also stood where she was.

'Dr Vernon and I have met several times on what you might call a professional basis,' Blake told her. 'Although with all due respect, I don't really see that it's any of your business, Miss Hunt.'

'No, you're right, it isn't,' Kelly confessed, some of the coldness having left her voice. 'I'm sorry, Mr Blake.'

He sighed.

'David,' he told her. 'Look, we have to work together for a day or two, we might as well make the time pass pleasantly.'

'David,' she agreed, smiling thinly.

They began walking again but more slowly this time.

'Why is it so important to you to know whether Vernon and I are friends?' he enquired.

'I was curious.'

'I'm *still* curious. When I arrived here, when we first spoke, everything was fine. Since I spoke to Vernon you don't want to know me.'

'It's difficult to explain,' she said, evasively.

'Then don't try,' Blake said, smiling.

Kelly looked at him, aware that she felt more than a passing attraction for this man.

Blake was not handsome but his finely chiselled features and sinewy frame, coupled with the easy-going personality he exuded, served their purpose well.

'Vernon said you'd been doing work on dreams,' he said.

'That's what I'm still working on,' Kelly explained as they reached her office. She ushered him inside and motioned for him to sit down but, instead, the writer wandered over to the window and looked out across the rolling lawns which surrounded the Institute. Kelly seated herself behind her desk, studying Blake's profile as he gazed out into the sunlit morning.

'The weather's too nice to work,' he said, quietly.

She smiled.

'Standing there isn't going to get your book written is it?' Blake turned and nodded.

'Quite right, Miss Hunt,' he said.

'Kelly,' she reminded him.

It was his turn to smile.

'How exactly *can* I help you?' she asked as he seated himself opposite her.

'I'd like to see the labs where you've been doing your research, ask you a few questions if that's all right but, otherwise, just give me free run of the library and I'll be happy. I'm not a difficult man to please.' He smiled that engaging smile once more and Kelly found herself drawn to him, to his eyes even though they were shielded behind his dark glasses. She felt a peculiar tingle run through her.

'Shall we start in the labs?' she said, getting to her feet again.

He nodded.

'Why not?'

Kelly led him out of her office.

The library at the Institute never failed to fascinate Blake. Built up, as it had been, over a hundred years, it had books which dated back as far as the sixteenth century. Before him on the table he had an original copy of Collin de Planncey's 'Dictionaire Infernale'. The pages creaked as he turned them, scanning the ancient tome, pleasantly surprised at how much of the French he could actually understand.

He'd been in the library for over four hours, ever since he'd left Kelly back in her office. Now, with the time approaching 5.15 p.m., he heard his stomach rumbling and realized that he hadn't eaten since early morning. The writer scanned what notes he'd written, realizing that he must check one or two discrepancies against his manuscript at the first opportunity. As it was, he replaced the old books in their correct position on the shelves, scooped up his pad and made for the stairs.

Kelly was on her way down.

'I was coming to see if you needed any help,' she said, the warmth having returned to her voice.

They had found it remarkably easy to talk to each other that morning. Their conversation had flowed unfalteringly and Kelly had felt her attraction for Blake growing stronger. She felt at ease in his company and she was sure the feeling was reciprocated.

'Did you find what you were looking for?' she asked him.

He smiled and ran appraising eyes over her.

'I think I found exactly what I was looking for,' he said.

She coloured slightly and waited on the stairs while he made his way up. They both walked out into the hall which was now much colder than when Blake had first arrived.

'Will you be back tomorrow?' she asked him.

'I got the information I needed,' he told her, 'with your help. But if I ever have a haunting you'll be the first one I get in touch with. You've really been very kind. Thanks.'

'Are you driving back to London now?'

'Not yet. I'm going to have something to eat first and then I thought I might take you out for a drink this evening if you're not doing anything else.'

Kelly chuckled, unable to speak for a moment, taken by surprise by the unexpectedness of his invitation.

'If I'm in a good mood, I might even let you buy a round,' Blake added.

'What if I am doing something else?' she asked.

'Then I'll have to wait for another evening won't I?'

She shook her head, still laughing.

'Can I pick you up about eight?' he asked.

'Eight will be fine,' she told him. 'But it might help if you knew where to pick me up *from*.' She scribbled her address and phone number on a piece of paper and gave it to him.

'Tell Dr Vernon I'll be in touch,' Blake said, and, for a moment, he saw a flicker of doubt cross Kelly's face. 'I'll phone him and thank him for letting me use the library.'

She nodded.

Blake turned and headed for the door.

'Eight o'clock,' he reminded her.

She watched him go, stood alone in the hallway listening as he revved up his engine. He turned the XJS full circle and guided it back down the driveway towards the road which led into Oxford itself.

Kelly smiled to herself and returned to her office.

From his office window, Dr Vernon watched as the writer drove away. He paused a moment then reached for the phone and dialled.

'Cheers,' said Blake, smiling. He raised his glass then took a hefty swallow from the foaming beer.

Across the table from him, Kelly did likewise, sipping her Martini and meeting the writer's gaze.

They were seated in the garden of 'The Jester', a small pub about a mile or so outside Oxford. There were three or four other people enjoying the evening air as well. It was still agreeably warm despite the fact that the sun was sinking, gushing crimson into the sky. When it got too chilly they could easily retire into the comfort of the lounge bar. Blake looked at his companion, pleased with what he saw. She was clad in a dress of pale lemon cheese-cloth, her breasts unfettered by the restraints of a bra. The writer noticed how invitingly her dark nipples pressed against the flimsy material. With the sinking sun casting a halo around her, drawing golden streaks in her brown hair she looked beautiful. He felt something akin to pride merely being seated there with her.

Kelly noticed how intently he was looking at her and smiled impishly.

'What are you looking at?' she asked him.

'A very beautiful young woman,' he told her. 'But, I was thinking too.'

'About what?'

He raised his eyebrows.

'No,' she said. 'Perhaps I'm better off not knowing.'

Blake laughed.

'I was wondering actually,' he began, 'how you came to be in the line of work you're in. It is unusual for a woman, especially of your age.'

'It was what I wanted to do when I left University,' she told him.

'How did your parents feel about it?' he wanted to know.

'They didn't say much one way or the other. I'd worked in a library for a few months before I joined the Institute. They'd probably have been just as happy if I'd stayed on there. Security is the be-all and end-all in our family I'm afraid.'

Blake nodded.

'What about you?' Kelly asked. 'Writing's a precarious business isn't it? What made you want to write?'

'Well, it wasn't because I needed to share my knowledge with others,' he said, tongue-in-cheek. 'Not in the beginning anyway. I wrote a couple of novels to start with.'

'Did you have any luck with them?'

He shook his head.

'Writing fiction successfully needs more luck than talent. You need the breaks. I didn't get them.'

'So you turned to non-fiction? The stuff you write now?'

'The ratio's different. It's fifty per cent talent and fifty per cent luck.'

'You sell yourself short, David.'

'No. I understand my own limitations that's all.'

'What about your parents. How do they feel about having a famous author for a son?'

'Both my parents are dead. My father died of a stroke five years ago, my mother had a heart attack six months after him.'

'Oh God, I'm sorry, David.'

He smiled thinly.

'You weren't to know,' he said. 'I just wish they could have lived to see my success that's all.'

A heavy silence descended, rapidly broken by Blake.

'Well, now we've got the morbid stuff out of the way,' he said, with a reasonable degree of cheerfulness. 'Perhaps we can carry on with this conversation.'

She sipped her drink and looked at him over the rim of the glass. Losing his parents within six months of each other must have been a crushing blow and obviously he didn't want to dwell on the memory.

'I suppose you must be reasonably secure as a writer now,' she said, attempting to guide the conversation in another direction.

'You can never be secure in my business,' he said. 'One flop and it's back to square one. It's like walking a tightrope in a pair of wellies.'

Kelly chuckled.

'Does it bother you living alone?' Blake asked.

'Not anymore,' she told him. 'It did to begin with but I'm used to it now.'

'And you've never felt like getting married?'

'No.' She dismissed the suggestion as if he'd just asked her to commit suicide. 'I'm not the settling down type, I don't think.'

'I know what you mean,' he confessed.

'You're not telling me *you* haven't been tempted. There must have been girls who you've been close too,' Kelly said.

'A couple. But none that I'd want to spend the rest of my life with.' He smiled. 'I'm a selfish devil. Sharing isn't one of my strong points.'

'Too much give and take, is that it?'

'You ask a lot of questions, Kelly,' he grinned.

'That's because I'm interested in you,' she told him.

'Now that *is* a compliment.'

They sat in silence for a time, looking at each other, enjoying the warmth of the dying sun, the smell of freshly cut grass and the gentle breeze. It stirred the trees which flanked the pub garden on one side. Birds nesting in the branches watched over the activity below them. Near to where Kelly and Blake sat, three sparrows were busily picking at a piece of bread thrown down by a young couple who were eating sandwiches. Somewhere in the distance Kelly could hear a cuckoo. She sat back in her seat feeling more relaxed than she had done for many months. The combination of the surroundings and Blake's company had a calming influence on her. She wondered if he felt the same way.

The writer downed what was left in his glass and looked at Kelly. She still had most of her Martini left.

'I'll have to bring you out more often,' he said, peering at the glass. 'If one drink lasts you this long you're going to save me pounds.'

They both laughed.

'You have another,' she said.

'Very generous,' Blake replied.

'Let me get it,' she offered, fumbling for her purse.

Blake looked indignant.

'Let a woman buy drink for me?' He winked at her. 'Good idea.'

She balled up a pound note and tossed it at him, watching as he retreated back into the bar to fetch another pint. It was a matter of moments before he returned, holding the glass in one hand and her change in the other. He sat down and supped a third of it immediately, wiping the froth from his lip with his thumb.

'Did Vernon say anything when you told him I'd left this afternoon?' the writer asked.

'No,' Kelly said, suspiciously. 'Should he have?'

Blake smiled, wryly.

'You know, Kelly,' he said. 'I could be forgiven for thinking you're a tiny bit paranoid about Dr Vernon.'

Kelly didn't answer.

'Every time I mention his name you go cold on me,' Blake continued. 'Why? Or is it my imagination?'

She took a sip of her drink.

'Perhaps it's *my* imagination,' she told him, wondering if that was the answer. Maybe she *was* becoming paranoid.

'What do you mean?'

She thought about mentioning what had been going on, her suspicions and suppositions but then decided against it.

'Forget it, David,' she asked. 'Please?'

He nodded.

Kelly finished her drink and pushed the glass away from her.

'Do you want another one?' the writer asked.

She smiled and shook her head.

'No thanks.'

There was another long silence between them then finally Kelly spoke.

'To tell you the truth, David,' she began, wearily, 'I'm a little bit concerned at the amount of interest Dr Vernon is showing in my research.'

Blake frowned.

'I don't understand,' he said. 'Surely he's got every right to be interested. He is Director of the Institute after all. It's only natural.'

'But he seems obsessed with my work.'

She told him about the incident with Maurice Grant, her trip to France and how Vernon had insisted on keeping her report.

Blake didn't speak, he merely finished the rest of his beer and put down the empty glass.

'Well,' she said, challengingly. 'Do you think I'm being paranoid now?'

'There's probably a perfectly reasonable explanation for it, Kelly,' he said.

'Don't try and humour me, David.' He was surprised at the vehemence in her words. 'There are other factors too. Things which don't make sense, which have no logical explanation.' She emphasised the last two words with scorn.

'Like what?' he wanted to know.

Kelly shivered as the slight breeze seemed to turn cold. She looked up and saw that the crimson of the setting sun had been replaced by a layered sky of purple. Kelly felt goose-pimples rise on her flesh and she rubbed her forearms.

'I don't feel comfortable talking about them here,' she told him, as if she feared some kind of surveillance in the peaceful garden.

'I'll take you home,' Blake said without hesitation.

They got to their feet and walked to the car park where the writer opened the passenger door of the XJS, allowing Kelly to slide in. He clambered in behind the wheel and started the engine, guiding the Jaguar out into the road.

'Are you all right?' he asked, glancing across at her, a little puzzled by her silence.

She nodded, feeling more at ease within the confines of the car. She even managed to smile at the writer who reached across and squeezed her hand gently. Kelly felt the coldness draining from her, as if Blake's touch had somehow restored her composure. She gripped his hand in return, reassured by his presence.

After a fifteen minute drive they reached her flat.

Kelly no longer felt the cold seeping through her and she looked at the writer almost gratefully.

'Home,' he said, smiling, and once more she found herself captivated by that smile of his. No, more than that. She was ensnared by it, drawn to him unlike any man before. He

159

exuded a magnetism which she found irresistible, almost in spite of herself.

'How do you feel now?' he asked.

'I'm OK,' she told him. 'Thanks, David.'

'For what?' he wanted to know.

'Just thanks.' She reached across and touched his hand with her slender fingers. If any emotion registered in his eyes she couldn't see it because his dark glasses now hid them even more completely. 'Would you like to come in for a coffee?'

Blake needed no second bidding. He climbed out of the Jag and locked his door then walked around and let Kelly out, watching appreciatively as she walked ahead of him, searching through her bag for her key. The writer enjoyed the gentle sway of her hips as she walked, the muscles in her calves tensing slightly with each step she took, perched on her backless high heels.

He followed her.

Her flat was, as he'd expected it to be both spotlessly clean and impeccably neat. At her bidding he seated himself in one of the big armchairs which flanked the electric fire. Kelly passed through into the kitchen and Blake heard water running as she filled a kettle.

She returned a moment later, crossing to the window to close the curtains. Then she flicked on the record player, dropping a disc onto the turntable.

'Do you mind some music?' she asked.

'Not at all,' he said.

The sound of Simon and Garfunkel flowed softly from the speakers.

'Coffee won't be a minute,' she told him, seating herself in the armchair opposite and, as she did so, she found once again that her gaze was drawn to the writer.

'Is this your own place?' Blake asked.

'It will be eventually,' Kelly told him. 'In another twenty years time probably.' She shrugged. 'By the time I'm an old, withered spinster at least I'll own my own flat.'

Blake smiled.

'I don't think there's much chance of you becoming an old withered spinster, Kelly,' he said.

'My mother keeps asking me why I'm not married yet.

Why I'm not knee deep in wet nappies and babies.' Kelly smiled. 'Parents love the idea of grandchildren until they actually have them. Then they complain because it makes them feel old.' Kelly felt a warm thrill run through her as she relaxed in the chair, feeling quite happy to let Blake look at her, to examine her with his eyes. Every so often she would see them flicker behind the dark screen of his glasses.

'Are you sensitive to light, David?' she asked him. 'I mean, the dark glasses.' She pointed to them.

'Slightly,' he said. 'I suppose that's what comes of squinting over a typewriter for five years.'

The kettle began to whistle. Kelly got to her feet and walked back into the kitchen, returning a moment later with two steaming mugs of coffee, one of which she handed to Blake. Then, she kicked off her shoes and, this time, sat on the floor in front of him, legs drawn up to one side of her.

'Kelly, I don't want to pry,' Blake began. 'But you said there were things about Vernon which you didn't understand. What did you mean?'

She sucked in a weary breath and lowered her gaze momentarily.

'From what you told me at the pub, I can't see any reason to suspect that Dr Vernon's up to something, especially not anything as sinister as you seem to think,' said Blake. 'What reasons would he have?'

'David,' she said, trying to keep her voice calm. 'I was responsible for what happened to Maurice Grant. What I did was wrong. It broke the rules of the Institute. The authorities could have closed the place. That Institute is Vernon's pride and joy. He could have lost it because of me and yet he didn't so much as give me a warning or suspend me.' She decided to put down her mug. 'Instead, he protected me when he had every right to dismiss me on the spot. Then, when I got back from France, he wanted to know everything that happened and he kept my report.'

Blake sat forward in his chair.

'You make Vernon sound like a monster when all he tried to do was help you,' he said.

'He's hiding something, David,' she said, angrily. 'John Fraser knew what it was. That's why he was killed.'

'Who's Fraser?'

She explained as much as she knew about the events of the last two days.

'But if Fraser was killed in a car crash, how could Vernon be involved?' the writer wanted to know. 'It was an accident, surely?'

'He knew about Vernon's secret.'

Another heavy silence descended, finally broken by Blake.

'I don't see how you can suspect Vernon of being involved in Fraser's death,' he said.

'David, he won't let *anyone* come between him and this research.'

'Does that include you?' Blake asked, cryptically.

It was at that point that the phone rang.

32

For long moments neither of them moved as the strident ringing filled the room. Then, finally, Kelly got to her feet and walked across to the phone, lifting the receiver tentatively, wondering why she felt so apprehensive. Blake watched her, noticing the hesitancy in her movements.

'Hello,' she said.

No answer.

'Hello,' she repeated, looking across at Blake as if seeking reassurance.

Words suddenly came gushing forth from the caller at the other end, some of which she didn't understand. Not merely due to the speed with which they were uttered but because they were in French.

'Who is this?' she asked, holding the phone away from her for a second as a particularly loud crackle of static broke up the line. 'Hello. Can you hear me? Who's speaking?'

'Kelly. It's Michel Lasalle.'

She relaxed slightly.

'Listen to me, you must listen,' he blurted, and Kelly was

162

more than aware of the high-pitched desperation in his voice. His breathing was harsh and irregular, as if he'd been running for a long time. 'I saw Madelaine,' he told her, his voice cracking. 'I saw her.'

'You had a nightmare, Michel, it's understandable ...'

He interrupted.

'No, I touched her, felt her,' he insisted.

'It was a nightmare,' she repeated.

'No. Joubert saw her too.'

Kelly frowned.

'What do you mean? How was he involved?' she wanted to know. She felt the tension returning to her muscles.

'He was there, with me,' the Frenchman continued, panting loudly. He babbled something in French then laughed dryly. A sound which sent a shiver down Kelly's spine. 'He watched me making love to her. She felt cold in my arms but it didn't matter, she is still mine. I still want her.'

Kelly tried to speak but couldn't.

'Joubert has not forgiven me,' the Frenchman said, softly. 'I don't think he ever will.'

'Forgiven you for what?' Kelly wanted to know.

'Writing that article.'

'Did he speak to you?' she asked, wondering whether or not she should humour the distraught man.

'He is always there, Kelly. Always. Watching.'

An uneasy silence fell, broken only by the gentle hiss of static burbling in the lines.

'Michel, are you still there?' Kelly finally said.

Silence.

'Michel, answer me.'

She heard a click and realized that he'd hung up. For long seconds she stared at the receiver then slowly replaced it.

'What was it?' Blake asked, seeing the concern on her face.

She walked slowly back towards him and seated herself on the floor once again, reaching for her coffee. It was cold.

'Kelly, who *was* that?' the writer persisted.

'Lasalle. One of the men from the Metapsychic Centre,' she told him, then proceeded to relay what the Frenchman had said to her.

163

'He's convinced that it was real,' she said.

Blake shrugged.

'Nightmares are usually vivid,' he said.

Kelly shook her head.

'But Lasalle won't accept that he had a nightmare,' she protested. 'He's convinced that what he experienced actually happened.' She sighed. 'I hope to God he's not heading for another breakdown. He had one when his wife died.' She looked up at Blake. 'And Joubert, he mentioned that Joubert was present in the nightmare. He sounded frightened of him.' She lowered her gaze once more. 'First Fraser, now Lasalle. One man's dead, another is close to a nervous breakdown and all because of the research I'm engaged in.'

'You can't blame yourself, Kelly,' Blake said, reaching out and gently lifting her head with his right hand.

She gripped that hand, aware of the combination of gentleness and strength in it but more conscious of the warmth which seemed to flow from it, from his entire being. She looked up at him, trying to see his eyes, searching for a glimmer behind the tinted screens which masked them. Kelly kissed his hand and moved closer to him, resting her own right hand on his knee as he slowly stroked the back of her neck beneath her hair. She squirmed beneath his subtle caresses, moving nearer, anxious to touch him fully. His other hand began gently kneading the smooth flesh of her shoulder and she closed her eyes.

'What if Vernon *is* responsible for Fraser's death?' she said, quietly, enjoying the sensations which were coursing through her.

'Then he's a dangerous man,' Blake said. 'You should stay away from him.'

'And Joubert?'

'Kelly. If there is any possibility that either of them have some kind of psychic power then you'd do best not to let them know you suspect.'

'But I must know the truth, David,' she protested, turning to face him.

As she did so, Blake leant forward and kissed her. Their lips brushed gently for a moment then, unhesitatingly, Kelly pressed her mouth to his. Blake responded fiercely, matching her passion with his own desire.

Kelly snaked her hand up around his neck, as if reluctant to break the kiss. When she finally did, she was panting softly, her eyes riveted to Blake. Her body was burning, as if fire were pouring through her veins. She felt her nipples, now stiff and erect, straining almost painfully against her dress and between her slender legs she felt a glowing moistness. Blake sensed her excitement and she could see that he felt similarly aroused by the contact they had enjoyed. Her hand strayed to the beginnings of bulge in his trousers, massaging and rubbing until Blake himself grunted under his breath.

Kelly moved away from him slightly, lying back on the carpet before him, inviting his attentions. The writer was not slow to respond and he joined her, his hands moving over the thin material of her dress until they came to her breasts. He rubbed gently, feeling the hardened points beneath his palms as she arched her back. Kelly felt as if she were floating, the warm glow between her legs becoming an all-consuming desire which filled every part of her. She took Blake's left hand and guided it up inside her dress, moaning as his fingers stroked the smooth flesh of her inner thighs, pausing there for agonisingly exquisite seconds before moving higher. She felt his probing digits reach her panties, his forefinger hooked, pulling down the flimsy garment. She lifted her buttocks to allow him to remove them, watching as he first kissed the sodden material before laying it on one side.

She pulled him close to her, their mouths locking once more as she thrust her pelvis towards his searching hand, almost crying aloud as his finger touched the hardened bud of her clitoris and began rubbing gently. She fumbled for his zip and freed his bulging erection, encircling it with her slender fingers, working up a gentle rhythm as she teased his stiff shaft. For three or four minutes they remained like that and then she suggested they undress.

It took them mere moments then, naked, they were free to explore every inch of the other's body. Blake lowered his head to her breasts and took first one nipple then the other between his teeth, rolling it gently as he flicked it with his tongue. Kelly felt his other hand trace a pattern across her belly before gliding through her soft pubic hair once more to search for her most sensitive area and she rolled onto her side, allowing him to push his heavily muscled thigh against her. She ground hard against him, eventually manoeuvering herself so that he was beneath her. She straddled his stomach.

'Take these off,' she said, quietly, reaching for his dark glasses. 'I want to see your eyes.'

Blake himself removed them and then turned to look at her.

Kelly felt as if the breath had been torn from her, as if someone had punched her hard and winded her.

Blake's eyes were the colour of a June sky. A deep blue which she found overwhelming in their intensity. She felt as if she were a puppet, suspended by wires which came from those eyes, her movements and feelings controlled by them. A renewed and much more powerful surge of emotion shook her and she bent forward to kiss him. But, he gripped her waist and almost lifted her up on to his chest, smiling as she rubbed herself against him. He felt the wetness spilling from her, dampening his chest. She moved a little further so that he could reach her with his tongue.

Kelly gasped as she felt it flicking over her distended lips, reaming her swollen cleft before fastening on her clitoris. She spoke his name, her head thrown back as she surrendered to the feelings which were sweeping over her. Kelly felt a tightening around her thighs, the first unmistakable sign of approaching orgasm. His hands reached up and found her swollen nipples, adding to her overall pleasure which was now building up like an impending explosion.

She twisted around so that she could reach his penis, lying on him in order to allow it to reach her mouth. She studied the bulbous head for a moment then took it into her mouth, wrapping her tongue around it, her free hand working away at the root, fondling his testicles. She felt him stiffen, realized that his excitement was a great as hers. But she needed him more fully. Kelly rolled to one side, kissing him briefly as she did so then she knelt over his groin, cradling his throbbing member in one hand, lowering herself slowly until it nudged her aching vagina. They both gasped as the union was completed. She sank down onto him, his shaft swallowed by her liquescent cleft.

Kelly knew that she would not be able to hold back any

longer. She stared into Blake's eyes and began moving up and down. The sensations began almost at once. She was aware only of the throbbing pleasure between her legs and his welcoming blue eyes which seemed to fill her entire field of vision. She could not look away from him and, as she speeded up her movements, she felt as though she were being joined with him, melting into him to form one entity.

The power of the orgasm made her cry out loudly. She bounced up and down on him, each wave of pleasure more intense than the one before. She had never felt anything so overwhelmingly wonderful in her life and that pleasure, almost impossibly, suddenly re-doubled as she felt him writhe beneath her as his own climax washed over him. Kelly moaned loudly as she felt his hot liquid spurt into her and she ground herself hard against him, coaxing every last drop from him. Shaking and bathed in perspiration, she slumped forward, kissing him gently, unable to look anywhere else but at his eyes.

They lay still, coupled together as he softened within her.

It was a long time before either of them spoke. The record player was silent, the record having finished long ago. Only the sound of the wind outside was audible.

'You don't have to drive back to London tonight do you?' Kelly asked him.

'You try getting rid of me,' he said, smiling.

They both laughed.

Kelly ran a finger across his lips then kissed him softly.

Her gaze never left his deep blue eyes and, once more, she felt that glorious sensation of floating. As if she had no control over her own body.

Blake smiled broadly.

PART TWO

'All human beings, as we meet them, are
commingled out of good and evil ...'
— *Robert Louis Stevenson*

'He who shall teach the child to doubt,
Shall ne'er the rotting grave get out.'
— *William Blake*

the entertainment industry.

He spotted Jim O'Neil sitting in one corner. He was on the
Bavarian set... European tour which ... to welcome him
and he...

33

London

The Waterloo Club, in the heart of London's Mayfair, was a
magnificent anachronism.

Founded a year after the battle of Waterloo by a group of
Wellington's infantry officers, the building was more like a
museum. There was a subdued reverence about the place,
much like that usually reserved for a church. It languished in
cultivated peacefulness and had defied all but the most
necessary architectural changes since its construction in 1816.
But, for all that, it retained an archaic splendour which was
fascinating.

David Blake sipped his drink and scanned the panelled
walls. The room seemed dark, despite the lamps which
burned in profusion, complimented by the huge crystal
chandelier which hung from the ceiling. There were a
number of paintings on view including excellent copies of
Denis Dighton's 'Sergeant Ewart capturing the Eagle of the
45th', a picture which Blake remembered from a history
book. Behind the bar was Sir William Allen's panoramic
view of Waterloo, a full fifteen feet in length. It hung in a gilt
frame, as imposing a piece of art as Blake had seen. On
another wall were two polished cuirasses, the breast plates
still carrying musket ball holes. Above them were the brass
helmets of Carabiniers, the long swords of the Scots Greys
and various original muskets and pistols.

Blake was suitably impressed with the surroundings
despite being somewhat perplexed as to why the BBC should
have chosen such a setting for the party to welcome Jonathan
Mathias to England. Other guests chatted amiably, some,
like himself, gazing at the paintings and other paraphernalia.
He guessed that there must be about two dozen people there,
most of whom he recognized from one or other branch of the

entertainment industry.

He spotted Jim O'Neil sitting in one corner. He was on the British leg of a European tour which had, so far, taken him and his band to ten different countries encompassing over eighty gigs. He was a tall, wiry man in his late twenties, dressed completely in black leather. The rock star was nodding intently as two young women chatted animatedly to him.

The writer was aware of other well-known faces too. He caught sight of Sir George Howe, the new head of the BBC, speaking to a group of men which included Gerald Braddock.

Braddock was the present Government's Minister for the Arts, a plump, red-faced man whose shirt collar was much too tight for him, a condition not aided by his tie which appeared to have been fastened by a member of the thugee cult. Every time he swallowed he looked as though he was going to choke.

Next to him stood Roger Carr, host of the chat show on which Mathias was to appear.

Elsewhere, Blake spotted actors and actresses from TV, an agent or two but, as far as he could see, he was the only writer who had been invited.

He'd been a little surprised by the invitation although he had written for the BBC in the past, most notably, a six part series on the paranormal. When he learned that Mathias was to be the guest of honour he'd accepted the invitation readily.

At the moment, however, there was no sign of the American.

'Do you get invited to many dos like this?' Kelly asked him, looking around at the array of talent in the room.

Blake had been seeing her for just over a week now, driving back and forth to Oxford, staying at her flat most nights and returning to his home to work during the day. When he'd told her about the invitation, initially she'd been apprehensive but now, as she scanned the other guests, she did not regret her decision to accompany him.

'There *aren't* many dos like this.' he told her, looking around, wondering where Mathias had disappeared to.

The psychic arrived as if on cue, emerging from the club

cloakroom like something from a Bram Stoker novel. He wore a black three-piece suit and white shirt, a black bow-tie at his throat. Cufflinks bearing large diamonds sparkled in the light like millions of insect eyes. The psychic was introduced to Sir George Howe and his group. All eyes turned towards the little tableau and the previously subdued conversation seemed to drop to a hush. It was as if a powerful magnet had been brought into the room, drawing everything to it.

'He looks very imposing in the flesh,' said Kelly, almost in awe. 'I've only ever seen him in photographs.'

Blake didn't answer her. His eye had been caught by more belated movement from the direction of the cloakroom as a late-comer arrived.

'Christ,' murmured the writer, nudging Kelly. 'Look.'

He nodded in the appropriate direction and she managed to tear her gaze from Mathias.

The late-comer slipped into the room and over to the group surrounding the psychic. Kelly looked at him and then at Blake.

'What's *he* doing here?' she said, in bewilderment.

Dr Stephen Vernon ran a nervous hand through his hair and sidled up beside Sir George Howe.

Blake and Kelly watched as the Institute Director was introduced. Words were exchanged but, no matter how hard she tried, Kelly could not hear what was being said. Gradually, the babble of conversation began to fill the room again.

Kelly hesitated, watching Vernon as he stood listening to the psychic.

'Kelly,' Blake said, forcefully, gripping her arm. 'Come on. Let's get another drink.'

Almost reluctantly, she followed him to the bar where Jim O'Neil now sat, perched on one of the tall stools. He was still listening to one of the girls but his interest seemed to have waned. As Blake and Kelly approached he ran an appreciative eye over Kelly whose full breasts were prominent due to the plunging neck-line of her dress. A tiny gold crucifix hung invitingly between them. O'Neil smiled at her and Kelly returned the gesture.

'Hello,' said O'Neil, nodding at them both but keeping his

eyes on Kelly.

The writer turned and smiled, shaking the other man's outstretched hand.

Introductions were swiftly made. O'Neil took Kelly's hand and kissed it delicately.

'Would you like a drink?' asked Blake.

'Make it a pint of bitter will you,' the singer asked. 'I'm sick of these bleeding cocktails.' He pushed the glass away from him.

The barman gave him a disdainful look, watching as the other man downed half of the foaming pint.

'Christ, that's better,' he said.

Kelly caught the sound of a cockney accent in his voice.

'No gig tonight?' Blake asked.

O'Neil shook his head.

'The rest of the band have got the night off,' he said, scratching bristles on his chin which looked as if you could strike a match on them. 'My manager said I ought to come here. God knows why.' He supped some more of his pint. 'I'm surprised they invited me in the first place. I mean, they never play any of my fucking records on Radio One.' He chuckled.

Kelly pulled Blake's arm and nodded in the direction of a nearby table. The two of them said they'd speak to O'Neil again later then left him at the bar ordering another pint.

The writer was in the process of pulling out a chair for Kelly when he saw Mathias and his little entourage approaching. The psychic smiled broadly when he saw Blake. Kelly turned and found herself looking straight at Dr Vernon. They exchanged awkward glances then Kelly looked at Mathias who was already shaking hands with Blake.

'It's good to see you again, David,' said the American. 'How's the book coming along?'

'I'm getting there,' the writer said. 'You look well, Jonathan.'

'I see there are no need for introductions where you two are concerned,' said Sir George Howe, smiling.

'We're not exactly strangers,' Mathias told him. Then he looked at Kelly. 'But I don't know you. And I feel that I should.'

The psychic smiled and Kelly saw a glint in his eye.

She introduced herself then stepped back, one eye on Vernon, as Sir George completed the introductions.

Blake shook hands with Gerald Braddock, wincing slightly as he felt the pudgy clamminess of the politician's hand.

Then came Vernon.

'This is Dr Stephen Vernon, an old friend of mine, he ...'

'We've met,' Blake told Sir George. 'How are you, Dr Vernon?'

'I'm very well,' said the older man. He looked at Kelly. 'I didn't expect to see you here tonight, Kelly.'

She didn't answer.

'Well, it seems as if everyone knows everyone else,' said Sir George, aware of the iciness in the air. His stilted laugh died away rapidly.

'How long are you here for, Jonathan?' Blake asked the psychic.

'Three or four days. Long enough to do the show with Mr Carr, and a couple of newspaper interviews, radio pieces. You know the kind of thing,' Mathias told him.

'I saw in the paper that you were coming to England,' Blake said. 'When are you doing the TV show?'

'It's being broadcast the day after tomorrow,' Roger Carr said, stepping forward. 'You should watch it, Mr Blake, I mean you deal in the same kind of tricks don't you? Only you write about them instead.' The interviewer smiled.

Blake returned the smile.

'You know, Mr Carr, there's something I've never been able to figure out about you,' the writer said. 'You're either stupid, in which case I'm sorry for you, or you're pig-ignorant. But I haven't been able to figure out which it is yet.'

Carr shot him an angry glance and opened his mouth to speak but, before he could, all eyes turned in the direction of the cloakroom.

There was an unholy din coming from there, a cacophony of shouts through which the high-pitched voice of a woman could be heard.

Seconds later, a figure dressed in a grey coat, spattered with rain, burst into the peaceful confines of the Waterloo Club. Her hair was wind-blown, her make-up streaked by the

174

rain. She stood panting in the doorway, her eyes fixed on Mathias.

'My God,' muttered Sir George. Then, to a green-coated doorman who had tried to stop the woman entering:

'Could you please eject this lady.'

'No,' Mathias said, raising a hand. 'Leave her.'

'David, who is she?' asked Kelly, noticing the look of recognition on Blake's face as he gazed at the woman.

'Toni Landers,' he said. 'She's an actress.' But the woman whom he had met in New York had been a radiant, sensuous creature. The woman who now stood in the doorway was pale and unkempt, her features haggard. She looked as though she'd aged ten years.

'Do you know this woman?' asked Sir George, looking first at Toni, then at Mathias who had not taken his eyes from her.

'Yes, I know her,' the psychic said.

'Could someone explain what the hell is going on?' Sir George demanded.

'Jonathan, I have to speak to you,' Toni said, her voice cracking. She leant against the bar for support.

Jim O'Neil was on his feet, ready to intervene. Toni looked ready to keel over. She sat down on a bar stool, her gaze still on the psychic.

'How did you find me?' he asked, moving towards her.

'I knew you were coming to England. I've been waiting for you. I found out which hotel you were staying in. They told me where you'd be tonight,' she admitted.

'She's bloody mad,' snapped Roger Carr, dismissively. 'Get her out of here.'

'Shut up,' Mathias rasped. 'Leave her.'

The doorman took a step away from Toni.

'Is this one of your theatrical tricks, Mathias?' Carr demanded.

Blake turned on him.

'Just for once, keep your bloody mouth shut,' he snapped. He motioned to the barman. 'Give her a brandy.'

The man hesitated, looking at Sir George.

'Come on, man, for Christ's sake,' Blake insisted.

'Give her the fucking drink. You heard him,' snarled Jim O'Neil, watching as the barman poured a large measure and handed it to Toni. She downed most of it, coughing as the fiery liquid burned its way to her stomach.

'Toni, what do you want?' Mathias asked her, quietly.

'I need your help, Jonathan,' she told him, tears glistening in her eyes. 'You're the only one who can help me now.'

'Why didn't you come to me before? What were you afraid of?'

She swallowed what was left in the glass.

'That you'd turn me away.'

He shook his head.

'Jonathan, I haven't been able to stop thinking about Rick. Every time I see a child I think about him.' The tears were coursing down her cheeks now. 'Please help me.' Her self-control finally dissolved in a paroxysm of sobs.

Mathias supported her and she clung to him, her body trembling violently.

'What do you want me to do?' he asked.

'Reach him,' she said, flatly. 'Now.'

Mathias didn't speak.

'Please, do I have to beg you?' Some of the despair in her voice had turned to anger. 'Contact my son.'

34

'This is a London club, not a fairground tent,' protested Sir George Ward as the massive oak table was dragged into the centre of the room by Blake, O'Neil and a third man.

'What I intend to do is no fairground trick,' Mathias told him, watching as a number of chairs were placed around the table.

The other guests looked on in stunned, anticipatory silence, Kelly amongst them. Every so often she cast a glance in Dr Vernon's direction, noticing that he was smiling thinly as he observed the proceedings.

Gerald Braddock plucked at the folds of fat beneath his jaw and shifted nervously from one foot to the other.

Toni Landers sat at the bar, the glass of brandy cradled in her shaking hand.

'What are you trying to prove by doing this, Mathias?' Roger Carr wanted to know.

'I don't have to prove anything, Mr Carr,' the psychic said, turning away from him. He held out a hand for Toni Landers to join him. She downed what was left in her glass and wandered across the room. 'Sit there,' the psychic told her, motioning to the chair on his right.

Blake watched with interest, aware that Kelly was gripping his arm tightly. He took her hand and held it, reassuringly.

'I cannot do this alone,' Mathias said, addressing the other guests. 'I must ask for the help of some of you. Not for my own sake but for this lady.' He motioned towards Toni. 'There's nothing to be afraid of. Nothing can hurt you.'

Jim O'Neil was the first to step forward.

'What the hell,' he said, sitting beside Toni then turning in his seat to look at the others.

Roger Carr joined him, sitting on the other side of the table.

Blake looked at Kelly and she nodded almost imperceptibly. They both stepped forward, the writer seating himself directly opposite where Mathias would be.

'Thank you, David,' said the psychic.

As if prompted by Kelly's action, Dr Vernon pulled up a chair and sat down next to her. She eyed him suspiciously for a moment then looked at Blake who had his eyes closed slightly.

'Sir George?' Mathias said, looking at the head of the BBC.

'No, I want no part of this,' said the bald man, defiantly.

Gerald Braddock, who had been rubbing his hands together nervously finally moved towards the table.

'What are you doing, Gerald?' Sir George asked him.

'It can't do any harm,' Braddock said, wiping his palms on his trousers. He looked at the others seated around the table and swallowed hard.

No one else in the room moved. Mathias walked to his seat between Toni Landers and Roger Carr. Opposite him was Blake. To *his* right, Kelly. At the writer's left hand sat Braddock then O'Neil.

'Could we have the lights turned off please?' Mathias asked. 'All but the one over the table.'

Sir George surveyed the group seated before him for a moment then with a sigh he nodded to the club's doorman who flicked off the lights one by one until the table was illuminated by a solitary lamp. Shadows were thick all around it, the other guests swallowed up by them.

'Could you all place your hands, palms down, on the table,' Mathias asked. 'So that your finger-tips are touching the hands of the person on either side of you.'

'I thought we were supposed to hold hands,' muttered Carr, sarcastically.

'Just do as I ask, please,' Mathias said.

Kelly looked up. In the half light, the psychic's face looked milk-white, his eyes standing out in stark contrast. She felt a strange tingle flow through her, a feeling not unlike a small electric shock. She glanced at Blake, who was looking at the psychic, then at Vernon, who had his head lowered.

'Empty your minds,' said Mathias. 'Think of nothing. Hear nothing but my voice. Be aware of nothing but the touch of the people beside you.' His voice had fallen to a low whisper.

The room was silent, only the low, guttural breathing of the psychic audible in the stillness.

Kelly shivered involuntarily and turned her head slightly looking at the others seated with her. All of them had their heads bowed as if in prayer. She too dropped her gaze, noticing as she did that Blake's fingers were shaking slightly. But then so were her own. Indeed, everyone around the table seemed to be undergoing minute, reflexive muscular contractions which jerked their bodies almost imperceptibly every few seconds.

Mathias grunted something inaudible then coughed. His eyes closed and his head began to tilt backward. His chest was heaving as if he were finding it difficult to breathe.

'Don't break the circle,' he muttered, throatily. 'Don't ... break ...'

He clenched his teeth together, as if in pain and a long, wheezing sound escaped him. It was as if someone had punctured a set of bellows. His body began to shake more violently, perspiration beading on his forehead, glistening in

178

the dull light. His eyes suddenly shot open, bulging wide in the sockets, his head still tilted backward.

He groaned again, more loudly this time.

The light above the table flickered, went out then glowed with unnatural brilliance once more.

'The child,' croaked Mathias. 'The ... child ...'

His groans became shouts.

Kelly tried to raise her head but it was as if there was a heavy weight secured to her chin. Only by monumental effort did she manage to raise it an inch or so.

Somewhere behind her one of the swords fell from the wall with a loud clatter but none of those seated at the table could move to find the source of the noise. They were all held as if by some invisible hand, aware only of the increasing warmth in the room. A warmth which seemed to be radiating from the very centre of the table itself.

'The child,' Mathias gasped once more.

This time Kelly recoiled as a vile stench assaulted her nostrils. A sickly sweet odour which reminded her of bad meat. She coughed, her stomach churning.

The feeling of heat was growing stronger until it seemed that the table must be ablaze. But, at last, she found that she could raise her head.

If she had been able to, she would have screamed.

Toni Landers beat her to it.

Standing in the centre of the table was the image of her son.

His clothes, what remained of them, were blackened and scorched, hanging in places like burned tassles. Beneath the fabric his skin was red raw, mottled green in places. The left arm had been completely stripped of flesh and what musculature remained was wasted and scorched. Bone shone with dazzling whiteness through the charred mess. The chest and lower body was a mass of suppurating sores which were weeping sticky clear pus like so many diseased eyes. But it was the head and neck which bore the most horrific injury. The boy's head was twisted at an impossible angle, a portion of spinal column visible through the pulped mess at the base of the skull. The head itself seemed to have been cracked open like an egg shell and a lump of jellied brain matter bulged obscenely from one of the rents. The bottom lip had been torn off, taking most of the left cheek with it, to expose ligaments and tendons which still twitched spasmodically. Blood had soaked the boy's upper body, its coppery odour mingling with the overpowering stink of burned skin and hair.

Toni Landers tried to raise her hands to shield her eyes from this abomination which had once been her son but it was as if someone had nailed her fingers to the table. She could only sit helplessly and watch as the apparition turned full circle in the middle of the table, meeting the horrified gaze of all those present before bringing its milky orbs to bear on her. One of the eyes had been punctured by a piece of broken skull and it nestled uselessly in the bloodied socket like a burst balloon.

The apparition took a step towards her.

It was smiling.

Kelly looked across at Mathias and saw that there was perspiration pouring down his face as he gazed at the sight before him. She then turned slightly and looked at Blake. He was not looking at the child but at the psychic, the writer's own body trembling convulsively.

The figure of the boy moved closer to Toni Landers, one charred hand rising before it as it reached the edge of the table.

Finally, by a monumental effort of will, Toni managed to lift her hands from the table.

As she covered her face she let out a scream which threatened to shake the building.

'Look,' urged Jim O'Neil.

Like the image on a TV set, the apparition of Rick Landers began to fade. Not slowly but with almost breathtaking suddenness until the table was empty once more. Above them, the light dimmed again.

'My God,' burbled Gerald Braddock. 'What *was* that?'

Even if anyone heard him, no one seemed capable of furnishing him with an answer.

Sir George Howe strode to the panel of switches behind the bar and snapped on the lights himself.

Mathias sat unmoved at the table, his eyes locked with those of Blake. The writer was breathing heavily, as if he'd just run up a flight of long steps. The two men regarded one another a moment longer then Mathias turned to Toni Landers who was sobbing uncontrollably beside him.

'Fuck me,' was all Jim O'Neil could say. His voice a low whisper.

Dr Vernon stroked his chin thoughtfully, looking at the spot on the table top where the apparition had first materialized. It still shone as if newly polished. He inhaled. There was no smell of burned flesh any longer, no cloying odour of blood. Only the acrid smell of perspiration.

Beside him, Kelly touched Blake's hand, seeing that the writer looked a little pale.

'Are you all right, David?' she asked, aware that her own heart was beating wildly.

Blake nodded.

'And you?' he wanted to know.

She was shaking badly and Blake put one arm around her shoulder, drawing her close to him.

Roger Carr sat where he was for a moment, looking at the others around the table, then he got to his feet and stalked across to the bar where he downed a large scotch in two huge swallows. Only then did he begin to calm down. He looked back over his shoulder at Mathias.

Not only was this man very good at what he did, the bastard was convincing too. Carr ordered another scotch.

Jonathan Mathias finally managed to quieten Toni Landers, wiping away some of her tears with his handkerchief. He helped her to her feet and led her outside into the rain soaked night. He told his chauffeur to take her home and then return.

As the psychic stood alone on the pavement watching the car disappear from view he looked down at his hands.

Both palms were red raw, as if he'd been holding something very hot. His entire body was sheathed in sweat but he felt colder than he'd ever felt in his life.

Blake hit the last full stop, pulled the paper from the
typewriter and laid it on top of the pile beside him.

Without the clacking of typewriter keys, the cellar was
once more silent.

The writer picked up the pages next to him and skimmed
through them. Another day or so and the book would be
finished, he guessed. He had submitted the bulk of it to his
publisher shortly after returning from the States. Now he was
nearing the end. He sat back in his chair and yawned. It was
almost 8 a.m. He'd been working for two hours. Blake
always rose early, completing the greater part of his work
during the morning. It was a routine which he'd followed for
the last four years. Down in the cellar it was peaceful. He
didn't even hear the comings and goings of his neighbours.
But, on this particular morning, his mind had been elsewhere.

As hard as he tried, he could not shake the image of Toni
Landers' dead child from his mind. In fact, the entire episode
of the previous night still burned as clearly in his consciousness as if it had been branded there. He remembered the
terror etched on the faces of those who had sat at the table
with him, the horrified reactions of those who had looked on
from the relative safety beyond the circle.

The gathering had begun to break up almost immediately
after the seance. Blake himself, rather than drive back to
Oxford, had persuaded Kelly to stay at his house for the
night. She had readily agreed. She was upstairs dressing. He
had woken her before he'd climbed out of bed, they had
made love and she had decided to take a long hot bath before
he drove her home.

He put the cover back on the typewriter and made his way
up the stone steps from the subterranean work room, locking
the door behind him as he emerged into the hall.

'What are you hiding down there? The Crown Jewels?'

The voice startled him momentarily and he spun round to see Kelly descending the stairs.

Blake smiled and pocketed the key to the cellar.

'Force of habit,' he said. 'I don't like to be disturbed.'

They walked through into the kitchen where she put the kettle on while he jammed some bread into the toaster. Kelly spooned coffee into a couple of mugs.

'Are you all right, Kelly?' he asked, noticing that she looked pale.

She nodded.

'I'm a little tired, I didn't sleep too well last night,' she told him.

'That's understandable.'

'Understandable, but not forgivable.'

He looked puzzled.

'David, I'm a psychic investigator. My reactions to the paranormal, anything out of the ordinary, should be ... well, scientific. But what I saw last night at that seance terrified me. I couldn't even think straight.'

'If it's any consolation,' he said. 'I don't think you were the only one.' He caught the toast as it popped up.

Kelly watched him as he buttered it, finally handing her a slice.

'I'd still like to know how Vernon managed to get an invitation,' she said.

'He's a friend of Sir George Howe, the old boy told us that.'

Kelly nodded slowly.

'I still don't trust him,' she said.

Blake leant forward and kissed her on the forehead.

'I don't trust anyone.'

The kettle began to boil.

It was 2.15 when Blake parked the XJS back in his driveway. The journey back from Oxford had taken longer than he'd expected due to a traffic hold up on the way back into the town. Now he clambered out of the Jag and headed for his front door, waving a greeting to one of his neighbours as she passed by with her two children.

Blake walked in and discovered that the postman had been

during his absence. There was a slim envelope which bore a familiar type-face. He tore it open and unfolded the letter, heading towards the sitting room as he did so. The writer perched on the edge of a chair and read aloud.

'Dear David, I'm sorry to have kept you waiting but I have only recently managed to read the manuscript of "From Within". I'm even sorrier to tell you that I do not feel that it matches the quality of your earlier work, which was based on solid facts and research. This latest effort seems comprised mostly of speculation and theorising, particularly on the subject of Astral travel and mind control. I realize that these subjects are open to question but the book does not convince me as to the validity of your statements. So how can we expect the public to believe it?

Despite the fact that you are well established and a proven top-seller, I feel that I cannot, as yet offer you a contract based on the manuscript in its present state.'

Blake got to his feet, still glaring angrily at the letter.

It was signed with the sweeping hand of Phillip Campbell, his publisher.

'I cannot offer you a contract ...' Blake muttered, angrily. He crossed to the phone and picked up the receiver, punching buttons irritably.

'Good morning ...'

He gave the receptionist no time to complete the formalities.

'Phillip Campbell, please,' he said, impatiently.

There was a click at the other line then another woman's voice.

'Phillip Campbell's office, good afternoon.'

'Is Phillip there?'

'Yes, who's calling?'

'David Blake.'

Another click. A hiss of static.

'Good afternoon, David.'

He recognized Campbell's Glaswegian accent immediately.

'Hello, Phil. I'd like a word if you can spare me the time.'

'Sure. What's on your mind?'

' "I cannot offer you a contract", that's what's on my mind,' Blake snapped. 'What the hell is going on, Phil? What's wrong with the bloody book?'

'I thought I told you that in the letter,' the Scot said.

' "Speculation and theorising" is that it?'

'Look, Dave, don't start getting uptight about it. If you can't stand a bit of criticism from a friend then maybe you're in the wrong game. What I wrote was meant to help.'

'You haven't seen the completed manuscript yet,' Blake reminded him.

'Fair enough. Maybe I'll change my mind once I have but, like I said, you need more concrete facts in it. Especially this business about someone being able to control another person's Astral Body. You're going to have trouble making the readers believe that.'

'Phil, I'm telling you, I know it can be done,' said Blake.

'Facts, Dave,' the publisher reminded him. 'Once I've seen the finished manuscript then maybe we can sort something out.'

There was a moment's pause then the Scot continued.

'David, I want this book in print as much as you do. We both stand to make a lot of money out of it but, in its present form, we'll be laughed out of court if we publish. You realize that.'

Blake sighed.

'Facts,' he said. 'All right, Phil, I'll get back to you.' He hung up. The writer stood there for a moment then he balled up the letter and threw it into a nearby waste-basket.

He headed back towards the cellar.

36

Oxford

The book fell from his hand and hit the bedroom carpet with a thud.

Dr Stephen Vernon sat up, disturbed from his light sleep. He yawned, retrieved the book and placed it on his bedside table. Then he reached across and flicked off the light. The hands of his watch glowed dully, showing him that it was almost 1.05 a.m. He pulled the sheet up to his neck and closed his eyes but the sleep which had come to him earlier now seemed to desert him. He rolled onto his side, then his back, then the other side but the more he moved the more he seemed to shed any desire to sleep.

He sat up again, reaching for the book.

He read three or four pages without remembering a single word and, with a sigh, replaced the thick tome. He decided that his best strategy was to get out of bed. He'd make himself a hot drink, that usually did the trick. Vernon clambered out of bed and pulled on his dressing gown. He left the bedside lamp burning and padded across the landing.

He was at the top of the stairs when he heard the faint knocking.

Almost instinctively he turned and looked at the door of the locked room but it took him but an instant to realize that the sound had originated downstairs.

He hesitated.

The knocking came again.

Vernon swallowed hard and moved cautiously down the first three or four steps.

Outside, in the darkness, he heard the sound of movement, the crunching of gravel beneath heavy feet.

Vernon peered over the bannister, down into the pit of blackness which was his hallway. The light switch was at the bottom, beside the large window which looked out onto the gravel drive and the front garden.

He glanced down, his heart quickening slightly.

He had neglected to draw the curtain across that window.

The movement seemed to have stopped so Vernon scuttled down the stairs, gripping the bannister with one hand in case he overbalanced in the gloom.

He was level with the window when he saw a dark shape three or four feet from the glass.

It moved rapidly back into the gloom and seemed to disappear.

Vernon felt himself perspiring as he reached the light switch, not sure whether to turn it on or not. If he did then *he* would be visible to anyone outside. His hand hovered over the switch but, eventually, he decided against it and moved cautiously into the sitting room, ears ever alert for the slightest sound.

From the brass bucket beside the fire-place he retrieved a poker then he turned and walked back into the hall, pausing at the front door, listening.

There was more movement outside.

Footsteps.

Should he call the police, he wondered? If it was burglars then there might be more than one of them. What if they should attack him?

What if he called the police but they didn't arrive in time?

What if ...

The sound was right outside the front door now.

Vernon, with excruciating care, slipped the bolt then the chain and fastened his hand around the door handle, raising the poker high above his head in readiness to strike. His heart was thudding madly against his ribs, his mouth as dry as parchment.

He pulled open the door.

Nothing.

Only the wind greeted him, a cool breeze which made him shiver. He exhaled almost gratefully and lowered the poker, squinting into the blackness in search of that elusive shape.

He saw nothing.

Vernon waited a moment longer then turned.

He almost screamed as the hand gripped his shoulder.

187

It appeared as if from nowhere and the older man tried to raise the poker once more but his co-ordination seemed to have deserted him. It fell from his grasp with a dull clang.

He turned to see the figure standing before him.

'You?' he gasped, one hand clutched to his chest. 'What do you think you're doing creeping about in the dark? I could have hit you with this.' He retrieved the poker. 'I wasn't expecting you so soon.'

Alain Joubert walked past Vernon into the house.

37

London

Toni Landers held the small bottle before her and read the label.

Mogadon.

She unscrewed the cap of the bottle and upended it, coaxing the contents into one hand. There were twelve of the white tablets, all that remained since she had begun taking them soon after Rick's death.

Rick.

The thought of his name brought a tear to her eye and she sat down on the side of the bath, still clutching the tablets, remembering the monstrous image which had appeared before her the night before, called by Mathias. That abomination, that disfigured, mutilated monstrosity had been her son.

She opened her hand and looked at the tablets again.

Would twelve be enough?

She had contemplated suicide only once since he'd been killed but, after what had happened the previous night, the prospect of ending her own life now seemed positively inviting. She wiped a tear from her eye and spread the tablets out on the ledge beside the sink.

It was after three in the morning but the house was not silent.

Across the landing she could hear the muted, muffled sounds of cautious lovemaking. An occasional stifled moan of pleasure, a whispered word. It only served to remind her of her own loneliness.

She had been staying with friends ever since Rick's death but she realized that she must go back to the States eventually. Back to her own home. The home she had shared with Rick.

She looked at the sleeping tablets once more and realized that there was no way she could return. Toni picked one up and held it between her fingers for a moment. It wouldn't be difficult. She'd take the tablets then wander back to bed and fall asleep. It was that simple. All she had to do was take the first tablet. Then the second. Then ...

She filled a beaker with water and got to her feet.

As she did so, she realized that the sounds of lovemaking had stopped. The house was silent again.

Toni heard footsteps, soft and light crossing the landing. She scooped up the Mogadon and pushed them back into the bottle, slipping it into the pocket of her housecoat. But, the footsteps receded momentarily and she guessed that whoever it was had gone into the nursery.

The baby was asleep in there, in the room close to her own.

The baby.

She felt tears welling up once more and, this time, they spilled down her cheeks. Her body was racked by a series of uncontrollable sobs which, no matter how hard she tried, she could not disguise. A second later there was a light tap on the bathroom door.

'Toni,' the voice asked. 'Are you all right?'

She choked back her sobs with a monumental effort and wiped her face with a flannel.

'Toni.' The voice was low but more insistent.

She crossed to the door and slid back the bolt, opening it slightly.

Vicki Barnes stood before her, her long, thick blonde hair uncombed, her eyes puffy from tiredness.

Even models could look ordinary at three in the morning.

'I was just checking on the baby,' Vicki whispered. 'I heard you crying.'

Toni shook her head.

'I'm OK now,' she lied, sniffing.

'Come on,' Vicki urged, taking her hand. 'Let's go downstairs. I'll make us both a cup of coffee. I can't sleep either.'

'I know,' Toni said, managing a slight smile. 'I heard you.'

Vicki raised her eyebrows and shrugged.

'Sorry,' she smiled. 'Paul says I should wear a gag when we have guests.'

The two women made their way across the landing, past the baby's room and down the stairs to the kitchen. Once there Vicki filled the electric kettle and plugged it in. In the cold white light of the fluorescents she could see how pale Toni looked, how dark her eyes were, the whites streaked with veins.

Vicki was two years younger than her friend. They'd met back in the mid-seventies when Vicki had been on a modelling assignment in New York. The bond between them had grown steadily since then and Toni had been Matron of Honour when Vicki had married a record producer three years earlier. The actress was also Godmother to their child, Dean, now almost fourteen months old.

'Vicki, do you ever think about dying?' asked Toni, staring straight ahead.

The model looked shocked.

'No,' she said, softly. 'Why do you ask?'

'I never used to, not until ...' The sentence trailed off as she bowed her head. Vicki got up and stood beside her friend, snaking an arm around her shoulder.

'Don't talk about it,' she said.

Toni reached for a tissue in her housecoat pocket and, as she did, the bottle of Mogadon fell to the floor. Vicki spotted it first and picked it up.

She understood immediately.

'Is this your answer, Toni?' she asked quietly, replacing the bottle on the table in front of the actress.

'I'm not sure I want to go on without Rick,' said the American, her voice cracking. She clenched her fists. 'He was all I had. He meant everything to me. Vicki, if you'd seen that ... thing the other night.'

'You mean at the seance?'

Toni nodded.

'He was there,' she paused for a moment, trying to compose herself. 'I know it was Rick. He looked the way he did when I had to identify him, just after it happened. After the accident. That was my son,' she said, tears running down her cheeks.

'No one's saying you haven't got a right to feel the way you do. But this isn't the answer.' Vicki held up the bottle of tablets. 'And before you beat me to it, I know it's easy for *me* to say.'

Toni didn't speak.

'Please Toni, for Rick's sake, think about it.'

The American nodded.

'I'm frightened, Vicki,' she admitted. 'When I get back to the States, I don't know how I'm going to be able to go inside that house again. There are too many memories there.'

'You'll do it. If I have to come with you, you'll do it.'

Toni smiled thinly. The other girl got to her feet and kissed her gently on the cheek. They held each other for long moments.

'Thank you,' Toni whispered.

'I wish there was more I could do,' Vicki said. She stepped back. 'Do you want to go back to bed now? If not I'll sit up with you.'

'You go, I'll be OK,' Toni assured her.

'And these?' Vicki held up the bottle of tablets.

'Take them with you.'

The model slipped them into her hand and made for the kitchen door.

'See you in the morning, Toni.'

The actress heard footfalls on the stairs as her friend made her way up the steps. For what seemed like an eternity, Toni sat in silence, sipping at her coffee then, finally, she got to her feet, rinsed the cup and wandered out of the kitchen, flicking the light off behind her.

As she reached the landing she trod more softly, not wanting to disturb her hosts. The house was silent. The only thing which she heard was her own low breathing.

Toni paused outside the nursery, looking at the door as if she expected to see through it. She reached for the handle, hesitated a second then turned it. She stepped inside and

191

closed it gently behind her.

The cot stood in the far corner of the room. On a table close to her was a small lamp which bathed the room in a warm golden glow. The walls were painted light blue, the lower half decorated with a kind of mural showing teddy bears riding bikes, flying aircraft and climbing trees. It had, she guessed, been painted by Vicki's husband.

A profusion of soft toys littered the floor near to the cot. A huge stuffed penguin in particular fixed her in the unblinking stare of its glass eyes and she saw her own distorted reflection in them as she approached the cot.

The child was awake but made no sound, he merely lay on his back gazing wonderingly up at her with eyes as big as saucers.

Toni smiled down at him, chuckling softly as he returned the gesture. She took one tiny hand in hers and shook it gently, feeling the little fingers clutching at her.

The baby gurgled happily and Toni reached down and ran her fingertips over the smooth skin of his chubby face, stroking the gossamer strands of his hair before moving her fingers to his mouth. She traced the outline of his lips with her nail, smiling at the little boy as he flailed playfully at the probing digit. His mouth opened wider and he gurgled.

Suddenly, with a combination of lightning speed and demonic force, Toni rammed two fingers into the child's mouth, pressing down hard as her nails raked the back of its throat.

The baby squirmed and tried to scream but the sound was lost, gurgling away into a liquid croak as blood began to fill the soft cavity.

With her free hand she clutched the child's head, holding it steady as she forced another finger into its mouth, hooking them inside its throat until it gagged on its own blood and the intruding fingers.

As Toni pushed a fourth finger into the blood-filled orifice, the soft skin at each side of the baby's mouth began to rip. Toni was pressing down so hard it seemed that she would push the child through the bottom of the cot.

Blood splashed her hand and flooded on to the sheet, staining it crimson and still she exerted yet more pressure, grunting loudly at the effort. The baby had long since ceased to move.

Toni lifted it from its cot, her fingers covered in blood, some of which ran up her arm to stain her housecoat. She held the child before her, gazing into its sightless eyes.

She was still holding the child when the door of the nursery was thrown open.

Toni turned slowly to face Vicki Barnes and her husband, both of whom stood transfixed by the sight before them.

Toni heard screams echoing in her ears but could not seem to comprehend that they were coming from Vicki who had dropped to her knees and was staring at the monstrous scene before her.

Then, as if someone had pulled a veil from her mind she was able to see herself just what she'd done. She held the bloodied bundle at arm's length, her expression a mixture of horror and bewilderment.

The next screams she heard were her own.

38

Oxford

The dining room table must have been fully eight feet long, perhaps half that in width and yet every single carefully polished inch of the surface seemed to be covered with pieces of paper. Some were still in the files they had originated in, others were scattered about like the pieces of some huge, unsolvable puzzle.

And to Dr Stephen Vernon, that was exactly what all these notes were. A puzzle. Yet somehow it had to be solved.

He looked across the table at Joubert who was making notes, scribbling down words and phrases, sifting through the mud in an effort to find those elusive nuggets of information. Since his arrival at Vernon's house the previous night, he had done little else. Now, as the clock ticked around to 6 p.m., he dropped his pen and sat back in the chair.

'There's something missing,' said the Frenchman, surveying the piles of paper, the type-written sheets, the crammed notepads, the EEG read-outs.

'But I thought you brought *all* your findings,' Vernon said.

'Lasalle must have some of the research material with him,' Joubert said, irritably.

'Then all of this is useless?' Vernon suggested.

'No, it isn't useless but there are other factors too,' the Frenchman said, getting to his feet and crossing to the phone.

Vernon watched him as he dialled, sucking enthusiastically on his cough sweet, enjoying the smell of menthol which filled the air around him.

Joubert drummed agitatedly on the side-board as he waited for the receiver to be picked up. Eventually it was and Vernon listened as the investigator rattled out some questions in French. In the middle of it all he caught the name Lasalle. Joubert muttered something and pressed the cradle down, dialling again. He waited for an answer.

'Lasalle,' he said, quickly, as the receiver was picked up. 'This is Joubert.'

'Alain, where are you? Why weren't you at the Centre, I ...'

'Listen to me, Lasalle,' he interrupted. 'Our notes on Astral projection, I need them. Do you have any?'

'That's what I wanted to tell you,' Lasalle said. 'All the files have gone from the Centre. Everything relating to that one project.'

'I know, I *have* them,' Joubert told him. 'But there are some missing.'

'You took them from the Centre?' he asked. 'But why?'

Joubert finally lost his temper.

'For God's sake. How many times do I have to say it? Shut up and listen to me,' he barked. 'Do you have any of the notes relating to that project?'

'Yes I have.'

'I'm going to give you an address, I want you to send everything you have to me. No matter how unimportant it may seem, I want the files. Do you understand?'

'Yes,' he answered, vaguely. His voice was almost subservient.

Joubert gave him the address of Vernon's house, his

194

irritation growing when he was forced to repeat it.

'Why are you in England?' Lasalle wanted to know.

'Send me those notes,' his companion snapped.

'Alain, you are needed here,' Lasalle said, weakly. 'There are newspaper and television people at the Centre every day. I can't cope with their questions. They want to know so much. I cannot work *and* answer them. I need help ... I feel overpowered ... trapped. Alain, please.'

'This fiasco is of your own making, Lasalle,' Joubert hissed. 'If you hadn't written that damned article none of this would be happening.'

'I need help here ...'

'And I need those notes,' he rasped and slammed down the phone. He stood motionless for a moment, the knot of muscles at the side of his jaw throbbing angrily. Vernon watched him in silence.

'He has what I need. I should have been more thorough,' the Frenchman said. He went on to tell Vernon what Lasalle has said about the press. As he did so, his face grew darker and finally, he slammed his fist down on the table top. '*I* should be the one being interviewed not him,' he snarled.

'Is the recognition *that* important to you?' Vernon asked.

Joubert sucked in a weary breath and nodded.

'Eight years ago I was working for the Metapsychic Centre investigating a series of hauntings in a hotel in the Hauts-de-Seine area of Paris.' He reached for a cigarette and lit it, drawing the smoke into his lungs. 'I was working with another man, named Moreau.' The Frenchman frowned, his eyes narrowing. 'We had been at the hotel for over two months, making recordings, taking statements from the people who stayed there. It seemed as if there *was* an entity of some kind present in the building. Eventually we managed to get a clear recording of its movements. The next night we even photographed it. A *true* haunting. As you know, most of those reported are either imagined or psychologically rooted but not this one. We had visual evidence.'

'What happened?' Vernon asked.

Joubert stubbed out what was left of his cigarette in the saucer and sat back in his chair.

'Moreau took the photographs and the tape recordings to the Director of the Metapsychic Centre. He claimed that *he*

195

had discovered the entity. Despite my protestations, he was credited with it. Now he's one of the Directors of the Parapsychology Laboratory in Milan. One of the most respected men in his field in Italy. After that happened, I swore that I would never share any such finding with anyone. What I worked on, what I discovered would be mine. No one else's. But look what has happened. The single most important breakthrough in the study of the paranormal for twenty years and Lasalle is being credited with it. When this is over, who will remember Alain Joubert?' He glared at Vernon. 'No one. Well, this time it will be different. I had kept things quiet until the time was right to reveal the discoveries. The only reason I agreed to help you was because I knew that you offered no threat, you wanted the secret for your own reasons. You would not take away the recognition which was rightfully mine.' His tone turned reflective. 'I underestimated Lasalle.'

'I don't see that there's much you can do,' Vernon said. 'If the press have the story then ...' He shrugged, allowing the sentence to trail off. 'What *can* you do?'

Joubert did not answer, he merely gazed past Vernon to the overcast sky outside.

Clouds were gathering.

39

Paris

He awoke screaming.

Lasalle sat up, as if trying to shake the last vestiges of the nightmare from his mind. He gulped in huge lungfuls of air, one hand pressed to his chest as his heart thudded madly against his ribs.

He had seen her once more.

His wife.

His Madelaine.

Or what had once been her.

He had been bending over the grave laying fresh flowers on it when a hand had erupted from the earth and gripped his wrist, pulling him down as she hauled herself free of the dirt. She had sought his lips with hers, only hers were little more than liquescent pustules. She had embraced him with those rotting arms, pulling him close in an obscene attempt to push her decaying body against him, writhing at the contact. He had felt pieces of putrescent flesh peeling off in his hands like leprous growths as he fought to push her away.

Lasalle got to his feet, holding his stomach. He scurried to the kitchen and stood over the sink feeling his nausea building. He splashed his face with cold water and the feeling passed slowly. The Frenchman found that he was shaking uncontrollably so he gripped the edge of the sink in an effort to stop the quivering. Perspiration beaded on his forehead and ran in salty rivulets down his face.

He remembered falling asleep at the table in the sitting room. He'd been slumped across it when he'd woken. Lasalle closed his eyes, but the image of his dead wife came hurtling into his consciousness. He filled a glass with water then walked back into the sitting room, fumbling in the pocket of his jacket for the tranquilizers. He swallowed one. Two. Three. The Frenchman washed them down with the water and sat motionless at the table, his hands clenched into fists.

On the sideboard opposite, the photo of his wife smiled back at him and Lasalle, unaccountably, felt tears brimming in his eyes. He blinked and one trickled down his cheek.

'Madelaine,' he whispered, softly.

He closed his eyes once more, trying to remember how he had come to fall asleep so early in the evening. It was not yet 9 p.m.

It must have been after the phone call, he guessed.

The phone call.

He swallowed hard. He had spoken to Joubert. That much he *did* remember.

Lasalle raised both hands to his head as if he feared it might explode. He could not seem to think straight. Thoughts and images tumbled through his mind with dizzying speed.

The phone call. The nightmare. Madelaine.

He exhaled deeply, wiping more sweat from his face.

The nightmare still stood out with unwelcome clarity. That monstrous vision filled his mind again and he shook his head but, this time, there was something else. Something which he only now remembered.

As the decomposing corpse of his wife had embraced him, he had heard soft malevolent laughter and he knew what had propelled him, shrieking, from the nightmare.

The laughter had been coming from the graveside.

From Joubert.

40

London

The young make-up girl smiled as she applied the last few touches of foundation to the face of Mathias. She then took what looked like a small paint brush and flicked away the residue. The layer of make-up was sufficiently thick to protect his face from the bright studio lights he would soon be facing.

Mathias returned her smile, watching as she gathered her brushes, powder pots and small bottles and slipped them back into a leather bag she carried. He thanked her then got to his feet and opened the door for her. She smiled and left.

As the psychic was about to close the door again he saw a tubby man approaching along the corridor. The man was dressed in jeans and a grey sweatshirt and he had a set of earphones around his neck.

'Are you ready, Mr Mathias?' he asked. 'There's two minutes before you go on.'

The psychic nodded and stepped back inside the dressing room for a moment to inspect his reflection in the large mirror, then he followed the tubby man along the corridor towards a door marked: STUDIO ONE.

As they drew closer he could hear the muted sounds of many voices coming from inside. An occasional laugh which signalled that the audience were settling down. There was a red light above the door and a sign which read: ON AIR.

The tubby man opened the door carefully and ushered Mathias through.

The sound of the audience was very loud now but Mathias paid it little heed as he was led to a chair behind the main set.

From where he sat he could see numerous spotlights suspended over the set but, other than that, he could see only crew members dashing furtively about, obeying the orders of the floor manager whose instructions they received via their headphones. High up above the studio was the room where the director and his assistants sat, watching everything on banks of screens, relaying information to the floor.

Mathias could hear Roger Carr's voice. He was speaking about the supernatural, dropping in the odd joke where he felt it necessary. The audience laughed happily. Mathias sipped at the glass of water on the table before him and shook his head.

The tubby man turned to him and held up one finger.

The psychic got to his feet.

Roger Carr turned towards the camera on his right hand side, noticing that a red light had just blinked into life on top of it. He smiled thinly at it, getting himself more comfortable in his leather chair.

'My last guest tonight,' he began. 'Many of you may already have heard of. Certainly in America, he's what you might call an institution. Some might even say he should be *in* an institution.'

The audience laughed.

'He's revered by millions as a healer, an expert on the supernatural. Someone even dubbed him "The Messiah in the Tuxedo".'

Another ripple of laughter.

'Whether his powers are genuine or not remains to be seen but there are countless Americans who claim that he is truly a miracle worker. Perhaps after this interview, you can form your own opinions. Saviour or charlatan? Messiah or magician? Judge for yourselves.' Carr got to his feet. 'Please welcome Jonathan Mathias.'

There was a sustained round of applause as the American walked onto the set. He glanced at the audience and smiled as he made his way towards Carr. The host shook hands with him and motioned for him to sit. The applause gradually died away.

' "The Messiah in a Tuxedo" ' said Carr, smiling. 'How do you react to comments like that?'

'I don't take much notice of criticism,' Mathias began. 'I ...'

Carr cut him short.

'But surely, some of the things you claim to have done do leave you open to it?'

'If I could finish what I was saying,' Mathias continued, quietly. 'Yes, I do receive criticism but mostly from people who don't understand what I do. Didn't someone once say that any fool can criticise and most do.'

There was a chorus of chuckles from the audience.

'You mentioned what you do,' Carr continued. 'You claim to be a faith-healer and ...'

'I've never claimed to be a *faith*-healer,' Mathias corrected him.

'But you do perform acts of healing? Non-medical acts.'

'Yes.'

'If that isn't faith-healing then what is it?'

'People come to me because they know I will help them. I have never claimed ...'

'You charge money for this "healing"?' Carr said.

'A small fee. Usually people donate money. I don't ask for much from them. They give because they want to. As a token of appreciation.'

Carr nodded.

'You also appear on American television, do you not?' he said. 'Presumably you are well paid for that?'

'I don't have a pay cheque on me right now,' Mathias said, smiling. 'But, yes, the pay is good. As no doubt yours is, Mr Carr.'

'You wouldn't deny then that your basic interests are commercial.'

'I have a talent, a gift. I use it to help others.'

'But you wouldn't perform for nothing?'

'Would *you*?'

There was a ripple of laughter from the audience.

'No,' Carr told him. 'I wouldn't. But then I don't exploit the fears and gullibility of sick people.'

'I wasn't aware that *I* did, Mr Carr.'

The interviewer shifted uncomfortably in his seat, angry that Mathias was taking his verbal assault so calmly.

'Then what do you class yourself as?' he asked. 'Surely not an ordinary psychic? The fact that you're a multi-millionaire seems to lift you out of the category of ordinary.'

'My powers are greater than an ordinary psychic ...'

Carr interrupted.

'Can you give me an example of your *power*?' he said. 'Read my mind.' He smiled.

'Would it be worth it?' Mathias japed.

The audience joined him in his amusement. Carr did not appreciate the joke. The veins at his temple throbbed angrily.

'If we wheel in a couple of cripples could you make them walk?' the interviewer hissed.

'I don't perform to order, Mr Carr,' the psychic told him.

'Only if the price is right, yes?'

The floor manager looked anxiously at the two men, as if expecting them to leap at one another. Mathias remained calm.

'How would you answer the charge of charlatan?' Carr said.

'It's for each individual to decide whether or not they believe in my powers,' the American said. 'You may believe as you wish.'

The two men regarded one another for long seconds, the interviewer seeking some flicker of emotion in the piercing blue eyes of his guest. Haw saw none. Not even anger. Carr eventually turned away and looked directly into the camera.

'Well, as you have heard, Mr Mathias invites us to make up our own minds as to his ... *powers*. Although, having seen and heard his answers tonight I, for one, will draw just one conclusion. And I think you know what that is. Goodnight.'

As the studio lights dimmed, Carr got to his feet and glared down at Mathias.

'Clever bastard aren't you?' he snarled. 'Trying to make me look like a prick in front of millions of viewers.'

'I don't think you needed my help on that score,' Mathias said. 'You were the one looking for the fight, not me.'

'Well, you can take your fucking powers and shove them up your arse,' he snapped.

As he stormed off the set, the floor manager shouted something about the director wanting to see him.

'Fuck him,' Carr retorted and disappeared through the exit door.

Mathias was getting to his feet when the floor manager approached him.

'The director told me to apologise to you for Mr Carr's remarks during the interview,' said the man.

Mathias smiled.

'No harm done,' he said.

The floor manager nodded and walked away.

Only then did the psychic's smile fade.

41

The bedroom window was open and the cool breeze caused the curtains to billow gently.

Roger Carr lay naked on his back, arms folded behind his head. He was gazing up at the ceiling, his eyes fixed on a fly which was crawling across the emulsioned surface. It eventually made its exit through the open window and Carr was left gazing at nothing but white paint. He lay there for a moment longer then rolled on to his side and reached for the bottle of beer which was propped on the bedside table. He tipped it up, discovering to his annoyance that it was empty. Carr tossed it away and it landed with a thud on the carpet, close to a pair of discarded knickers. The owner of the garment was out of the room at present. Carr thought about shouting to her to fetch him another bottle of beer. Instead he rolled over once more and returned to gazing at the ceiling.

With his hands behind his head, the ticking of his watch

sounded thunderous in the silence. The hands had crawled round to 12.18 a.m.

He wondered what Mathias was doing.

Bastard.

Flash Yank bastard.

Carr had been surprised by the American's composure during the interview earlier in the evening. Most people usually crumbled beneath such a concerted verbal onslaught, but Mathias had managed to remain calm throughout.

Fucking bastard.

Carr realized that the psychic had bettered him during the argument. It could scarcely be called a discussion after all. In front of millions of viewers and the studio audience, Carr had met his match and that hurt him deeply. The image of Mathias flashed into his mind and he sat up, his breath coming in short, angry grunts. He swung himself off the bed and walked across to the window where he inhaled the cool night air and looked out into the darkness.

The street was quiet, but for the barking of a dog. The house was less than five minutes drive from the BBC and Carr had chosen it for its peaceful surroundings. He didn't like noise, he didn't like interference. He was a solitary person once he left the studio. He liked to pick and choose whose company he kept, therefore few people ever got close to him. Or wanted to for that matter.

Since his wife had walked out on him over three years earlier, Carr had become even more embittered and antagonistic in his dealings with others. At the time she had tried to force him into a reconciliation but Carr was not a man to be forced into anything. He'd even packed one suitcase for her before hurling her car keys at her and showing her the door. She had told him she would give him another chance if he could try to change his ways. Four affairs in as many years had been too much for her.

Carr hadn't wanted another chance.

He smiled as he remembered that night she left but the smile faded as he found himself thinking again about Mathias.

Once offended, Carr would stop at nothing to make things even. He bore grudges almost gleefully.

'Yank bastard,' he said, aloud.

'First sign of madness.'

The voice startled him, he hadn't heard her footfalls on the stairs. Carr spun round to see Suzanne Peters perched on the edge of the bed with a glass of milk in her hand.

'What did you say?' he asked, irritably.

'I said it's the first sign of madness,' she told him. 'Talking to yourself.'

Carr didn't answer her, he merely turned around and walked back to the bed, flopping on it lazily.

Suzanne muttered something to him as she almost spilt her milk. She placed it on the table beside the bed and stretched out beside him pushing her naked body against his, allowing her ample breasts to press into his side while her left hand snaked across his chest.

At twenty-two, Suzanne was almost half his age. She worked as a receptionist at Broadcasting House and had done for the past ten months. During that time, she and Roger Carr had become lovers although it was a term Carr disliked because, to him, it implied that there was some emotion involved in the relationship. In his eyes that was certainly not the case.

She nuzzled his chest, kissing it as she allowed her hand to reach lower towards his penis. She took his organ between her fingers and began to rub gently. He stiffened slightly but then she felt his own hand close around her tiny wrist, pulling her away from him. Suzanne sat up, sweeping her thick blonde hair back and looking at her companion with bewilderment.

'What's wrong with you tonight?' she wanted to know.

Carr didn't even look at her.

'I've got something on my mind,' he said.

'That's obvious. Is it anything *I* can help with?'

Carr eyed her almost contemptuously.

'*You*, help me? Give it a rest.'

He returned to staring at the ceiling.

'I only asked,' she said, lying down beside him once more. She ran one finger through the thick hair on his chest, curling it into spirals.

'That bastard Mathias made me look like an idiot,' Carr said, angrily. 'He's a bloody con-man.' The interviewer's voice took on a reflective tone. 'I'll have him for what happened tonight. One way or another I'll fix that shitbag.'

Once more Suzanne allowed her hand to reach lower towards his groin. She enveloped his penis in her smooth grip and, this time she felt him respond. He stiffened in her hand and she kissed his chest, nipping the flesh of his stomach as she moved down onto his growing erection. Suzanne flicked at the bulbous head with her tongue, watching as a drop of clear liquid oozed from it. Her lips closed around his throbbing shaft and she felt him thrusting his hips upwards trying to force himself further into the velvet warmth of her mouth. Her hand continued to move expertly on his root and she sensed an even greater swelling as his penis grew to full stiffness.

Carr gripped her by the back of the neck and pulled her off, dragging her across him, kissing her hard. His hands found her breasts and she almost cried out as he kneaded the soft mounds with furious vigour, but the discomfort was tempered by an overriding pleasure and her nipples grew into hard buds as he rubbed them with his thumbs.

She felt his knee rise to push against her pubic mound as he rolled her over first onto her back and then her stomach. She felt him grip her hips and she arched her back to allow him easier access. He thrust into her violently, a deep angry grunt accompanying his almost frenzied penetration of her. Suzanne gasped, both at the pleasure and the power of his movements. She knelt, feeling his heavy testicles against her buttocks as he moved inside her. Suzanne ground herself back to meet his every thrust and, as they formed a rhythm, she felt her own excitement growing.

Carr gripped her hips, clinging onto her soft flesh so hard that he left red welts where his fingers had been. He pulled her onto his throbbing shaft, grunting more loudly now.

She could not suppress a whimper of pain as he grabbed a large hunk of her hair and pulled, tugging her head back with a force which threatened to snap her neck. He held her like that, still spearing her unmercifully, only now her pleasure had given way to pain. Carr made a guttural sound, deep in his throat and pulled harder on her long hair. Some of it came away in his hand.

'No,' she managed to squeal, breathlessly.

He ignored her complaint, his own climax now drawing

closer. The speed of his thrusts increased.

She could no longer bear his weight so she lowered herself until she was lying face down on the bed, her legs still splayed wide as Carr drove into her relentlessly.

Suzanne felt a sudden, unaccountable flicker of fear as he fastened first one, then two hands around her throat.

He began to squeeze.

She let out a wheezing gasp and tried to claw at his hands to release the increasing pressure but the more she tugged at those twin vices, the harder he pressed. She felt his nails digging into her flesh as he crushed her windpipe and, all the time, he continued his violent movements which threatened to split her in two.

White light danced before her eyes and she flailed helplessly behind her, trying to scratch Carr. Anything to relieve the unbearable pressure on her throat. It felt as if her head were going to explode.

Roger Carr grinned crookedly, his face a mask of rage and triumph as he held her beneath him.

Suzanne felt herself growing weaker. It seemed only a matter of moments now before she blacked out.

With one last vigorous thrust he felt the pleasure build to a peak then, gasping loudly, he pumped his fluid into her. Carr shuddered as the sensations gradually subsided. He withdrew from her and lay on one side.

He wondered why she wasn't moving.

Suzanne coughed, horrified to see spots of blood mingling with the sputum which stained the pillow. Still lying on her stomach she raised one quivering hand to her throat and tentatively felt the deep indentations there. She felt Carr's hands on her shoulders, turning her over and, despite her pain she found the strength to push him away. He looked down at her ravaged neck and raised both hands to his head. In the semi-darkness his eyes looked sunken, only the whites standing out with any clarity.

She coughed again and tried to sit up, her head spinning. Carr reached out to touch the welts on her flesh, his gaze straying to those on her hips too. She slapped his hand away and staggered to her feet.

'You stay away from me,' she croaked, pointing at him with a shaking finger. 'I mean it.'

Carr got to his feet and moved towards her.

'Suzanne, I ...'

'Get away you ...' She coughed and more blood-flecked spittle dribbled over her lips. 'You're mad. You could have killed me.'

He hesitated, listening as she crossed the landing to the bathroom.

Carr sat down heavily on the edge of the bed, head bowed. He was drenched in perspiration but he felt almost unbearably cold. He found his dressing gown and pulled it on. His fingers, he noticed, had some blood on them so he hurriedly wiped it off with the corner of a sheet. His initial bewilderment by now had turned to fear. Carr rubbed his face with both hands, aware that his chest was heaving from the effort of trying to slow his rapid breathing. He looked at his hands as if they were not his own, as if they had been guided by a will other than his.

Suzanne returned from the bathroom and gathered up her clothes.

'Look, I don't know what to say ...' he began.

She interrupted.

'Don't say anything,' she told him.

'I don't know what came over me, I ...'

'Just leave me alone,' she demanded, picking up the last of her clothes. He watched as she hurried from the room, listening as she made her way down to the ground floor.

Carr shuddered once more as a chill ran through him.

He found her pulling on her jeans, tears trickling down her cheeks to smudge her make-up.

'Suzanne,' he said, almost apologetically. 'Honest to God, I don't know what happened.'

'I do,' she snapped, fastening the button at the waist. 'You tried to kill me.'

'I didn't know what I was doing.'

She pointed to the angry red marks on her neck.

'How am I supposed to explain these away?' Suzanne asked.

She pulled on her coat and turned towards the door which led through to the kitchen. 'I'll go out the back way, I don't even want anyone to know I've been with you.'

He followed her, slapping on the light.

'Stay away from me, Roger,' she said, a note of concern in her voice. 'I mean it.'

'You have to believe me,' he said. 'I didn't know what I was doing.' Again he felt that cold chill sweeping through him.

He caught her by the arm, spinning her round.

'Let go,' she shrieked and struck out at him, raking his cheek with her nails, drawing blood.

Carr's nostrils flared and his face darkened. With a roar he hurled Suzanne across the kitchen.

She slammed into the cooker and lay motionless for a moment but, as she saw Carr advancing on her, she managed to claw her way upright. He overturned the table in his haste to reach her.

Suzanne made a lunge for the door but Carr grabbed her by the collar. The material of her blouse ripped, the buttons flying off. Her large breasts were exposed but she cared little for that. Her only thought was to get out of the house.

But Carr moved too quickly. He shot out a grasping hand and tugged her back by her hair, slamming her head against the fridge as he did so. A cut opened just above her hairline, crimson fluid running down her face and staining the white door of the fridge as she lay against it.

As he lunged for her once more she flung open the fridge door and rammed it against his legs, struggling to get to her feet.

Carr snarled angrily and almost fell but he recovered in time to see her pull a long serrated blade from the knife rack on the wall nearby. She turned on him, the vicious blade glinting wickedly. He did not hesitate, he grabbed for her, his hands aimed at her throat but Suzanne struck out with the knife.

The combined force of his momentum and her own upward thrust was devastating.

The blade punctured the palm of Carr's right hand and erupted from the back, sawing through several small bones as it did so. Blood burst from the wound and Suzanne tore the knife free, nearly severing his thumb as she did so. He roared in pain and held up the mutilated limb almost as an accusation, watching the tendons and muscles beneath the skin moving frantically. It felt as if his arm were on fire but, despite the severity of the wound, Carr did not hold back. He reached for a chair and lifted it above his head, bringing it down with bone-crushing force across Suzanne's outstretched arm.

The knife was knocked from her grasp and she fell backwards, blood now flowing more freely from the rent in her scalp.

Carr grinned maniacally and struck again.

So violent was the impact this time that the chair broke as he brought it down across her face and upper body. Her bottom lip exploded, her nose merely collapsed as the bones in it were obliterated. In one fleeting second, Suzanne's face was a bloody ruin.

Carr dropped to his knees, one hand groping for the discarded knife. He gripped it in his gashed hand, ignoring his own pain as he took hold of a hunk of Suzanne's hair and lifted her head.

She tried to scream but her bottom jaw had been splintered and the only sound she could make was a liquid gurgle.

Carr pressed the knife to her forehead, just below the hairline, using all his strength as he moved the serrated blade quickly back and forth, shearing through the flesh of her scalp. He slid it in expertly towards her ear, slicing off the top of the fleshy protuberance as he did so and, all the time, her body jerked violently as waves of pain tore through her.

The knife grated against bone as he sawed madly at her head, tugging on her hair as he did so until finally, with a loud grunt, he tore most of it free.

Like some bloodied wig, the hair came away in his hand, most of the scalp still attached.

Suzanne lay still.

Carr staggered upright, the grisly trophy held before him.

There was loud banging from the direction of the front door, growing louder by the second.

Carr closed his eyes tightly, suddenly aware of an unbearable pain in his right hand. The entire limb was going numb, he could hardly lift it. He staggered back, seeking support against the sink and, gradually, a vision plucked raw and bloody from a nightmare swam before him. Only he wasn't dreaming.

He looked down in horrified disbelief at the scalped body of Suzanne Peters, almost shouting aloud as he recognized the matted mass of hair and flesh which he held. He dropped it hurriedly.

'No,' he murmured, quietly. 'Oh God, no.' His voice began to crack and he edged away from the girl as if she were somehow going to disappear. He continued to shake his head, not able to comprehend what had happened. Or how.

The banging on the front door intensified but all Roger Carr was aware of was the agonising pain in his hand, the stench of blood which hung in the air like an invisible pall.

And the icy chill which had wrapped itself around him like a frozen shroud.

42

The restaurant was small, what the owners liked to refer to as intimate. But, due to the number of people crowded into it, the place looked more like a gigantic rugby scrum. Not at all intimate, thought David Blake as the waiter led him through the melee towards the appropriate table.

Amidst the sea of lunch-time faces, the writer spotted Phillip Campbell immediately.

The Scot was sitting near to the window, sipping a glass of red wine and poring over a thick pile of A4 sheets, scribbling pencilled notes on the pages every so often. He was dressed in a light grey suit which seemed to match the colour of his hair. A red rose adorned his button-hole as it did on every occasion that Blake saw him. He wondered, at times, if Campbell was propagating the flowers in the breast pocket of his jacket. As each new one came up. Snip. Into the button hole.

He looked up as Blake reached the table, rising to shake hands with the writer.

They exchanged pleasantries and the younger man sat

down, loosening his tie as he did so. The waiter scuttled over and placed a large glass before him.

'Thank you,' said Blake, looking rather surprised.

'Vodka and lemonade,' Campbell told him, smiling. 'You haven't started drinking something else have you?'

The writer chuckled, shook his head and took a sip from the glass.

'I make a point of knowing all my author's requirements,' the Scot said, raising his glass. 'Cheers.'

Both men drank. The waiter arrived with the menus and left them to decide.

'What do you think of the completed manuscript now that you've read it?' Blake asked, indicating the A4 sheets.

'You're no closer, David,' Campbell told him. 'I'm still not convinced about half the things you claim in here.' He tapped the pile of typewritten pages.

The writer was about to speak when the waiter returned. The two men ordered and he hurried off through the throng to fetch their first course.

'It's too muddled,' Campbell continued. 'You don't name any sources for some of the theories you've put forward, especially the ones to do with Astral projection. *Control* of the Astral body.'

'I met a girl at the Institute of Psychical Study,' Blake said. 'She's conducted laboratory tests into this kind of thing.'

'Then why isn't she named as a source?'

'Her superior is keeping a pretty tight rein on the research they're doing. I don't think he'd be too pleased if her findings turned up in my book.'

'How well do you know this girl?'

'We're pretty close,' Blake told him.

Campbell nodded.

'The Astral body can be activated by artificial stimulus like drugs or hypnosis, she told me.'

'Then use her name for Christ's sake,' snapped Campbell. 'Can't you speak to her superior about this information? Maybe he'll release some details.'

The waiter returned with the first course and the two men began eating.

'I can't use her name or her findings and that's final,' Blake told him.

211

'Then you've still got nothing concrete and until you have, this manuscript is no good,' said Campbell, pushing a forkful of food into his mouth.

'I take it that means you're not ready to negotiate a contract?' Blake said.

Campbell nodded.

Blake smiled humourlessly.

'You could do with a demonstration, Phil,' he said.

The Scot took a sip of his wine.

'That I could,' he smiled. 'See if you can arrange it, eh?'

Blake chuckled. Behind the tinted screens of his dark glasses his eyes twinkled.

43

Gerald Braddock reached forward and wound up the window of the Granada. It was warm inside the car but he decided that the heat was preferable to the noxious fumes belching from so many exhaust pipes. The streets of London seemed even more clogged with traffic than usual. High above, in the cloudless sky, the sun blazed away mercilessly.

The politician fumbled for the handkerchief in his top pocket and fastidiously dabbed the perspiration from his face. He thought about removing his jacket but decided against it, realizing that they were close to their destination. The driver threaded the car skilfully through the traffic, hitting the horn every so often to clear offending vehicles out of the way.

Braddock sat back and closed his eyes but he found it difficult to relax. The events of two nights before were still uncomfortably fresh in his mind.

He had told no one of what he had witnessed at the seance, least of all his wife. For one thing she would probably never have believed him and, if she had, Braddock realized that mention of it may well have disturbed her. For his own part, the image of that maimed and burned child had surfaced, unwanted, in his mind on a number of occasions since. Albeit fleetingly. He wondered how long it would take to fully erase the image and the memory. He was thankful that nothing about the incident had appeared in any of the papers. Even the gutter press had so far remained blissfully ignorant of what would, for them, have been front page fodder. Braddock was grateful for that because he knew that the Prime Minister would not have looked kindly on his participation in such a fiasco.

He had held the post of Minister of the Arts in the last two Conservative administrations. Prior to that he had served as a spokesman on Finance in a career in the House of Commons which spanned over twenty years. Some had seen his appointment as Arts Minister as something of a demotion but Braddock was happy with his present position as it removed some of the pressure from him which had been prevalent when he'd been with the Exchequer.

As traffic began to thin he decided to roll down the window slightly. A cooling breeze wafted in, drying the perspiration on him. He glanced to his right and saw a sign which read: BRIXTON ½ MILE.

Another five minutes and the Granada began to slow up.

As Braddock looked out he saw that there was already a sizeable crowd gathered in the paved area which fronted the new Activity Centre. The building had been converted from four derelict shops, with the help of a two million pound Government grant. The minister scanned the rows of black faces and felt a twinge of distaste.

As the driver brought the car to a halt he saw two coloured men approaching. Both were dressed in suits, one looking all the more incongruous because, perched on his head, was a multi-coloured woollen bonnet. His dreadlocks had been carefully pushed inside. Braddock smiled his practised smile and waited for the driver to open the car door.

He stepped out, extending his hand to the first of the black men.

Braddock cringed inwardly as he felt his flesh make contact with the other man and he hastily shook hands with the Rastafarian, allowing himself to be led across the concrete piazza towards a make-shift platform which had been erected in front of the entrance to the Activity Centre.

213

As he made his way up the three steps the crowd broke into a chorus of applause.

Braddock scanned the faces before him, some white but mostly black. He continued to smile although it was becoming more of an effort. The first of the organisers, who had introduced himself as Julian Hayes, stepped forward towards a microphone and tapped it twice. There was a whine from the PA system and Hayes tapped it again. This time there was no interference.

'It's been more than two years since building first started on this Centre,' Hayes began. 'And I'm sure we're all happy to see that it's finally finished.'

There was some more clapping and the odd whistle.

Hayes smiled broadly.

'As from today,' he continued. 'We shall all be able to use the facilities. I would like to call on Mr Gerald Braddock to officially open the Centre.' He beckoned the politician forward. 'Mr Braddock.'

There was more applause as the minister reached the microphone. Beside it he noticed there was a small table and on it lay a pair of shears with which he was meant to cut the gaily coloured ribbon strung across the doors of the centre.

He paused before the microphone still smiling, scanning the rows of dark faces. Braddock felt the disgust rising within him. He coughed, suddenly aware of a slight shiver which ran down his spine. The sun continued to beat down relentlessly but, despite the heat, the politician felt inexplicably cold.

'Firstly,' he began, 'I would like to thank Mr Hayes for asking me to declare this new centre open. He must take credit for so much of the organisation which went into ensuring that the project was completed.'

There was more vigorous clapping.

Braddock smiled thinly and gripped the microphone stand.

'The cutting of the ribbon is symbolic,' he said, 'in as much as it marks the cutting of ties between you people and my Government. We have pumped over two million pounds into the development of this Centre. I hope that it will be put to good use.'

Hayes looked at his Rastafarian companion who merely shrugged.

'In the past we have tried to help this area but, up until

214

now, that effort has been largely wasted,' Braddock continued. 'Our good faith has not been repaid. I sincerely hope that it will not be the case this time.' The politician's voice had taken on a dictatorial tone, one not unnoticed by the crowd.

There were one or two disapproving comments from the assembled throng. A babble of unrest which grew slowly as Braddock pressed on regardless.

'There are many deserving causes to which we could have given a grant such as the one received to convert these old shops into this fine new Centre,' he said, 'most of which would normally come higher on our list of priorities. Nevertheless, partly through pressure from leaders of your community, we decided to furnish your committee with the appropriate funds.'

Julian Hayes looked angrily at Braddock's broad back then at the crowd who were muttering amongst themselves, angered by the politician's remarks.

'You seem to think that you qualify as a special case,' Braddock said, vehemently, 'because you're black.'

'Steady, man,' the Rastafarian rumbled behind him.

Hayes raised a hand for him to be silent although his own temper was becoming somewhat frayed as the minister ploughed on.

'It will be interesting to see how long this Centre remains intact. How long before some of you decide to wreck it. As it is, one of the few advantages that I can see is that it will give some of you a place to go, instead of hanging idly around on street corners.'

The crowd, by this time, were now gesturing menacingly at Braddock. Someone shouted something from the rear of the crowd but the minister either didn't hear it or ignored it. His own face was flushed, perspiration running in rivulets over the puffy flesh, yet still he felt himself encased in that invisible grip which seemed to squeeze tighter, growing colder all the time.

'Perhaps now,' he hissed, 'with your own Centre, you will stop bothering the decent white people who are unfortunate enough to have to live in this filthy "ghetto" you have created in Brixton.' He was breathing heavily, rapidly. His eyes were bulging wide and, when he spoke it was through clenched teeth.

'That's it,' snapped the Rastafarian, stepping forward. 'Who the hell do you think you are, man?'

Braddock spun around, his eyes blazing.

'Get away from me you stinking nigger,' he roared, his voice amplified by the microphone.

The crowd raged back at him.

'Mr Braddock ...' Julian Hayes began, moving in front of his colleague to face the politician. 'We've heard enough.'

'You black scum,' rasped the minister.

In one lightning movement, he snatched the shears from the table and drove them forward.

The twin blades punctured Hayes' stomach just below the navel and Braddock tore them upwards until they cracked noisily against the black man's sternum. Blood burst from the hideous rent and Hayes dropped to his knees as a tangled mess of purplish-blue intestines spilled from the gaping hole. Hayes clawed at them, feeling the blood and bile spilling on to his hands and splattering down the front of his trousers. He whimpered quietly as he attempted to retain his entrails, pushing at them with slippery hands.

In the crowd someone screamed. Two or three women fainted. Others seemed rooted to the spot, not sure whether to run or try to confront Braddock who stood on the platform facing the Rastafarian, the dripping shears now held in both hands.

'Motherfucker,' rasped the black man and lunged forward.

Braddock sidestepped and brought the razor sharp blades together once more.

They closed with ease around his opponent's neck and, with a movement combining demonic force and seething anger, the politician snapped the blades together.

Two spurting crimson parabolas erupted from the Rastafarian's neck as the shears bit through his carotid arteries, slicing through the thick muscles of his neck until they crushed his larynx and met against his spine.

Braddock roared triumphantly, exerting more force on the handles until the black man's spinal column began to splinter and break. He was suspended in mid-air by the shears, held there by Braddock who seemed to have found reserves of strength he hadn't formerly been aware of. Blood gushed

216

madly forth, much of it covering the politician himself, but he ignored the crimson cascade, grunting loudly as he finally succeeded in severing his opponent's head. It rose on a thick gout of blood as the body fell to the ground, twitching slightly.

The head rolled across the platform, sightless eyes gazing at the sky as torrents of red fluid poured from the stump of the neck.

Some of the crowd, by now, had scattered, others had surrounded the platform but, understandably, seemed reluctant to approach Braddock.

The politician had lowered the shears and his breathing seemed to have slowed. He stood motionless, like a child lost in a supermarket. Those watching saw him raise one bloodied hand to his forehead and squeeze his eyes tightly shut. When he opened them again his expression had changed from one of anger to utter horror. He looked at the headless corpse at his feet, then at Julian Hayes who was rocking gently back and forth clutching at his torn belly.

Finally, Braddock lifted the shears before him, staring at the sticky red fluid which covered them. And him.

He dropped the weapon and staggered backward, his face pale and drained.

Somewhere in the distance he heard a police siren.

As the sun burned brightly in the sky, he shivered, his entire body enveloped by an icy chill, the like of which he had never experienced before.

Gerald Braddock took one more look at the carnage before him then vomited.

The dashboard clock showed 6.05 p.m. as Kelly pulled the Mini into Blake's driveway. She tapped the wheel agitatedly, wondering, when she didn't see his XJS, if he was out. She decided that he might have put it in the garage, hauled herself out of her own car and ran to his front door, clutching the two newspapers which she'd gathered from the back seat.

The sun was slowly sinking and the air was still warm from the daytime heatwave. Kelly felt her blouse sticking to her. The drive had been a long and tortuous one, especially once she'd reached inner London. Now she banged hard on Blake's front door, almost relieved that she'd completed the trip.

She waited a moment but there was no answer.

Kelly banged again, this time hearing sounds of movement from inside. The door swung open and she saw Blake standing there.

'Kelly,' he beamed. 'What a great surprise. Come in.' He ushered her inside, puzzled by her flustered appearance and look of anxiety.

'Is something wrong?' he asked. She had still not smiled.

'Have you seen the news today?' she asked. 'Or watched TV at all?'

Blake shook his head in bewilderment.

'No. I had lunch with my publisher. I've been working since I got back. I haven't had time to look at the papers. Why?'

She held two newspapers out before him, both were folded open to reveal headlines. He looked at one, then the other:

ACTRESS KILLS BABY

Blake read it then looked at Kelly.

'Read the other one,' she told him.

TELEVISION PERSONALITY CHARGED WITH MURDER

Below it was a photograph of Roger Carr.

The writer looked at the first article once more and noticed the name Toni Landers.

'Jesus Christ,' he murmured, sitting down on the edge of a chair. 'When did this happen?'

'Last night they found Roger Carr in his house with the body of a girl,' said Kelly. 'The night before, Toni Landers killed the baby. The article said it belonged to her friend.'

Blake frowned and skimmed the articles quickly.

'That's not all,' Kelly told him. 'When I was driving home from the Institute today, I had the radio on. Do you remember Gerald Braddock?'

Blake nodded.

'According to the radio he went crazy this afternoon and killed two people,' Kelly told him.

The writer hurriedly got to his feet and switched on the television.

'There might be something on here about it,' he said, punching buttons until he found the appropriate channel.

'... Mr Braddock today. The Arts Minister is now in the Westminster Hospital, under police guard, where he was treated for shock prior to being charged.' The newsreader droned on but Blake seemed not to hear the rest.

'Treated for shock?' said Kelly. 'That's a little unusual isn't it? Do murderers usually go into a state of shock after committing the crime?' She exhaled deeply.

'I wish I knew,' said Blake. 'I know less than you do.' He scanned the papers once more. 'As far as I can make out Toni Landers and Roger Carr can remember nothing about the murders they committed. Yet they were both found *with* their victims.'

'So was Gerald Braddock,' Kelly added. 'Only there were witnesses in his case.'

'Three respected people suddenly commit murder for no apparent reason,' Blake muttered. 'They can't remember doing it and nothing links them.'

'There *is* a link, David,' Kelly assured him. 'They were all at the seance the other night.'

The two of them regarded each other warily for a moment then Blake got to his feet once more and picked up the phone. He jabbed the buttons and got a dial tone.

'Can I speak to Phillip Campbell, please?' he asked when the phone was finally answered. He waited impatiently while the receptionist connected him.

'Hello, David,' the Scot said. 'You were lucky to catch me, I was just about to leave.'

'Phil, listen to me, this is important. Do the names Toni Landers, Roger Carr and Gerald Braddock mean anything to you?'

'Of course. Toni Landers is an actress, Carr's an interviewer and Braddock's a politician. Do I get a prize for getting them all right?'

'In the past two days, each one of them has committed a murder.'

There was silence from Campbell's end.

'Phil, are you still there?' Blake asked.

'Yes, look, what the hell are you talking about, David?'

'It's all over the papers, on the TV as well.'

'But I know Braddock,' Campbell said in surprise. 'He couldn't fart without help, let alone murder anyone.'

'Well, all that changed today,' Blake said. He went on to explain what had happened to Toni Landers and Roger Carr. 'None of them could remember what they'd done. It's almost as if they were in some kind of trance. In my book I've discussed the possibility of some kind of unconscious reaction to an external stimulus ...'

Campbell interrupted.

'If you're trying to use three random killings to justify what *you've* written, David. Forget it,' snapped the Scot.

'But you'll admit it's a possibility?'

'No. Christ, that's even more bloody conjecture than you had before. Ring me when you've gathered some *real* evidence.'

Blake exhaled wearily and dropped the receiver back into place.

'What did he say?' Kelly asked, tentatively.

The writer didn't answer. He was staring past her, his eyes fixed on the twin headlines:

ACTRESS KILLS BABY
TELEVISION PERSONALITY CHARGED WITH MURDER

Outside, the dying sun had coloured the sky crimson.

Like cloth soaked in blood.

The smell of roast meat wafted invitingly through the air as Phillip Campbell stepped into the sitting room of his house.

The television was on and, through the open kitchen door, he could hear sounds of movement. As he drew closer, the smell grew stronger, tempting him toward the kitchen like a bee to nectar. He paused in the doorway and smiled. His daughter had her back to him, busily inspecting the dials on the cooker. Her black hair was long, spilling half-way down her back, almost to the waist band of her jeans. She looked a little too large for the pair she wore, possessing what were euphemistically known as 'child-bearing hips'. But her legs were long and relatively slender. She wore a baggy sweater, cut off at the elbows, which she'd knitted herself during her last break from University. She always came home during the holidays, only this time she had felt it as much out of duty as a desire to be with her parents.

Campbell's wife was in Scotland and had been for the past two weeks. Her mother was terminally ill with colonic cancer and was being nursed through her final few weeks by her family. Campbell himself had been up to see her twice but, after the second visit, he had been unable to bear the sight of the old girl wasting away. His wife phoned every other night and the presence of his daughter in some way compensated for her absence.

'Whatever it is it smells good,' the publisher said, smiling.

Melissa spun around, a look of surprise on her face.

'I didn't hear you come in, Dad,' she told him. 'You must be getting sneaky in your old age.' She grinned.

'You cheeky little tyke,' he chuckled. 'Less of the old age.'

Her mood changed slightly.

'Mum phoned earlier,' Melissa told him.

Campbell sat down at the carefully set table.

'What did she say?' he wanted to know.

'Not much. She sounded upset, she said something about being home next week.'

'Oh Christ,' Campbell said, wearily. 'Well, perhaps it's a kindness if her mother does pass on. At least it'll be the end of her suffering.'

There was a moment's silence between them then Campbell got to his feet.

'I'm going to get changed before dinner,' he said.

'You've got about five minutes,' Melissa told him. 'I don't want this to spoil.'

'You cooks are really temperamental aren't you?' he said, smiling.

The cuckoo clock on the wall of the kitchen burst into life as the hands reached 9 p.m.

Campbell set down the plates on the draining board and picked up a tea-towel as Melissa filled the sink with hot water.

'I'll do the washing up, Dad,' she told him. 'You go and sit down.'

He insisted on drying.

'Are we going to be seeing any more of this young fellow Andy or whatever his name was, next term?' Campbell asked, wiping the first saucepan.

'I don't know. He's gone grape-picking in France for the summer,' she chuckled.

'You were keen on him though?'

'You sound as if you're trying to get me hitched.'

'Am I the match-making type?' he said with mock indignation.

'Yes,' she told him, handing him a plate. 'Now, can we change the subject, please?'

Her father grinned.

'What sort of day have *you* had?' Melissa asked him.

They talked and joked while they cleared away the crockery, pots and pans and cutlery then Melissa decided to make coffee.

'I've got a few things to read before tomorrow,' he told her.

'I thought you didn't usually bring work home with you?'

'Sometimes it's unavoidable.'

'I'll bring your coffee in when it's ready,' she said.

He thanked her then wandered through into the sitting room, searching through his attaché case for the relevant material. Seated in front of the television, Campbell began scanning the synopses and odd chapters which he had not found time to get through at the office. There was work from established authors, as well as unsolicited efforts from those all too anxious to break into the world of publishing. The mystique which seemed to surround the publishing world never ceased to amaze the Scot.

Melissa joined him in the sitting room and reached for the book which she had been reading. They sat opposite one another, undisturbed by the television. Neither thought to get up and turn it off.

It was approaching 11.30 when Melissa finally put down her book and stretched. She rubbed her eyes and glanced at the clock on the mantlepiece.

'I think I'll go to bed, Dad,' she said, sleepily.

Campbell looked up at her and smiled.

'OK,' he said. 'I'll see you in the morning.'

He heard the door close behind her as she made her way upstairs. The Scot paused for a moment, his attention taken by a photograph of Gerald Braddock which had been flashed up on the TV screen. He quickly moved forward and turned up the volume, listening as the newscaster relayed information about the horrific incident in Brixton that afternoon. Campbell watched with interest, remembering his phone conversation with Blake. He shook his head. How could there possibly be any link between Blake's theories and Braddock's demented act? He dismissed the thought as quickly as it had come, returning to the work before him. Campbell yawned and rubbed his eyes, weariness creeping up on him unannounced. He decided to make himself a cup of coffee in an effort to stay awake. There wasn't much more to read and he wanted everything out of the way before he eventually retired to bed. He wandered into the kitchen and filled the kettle, returning to his chair in the sitting room. He slumped wearily into it and decided to watch the rest of the late news before continuing.

He yawned again.

Phillip Campbell made his way quietly up the stairs, pausing when he reached the landing. He heard no sounds from Melissa's room and was certain that he hadn't disturbed her. The Scot slowly turned the handle of her door and edged into the room. He smiled as he looked at her, sleeping soundly, her long black hair spread across the pillow like a silken smudge. She moved slightly but did not awake.

Campbell paused for a moment running his eyes over the numerous pen and ink, watercolour and pencil drawings which were displayed proudly in the room. Beside the bed was a plastic tumbler crammed with pieces of charcoal, pens and pencils and, propped against the bedside table was an open sketch-pad which bore the beginnings of a new drawing.

Campbell moved closer to the bed, his eyes fixed on his sleeping daughter. Even when he stood over her she did not stir.

He bent forward and, with infinite care, pulled down the sheets, exposing her body. She wore only a thin nightdress, the dark outline of her nipples and pubic mound visible through the diaphanous material. Campbell felt his erection growing, bulging urgently against his trousers. Without taking his eyes from Melissa, he unzipped his flies and pulled out his rampant organ.

It was then that she rolled on to her back, her eyes opening slightly.

Before she could react, the Scot was upon her, tearing frenziedly at the nightdress, ripping it from her, exposing her breasts. He grabbed one roughly, using his other hand to part her legs. She clawed at his face then attempted to push him off, using all her strength to keep her legs together but he knelt over her and struck her hard across the face. Still dazed from sleep, she was stunned by the blow and her body went momentarily limp. Campbell took his chance and pulled her legs apart, forcing his penis into her.

Melissa screamed in pain and fear and bit at the hand which he clamped over her mouth but he seemed undeterred by her feeble assaults and he struck her once more, harder this time. A vicious red mark appeared below her right eye.

With a grunt of triumph he began to thrust within her, using one forearm to hold her down, weighing heavily across

224

her throat until she began to gasp for air. She flailed at him weakly and he slapped her hands away contemptuously as he speeded up his movements, thrusting harder into her.

With his free hand, Campbell reached for the bedside table and pulled a pencil from the pastic container. The point had been sharpened repeatedly to a needle-like lead tip and he gripped it in one powerful hand.

Melissa, who was already on the point of blacking out now seemed to find renewed strength as she saw him bringing the pencil closer, but the weight on top of her prevented her from squirming away from her father.

He guided the pencil inexorably towards her ear.

She tried to twist her head back and forth but he struck her again and she felt the pressure on her throat ease as he held her head steady.

With fastidious precision, Campbell began to push the needle sharp pencil into her ear, putting more weight behind it as the wooden shaft penetrated deeper.

He felt his daughter's body buck madly beneath him and her eyes bulged wide as he pushed the pencil further, driving it into the soft grey tissue of her brain, forcing it as far as it would go. Almost a full half of the length had disappeared before she stopped moving but still Campbell forced the object deeper, as if he wished to push it right through her skull, to see the bloodied point emerge from the other side.

The Scot grunted in satisfaction and continued to pound away at her corpse, a crooked smile of pleasure on his face.

Phillip Campbell awoke with a start, his body bathed in perspiration. He was panting like a carthorse, his heart thudding heavily against his ribs. He looked across at the empty chair opposite him.

'Melissa,' he breathed, a note of panic in his voice.

He hauled himself out of his chair and bolted for the stairs, taking them two at a time, stumbling as he reached the landing. He threw open the door of his daughter's room and looked in.

She was sleeping soundly but, as he stood there, breathless, she murmured something and opened her eyes, blinking myopically at the figure silhouetted in her doorway.

'Dad?' she said, puzzlement in her voice. 'What's wrong?'

He sucked in a deep, almost painful breath.

'Nothing,' he told her.

'Are you all right?'

The Scot wiped his forehead with the back of his hand.

'I must have dozed off in the chair,' he said, softly. 'I had a nightmare.' He dare not tell her about it. 'Are *you* OK?' he added, his voice full of concern.

She nodded.

'Yes, of course I am.'

Campbell exhaled.

'I'm sorry I woke you,' he croaked, and pulled the door shut behind him.

He walked slowly back across the landing, pausing as he reached the top step.

There was a sticky substance on his underpants, a dark stain on his trousers. For a moment he thought he'd wet himself.

It took but a second for him to realize that the substance was semen.

46

How long the phone had been ringing he wasn't sure but the discordant tone finally woke him and he thrust out a hand to grab the receiver.

'Hello,' Blake croaked, rubbing a hand through his hair. He glanced at the alarm clock as he did so.

It was 12.55 a.m.

'David, it's me.'

Blake shook his head, trying to dispel some of the dullness from his mind.

'Sorry, who is it?' he asked.

Beside him, Kelly stirred and moved closer to him, her body warm and soft.

'Phillip Campbell,' the voice said and finally Blake recognised the Scot's drawl.

'What do you want, Phil?' he said, with surprising calm.

'I had a dream ... a nightmare. It was so vivid.'

'What about?'

Campbell told him.

'So now you believe what I've been telling you about the subconscious?' Blake said, almost mockingly.

'Look, we'll sort out the contract in a day or two. All right?'

'That's fine.'

Blake hung up.

Kelly, by now, was partially awake.

'What was that, David?' she purred. Her voice thick with sleep.

He told her of Campbell's insistence on going ahead with the book.

'I'm glad he's decided to publish the book, I wonder why he changed his mind?' she said.

Blake didn't speak. He merely kissed her gently on the forehead then lay down again.

Kelly snuggled up against him and he pulled her close.

In no time they had both drifted off to sleep again.

47

Paris

The full moon was like a huge flare in the cloudy sky, casting a cold white light over the land. The breeze which was developing rapidly into a strong wind, sent the dark banks scudding across the mottled heavens.

Michel Lasalle stopped the car and switched off the engine, sitting motionless behind the wheel. Despite the chill in the air he was sweating profusely and wiped his palms on his trousers before reaching over onto the back seat where the shovel lay. He pushed open his door and clambered out.

The gates of the cemetary, as he'd expected, were locked but Lasalle was undeterred by this minor inconvenience. He tossed the shovel over the wrought iron framework where it landed with a dull clang. He stood still, looking furtively around him in the darkness then, satisfied that no one was around, he jumped and managed to get a grip on one of the gates, hauling himself painfully upward until he was in a position to swing over the top.

The impact jarred him as he hit the ground but the Frenchman merely rubbed his calves, picked up the shovel and headed across the darkened cemetery towards the place he knew so well. Trees, stirred by the wind, shook their branches at him, as if warding him off, but Lasalle walked on purposefully, a glazed look in his eye.

The gendarme had heard the strange noise and decided that his imagination was playing tricks on him. But, as he rounded a corner of the high wall which guarded the cemetery, he saw Lasalle's car parked outside the main gates. The uniformed man quickened his pace, squinting at the vehicle through the gloom in an attempt to catch sight of anyone who might be inside. He moved slowly around the car, tapping on two of the windows, but received no response.

As the moon emerged from behind the clouds he peered through the gates of the graveyard.

Illuminated in the chilly white glow was a figure.

A man.

The gendarme could see that he was busy digging up the earth of a grave.

The uniformed man looked up and saw that the walls were covered by barbed wire, his only way in was over the metal gates. He leapt at them, gained a grip, and began to climb.

Lasalle had dug his way at least three feet down into the earth of his wife's grave when he looked up and saw the gendarme approaching. Lasalle murmured something to himself and froze for precious seconds, not sure what to do.

He bolted, still clutching the spade.

'Arrêtez!'

He heard the shout and looked over his shoulder to see that the gendarme was pursuing him.

Lasalle didn't know where he was going to run. The

uniformed man had blocked his only way out of the cemetery. He had no chance of scaling the wall at the far side and, more to the point, the other man was gaining on him. Weakened by the exertions of his digging, Lasalle stumbled, peering round a second time to see that his pursuer was less than ten yards behind. The uniformed man shouted once more and Lasalle actually slowed his pace.

He spun round, the shovel aimed at the gendarme's head.

A blow which would have split his skull open missed by inches and cracked into a tree.

The uniformed man hurled himself at Lasalle and succeeded in bringing him down. They crashed to the ground, rolling over in the damp grass. The gendarme tried to grip his opponent's arms but, despite Lasalle's weakness, he found a reserve of strength born of desperation and, bringing his foot up, he flipped the other man over. The gendarme landed with a thud, the wind knocked from him as he hit a marble cross which stood over one of the graves.

Lasalle snatched up the shovel again and brought it crashing down.

There was a sickening clang as it caught the other man on the back, felling him as he tried to rise.

Lasalle hesitated a moment then sprinted back the way he had come, towards the grave of his wife.

The gendarme hauled himself to his feet and spat blood, trying to focus on his fleeing quarry. He tensed the muscles in his back, wincing from the pain where he'd been struck but there was a determined look on his face as he set off after Lasalle once more.

It only took him a moment to catch up with the running man.

Again, Lasalle swung the shovel, his blow shattering a marble angel, the head disintegrating to leave a jagged point of stone between the wings.

The swing set him off balance and the gendarme took full advantage, hitting the other man with a rugby tackle just above the knees.

Lasalle grunted. The sound turning to a scream as he toppled towards the broken angel.

The moon shone brightly on the jagged stone.

The point pierced Lasalle's chest below the heart, snapping ribs and tearing one lung. Wind hissed coldly in the gaping wound as he tried to suck in an agonised breath. Impaled on the marble angel, he tried to pull himself free but blood made the stone slippery. He tasted it in his mouth, felt it running from his nose as his struggles became weaker.

The gendarme rolled free and attempted to pull the other man clear, the odour of blood filling the air around them.

Lasalle finally freed himself and toppled backward, blood pumping madly from the gaping hole in his chest. His body shook once or twice but, even as the uniformed man knelt beside him, he heard a soft discharge which signalled that Lasalle's sphincter muscle had given out. A rancid stench of excrement made him recoil.

The moon shone briefly on the dead man's open eyes.

The gendarme shuddered as the wind hissed through the branches of a nearby tree.

It sounded like a disembodied voice.

A cold, invisible oration spoken for the man who lay before him.

The last rites.

48

Oxford

The sun shone brightly, pouring through the windows of her office and reflecting back off the white paper before her. She told herself that was the reason she found it so hard to concentrate. She had read the same two pages half-a-dozen times but still not a word had penetrated. It was the heat. It had to be the heat that was putting her off.

Kelly sat back in her chair and dropped the wad of notes.

She sighed, knowing full well that her lack of concentration had nothing to do with present climatic conditions.

Since arriving at the Instiute that morning she had been able to think of nothing but Blake. Even now, as the vision of him drifted into her mind she smiled. For a moment she rebuked herself, almost angry that she had become so strongly attached to him. She felt almost guilty, like a schoolgirl with a crush on a teacher but, the more she thought about it, the more she realized how close to love her feelings for Blake were becoming. Was it possible to fall in love with someone in such a short time? Kelly decided that it was. She was certain that he felt the same way about her. She felt it in his touch, in the way he spoke to her.

Kelly shook her head and chuckled to herself. She could hardly wait for the evening to see him again.

Once more she began reading the notes before her.

There was a light tap on the door and, before she could tell the visitor to enter, Dr Vernon walked in.

Kelly's eyes widened in unconcealed surprise.

Standing with the Institute Director was Alain Joubert.

He and Kelly locked stares as Vernon moved into the room.

'I believe you already know Alain Joubert,' he said, motioning to the Frenchman.

'Of course,' Kelly told him, shaking hands with Joubert curtly.

'How are you, Miss Hunt?' Joubert asked, his face impassive.

'I'm fine, I didn't expect to see you again so soon. Is Lasalle here too?'

Joubert opened his mouth to speak but V rnon stepped forward. His face was suddenly somehow softer and Kelly noticed the difference in his features.

'Kelly, you were a friend of Lasalle's weren't you?' he said, quietly.

'What do you mean "you were"? Why the past tense?' she asked.

'He was killed in an accident last night.'

'What kind of accident?' she demanded, her voice a mixture of shock and helplessness.

'We don't know all the details,' Vernon explained. 'The Director of the Metapsychic Centre informed me this morning. I thought you had a right to know.'

She nodded and brushed a hand through her hair wearily.

'He was dying anyway,' Joubert said.

'What do you mean?' Kelly snapped, looking at the

231

Frenchman.

'He was cracking up. Taking more of those pills of his. He was dying and he didn't even realize it.'

Kelly detected something close to contempt in Joubert's voice and it angered her.

'Doesn't his death mean anything to you?' she snapped. 'The two of you *had* worked together for a long time.'

The Frenchman seemed unconcerned.

'It's a regrettable incident,' Vernon interjected. 'But, unfortunately, there's nothing we can do.' He smiled condescendingly at Kelly, the tone of his voice changing. 'That wasn't the real reason I came to speak to you, Kelly.'

She looked at him expectantly.

'You're probably wondering why Joubert is here?' he began.

'It had occurred to me,' Kelly said.

'I want you to work with him on the dream project.'

Kelly shot a wary glance at the Frenchman.

'Why?' she demanded. 'I can handle the work alone. I've been doing it since John Fraser ... left,' she emphasised the last word with contempt.

'Joubert is more experienced than you are. I'm sure you appreciate that,' Vernon said. 'In fact, I felt it only fair to put him in charge of the project.'

'I've been involved with the work from the beginning. Why should Joubert be given seniority?'

'I explained that. He's more experienced.'

'Then you don't leave me much choice, Dr Vernon. If you put Joubert over me, I'll resign.'

Vernon studied Kelly's determined features for a moment.

'Very well,' he said, flatly. 'You may leave.'

Kelly tried to disguise her surprise but couldn't manage it.

'If that's the way you feel, then I won't try to stop you,' Vernon continued, unwrapping a fresh menthol sweet. He popped it into his mouth.

She got to her feet and, without speaking, picked up her leather attaché case and fumbled for the notes on the desk.

'Leave the notes,' said Vernon, forcefully.

She dropped them back on to the desk.

'I'm sorry you couldn't have accepted this situation,' Vernon told her. 'But, as you know, the work of the Institute comes first.'

'Yes, I understand,' she said, acidly. 'I hope you find what you're looking for.' She glanced at Joubert. 'Both of you.'

Kelly felt like slamming the door behind her as she left but she resisted the temptation. As she made her way up the corridor towards the entrance hall she felt the anger seething within her.

She stalked out into the bright sunshine but paused for a moment, narrowing her eyes against the blazing onslaught. She found that the palms of her hands were sweating, her breath coming in short, sharp gasps. She marched across to her waiting car and slid behind the wheel, sitting there in the cloying heat, not allowing herself to calm down. She thumped the steering wheel in frustration, looking to one side, towards the Institute.

How could Vernon let her walk out just like that? She inhaled and held the breath for a moment.

And Joubert.

The arrogant bastard. She wondered if his research was the only reason for being in England.

The reality of the situation suddenly seemed to hit her like a steam train and she felt tears welling in her eyes.

Tears of sadness for Lasalle.

Tears of frustration for herself. Of anger.

Her body shook as she felt the hot, salty droplets cascading down her cheeks and she reached for a tissue, hurriedly wiping them away.

She wondered if Joubert and Vernon were watching her.

The seed of doubt inside her mind had grown steadily over the past few weeks until now, it had become a spreading bloom of unquenchable conviction.

There was, she was sure, a conspiracy taking place between the Frenchman and the Institute Director. Nothing would dissuade her from that conclusion now.

First John Fraser, then Michel Lasalle. Both had been involved with the projects on Astral projection and both were now dead.

Coincidence?

She thought about what had happened over the past couple of days as she started the engine and drove off.

The seance.

233

Toni Landers. Roger Carr. Gerald Braddock.

She glanced over her shoulder at the gaunt edifice of the Institute.

Even in the warm sunshine it looked peculiarly menacing.

She rang Blake as soon as she got in. She told him what had happened that morning. He listened patiently, speaking softly to her every now and then, calming her down. She felt like crying once more, such was her feeling of helplessness and rage.

He asked her if she was OK to drive and, puzzled, she said that she was.

'Will you come and stay with me?' he wanted to know.

Kelly smiled.

'You mean move in?'

'Stay as long as you like. Until this is sorted out or, you never know, you might even decide that you can put up with me for a few more weeks.'

There was a long silence between them finally broken by Blake.

'Best food in town,' he said, chuckling.

'I'll start packing,' she told him.

They said their goodbyes and Kelly replaced the receiver, suddenly anxious to be with him. She hurried through into the bedroom, hauled her suitcase down from the top of the wardrobe and began rummaging through her drawers for the items she would need.

She felt a slight chill but disregarded it and continued packing.

49

London

The crushed lager can landed with a scarcely audible thud on the stage in front of the drum riser. A roadie, clad in jeans and a white sweatshirt, scuttled to pick up the debris and remove it. On the far side of the stage two of his companions were dragging one of the huge Marshall amps into position alongside three others of the same size. Each was the height of a man.

Jim O'Neil picked up another can of drink and downed half in one huge swallow. He wiped his mouth with the back of his hand and wandered back and forth behind the curtain. From the other side he could hear the sound of almost 2,000 voices muttering, chatting expectantly. Whistles punctuated the gathering sea of sound.

He guessed that the theatre was full to capacity and the crowd were growing restless as the minutes ticked away until the curtain rose. The place smelled of sweat and leather.

O'Neil himself looked like something from a gladiatorial arena clad as he was in a pair of knee boots, leather trousers and a waist-coat decorated with hundreds of studs. On both arms he wore leather wrist-bands which covered his muscular forearms, the nickel-plated points glinting in the half-light.

There was a burst of sound from his left and he turned to see his lead guitarist, Kevin Taylor, adjusting his amps.

A loud cheer from the other side of the curtain greeted this involuntary action and when the drummer thundered out a brief roll there was even more frenzied shouting from the waiting crowd.

O'Neil wandered over towards Kevin Taylor and tapped the guitarist on the shoulder. He turned and smiled at the singer. At twenty-four, Taylor was almost five years younger than O'Neil but his long hair and craggy face gave him the appearance of a man much older. He wore a white tee-shirt and striped trousers.

'Go easy on the solos tonight,' O'Neil said to him, taking another swig from his can of lager. 'There are four of us in the band you know.'

'I don't know what you mean,' said the guitarist, a slight Irish lilt to his accent.

'At the last gig you nearly wore your fucking fingers out you played so many solos.'

'The audience seems to enjoy it,' Taylor protested.

'I don't give a fuck about the audience. I'm telling you, don't overdo it and keep it simple. Nothing fresh. Right?'

'You're the boss.'

'Yeah,' O'Neil grunted. 'I am.' He finished the lager, crushed the can in one powerful hand and dropped it at the Irishman's feet.

O'Neil walked away, wondering if he was the only one who felt cold.

'Two minutes,' someone shouted.

The singer moved towards the front of the stage and tapped the microphone then, satisfied, he retreated out of view and waited for the curtain to rise. The lights were lowered until the theatre was in darkness and, as the gloom descended, the shouts and whistles grew in intensity finally erupting into a shattering crescendo as the curtain began to rise and the coloured lights above the stage flashed on and off. As the band opened up with a series of power chords which would have registered on the Richter scale, even the swelling roar of the audience was eclipsed. The explosion of musical ferocity swept through the hall like a series of sonic blasts, the scream of guitars and the searing hammerstrokes forged by the drummer merged into a force which threatened to put cracks in the walls.

O'Neil took the stage, his powerful voice soaring like an air raid siren over the driving sound of his musicians.

As he sang he ran from one side of the stage to the other, grinning at the hordes of fans who clamoured to get closer to the stage, occasionally pausing to touch their upraised hands. Like some leather clad demi-God he strode the platform, his disciples before him, fists raised in salute and admiration.

The heat from the spotlights was almost unbearable but still O'Neil felt an icy chill nipping at his neck, spreading slowly through his entire body until it seemed to fill him. He gazed out at the crowd, their faces becoming momentary blurs to him as he spun round and moved towards Kevin Taylor.

O'Neil raised the microphone stand above his head, twirling it like a drum-major's baton, much to the delight of the crowd.

Even Taylor smiled at him.

He was still smiling when O'Neil drove the stand forward like a spear, putting all his weight behind it, forcing the metal tube into Taylor's stomach. The aluminium shaft tore through his midsection and, propelled by O'Neil, erupted from the guitarist's back just above the kidneys. Blood burst from both wounds and Taylor croaked in agony as he was forced back towards the stack of amps behind him. O'Neil let go of the mike stand as Taylor crashed into the speakers.

There was a bright flash as they shorted out and, the guitarist, still transfixed, began to jerk uncontrollably as thousands of volts of electricity ripped through him.

There was a blinding white explosion as the first amp went up.

The PA system began to crackle insanely as a combination of feed-back and static accompanied the short circuit.

Another amp exploded.

Then another.

Rigged to the same system, it was like dropping a lighted match into a full box.

Flames began to lick from the first amp, devouring Taylor's twitching body hungrily, writhing in his long hair like yellow snakes. He looked like a fiery Gorgon. On the far side of the stage the other banks of speakers began to blow up, some showering the audience with pieces of blazing wood.

Those in the front few rows clambered back over their seats, anxious to be away from the terrifying destruction before them but those behind could not move fast enough and many were crushed in the mad stampede to escape. Anyone who fell was immediately trodden underfoot as fear overcame even the strongest and panic rapidly became blind terror. On the balcony, some stared mesmerised at the stage which was rapidly becoming an inferno.

Flames rose high, destroying everything they touched. The other musicians had already fled the stage and a roadie who dashed on to help was crushed beneath a falling amp, pinned helplessly as he burned alive, his shrieks drowned out by the deafening crackle coming from the PA and the horrified shouts of the crowd.

The curtain was lowered but flames caught it and it became little more than a canopy of fire, suspended over the stage like some kind of super-nova. Dozens of lights, unable to stand up to the heat, shattered, spraying glass on to those below. A large frame holding eight football-sized spotlights came free of its rigging and plummeted into the audience where it exploded. Dozens were crushed, others were burned or sliced open by flying glass which hurtled around like jagged crystal grapeshots.

Motionless on the stage, framed by fire, stood Jim O'Neil, his face pale and blank as he gazed uncomprehendingly around him at the destruction. He saw people in the audience screaming as they ran, he saw others lying on the floor, across seats. Bloodied, burned or crushed.

A roadie ran shrieking across the stage, his clothes and hair ablaze. The acrid stench of burned flesh filled O'Neil's nostrils and he swayed as though he were going to faint.

Behind him, still impaled on the microphone stand, the body of Kevin Taylor was being reduced to charred pulp by the searing flames which leapt and danced all around the stage.

O'Neil could only stand alone and shake his head. Like some lost soul newly introduced to hell.

Sweat was pouring from him but, despite the blistering temperatures, he felt as if he were freezing to death.

50

As darkness crept across the sky, Blake got to his feet and crossed the room to draw the curtains. Kelly watched as he shut out the gloom, feeling somehow more secure, as if the night were comprised of millions of tiny eyes — each one watching her.

The writer paused by the drinks cabinet and re-filled his own glass. Kelly declined the offer of a top-up. She felt that she had already consumed a little too much liquor since arriving at Blake's house earlier in the day.

Throughout the journey to London she had felt an unexplained chill, an inexplicable sense of foreboding which only seemed to disappear once she saw Blake. She felt safe with him. But, more than that, she was now even more convinced that she was falling in love with him.

He returned to his chair and sat down, glancing across at Kelly.

Barefoot, clad only in a pair of skin tight faded jeans and a tee-shirt, she looked more vulnerable than he had ever seen her before. And also, perhaps because she was unaware of it, more alluring. Yet he knew, beneath that apparently anxious exterior, she still retained the courage and determination which had first drawn him to her.

'Are you feeling all right?' he asked, noticing how intently she stared into the bottom of her glass.

'I was just thinking,' she told him, finally gracing him with her attention. 'I know we've been over this dozens of times but I can't seem to get it out of my mind. I'm convinced that someone at that seance is responsible for what's been going on, for these murders.'

'Go on,' he prompted her.

'The only one who knew all five victims ...'

Blake interrupted.

'How can you call Braddock and the other two, *victims*

when they were the ones who committed the murders?'

'They did them against their will. They were used.' She looked intently at him. 'And I'm sure that the same person who influenced them was also responsible for the deaths of Fraser and Lasalle. It has to be Dr Vernon.'

Blake shook his head.

'Fraser was killed in a car crash, right? You've already told me that Lasalle was starting to crack up again. What proof is there that Vernon had anything to do with *their* deaths?' he said. 'Who's to say that both men didn't die in bona fide accidents?'

'Whose side are you on?' she snapped.

'It's nothing to do with sides, Kelly,' he said, angrily. 'It's a matter of practicality. You can't go accusing someone like Vernon without proof. Besides, if it were true, how the hell are you going to prove it? There isn't a policeman in the country who'd believe you. The whole idea of controlling someone else's Astral personality is difficult enough to understand, even for people like you and I, let alone for someone with no knowledge of the subject.'

'Are you saying we're beaten?' she muttered.

'No, I'm just trying to be practical,' Blake explained.

'Three of the people involved in that seance have already commited murder. What about the rest of us? How long before something happens to us?'

Blake picked up the phone.

'I'm going to call Mathias and Jim O'Neil,' he said. 'I want to know if they're aware of what's been happening. They could be in danger too.'

'And so could we,' Kelly added, cryptically.

Blake didn't answer.

'Grosvenor House Hotel. Can I help you?' said a female voice.

'I'd like to speak to Mr Jonathan Mathias,' said Blake. 'He has a suite at the hotel. My name is David Blake.'

There was a moment's silence and, from the other end of the line, Blake heard the sound of paper rustling.

Kelly kept her eyes on him as he stood waiting.

'I'm afraid Mr Mathias checked out this morning,' the voice told him.

'Damn,' muttered the writer; then to the receptionist,

240

'Have you any idea where he is? Where he went? It is important.'

'I'm sorry, I can't help you there, sir,' she said.

Blake thanked her and pressed his fingers down on the cradle.

'No luck?' Kelly asked.

'He's probably back in the States by now,' the writer said, reaching for a black notebook which lay close to the phone. He flipped through it, running his finger down the list of names and numbers. He found what he was looking for and tapped out the correct number, listening as the purring tones began.

'Come on,' he whispered, impatiently.

'Are you calling O'Neil?' Kelly wanted to know.

Blake nodded.

'He's probably on stage at the moment but perhaps if I can talk to one of his crew I can get him to ring me back.' The purring went on. Blake jabbed the cradle and pressed the numbers again.

Still no answer.

'What the hell are they playing at?' he muttered.

He flicked the cradle and tried yet again.

A minute passed and he was about to replace the receiver when he heard a familiar click from the other end.

'Hello, is that the Odeon?' he blurted.

The voice at the other end of the line sounded almost unsure.

'Yes. What do you want?'

Blake detected a note of unease in the voice. Fear perhaps?

'Is Jim O'Neil still on stage? If ...'

The man at the other end cut him short.

'Are you from a newspaper?' he asked.

'No,' Blake told him, puzzled. 'Why?'

'I thought you might have heard about the accident. No press allowed. The police won't let any of them through.'

'What's happened there?' the writer demanded. 'I'm a friend of O'Neil's.'

'There was an accident, a fire. God knows how many people are dead.' The man's voice began to crack. 'O'Neil killed one of his band. It happened on the stage. I ...'

241

'Where's O'Neil now?'

Kelly got up and walked across to the table. Blake picked up a pencil and scribbled a note on a piece of paper. She read it as he continued speaking: O'NEIL HAS KILLED. FIRE ON STAGE. PEOPLE IN AUDIENCE KILLED.

'Oh my God,' murmured Kelly.

'Where is O'Neil at the moment?' the writer repeated.

'The police took him away,' the other man said. 'I've never seen anything like it. He looked as if he didn't know what was going on, he ...'

The phone went dead.

Blake flicked the cradle but could get no response. He gently replaced the receiver.

For long moments neither he nor Kelly spoke, the silence gathering round them like an ominous cloud.

'Toni Landers. Gerald Braddock. Roger Carr and now O'Neil,' Kelly said, finally. 'Who's going to be next?'

Her words hung, unanswered, in the air.

51

New York

Jonathan Mathias raised both arms above his head and stood for a moment, surveying the sea of faces before him. All ages. All nationalities. But with a single purpose.

To see him.

The hall in the Bronx was the largest that he used and as he ran an appraising eye over the throng he guessed that somewhere in the region of 2,000 people had packed into the converted warehouse. They stood in expectant silence, waiting for a sign from him.

'Come forward,' Mathias said, his powerful voice reverberating around the crowded meeting place.

Men working for the psychic, dressed in dark suits, cleared an aisle through the middle of the horde, allowing the procession of pain to begin. First came the wheelchairs, some of their occupants looking expectantly towards the stage where Mathias stood. He saw a young woman being brought forward by two men who had laid her on a stretcher. She lay motionless, sightless eyes gazing at the ceiling, her tongue lolling from one corner of her mouth.

Dozens hobbled towards the psychic on crutches, many struggling with the weight of the callipers which weighed them down. Others were supported by friends or relatives.

Mathias counted perhaps twenty or more figures moving slowly behind those on crutches. Most carried the white sticks which marked them out as blind, others were led forward by members of the crowd or by the dark-suited stewards. One of them, a man in his forties, stumbled and had to be helped up, but he continued on his way, anxious to reach the figure whom he could not see but who he knew would help him.

As the last of the sick passed through the midst of the crowd, the gap which had opened now closed. The people drifting back to their places. From where Mathias stood, it looked like one single amoebic entity repairing a self-inflicted rent in itself. The sea of faces waited as the lights in the hall dimmed slightly, one particularly bright spotlight focusing on the psychic, framing him in a brilliant white glow.

The psychic had still not lowered his arms. He closed his eyes for a moment and stood like some finely attired scarecrow, his head slightly bowed. In the almost palpable silence, even the odd involuntary cough or whimper seemed intrusive.

Without looking up, Mathias nodded imperceptibly.

From the right of the stage, a woman put her strength into pushing a wheelchair up the ramp which had been erected to facilitate the countless invalid chairs. A steward moved forward to help her but Mathias waved him back, watching as the woman strained against the weight contained in the chair. Eventually, she made it and, after a swift pause to catch her breath, she moved towards the psychic who fixed both her and the boy in the wheelchair in his piercing gaze.

The occupant of the chair was in his early twenties, his ruddy features and lustrous black hair somehow belying the fact that his body was relatively useless. The boy had large, alert eyes which glistened in the powerful light and he met Mathias' stare with something akin to pleading. He still wore a metal neck-brace which was fastened to his shattered spine by a succession of pins. Paralysed from the neck down the only thing which moved were his eyes.

'What is your name?' Mathias asked him.

'James Morrow,' the youngster told him.

'You're his mother?' the psychic asked, looking at the woman fleetingly.

She nodded vigorously.

'Please help him,' she babbled. 'He's been like this for a year and ...'

Mathias looked at her again and, this time, his gaze seemed to bore through her. She stopped talking instantly and took a step back, watching as the psychic gently gripped her son's head, circling it with his long fingers, their tips almost meeting at the back of the boy's skull. He raised his head and looked upward, momentarily staring at the powerful spotlight which held him like a moth in a flame. His breathing began to degenerate into a series of low grunts and the first minute droplets of perspiration started to form on his forehead. The psychic gripped the boy's head and pressed his thumbs gently against his scalp for a moment or two, passing to his temples, then his cheeks.

James Morrow closed his eyes, a feeling of welcome serenity filling him. He even smiled slightly as he felt the psychic's thumbs brush his eyelids and rest there.

Mathias was quivering violently, his entire body shaking madly. He lowered his head and looked down at Morrow, his own teeth now clenched. A thin ribbon of saliva oozed from his mouth and dripped on to the blanket which covered the boy's lower body.

The psychic gasped, a sound which he might have made had all the wind suddenly been knocked from him. He felt his hands beginning to tingle but it wasn't the customary heat which he experienced. It was a searing cold, as if someone had plunged his hands into snow.

James Morrow tried to open his eyes but was unable to do so due to the fact that Mathias' thumbs held his lids closed. The boy felt a slight increase of pressure on the back of his head as the psychic gripped harder.

Mathias felt the muscles in his arms and shoulders throbbing as he exerted more force, pushing his thumbs against Morrow's closed eyes. He was aware of the youngster trying to pull his head back and, as if from a thousand miles away, Mathias heard him groan slightly as the fingers and thumbs dug into him.

The psychic looked down at him and smiled thinly, his face appearing horribly distorted by the blinding power of the spotlight.

Even if Morrow had been aware of what was happening, there was nothing he could have done to prevent it. All he felt was the steadily growing pain as Mathias gripped his head with even more force, a vice-like strength which threatened to crack the bones of his skull. But, as it was, all he could do was remain helpless in the wheelchair, unable to sqirm away from those powerful hands which felt as if they were intent on crushing his head.

The pressure on his eyes became unbearable as Mathias' thumbs drove forward.

Mathias felt some slight resistance at first but then he grunted triumphantly as he felt Morrow's eyes begin to retreat backward beneath the force he was exerting. Blood burst from the corner of the left one and cascaded down the younger man's cheek. Mathias felt the glistening orb move to one side, his thumb slipping into the crimson wetness which was the socket. His nail tore the lid of Morrow's right eye, scraping across the cornea before puncturing the entire structure. The psychic felt his other thumb tearing muscle and ligaments as he began to shake his paralysed victim.

With both thumbs embedded in Morrow's eyes, Mathias forced him backwards, aided by the motion of the wheelchair.

The watching crowd were stunned, not quite sure what was going on. They saw the blood, they saw Morrow's mother running forward but still they looked on in dumb-struck horror.

It was Morrow's keening wail of agony which seemed to galvanise them into action.

In the watching throng, a number of other people screamed. Shouts rose. Shouts of fear and revulsion.

One of the screams came from James Morrow's mother

who ran at the psyshic, anxious to drag him away from her son, who sat motionless in his wheelchair as the psychic continued to gouge his thumbs ever deeper into the riven cavities of his eye sockets. Blood was running freely down the boy's face now, staining his shirt and the blanket around him.

Mathias finally released his hold, turning swiftly to strike the approaching woman with one bloodied hand. The blow shattered her nose and sent her sprawling.

The body of James Morrow, sitting upright in the chair, rolled towards one side of the stage where it tipped precariously for a second before toppling over. The lifeless form fell out and the psychic watched as Mrs Morrow, her face a crimson ruin, crawled helplessly towards it, burbling incoherently.

Mathias blinked hard, aware that people were moving away from the stage. Away from *him*. He glanced down at the struggling form of Mrs Morrow, draped over her dead son like some kind of bloodied shroud. He took a step towards the carnage then faltered, his head spinning, his eyes drawn to the twin gore-filled holes which had once been James Morrow's eyes.

The psychic looked down at his own hands and saw that they were soaked with blood. A fragment of red muscle still clung to one thumb nail. The crimson fluid had run up his arms, staining the cuffs of his shirt.

He shook violently, struggling to breathe as he surveyed the grisly scene before him.

The spotlight pinned him in its unremitting glare but, despite the heat which it gave off, Mathias found that he was shivering.

52

Kelly slipped off her jeans and shivered momentarily before climbing into the large bed in Blake's room. She heard the sound of footfalls approaching across the landing.

Blake entered the room and pulled the door closed behind him. He began unbuttoning his shirt.

'I'll drive to the Institute tomorrow,' he said. 'Confront Vernon. I'll mention his wife. Anything I have to in order to get him to respond.'

He walked to the bedside cabinet and knelt down. The bottom drawer was locked but a quick turn of the ornate gold key and the writer opened it. He reached inside and lifted something out, hefting it before him.

It was a .357 Magnum. A snub-nose model. Blake flipped out the cylinder and carefully thumbed one of the heavy grain bullets into each chamber then he snapped it back into position. He laid the revolver on top of the cabinet.

Kelly regarded the gun warily.

'If Vernon does respond,' said Blake slipping into bed beside her, 'then, at least you'll know you were right. If he doesn't, then you can start looking for another suspect.'

'That narrows the field down quite a bit,' Kelly said, cryptically. She moved close to him, nuzzling against his body, kissing first his chest then his lips. 'Please be careful,' she whispered.

Blake nodded, glanced one last time at the Magnum then reached over and flicked off the lamp.

She was blind.

Kelly thrashed her head frantically back and forth, the terror growing within her.

She could see nothing.

247

She tried to scream but no sound would come forth.

It took her a second or two to realize that she had been gagged. A piece of cloth had been stuffed into her mouth, secured by a length of thick hemp which chafed against the soft flesh of her cheeks. Her eyes had been covered by more, tightly fastened, strands of knotted material, sealed shut as surely as if the lids had been sewn together.

She felt someone moving beside her, felt a hand gently stroking her flat stomach before first moving upwards to her breasts and then down to her pubic mound.

Kelly attempted to move but, as she did, red hot pain lanced through her wrists and ankles as the rope which held her to the bed rasped against her skin. She made a whimpering sound deep in her throat, aware that her legs had been forced apart. She lay spreadeagled, her body exposed to whatever prying eyes chose to inspect it. Her legs had been pulled apart to such an extent that the muscles at the backs of her thighs felt as if they were about to tear. Pain gnawed at the small of her back, intensifying as she struggled in vain to free herself. The rope which was wound so tightly around her wrists and ankles bit hungrily into her flesh until she felt a warm dribble of blood from her left ankle.

Kelly was aware of movement, of a heavy form positioning itself between her legs.

She felt fingers trickling up the inside of her thighs, seeking her exposed vagina.

In the darkness she felt even more helpless, unable to see her assailant because of the blindfold.

Something nudged against her cleft and she stiffened.

Whatever it was, it was excruciatingly cold on that most sensitive area. She lay still as the freezing object probed deeper and, again, she tried to scream.

Kelly heard soft chuckling then a guttural grunt of pleasure.

It was followed by a rapid, rhythmic slopping sound which seemed to keep time with the low grunts.

She realized that her invisible assailant was masturbating.

The cold object between her legs pushed deeper, now adding pain to the other sensation she was feeling.

Another second and Kelly felt warm fluid spilling onto her belly in an erratic fountain. The grunts of her captor grew louder as he coaxed the last droplets of thick liquid from his penis.

Light flashed into her eyes as the blindfold was torn free and, in that split second, she saw the face of her attacker.

His penis still gripped in one fist, the other hand holding the gun against her vagina, he grinned down at her.

She heard a noise which she knew to be the pulling back of the revolver's hammer but her senses were already reeling as she stared with bulging eyes at the man who hovered above her.

David Blake smiled down at her, his face twisted into an unearthly grimace.

Kelly awoke from the nightmare bathed in perspiration. She let out a moan of terror and sat up, looking around her, trying to convince herself that what she had experienced had been the work of her imagination.

The room was silent.

Blake slept soundly beside her, his chest rising and falling slowly.

She let out a long, almost painful breath and ran her hands through her sweat-soaked hair.

As she did so she became aware of a slight tingling in her hands and feet so she pulled the sheet back and glanced down.

Kelly stifled a scream.

On both her wrists and ankles, the flesh was puffy and swollen. Ugly, vivid red welts disfigured the skin.

They were very much like rope burns.

The sound of the alarm shattered the silence and shocked Blake from his slumber. He shot out a hand and silenced the insistent buzzing before lying back for a moment to rub his eyes. He took two or three deep breaths and blinked at the ceiling before easing himself slowly out of bed.

Beside him, Kelly did not stir.

The writer gathered up some clothes and crept out of the room in an effort not to wake her. He paused once more when he reached the bedroom door, satisfied that Kelly had not been disturbed.

He showered and dressed, returning to the bedroom once more to retrieve the Magnum. He then made his way downstairs where he slipped the revolver into his attaché case and clipped it shut.

Blake ate a light breakfast then he got to his feet and, case in hand, headed out to the waiting XJS.

The drive to Oxford should take him a couple of hours.

Kelly watched from the bedroom window as Blake climbed into the Jag and started the engine.

She remained hidden in case he looked round but she need not have worried. The sleek vehicle burst into life and the writer guided it out onto the road.

Kelly had heard the alarm clock earlier but had lain awake, eyes still closed, while he had slipped away. She had feigned sleep, aware of his presence in the room. She had heard him moving about downstairs and then, finally, she'd listened as he had walked out to the car. Only at that point had she clambered, naked, out of bed and crossed to the window to watch him leave. Now she returned to the bed and sat down on the edge.

First she inspected her ankles, then her wrists

They were unmarked.

She told herself that she should have woken Blake immediately after she'd had the nightmare but it had frightened her so much that she had decided to remain silent. Even now, in the light of day, she could not find the courage to speak to him about it. That was why she had chosen to give him the impression she was still sleeping when he left.

The dream had been so vivid. Too vivid. Parts of it still burned brightly in her mind like a brand. Ugly and unwanted.

Kelly dressed and made her way downstairs where she found a note propped up on the kitchen table.

SEE YOU LATER, SLEEPYHEAD.

It was signed with Blake's sweeping signature.

She smiled, folded up the note and slipped it into the pocket of her jeans. As she waited for the kettle to boil she put two pieces of bread in the toaster and propped herself against the draining board, waiting.

Should she tell Blake about the dream when he returned? She ran a hand through her hair and decided that she shouldn't. After all, it had been only a dream, hadn't it?

She looked at her wrists and remembered the rope burns which she'd seen the previous night.

Kelly sighed. She wasn't even sure she *had* seen them.

The toast popped up and she buttered the slices, chewing thoughtfully.

She heard a noise from the front of the house and wandered through the sitting room in time to see the postman retreating back up the path. Kelly walked through into the hall and picked up the mail he'd pushed through. As she straightened up she glanced across at the door which led to Blake's underground workroom.

The key was in the lock.

Kelly placed the mail on a nearby table and wandered across to the cellar door. She turned the handle and found that the door was unlocked anyway. She pushed it, reaching for the light switches inside. Kelly slapped them on and the cellar was bathed in the cold glow of fluorescents.

Apart from the steps which led down to the work area itself, the floor had been carpeted. She scurried down the stairs, the coldness of the concrete on her bare feet giving her added speed. Finally she stood at the bottom, glad of the

251

warmth from the carpet. The cellar was large, stretching away from her in all four directions. A huge wooden desk occupied central position and she noticed that there was a typewriter on it. A small waste bin, overflowing with scraps of balled up paper stood nearby. There was a telephone too. The entire cellar had been decorated in white; it positively gleamed and, as she moved around, Kelly detected the scent of an air freshener. Bookcases lined two walls, huge, dark wood creations creaking with hundreds of volumes but, unlike those which Blake displayed on his shelves upstairs in the sitting room, these books were more in the manner of research material. A great many were bound in leather and, as Kelly drew closer, she realized that most were very old.

She reached up and took one.

The gold leaf title was cracked and barely readable so she opened the book and scanned the title page: *Inside the Mind*. She checked the publication date and saw that it was 1921. Replacing it she found another, this one even older: *Psychiatry and the Unknown*. It was dated 1906.

No wonder Blake kept these books hidden away, Kelly thought, scanning more titles. They must be worth a fortune. She ran her index finger along the shelf, mouthing each title silently as she went.

She came to a shelf which consisted entirely of ring binders, each one labelled on the spine. She recognised Blake's writing on the labels.

'*Dreams*,' she read on the first and took it down, flipping through quickly.

Some of the pages were typed, others hand-written. Here and there she spotted a photograph. There was one of Blake's house and, beside it, a rough drawing of the same building. It was almost childlike in its simplicity, drawn, as it was, with a thick pencil. However, the similarity was unmistakable. Kelly replaced the file and reached for another.

'*Hypnosis*,' she murmured.

There was a photo of Mathias inside.

Kelly turned the page and found one of Blake himself but apparently he was sleeping. It must, she reasoned, have been taken with an automatic timer. She was puzzled as to why he should have taken such a shot though. Kelly scanned what was written beneath the photo but saw only a date. The photo, it seemed, had been taken over a year ago. She wondered if Blake had, perhaps, asked someone else to take it but she still couldn't understand why he would need such a photograph.

She reached for another file marked 'Astral Projection' and skimmed through that.

There were more photos.

Of Mathias. Of Blake himself.

Of Toni Landers.

She turned a page.

There was a newspaper clipping which featured Roger Carr.

Kelly swallowed hard and perched on the edge of the desk as she read one of the typewritten sheets in the file.

'*December 6th,*' she read, keeping her voice low, as if she were in a library.

'*The Astral body is a separate entity. I am sure of that now. From what I have observed and read, but, more importantly, from experimentation upon myself, I know that it can be summoned in tangible form. By a long and tortuous process I have actually managed to separate my Astral body from my physical body at will. To unlock the part of the mind previously unexplored by scientists and psychologists. I now feel confident enough to use this process on others.*'

Kelly swallowed hard and read on:

'*In order to confirm that tangible Astral projection is possible, I conducted the following test. While in a self-induced trance, I inflicted injury upon my own Astral body and discovered that this injury was subsequently manifested on my physical body.*'

There were two photographs beneath. One showed Blake looking at the camera, the other, identical in appearance, highlighted a small scar on his left shoulder. The photos were marked with dates and times. The unblemished one bore the legend: *December 4th 7.30 p.m.* The second: *December 5th 8.01 a.m.*

'*This proved two important things, firstly that it is possible to possess two centres of consciousness simultaneously and also that any injury sustained in the Astral state will manifest itself on the host body. The proof is irrefutable. Tangible*

Astral projection is possible, so too is the manipulation of another person's subconscious mind.'

Kelly closed the file, got to her feet and replaced it. For long seconds she stood motionless in the silent cellar then she scurried back up the steps, aware of the icy chill which seemed to have enveloped her.

She closed the cellar door behind her, noticing that her hand was shaking.

54

It was almost 3.15 p.m. when the XJS came to a halt outside the house.

Kelly, watching from the sitting room, peered out and saw Blake lock the vehicle before gathering up his attaché case. He headed for the front door and, a moment later, she heard the key turn. As it did she moved across to the sofa and sat down, her eyes on the hall door.

Blake smiled at her as he entered.

She watched as he laid the attaché case on the coffee table and flipped it open, removing the Magnum which he placed beside it.

'Vernon didn't try anything?' she said, looking at the gun.

The writer shook his head.

'If he has acquired some kind of power then he knows how to control it,' he said, crossing to the drinks cabinet and pouring himself a large measure of Haig. He offered Kelly a drink and she accepted a Campari.

'Did he say anything at all?' she wanted to know.

'Nothing that I found incriminating if that's what you mean,' Blake told her. 'I mentioned his wife. You were right, he does get touchy about *that*. He wanted to know how I knew about her, what I knew about her. When I mentioned John Fraser he threatened to have me thrown out or arrested.' The writer downed a sizeable measure of the fiery liquid.

'You didn't accuse him of killing Fraser did you?'

'Not in so many words. I just told him what *you'd* told *me*. He didn't react very favourably.'

There was a long silence, finally broken by Blake.

'I don't know where we go from here,' he said.

Kelly didn't speak for a moment then she sucked in a long breath and looked at Blake.

'David, how much do *you* know about Astral projection?' she asked.

He sipped at his drink, his eyes glinting behind the dark screen of his glasses.

'Why do you ask?' he said, his voice low.

'I was just curious,' she told him. She opened her mouth to speak again but couldn't seem to find the words.

Blake sat beside her on the sofa and placed one arm around her, drawing her to him. He smiled reassuringly. She moved closer to him, aware of an icy chill which surrounded her.

He held her firmly and only when her head was resting on his shoulder did his smile disappear.

He looked across at the Magnum.

55

Oxford

The strains of 'God Save the Queen' died away gradually to be replaced by a rasping hiss of static, so loud that it jolted Dr Stephen Vernon from his uneasy dozing. He moved to get up, almost spilling the mug of cocoa which he held in one hand. He switched off the television and stood silently in the sitting room for a moment. He was alone in his house. Joubert was at the Institute and would be for the remainder of the night, going through reams of notes so far untouched.

Vernon gazed down into his mug of cold cocoa and winced as he saw the film of skin which had covered the surface. He put it down and headed for the sitting room door, turning off lights as he went.

He had reached the bottom of the staircase when he heard the noise.

Vernon froze, trying to pinpoint the direction from which it had come. He felt his heart begin to beat a little faster as he heard it once more.

A dull thud followed by what sounded like soft whispering.

He turned, realizing that it came from the study, behind him to the left. The white door was firmly shut however, hiding its secret securely.

Vernon hesitated, waiting for the sound to come again.

He heard nothing and prepared to climb the stairs once more. He'd left the window in the room open. A breeze might well have dislodged something in there, knocked it to the floor, caused ...

He heard the sound like whispering again and, this time, turned and approached the door.

Vernon paused outside, his ear close to the wood in an effort to detect any sounds from within. His hand hovered nervously over the knob, finally closing on it, turning it gently.

He tried to control his rapid breathing, afraid that whoever was inside the study would hear his approach. Also, as he stood there waiting for the right moment to strike, he felt suddenly vulnerable. He released the door knob and looked around the darkened hallway for a weapon of some kind.

There was a thick wood walking stick propped up in the umbrella stand nearby; Vernon took it and, for the second time, prepared to enter the study.

Beyond the closed door all was silent once again, not the slightest sound of movement disturbed the solitude. A thought occurred to Vernon.

What if the intruder was aware of his presence and, at this moment, was waiting for *him*?

He swallowed hard and tried to force the thought from his mind.

He gripped the knob and twisted it, hurling open the door, his free hand slapping for the light switches just inside.

As the study was illuminated, Vernon scanned the area before him, the walking stick brandished like a club.

His mouth dropped open in surprise as he caught sight of

the intruder.

Hunkered over the large table, one of the files open before him, was David Blake.

'You,' gasped Vernon, lowering his guard.

That lapse of concentration was all that Blake needed. He flung himself across the table, catapulted as if from some gigantic rubber band. He crashed into Vernon, knocking the walking stick from his hand, rolling to one side as the older man lashed out at him. Vernon managed to scramble to his feet, bolting from the room but Blake was younger and quicker and he rugby-tackled the doctor, bringing him down in the hallway. They grappled in the gloom and Vernon found that his fear gave him added strength. He gripped Blake's wrists and succeeded in throwing him to one side. The younger man crashed against a nearby wall but the impact seemed only to slow him up for a moment. He scrambled to his feet and set off after the older man again, following him into the kitchen this time.

Vernon tugged open a drawer, the contents spilling across the tiled floor. Knives, forks, spoons, a ladle — all rained down around his feet with a series of high pitched clangs. He snatched up a long carving knife and brandished it before him.

Blake hesitated as he saw the vicious blade winking at him and, for what seemed like an eternity, the two men faced one another, eyes locked. Like two gladiators, they both waited for the other to move first.

'What do you want?' asked Vernon, the knife quivering in his grip.

The younger man didn't answer, he merely edged forward slightly.

'I'll kill you, Blake, I swear to God I will,' Vernon assured him, making a sharp stabbing movement with the blade.

Blake was undeterred. He took another step forward, something on the worktop to his right catching his eye.

It was a sugar bowl.

With lightning speed, he picked it up and hurled the contents into Vernon's face. The tiny grains showered him, some finding their way into his eyes, and he yelped in pain, momentarily blinded by the stinging shower of particles. Blake took his chance. Dropping to one knee, he grabbed a corkscrew and hurled himself at Vernon who somehow managed one last despairing lunge before Blake reached him.

The blade sliced through the younger man's jacket and laid open his left forearm just above the wrist. Blood spurted from the cut and plashed on to the tiles. But Blake slammed into Vernon with the force of a pile-driver, knocking him back against the sink. He snaked one arm around the older man's neck and held him firmly, bringing the corkscrew forward with devastating power.

The sharp point pierced Vernon's skull at the crown and he screamed in agony as Blake twisted it, driving the curling metal prong deeper until it began to churn into the older man's brain. White hot pain seared through him and he felt himself blacking out but, just before he did, Blake tore the corkscrew free, ripping a sizeable lump of bone with it. Greyish red brain matter welled up through the hole and Vernon fell forward on to the tiles as Blake struck again. This time driving the corkscrew into the hollow at the base of his skull, ramming hard until it erupted from Vernon's throat. There was an explosion of crimson as blood spouted from both wounds and his body began to quiver uncontrollably as Blake tore the twisted weapon free once more

He stood there for a moment, gazing down at the lifeless body before him, now surrounded by a spreading pool of red liquid. Then, almost contemptuously, he tossed the corkscrew to one side, stepped over the body and headed back towards the study.

Kelly let out a strangled cry as she sat up, the last vestiges of the nightmare still clinging to her consciousness like graveyard mist.

She closed her eyes tightly for a moment, aware that her heart was thundering against her ribs. But, gradually, she slowed her breathing, aware that the dream was fading.

Blake was sleeping peacefully beside her. Apparently he had not heard her frightened outburst. She thought about waking him, telling him what she had dreamt but she thought better of it. Kelly could hear his gentle, rhythmic breathing beside her and she looked down at his still form.

The breath caught in her throat.

There was a small dark stain on the sheet.

She prodded it with her finger and found that it was still damp. Kelly noticed that whatever the substance was, it also coloured her finger. In the darkness of the bedroom it looked black but, as she sniffed it, she caught the unmistakable odour of blood.

Blake moved slightly, turning on to his side.

Kelly pulled the sheet back further and ran her gaze over his body.

On his left forearm, just above the wrist, there was a cut.

She stood in the bedroom doorway for a full five minutes, her eyes riveted to Blake's sleeping form then, certain that she had not disturbed him, she crept downstairs to the sitting room.

Kelly did not turn on the light, not even one of the table lamps. She found the phone and selected the appropriate number, waiting for the receiver to be picked up, hoping that she had remembered Dr Vernon's number correctly.

She didn't have to wait long for an answer.

'Yes.' The voice sounded harsh and she realized that it wasn't the doctor.

'Can I speak to Dr Vernon, please?' she whispered, casting a furtive glance towards the door behind her.

'Who is this?' the voice asked.

'I'm a friend of his,' she persisted. 'Could I speak to him please?'

'That isn't possible. Dr Vernon was murdered earlier tonight.'

Kelly hung up, banging the phone down with a little too much force. She wondered if Blake had heard her but the thought swiftly vanished. There was no sound of movement from upstairs. She stood alone in the dark sitting room, perspiration forming droplets on her face and forehead.

Vernon murdered.

She sat down on the edge of the sofa, her head cradled in her hands, still not fully comprehending what she had heard.

She thought of the blood on the sheet. Of her nightmare. The cut on Blake's wrist.

And of what she had read earlier in the day;

'An injury sustained in the Astral state will manifest itself on the host body.'

Kelly suddenly felt more frightened than she could ever remember.

56

Kelly brought the Mini to a halt and sat behind the wheel for a moment, scanning the area in front of Dr Vernon's house. In addition to the doctor's Audi, there was a dark brown Sierra in the driveway and, by the kerbside itself, a Granada. She could see two men seated in that particular car. One was eating a sandwich while the other, the driver, was busy cleaning his ears out with one index finger. Both men wore suits despite the warmth of the early morning sunshine.

She wound down the window a little further, allowing what little breeze there was to circulate inside the car. She was perspiring, but not all of it was due to the heat of the day.

The drive from London had taken over two hours. She'd told Blake that she wanted to pick up some more clothes from her flat. He'd seen her off like the dutiful lover he'd become, then retired to his workroom for the day. She had not mentioned anything to him about either her nightmare or the phone call to Vernon's house. She had not slept much the previous night, not after returning to bed. What was more, she'd been mildly disturbed to find that the bloodstains on the sheet had all but disappeared and, that morning, Blake's wrist appeared to be uninjured but for a minute red mark which looked like little more than a cat-scratch.

Now Kelly sat in the car staring across the road at the Granada and the house beyond it, realizing that, sooner or later she was going to be forced to make her move. Her palms felt sticky as she reached for the door handle and eased herself out of the Mini. She sucked in a deep breath then headed across the road towards the driveway.

She was a foot or two beyond the Granada when a voice called her back and she turned to see one of the men getting out, his cheeks bulging, hamster-like, with the last remnants of his sandwich.

'Excuse me, Miss,' he said, trying hurriedly to swallow what he was chewing.

Kelly turned to face him, noticing as she did that he was reaching inside his jacket. He produced a slim leather wallet and flipped it open to reveal an ID card which bore his picture. It was a bad likeness, making his thick brown hair appear ginger.

'I'm Detective-Sergeant Ross,' the man told her. 'May I ask what you're doing here?'

'Police?' she said, feigning surprise.

He nodded and succeeded in forcing down the last of his food.

'What are you doing here?'

Ross smiled thinly.

'*I* asked first, Miss,' he said.

The lie was ready on her tongue.

'I've come to see my father,' she told him.

Ross's smile faded suddenly and he almost took a step back.

'We weren't aware that Dr Vernon had any close family,' he told her.

Kelly felt her heart beating a little faster.

'Is something wrong?' she wanted to know, hoping that her little act was working.

'Could you come with me please, Miss?' the DS said and led her up the driveway towards the house. As they drew nearer, Kelly tried frantically to slow her rapid breathing. She had suddenly begun to doubt the success of her little venture. The front door opened and a man dressed in a grey suit, carrying a black briefcase, emerged.

He exchanged brief words with Ross then climbed into the Sierra, reversed out of the driveway and sped off.

'You still haven't told me what's going on?' Kelly insisted, not trying to disguise the mock concern in her voice.

They were inside the house by now and Ross ushered her into a sitting room where she sat down on one of the chairs.

'I'll be back in a minute,' he told her and disappeared.

Kelly looked around the room, hands clasped on her knees. She swallowed hard and attempted to stop her body quivering. Her roving eyes scanned the shelves and tables for photos. If there was one of Vernon's daughter then she was finished. Although Ross had told her that the police were unaware he'd had a family, it did little to comfort her. She was still in the process of composing herself when Ross returned, accompanied by a taller, older man with a long face and chin which jutted forward with almost abnormal prominence. He introduced himself as Detective Inspector Allen.

'You're Dr Vernon's daughter?' he asked, eyeing her up and down.

'Yes,' she lied.

Allen looked at his companion then at Kelly. He cleared his throat self-consciously and proceeded to tell her what had happened the previous night. Kelly reacted with all the rehearsed shock and grief she could muster.

'As far as we know, nothing was stolen,' Allen continued. 'There was still money in one of the drawers upstairs and your father's wallet was in his jacket which is hanging in the hallway.'

'So why was he killed?' Kelly asked, reaching for a handkerchief which she clutched between her hands in mock despair, tugging at it most convincingly.

'We were hoping you might be able to shed some light on that,' Allen said. 'Did he have any enemies that you know of?'

Kelly shook her head.

'He kept himself to himself,' she said, lowering her eyes slightly.

'Did you know that there was someone living in the house with him?' the DI wanted to know. 'One of the guest rooms is occupied.'

'I didn't know that,' she said, with genuine surprise.

Allen frowned.

'How often did you see your father, Miss Vernon?'

Kelly licked her lips self-consciously. She was going to have to tread carefully.

'Not regularly. I live in London at the moment. But that's not my permanent address.'

'Alone?'

'What?'

'Do you live alone?'

She paused a second or two longer than she should have and, what was more, she was aware of that fact. Kelly realized that she was on the verge of blowing the entire facade wide open.

'You'll have to excuse me,' she said, pressing the handkerchief to her eyes. 'I can't seem to think straight. After what you've told me about my father I ...' She allowed the sentence to trail off.

Allen nodded comfortingly.

'I realize it must be difficult,' he said, softly. 'Take your time.'

How many more questions, she wondered?

She was spared the trouble of answering by Ross who popped his head around the corner and called to his superior. Allen excused himself and left the room for a moment. Kelly let out an audible sigh of relief, grateful for the momentary respite. She heard voices in the hallway, one of which she was sure she recognised.

A moment later, Alain Joubert entered the sitting room, followed by Allen.

The Frenchman stopped in his tracks when he saw Kelly, who shot an anxious glance in the policeman's direction, thankful that he hadn't noticed her reaction. He did, however, glimpse the surprised expression of Joubert.

'Do you two know each other?' Allen asked.

'We ...'

Kelly cut him short.

'My father introduced us about a month ago,' she said, stepping forward. 'How are you, Mr Joubert?'

The Frenchman managed to conceal his bewilderment and Kelly prayed that he wouldn't give the game away.

'I'm sorry to hear what happened,' Joubert said, flatly.

Kelly nodded.

'Were you aware that Mr Joubert had been staying at your father's house for the past two weeks?' asked the policeman.

'No,' Kelly said. 'But I knew that he was working on a new project with someone. I wasn't aware it was Mr Joubert though. My father likes to keep his work to himself.'

'You claim that you've been at the Research Institute all night?' Allen said to the Frenchman.

'Yes I have,' Joubert told him. 'The night-watchman will

verify that if you ask him.'

'As far as we can see, nothing of Dr Vernon's was taken, but you might like to check your own belongings,' the DI suggested.

Joubert nodded.

'It would be more convenient for all of us if you could leave the house for a day or two, sir,' Allen said. 'While the lads from forensic go over the place.'

Joubert nodded.

'I'll book into a hotel,' he said. 'I'll get some things from upstairs.' The Frenchman glanced once more at Kelly then left the room.

'How *was* my father killed?' Kelly asked.

'He was stabbed,' said Allen, hastily.

'Knifed?'

The policeman swallowed hard.

'No. He was stabbed with a corkscrew. I'm sorry.'

Kelly closed her eyes for a moment, the details of her dream suddenly flashing with neon brilliance in her mind. She felt a twinge of nausea but fought it back. Allen moved towards her as if he feared she would faint but she waved him away.

'I'm all right,' she assured him, smiling thinly.

Joubert returned a moment later carrying what looked like an overnight bag.

'There is one more thing I'd like to check on before I leave,' he said, entering the study.

Kelly and DI Allen followed him.

The Frenchman muttered something in his own tongue as he surveyed the empty table in the study.

'The files,' he said, wearily. 'They've been taken.'

'What files?' Allen demanded.

'The project that Dr Vernon and I were working on,' Joubert snapped. 'All the information was compiled in half a dozen files. They're gone.'

'What kind of information?' the policeman persisted.

'Just research notes, of no importance to anyone but us.' He cast a sly glance at Kelly.

'Are you sure they've been taken?' said Allen.

'They were here,' Joubert snapped, tapping the table top.

'Can you describe them?' asked Allen.

The Frenchman shrugged.

'Six plain manilla files, what more can I tell you?'

'Whoever took them knew what they were looking for,' Kelly interjected.

Joubert nodded and looked at her once more.

'Damn,' he said, under his breath.

'Well,' Allen told him. 'It's not much to go on but, we'll do our best to trace them.' He paused for a moment. 'I'd like the name of the hotel you're staying in, Mr Joubert, if you could phone me at the station as soon as you've booked in.' He handed the Frenchman a piece of paper with a phone number on it. 'And you, Miss Vernon, I'd appreciate an address where I can reach you.'

She gave him that of her flat in Oxford.

'I don't think we need keep you any longer,' the DI told them. 'But we'll be in touch.'

Joubert was the first to turn and head for the front door.

Kelly followed, catching up with him as he reached his car. She glanced round, making sure they were out of earshot.

'Did Lasalle know what was in those files?' she asked.

'What the hell has *he* got to do with all this?' Joubert barked. 'And you are taking a chance posing as Vernon's daughter aren't you?'

'Joubert, I have to speak to you. But not here.'

His expression softened somewhat.

'It's important,' she persisted.

'Very well. Perhaps you could recommend a hotel.' He smiled humourlessly.

'I've got my car,' she told him. 'Follow me into the town centre. We must talk. There's a lot that needs explanation.'

He regarded her impassively for a moment then nodded, climbed into his Fiat and started the engine. Kelly scuttled across the road to her own car and twisted the key in the ignition. She waited until Joubert had reversed out into the street, then she set off. He followed close behind. Kelly could see the trailing Fiat in her rear view mirror as she drove.

She wondered if finally she would learn the answers to the questions which had plagued her for so long.

265

There were only a handful of people in the bar of 'The Bull' hotel. It was not yet noon and the lunchtime drinkers had still to appear.

Kelly sat over her orange juice, waiting for Joubert to join her. When he finally sat down opposite her she noticed how dark and sunken his eyes looked, a testament to the fact that he had been working all night. He sipped his own drink and watched as Kelly did the same.

'You said you wanted to talk,' the Frenchman said. 'What had you in mind?'

'For one thing, I'd like to know what the hell you and Vernon had been up to for the past month or so,' she said, challengingly. 'Ever since the two institutes began work on Astral projection and dream interpretation it's been more like working for MI5 than a psychic research unit. What were you and Vernon working on?'

'What happened to the famous English quality of tact?' he said, smiling. 'What do you want to know?'

'If I asked all the questions that are on my mind we'd be here until this time next year. Right now I'll settle for knowing why you and Vernon were so secretive about the research findings.'

Joubert sipped his drink once more, gazing into the glass as if seeking inspiration.

'How much did you know about Vernon?' he asked.

'Personally, not a great deal. Professionally he seemed obsessed with the work on Astral projection and mind control,' Kelly said.

'He was. But with good cause, as I was. We both had reasons for wanting the findings kept quiet until a suitable time.'

'Reasons worth killing for?' she asked.

Joubert looked aghast.

'Certainly not,' he said, indignantly. 'Why do you say that?'

'The death of Lasalle didn't seem to make much of an impression on you.'

'You thought I was responsible for Lasalle's death?' he said, although it sounded more like a statement than a question.

She nodded.

'He was cracking up, close to insanity when he died,' said Joubert. 'No one could have helped him, least of all me. He was afraid of me.'

'You gave him cause to be. I noticed the hostility between you.'

'It was nothing personal. I was angry with him for revealing our findings so early. That was all.' The Frenchman lowered his voice slightly. 'Lasalle was a good friend of mine,' he said, reflectively. 'But he did a lot of damage to our research with that article he wrote. It brought too much media attention to a project which should have been fully completed before being put up for scrutiny. And, he ruined my chances of making a name for myself in our field.' He went on to recount the story he had told Vernon, about how the limelight had been snatched from him once before. 'So, perhaps you can understand *my* reasons for secrecy. That was why I was unco-operative with you. I didn't want anybody or anything to interfere with my chances of making the breakthrough. *I* wanted to be the one who was remembered for making one of parapsychology's greatest finds.'

Kelly exhaled.

'And Vernon?' she said. 'Why was he so fascinated by mind control?'

'His reasons were even more genuine than mine,' said the Frenchman.

'One of my colleagues said that he was hiding something about his wife. He ...'

Joubert interrupted.

'Vernon's wife has been irretrievably and irreversibly insane for the past six years. When you masqueraded as his daughter this morning you took a bigger risk than you could have imagined. Vernon *has* a daughter. Admittedly, he hadn't seen her for six years and, as far as she is concerned, he had no place in her life but she exists nevertheless.'

Kelly raised her glass to her lips but she lowered it again, her full attention on Joubert as he continued.

'He had a Grandson too. As he explained it to me, the child, who was less than a year old at the time, was being cared for by Mrs Vernon. She doted on the boy, worshipped him as if he were hers. Vernon himself has always been a nervous man, afraid of burglars and intruders. He and his wife owned two Dobermans. They were kept in a small compound during the day and released at night.' He sighed. 'This particular day, they escaped. The baby boy was crawling on the lawn. There was nothing Mrs Vernon could do. The dogs tore the child to pieces before her eyes.'

'Oh God,' murmured Kelly.

'She went into a state of shock and then slipped into a catatonic trance. Vernon thought that if he discovered a way to unlock the subconscious mind, he could use it to cure his wife. That was his *secret*. Nothing sinister.'

Kelly shook her head almost imperceptibly.

'If only he'd said something,' she whispered.

'He never intended the truth to be revealed,' Joubert said. 'But now it doesn't matter.'

'Who would want to kill him?' she asked, as if expecting the Frenchman to furnish her with an answer.

'The same person who would want to steal those files,' he said. 'I can't think what possible use they would be to anyone not acquainted with the paranormal. Besides, who else but Vernon and myself even knew they were at the house?' He shook his head.

'I saw Vernon murdered,' Kelly said, flatly.

Joubert looked at her aghast.

'In a dream,' she continued.

'Have you had precognitive dreams before?' he asked, somewhat excitedly.

'Never.'

'Did you see who killed him?'

Kelly took a long swig from her glass, wishing that it contained something stronger. She nodded.

'His name is David Blake,' she said. 'The man I'm living with.'

Joubert watched her across the table, aware that she was quivering slightly.

'Could there have been some mistake?' he asked.

She shrugged.

'I don't know what to believe any more.'

'Kelly, if it's true then you could be in a great deal of danger.'

'He doesn't know I suspect him,' she said, her voice cracking. 'Besides,' Kelly wiped a tear from her eye corner, 'I love him.' Her eyes filled with moisture which, a second later, began to spill down her cheeks. 'Oh God it can't be Him. It can't.'

Joubert moved closer and curled one comforting arm around her shoulder.

'He wouldn't hurt me though, I know he wouldn't,' she murmured.

'How can you be sure?'

She had no answer.

58

London

It was late afternoon by the time Kelly drew into the driveway outside Blake's house. There was no sign of his XJS. He was either out for a while or the car was in the garage. She left her Mini where it was, locked it, then headed for the front door.

As she stepped inside the hall, the silence seemed to envelop her like an invisible blanket and she stood motionless for a moment as if reluctant to disturb the solitude. She glanced across at the cellar door.

It was open slightly.

Kelly approached it silently, listening for the noise of a clacking typewriter from below but there was none.

'David,' she called and her voice sounded hollow in the stillness.

No answer.

She walked back to the sitting room door, opened it slightly and peered in, calling his name as she did so.

Nothing.

Kelly wandered to the bottom of the staircase and looked up.

'David, are you up there?'

The silence reigned supreme.

She opened the cellar door wider and gazed down into the subterranean chamber.

Kelly began to descend.

Half way down the stairs she called his name once again, now satisfied that the house was empty. The extractor fan was on, a slight whirring sound filling the calmness. Kelly felt that all too familiar ripple of fear caress her neck and spine. The cellar looked vast, stretching out all around her, making her feel vulnerable and exposed. She moved towards his desk, her pace slowing, her jaw dropping open.

Perched on top of the typewriter were the six manilla files.

Kelly froze for a second then reached forward and picked one up, flipping it open. She recognised Lasalle's handwriting on the first page.

'Found what you're looking for?'

The voice sounded thunderous in the silence.

Kelly spun round, almost dropping the file, her eyes fixed on the figure at the top of the stairs.

Blake stood there motionless for a moment then slowly descended the steps.

His face was expressionless as he approached her, one hand extended. He motioned for her to give him the file which she did, not shifting her gaze from his eyes, trying to look through those twin dark screens which covered them.

'Why did you kill Dr Vernon?' she asked, falteringly.

'Kelly,' he said, softly. 'You shouldn't have come down here. What goes on in this room is my business.'

'You did kill him didn't you, David?' she persisted.

'Yes,' he said, unhesitatingly. 'I needed the files.'

'I've been to his house today. I've spoken to Joubert.'

Blake chuckled.

'Not so long ago you were convinced that Vernon and Joubert were responsible for these events,' he said.

'Tell me why you did it,' she said. 'Why you caused all those deaths.'

He didn't answer.

'Why?' she roared at him, her voice a mixture of fear and desperation.

He saw a single tear trickle from her eye corner. She wiped it away angrily.

'Ever since I can remember, even before I began writing about the paranormal, the idea of Astral projection has fascinated me,' he began, his tone measured and calm. 'Not just travelling through space on an ethereal level, but actual *physical* movement of the Astral body through time. The tangible realization of that movement which meant I could literally be in two places at once. In control of *two* centres of consciousness. I made it work. It took years to master but I learned how to do it and the more I learned, the more I realized that it was possible to manipulate the subconscious personalities of others as well. To use them.' He regarded her with no hint of emotion on his face.

'Like Toni Landers and the rest?' she said.

'I learned to control the Shadow inside them.'

'The Shadow?' Kelly said, looking vague.

'The alter-ego. What you know as the subconscious. That part of the mind which controls our darker side, that's the Shadow. I found a way to release it.'

'How?' she wanted to know. 'Is it by a form of hypnosis?'

'Yes, combined with my own ability to absorb the energy which the Shadow radiates. It's like an infra-red beacon to me. I can tap into it. Feed on it. It increases my own power. Everyone, no matter who they are, has this darker side to their nature. Most people are able to control it, and it's kept in check by their code of morals or by the law. But when the force is released, they act out thoughts and desires which had previously been hidden.'

Kelly shook her head.

'Why did you do it, David?' she asked, tears brimming in her eyes once again. 'What did you hope to achieve by having Toni Landers kill that baby, or Roger Carr murder that girl. Or Braddock or O'Neil. Why did they have to kill?'

'I had to be sure of my own abilities. Now I am,' he said, impassively. 'The seance gave me a perfect opportunity to use that power, to prove once and for all that I could influence other people's alter-egos. Use them. Can't you appreciate what this means?' His voice had taken on a note of excitement. 'Politicians could be manipulated. Leaders of the Church, Heads of State.'

'You're mad,' she said, taking a step back.

'No, Kelly, I'm not mad,' he said. 'This power is too great to be wasted. Think about it. There need be no more wars, no more civil unrest, because those who provoke such incidents could be found and destroyed before they were able to create trouble. Any trace of evil inside their minds would be visible to someone like me who knew how to use the power of the Shadow.'

'And if you did discover some evil inside them?'

'I told you, they would be destroyed. Executed. This knowledge gives me the power of life and death over anyone I choose. It's a weapon too.'

'For selling?' she asked, cryptically.

'If necessary,' he told her. 'There's no weapons system on earth to match it.'

'But why use it to kill?'

'Every discovery has its sacrifices,' he said, smiling. 'You should know that.'

'No one will believe it.'

Blake smiled and crossed to his desk. He pulled open one of the drawers and took out a letter. Kelly watched him, warily.

'If you'd searched my office more thoroughly,' he said. 'You'd have found this.' He unfolded the letter. 'It arrived two days ago, from Thames TV. I've been invited onto a discussion programme. Myself and two other "experts" are supposed to discuss whether or not the supernatural is real or imaginary. Nice of them to include me don't you think?'

'What are you going to do?'

His smile faded.

'I'm going to prove, once and for all, exactly how powerful the Shadow is,' Blake told her.

Kelly took another step back.

'I loved you, David,' she said, softly, tears rolling down her cheeks.

'Then stay with me,' he said, moving towards her.

'You're a murderer. I saw you kill Vernon.'

'Ah, your dream,' he said, that chilling grin returning. 'I had already been probing your mind for a week or two prior to that little incident. Can't you see, Kelly, you and I are one. We belong together. You can share this power with me. Learn how to use it.'

'Learn how to kill, you mean?' she said, vehemently.

'All right then, leave. Go to the police. Tell them I killed Dr Vernon but who the hell is going to believe you? How could I have killed him?' he added, mockingly. 'I was in bed with you last night.'

She swallowed hard, realizing he was right.

'Go. Get out,' Blake roared. 'I offered you the chance and you refused. Leave here.'

He watched as she turned and hurriedly climbed the stairs, disappearing into the hall. A moment later he heard the front door slam behind her. His expression darkened as he gripped the file. He clutched it a second longer then, with a grunt, hurled it across the room.

Kelly knew Blake was right.

As she started the engine of the Mini she realized she would never convince the police of his guilt. She was helpless, something which made her feel angry as well as afraid.

She guided the car out into traffic, wiping more tears away with the back of her hand. Combined with that feeling of helplessness was also one of loss, for somewhere inside her, despite what she knew, she retained her affection for Blake. Kelly felt as if the world were collapsing around her.

She knew that she must tell Joubert what she had learned. There was a phone box on the corner of the street. Kelly slowed down and prepared to swing the car over. She checked her rear view mirror.

She could not supress a scream.

Reflected in the mirror, glaring at her from the back seat, was the face of Blake.

Kelly twisted the wheel, her eyes riveted to the visage in the mirror.

All she heard was the loud blast of the air horns as the lorry thundered towards her.

273

It was enough to shake her from her terror and now she looked through the windscreen to see the huge Scania bearing down on her. The driver was waving madly for her to get out of his way.

She pushed her foot down on the accelerator and the Mini shot forward, swerving violently, missing the nearest huge wheel by inches. Kelly yelped as the car hit the kerb with a bone jarring bump before skidding across the pavement and coming to rest against the hedge of the garden opposite.

A car behind her also came to a grinding halt and the lorry pulled up a few yards further on, the driver leaping from the cab.

Kelly shook herself and twisted in her seat.

The back seat was empty.

There was no sign of Blake.

She felt sick, the realization of what had just happened slowly dawning on her. She heard footsteps approaching the car then her door was wrenched open.

The lorry driver stood there, his face flushed.

'Are you all right?' he asked, anxiously.

She nodded.

'What the hell were you doing? You pulled straight in front of me. I could have killed you.'

Kelly closed her eyes tightly for a moment.

'I'm sorry,' she whispered.

The driver of the other car had arrived by now and he reached in to undo Kelly's seatbelt. The two men helped her from the car, standing beside her as she sucked in deep lungfuls of air.

'I'll phone for an ambulance,' said the truck driver.

'No.' Kelly caught his arm. 'I'll be OK. I wasn't hurt.'

'You look pretty shaken up,' he told her.

'Please. No ambulance.'

She wasn't sure what had disturbed her the most. Nearly being hit by the lorry or the sight of Blake's leering face.

'I'm fine, really,' she assured them both.

Other vehicles slowed down as they drove by, glancing at the roadside tableau.

Kelly eventually clambered back into the Mini and strapped herself in. The two men watched as she guided her car off the pavement back on to the road.

'Thanks for your help,' she said and drove off, leaving the two men shaking their heads as she disappeared into traffic.

After another mile or so and Kelly came to a second phone box. Glancing somewhat nervously into her rear-view mirror she signalled then pulled in, clambering out of the car and reaching the box moments before two young girls, who began muttering to each other and pacing up and down outside.

Kelly fumbled for some change and dialled the number of Joubert's hotel. She tapped agitatedly on one glass panel of the phone box as she waited to be connected. Finally she heard the Frenchman's voice.

Scarcely had he identified himself than she began babbling her story to him. About Blake. About Vernon's death. The murders committed by Toni Landers and the others. Blake's TV appearance.

The power of the Shadow.

The Frenchman listened in stunned silence, only his low breathing signalling his presence on the other end of the line.

The rapid pips sounded and she pushed in another coin.

'Kelly, you must get away from there,' Joubert said, finally.

'I can't leave now,' she told him.

'For God's sake, he could kill you too.'

'He must be stopped.'

'But Kelly ...'

She hung up, paused a moment then walked back to her car. As she opened her hand she glanced at the bunch of keys resting on her palm.

One of them unlocked the front door of Blake's house.

The thought hit her like a thunderbolt. She scrambled behind the steering wheel and started the engine.

It was 5.56 p.m.

She had time but it was running out fast.

PART THREE

'We'll know for the first time,
If we're evil or divine ...'
　　　　　　　　— *Ronnie James Dio*

'The evil that men do lives after them ...'
　　　　　　　— *Julius Caesar, Act III, Scene II*

At 6.35 David Blake walked from his house, climbed into the waiting XJS and started the engine. Despite the relative warmth of the evening, the sky was a patchwork of mottled grey and blue. Away to the north clouds were gathering in unyielding dark formations and Blake wondered how long it would be before the impending storm arrived. As if to reinforce his supicions, a distant rumble of thunder rolled across the sky.

He guided the Jag out into the street and swung it right.

He didn't see Kelly.

She had been standing about twenty yards further down the street for almost an hour, watching and waiting, the key to Blake's front door clutched in her hand.

Now she watched as the XJS pulled away, disappearing around the corner.

As if fearing that he might return, she paused for another five minutes then began walking briskly towards the house, not hesitating as she made her way up the path, attempting to hide the anxiousness in her stride. She reached the front door and pushed in the key.

'He's just gone out.'

She gasped aloud as she heard the voice, turning to discover its source.

Kelly saw the middle-aged man who lived next door to Blake. He was struggling to hold his Alsatian under control, the large dog pulling on its leash as if threatening to tug the man off his feet. He stood there, watching as Kelly turned the key in the lock.

'I don't know where he's gone,' the man persisted.

She smiled as politely as she could manage.

'It's all right, I'll wait,' she told him and stepped inside.

Through the bevelled glass of the front door, Kelly could see the distorted image of the man next door. He appeared to be standing staring at the house but, after a moment or two, he moved on. She sighed and moved quickly across the hall to the staircase, scuttling up the steps towards Blake's bedroom.

She paused outside the door, aware of a slight chill in the air but she ignored it and walked in. The silence swallowed her up and she was aware only of the sound of her own heart beating.

Kelly moved around the bed to the cabinet, her eyes fixed on the ornate gold key in the lock of bottom drawer. She dropped to her knees and turned it.

It was almost seven o'clock by the time she left the house. As she clambered into the Mini she guessed that the drive across London would take her forty-five minutes if she was lucky. She prayed that the traffic wouldn't be too heavy. Her heart was still thumping hard against her ribs and she took a tissue from her handbag to wipe the moisture from the palms of her hands.

As she dropped the bag on to the passenger seat she noticed how heavy it was.

The .357 Magnum nestled safely inside.

Blake turned up the volume on the casette and drummed on the steering wheel as he waited for the lights to turn green. Traffic in the centre of London was beginning to clog the roads but the writer seemed unperturbed by the temporary hold-up. The show he was due to appear on was going out live but he looked at his watch and realized he'd make it in time. He smiled as he saw the traffic lights change colour.

Another fifteen minutes and he would be at the studio.

Another ominous rumble of thunder shook the heavens. The storm was getting closer.

Kelly looked first as the dashboard clock and then at her own watch. She drove as fast as she was able in the streams of traffic, slowing down slightly when she saw a police car cruise past in the lane next to her. Almost without thinking, she reached over and secured the clasp on her handbag, ensuring that the revolver didn't fall out. Kelly could feel the perspiration on her back and forehead, clinging to her like dew to the grass.

She guessed that Blake must have reached his destination by now.

Another glance at her watch and she estimated it would be over ten minutes before she caught up with him.

The first spots of rain began to spatter her windscreen.

60

By the time Kelly reached the Thames Television studios in Euston Road the rain was falling in torrents. Large droplets of it bounced off the car and she squinted to see through the drenched windscreen. Her wipers seemed quite inadequate for the task of sweeping away the water which poured down the glass.

She found a parking space then jumped out of the car, picking up her handbag. She sprinted towards the main entrance, slowing her pace as she saw a uniformed doorman barring the way. A thought crossed her mind.

What if he wanted to search her bag?

She held it close to her and looked at him warily but his only gesture was to smile happily at her. Kelly smiled back, as much in relief as anything else. The man opened the door for her and she walked inside the vast entry-way.

'Could you tell me which studio David Blake is in?' she asked.

'Who?' he said.

'David Blake,' she repeated. 'He's a writer. He's taking part in a discussion programme tonight at eight. I hope I'm not too late.'

'Oh yes, that's Studio One, they started about ten minutes ago. It's that way.' He hooked a thumb in the general direction.

Kelly walked past him.

'Just a minute, Miss,' he called.

She froze.

'Have you got a ticket?' he wanted to know.

She opened her mouth to speak but he continued.

'There's a few seats left. If you see that young lady behind the desk, I'm sure she'll be able to help you.' He smiled and indicated a woman who was sitting beneath a large framed photo of a well-known comedian.

Kelly asked for a ticket.

'I'm afraid that the programme in Studio One is being transmitted live,' said the other woman, apologetically. 'It's not normal policy to allow members of the audience in while the show is on.'

'Damn, my editor will kill me,' said Kelly, with mock exasperation. 'I'm supposed to cover this show for the paper, talk to the guests afterwards. We're doing a feature on one of them this week.'

'Do you have your press card with you?' asked the receptionist.

'No, I don't, I was in such a rush to get here I ...' She shrugged, wondering if the ruse would work.

The woman ran an appraising eye over her.

'Which paper?' she asked.

'*The Standard*,' Kelly lied. 'It is very important.' She played her trump card. 'You can call my editor if you like.'

The woman thought for a moment then shook her head.

'No, that won't be necessary. I think we can get you in.' She called the doorman over. 'George, can you show this lady into Studio One. But they are on the air at the moment.'

The doorman nodded, smiled politely at Kelly and asked her to follow him. She swallowed hard, trying to control her breathing as they made their way up a long corridor. The walls on either side bore framed photographs of celebrities past and present. Kelly felt as if she were being watched, scrutinised by each pair of monochrome eyes, all of whom knew her secret. The .357 suddenly felt gigantic inside her handbag and she hugged it closer to her, watching as the doorman paused beneath a red light and a sign which proclaimed: STUDIO ONE. He opened the door a fraction and peered inside.

'Keep as quiet as you can,' he whispered and led Kelly into the studio.

Apart from the area which made up the studio floor, the

281

entire cavervous room was in darkness. Kelly saw rows and rows of people before her, their attention directed towards the four men who sat in front of them.

She caught sight of Blake.

The doorman ushered her towards an empty seat near the back of the studio where she settled herself, mouthing a silent 'Thankyou' to him as he slipped away. A man seated in front of her turned and looked at her briefly before returning his attention to the discussion being conducted by the four men.

Kelly glanced around the studio.

Cameras moved silently back and forth. She saw a man with headphones hunched close to the interviewer, a clipboard clutched in his hand. He was counting off seconds with his fingers, motioning a camera forward as one of the four men seated amidst the modest set spoke.

Blake was seated between the interviewer and an elderly priest who was having trouble with a long strand of grey hair which kept falling over his forehead. He brushed it back each time he spoke but, within seconds, the gossamer tentacle had crept back to its original position.

Arc lights burned brightly, pinpointing the men in their powerful beams while sausage-shaped booms were lowered carefully by the sound engineers, all of whom were intent on staying out of camera shot. The sound was coming through loud and clear but Kelly seemed not to hear it. Her gaze was riveted to Blake who was in the process of pouring himself some water from the jug on top of the smoked-glass table before him. He smiled cordially at a remark made by the old priest and sipped his drink.

Kelly watched him, unable to take her eyes from the writer's slim frame. She heard his name spoken then his voice filled the studio.

'In the course of my work I've come across all manner of religions, each one as valid as the next,' he said.

'But you mentioned voodoo earlier,' the old priest reminded him. 'Surely you can't class that as a religion?'

'It's the worship of a God or a set of Gods. As far as I'm concerned that makes it a religion.'

'Then you could say the same about witchcraft?' the priest countered.

282

'Why not?' Blake said. 'The deities worshipped by witches were thought to be powerful in their own right. A God doesn't have to be benevolent to be worshipped.'

'Do you have any religious beliefs yourself, Mr Blake?' asked the interviewer.

'Not in God and the Devil as we know them, no,' the writer told him.

Kelly sat motionless, watching him, her eyes filling with tears once more. She touched the Magnum inside her handbag but, somewhere deep inside her, she knew that she could not use the weapon. What she should be feeling for Blake was hatred but, in fact, she felt feelings of love as strong for him now as she had ever known. Could this man really be evil? This man she felt so much for?

'What do you believe in then?' the interviewer asked Blake.

'I believe that there is a force which controls everyone's lives but I don't believe that it comes from a God of any description,' the writer said. 'It comes from here.' He prodded his own chest.

'Don't you, in fact, use this theory in your forthcoming book?' the interviewer said. 'This idea of each of us having two distinct sides to our nature. One good, one evil.'

'That's hardly an original concept,' said the psychiatrist, haughtily. 'Surely every religion in the world, in history, has revolved around the struggle between good and evil.'

'I agree,' said Blake. 'But never before has it been possible to isolate the evil side of man and make it a tangible force independent from the rest of the mind.'

Kelly shuddered, her mind suddenly clearing as if a veil had been drawn from it.

She slid one hand inside her handbag, her fist closing around the butt of the .357. She slowly eased back the hammer, glancing around furtively to see if anyone else had noticed the metallic click.

There was a man standing directly behind her.

He wore a short sleeved white shirt and dark trousers and, Kelly caught a quick glimpse of the badge pinned to his chest: SECURITY.

She took her hand off the Magnum and hurriedly turned to

face the studio floor once again, her heart beating madly against her ribs. She glanced at Blake.

A camera was moving closer towards him.

She realized the time had come.

'What exactly are you suggesting?' the interviewer asked, smiling.

Blake looked into the camera.

'Everyone can be *made* to commit acts normally abhorrent to them,' he said.

The camera zoomed in on him.

Kelly allowed her hand to slip back inside the handbag, and, once more, she gripped the revolver. She could hear the low breathing of the security guard behind her but she realized that she had no choice.

She began to ease the gun slowly from its place of concealment.

Behind her, the security man moved and Kelly swallowed hard as she heard his footsteps gradually receding. The next time she saw him he was a good fifty feet away, to the left of the studio's set. Kelly watched him for a moment longer then turned her attention back to Blake.

He was staring into the camera, motionless in his chair.

The other three men looked at him in bewilderment and, after a minute or so of silence, some impatient mutterings began to ripple through the audience but Blake merely sat as he was, his eyes fixed on the camera as if it were a snake about to strike him.

The cameraman was not the only one in the studio to feel as if iced water had been pumped through his veins. He shivered.

Kelly too felt that freezing hand grip her tightly but the tears which ran down her cheeks were warm.

She could not take her eyes from Blake and now the cold seemed to be intensifying, growing within her until it was almost unbearable.

She slid the Magnum from her handbag and stood up, holding the gun at arm's length, fixing Blake hurriedly in the sights.

The man in front of her turned and opened his mouth to shout a warning.

From the studio floor, the security guard spotted her.

He raced towards her, his eyes fixed on the gleaming Magnum.

The noise was thunderous.

As Kelly squeezed the trigger, the .357 roared loudly. The savage recoil nearly knocked her over and she winced as the butt smashed against the heel of her hand. The Magnum bucked violently in her grip as it spat out the heavy grain bullet. The barrel flamed brilliant white for precious seconds and, in that blinding illumination, members of the audience dived for cover, most of them unaware of what had made the deafening blast.

The bullet hit the floor and drilled a hole the size of a fifty pence piece in the hard surface.

Kelly fired again.

The second shot shattered the smoked glass table in front of Blake who turned and looked up into the audience, the muzzle flash catching his eye. Shards of glass sprayed in all directions and the old priest yelped in pain as one laid open his cheek. He felt himself being pulled to one side by the psychiatrist.

Blake rose, his arms outstretched.

The writer presented a much bigger target and, this time, Kelly didn't miss.

Moving at a speed of over 1,430 feet a second, the heavy grain slug hit him squarely in the chest. It shattered his sternum and tore through his lung before erupting from his back, blasting an exit hole the size of a fist. Lumps of grey and red viscera splattered the flimsy set behind him and Blake was lifted off his feet by the impact. He crashed to the floor and rolled over once, trying to drag himself away, but Kelly fired once more.

The next bullet hit him in the side, splintering his pelvis, decimating the liver as it ripped through him.

He clapped one hand to the gaping wound as if trying to hold the blood in. His chest felt as if it were on fire and, when he coughed, blood spilled over his lips and ran down his chin, mingling with that which was already forming a pool around him.

Nevertheless, fighting back the waves of agony which tore

through him, he managed to claw his way across the set and he was on his knees when the third bullet hit him. It smashed his left shoulder and spun him round, fragments of bone spraying from the exit wound, propelled by the eruption of blood which accompanied the blast.

He sagged forward across the chair, hardly feeling any pain as another round practically took his head off. It caught him at the base of the throat, the massive force throwing him onto his back where he lay motionless, a crimson fountain spurting from the large hole.

Kelly stood at the back of the studio, the gun hot in her hand, her palms stinging from the constant recoil. The smell of cordite stung her nostrils but she seemed not to notice it and, as the security man approached her, one eye on that yawning barrel, she merely dropped the Magnum and looked blankly at him.

He slowed his pace as he drew closer and she saw his lips moving as he spoke but she heard nothing. Only gradually did the sounds begin to filter back into her consciousness.

The screams. The shouts.

She shook her head then looked in bewilderment at the security man, her eyes wide and uncomprehending. She looked down at the gun which lay at her feet then back at the set.

Kelly saw two or three people gathered around a body and it took her a moment or two to realize it was the body of Blake.

She saw the blood. Smelled the cordite. Her ears were still ringing from the explosive sound of the gunshots.

First aid men scurried on to the set to tend to Blake but she saw one of them shake his head as he felt for a pulse and heartbeat. Another man removed his jacket and laid it over Blake's face.

She realized that David Blake was dead.

The security guard took her by the arm and she looked at him, her eyes wide and questing. She shook her head, glancing down once more at the gun.

In that instant, as she was being led away, Kelly felt as if her entire body had been wrapped in freezing rags.

61

The room inside Albany Street police station was small. Despite the dearth of furniture it still appeared miniscule. Less than twelve feet square, it contained two chairs, one on each side of a wooden table. A cracked wash-basin was jammed into one corner near the door and there was a plastic bucket beneath it to catch the drips which dribbled through the chipped porcelain. The room smelt of perspiration and cigarette smoke, but the windows remained firmly closed. Powerful banks of fluorescents, quite disproportionately bright for the size of the room, blazed in the ceiling.

Inspector Malcolm Barton lit up another cigarette and tossed the empty packet onto the table in front of Kelly.

'How well did you know David Blake?' he asked.

'I've already told you,' Kelly protested.

'So tell me again.'

'We were lovers. I was living at his house. I had been for about a fortnight.'

'Then why did you kill him?'

'I've told you that too.'

Barton blew out a stream of smoke and shook his head.

'You can do better than that, Miss Hunt,' he said. 'First you told me you intended to kill Blake then you said you didn't remember pulling the trigger. Now, I'm just a thick copper. I like things plain and simple. Tell me why you shot him.'

Kelly cradled her head in her hands and tried to keep her voice calm. She had been at the police station for over an hour, taken directly there from the Euston Road studios.

'He was dangerous,' she said.

'He never seemed like a nut-case to me the odd times I saw him on the box. What gave you this special insight?' The policeman's voice was heavy with scorn.

'He told me about his powers,' said Kelly, wearily.

287

'Of course, his *powers*. I'd forgotten about them.'

'If you won't believe me then at least let someone else back up what I've told you. Blake had the ability to control people's minds, to make them act out their worst desires. That was his power.'

'And you know of someone who'll verify that do you?' Barton chided. 'I'd be interested to meet him.'

'Then let me make a bloody phone call,' Kelly snapped. 'Like you should have done when you first brought me here.'

Barton pointed an accusatory finger at her.

'Don't start giving me orders, Miss Hunt, you're not in a bargaining position,' he hissed. 'Jesus Christ you were seen by dozens of people. You told me yourself that you had to kill Blake.'

'Have I ever denied I shot him?' she said, challengingly.

'You said you didn't remember pulling the trigger.'

'I didn't. I wasn't even sure what had happened until I saw him lying there.'

There was a moment's silence then Barton crossed to the glass panelled door behind him.

'Tony, bring the phone in here will you,' he called, then turned back to face Kelly. 'All right, you make your phone call.'

A tall, slim man in a sergeant's uniform entered the room carrying a trimphone which he plugged into a socket in the wall near Kelly. He hesitated a moment then walked out.

'Go on,' urged the Inspector, nodding towards the phone.

Kelly picked up the receiver and dialled the number of the hotel where Joubert was staying. She wiped perspiration from her face with her free hand, looking up occasionally at Barton who was rummaging through his pockets in search of another packet of cigarettes. He found one and lit up.

On the other end of the line, Kelly heard the sound of Joubert's voice.

'Blake made the broadcast,' she told him. 'I couldn't stop him in time.'

He asked where she was.

'I killed Blake. The police are holding me here now. Please Joubert, you must come to London. It might already be too late.' She gave him instructions on how to reach the police station then hung up.

'Too late for what?' Barton wanted to know.

'Everyone who watched that programme,' she said.

'He might have been bluffing,' said Barton, disinterestedly.

'I wish to God he had been,' Kelly said, quietly.

There was a knock on the door and the tall, slim sergeant entered, carrying a piece of paper. He passed it to Barton. The Inspector read it, glancing occasionally at Kelly as he did so. He sucked hard on his cigarette.

'What do you make of it, guv?' said the sergeant.

'When did these reports come in?' Barton wanted to know.

'These were the first three, they came in less than an hour ago.'

Barton looked puzzled.

'What do you mean, the first three?' he asked.

'We've had five more reports since,' the sergeant told him.

'I suppose you'd take this as proof of your little story would you, Miss Hunt?' the Inspector said, tapping the piece of paper.

'What is it?' she asked.

'At 8.07 a pet shop owner in Kilburn slaughtered every single animal in his shop with a knife. One of our constables found him in the street outside the shop. He'd just gutted a couple of kittens. At 8.16 a woman in Bermondsey held her eight-week-old child against the bars of an electric fire until it died. At 8.29 a man in Hammersmith killed his wife and daughter with a chisel.'

Kelly closed her eyes.

'Oh God,' she murmured.

'Go on then, tell me it was your friend Blake who caused these killings.'

'It doesn't matter any more,' said Kelly, wearily. 'It's already begun and there's no way to stop it.'

This time Barton did not add a sarcastic remark.

He felt inexplicably afraid as he lit up another cigarette.

And he wondered if he was the only one who felt the peculiar chill in the room.

62

8.36 p.m.

The scissors fell to the carpet with a dull ring as Laura Foster knocked them off the arm of the chair. She reached down and retrieved them; replacing them next to her. Her husband, Paul, got to his feet as she handed him the trousers she'd finished turning up. He pulled them on and strutted around the sitting room happily.

'They're OK aren't they?' he asked.

'They are now,' Laura told him. 'You'd have worn them without me turning them up. They looked like concertinas on your shoes.'

Paul slipped them off again and walked across to her chair, bending down to kiss her. She giggled as he slipped one hand inside her blouse and squeezed her unfettered breasts.

'Shall I bother putting my others back on?' he asked.

Laura chuckled again, pointing out how comical he looked in just his socks and underpants.

He moved closer, kissing her fiercely and she responded with equal fervour, one hand straying to the growing bulge in his pants. She slipped her hand beneath his testicles and fondled them, feeling his erection throbbing against her fingers.

Paul closed his eyes as she pulled his pants down, freeing his stiff organ.

The next thing he felt was an unbearable coldness as the scissor blades brushed his testicles. His eyes jerked open and, for interminable seconds he found himself gaping at Laura. Her own eyes were glazed, almost unseeing. Her face was expressionless.

The blades snapped together.

Laura sat impassively as he dropped to his knees, hand clutching his scrotum. Blood sprayed from the neatly severed veins and Paul found that his agony was mixed with nausea as he saw one egg-shaped purple object glistening on the carpet before him.

As he fell backward he heard laughter and, just before he blacked out, he realized that it was coming from the television.

Liverpool

8.52.

The child was small and it had been common sense to keep him in plain view at all times since his premature birth two weeks earlier. Now he gurgled happily in his carry-cot, his large brown eyes open and staring at the multi-coloured TV screen nearby.

Terry Pearson looked down at the child and smiled.

'Is he all right, love?' asked his wife, Denise, who was glancing through the paper to see what other delights the networks were offering for the remainder of the evening. She and Terry had been watching the screen since six that evening. Though Denise doubted if there'd be anything else to match the excitement of what had happened on the chat show they'd been watching.

'I suppose there'll be something on *News at Ten* about that fella getting shot,' she said, putting down the paper and crossing to the carry-cot.

Terry nodded, not taking his eyes from his son. Denise also gazed down at the baby, both of them mesmerised by it.

It looked so helpless. So tiny.

Terry reached into the cot and, with contemptuous ease, fastened the fingers of one powerful hand around the baby's neck, squeezing tighter until the child's face began to turn the colour of dark grapes. He held it before him for a moment longer, watched by Denise, then, with a grunt, he hurled the child across the room as if it had been a rag doll.

The baby hit the mirror which hung on the far wall, the impact bringing down the glass which promptly shattered, spraying the carpet with needle-sharp shards of crystal.

Terry crossed the room and prodded the tiny body. There was blood on the wall and a sickly grey substance on the

291

carpet.

He reached for a particularly long piece of mirror, ignoring the pain in his hand as it cut into his palm. Blood dribbled down his arm, the flow increasing as he put his weight behind the rapier-like implement.

Denise chuckled as she watched her husband tear her child's flesh and raise it to his lips.

Then she held the tiny body still as Terry set about hacking the other leg off.

Norwich

9.03.

The book fell from her grasp and she awoke with a start, picking the paperback up, muttering to herself when she saw that she'd lost her page. Maureen Horton found her place and folded down the corner of the page, checking that Arthur wasn't looking. He hated to see books being mistreated and, as far as he was concerned, folding down the corner of a page was a particularly heinous crime. He'd reminded her time and again what bookmarks were for. Well, she didn't care. This was one of *her* books. A good old romance. Not that pompous Jeffrey Archer stuff that Arthur always had his nose in.

Arthur.

She looked across to his chair but he was gone.

Probably out making a cup of tea, she reasoned. He'd left the TV on as usual. She was always nagging him about wasting electricity. What was the point of having the television on if they were both reading she insisted? Arthur always tried to tell her he preferred what he called 'background sound'.

She smiled to herself and leant forward to turn up the volume. The news had just started.

She heard a slight whoosh then felt a numbing impact across the back of her head as her husband struck her with the petrol can.

Arthur Horton grabbed his semi-conscious wife by the hair and dragged her back into her seat.

She lay there, twitching slightly, watching him through

pain-racked eyes. Maureen could feel something warm and wet running down her back, pouring freely from the cut on her skull.

He moved to one side of her and she heard the noisy squeaking of the cap as he unscrewed it. Arthur gazed down at her with glassy eyes, the aroma of petrol stinging his nostrils. He upended the can, emptying the golden fluid all over his wife and the chair, watching as she tried to move. Maureen opened her mouth to scream but some of the petrol gushed down her throat and she gagged violently.

He struck the match and dropped it on her.

Maureen Horton disappeared beneath a searing ball of flame which hungrily devoured her skin, hair and clothes. She tried to rise but, within seconds, the searing agony had caused her to black out. Her skin rose in blisters which burst, only to be replaced by fresh sores. Her skin seemed to be bubbling as the flames stripped it away, leaving only calcified bone.

Arthur Horton stood motionless as his wife burned to death, the leaping flames reflected in his blank eyes.

63

London

9.11 p.m.

Kelly coughed as Inspector Barton stubbed out his half-smoked cigarette, the plume of grey smoke rising into the air. The entire room seemed to be full of fumes, so much so that she felt as if she were looking at the policeman through a fine gauze.

'Is there anything in this statement you want to amend?' he said, tapping the piece of paper before him with the end of his pen.

'What's the point?' she wanted to know.

'The point *is*, that you're looking at a twenty year stretch or murder, that's what the point is.'

'Perhaps I should plead insanity,' she said, cryptically.

'Looking at some of the things that are in this statement you'd probably get away with it too,' snorted Barton.

'Why can't you understand?' Kelly rasped. 'Blake had the ability to reach people on a massive scale. For him, this TV show provided the ultimate opportunity to display his ability to control the minds of those watching, to summon their evil sides. From the amount of reports you've been getting, it looks as if he succeeded.'

'It's coincidence,' said Barton, although he sounded none too convinced.

'No, Inspector,' Kelly sighed. 'It isn't coincidence and, so far, the reports have been restricted to a small area of London. That show was networked, nationwide.'

'So you're telling me there are people carving each other up from one end of Britain to the other?'

'Anyone who saw that programme is at risk,' Kelly said.

'That's bollocks,' snapped Barton, getting to his feet. He left the statement lying on the table in front of her. 'You read that over again, I'll be back in a while, perhaps you'll have some more convincing answers for me then.' He closed the door behind him. Kelly heard the key turn in the lock.

She slumped back in her chair, eyes closed. Where the hell was Joubert? It had been over an hour since she'd phoned him. She opened her eyes and looked down at her hands. The hands which had held the gun. Kelly found that she was quivering.

She remembered reaching into her handbag for the pistol but, after that, her mind was a blank. Nothing remaining with any clarity until the point when she was grabbed by the security guard. She wondered if Toni Landers, Roger Carr, Gerald Braddock and Jim O'Neil had felt the same way after committing *their* crimes.

She glanced at her statement, aware of how ridiculous the whole affair must appear to someone like Barton.

Alone in that small room she felt a crushing sense of desolation.

Blake had released a wave of insanity which was now unstoppable.

64

Glasgow

9.23 p.m.

The shrill whistling of the kettle sounded like a siren inside the small flat.

Young Gordon Mackay got slowly to his feet and wandered through from the sitting room, glancing back at the television as he did so.

'Turn it off, Gordon,' shouted his younger sister, Claire. 'It'll wake the baby up.'

He nodded wearily and switched off the screaming kettle.

'Why couldn't you do it?' he asked Claire who was sitting at the kitchen table with three or four books spread out in front of her.

'Because I'm doing my homework,' she told him. 'Anyway, all you've been doing all night is sitting in front of the television.'

'Fuck you,' grunted Gordon, pouring hot water on to the tea bag in his mug. He stirred it around then scooped the bag out and dropped it into the waste-disposal unit of the sink. As he flicked it on it rumbled into life, the vicious blades churning noisily as they swallowed the solitary tea-bag. That was one of the perks of baby-sitting, Gordon thought. Normally his mother wouldn't let him near this lethal device but, when she and his father left him to mind the other three kids, it was like a new toy to him. He took some withered flowers from a vase on the window sill and watched as they were gobbled up by the hungry mouth of the machine.

'Mum said you weren't to use that,' Claire bleated.

Gordon ignored her, feeding more refuse into the gaping hole.

Claire got to her feet and crossed to the sink.

'Turn it off, Gordon,' she said, angrily.

He ignored her.

Claire reached across him for the button which controlled the machine.

Gordon grabbed her arm tightly.

'Let go,' she shouted, striking him with her free hand, trying to pull away.

As he turned to look at her, his eyes were glazed, as if he didn't see her at all. Claire was suddenly afraid.

With a strength that belied his size, Gordon wrenched her towards the sink, guiding her hand towards the churning blades of the waste-disposal unit.

Claire began to scream as her finger tips actually brushed the cold steel of the sink bottom. She clenched her hand into a fist but it only served to prolong the moment for precious seconds.

Gordon thrust her hand into the machine, forcing her arm in as far as the wrist.

Blood spurted up from the razor sharp blades, spewing up crimson fountains as the limb was first lacerated then crushed. He heard the noise of splintering bone as her arm was dragged deeper into the yawning hole, the skin being ripped away as far as the elbow. The stainless steel sink flooded with thick red fluid and, as Claire's shrieks of agony grew shrill, the noise of the machine seemed to be deafening. Her hand was torn off and she fell back, blood spurting from the shredded stump that was her arm. Gordon looked down at her, at the pulped flesh and muscle and the spreading puddle of crimson which formed around the mutilated appendage.

He didn't realize that bone was so white. It gleamed amidst the crimson mess, fragments of it floating on the red puddle.

The sound of the waste-disposal unit filled his ears.

Southampton

9.46.

The garage door opened with a distressing creak and Doug Jenkins peered from beneath the bonnet of his car to see who had come in. He saw the door close and the sound of footsteps echoed throughout the garage as Bruce Murray approached the old Ford Anglia.

'Sorry, Doug,' Murray said. 'That all night spares place doesn't carry the parts for a car as old as this. I rang them before I came over.'

Jenkins cursed under his breath.

'Why the hell don't you buy a new car?' Murray wanted to know. 'This one's twenty years old at least.'

'I've had this since I was eighteen,' Jenkins protested. 'I've got a soft spot for it.'

'The best spot for it would be the bloody junk yard,' Murray chuckled as he stepped forward to inspect the engine. 'Have you been working on it all night?'

'No, only for the past hour or so, I've been watching TV.'

Jenkins stepped back, wiping his hands on an oil-covered rag. He shuddered, despite the warmth inside the garage.

'Pass me that wrench will you, Doug?' said Murray, holding out a hand.

His companion selected one from the dozens which hung on the wall and passed it to Murray. The wall was like something from a hardware store. Hammers, spanners, saws, wrenches, hatchets and even a small chainsaw were hung neatly from nails, all of them in the correct order. Doug Jenkins was nothing if not methodical. He rubbed his eyes with a dirty hand, leaving a dark smudge on his face. The cold seemed to be intensifying.

'I heard there was some trouble on TV earlier,' said Murray, his back to his friend. 'Somebody got shot in full view of the camera or something. Did you see it?'

Silence.

'Doug, I said did you see it?' he repeated.

Murray straightened up and turned to face his companion.

'Are you going deaf, I ...'

The sentence trailed away as Murray's jaw dropped open, his eyes bulging wide in terror. A sound like a revving motorbike filled the garage.

'Oh Jesus,' Murray gasped.

Jenkins advanced on him with the chainsaw, holding the lethal blade at arm's length, its wicked barbs rotating at a speed of over 2,000 rpm.

'What are you doing?' shrieked Murray, gazing first at his friend's blank eyes and then at the murderous implement levelled at him.

Jenkins drove it forward.

Murray tried to knock the blade to one side with the wrench but fear affected his aim. The chainsaw sliced effortlessly through his arm just below the elbow. He shrieked as blood spouted from the stump and he held it up, showering both himself and Jenkins with the sticky red fluid.

Jenkins brought the spinning saw blade down in a carving action which caught Murray at the point of the shoulder. There was a high pitched scream as the chainsaw cut through his ribs, hacking its way deeper to rupture his lungs which burst like fleshy balloons, expelling a choking flux of blood and bile. The churning blade chewed easily through muscle and sinew, finally severing Murray's bulging intestines. Like the glutinous tentacles of some bloodied octopus, his entrails burst from the gaping rent in his stomach, spilling forth in a reeking mass.

As he fell forward into a pool of blood and viscera, his body jerked uncontrollably as the final muscular spasms racked it.

Jenkins switched off the chainsaw and, in the silence, looked down at the corpse of Murray.

He looked on disinterestedly as blood washed over his shoes.

London

9.58.

The diesel was picking up speed.

As the train hurtled through Finsbury Park station, people on the platforms appeared only as rapid blurs to Derek West. He had only been driving for about five or ten minutes, since picking up the diesel at the Bounds Green Depot earlier on. Up until then he and five or six of the other drivers and guards had been sitting idly around reading the papers or watching TV. Derek had consumed yet another mug of strong tea then clambered into the cab and started the powerful engine. The diesel was pulling eight tankers behind it. Each one containing almost 71,000 litres of liquid oxygen.

Now, Derek felt the massive engine throbbing around him

as he glanced down at the speedometer.

As the train roared through the last tunnel it was travelling at well over ninety miles an hour.

Up ahead of him, Derek could see the massive edifice which was King's Cross, lights gleaming in the darkness.

He smiled thinly.

Out of his eye corner he caught sight of a red warning light but he paid it no heed.

The needle on the speedo touched ninety-five.

The diesel thundered on, travelling as if it had been fired from some gigantic cannon. It swept into the station, the air horn sounding one last defiant death-knell which echoed around the cavernous interior of the station.

It struck the buffers doing ninety-eight.

Concrete and metal seemed to dissolve under the crushing impact of the hundred ton train. The huge machine ploughed through the platform, sending lumps of stone and steel scything in all directions like shrapnel. Such was the power with which it hit, the engine buckled and split open, the top half of it somersaulting, blasting massive holes in the gigantic timetable a full fifty feet from the buffers. Screams of terror were drowned as the engine exploded, followed, a second later, by a series of devastating detonations as the liquid oxygen tanks first skewed off the track and then blew up.

An eruption of seismic proportions ripped through the station as a screaming ball of fire filled the giant building, melting the glass in the roof and roaring upward into the night sky like a searing, monstrous flare which scorched everything around it. Concrete archways were simply brushed aside by the incredible blast and part of the great canopy above fell inward with a deafening crash. It was impossible to hear anything over the high-pitched shriek of the flames which shot up in a white wall. People not instantly incinerated by the fireball were crushed by falling rubble or flattened by the shock wave which ripped the station apart as if it had been made of paper. The searing temperatures ignited fuel in the engines of other trains and more explosions began to punctuate the persistent roar of the main fire. Wheels, buffers, sleepers and even lengths of rail flew through the air, those that hadn't already been transformed to molten metal by the fury of the temperatures.

The glass front of the station exploded outward, blown by the incredible shock wave, and the street beyond was showered with debris. Taxis waiting in the forecourt were overturned by the blast.

It was as if the station had been trodden on by some huge invisible foot. Huge tongues of flame still rose, snatching at the darkness, melting everything near them with the blistering heat. Platforms had been levelled, people inside the once proud building had been blasted to atoms, pulverised by the ferocity of the explosion. The entire building had become one massive ball of fire.

It looked as if a portion of Hell had forced its way up through the earth.

65

Mere seconds after she heard the loud bang, Kelly felt the floor move. She gripped the table and looked anxiously around her as if fearing that the roof were going to fall in on her. She heard the unmistakable sound of shattering glass and was thankful that the room had no windows. There were shouts and curses from the rooms beyond hers.

She guessed that the violent vibrations continued for a full fifteen seconds then the room seemed to settle once again. A couple of pieces of plaster fell onto the table and she cast an anxious glance at the ceiling once more.

Kelly was aware that there had been a massive explosion somewhere close but she could not have imagined it was as close as King's Cross.

Phones began to ring. It sounded like pandemonium beyond the locked door.

She closed her eyes, wondering what could have caused the blast, her mind tortured by the fact that the perpetrator was more than likely acting out some maniac scheme previously hidden deep within his subconscious.

Until tonight.

Until Blake had ...

She got to her feet and paced up and down for a moment, till partially stunned by the bang and its subsequent tremor.

Even she had not fully believed that anyone could possess such an awesome power as Blake had claimed. Now, she had been given ample proof. Kelly wondered what would have happened if she had arrived at the studios earlier. If she had not walked out on him. If she had joined him.

If she had killed him earlier.

The questions were immaterial now. The final act had been completed. The horror unleashed.

She glanced up at the clock, then at her own watch.

Where was Joubert?

Had he been butchered by some demented victim of Blake's master plan? she wondered, but then hurriedly pushed the thought to the back of her mind. He would come. She knew he would come. How foolish she had been to doubt him. Those suspicions stung even more now as she remembered how she had confided in Blake, never suspecting the man she had trusted, lived with. Loved.

She sat down once more, her head cradled in her hands, eyes fixed on the statement before her — her admission of guilt, although she still did not remember pulling the trigger and blasting the writer into oblivion. All she remembered was the feeling of cold, a sensation she had experienced many years earlier whilst in a haunted house. The coldness which comes with absolute evil.

Kelly slumped forward on the desk, tears trickling down her face.

She didn't raise her head when she heard the footsteps from the direction of the door.

'What happened?' she asked. 'I heard an explosion.'

Silence greeted her enquiry.

'I asked you what happened,' Kelly said, wondering why her companion was silent. She looked up.

Had she been able to, Kelly would probably have screamed. As it was, she felt as if someone had fastened a cord around her throat and was slowly twisting it, tighter and tighter, preventing her from making any sound. She shook her head slowly from side to side.

301

Standing before her was David Blake.

66

For long seconds, Kelly could not speak. Her eyes bulge
madly in their sockets as she gazed at Blake.

Or was it Blake? Was she too losing her grip on sanity?

He reached forward and touched her hand and she felt
shiver run through her. It seemed to penetrate her soul.

'How?' was all she could gasp, her voice a horrifie
whisper. 'I saw you die.' She screwed up her eyes until the
hurt then looked again.

Blake remained opposite her.

'Tell me how,' she hissed.

'The power of the Shadow,' he told her, quietly. '
enabled my Astral body to live on after death. Only tot;
destruction of my physical form can cause my Astral body t
disappear.'

She ran both hands through her hair.

'How will it end?' she asked him.

Blake didn't answer.

'Did you use hypnosis?' she said.

'A form of hypnosis, but the word is inadequate.'

'Stop it now, please,' she begged. 'Let it end.'

'It's only just beginning,' he whispered.

Kelly finally did manage a scream, a long wild ululation c
despair. Tears were squeezed from her eyes as she closed th
lids tightly. She slumped forward on the table, sobbing.

'Make it stop,' she whimpered. 'Please, make it stop.'

She raised her head.

Blake was gone. She was alone once more.

The door to the room was flung open and Barton dashed ir

'What's wrong?' he asked, seeing how distraught sh
looked. 'We heard you scream.'

Kelly could not answer him. Tears dripped from her fac

and stained the statement sheet below. She saw Barton motion to someone behind him and, a second later, Joubert entered the room.

'They told me what happened,' said the Frenchman, watching as she wiped the tears from her face. She looked at Barton.

'Where was Blake's body taken after he was shot?' she asked.

Barton looked bewildered.

'Great Portland Street Hospital,' he said. 'What the hell does that matter?'

'It has to be destroyed,' Kelly told him. 'Burned. Dismembered. Anything. But please, Inspector, you must destroy Blake's body.'

'You *are* off your head,' the policeman said.

She turned to Joubert.

'Blake was here. In this room. Not two minutes ago,' she babbled. 'He's found a way for his Astral body to survive beyond death. These atrocities will continue unless the physical form can be destroyed.'

'Hold up,' Barton interrupted. 'Are you trying to say that Blake isn't dead, because if he's not, who's the geezer laid out at Great Portland Street ...'

'*I* understand what she means, Inspector,' Joubert interrupted.

'Well I fucking well don't,' snapped the policeman. 'Now one of you had better start making some sense, and fast, because I'm not known for my patience.'

'Just destroy the body,' Kelly said, imploringly.

'Forget it,' said Barton. 'Who the hell do you think I am? The body's at the hospital and it stays there until it's buried.'

He turned and left the room, slamming the door behind him.

Kelly and Joubert looked at each other and, if defeat had a physical face, then it was mirrored in their expressions.

The light flickered once then died.

'Sod it,' muttered Bill Howard getting to his feet. He put down his copy of *Weekend* and fumbled his way across to the cupboard set in the far wall. He banged his shin on one of the slabs and cursed again, rubbing the injured area.

There was some light flooding into the basement area but it was largely dissipated by the thick glass and wire mesh which covered the ground level window, the only window in the morgue of Great Portland Street Hospital.

Bill had worked there for the past thirty-eight years, ever since he'd been de-mobbed. He'd tried a spell as ward orderly but his real niche had been down below in the morgue. He felt curiously secure within its antiseptic confines. He knew it was a place where he would not be disturbed by the day-to-day running of the hospital. As long as he did his job then things went along fine. Clean up the stiffs, make sure they were ready for the post-mortems which were carried out in the room next door. Not once, in all his years at the hospital, had the task bothered him. Hardly surprisingly really, he reasoned, after having spent six years in the army medical corps treating all manner of wounds, gangrene, dysentery and other illnesses from Dunkirk to Burma. He'd seen sights which made his present job positively tame.

His wife had died three years earlier after a long battle with cancer but now Bill lived quite happily with his dog in a nice little flat not far from the hospital. Another half an hour and he'd be able to go home.

Bill found his way to the cupboard and opened it, peering through the gloom in search of the strip-light he required. In the dark confines of the morgue he had but one companion.

Bill had been informed that the body would be removed the following day by the police. It had been brought in at about 8.30 that evening, the man had been shot, so Bill had been told. He'd waited until the police and hospital officials had left then he'd lifted the plastic sheet which covered the body and glanced at it. They had left it clothed and the name tag pinned to the lapel of the man's bloodied jacket read 'David Blake'.

Now Bill took the light tube from its cardboard casing and went in search of a chair to stand on.

As he passed the body he shuddered involuntarily. The morgue was usually cold but tonight it seemed positively wintry. Bill saw his breath form gossamer clouds in the air as he exhaled. He wouldn't be sorry to get home in the warm. He would not have to return until nine the following morning.

Bill clambered up onto the chair and removed the old light and slotted in the replacement.

He heard a faint rustling sound.

Bill froze, trying to detect where the noise was coming from. He realized that it was coming from the direction of his desk. He paused a moment, ears alert.

Silence.

He stepped down off the chair.

The rustling came again.

Bill hurried across to the light switch, his hand poised over it but, as he was about to press it, he saw what was making the noise. A slight breeze coming from the half open door was turning the pages of his magazine. He smiled.

Getting jumpy in your old age, he told himself.

Bill almost gasped aloud as he felt a particularly numbing sensation on the back of his neck. It felt as if someone had placed a block of ice against his back. He felt his skin pucker into goose-pimples.

Bill switched on the light and turned.

He suddenly wished he hadn't.

68

The night was alive with the sound of sirens as dozens of accident and emergency vehicles raced towards the blazing inferno which was King's Cross. For miles around flames could still be seen leaping through the fractured roof, turning the clouds orange. A dense pall of smoke hung over the ruins raining cinders down on all those nearby.

Inside Albany Street Police station Sergeant Tony Dean was hurriedly, but efficiently, answering phone calls and barking instructions into the two-way radio on his desk. The tall sergeant was sweating profusely due to his exertions.

'How's it going?' asked Inspector Barton.

'I've called in the blokes who were off duty tonight,' Dean told him. 'And we've got every available man at the scene.'

'Don't spread us too thin, Tony,' Barton reminded him. 'With so many coppers in one place, the villains could have a field day.'

'Scotland Yard have been on the blower, they've sent an Anti-Terrorist squad to the station to check it out.'

'It must have been a bloody big bomb then,' said Barton sceptically, remembering the devastating explosion. He looked warily at the sergeant. 'Have there been any more reports in like the ones we had earlier? You know, the murders.'

Dean nodded.

'Another six since nine o'clock,' he said. 'I checked with a couple of other stations as well. It's happening all over the city, guv.'

Barton didn't answer, he merely looked towards the door which hid Kelly and Joubert from his view. He decided he'd better check on them. As he turned he heard Dean's voice loud in his ear:

'You took your bleeding time, didn't you?'

The Inspector saw PC Roy Fenner hurrying through the

306

door towards the desk where he stood.

'Sorry, Sarge, I got held up, there was loads of traffic,' he babbled. 'Evening, Inspector,' he added.

'Get your uniform on and get back out here,' Dean told him.

'What's been going on anyway?' Fenner wanted to know. 'I've been watching telly all night. First this bloke got shot. In full view of the camera, I thought it was a gimmick but ...'

'Move yourself,' bellowed Dean and the PC disappeared into the locker room to change.

Barton stroked his chin thoughtfully, a flicker of uncertainty passing across his eyes.

'Something wrong, guv?' the sergeant asked him.

He shook his head slowly.

'No,' he murmured then passed through the door which led him to Kelly and Joubert.

Dean snatched up the phone as it rang again and jammed it between his shoulder and ear as he scribbled down the information.

'Christ,' he muttered, as he wrote. 'What was that again? Some bloke's killed his wife by pressing a red hot iron into her face. Yes, I got it. Where was this?' He scrawled down the location. 'Gloucester Place. Right. Have you called an ambulance? OK.' He hung up. Dean stared down at what he'd written and shook his head, then he turned towards the door of the locker room.

'What are you doing, Fenner? Making the bloody uniform?'

The door remained closed.

'Fenner.'

There was still no answer.

Dean opened the door and poked his head in.

'For Christ's sake, what ...'

His sentence was cut short as Fenner leapt forward, bringing his hard-wood truncheon up with bone-crushing force.

The impact lifted the sergeant off his feet and the strudent sound of breaking bone filled his ears as he heard his lower jaw snap. White hot agony lanced through him and he felt consciousness slipping away from him. But, through a haze of pain, he saw the constable advancing. Dean tried to speak but as he did, blood from his smashed jaw ran down his face and neck and the sound came out as a throaty croak. He could see Fenner looking at him, but the constable's eyes did not seem to register his presence. He looked drunk.

Dean managed to scramble to his feet as Fenner brought the truncheon down again.

The sergeant succeeded in bringing his arm up and the solid truncheon cracked against his forearm but he managed to drive one fist into Fenner's face, knocking him backward. He fell with a crash, the truncheon still gripped in his fist.

All three of them heard the sounds from beyond the door but Kelly was the first to speak.

'What's happening out there?' she asked.

Barton hesitated a moment, looking first at Kelly, then at Joubert. They stood motionless for a moment then there was another loud crash, like breaking wood. Barton turned and scuttled through the door.

'We have to get out of here,' said Kelly.

'But how?' Joubert wanted to know.

'There has to be a way. We must find Blake's body and destroy it.' She was already moving towards the door which she found, to her relief, was unlocked.

'No,' said Joubert, stepping ahead of her. 'Let me go first.' He pulled the door open and both of them saw that a narrow corridor separated them from another, glass panelled door about twenty feet further away. Through the bevelled partition they could see the dark outlines of moving figures. Shouts and curses came from the room beyond and Kelly swallowed hard as they drew closer.

They could have been only a yard away when they heard a demonic shout.

A dark shape hurtled towards the glass-panelled door.

Inspector Barton crashed through the thick glass, his upper body slumping over the door which swung under the impact. Shards of glass flew towards Kelly and Joubert, one of them slicing open the Frenchman's left ear; he clapped a hand to the bleeding appendage, using his body to shield Kelly from the worst of the flying crystal. Barton lay across the broken shards, one particularly long piece having pierced his chest. The point had burst from his back and now hel-him there, blood running down it.

Joubert pulled the door open a fraction more, edging through.

Kelly followed.

She was almost through when she felt a bloodied hand close around her wrist.

Joubert spun round as she screamed and he saw that the dying Barton had grabbed her as she passed. Impaled on the broken glass, the policeman raised his head as if soliciting help. Crimson liquid spilled over his lips and he tried to lift himself off the jagged points but, with one final despairing moan, he fell forward again.

Kelly shook free of his hand and followed Joubert through the door.

Albany Street Police station resembled a bomb-site.

Filing cabinets had been overturned, their contents spilled across the floor. Furniture was smashed and lay in pieces everywhere. The windows were broken. Kelly saw blood splashed across the floor and on the far wall.

Close by lay the body of Sergeant Dean, his face pulped by repeated blows from the truncheon. A foot or so from him, the leg of a chair broken across his head, lay PC Fenner.

'Come on, let's get out of here,' said Joubert and the two of them bolted. They dashed out into the rainy night, pausing momentarily to gaze at the mushroom cloud of dark smoke and orange flame which still ballooned upward from the blazing wreckage of King's Cross. Then, Joubert pulled her arm, leading her towards his car.

They scrambled in and he started the engine.

'How far is Great Portland Street Hospital from here?' the Frenchman asked, guiding the Fiat into traffic.

'Not far,' she told him.

Joubert glanced at her but Kelly was looking out of the side window.

If they could get to Blake's body, perhaps they still had a chance to stop the horror he had released.

Perhaps.

'There,' Kelly shouted, pointing to the dimly lit sign over the hospital entrance.

Joubert waited for a break in the stream of traffic then swung the Fiat across the street and parked it outside the large building. Apart from the dozen or so lights which burned in the big windows, the hospital appeared to be in darkness. Kelly scrambled out of the car and hurried up the stone steps to the main entrance, Joubert following closely behind.

The entry-way was bright but the light was not welcoming. It reflected off the polished floors as if they were mirrors, causing Kelly to wince. There was a desk directly opposite, a steaming mug of coffee perched on it. Whoever it belonged to was nowhere in evidence. For fleeting seconds a terrifying thought crossed Kelly's mind.

What if one or more of the patients had seen the programme earlier in the evening? Even now, the wards could be full of butchered, helpless invalids. She shuddered and tried to push the thought to the back of her mind but it refused to budge.

'Kelly, here,' said Joubert, pointing to a blue sign which proclaimed: MORTUARY. A white arrow pointed down a flight of stone steps and, moving as quickly and quietly as they could, the two of them made their way towards the morgue.

As they descended, the darkness seemed to grow thicker until it swirled around them like a cloud, hardly broken by the low wattage lights set in the walls. As they reached the bottom of the stairs a long corridor faced them and, almost unconsciously, both slowed their pace, suddenly not so eager to reach their destination. The lights in the corridor flickered ominously for a second then glowed with their customary brilliance once more. Kelly swallowed hard as she advanced towards the door of the morgue, her heels clicking noisily in the cloying silence.

They drew closer.

It was Kelly who noticed that the door was ajar.

There were some spots of dark liquid on the polished floor which Joubert knelt and touched with his finger. He sniffed it.

'Blood,' he told Kelly, softly.

Inside the morgue itself, apart from the half-light coming through the street-level window, everything was in darkness.

The door opened soundlessly and the two of them stepped inside, glancing to left and right for any sounds or movements.

There was a faint humming in the background which Kelly took to be the hospital generator. Other than that, the morgue was unbearably silent. She heard the blood singing in her ears, her heart thumping noisily as she tip-toed towards the one slab which bore a body.

Covered by a sheet, it looked shapeless in the gloom.

They both approached it slowly, their eyes not leaving the motionless body.

There was more blood on the floor beside the slab.

A dark shape suddenly passed over them and Kelly spun round in panic.

It was a second or two before she realized that it had merely been the shadow of a person walking by outside.

Joubert looked at her and she nodded slowly in answer to his unspoken question.

The Frenchman gripped one corner of the sheet which covered the body.

Kelly moved closer.

There was a soft click behind them and, this time, Joubert felt his heart skip a beat. He squinted through the gloom to see that a slight breeze had pushed the morgue door shut. The Frenchman used his free hand to wipe a bead of perspiration from his forehead.

He took hold of the sheet more firmly, aware of the biting chill which seemed to have filled the room.

Kelly nodded and, gritting his teeth, he whipped the sheet away.

Lying on the slab, glazed eyes bulging wide in terror, was

the body of Bill Howard.

Kelly and Joubert exchanged anxious glances, the Frenchman touching the face of the dead man with the back of his hand.

'He hasn't been dead long,' he told Kelly, keeping his voice low.

She took a step back, allowing an almost painful breath to escape her lungs.

Bill Howard had obviously died in agony and it showed in his contorted features. A long metal probe had been rammed into his mouth, puncturing his tongue before being driven through the base of his skull above the hollow at the back of his neck.

A question burned brightly in her mind.

Where was Blake's body?

As the two of them emerged from the stairway into the hospital entry-way, they were surprised to find it still deserted. Once more Kelly wondered if the patients had been butchered in their beds, maybe the staff as well. She slowed her pace slightly, her eyes shifting to the solitary mug of tea which still stood on the desk. It was no longer steaming. Whoever had put it there had not returned to claim it.

'Kelly, come on,' Joubert urged, making for the main door. She hesitated a moment longer then followed him out to the car.

'Where to now?' he asked.

She gazed ahead of her, her voice soft but determined.

'There's only one place left where the body could be.'

Joubert understood.

The traffic was surprisingly light in the city centre. The drive to Blake's house took less than thirty minutes. Joubert brought the Fiat to a halt and switched off the engine, peering through the side window at the large building.

Rain coursed lazily down the windows of the car and, overhead, a loud rumble of thunder was instantly answered by a vivid but soundless flash of lightning.

Kelly brushed fingers through her hair, noticing that her hand was shaking. She clenched her fists together for a moment, drawing in a deep breath.

'What if the body *isn't* in the house?' asked Joubert, cryptically.

'It has to be there,' she said. 'Blake would feel safe hiding it there.'

They both clambered out of the Fiat, ignoring the rain as they stood facing the house. A single light burned in the porch. Far from looking forbidding, Blake's house seemed positively inviting. It beckoned to them and they responded, moving quickly but cautiously towards the dwelling, never taking their eyes from it. Once more Kelly felt a shiver run up her spine.

They paused at the end of the short driveway.

'It'd be better if we split up,' Kelly said. 'That way we'll have a better chance of finding the body. And it won't take so long.'

Joubert regarded her warily for a moment.

'I'll check inside the house,' she said, producing her key ring and showing him the key to Blake's front door which she still possessed. 'You search the garden and garage.'

The Frenchman nodded.

A particularly brilliant flash of lightning lashed across the rain-soaked heavens, bathing the two investigators in cold white light. For fleeting seconds they resembled ghosts, their faces distorted and white in the flash.

Kelly hesitated a moment longer then, with a final look at Joubert, she headed towards the front door.

He waited until she was inside then he moved cautiously forward, his sights set on a door at the side of the garage.

Kelly stepped into the hall and quickly looked around her, searching the darkness with uncertain eyes. She raised her hand, wondering whether or not she should put on the light, but she felt simultaneously exposed *and* safe in the glow. She eventually decided to switch it on.

Nothing moved in the hallway.

To her right, the sitting room door was slightly ajar.

Ahead of her, the stairs disappeared upward into the impenetrable darkness of the first floor.

On the left, the door of the cellar was closed and, this time, there was no key in it. She decided to leave it until last and moved towards the sitting room, pushing the door wide open. Light from the hall offered her sufficient illumination to find the nearest table lamp. This she also switched on.

Standing in the sitting room, Kelly could feel the silence closing in around her as if it were a living thing.

Outside, the storm was reaching its height.

Joubert found that the door which led into the garage was unlocked but the catch was rusty and he needed to put all his weight behind it to shift the recalcitrant partition.

It swung open with a despairing shriek and the Frenchman practically fell into the dark abyss beyond. He stumbled but managed to keep his feet, looking round for a light switch. He found one close to the door and flicked it on. The fluorescents in the ceiling sputtered into life and Joubert scanned the inside of the garage. The floor was spotted with congealed patches of oil and slicks of petrol but, apart from a small toolbox shoved into one corner, the place was empty. There was certainly nowhere to hide a body.

He took one last look then retraced his steps, flicking off the light as he did so.

Outside in the rain again he wiped some of it from his face and decided which direction to follow next.

There was a narrow passageway beside the garage and the

side of the house which, he suspected, led to the back garden. Joubert moved cautiously towards it, attempting to see through the short, but darkness-shrouded, passageway. It was less than four feet wide, perhaps three times that in length and it was as black as the grave in there. He put out one hand and fumbled his way along the stone wall, unable to see a hand in front of him.

There was a loud clap of thunder and Joubert prayed for a flash of lightning which would at least give him a few seconds of light. Enough to reach the end of the passage or perhaps alert him if he were not alone in the gloom.

He tried to force that particular thought to the back of his mind but it would not budge.

Inch by inch he edged onward, deeper into the blackness.

Something touched his leg.

Something solid.

Joubert jumped back, not knowing what he was going to do, fear overwhelming him.

In that split second there was an ear-shredding whiplash of lightning which lit up the entire passage.

A foot or so from the end of it, there was a wooden gate. He had walked into it in the blackness, unable to see the object.

Joubert closed his eyes for a second and smiled thinly, moving forward once again. He succeeded in slipping the catch on the gate and passed through and out of the passage. The Frenchman found himself in the back garden. The rain continued to pelt down, plastering his hair to his face, streaming into his eyes. Another crack of lightning lit the heavens and Joubert saw that, ten or twelve yards further on, nestling in some trees at the bottom of the garden, was what looked like a wooden shed. He trod quickly over the sodden grass towards the small hut and tugged on the handle.

It was locked.

He pulled on it again, finally using his foot to dislodge the timber door. It swung open, a pungent smell of damp and decay billowing out to greet him. He coughed and stepped inside.

There was no light in the hut.

The bulb was still in place but it was broken. He narrowed his eyes in an effort to see around the confines of the small structure, which seemed, to all intents and purposes, like a garden shed. He saw a lawn-mower, a roller and sundry other garden implements.

Joubert even spotted a large, double-handed axe. Blake had obviously intended chopping down some of the over-hanging branches which grew around the shed, Joubert assumed. He moved forward and picked up the axe, glad of a weapon though he wondered if it would be of any help if the need arose.

The rain was pounding the shed so violently now that it reminded the Frenchman of waves breaking continually on rocks. He shivered in his wet clothes and took one last look around the tiny hut.

Hidden behind a pile of boxes and encrusted with grime as it was, he almost failed to see the freezer.

It was long, perhaps six feet and at least half that in depth. Quite large enough ...

·Gripping the axe tighter, he moved towards it, pulling the boxes aside in his wake until he could reach the old freezer without any trouble. He hooked his fingers beneath the rim and prepared to fling it open.

There was a harsh crack as the wind blew the shed door shut, plunging Joubert into darkness.

He muttered something in French and hurried across to the door, pushing it open once again, allowing the rain to lash his face for a second, then he returned to the freezer. He dug his fingers under the filthy lid and lifted.

It was empty.

Only a large spider and some woodlice scuttled about inside.

Joubert slammed the lid down again, his heart still beating fast. He wiped his face with the back of his hand and leant back against the empty freezer to catch his breath.

The lights inside the house dimmed for a moment then glowed once more as thunder continued to roll across the heavens. Kelly stood quite still in the darkness, her eyes darting back and forth, ears alert for the slightest sound. But all she heard was the driving rain and the fury of the storm outside.

As the lamp in the sitting room came on she moved slowly

towards the kitchen.

The door was open.

Kelly stopped for a second and glanced over her shoulder before entering the next room. She flicked on the lights and looked around. There were a couple of dirty mugs in the sink but, apart from that, everything seemed to be in its place.

The lights went out again.

She waited for the brightness to return, her heart thudding more rapidly in her chest.

She waited.

Outside the thunder roared loudly.

Waited.

'Come on, come on,' she whispered, trying to steady her breathing.

Waited.

The house remained in darkness.

From inside the garden shed, Joubert had seen Kelly turn on the kitchen lights and now, as he stood looking at the house, he too wondered how long it would be before the power supply was restored. The Frenchman decided that he would be better employed aiding Kelly in her search of the house. Carrying the axe with him, he headed for the door.

A gust of wind slammed it in his face.

He gripped the rusty knob irritably and tugged it open.

Joubert found himself face to face with David Blake.

Before the Frenchman could move, he felt powerful hands grabbing for his throat, hands which felt like blocks of ice as they squeezed. He struck out vainly at Blake who finally hurled the intruder to one side where he crashed into a pile of boxes. As he tried to rise he felt an incredible pressure on his skull as Blake gripped him in a vice-like grip, his fingers resembling talons as they threatened to plunge through the Frenchman's skull.

Joubert felt the cold filling his head, his torso. His entire body.

He screamed but the sound was lost as thunder tore open the dark clouds and the rain lashed the hut unmercifully.

He felt himself being hurled to the floor where he landed with a jarring impact. When he opened his eyes there was no sign of Blake. Joubert didn't know how long he'd been

317

unconscious. A minute? An hour?

The Frenchman got to his feet, picking up the axe as he did so. He held it before him, studying the heavy, wickedly sharp blade. He looked towards the house and thought of Kelly. The axe felt as if it were a part of him, an extension of his arms.

He kicked open the door and trudged across the lawn towards the darkened house, the large, razor-sharp weapon held before him.

A smile creased his lips.

71

When the power inside the house went off, Kelly could hear nothing but the rumbling of thunder. The electric wall clock stopped ticking and she was deprived of even that welcome sound.

Now she stood alone in the darkness, praying for the light to return. The thought that the fuse box might have blown began to creep into her mind.

Or had someone in the house turned the power off?

She spun round, her imagination beginning to play tricks on her. Had she seen movement in the sitting room behind her?

The lights came back on so suddenly she almost shouted aloud in surprise and relief.

Kelly licked her lips but found that her tongue felt like old newspaper. She quickly checked in the pantry then turned, intent on heading back through the house to look upstairs.

In the light flooding from the kitchen windows, she saw Joubert approaching across the small lawn.

She breathed an audible sigh of relief and knelt to undo the bolt on the back door, preparing to turn the key in the lock to let him in. He obviously hadn't found anything, she reasoned, except for the axe which he carried. He had almost reached the back door.

She turned the key in the lock, her hand resting on the knob.

As he saw the door opening, Joubert uttered a high-pitched yell of fury and swung the axe with all his strength. It scythed through the wooden door, ripping it free of one hinge. Kelly's own scream mingled with the shriek of splintering wood. She turned and ran for the sitting room as Joubert stove in the remainder of the door and crashed into the kitchen.

Kelly slipped and fell as she reached the hall, looking over her shoulder in time to see him emerge from the kitchen.

He looked like something from a nightmare with his hair plastered down, his face scratched and bruised and his mouth spread in a kind of rictus. He hurdled a coffee table and hurried after her.

Kelly leapt to her feet, slamming the hall door behind her, darting towards the stairs.

She took them two at a time, stumbling once again at the top.

Below her, Joubert flung open the door and hurried across the hall, pausing on the bottom step before ascending slowly.

Kelly was faced by four doors.

She raced towards the first, hearing his heavy footfalls on the stairs as he climbed higher.

The door was locked.

Kelly hurried to the second one, praying that it was open.

She pulled open the door and ran inside, flinging herself beneath the bed.

Through the half-open door, she could see when Joubert reached the landing. He stood at the top of the stairs for what seemed like an eternity, only his feet visible to Kelly but she realized that he must be deciding which door to try first.

He moved towards the room on her left.

The locked one. She heard him twisting the handle then she heard the sound of shattering wood as he smashed off the knob and kicked the door open.

Kelly closed her eyes, wondering if this was all a nightmare. If she would wake up in a second. She tried to swallow but her throat was constricted.

She heard his footsteps, saw his feet as he stood in the doorway of the room in which she hid.

He took a step inside.

Kelly bit her fist to stifle a cry.

He moved closer towards the bed.

If only she could roll out on the other side, run for the door ...

But what if she slipped? What if he reached the door before her?

What if ...?

He was standing beside her now, his feet together.

She imagined that axe poised over the bed.

With a strength born of terror, Kelly snaked her arms out, fastened them around Joubert's ankles and tugged. She succeeded in pulling his legs away from him and he went down with a heavy thump, the axe falling from his grip.

She rolled over, scrambling clear of the bed, jumped to her feet and ran for the door.

Joubert was up in a second. He flung out a hand and managed to grab a handful of her hair. Kelly yelped as some of it came out at the roots and she felt herself overbalancing. She grabbed for the door frame and managed to retain her stance but he had slowed her up and, as she reached the landing, the Frenchman hurled himself at her, bringing her down in a pile-up which knocked the wind from them both.

Kelly struck out with her nails, raking his face. Joubert bellowed in pain and tried to pull her down again but Kelly got to her feet and kicked him hard in the side, bringing the heel of her shoe down on his outstretched hand so hard that it penetrated. Blood welled from the puncture and Joubert rolled to one side. But, he was still between Kelly and the stairs.

As the Frenchman struggled to his knees, Kelly ran at him and lashed out again with a kick which caught him firmly in the solar plexus. He fell backward, clutching at empty air for a second before tumbling down the stairs, thudding to a halt at the bottom with his head at an unnatural angle.

She gazed down at his motionless form realizing that his neck must be broken. Kelly ran into the bedroom and picked up the double-handed axe, moving quickly from bedroom to bedroom in search of Blake's body.

The rooms were empty.

Kelly began descending the stairs, the axe held firmly in

her hands. She paused beside the body of Joubert, holding the razor sharp blade above his head as she felt for a pulse.

Nothing. As she'd thought, his neck had been broken in the fall.

She suddenly felt overwhelmed by sadness, not just for his death but for all the other people who had died that night and who would die if she did not complete her task. Her grief slowly became anger as she realized that all of the carnage, all of the suffering had been caused by Blake.

There were two more rooms in the house to be searched.

She went through the dining room quickly. That left the cellar.

The door was locked but that did not deter Kelly. She brought the axe down twice, shattering the lock, knocking the door wide open. She slapped on the lights and slowly descended into the subterranean room.

The silence crowded around her, an almost physical force. She stood still at the bottom of the steps, her eyes searching.

Next to one of the large bookcases, almost invisible on first glimpse, was a small door, no bigger than three feet square, its handle also painted white to make it even more inconspicuous. Kelly bent and tugged on the handle.

It opened effortlessly and she recoiled as a rancid smell of rotten wood and damp earth rose from the tiny compartment. But, if the door was small then what lay beyond it was not. The space behind the door looked as though it had been made many years earlier. It stretched back into darkness, she wasn't sure how far. The walls were soft and slimy and she had to duck low to avoid scraping her hair on the dripping ceiling. The stench was almost overpowering.

Lying undisturbed, covered by a blanket, amidst the muck and filth, was the body of Blake.

Kelly grabbed both ankles and, using all her strength, pulled. Inch by inch, the corpse came clear of its resting place until it lay in full view in the cellar. Kelly noticed that the eyes were still open. They seemed to fix her in a reproachful stare and, for a moment, she was rooted to the spot.

There was another deafening clap of thunder, audible even in the depths of the cellar.

The room was plunged into darkness as the lights flickered then died.

A second later they came back on again and Kelly finally managed to tear her gaze from the body of Blake.

She reached for the axe and raised it above her head, knowing what she must do, praying for the strength to perform this final act of destruction. Tears welled up in her eyes then trickled down her cheeks and the axe wavered in the air. Kelly squeezed her eyes tightly shut for a moment, anxious to avoid the reproachful stare of Blake's dead eyes.

The lights began to flash on and off, blinking wildly as the thunder now seemed to become one continual salvo of sound.

Kelly screamed as she brought the axe down.

The blade buried itself in the right shoulder of the corpse and she heard a loud cracking of bone as the scapula was shattered. Kelly wrenched it free and struck again, her aim slightly off but the weight of the weapon was enough. It severed the right arm. She lifted it again and, after two more powerful strokes, succeeded in hacking off the other arm. Tears were now pouring freely down her cheeks and the storm offered a macabre accompaniment to her own sobs and the thick, hollow sound the axe made as it sheared through dead flesh.

She changed position to attack the right leg, the axe skidding off the pelvic bone and shaving away a portion of thigh. Kelly recovered her balance and struck again, forced to stand on the torso to pull the blade free. Her next blow exposed the femur and, with a despairing grunt, she smashed the thick bone and managed to hack the leg off. The remains of the body shuddered beneath each fresh impact but Kelly continued with her grisly task, perspiration soaking through her clothes. It took five attempts to sever the left leg.

Panting like a carthorse, she took a step back, realizing that she had still not completed the monstrous task.

With a blow which combined horrified determination and angry despair, she struck off the head. It rolled for two or three feet across the floor, coming to rest on the stump. She noticed with relief that the sightless eyes were facing away from her.

Kelly stood amidst the pieces of dismembered corpse and dropped the axe, shaking her head gently. Her breath came in great choking gasps which seared her throat and lungs. She

322

leant back against the nearest wall for support, closing her eyes for a moment.

The cellar door slammed shut and Kelly shot an anxious glance towards it.

At the top of the stairs stood David Blake.

Kelly shuddered as the room seemed to fill with icy air, as if someone were sucking all the warmth from the cellar and replacing it with the bone-chilling numbness she now felt.

Blake began to descend, his eyes fixed, not on her, but on the hewn corpse.

'It's over, Blake,' she said, her voice a harsh croak.

He didn't answer. He merely continued his purposeful stride, his face impassive until he reached the bottom of the stairs. Then, his nostrils flared. With a roar of rage he ran at her.

Tired from her exertions, Kelly could not move fast enough to avoid his fearsome lunge. He grabbed her by the throat, lifting her bodily from the ground.

Kelly found herself looking deep into his eyes — into bulging orbs which were pools of sheer hatred. But there was something else there too.

Fear?

She felt the cold seeping through her like gangrene through a rotting limb but Blake's powerful grip was beginning to weaken. With a grunt he lowered her to the floor where she sprawled before him, gazing up at his contorted features. He took a step back, almost tripping over the mutilated remains of the corpse. *His* corpse.

The Astral body of David Blake, the tangible embodiment of his evil, staggered drunkenly for a second, one hand held towards Kelly in a last act of defiance.

With a despairing groan, he dropped to his knees, his eyes still fixed on the girl who was cowering a few feet from him. Kelly saw him open his mouth to scream but the sound, when it came forth, was like nothing human. The thunderous ululation rattled around the cellar, causing Kelly to cover her ears for fear that they would be damaged. The lights in the room went out for a moment then came back on with an increased brilliance.

Blake's scream died away as his face began to split open. Huge, jagged fissures opened in his flesh, as if his mirror

323

image had been broken. An evil-smelling, yellowish-white substance bubbled up from the rents which were now spreading all over his body. He clawed at his chest, pulling his shirt open, a large lump of skin coming with it, exposing the bloodied internal organs beneath. His fingers seemed to shrivel like dying flowers and Kelly saw more of the pus-like fluid oozing from the deep cuts which were spreading along his arms and legs like rips in fabric.

He fell forward, his head disintegrating as he hit the ground. It split open, pus and blood bursting from the ruptured skull. A tangle of intestines snaked upward, as if propelled by some inner force as his stomach burst.

Kelly looked away, feeling her stomach somersault. The odour of corruption, that rank and fetid stench which floated in the air like an invisible cloud, surrounded her. She coughed and thought she was going to be sick. But the feeling passed.

The room was plunged into darkness again as the lights dimmed for fleeting seconds and a massive thunderclap shook the house.

Kelly managed to look back at the decaying form of Blake. The last moments lit by the faintly glimmering lights which seemed to act like strobes as they flickered.

As the electrical power was restored, the cellar was bathed in the cold white light of the fluorescents.

Blake had vanished.

Nothing remained.

No blood. No pus.

Nothing.

Only the dismembered corpse lay before her.

Kelly got slowly to her feet, swaying uncertainly for a moment. She was soaked with sweat. Every single muscle in her body ached and it took a monumental effort for her to even walk. She was completely drained. As close to collapse as she could ever remember but, somewhere amidst that exhaustion, there was a feeling of triumph. She had succeeded in stopping Blake. Now she prayed that she had been able to end the reign of terror he'd unleashed. There was no way of knowing yet.

All she could do was wait.

And hope.

She knew that there was one more thing which had to be done.

Crossing to the phone on the nearby desk, she lifted the receiver and pressed out three nines. She had no choice but to tell the police. Kelly heard the purring at the other end of the line.

The lights flickered once more and she muttered under her breath as she heard the phone go dead.

She was about to try again when the hand closed on her shoulder.

She spun round, the scream catching in her throat.

The figure which faced her was identical in every respect. A mirror image of herself.

And it held the axe.

Her alter-ego smiled as it brought the vicious weapon down with incredible force. The blade aimed at Kelly's head.

It was the last thing she saw.